Blackthorn
Winter

Carol Townend

HEADLINE

First published in 1993
by HEADLINE BOOK PUBLISHING PLC

First published in paperback in 1993
by HEADLINE BOOK PUBLISHING PLC

10 9 8 7 6 5 4 3 2 1

ISBN 0 7472 4148 1

Typeset by Avon Dataset Ltd, Bidford-on-Avon

Printed and bound in Great Britain by
HarperCollins Manufacturing, Glasgow

HEADLINE BOOK PUBLISHING PLC
Headline House
79 Great Titchfield Street
London W1P 7FN

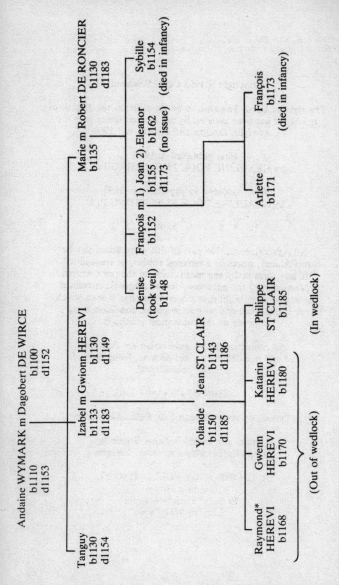

Andaine WYMARK m Dagobert DE WIRCE
b1110   b1100
d1153   d1152

Tanguy
b1130
d1154

Izabel m Gwionn HEREVI
b1133   b1130
d1183   d1149

Marie m Robert DE RONCIER
b1135   b1130
             d1183

Denise
(took veil)
b1148

François m 1) Joan 2). Eleanor
b1152   b1155   b1162
         d1173   (no issue)

Sybille
b1154
(died in infancy)

Arlette
b1171

François
b1173
(died in infancy)

Yolande   Jean ST CLAIR
b1150   b1143
d1185   d1186

Raymond*   Gwenn   Katarin   Philippe
HEREVI   HEREVI   HEREVI   ST CLAIR
b1168   b1170   b1180   b1185

(Out of wedlock)   (In wedlock)

*AKA Gwionn Leclerc

Author's Note

The blossom of the blackthorn often appears in March when the east winds can blow very chill. Traditionally, a cold – or late – spring was known as 'a blackthorn winter'.

In 1162, Aubrey de Vere, first Earl of Oxford, who had married two wives and had no children, betrothed himself to Agnes of Essex. Agnes was about eleven, the earl was in his forties. Then, in 1163, Agnes's father, Henry Earl of Essex, fell into disgrace and forfeited his lands. Thus Agnes's value as a bride plummeted. Aubrey de Vere decided to set the arrangement aside.

The earl reckoned without Agnes, who was determined she would marry him and thus save her own and her family's name from further shame. Agnes appealed to Rome. The earl shut her up in a tower in the hope that she would give way. She did not, and the case dragged on for years, not being resolved until 1172, when the earl received judgement from Rome. He was to marry Agnes and treat her appropriately within twenty days or face excommunication.

The earl complied. By then he was about sixty, and Agnes a little over twenty . . .

Part One

The Dutiful Daughter

I, the Lord your God, am a jealous God, punishing the children for the sin of the fathers to the third and fourth generation.

Exodus 20:5.

Chapter One

December 1173. Huelgastel — High Castle — in Southern Brittany

With the benefit of hindsight, it was easy for Arlette to pinpoint Advent Sunday in 1173 as the day when her life went awry. It was to be over twenty years before she found her path again and could finally say that she had won her long battle with fate and become mistress of her own destiny . . .

That December, Arlette had possessed the typical arrogance of a loved and cosseted child. A wilful, red-headed bundle of energy, with sparkling blue eyes, the two-and-a-half-year-old granddaughter of the powerful Count Robert de Roncier had been confident that she was the brightest star on her mother's horizon. A nursemaid's nightmare, not only did Arlette have the run of the solar — the women's domain — she had the run of castle and bailey too.

But something happened that Sunday morning which completely changed her life.

Being the first Sunday in Advent, it was most unusual for Arlette's mother, Lady Joan, not to put in an appearance at Mass. After the service, the child gave her nursemaid Agata the slip. She raced along the chapel corridor, and crawled up the twisting stone stairs to her mother's bedchamber. Arlette could crawl more rapidly than most folk could walk.

She found her mother in bed, amidst a heap of furs and shawls which hid her swollen belly. Lady Joan de Roncier's hair was midnight dark, it was not from her that Arlette had inherited her flaming colouring. Lady Joan was eighteen, pregnant, and the birth was imminent. Everyone hoped for a son, an heir for Count Robert's heir, François de Roncier.

Arlette hovered in the doorway for a moment, watching. She was happily oblivious of her mother's condition, and could not understand why her mother's much-loved wolfhound, Gabriel, was not in the bedchamber as was his habit.

The chamber boasted a small fire, but today apparently this luxury was not enough, for a tall brazier had been brought up and it glowed on its ashpan in the centre of the room. Next to the brazier stood a wooden screen, all white and gold with long robed angels flying across it. The angels' golden tresses streamed behind them as they soared through the heavens. Each one held a shining trumpet to their rosy lips.

Lady Deneza, wife to Sir Hamon le Moine, the castle seneschal, stood staring at a poker which was lodged in the bright heart of the brazier. Fifteen years older than the woman in the bed, Lady Deneza's knowledge of the healing arts was comprehensive. She was serving as Lady Joan's midwife, and she was preparing an infusion of the dried root of herb-bennet in red wine. She hoped it would take the edge off Lady Joan's pains.

Wine goblet in one hand, Lady Deneza pulled the poker from the brazier and thrust it, steaming and hissing into the dark liquid. A warm, spicy, clove-like aroma filled the chamber. Immersed in stirring the concoction, Lady Deneza ignored the child skipping across the rush matting.

'Mama!' Arlette cried, delighted to have found her mother so easily. 'Mama sleepy?' She was talkative for her age.

4

Lady Joan smiled through her discomfort and reached out her hand to her daughter. As always, Arlette's copper curls refused to be confined in their stubby braids and hung, a shining cloud, about the small, pale face; for Arlette had the delicate, milk-white complexion that usually partnered that fiery-coloured hair. 'No, Arlette. I'm not sleepy. But I do need a cuddle. Come here. Come and give your mother a hug.'

Happily, Arlette clambered on to the high, wide, canopied bed, and dived under the covers, a small bump snuggling close to her mother's body.

Her nursemaid, Agata, came to lean in the doorway. At forty, plump and out of condition, she was short of breath, and holding her sides.

'Oh, my lady! I'm sorry. She moves that fast, I can't catch her.' Walking with surprising softness, given the solidity of her frame, Agata approached Lady Joan's bed. 'Come out of there, young mistress. Fancy pestering your poor mother at a time like this! Come out! Leave Lady Joan alone.'

The hump in the bed that was Arlette wriggled, and then was still.

Lady Joan bit her lip as a contraction, the fiercest one yet, gripped her belly. When it had eased, she raised smiling eyes to Agata's. Like her daughter's Joan's eyes were blue, but her irises were ringed with grey. 'Arlette's not pestering me, Agata. I invited her in. I want to explain what's happening. I don't want her to be afraid.'

Agata threw a swift, assessing look at Lady Joan. Moisture was pearling the wide, unlined brow, the tendrils of hair at her lady's temples were dark with sweat, and there were tiny lines of tension at the corners of her mouth. Agata folded her hands under her large bosom. A mother of two herself, though hers were now grown and had long since flown the nest, she recognised Lady Joan's travail was heavy on her.

5

'But, my lady—'

'Excuse me, Agata.' With unassuming authority, Lady Deneza stepped up to the bed, goblet in hand, as the nursemaid withdrew to warm her hands by the brazier.

'I think you should drink this, my dear,' Lady Deneza said.

Wrinkling her nose, Lady Joan waved the goblet aside. 'My thanks, but no—'

'It will ease you—'

'It clouds my mind, and today, of all days, I need it clear. Besides, I hate cloves.'

'It is herb-bennet: no cloves have been near that wine, my lady.' Lady Deneza sighed. 'But as you wish. It's waiting for you, in case you should need it.'

'Thank you, Deneza.' A spasm crossed Lady Joan's face, and her hand plucked at the bedcovers. 'Arlette?'

A red head bobbed up beside her, face grinning. 'Mama?'

The child began to jig up and down on the mattress.

'Keep still, Arlette,' Joan stifled a groan. 'I've something to tell you.'

'Mama?' The child stopped jiggling and, reaching for her mother's brown plait, she began playing with the ribbon, putting the end of it in her mouth and sucking it noisily.

Agata tutted.

'Let her be, Agata,' Lady Joan said, smiling tolerantly. Another spasm wiped the smile from her face. Gripping her belly, Joan went sheet-white with the shock of the pain.

'Mama?' Arlette dropped her mother's plait. The ribbon had unravelled, but no one noticed. 'Mama hurting?'

'Ah, God! Yes. It hurts.' Lady Joan gasped.

Agata came and plucked Arlette from the bed.

'Have the drink, my lady,' Lady Deneza waved the rejected goblet under Joan's nose. 'Why suffer?'

6

'Later. I'll drink it later. Where's Arlette? Agata, wait.'

There was a stir in the doorway, and Arlette's grandmother, Marie de Roncier, strode into the room, followed by her maid. Like Lady Deneza, Countess Marie de Roncier had an air of authority, but her authority was anything but unassuming. 'Shut that door,' the countess rapped.

Like a scalded cat, her maid leapt to do her bidding.

Tall and thin, Countess Marie had black eyes, a strong, lined face, and a nose that friends might term imperial, but most folk would liken to the beak of a bird. An intimidating woman, the countess kept most people at arm's length.

'What *is* that child doing in here?' Countess Marie's sharp eyes had taken in the scene at one glance. 'Agata, remove her.'

Agata bobbed a curtsey in the countess's direction, and edged past her, Arlette clutched to her bosom.

'Agata, wait,' the girl in the bed cried out.

'What's this, Joan?' the countess spoke in bracing tones. 'You're not going to make a fuss, are you? You were so good when Arlette was born.'

'Countess, you misunderstand, I wanted to explain to Arlette . . . ah!' Joan began to pant.

Lady Deneza dragged back the bedcovers and, flicking her veil impatiently over her shoulders, the countess bent to watch the examination.

'A little way to go yet,' Deneza pronounced.

The countess nodded, and unpinned her veil, lest it got in the way. 'I came at the right time, I see,' she said. 'Agata, remove that child.'

Joan groaned. 'Agata . . . you explain . . . please?'

'I'll tell her, my lady,' Agata answered and, relieved to escape Lady de Roncier's chamber, Agata lifted the latch and carried Arlette to the solar below.

* * *

The next morning, when Agata had finished dressing her wriggling charge, Arlette's father, François de Roncier, strode into the cramped, round tower room that served as the nursery. His copper-coloured hair stood up on end. Lady de Roncier's labour had been a protracted one, and her husband had spent the night in the hall in the company of his father, Count Robert, diligently emptying a wine-keg.

'You've a brother, Arlette!' he cried, hazel eyes alight with triumph, ruddy cheeks a-glow. He picked his daughter up and tossed her high in the air.

'Brother?' The little girl smiled. She was delighted to see her father, who never normally visited her room. Arlette could see the reddish overnight stubble on her father's chin, and smell sweet wine on his breath.

François yawned and nodded. 'Aye. You've a baby brother.' François tweaked one of his daughter's short braids. 'Your mother wants to call him François—'

'Papa's François,' Arlette pointed out.

'Mmm.' François gripped his daughter's hand. 'Come on, daughter. You're to attend a service of thanksgiving in the chapel with me. And after that, we'll go and see little François.'

'And Mama?' the little girl asked.

'And Mama.'

François de Roncier was something of a stranger to his daughter, but Arlette knew him well enough to marvel at the way he tiptoed into the bedchamber where Lady Joan lay recovering from her confinement. She had never seen her father tiptoe anywhere. The room was stifling hot, and did not smell comfortably of Arlette's mother. It smelt different; unfamiliar and oppressive. Lady Deneza was warming her hands at the brazier; her mother's faithful wolfhound, Gabriel, banned to the kennels for the duration of Lady Joan's confinement, had resumed

8

his usual place at the foot of the bed. He lifted his great grey head from his paws as they entered.

'Mama!' Arlette rushed to the bed, but she was prevented from climbing up by her father.

'No, Arlette,' François whispered in her ear. 'Your mother needs rest.'

Lady Joan was lying against a bank of pillows, eyes closed. Arlette hardly recognised her. Her mother's face was youthful no longer. She had aged twenty years; her skin looked drawn and fragile. She was pale as a lily. A woman Arlette had not seen before, her brother's wet-nurse, was seated on the other side of her mother's bed, rocking a bundle in her arms.

'Mama?'

Lady Joan opened her eyes and smiled weakly at Arlette. Her hand crept across the bedcovers. Instinctively, Arlette reached for the hand, but her father grasped it first.

Arlette thrust her thumb in her mouth and, sucking hard, looked up at her father. He was regarding Joan with a perplexed expression which had set a deep pleat between the russet brows.

'Deneza—' François voiced his daughter's thoughts — 'she's very washed out . . .'

Lady Deneza's skirts swished across the matting. 'It was a punishing confinement, my Lord. There was much blood lost. Your wife needs rest—'

'I don't remember her looking like this after Arlette was born. Surely it should be easier the second time?'

Lady Deneza nodded. 'That is usually the case, my lord. But that's no guarantee. I'm sure that if she's allowed some rest . . .' Her voice trailed off.

François eyed Lady Deneza keenly. 'You want us out of the way?'

'Aye, my lord. You can show Arlette the babe, but then you must go.'

Taking his daughter by the hand, François grinned down at her. 'See how these women order me about, Arlette?'

'Where's baby?' Arlette asked.

'Here.' François led his daughter round the bed to where the strange woman was seated. At her feet was a wooden crib. The crib had been intended for Lady Joan's baby, but because the infant François was having difficulty feeding, and the Lady Joan had a strong desire that he should be kept near her, the wet-nurse had temporarily placed her own child in the de Roncier crib. Her child was sound asleep.

'You want to see your brother, sweetheart?' the woman asked. One of her front teeth was missing.

Arlette nodded. Tenderly, the woman folded back the woollen shawl and Arlette was given a glimpse of a shock of dark hair, a tiny, squashy face, and a rosebud mouth. The baby's eyes were open, and he whimpered fretfully. Her brother, Arlette realised, was the source of the unfamiliar smell that pervaded the chamber.

'François . . .' Gently, Arlette stroked her brother's cheek. She frowned, perceiving at once that there was something not quite right about her little brother. He seemed to be having difficulty breathing, and there was a blue tinge to his pretty lips, but though Arlette was sensitive enough to see that all was not well, she was too young to be able to express her concern in words.

Afraid her touch might hurt her new brother, Arlette withdrew her hand. She stepped back, catching her foot on the wooden crib. At once, the crib filled with loud, indignant wails. There was nothing wrong with the wet-nurse's child.

'François is sick,' Arlette muttered as she stared, fascinated, at the pink and white fury in the crib. This was what a baby should look and sound like. 'François is sick.'

10

'Nonsense, Arlette. He's just sleepy,' her father answered with a dismissive laugh. 'Come along. We've been given our marching orders.'

Arlette's diagnosis of her brother's condition proved correct.

Her brother was sick. He grew even sicker before the end; but that one, brief glimpse was all Arlette ever had of him, for the infant was not the only invalid. Lady Joan's condition was causing concern, and Arlette was banned from the sickroom.

The infant François clung to life for three days.

After his death, the wet-nurse shouldered her belongings, picked up her own, shockingly healthy child, and came to the nursery to bid adieu to Agata, who was a distant relative of hers.

'A weakling,' she pronounced, sticking her tongue through the gap in her teeth. 'I could see it at once, and I'm sure *she* − ' a thumb discreetly jabbed at Arlette who was sitting on the floor absorbed in unpicking the rushes from the matting − 'knew it too. That child is twice as perceptive as her father. Mind you, my lord was half pickled at the time. Is he often like that?'

Agata grimaced, and glanced at Arlette, before making an extraordinary gesture that was mid-way between a nod and a shake, and could have meant anything. 'Children often know things before we do,' she said.

'That's true.' The wet-nurse sighed, and lowered her voice. 'Shame though, he had the makings of a bonny babe. Her ladyship's distraught. She's ill. Mortal ill—'

'Not mortal ill, surely?' Agata's brown eyes were round as pennies.

'Aye. I've seen it enough times. Her blood's been poisoned. Wouldn't be surprised if she doesn't follow her son, and soon.'

'Sweet Jesus!' Agata crossed herself.

11

Arlette toddled up and clutched at her nurse's skirts. Agata frowned at the wet-nurse. 'Hush, Ella! The child . . .'

Arlette was never to see her mother again, for Lady Joan outlived her son by only a day, dying in the small hours on the feast of St Nicholas.

Lady Joan de Roncier and her son were to be buried together in the family vault, and Countess Marie instructed Agata to keep Arlette in her tower room while the funeral was conducted. As yet the child had no idea that her mother had died.

'I don't want my granddaughter informed of her mother's death until it's over, Agata,' the countess said baldly. 'I don't want any scenes. See she keeps to her room. My son is taking this badly, and it's best his daughter stays out of sight. I can't be doing with a hysterical child.'

Agata gazed blankly at Marie de Roncier's stony features and tried to feel pity for the woman who had — if the rumours were true — reserved all of her affection for a husband who did not truly love her, and had not done so even in her youth. Robert de Roncier had apparently loved Marie's elder sister, the beautiful Izabel Herevi. Count Robert's second choice, Marie had never managed to capture his heart. He had married her out of duty. Over the years Count Robert had come to be fond of his wife, but everyone knew that he had never been able to gift her with the adoration he had felt for her sister.

Bitter disappointment had made Marie de Roncier cold-hearted.

The countess was not an easy woman to like, and with her dark eyes, and proud beak of a nose, she was a daunting figure. Agata would have hesitated to argue with such a woman even if they held the same station in life. Privately Agata thought the most healthy course would

12

have been for father and daughter to learn to comfort each other in their mutual sorrow. But for a nursemaid to disagree with a countess . . . Agata loved her work as Arlette's nurse. She doted on her charge, and was frightened of the consequences if she spoke her mind. She kept her rebellious thoughts concealed.

'Yes, Countess,' Agata agreed meekly.

On the morning of Lady Joan and her son's funeral, Agata duly tried to keep Arlette in the nursery, but Arlette had other ideas. Though Arlette was young, she had a will of iron, and was brimming with life.

'Walk, Agata?' the child asked, catching her hand.

'No, *mignonne*. Your grandmother has told us to stay here this morning.'

Arlette pulled her red-gold brows together in a scowl, and Agata braced herself for a tantrum. Fortunately, these were rare, but Arlette had been known to indulge in one if she thought one would get her her way. If mishandled, Arlette could be a tyrant, a two-year-old tyrant.

'Arlette walk,' the child insisted, going over to the door and trying to reach the latch. But she was two inches too short, and not stupid, and after a moment she realised she could not undo it.

Quickly, Agata scrabbled for her work-bag which was under Arlette's bed. She had made a soft ball from gaily coloured patches of cloth, and she had been saving it for just such a moment. It would distract the child.

Meanwhile, Arlette toddled towards her. The child had banished her scowl, and had replaced it with what Agata recognised was her sunniest, most charming smile.

'Agata do door. Agata open. Please . . .'

'No, *mignonne*. We have to stay here this morning. Look . . .' Drawing out her bag, Agata produced the ball. 'I made you this. Isn't it pretty?'

13

'Pretty,' Arlette agreed, taking the ball from her, her mouth a round 'O' of delight.

'Now, what should you say?'

Bright blue eyes sparkled up at Agata. 'Thank you, Agata.'

Agata's heart twisted. Poor lamb; poor, motherless lamb. 'There's a good girl,' she said. 'Now you stand over there, that's right, and throw the ball to me. Good girl. That's it.'

The de Roncier family vault was situated in especially consecrated ground outside Huelgastel, in the shadow of the castle walls.

While Agata and Arlette played ball in the restricted space of the round tower room, the noises of the funeral train assembling in the bailey floated through the window. With one half of her mind on the game she was playing, Agata found the other half was straining to interpret the various sounds. That tramping would be the castle guard as they assembled to pay Lady Joan and her dead son their last respects. And that low rumbling sound must be the waggon upon which the bier would be placed. That clattering must be the hooves of Lady Joan's last escort. Poor lady. Poor Arlette.

Carefully, Agata threw the dead noblewoman's daughter the soft, coloured ball. Arlette failed to catch it, and scuttled the few yards to the wall to retrieve her toy. She threw the ball back to Agata, but the child's aim was as poor as her catching, and the ball sailed on to the bed.

All at once, for no reason that Agata could see, the child lost interest in the game.

'Want Mama,' Arlette said, very firmly. She came to stand in front of her nurse, looking very small and very vulnerable; nothing but huge blue eyes and disordered red hair. 'Want Mama.'

Agata swallowed, and thought rapidly. She had not forgotten Countess Marie's strict instructions that her granddaughter should not be told of her mother's death till after the funeral. And who did the countess intend would tell the child? Her father? Agata did not think so. Ever since Lady Joan's death François de Roncier had been drowning his sorrows in a sea of wine. The way he was carrying on, it did not seem likely that he would come to his senses for at least a week.

The countess, then. She must have decided to break the news to Arlette herself. Inwardly, Agata's kind heart shied away from that thought. Countess Marie de Roncier may be a strong woman, an ideal albeit unloved mate for Count Robert, but she stifled her own feelings and had no time for emotions in others. The countess was impatient, and not good with children. Agata did not like to think of her being the one to tell young Arlette.

Going down on her haunches so as to be at Arlette's level, Agata stroked back the unruly curls with a loving hand, and took a deep breath. It would have to be her. And it would have to be now. The funeral was not over, but the countess would never know that Agata had broken the news too soon.

Down in the bailey, the iron-bound waggon wheels ground to a halt. The pall-bearers would be loading Lady Joan's coffin . . .

'You can't see Mama,' Agata said.

'Why?'

'She . . . she's dead, *mignonne*. That's why.'

'Dead?'

Arlette had never encountered death, she had no idea what it was. Agata struggled to find words that the child could understand.

'Your mama has gone to sleep. She's resting. We can't see her.'

The red-gold brows drew together. 'She'll wake. Soon.'

'No, *mignonne*.' Agata took the child by the hands, and met the confused blue gaze directly. 'She won't waken.'

15

'Never?'

'Never.'

'No! I want her. Want Mama . . .'

The plaintive cry tugged Agata's heartstrings. It would surely have been easier for Arlette to come to terms with Lady Joan's death if she had been taken to see her mother's body, if she had seen for herself that her mother was not going to wake up.

'Arlette want to see Mama,' the child insisted.

'No, *mignonne*. It's not possible. She's dead.'

'Want to see. Want to see.'

There was a hunger in Arlette's wide blue eyes, an irresistible hunger. Outside, in the bailey, the waggon wheels were rumbling, heading for the drawbridge and the hallowed ground. Agata sighed, and came to a decision. She was going to disobey the countess. She stood up.

'I'll show you where your Mama is, if you promise to be quiet as a mouse.'

The red head nodded. The short braids bounced, and trustingly the child held out her arms.

With Arlette clinging like a leech, Agata climbed the stairs at breakneck pace. She wanted to reach the roof before the funeral train had gone out of sight. She would take Arlette to the vault later, but if the child saw the coffin, and the sad, ceremonial procession, it might help her understand.

They reached the top as the cart rolled on to the drawbridge. Heart pounding with the strain, Agata sat Arlette in a machicolation, held her fast with one hand, and pointed while she caught her breath. She didn't have to say anything. Those wide, tragic blue eyes went straight to the black-draped bier.

Father Josse, the tall young castle priest, set the pace, walking slowly on foot in front of the waggon. Arlette's father rode bareheaded behind his wife's coffin, slumped on his great charger, but holding the beast in check with

16

the easy familiarity of one brought up in the saddle. Even at this distance Agata could see that François de Roncier's ruddy face was blurred with grief. Lady Joan's shaggy wolfhound, Gabriel, paced alongside the count's two powerful mastiffs, tail down.

'Papa crying,' Arlette observed.

And so he was, openly, unashamedly. It was not uncommon for men to display their emotions, but nonetheless Agata felt a little shock of surprise. François de Roncier was the son of a count, and she had thought him to be out of reach of the great emotions that wreaked havoc in ordinary people's lives. Had François de Roncier loved his wife? she wondered. Like all Huelgastel's servants, Agata knew that François had married Lady Joan for the large dowry she had brought him. Not once had she seen them make a public show of affection. Everyone had assumed that their marriage was in every way a duty marriage. All bluff and bluster, Agata had never considered François de Roncier to be capable of feeling much for anyone save his haughty, domineering mother. She thought it more likely that he was mourning the loss of his son, the loss of his heir, but perhaps she misjudged him.

A stiff breeze was blowing across the parapet. Glancing with fond concern at the red head leaning through the machicolations, it occurred to Agata that perhaps everyone, even noblemen, could come to feel affection for those with whom they were in close contact.

The count and countess rode behind their son. Not for them the casual slump in their ornate horned saddles. They sat straight-backed and proud. If the count and countess felt any grief for their dead daughter-in-law and grandson, they were not parading it.

'Mama?' Arlette said, uncertainly, eyes going back to the bier.

Agata had a lump in her throat the size of a gull's egg. 'Yes, *mignonne*,' she said. 'Your mama's coffin is on the waggon. Your mama will sleep in that.'

'For ever?' A red curl lifted in the breeze.

'For ever.'

'Where's Mama going?'

'When people die in your family, they go to sleep in the vault. Your papa is taking your mama to the vault.'

'Vault,' Arlette said, trying the new word out on her tongue. 'Vault.'

'Yes, *mignonne*. You can't go inside, but I can show you where it is, later.'

Arlette turned back to watch the funeral procession. 'Baby François dead,' she announced. 'With Mama?'

'Yes.' Agata swallowed. 'He's with your mama.'

The child looked at her weeping father. 'Papa sad.'

'He has you, *mignonne*. He's a lucky man.'

Arlette smiled doubtfully, and held out her arms. Her nose had gone red in the cold December air.

'You want to go inside?'

The child nodded. Her smile grew. 'Wait for Papa. I'll love him better.'

'There's my girl,' Agata said, inwardly marvelling at the child's calm. It was unnatural, and she feared that Arlette had not taken her mother's death in at all.

Agata was wrong. Arlette *had* taken her mother's death in. Inside she was howling with all the force of her passionate nature. The moment her eyes had lit on the long box with its ugly black shroud, Arlette had known that her life had changed irrevocably.

Up until that cold December morning, Arlette had known only love and security. Lady Joan had ensured that her daughter had known her place in the world. The loss of her mother was a blow almost too great to contemplate, but the instinct for survival was strong in Arlette, and that instinct enabled her to contain her grief.

Put simply, the child had lost one anchor, and knew she must find another.

18

Where better to start than with her father?

That afternoon, Arlette was permitted to leave the nursery in search of a warm cup of milk and honey. With her grief suppressed, and full of pent-up energy, Arlette charged through the cavernous hall, the faithful Agata panting in her wake. The little girl shot through the studded oak doors and into the bailey. So eager was she for a taste of fresh air, that she failed to notice her father, hunched over a pottery wine-cup at the family table which was permanently set up on a high dais in front of a vast, roaring fire.

Outside, in the inner bailey, which was unusually quiet and deserted, the wintry light was failing, and one or two of the wall torches had been lit. Rooks, returning late to their leafless roosts, flapped clumsily across a cold, dull, pewter sky. Beyond the confines of the castle walls, a dog was howling, sounding like a wolf in pain.

The dairy, scarcely more than a shack leaning against the curtain wall, was situated in the outer bailey. Arlette dashed through the arch in the inner wall, and headed straight for it.

A quarter of an hour later, with her stomach full of comforting milk, and a white ring of it around her mouth, Arlette allowed Agata to shepherd her into the hall.

'Hold still, *mignonne*,' Agata steered her charge under a wall-sconce in order to wipe the milk from her mouth. 'There. That's better, isn't it?'

The child didn't respond. Her eyes were on her father sitting at the high table. One upturned wine-jug lay at François de Roncier's elbow, and a brimming one stood before him. His black mastiffs, never far away, were dozing before the fire. There was no sign of Gabriel. Arlette's father had been drinking heavily ever since the funeral party had returned. The count and countess were not with their son; he was the only member of his family

19

who chose to drown his sorrows.

The bright flames crackled in the hearth behind him. Lights flickered in iron wall-sconces. Along the white-washed walls was ranged a display of ancient spears and pikes, the centre-piece being a pair of straight shining Saracenic swords heavily inlaid with gold and silver — these last being booty brought back from a crusade in Palestine by one of Arlette's forebears. Rushes covered the granite flagged floor.

The child gazed across the massive hall at the dejected figure of her father. Suddenly she felt impelled to close the gap and ran, straight as an arrow, across the rushes. 'Papa!'

The copper head lifted, and red-rimmed, bleary hazel eyes blinked at her. 'If it isn't my little heiress,' François said. His tone was not pleasant. 'Why couldn't you have been an heir, eh? Why couldn't you have been a boy?'

'Papa? Papa sad?' Arlette laid a hand on her father's sleeve, and her blue eyes fastened on the haggard face in a look of silent appeal and sympathy that would have melted the heart of the devil himself. This man was her father and more than ever she needed his love.

François frowned down at the diminutive hand; but made no move either to accept or reject his daughter's gesture. The hand stayed where it was.

'Papa's sad,' he acknowledged, slightly slurring his words. Reaching for the upright jug, François replenished his cup. He emptied it in one draught, and poured again, not very accurately. Some wine splashed on his daughter's face. She wiped it away, and continued to stare soulfully at her father. 'Papa is *very* sad.'

'Arlette sad too,' his daughter said.

Agata, who had drawn nearer to her charge, hovered uncertainly behind François' high-backed throne of a chair. She did not like de Roncier's expression, but hesitated to intervene. Father and daughter should be able to comfort each other.

Glancing at her father's hounds, Arlette asked, 'Where's Gabriel, Papa?'

'By the vault, howling. Brute won't budge,' François said, tossing back another cupful of wine. Dropping an elbow on to the table, he leaned wearily on his hand. From under heavy, drink-laden lids he studied his daughter's face. 'You don't look much like your mother, thank God,' he decided, frowning as though he were having difficulty focusing. 'You won't remind me of her, at least. True, your nose has her shape, and there's something about the contours of your face, but you've got to search to find the resemblance . . .' Straightening, François groped for the wine-jug, and missed.

'Allow me, my lord.' Agata poured the wine. She was well aware that de Roncier had already swallowed several more quarts of his favourite Gascon wine than was wise, but it was not her place to stop him. He looked to be in a dangerous mood. He would only listen to his parents. It occurred to Agata that she could fetch his mother, Countess Marie. She would put a stop to this.

So, when François' cup was full, Agata bobbed him a swift curtsey, and headed for the solar stairs. It would only take her a moment to find the countess, and Arlette would be safe with her father.

'Why couldn't you have been a boy?' François said, unaware the nurse had left, and becoming more bitter and aggressive with every mouthful. He drained his cup again and, wiping his mouth with the back of his hand, raised his voice. 'Why?'

Arlette's huge eyes began to fill with tears.

An expression of disgust and irritation flashed across her father's face. Removing Arlette's hand from his sleeve, he flung it aside.

'Oh, Jesus. That's right. Start snivelling, like the blubbering girl you are.' It was a matter of hours since François himself had wept openly over his wife's bier, but

21

this fact conveniently slipped his mind. 'I wanted a son.' Maddened by shock, and grief, and too much wine, François was working himself into a royal rage. He found it easier to be enraged than to stop and acknowledge the pain twisting inside him. 'I wanted an heir to continue the family line. And what am I left with? A cry-baby. A useless, stupid cry-baby girl. Why couldn't you have been a boy, damn you?'

His question was punctuated by a mournful howl from Gabriel outside.

Supporting himself with his hands on the table, François hauled himself to his feet. By the fire, the mastiffs lifted their heads from their paws and growled softly.

'It's your fault your mother's dead!' François shouted. He felt better when he shouted. It hurt less, and once started he couldn't seem to stop. 'Your fault!' He jabbed his forefinger at Arlette's small chest to punctuate his words. 'If you'd been a boy this need never have happened. Christ! I can't bear to look at you a moment longer.'

And, pushing past his stunned child, François de Roncier called for his dogs and stormed down the hall and into the bailey where, beside himself with both anger and anguish, he commanded a startled groom to saddle up his destrier. He leapt on to its back, and was soon thundering across the drawbridge and into the deepening twilight. His dogs loped after him. The nearby port of Vannes boasted a multitude of anonymous hostelries — there were plenty of places where he could lose himself and his sorrows.

When the countess swept into the hall with Agata, she found Arlette standing dejectedly by her father's chair, staring down at her kid shoes.

'Where's Papa?' Countess Marie asked, voice sharp as a needle. Her black eyes took in the empty wine-jugs, made note of the spills on the table, missed nothing but

22

her granddaughter's deep distress.

Arlette lifted her head. 'My fault,' she murmured.

The countess tutted. 'Come along child, speak up. Where's your father?'

Arlette gave a tiny shudder and pointed at the double doors. 'Gone.' The fiery head dropped, and the child resumed her contemplation of her shoes. 'Quite gone.'

Gabriel did not quieten, and would not shift from his mournful watch over the family vault, even though the countess ordered one of the grooms to try and bribe him with fresh meat. The noise was driving everyone mad.

Eventually, Agata remembered the dog had a fondness for Arlette. The child was taken outside. She regarded the cold stone tomb with hollow eyes, shuddered, and called her mother's dog by name. The dreadful howling stopped. Reluctantly, Gabriel allowed the child to lure him away. He trotted with Arlette and Agata to the nursery.

Once there, Agata did her best to undo the damage she suspected François had done.

'What did your Papa say, *mignonne*?'

Arlette sat on the rush matting, quivering with emotion. When Gabriel came to sit beside her, she wrapped her arms around him and hid her face in the rough fur. 'He wants a boy,' she murmured. 'My fault.'

'Your fault? What's your fault?'

'Mama's dead. My fault.'

Agata shook her head, and stroked the child's hair. 'No. No. Your Papa didn't mean it. He grieves. He loves you just as you are, I'm sure.'

But Arlette's blue eyes were unresponsive. Agata could see that the child did not believe her. What had de Roncier said to her? She knew she would probably never find out, but she could see that Arlette had been left with the impression that she was to blame for her mother's death. It was a heavy burden to put on a child.

23

'Listen, *mignonne*,' Agata spoke firmly. 'Your mother died, but it was not your fault. Do you hear me?'

The blue eyes remained blank.

'It's not your fault.'

'I want to be a boy.'

Agata frowned. '*Mignonne*, that's impossible—'

'I'm a boy. Papa wants a boy.'

'Your papa can remarry. Then he can have a boy. You're his little girl.'

'He wants a boy.' The child pointed at her own chest, staring up with painful determination at her nursemaid. 'I'm his boy,' she said again.

Chapter Two

In the round tower room where Arlette continued to share a bed with the faithful Agata, excitement had wakened the child. At her side, Agata snored gently. Arlette yawned, and did not rise at once: dawn was not yet even a faint glow behind the narrow window-slits set high in the wall. The child had turned seven, and since her mother's death she had been waging a ceaseless, and to date unsuccessful, campaign to win her father's favour and interest. She still felt the loss of her mother as a scar on her brain.

After Arlette's mother had died, her father had mourned her for two years. Then he had remarried.

His bride, an other-worldly French noblewoman, Eleanor d'Etoile, had reached seventeen; without even trying, she had won most of François de Roncier's attention. But for some weeks of late, a sudden interest in matters of estate had kindled in François' heart, and he had taken to beating the bounds of the family domain with Count Robert. The reason for this was plain. Arlette's step-mother was easily old enough to provide her father with the male heir that he craved, and François was learning all he could about the county that he would one day pass on to his son.

Knowing that she was not likely to see her father till the end of the week, Arlette was determined to use these few days to achieve a secret aim. She didn't want to waste a

25

moment. This time, when she showed her father her latest accomplishment, she was certain he would be bowled over by her achievement.

She had not quite perfected her new skill. But today, with the help of her young friends, Jehan and Aubrey, she would. By the time François de Roncier returned, he would be astounded to find that not only had his seven-year-old daughter mastered the art of riding bareback; but he would also be given a fine display of horsemanship. Arlette was learning to stand on her pony's back, and she could almost complete three whole circuits standing, with Jehan holding the leading rein. Almost. Today she would succeed.

This time, her father could not fail to be impressed. Why, not all of the mercenary horse-soldiers her grandfather employed could ride their horses standing on their backs! Not only would François be forced to admire his daughter's skill, but, more importantly, he would be proud of her. Arlette was determined to make her father proud of her, if it was the last thing she did.

Moving as surreptitiously as she could, Arlette edged out from under the down quilt. No sooner had her toes touched the matting than Gabriel's wet nose pushed into her palm. Gabriel, while not a young dog at the time of his mistress's death, had attached himself to Arlette. The two were inseparable.

Gabriel whimpered, and Arlette could hear his tail thump-thump against the floor. This was not the first jaunt that Arlette had undertaken before the rest of the household stirred, and the dog knew that if his little mistress was rising early, something unusual and interesting was afoot. Gabriel could sense Arlette's excitement.

Arlette groped for Gabriel's muzzle — it was black as pitch in her room, and put both hands round the animal's jaw. 'Hush, Gabriel.'

26

Agata snored on.

Tiptoeing across the matting, Arlette felt her way to the door, bent to scoop up the bundle of clothes and food she had left ready the night before, and lifted the latch. Apart from Agata's snoring and Gabriel's snuffling, all was quiet.

On the stairwell outside, Arlette stopped to dress in the unsteady light of a dying flambeau. Without her mother's loving hand to guide her, Arlette had run wild, and no one apart from her nurse Agata had ever made the slightest attempt to bring her to heel.

Most of the time Arlette dressed as a boy, and today was no exception. She dragged on a pair of simple brown breeches, which tied at the waist, and tucked in the crumpled cream linen chainse, or shirt, which she had slept in. This was her normal summer attire. In the winter she would fling a short woollen tunic over her shirt, and never failed to grin when she was − as was often the case − mistaken for a boy by strangers visiting Huelgastel.

Should the occasion merit it, Arlette had been known to agree to making a half-hearted concession to her femininity by donning a longer girl's tunic over her chainse and breeches. She had a long leather belt with silver tips at the ends which had once belonged to her mother, and when she belted in her long tunic with this, the silver tips almost reached the floor.

The one other concession Arlette made to her sex was her copper-coloured hair. Thick and shining, she was growing it to please Agata, who had set views about girls and hair. Arlette's hair reached down below her shoulders, and grew like a weed. It was wavy when loose, but Arlette usually caught it back with a leather thong, and wore it hanging down her back like her pony's tail, much to Agata's disgust. Agata might give in as far as Arlette's clothing was concerned − after all the child was young − but the matter of her hair was a constant bone of

27

contention between them. Every morning Arlette would submit to the ritual plaiting, and Agata would give rein to her dormant artistic nature by intertwining silken ribbons with the bright tresses, as the nurse deemed seemly for Count de Roncier's granddaughter. And every morning, Arlette would skip off and, as soon as Agata's back was turned, the plait would be unwound, the ribbons lost, and the leather thong and the pony's tail would replace Agata's delicate arrangement.

Arlette looked more like a pedlar's child than a count's granddaughter. She had never yet worn a veil.

She thrust her feet into her short kid boots, and laced up the sides. Picking up the cloak in which she had wrapped the food, she made her way down the curling stairs, with Gabriel padding softly at her side.

Outside, Arlette put her hand on Gabriel's collar, and paused at the top of the hall steps to take stock of the shadowy, pre-dawn courtyard. She did not want to be spotted by the castle guard.

The morning star rested on the edge of the curtain wall. A light glowed in the cookhouse, and the smell of fresh-baked bread made her nose twitch and her mouth water. Unconsciously, the child sighed. There was nothing she loved more than to break her fast with a chunk of wholesome bread, still warm and steaming from being in Martha's brick oven, with a generous dollop of golden butter melting into it. But if today's expedition was to remain secret, Arlette and her co-conspirators would have to make do with yesterday's bread.

A sentry tramped along the guard's walkway. Was his helmeted head turned to the outside world? It was too dark to see. Jehan had assured Arlette the men were not trained to watch the inner bailey, they were on the watch for trouble from without but, just to be sure, she waited till the man's perambulation took him out of her line of vision around the side of the tower, and then she scurried

28

across the yard, the faithful Gabriel at her heels.

Jehan and Aubrey — Sir Hamon and Lady Deneza's sons, and Arlette's two best friends — were waiting for her in the stables. Jehan le Moine was twelve, a slender lad in a green tunic with shining dark eyes and a mop of unruly black hair. A clever boy, Jehan had taken care to win a reputation for being responsible. He had a secure place in the castle guard. His brother Aubrey was nine. Skinnier even than his brother, Aubrey had light brown eyes and straight, fine hair. His tunic and trousers were black. He helped out in the stables. The friendship had sprung up between Arlette and the seneschal's boys quite naturally, and as Jehan was known to be sensible, and the two boys came from knightly stock, no-one objected to Arlette spending hours in their company, particularly if it saved someone else the task of minding her. Within the castle, the two boys were nearest to Arlette's age. She thought of them as her brothers.

'Did you remember the bread?' Jehan demanded when she stepped into the stalls.

Arlette waved yesterday's wheat loaf, sadly cold, under Jehan's nose. 'Of course I did! And I've apples, and a great wedge of cheese! You're not the only one who gets hungry. Have you a plan?'

The children needed a plan to sneak Arlette out of Huelgastel, for though Count Robert's granddaughter was allowed outside the confines of the castle when taking riding lessons with Jehan or a groom, her leaving the bailey at this hour would not be countenanced. And because Arlette wanted to surprise her father with her new achievements, she did not want anyone apart from Jehan and Aubrey to be in on her secret lessons.

'Yes, I've a plan, but it will entail you keeping still for at least a quarter of an hour.' Jehan's dark eyes twinkled. 'Do you think you can manage that?'

'Watch me. What do I have to do?'

29

Ten minutes later, when the morning star was fading and the sky brightening, Job, the gatekeeper whose turn on guard was almost over, stood outside the gatehouse, blinking at an extraordinary sight.

Jehan le Moine had the Little Lady's pony, Honey, on a leading rein — despite her unladylike qualities, Count Robert's vassals referred to Arlette as the Little Lady in order to distinguish between her and the Lady Eleanor. Honey was dragging a small litter piled untidily with sacking, and lounging like a lord on the litter was the Little Lady's grizzled wolfhound. Jehan's brother Aubrey walked alongside the litter.

'What are you lads up to?' Job inquired, lazily picking his nose.

'We're to fetch Mother some herbs and medicines from the apothecary's in Vannes,' Jehan said. 'Honey can carry them for us, and Gabriel needs the exercise.'

Job laughed. 'You'd do better to take a packhorse than that litter. And that hound won't get much exercise that way.'

'He will, later. It's a game.' Jehan said.

'Does the Lady Arlette know you've got her pets?'

Young Aubrey made a choking sound in his throat, and his cheeks went as bright as a cockerel's comb.

'She knows,' Jehan said, glowering at his brother. 'We have her blessing.'

Wiping his hand on his breeches, Job waved them on. 'You'd best be off if you intend to walk to Vannes and back. It's five miles if it's a mile, and with Aubrey's short legs the walk alone will take you the best part of the day.'

'We like walking,' Jehan told the guard, grinning. 'Don't fret. We'll be back before dark.'

'Crazy,' Job pronounced, indulgently. And he smiled, glad to see that the seneschal's so-sensible eldest son had his moments of madness. The two boys led Honey across the drawbridge, and Job kept his eyes on the peculiar procession till it had straggled down the hill and reached the forest and the Vannes road. It would take them a month if they went on at that rate, he thought. At the bottom of the hill the Little Lady's hound jumped off the litter and loped into the trees. A moment more, and both boys and litter were screened by the forest. 'Crazy,' Job repeated. And he went back into the gatehouse, where he intended to sit down and rest his throbbing feet until his replacement appeared.

Half a mile on, the Vannes road wound through a heavily wooded area which stretched a little way south and a long way north. A narrow trackway led from the road to an enclosed clearing; a clandestine, little-frequented spot, the clearing was the ideal place to put the polish on Arlette's riding technique.

'We're here. You can come out now,' Jehan said.

A tousled red head emerged from under the sacking. Arlette's face was as bright as her hair. 'That's a mercy!' she gasped. 'I was suffocating under there! Have you got the lunge rein?'

'It should be under the sacks,' Jehan said.

Aubrey began unbuckling the litter from Honey's harness, and shortly afterwards, Arlette's lesson began. It had been agreed that Jehan was in charge but, not to be outdone, Aubrey shinned up a nearby oak and oversaw the proceedings from a large branch. From this perch he alternately called out encouragements and criticisms. He rather resembled an oversized crow in his black breeches and tunic.

'Right,' Jehan said, adopting workmanlike tones. 'Keep your back straight. No, not like that—'

'No, *no*!' Aubrey interrupted from his tree. 'Ease up on the reins, Arlette. You're using poor Honey's mouth to keep your balance. Think how your pony must feel.'

31

There was a pause while Arlette attempted to comply with both her instructors.

'That's better,' Aubrey approved, his voice floating down into the clearing. 'Much better.'

'Thank you, Aubrey.' Jehan took over once more. 'Remember what you learnt last time, Arlette. Tighten your knees. That's it. Heels down. And watch your hands!'

Trusting in Jehan's competence — he was after all the son of a knight who, though aged now, had the reputation of having been a horseman to rival her grandfather — Arlette put herself completely in Jehan's hands. She kept her back straight and her heels down, and when Honey's harsh coat began to chafe the flesh of her thighs through her breeches, she bit her lips and never complained. When she fell off, which she did from time to time, she rubbed her bruises and hauled herself back on to Honey's back without a murmur.

By mid-afternoon she was exhausted.

'One more time standing up,' Jehan insisted, with the quiet ruthlessness of someone who would always achieve what he set out to do in life. 'Then you'll be sure of it.'

'You're a slave-driver,' Arlette groaned, tired, but triumphant, because she had achieved her target. She could ride Honey bareback, and with the pony on the long lunge rein had managed to stand and complete the three circuits.

She held Honey still while Jehan checked the buckle of the leading rein.

'Off you go,' Jehan said.

Arlette kicked Honey to a walk, put the reins in her mouth, and carefully brought her feet up. Then in one deft, practised movement, she stood upright, arms outstretched for balance.

Honey walked steadily on. One circuit. Two. Three. Four! *Four*. Aubrey swung down from his tree, and silently applauded her.

32

Having exceeded her aims, Arlette felt justified in dropping into a sitting position.

Aubrey pounced immediately. 'Not like that! You'll give Honey backache, flopping down like a sack of meal.'

Aubrey always thought of everything from the animals' point of view. Animals were less complex than human beings; the boy found them easier to understand.

Arlette dismounted and went to Honey's head. 'I'm sorry if I hurt you,' she said, petting the pony. 'But I did it!' She smiled at her friends. 'Thank you, both of you, for your help. Now I've really got something to show Father when he gets back!'

Two evenings later, Jehan was on duty on the curtain wall when he spotted Count Robert, his son, and their escort at the bottom of the hill, coming towards the castle.

Putting his forefinger and thumb to his lips, he blew a piercing whistle; at this pre-arranged signal, Aubrey, who had been mucking out some of the stalls, emerged from the stables which leaned up against the outer walls. Fork in hand, Aubrey craned his neck to look up to his brother above him on the walkway.

'You can see them? They're back?' Aubrey asked.

Jehan nodded. 'Tell Arlette. She'll be in the solar, most likely. She wants to be ready the moment they ride in.'

Aubrey sped across the yard and dived into the hall.

François rode through the gaping mouth of Huelgastel portcullis at Count Robert's right hand. François had never been able to tolerate much sun, and after several days in the saddle, despite wearing a wide-brimmed blue felt hat, his pale skin was burned to an angry red. He removed his hat and, wiping the sweat from his brow with his sleeve, eased his shoulders. He was sticky all over, his throat was full of grit, and he was covered with dust.

For the past four miles he had been looking forward to

seeing his young wife, Eleanor. There was nothing like a tour of the lands that would one day be his to remind a man of his duties. One day, François would be able to show his son their lands, in the same way that his father had shown them to him.

When he had refreshed himself – he might even bathe – François was looking forward to setting about getting Eleanor with child. So far Eleanor's responses to François' advances left something to be desired. It was not that she had ever rejected him. Eleanor was a lady. A dutiful wife, she knew her role. One day, God willing, Eleanor would be his countess, and this title was to be her reward for providing the de Roncier family with a male heir. François had a daughter, but a daughter was not good enough. François must have a son, and Eleanor had been selected from among the cream of the French nobility to be that son's mother.

No, Eleanor knew better than to reject François. But she had never encouraged him either. She never made it easy for him. François wished that Eleanor could occasionally try to forget she was a lady for an hour or so . . . Joan had managed it. So why not Eleanor?

He and Eleanor had been married for three years, and so far she had not got the trick of it. In the great canopied bed that François had once shared with Joan, Eleanor would smile her vague, dreamy smile, and she would lie back and spread her legs, and permit him to do whatever he wanted. But never, not once, had she shown François any warmth. She never encouraged him, never initiated anything. To date, François had not pushed Eleanor for a response. After all, she had been young when they married, only fourteen, and he had hoped that when she was fully grown, she would be able to respond to him. But Eleanor was seventeen now. Old enough. It was time she got the trick of it, like Joan.

There were times, dreadful times, when François would

remember Joan. He tried not to, but he could not help himself. His lovely, earthy Joan had had a passionate nature which had been most unsuitable in a future countess, as François' mother had never tired of telling him. But François had not cared. He had loved Joan. And he had married her despite his mother's objections.

Riding into the bailey that evening, François tossed his reins to a groom and dismounted. He glanced through the arch to look at the hall entrance, hoping to see Eleanor waiting for him on the top steps. She was not there, but his daughter, dressed like a street urchin, was running towards him.

'A moment, Olier,' François said. 'I must get something from my saddlebag.'

While François rummaged in his pack for the expensive gift he had bought his young wife in the hope that it would encourage her to view him in a warmer light, Count Robert heaved himself out of the saddle.

'Jesu, I'm not the man I was,' the count complained, shaking his legs and briskly rubbing his thighs. He removed his hat and ran his hand through a fine head of silver hair. The count's hair had once been as dark as night, but the only trace of this remained in the black brows which arched over a pair of piercing blue eyes.

François drew out his gift, which was safely wrapped in a piece of unbleached linen. It was a silver trinket box with a lock and a solid gold key. François had had the de Roncier coat of arms — a cinquefoil in a circlet of black thorns — engraved upon the lid. The box was lined with purple velvet. Its key was most intriguing, being a rose gold ring which François guessed would fit the middle finger of Eleanor's hand. The key could only be used when removed. The box and its key had cost François a fortune in deniers, but he considered it a small price to pay if it encouraged Eleanor to respond to him a little; perhaps then he would be able to shed the burden of grief that had weighed him down ever since Joan had died.

'Papa! Papa!' Arlette clamoured for his attention as she led her pony, Honey, to the mounting-block by the stable door.

The seneschal's youngest, Aubrey, who enjoyed playing at being a groom, was mucking out one of the stables, forking soiled straw into a cart for removal from the bailey.

Silver box safely in hand, François wiped his clammy brow. 'Daughter?' Disdaining the mounting-block, Arlette jumped astride her pony. Her cheeks were flushed, her blue eyes sparkled and her nose looked more like Joan's than ever. His stomach twisted. François looked away, back through the arch. No Eleanor.

'Watch me, Papa! Watch what I can do!'

Aubrey dropped his fork and clipped a leading rein to his daughter's pony. Clearly, Arlette had some new foolery to show him.

'May we, my lord?' Hamon's boy looked to François for permission to proceed.

Absently, François nodded. Where *was* Eleanor? He wanted to see her face when she unwrapped her gift. He decided it would be wasted if he gave it to her immediately. He would wait until he had bathed and eaten. He would wait until they were in bed.

'My lord?' Aubrey drew his attention back to his daughter.

'Get on with it.'

Count Robert came to stand by his son. 'She has the makings of a good horsewoman, François,' he said, smiling indulgently as he watched Arlette. 'She's got to grips with riding bareback while we've been away.'

'Mmm?' The hall doorway remained empty.

Count Robert tapped his son on his shoulder. 'What are you looking over there for, François? Look at your girl, for God's sake. By Christ, she's climbing to her feet! She

36

can ride, can my little granddaughter. Now there's a chip off the old block, eh?'

'Not bad,' François acknowledged with a yawn. He noticed that his daughter's shirt was torn. It had a grass stain on the back of it, and her boots were dull with dust. He would have to have a word with old Agata. Joan had liked the woman — Agata had been her choice for Arlette's nursemaid — but Agata was obviously not strong enough to be in charge of his daughter. Either Agata was slacking, or else she was getting too old. She should not let Arlette run so wild. How old was his girl now? Seven or so. It was time something was done about her appearance and her behaviour. Both were a disgrace.

Just then there was a stir in the hall doorway, and at last Eleanor was standing on the top step, waiting to greet him. A slender wand of a girl, Eleanor was a cool and immaculate figure in a cream pleated linen bliaud and ivory tunic. Her belt bore a silver buckle, and her fine fair hair and slim neck were concealed beneath a spotless white wimple and drifting muslin veil. His snow queen. His beautiful snow queen.

Involuntarily, François took a step towards the inner bailey.

'Look, Papa! Look at me!'

Reluctantly, François tore his gaze from his wife and regarded his daughter. She was standing upright on her pony's back, and her springy red hair leapt free of its ribbon so the riotous curls flew like bright flames about her face. It exhausted him to look at her.

Honey was walking in steady circles round Hamon's youngest, like a mule turning a mill-wheel. Arlette craned her head to catch his eyes.

'Look, Papa! Look what I can do!'

Behind him, a boy's voice offered advice from the guard's walkway which ran the length of the curtain wall.

'Steady, Arlette. Remember, take it gently, or you'll lose your balance . . .'

It was Jehan who had spoken. He crouched on his haunches, spear in hand, at the edge of the wooden platform, apparently intent on Arlette's progress. Surmising that by rights the boy should be standing guard above the gatehouse, François threw him a dark glance. Jehan flushed and withdrew to his post.

Turning back to his daughter, still precariously balanced on her pony, François saw out of the corner of his eye that Eleanor had crossed the inner bailey and was standing under the arch of the bailey wall absorbing the scene.

Her pale blue eyes met his, and she gave him one of her subtle smiles. 'Welcome home, my lord,' she said.

François moved towards her.

'Papa! *Papa!*'

At that moment Arlette's pony caught a hoof on a sun-dried rut and wrong-footed. Arlette screeched like a jay and went flying through the air. She landed softly; half in, half out of Aubrey's muck cart. She sat up, straw and manure entangled with her hair, and cheeks as bright as the breast of a robin. She looked at François and burst into tears.

Aubrey dropped Honey's leading rein and ran towards her, but François held out his arm to his wife who, after a momentary hesitation, threaded her hand through it. They began walking towards the hall.

'I never know what Arlette will do next,' Eleanor said in her soft voice.

'No, she's becoming a problem. I think it's time someone took her in hand. Just look at her: hair all over the place; clothes torn and dirty, and all but falling off her. She's outgrown Agata—'

'They're very fond of each other, my lord,' Eleanor commented.

'Fond? Pah! I think I'll have a word with Mother.'

'I'll help, if I can.'

'You would?'

'Assuredly, my lord. Your daughter is my daughter now, isn't she?'

François smiled.

In the outer bailey, Count Robert strode up to his granddaughter and plucked her, sobbing, from the cart. 'Come along, my girl, this won't do.'

'But I can do it, Grandpapa, really I can,' Arlette scrubbed her eyes with a frayed sleeve. 'Why didn't Father wait to see?'

'I'll watch you,' the count said, and leaned against the mounting-block. 'Try again, and if you manage it, I've something for you.'

Arlette sniffed, and gave her grandfather a watery smile. 'What? What have you got me? Let me guess. Spanish almonds? The sweet ones?'

The count patted his scrip, and his blue eyes crinkled up at the corners. 'Wait and see. When you've done a couple more circuits, you'll find out.'

Arlette went to her pony and clambered up. 'You know something, Grandfather?'

'Mmm?'

'Sometimes I think Papa will never love me.'

The count straightened. 'What? That's nonsense.'

'I feel as if I'm trying to hold on to a shadow.'

The count snorted. 'Hold on to a shadow? What fairy tale have you been listening to? You can't hold shadows.'

'Exactly,' Arlette muttered. She gripped Honey's reins, and climbed to her feet, and completed two circuits without mishap.

Face aglow with triumph, Arlette slid from Honey's back. 'There! You saw it, didn't you?'

Count Robert tweaked a hectic curl. 'I saw it. And here's your reward. I know you love them.'

He handed her a small box which contained a pound of the coveted Spanish almonds.

'Honeyed almonds! Thank you, Grandpapa!'

'You did well, girl.' He straightened. 'Now I regret, but I must leave you.'

'You want to see Sir Hamon?'

Arlette knew that whenever her grandfather left Huelgastel, he delegated all the administration and justice to his seneschal and friend, Sir Hamon le Moine. On his return, it was his habit to speak to Sir Hamon and catch up with events before he did anything else.

'Aye.'

'I saw him go into the armoury.'

'My thanks. Keep practising, child, you're doing well.'

And with that, Count Robert stamped his feet to get the circulation going, and stumped off to the armoury. 'Hamon! *Hamon!*'

That evening the de Roncier family ate, as usual, at the high table, backs to the huge fireplace, facing a vast, noisy array of retainers, servants, soldiers and mercenaries who jostled shoulders on the benches alongside the trestle tables which were dragged from the walls and put up at mealtimes. Being June the fire was low. It smoked, and a regular stream of misty grey clouds floated up to the rafters.

Meals in Huelgastel were chaotic affairs, particularly for those ranked low enough to be seated at one of the trestles at the draughty end of the hall near the large double doors. At that end it was very much each man for himself. Great bowls and platters were dumped without ceremony on the trestles' bare boards. Loaves were tossed down willy-nilly. Hands shot out, grabbed, looted. Knives glittered. Men and dogs growled. At that lower end of the hall the woman had the choice of salvaging what they could from the scraps that were left, or using their wiles to ensure some chivalrous male saw to their needs. If they were young and pretty, they flashed their eyes and stuck out their chests, and prayed their chevalier was stronger than the next man. If they were ugly, or old and grey, they resorted to trickery, snatching food from other trenchers when someone wasn't watching, or taking the crumbs no one else wanted. The children relied on speed, or their parents.

'That's mine!'

'Too late, Dewi. It's mine!'

'Get your hoofs out of the trough, Rojer!'

The high table preserved a more dignified air. The scrubbed board was spread with a white linen cloth. The women and children at the top end of the hall were specifically catered for. Servants with bleached napkins draped over their arms moved solemnly along the table, offering the platters to each couple in turn — those on the top table ate in pairs. Even the children were offered food; though as the children were last in line, there was little choice by the time the platter reached them and they had to take what was left. There was usually enough. That evening, braised chicken with raisins was being served. The bread had been placed in baskets at intervals along the table: there was plenty of it, so nobody had to fight to get their share.

The count and countess occupied the central position on the dais, sharing a trencher, while François and his lady shared another trencher on the count's right hand. Father Josse sat next to them, and ate alone, so he had a trencher to himself. Sir Hamon and Lady Deneza took the place on Count Robert's left hand. The children, Arlette and the le Moine brothers, occupied the far end of the table. All were drinking wine, even the children, though theirs was watered.

François waited till everyone had their food before drawing his mother's attention to Agata's inadequacies.

Agata was lost in the throng some distance down the hall, well out of hearing.

'You should have seen Arlette when we rode in this evening, Maman. She looked a complete shambles. Hair like a bush, filthy as a peasant – and a boy at that. I've been remiss, I admit, with regard to my daughter's upbringing. I've had other things on my mind, but she can't be allowed to carry on the way she does now.'

Count Robert looked up from his meat. 'She was showing off her new trick, François. You can't expect her to do that in a skirt, surely?'

Eleanor gave François one of her cool smiles. Why couldn't Arlette be more like Eleanor? François thought. She should learn to be more feminine. 'I've no notion why Arlette has to try such antics in the first place,' he said. 'Why can't she behave like . . . like the girl she is?'

Countess Marie shared her peers' disdain of her own sex and her black eyes slowly travelled the length of the table to where her granddaughter was sitting. Arlette was happily oblivious of the fact that she was the subject of her elders' conversation. Her red head rested against Jehan's dark one. The children were feeding scraps to Gabriel under the table. They were laughing. Marie could see that an attempt had been made to plait Arlette's hair, but already it was unwinding. Since the child was seated, Marie could not see if her granddaughter was clad in a girl's tunic or her boy's breeches.

'I believe you're right, François,' Marie said, spearing a braised chicken-leg with her knife and peeling the flesh from the bone with her fingers. 'Agata has no idea of discipline, and your daughter needs disciplining if she's going to make a good alliance for us.' The countess was a leisurely eater, for her teeth were no longer sound. Cutting her meat into minute slices, she popped a sliver between her thin lips, and masticated slowly.

Eleanor's pale eyes lifted from her trencher. 'Perhaps

Arlette needs more female companionship,' she suggested softly.

'Female companionship?' Count Robert scowled. 'Rot, I can't see what you're all getting so heated about. Arlette's a grand girl. Why, she can ride as well as any boy her age, she's showing an interest in archery, and—'

'Father, you merely give weight to my point,' François cut in. His hand moved to cover Eleanor's. 'As yet I have but one child, a daughter, and as such her usefulness lies solely in the marriage that she will make – in the allies that her marriage will bring us. It's time she learnt to find pleasure in the more feminine accomplishments. I hope to make her a good match, but at the moment all she's learning are tumbler's tricks – useful if she's going to run off with a troupe of travelling players, but not in a girl whom, God willing, I'll marry to a count.'

Eleanor fingered the large silver cross which she wore on a heavy chain round her neck. 'I would be happy to spend more time with Arlette, my lord,' she said.

'That would help. Though something will have to be done about Agata.'

Count Robert's silver head shook. 'I think you should reconsider what you do about Agata—'

'That woman's going,' François said firmly. 'She's too soft with her, and it's having a bad effect on my daughter.'

Robert raised his wine to his lips and regarded his granddaughter over the rim of his goblet. He set the cup down. 'I think you're making a mistake over Agata,' he repeated. 'But she's your girl, and I'll not dictate how you should bring her up.'

'I have an idea,' Marie said, slicing another piece of chicken from the bone. 'I'll have Clemence brought to the castle.'

'Clemence!' François' hazel eyes widened and his florid cheeks took on more colour. 'You'd bring Clemence here,

Maman? A girl about whose background we know nothing?'

'Clemence?' Eleanor wrinkled her delicate nose. 'Who is Clemence, my lord?'

Marie answered for her son. 'Clemence is an orphan lodged at my daughter's convent. Some time ago Denise asked me to take an interest in her welfare.'

Eleanor knew that Denise de Roncier, Robert and Marie's eldest child, had taken the veil, and that Marie often visited her at St Anne's Convent, near by. Though young, Denise must be suited to the conventual life for she had recently been elected to the position of Mother Superior. This was the first time that Eleanor had heard the name Clemence mentioned.

Count Robert smiled. 'Clemence is one of my wife's charities. Marie pays for her upkeep at St Anne's.'

Countess Marie nodded. 'Yes. While you were away, Robert, I saw Denise, and I asked her how Clemence was doing. I was able to speak to her.' Her beady black eyes sought François' hazel ones. 'Clemence is almost eleven. She's blonde and comely, and has a liking for pretty clothes that cannot be satisfied in a convent. Denise has been unable to find any sense of vocation in her. I should think Clemence might be just the influence we need for Arlette. Well, François? What do you say? Shall I have Denise send the girl over?'

François spread his hands, faint colour still staining his cheekbones. 'If you're happy to have Clemence under our roof, Maman . . .'

'Absolutely. I like her.'

'And you think she's biddable?'

Marie smiled. 'For the cost of a bolt of Persian silk with ribbons to match, that one would do anything.'

'Good. Will you send for her?'

'I will. And I'll instruct her as to her duties. Shall we say something between a lady's maid and a companion?

Do you think that would work?'

'Thank you, Maman. That should work very well.'

In a fever to get to his bedchamber, François did not hang back in the hall after the ladies and children had retired. He called for a pitcher of wine and two goblets and, turning a blind eye on the knowing glances Sir Hamon and his father were flinging in his direction, he strode directly to his bedchamber.

The bed was empty, the sheets turned back. The fire in the hearth was unlit, and would be till autumn. The chamber was lit by a couple of cresset lights, and a slim candle which had been set on the coffer that had sat by François' bed since Joan's time.

François put his wine on the coffer next to the candle. After Joan's death he had thought long and hard before choosing Lady Eleanor d'Etoile, a woman ten years younger than he, as his second wife. François had private reasons for his choice, reasons that touched on his personal ambitions: Lady Eleanor was the youngest daughter of a lord high in the favour of the pious Louis of France. He wanted to gain his wife's favour not only because he was desperate to recapture something of the richness of the emotion he had shared with Joan, but also because one day he might come close to achieving his ambition, and then he would need her to intercede for him.

He had bathed to rid himself of the dust of the road before dinner but, notwithstanding this, François removed his chainse, or shirt, and washed himself with more than usual care in the ewer that had been placed on a stand. About to remove his braies, he remembered his wife's modest nature and left them on, sliding between the clean linen sheets. He sighed. It was good to be in his own bed again. He rested his arms on his head, and waited for his bride. He had his gift ready, under the bed, to produce at an opportune moment.

The wall opposite the bed had been empty when he had left, save for a small carving of the family coat of arms. It was now dominated by a vast painted crucifix, placed next to, and completely overshadowing, the coat of arms. Anyone lying in the bed could not help but look at the cross. Idly, François studied the figure. He knew that his wife prayed regularly, but he had never thought to see such a cross in their chamber. He shuddered. It was a very realistic interpretation – the Son of God in his death throes. The limbs of the Christ figure twisted and writhed in the jumping candlelight, and every muscle on the broken body seemed to be straining to escape. He was crowned with a vicious, spiky crown of nail-sized thorns which had been thickly coloured with the blackest of pigments. Several dark thorns bit into the Christ's forehead, and thin rivulets of blood trickled down His face. The blood dripping from the thorns and oozing from the Christ's hand and feet was the reddest François had seen. It was not a cross that he would have chosen to put up in his bedchamber.

He transferred his gaze to the family coat of arms, and looked at the circlet of thorns thereon. It was odd how this smaller circlet appeared darker than he remembered. It looked more prominent. Puzzled, François' eyes moved back to the cross. The same colour? Surely not. But it was very close. It must be a trick of the light.

The door opened, and thorned circlets were forgotten as Eleanor glided in. She held a candle in one hand, and her gold-embossed missal in the other.

'Oh, my lord! I'm sorry if I've kept you waiting,' she said. 'I've been in the chapel. I thought you were downstairs with your father.'

'I wanted to see you, Eleanor. It seems a long time.'

'Ten days,' she said, and carefully set both missal and candle down on the ledge of the narrow window. She put out her candle, and moved slowly round the chamber to extinguish the cresset lights. She reached the coffer by her husband's side of the great bed, and bent to pinch the bedside candle.

François caught her wrist, and his wife's light eyes, huge in the pale oval of her face, turned to him.

'Leave it.'

'But my lord, I wish to disrobe.'

'Leave it.'

The light eyes shifted away from him. 'As you wish, my lord.'

François leaned back in the pillows, and watched Eleanor. 'Where's Thérèse?'

Thérèse was Eleanor's maid, whom she had brought from France.

'I sent her to bed. I can manage.'

Eleanor kept her belongings in a hefty travelling chest to the right of the bed. A shelf on the wall by the chest held her hand mirror of polished brass, and her ivory-backed brush and comb. There was a wooden stool by the chest. Eleanor sat on it, and methodically unpinned her veil, placing the pins in a dish on the chest.

When she had removed her veil and wimple, François saw that her hair was bound up in a bun. François loved his wife's hair. It was very fine, pale yellow in colour, and very soft.

'Let me undo that,' he said.

But Eleanor's nimble fingers were already at the bun, pulling out the hairpins. 'No need, my lord, it's already done.' She brushed her hair, wound it into a loose plait, and rose to drift behind the angel screen which, like the bed, was a relic from Joan's time. After a pause her tunic and bliaud were flung over the top of the screen. She emerged clad in her undergown, and approached the bed.

François wanted to speak to her. He wanted to tell her how beautiful she was, but something in his wife's manner

47

prevented him. Silently, Eleanor got in beside François. She lay on her back like a marble statue with her eyes turned upwards towards the crimson bedhangings. She looked very remote.

François sighed, and he leaned up on his elbow. 'I . . . I missed you, Eleanor,' he managed. He wondered where he had gone wrong. Why was this so difficult? Eleanor was his wife. She would never deny him his right to couple with her, yet without saying a word she succeeded in making him feel like a barbaric rapist.

'Did you, my lord?' The pale eyes remained pinned on the bed-hangings.

He tried again. 'I . . . I've been looking forward to seeing you.'

'Have you, my lord?'

'I brought you a present.' He leant down and retrieved the gift from its hiding place.

Her head angled towards him.

'Look.'

Eleanor sat up to unwrap the present, her expression barely altering at the sight of the silver box. 'Why, thank you, my lord,' she said politely. 'It's very pretty.'

'It's for putting your jewels in, he said, dismayed by her indifference. 'I know you don't have many, but I shall rectify that.'

'Thank you, my lord.'

'Eleanor?'

'My lord?'

'You know my name. Use it.'

Eleanor drew in a breath, her slight breast heaved, but she made no answer.

'Try, Eleanor. Please.'

The proud nostrils flared.

Under the bedcovers, François clenched his fist. 'Eleanor, for God's sake. You could manage it when we're in bed surely?'

She lay back on the pillows. 'As you wish, François.'

His wife's whispered submission brought him no satisfaction. Uncertain how to proceed, François placed a hand on Eleanor's head to stroke her hair. He unwound her plait, gently spreading the fine golden strands about her face. He was careful to move slowly, gently, with a consideration that was rare for him, but nonetheless he saw a tell-tale muscle clench in Eleanor's jaw. He decided to override her distaste. For all her coolness, for all her icy disdain, he desired her. She was his wife, and he had married her to get an heir. She needed breaking in, that was all. He would try and treat her carefully.

'You are beautiful,' he muttered, pressing his lips to his wife's cool cheek.

Silence. She was looking past him at the gruesome crucifix on the opposite wall.

Drawing in a long breath, François slid his hand round his wife's slender waist. Her body tensed, and was still.

Turning her face to his, François kissed Eleanor's mouth. She did not resist him, but she did not encourage him either.

'Open your mouth.'

She opened her mouth, lying beside him like a graven image.

François kissed her thoroughly. She gasped when his tongue encountered hers, but he held her head in place and took his time. He pushed a leg between hers, and his hand found its way to her breast. He began stroking it, tugging at her nipple through the fabric of her gown, trying to elicit some response from her. At last he felt her nipple tighten, but given the way Eleanor was lying like a dead thing in his arms, could not convince himself that she was moved with delight. Tugging persistently at his wife's small breast, he lifted his head. His breathing was ragged and, pressed against her as he was, she could not fail to have noticed his arousal. Eleanor's eyes were fastened on the cross on the wall as though her life depended on it. She was pale as marble.

'Holy Christ, Eleanor, you might look at me! You might at least pretend!'

'My lord?'

Something snapped inside François. He rolled over, and snuffed out the candle. 'I'll be damned if I'll watch you lying under me like a blessed martyr,' he said through the darkness. 'You won't put me off. I'm sorry you don't like it, but I'm going to have you. Remove your gown.'

'As you wish, my lord.'

'François, my name's François.'

'As you wish, François.'

While he pushed his braies down, a rustling noise confirmed that she was obeying him.

He reached for her. Her skin was chilled, as though it were mid-winter. He did not have to ask her to spread her legs.

Silently, François levered himself over her. He did not enter her immediately, but pressed his manhood against her, containing his desires long enough to lie motionless for a moment or two. If his body warmed hers, perhaps she would like it. He was hoping against hope that she would put her arms about his neck without him having to ask her. She did not.

He ran a hand over her breasts. Her nipples were both taut. With cold? He sighed, eased away a fraction and explored between her legs. She felt dry, unwelcoming. He moved his fingers, rubbing up and down and around her womanhood in the way that had never failed to tantalise Joan. No response.

'Hold me, Eleanor.'

Two icy hands took hold of his shoulders.

'Tightly. Hold me tight.'

Two cold arms went round his neck.

François pressed home. She gave a little moaning gasp

50

when he entered her, which he ignored. She was dry inside, all the way in. He pushed in and out, in and out. Then he stopped.

'If you were to relax, Eleanor, you'd find it hurt you less.'

Silence.

He pressed home once more. In and out, in and out.

She did not moan again. Once François got used to the lack of response, she felt quite good inside. Firm and tight. It was not his fault if she was frigid. He had done his best. Feeling his climax approaching, François abandoned all thought of giving his wife pleasure, and rocked himself into oblivion.

Chapter Three

One bright morning two weeks later, Arlette wandered into the castle mews, Gabriel padding alongside her. She was still quite oblivious of her father's plans with regard to Agata.

Count Robert's hawks were in the middle of their summer moult, and Arlette reasoned that time would be hanging heavily on the hands of Morgan le Bihan, the castle falconer. She wanted to ask him a favour.

'Morgan!' she called as she entered the weathering ground. 'Where are you?'

The mews were sited at the north end of the outer bailey, in the broader, grass-covered section of ground, next to where the archers set up their butts. In order to keep the birds settled, the mews were fenced off from the shooting range and the rest of the bailey by a six-foot wattle fence. Count Robert's falcons were housed in two rows; the hawks standing on ring or bow perches, while the falcons stood on blocks. The birds sat on their perches blinking angrily at anyone who walked past them. They were always more irritable when they were in moult. Arlette skipped between the two rows of birds.

A hand, which was clutching something red and extremely bloody looking, waved at her from down one of the lines.

'Over here, my lady.' Morgan le Bihan spoke quietly, so

as not to startle the grey-backed hawk which sat feeding on his gloved right hand.

By the time Arlette reached him, Morgan was sitting cross-legged on the ground in front of the hawk's perch. The bird's dark crown was bowed over a strip of raw lamb's liver, firmly clutched in wicked yellow talons. Red blood spots mingled with the black dots on the bird's white belly. It was a large peregrine falcon, a female, still leashed to its block, and Arlette recognised her as belonging to her father. A leather pouch which contained some of the meat for the hawks in the mews sat on the floor just outside the range of the peregrine's leash.

At seventeen, Morgan was short for his age. Born and brought up in Huelgastel, the castle falconer had been small even as a child, hence his name, Bihan, Breton for small. Morgan's mother had died when he was born. His father had been a mercenary who had been killed while in service with Count Robert. Count Robert had had the mercenary's five-year-old orphan farmed out with Gradlon the castle smith, and Gradlon had brought Morgan up alongside his own sons. Morgan could still remember his father, who had loved him.

Morgan's shoulders were beginning to fill out. He had thick, glossy black hair which always needed trimming, and on seeing the count's granddaughter, he flicked his overlong fringe out of his eyes and grinned. An expert with his birds, Morgan was shy and withdrawn with most people, especially girls, but he liked young Arlette. He found children easier than adults, generally they were less critical of his awkwardness with words, but it was more than that with Arlette. Morgan liked Count Robert's granddaughter because she made him feel clever. She put him at ease.

'What are you after today, Little Lady?' he asked. Morgan's eyes were a muddy green, fringed with long dark lashes. Like Arlette he had freckles running over the bridge of his nose. His right cheek was scarred where two years earlier one of the hawks had taken a chunk out of it. There were other similar scars on his left, ungloved hand.

'I'd like you to teach me how to make a hood and a set of jesses,' Arlette said.

'You would? And why would you be wanting to learn that?'

Arlette tossed her head. 'One day I should like to train a hawk of my own. And I should practise making equipment for it.'

The falcon had finished her liver. Dark eyes flashed. Thus prompted, Morgan dipped his hand in the meat pouch and drew out another long red ribbon of flesh. 'And that's your lot, my friend, or you'll never take wing again,' he said. Morgan always spoke to his birds.

Gabriel sat down close to the bag, nose twitching. Noticing this, Morgan fastened the buckle on the pouch. 'So you're after a hawk, Little Lady.' He smiled. 'You won't be able to handle one like this.'

Arlette watched, fascinated, as the peregrine's sharp beak tore its way through its titbit. 'I know that. But Grandfather said that when I was older I might have a merlin. Do you think I could manage a merlin when I've grown a bit, Morgan? Next year perhaps?'

Morgan set her father's falcon back on its block, and considered. He liked the way Arlette asked him questions. He liked the way she listened attentively to his answers. The peregrine screamed and pecked angrily in the direction of his gloved hand. 'No, you're not getting any more out of me,' he said to the bird. He winked at Arlette. 'Your father would have me flayed alive if his favourite hawk was too fat to fly when the hunting season starts. But does she — ' he jerked his head at the falcon — 'care? No, she'd eat an entire flock of pigeons given half a chance. They get very bored when they're in moult. I have to watch them.'

'Morgan, about the hood . . .'

'Ah, yes.' Moving to the next bird in the line, Morgan dragged the meat bag with him. 'Show me your hands, Little Lady.'

Arlette held out her hands.

The falconer regarded them gravely, and shook his head. 'You're too young, Arlette. Compare the size of your fingers with mine.'

'Yours are bigger.'

'Stronger. I doubt that your little fingers have the strength to push the awl through the leather.'

Arlette's face clouded. 'Oh, Morgan. Don't say that. I do so want to try. Let me try. Please.'

'I'll make you a hood if you like.'

'But I want to do it. I want to learn.'

Morgan gave Arlette's chin an affectionate pinch. 'Why can't you wait till you grow? You're a stubborn girl. Look, if I prove to you that your fingers are not yet strong enough, will you agree to wait a year or two?'

'I suppose I'll have to.'

'Wait here. I've leather in my workshop, I'll fetch it. And don't let that hound of yours start poking around. I've day-old chicks in there, and they're intended for my hawks.'

Arlette absorbed this fact without a qualm. As a tiny child, when she had first seen Morgan feeding the sad yellow bundles of fluff to his hawks, she had been revolted, and had demanded that Morgan feed them with liver or meat such as they ate in the castle. But Morgan had explained to her that God had designed hawks to feed on whole carcasses. They needed a quantity of bone and feather in their diet or they became ill.

'It's natural for hawks to kill small birds and eat them,' he had said.

'But those poor chicks . . . they're not even a day old!'

Practically, Morgan had shrugged aside her

56

protestations. 'They're male chicks. No use to us, for they'll never lay. And my hawks have a right to be fed. You like my hawks, don't you?'

'Yes. It's just that it seems very cruel.'

'It's natural.'

Arlette had finally accepted this; now the idea of the hawks being fed day-old chicks no longer distressed her.

While Morgan marched towards his workshop by the entrance to the mews, Arlette looked at the hawk beside her father's. Another peregrine, a tiercel gentle, or male, and thus smaller than François' bird, this one belonged to Count Robert. The tiercel stood on its block, glassy eyes fastened on the meat bag.

'Are you hungry too?' Arlette murmured. 'He won't be a moment.'

Arlette stared at the falcon, and the falcon stared at the meat bag. All at once the tiercel hopped clumsily from its block, waddling into the shallow bowl of water that served both as bath and drinking water. It always amazed Arlette that a bird who could fly through the air with the grace of an angel should have so inelegant a gait when grounded.

The game pouch containing the chicks lay beyond the bath. Straining against the leash, the tiercel tried to peck at it.

'Don't do that! The leash will hurt your foot! Stop it!'

Arlette stooped to drag the pouch further out of reach, but Gabriel got there before her, his strong white teeth sinking into the soft leather. Arlette made a grab for the bag, but Gabriel began to growl as his nostrils filled with the tantalising smell of fresh meat.

'Gabriel, let go! Gabriel! Bad boy!'

Arlette yanked wildly at the bag until, realising she was not playing, Gabriel abruptly released his grip on the bag. Arlette stepped backwards, caught her foot on the peregrine's bath, and sat down with a thud. Count Robert's tiercel squawked, and beat its wings in a vain attempt to become airborne. A beak that was curved like a sabre stabbed out.

Arlette yelped, and hopped smartly out of the tiercel's bath, clutching the back of her neck. The seat of her breeches were soaking. Cold water ran down her legs. She dropped the game pouch to the grass, and turned accusing blue eyes on her grandfather's tiercel.

'You bit me, you wretch!'

Morgan was back in the weathering ground. He took one look at Arlette's face and broke into a run. 'What's happened? You're not hurt? Here, let me see.'

Dropping the leather scraps, Morgan drew Arlette well out of the tiercel's range, and peeled her hand from her neck. It came away bright and shiny with blood. Brushing the red tangle of hair aside, he examined the wound. He swore. 'Jesu, Little Lady, that's a deep one. How did you get so close? You weren't trying to handle the tiercel, were you? You weren't trying to feed her?'

Arlette could feel tears of pain rising, but her indignation that Morgan should think her so foolish was sufficient to hold them back. 'Feed her? I know better than that. I remember you showing me your scars, and telling me that you should always wear a glove when handling hawks. It was an accident. Gabriel . . .' The bite throbbed in time with her heartbeat ' . . . Oh, Morgan it does hurt. I want to see Agata.'

'I'll take you to her. Come on.'

'But your hawks—'

'I'll finish feeding them later. That gash needs washing and dressing, it might be infected. You'll need a clean tunic too, that one's covered in blood. This must be the last time that you bring that blasted hound into the weathering ground.'

'I'm sorry, Morgan. He thought I was playing. It was a mistake.'

'Next time, leave him outside. Understood?'

58

Arlette nodded, and flinched at the pain in her neck. 'You should feed your hawks more, Morgan,' she said, with a poor attempt at humour. 'Then perhaps they wouldn't try to eat people.'

Shaking his head, Morgan pressed the cloth of Arlette's tunic to her wound to staunch the flow, and steered her into the bailey.

Morgan and Arlette didn't find Agata in the hall.

'She might be in the solar,' Arlette suggested.

Morgan hesitated. The solar was normally out of bounds for the castle falconer, and he felt nervous about going there. He lifted his hand from Arlette's neck. The gash still bled freely. Arlette's face was drained of colour, making her freckles stand out starkly against a pallor that was unnatural even for her. Brave as she was, Arlette was only a child and Morgan could not leave her to find her nurse in this state. He would have to accompany her. The Little Lady was not one to swoon, but she had had a shock. He replaced his hand on the tear in her neck, pressing firmly to stop the flow. Arlette had been hurt in his mews, and it was his responsibility to see her safely to her nurse.

To Morgan's dismay, Agata was not in the solar either. His jaw dropped as he gazed at luxury such as he could never have imagined. A frieze of life-sized herons stalked around the walls at ground level. Above the herons the stonework was whitewashed and the pointing picked out in red. Bold, multi-coloured chevrons had been painted on the intricate array of roof beams. There were thick wool tapestries. There was a polished side-table, and a silver salver with crystal glasses stood upon it. There were brightly coloured silk cushions on the window seat. There was a wide stone fireplace . . .

A fish out of water, Morgan brushed back his hair, and straightened his tunic.

'Agata must be in our room,' Arlette said.

Pulse beating in his head, and praying that they were not about to run across a member of Arlette's family, Morgan marched Arlette briskly through the solar.

'Which way?' he demanded. The sooner he was back in his mews, the happier he would feel.

'Along that passage and up the stairs.'

As they rounded the last turn in the stairs, the light streaming through the loophold of the turret wall made a black silhouette of someone emerging from Arlette's chamber. The figure paused on the large triangular step that formed the landing outside the chamber door, and looked back into the room.

Recognising François de Roncier by his stance and the cut of his hair, Morgan cursed his ill-luck for being discovered in the family's private quarters. He snatched his hand from Arlette's neck as though stung, and hung back while the Little Lady ascended the remaining stairs to the landing.

'When you've unpacked your things,' de Roncier was saying, addressing someone inside the turret room whom Morgan could not see, 'come down to the solar. Jehan should have found her by then, and you can meet her.'

'Papa!' Ignoring the throbbing in her neck, Arlette skipped forwards, a delighted smile on her lips. 'Did you want me, Papa?'

De Roncier swung round on his heel, and put his hands on his hips. 'There you are, and about time.'

At his tone, Arlette's smile faded.

'Where have you been? I sent Jehan to look for you, but he's been an age.' Arlette's father caught sight of Morgan, hovering two steps below. 'Le Bihan? What on earth brings you here?'

'I'm sorry, my lord, but your daughter visited the mews and the count's tiercel took a peck at her. I thought it best I brought her back so Agata could look at the wound.'

60

'One of the hawks took a peck at her? Where?' Impatiently, François took his daughter by the shoulders and turned her face to the light.

'My neck, Papa. Here.'

'Hmm.' Lifting his daughter's bright hair, de Roncier pursed his lips. 'It does need attention. Might need a stitch. Clemence should know how to do it, she'll sort you out.'

Arlette looked up at her father. 'Clemence, Papa? Who's Clemence?'

But she may as well not have spoken, for de Roncier was scowling at Morgan. 'How did it happen?' he demanded. 'You're not responsible for this, le Bihan?'

'No, my lord, I . . . I . . .' Morgan stuttered to a halt. He had done nothing wrong, but he couldn't think what to say that would not put Arlette or her beloved dog in a bad light.

'No, Papa,' Arlette put in quickly. 'It was my fault. I got too close to Grandpapa's hawk. I made a stupid mistake.' She was wondering who Clemence was, and why her father thought this Clemence should tend to her and not her Agata.

De Roncier's hazel eyes bored into Arlette. 'Hawks are not toys,' he said sternly. 'Your fault, you say?'

Arlette hung her head. 'Yes, Papa.'

'Your breeches are wet.'

'I know.'

Sighing heavily, de Roncier gripped his daughter's arm and pulled her into her room. 'I see I had Clemence brought here not a moment too soon. You're a disgrace, and I'll stand it no more.'

Uncertain as to whether he was dismissed, Morgan stepped up to the landing, and peered curiously into the Little Lady's room. He saw a poky chamber with curved walls which was almost completely filled by a feather bed, a couple of chests, and a rush mat. A shelf on the wall held a branched candlestick. The bed, though half the size of the one that François shared with Eleanor, had a carved walnut headboard which nevertheless was finer and grander than any Morgan had seen.

Morgan gaped, but he was not looking at the bed, grand though it was. Sitting on the bed was a stranger, a girl-child with hair like spun gold. She was the prettiest girl Morgan had ever seen. A vision.

As Arlette and her father moved towards the bed, the vision rose gracefully to her feet. She was wearing a pale blue bliaud, a costly one – Morgan was ignorant as far as ladies' clothing went, but even his inexperienced eyes recognised silk when they saw it. The colour suited her. The girl was young; Morgan estimated her to be eleven or twelve years old. She was not tall; in a year or two Arlette would outreach her. The girl's face was softly rounded, her cheeks were a delicate pink – all peaches and cream. Her mouth was rosy and curved like a bow. Two long blonde plaits hung over her burgeoning breasts, but it was the girl's eyes that caught Morgan's attention. For an instant her gaze rested on Morgan, and he felt the impact of it in his belly. Her eyes were large and limpid, a soft blue-grey.

The vision looked at de Roncier, and curtseyed. 'Is this your daughter, my lord?'

Her voice was soft, and gentle on the ear. She was enchanting.

De Roncier nodded. 'This is Arlette. Arlette, this is Clemence, your maid and companion.'

'Clemence? My maid and companion?' The Little Lady sounded confused. 'But I don't need a maid,' she went on. 'Agata looks after me.'

The vision took Arlette by the shoulders and kissed her on both cheeks. 'Your father has explained it all to me,' Clemence said. 'You're growing up fast. You need a proper maid. I'm looking forward to getting to know

62

you. I'm sure we shall be friends.'

Arlette's eyes went from her father to the smiling girl, and back to her father. 'But Papa! Where's Agata?' A diminutive, blood-stained hand fluttered to the gash in her neck. 'I want Agata.'

De Roncier made an impatient movement. 'Don't be difficult, Arlette. You're embarrassing Clemence.'

'But where's Agata, Papa?' Arlette insisted on a rising note. 'Why won't you tell me where she is?'

Morgan stood transfixed in the doorway. He had the feeling that he ought not to be witness to this. He ought to go back to the mews, but his feet would not move.

'Agata's gone,' de Roncier said, harshly.

'Gone? Where?'

'Into service with Sir William Ricarde.'

'Agata's left us? No. *No!* I don't believe it! She wouldn't go without saying goodbye—'

'Arlette, I'm warning you . . .'

Arlette backed to the door. 'I want Agata! I want Agata!'

One stride carried de Roncier to his daughter. He caught the front of her tunic and hauled her back to face her new maid. 'Clemence will see to your needs from now on. Clemence will look after you. Clemence will show you how to be a lady.'

Arlette gave Clemence and her fine blue silk bliaud a dismissive look. 'A lady?' she sounded puzzled. 'But why should I want to be a lady?'

Fascinated, Morgan watched a muscle clench in de Roncier's jaw. 'You should want to be a lady, my girl, because I expect it of you. You've run wild long enough. It's time you toed the line. You're to learn to be a lady, and Clemence will help you.'

'I want Agata! I don't wany any poxy maid.'

Morgan flinched at Arlette's choice of words. No doubt she had picked up that expression from the guardhouse.

He doubted she knew what it meant, but it had a marked effect on her father. His lips worked, and the veins stood out on his neck.

A grim silence fell over the group in the turret room. Clemence flushed dark pink, and clenched her hands. She hid her hands in the folds of her gown.

'Lady Arlette,' Clemence said softly, 'let me help you. Let me look at your neck.'

Eyes haunted, Arlette backed towards the door, and Morgan realised she was about to fly for it.

'Keep away! Don't touch me!' Arlette cried, flinging Morgan a look which twisted his heart.

Feeling like a Judas, Morgan steeled himself to catch her. He did not want to stop her flight, but he had found his niche as castle falconer, and it was more than his life was worth to let her slip past him under the hard and watchful gaze of her father.

Fortunately, Morgan was not put to the test, because de Roncier reached his daughter in one long stride. He kicked the door shut.

Through three inches of oak, Morgan heard a sharp slap, then a startled yelp. One of Morgan's hands flew to the latch.

De Roncier's words fell on his ears like cold stones. 'You'll obey me, my girl, or by God I'll give you the hiding you deserve . . .'

Morgan heard another slap, and another indignant cry.

'Don't, my lord!' Though he had only heard her utter a phrase or two, Morgan recognised Clemence's voice. It was high and sharp with distress. 'Leave Lady Arlette with me, my lord! We'll manage. We'll be fine now. Oh, my lord, not your belt! Please don't . . . !'

Morgan closed his eyes, battling with a rash and overpowering impulse to fling open the door and wrest the Little Lady from her father's hands. Lest he should be tempted to give into it, Morgan shut his ears to the muted whimpering, and blindly made his way back to the mews.

At last de Roncier released his grip on Arlette's arm, and flung her, limp as a rag doll, across her bed. Buckling his belt back about his waist he strode through the door without so much as a backward glance.

Clemence laid a light hand on her new mistress's back. 'My lady?'

Arlette flinched.

Clemence withdrew her hand. 'My lady, shall I fetch you some water?'

Taking the ensuing silence for consent, Clemence slipped from the room. A couple of minutes later she reappeared with an earthenware pitcher and cup. Her mistress had not moved.

'My lady, can you sit up?' Shocked to her core, Clemence noticed dark streaks were flowering on the back of Arlette's ragged tunic. Arlette's father had drawn blood. The gash in her mistress's neck was now a minor consideration. Clemence ought to examine her back. She sat on the edge of the mattress.

'Can you sit up, mistress?'

Clemence heard a whimper, quickly suppressed, and her soft heart was moved. For years, in the convent, Clemence had longed for parents, longed to know what her mother and father had been like. It came to her now that there were worse things than not knowing who your father had been.

When Mother Denise had come to tell Clemence that the Countess Marie de Roncier had requested her as a maid for her granddaughter, she had been pleased. It was not that they had been cruel to her at St Anne's. The convent was a good place to be. Clemence was only an orphan, and where else would a penniless orphan have been so well fed and cared for? The good sisters had, in their way, tried to fill the gap in Clemence's life. They had tried to love her. It was not their fault if Clemence had no vocation. They could not help it if the endless round of services and the plain workaday clothes had bored and depressed her. Clemence had tried to make a good novice, but God had not created her in a nun's mould. Clemence was for the world. She had come to understand that, and now, thankfully, it seemed that Mother Denise understood it too, for Clemence was to leave St Anne's with Mother Denise's blessing.

The idea of coming to Huelgastel had delighted her. The countess had promised, and had given her, beautiful fabrics, one of which she had used to make the blue silk gown that she wore today, thinking to impress her new mistress. She had been looking forward to meeting Arlette, looking forward to making friends with her.

Clemence eyed the stiff-backed, battered child on the bed and, gently easing her up to a sitting position, held the cup to her lips.

Arlette shot her a haunted look, and drank.

Making friends with Lady Arlette was not going to be as easy as she had imagined. Before Clemence had arrived at Huelgastel, she had held a clear picture of the countess's granddaughter in her head. She had been expecting a girl who was nearer to her own age. She had imagined that she and Arlette de Roncier would sit sewing together. They would laugh and talk and . . .

Stroking the unruly red curls from her mistress's face, Clemence looked reality in the face. Arlette was a child. Her cheeks were white as milk, and blotched with drying tears. After that first, startled yelp, she had wept silently while her father had taken his belt to her. Was this the first time that François had beaten his daughter? Clemence wondered. Arlette de Roncier was a hurt and wounded child, and though twelve-year-old Clemence could not begin to understand how she felt, she did know that she was going to require careful handling.

'Is that better, mistress?' Clemence asked.

Arlette de Roncier turned her huge eyes on Clemence and folded her lips together.

Undaunted, Clemence gave her a warm smile. Lady Arlette was not going to give Clemence her friendship easily. This was going to be more of a challenge than she had thought. But for all that, Clemence was not displeased. She may have been bored at the convent, but she did not think she was going to be bored at Huelgastel.

'Let me look at your back, my lady.'

Arlette hugged herself, hung her head, and pressed her lips more closely together.

'My lady, please. Your back needs attention.'

Silence.

'My lady.'

'Go away. I want Agata.'

'I know you want Agata. And I regret it, but I can't fetch her for you. Your father has sent her away. You'll have to make do with me.'

'I don't want you. Go away.'

Wise beyond her years, Clemence stood up and went to the door. 'Very well. I'll go. But it will have to be you who tells your father that I'm not satisfactory. No doubt he'll find you another maid.'

Arlette's bright head lifted.

Clemence walked through the door and on to the landing. She heard a sob.

'C . . . Clemence . . . please don't go.'

It was a ghost whispering, but it was enough.

Clemence retraced her steps. 'Will you let me look at your back?'

The fiery head dipped in grudging assent.

'I'm so glad. Here, let me help you with that tunic and, when I've seen to your back, I'll deal with the cut on your neck.'

67

* * *

'My thanks, Clemence,' Arlette said when her back had been washed, and salve spread over it. The cut on her neck had stopped bleeding, and Clemence had pronounced that it did not, after all, require stitching. Arlette reached for her shabby brown tunic.

'No. Not that. Why don't you try this?' Clemence said, lifting an unbleached linen undergown and indigo bliaud from one of the coffers and spreading it on the bed for Arlette's approval. 'This dark blue will be very pretty with your colouring.'

'Pretty?' Arlette curled her lips. 'Pretty?'

'Your father had it made for you.'

'He did?' Arlette picked up the bliaud and held it to her. 'The material's very smooth.'

'It's silk. Do wear it, mistress. It will please your father.'

Arlette's blue eyes filled, and she tossed the gown down. 'Please Papa? Oh, Clemence, if only you knew how I've tried . . .' Her voice faltered, and she turned her face to the wall.

'Tell me. I'll help you, if I can. I want to be your maid.'

'Agata understood,' Arlette spoke to the wall in a muffled voice. 'Agata was my friend.'

'I know. And I'm sorry she's been sent away. But your father wished it. If you want to please him, you'll accept what he has done. Do try this on, my lady, and while you do you can tell me all about it. I want to be your maid. I'm willing to work hard.'

There was a pause, and the red-gold head turned. 'Why? Why is it so important to you that you become my maid? You don't even know me.'

Clemence shrugged. 'If you don't accept me, they'll send me back to the convent. I hate the convent.'

'Why? What's it like?'

Clemence was not stupid. 'I shan't tell you, not unless

you agree to give me a chance. Will you give me a chance, mistress?'

'I don't need or want a maid — ' Clemence's heart sank — 'But I need a friend. Shall we try and be friends instead, Clemence?'

Clemence relaxed. 'Yes, please.' She held up the indigo bliaud. 'And this?'

'I'll try it on, to please Papa.'

'There are more gowns for you to try later,' Clemence said, easing the undergown over Arlette's head.

Shift in place, Arlette glanced at the coffer, which was brimful of brightly coloured stuffs.

'He's had all those made for me?'

'Yes, mistress. Here, let me fasten this belt . . .' Clemence drew back and examined her mistress with a critical eye.

'Well? How do I look? I feel like a doll. I hate long robes — the skirts get in the way when I walk.'

'Take smaller steps. You'll get used to it. You look lovely, your father will be proud. We'll have to tidy your hair, of course.'

The bright head lowered, and Clemence heard a soft sigh.

'Mistress?'

'Do you like being a girl, Clemence?' This in incredulous tones.

'Why, yes.'

Another soft sigh. 'I'm not going to find it easy, Clemence. But if it's what my father wants.'

'It is.'

'I thought he wanted a boy, Clemence. I was trying to please Papa. And Papa hit me. Why did he do that? I was only trying to please him.'

'You're his girl. You can please him best by learning to be a lady.'

'Boys have more fun. And when they grow up they have

all the authority. I want power, Clemence.'

'Power?' Clemence gave a bubbling laugh. 'Power sounds very cold, mistress, very lonely. I think I'd rather have love.'

'You can't trust love. Love can betray you. I loved my mama and she died. I loved Agata, and she's gone too.'

'But mistress, your mama didn't choose to die. Agata didn't choose to go away. Neither of them deliberately betrayed you.'

'Didn't they?' Arlette asked in a tight, unhappy voice.

Deciding she had made enough headway for one day, Clemence chose not to probe any further.

Summer was all but gone by the time the two girls had really begun to understand and trust one another. They came to an agreement; each was learning to help the other, so both benefited.

Having convinced Arlette that it would be in her best interests to try and become the lady her father wanted her to be, Clemence achieved her aim of staying out of the convent.

Becoming a lady was not quite the hard grind that Arlette had feared, for she discovered that Clemence could not ride, and leapt at the opportunity to teach her. This she enjoyed, for she could escape Huelgastel solar and the endless stitchery that Clemence seemed to think a lady should devote most of her waking hours to. Clemence could not say that she looked forward to her lessons, but she agreed to them because she knew that Arlette derived great pleasure from being free of the castle.

Another advantage of the riding excursions was that Arlette's father approved of them. All ladies rode. It was only peasant girls who could not ride, and that because horses were costly creatures reserved for the nobility. Most of the nuns in St Anne's Convent were drawn from the nobility, and they had often gone hunting and hawking, particularly if the bishop were visiting. Unfortunately, Clemence − being an orphan − had never been included in these expeditions. Arlette had been quick to point out that if Clemence was to be Arlette's companion, she would have to learn the rudiments of riding, like other ladies.

It was a warm and golden morning when they rode out for one of Clemence's lessons. The dew had not lifted, and it hung like fairies' gossamer on the cobwebs the spiders had slung across the brambles. The ripening blackberries gleamed like jewels. On either side of the road the tall oaks towered, their leaves beginning to turn yellow. Autumn was fast approaching and the earth was damp under the ponies' hoofs; only last week the sun would have dried it to dust by this hour.

The two girls rode abreast; Arlette with casual confidence, and a white-faced Clemence bravely clinging to her pony's saddle horn. Aubrey, who was acting as their groom, brought up the rear, and Gabriel loped alongside weaving circles round them all. They needed no other escort, for Clemence was yet to relax on horseback and she tired easily. They were not likely to go far from the castle.

Chafing at the pace, Aubrey watched a brown speckled butterfly sunning itself on a blade of grass and listened to the girls' conversation.

Once down the hill, they had not gone more than half a mile when Clemence, who was still clinging to the front of her saddle, made an announcement. 'I've got a stone in my boot. Can we stop while I dismount and take it out?'

Aubrey sighed and irritably flicked a fly away with his hand. He was longing for a gallop. If he and Arlette had been riding out on their own, they would be racing by now. But lately, Arlette had not been allowed to ride alone with him. Always they had to take Clemence with her.

And Clemence was a slow learner. Aubrey did not think she would ever learn to gallop, not if she lived to be a hundred.

'We'll stop at that curve in the road,' Arlette said. Her eyes danced. 'Unless you think you could manage to take your boot off without dismounting?'

Clemence flung Arlette a harassed look. 'Without dismounting? Holy Mother! Could you?'

Aubrey spurred forwards. 'I helped the Little Lady to learn to ride bareback,' he said, with pride. 'If you would relax a little, I'm sure we could help you.'

'Ride bareback?' Clemence squeaked like a mouse. 'I could never ride bareback.'

A realist, Aubrey knew this. 'No, but it would help if you could learn to get your balance.' He spotted Morgan le Bihan coming round the bend on a grey gelding, a merlin on his left wrist. Aubrey pointed at the falconer. 'One day you might want to go hawking.'

'He's right, Clemence,' Arlette put in. 'You'll have to become confident enough to handle a hawk on horseback. You'll have to try and let go of the saddle. How about trying it today?'

A strand of flaxen hair floated across Clemence's eyes. Without loosing her grip on the pommel she shook her head and tried to blow it out of the way. 'Can I stop for a moment? I'm sure I'll be better when I've got the stone out of my boot.'

Aubrey and Arlette exchanged glances.

'I'm sorry,' Clemence said, in a small voice. 'I'm useless, aren't I?'

'No, you're not. You need practice, that's all,' Arlette said, soothingly.

'I'm holding you back.'

'No.'

Morgan rode up, and they all reined in, except Clemence who was clinging like a burr to her pommel. She gave a little wail of frustration as her pony wandered on down the road.

The falconer wheeled round, and caught hold of her pony's reins. 'Are you all right, mistress?' Morgan asked.

Clemence gritted her teeth. 'No, I'm not. I'm holding them up. They want to race. Will you stay with me while I get a stone out of my boot, and then they can have their race?'

Morgan gazed into the blue-grey eyes. There was nothing he wanted more. 'Assuredly,' he said. 'If I know Aubrey he won't be worth knowing till he's had the wind through his hair.'

Unaware of the effect she had on the falconer's pulse, and pleased to have found someone who understood how she felt, Clemence gave him a relieved smile.

Morgan led Clemence back to the others. 'Good morning, Little Lady,' he said.

Clemence was struggling to dismount and, after a moment, Morgan swung down, merlin still on his wrist, and went to assist her.

'Yesterday her hair was falling down,' Aubrey muttered, impatiently. 'Today it's a stone in her boot.'

'Aubrey!' Arlette said, chidingly.

Morgan's eyes met Arlette's. 'I'll stay with Mistress Clemence for a few minutes if you and Master Aubrey want a gallop.'

Aubrey's face lit up.

'Would you, Morgan? My thanks.' Arlette grinned at Aubrey. 'To the shrine and back?'

'The shrine,' Aubrey agreed.

Arlette dug in her heels. 'We won't be long.'

'Take as long as you like,' Morgan said.

As Arlette and Aubrey thundered up the road, the castle falconer smiled shyly at Clemence.

Clemence blushed.

Chapter Four

January 1183. Huelgastel

More than four years had gone by since Clemence had arrived at Huelgastel. Arlette had shot upwards, and her wolfhound Gabriel had become old and grey and lame. Unable to climb the stairs to Arlette's turret room, he slept in a straw bed in the stables. He had not moved in days.

François de Roncier asked his daughter to meet him in the stables.

'Arlette, Gabriel's your responsibility. *You* can put him out of his misery . . .' François thrust his hunting knife at his eleven-year-old daughter, and waited.

Knowing her father was watching her like a hawk lest she betray the smallest sign of weakness, Arlette turned her face into the shadows praying his hard, hazel eyes would miss the gesture.

'Why the delay, daughter?' François de Roncier demanded, pitilessly, while the chill air made clouds of his breath. 'Get on with it. The blade's sharp.'

Looking helplessly at her sire, Arlette noted that the florid, cobwebby veins which coloured his cheeks were more pronounced than usual. A dangerous sign that, as she knew from experience. Arlette was conscious that her own eyes must be glassy with unshed tears, but for once she was unable to conceal them, for all that she knew her father would make her suffer for her softness later. But how could she help herself when it was Gabriel they were talking about? Gabriel.

In the straw by the hem of Arlette's gown — she always dressed as a girl these days — lay her much-loved wolfhound. He was panting for breath as though he had galloped in from Rome, though everyone in the bailey knew he had not stirred in over three days. Gabriel would never run with the pack again. He was dying. Arlette knew it. But kill him? She could not.

'Oh, Papa. Can't you do it? Gabriel's my friend. He's been with me since Mama died — practically all my life . . .'

'All the more reason to do him this service,' the inflexible voice insisted. 'A faithful hound should be rewarded. Do you want him to suffer?'

'He . . . he's not suffering . . .'

'Not suffering? Listen to him. He can barely draw breath. Get on with it.'

Arlette sighed and bent her head. Two dark red plaits swung out from her muslin veil and hung down her childish breast. A stray sunbeam filtering through the stable door burnished François de Roncier's cropped copper hair, and made slender tongues of fire of Arlette's neat, waist-long plaits. Slowly, she turned the knife in her hand. 'Please, Papa. Gabriel's only resting. I'm certain he's in no pain. Can't we let him go in his sleep?'

Her father's foot tapped. The cobwebby veins filled with bright blood. 'In his sleep? That could take days . . .'

'I . . . I don't think so—'

'I'm not wasting good meat on an animal that no longer earns its keep. Do it now, girl, or I swear your backside will smart for a month.'

Arlette threw a last, desperate glance at her father's face, but his implacable look was firmly in place, and his colour was rising by the second. With swift grace, she

76

knelt beside her dog in the straw. She loved Gabriel, and would have to do it well. She ran her forefinger along the shining blade, and a thin crimson line leapt across her skin.

De Roncier snorted. 'What did you do that for? I told you it was sharp.'

Arlette bent over Gabriel. She hugged him. She looked lovingly into the dark, doggy eyes that were clouded with age and coming death. She knew her father was wrong, and that it would not take days for Gabriel to die. If only he would permit her to let Gabriel be, her dog would be gone by evensong. But her father would not permit that. She had to kill him. She whispered in Gabriel's ear, 'I love you.' The dull eyes brightened, and a grey-streaked tail swished feebly, valiantly through the straw. 'Sweet dreams, Gabriel.'

The knife flashed. Gabriel whimpered.

Clasping her hound tight as fury to her chest, Arlette felt his back legs twitch. She held him until all movement had ceased, before she rocked back on her heels. Gabriel's blood was seeping out over the straw. She tossed back her veil and forced herself to lift her head.

'There you are, Papa. I've done it.'

Her father smiled. 'Good girl. I knew you could. It wasn't that bad, was it?'

Arlette turned her eyes away.

François de Roncier thrust back the door, and hailed one of the grooms. 'Olier! Olier!'

'Mon seigneur?'

'Get this stable cleaned. There's a carcass for the midden.'

'Aye, mon seigneur.'

François de Roncier glanced back at his daughter, hazel eyes softer and warmer than she'd seen them in years, now that she had done his bidding. 'I know what it is to lose a good dog, Arlette. One of my bitches is in pup. I'll

77

see you get the pick of the litter.'

Arlette could not find a response, but that did not matter, for it seemed her father did not expect one. Already he was striding towards the mews, bellowing for Morgan le Bihan.

When Olier's shadow fell across the blood-stained straw, the groom found Count Robert's granddaughter vomiting quietly and efficiently into a leather feed bucket.

After dinner, when the trestles in Huelgastel hall had been cleared of soggy trenchers and empty platters, Count Robert de Roncier stroked his white moustache and motioned to a servant to remove the cloths. He addressed his granddaughter. 'A game, Arlette?'

Kindred spirits, it had become customary for Count Robert and Arlette to play chess at the high table. Arlette found a sympathy in her grandfather that was entirely lacking in her father and grandmother.

The fire was roaring that evening, but while long flames devoured the dry logs with a greedy hunger, they could not hope to warm the hall which had the proportions of a cathedral. The high table was sited in the warmest spot, although when the wind came from the north-east, it blew clouds of eye-stinging smoke around those on the dais. The display of arms on the whitewashed walls winked in the torchlight, and the polished blades of the Saracens' swords − the booty brought back by one of Count Robert's ancestors from Palestine − gleamed like silver.

'I'd like that, Grandpapa.'

In the past, Count Robert had possessed more than his fair share of good looks. He remained a handsome man. His hair and moustache were no longer black as pitch as they had been in his prime. They had been bleached by the years till they were as white as snow, but the count's white locks still curled vigorously across a broad, lined brow. The skin that stretched across his hollow cheeks was grey like dirty parchment, for his blood no longer raced hot and fierce through his veins. His nose was long and straight, and gave him a noble profile, but if one gazed only at his profile one would miss his eyes. And Count Robert's eyes were extraordinary. Of a deep, dark blue, they were arresting – utterly beautiful, and very like his granddaughter's.

The passing years had added weight to Robert de Roncier's once lean body. His waist had thickened, his belly was no longer flat. Count Robert was now in his mid-fifties: in an era when forty was considered aged, the count was deemed to be well-stricken in years. He could still sit astride his charger, but he no longer toured his estate; such matters he had recently delegated to his son.

Robert de Roncier managed a short ride most days, but often he chose to use the mounting-block to heave himself into the saddle: at such times the Huelgastel grooms would exchange knowing glances and bite their tongues. The grooms did not think it would be long before Count Robert stopped riding altogether. And what would happen to him then? Apart from his granddaughter, on whom the old man doted, his horses and his hunting gave him most joy. The grooms wondered what would happen to the ageing count when his body finally wore out, for his mind was lively as a child's, and he retained the will to continue with his favourite pastimes, even if he were losing the strength to pursue them.

He reached for the chess-board, and Arlette began setting out the ivory pieces.

'Have you been crying?' the count asked abruptly.

Arlette set a bishop on the wrong square. 'No.'

'Something's on your mind. What is it?' A gust of smoke lodged in the back of his throat, and Robert coughed and reached for his goblet of wine, noting with a frown the tell-tale white clouds that were gusting out of the fireplace and drifting towards the high roof-beams.

They were in for another bitter night.

'I . . . I'd rather not say.' Arlette picked up a castle and clenched her fingers round it.

'You've not been quarrelling with your father?'

'No.'

A jangle of curtain rings marked the entrance into the hall of a brace of giggling servant girls with swathes of milk-white linen draped over their arms. They brought with them a stronger draught which blew out the lights in the wall-sconces that flanked the fire.

'Lena!' The count gestured at the older of the two maidservants, a pale, pretty girl with light brown hair confined behind a veil and wimple, and intelligent grey eyes.

'Mon seigneur?' Lena curtseyed, and moved gracefully towards him.

Robert knew that his son had taken to having relations with Marie's maidservant, and he eyed her speculatively. The girl's gown was simple, and gave Count Robert no clue as to what lay beneath it, but privately, François had let slip that she had the body of a goddess . . . 'See to those lights, would you, Lena? And bring us some candles. We can't tell the pawns from the knights in this murk.'

Turning back to his granddaughter, the count gently prised the castle from her hand. 'What is it, Arlette? Is it Gabriel? I heard he died today.' Count Robert saw tears well in Arlette's eyes, but they did not brim over, and nor did he expect them to, not in the hall. His granddaughter had learnt how to control herself, and would certainly do so while they were seated in so public a place as Huelgastel high table.

'Aye, he died,' Arlette said, in a tight, sad voice.

'I'm sorry, girl. You can have another—'

'Another!' Arlette's blue eyes flashed. 'You sound just like Papa! He thinks Gabriel can be replaced as easily as

80

an out-grown dress. But he can't. I love Gabriel. He's been part of my life for as long as I can remember . . .'

Robert de Roncier enfolded one of his granddaughter's small, young hands in his gnarled, worn one. After his marriage to Marie, Robert had tried to love his wife. In that he had failed, Marie would never replace Izabel in his heart. But he had a great fondness for Arlette, and did not like to see her distressed. 'Hush, child, hush. Of course you loved Gabriel, no one questions that. But he was getting on in years, and everything mortal must die some time . . .' He laughed. 'Why, I'm growing old too, and one day even I'll have to go . . .

'Don't, Grandpapa. I can't bear to think of you dying. I *won't* think about you dying.'

Robert gave her a straight look. 'It'll happen, and you'd best prepare yourself . . .'

Arlette's youthful face creased in concern. 'Grandpapa, you've been feeling poorly again, and you've not told me. You *promised* you'd tell me if it happened again. Was it one of your dizzy spells?'

Count Robert *had* had a dizzy turn, that afternoon, but he wasn't about to disclose that. He dropped Arlette's hand, and finished setting up the pawns. 'I'm fit as a flea. Haven't felt as good in years. Put my dizzy spells out of your mind, and tell me what happened between you and your father. You're always at each other's throats. You two must learn to get on.'

'Papa forced me to kill Gabriel.' Arlette's soft voice was scratchy with hatred, and she looked towards the rush matting in front of the fireplace where her hound had liked to lie.

'He made *you* slay him?'

'Aye.'

Robert rubbed the bridge of his nose. What Arlette had told him had not surprised him. His son had grand designs planned for his only child, and Arlette's strict upbringing since the age of seven had been designed to ensure that she did not disgrace the family when the time came. Robert did not believe that François treated his daughter harshly for cruelty's sake, but in order that Arlette would become fitted to the great task ahead of her. She had to have the softness hammered out of her. She may have been a tomboy before Clemence had been brought to the castle, but she possessed a soft heart. It had to be strengthened, like tempered steel.

The count wondered if his son realised that his stern handling of Arlette might be hardening her heart against him. He was not certain if François' methods were working either. This hound of hers was a typical example. But had it really been necessary for François to make his girl kill the animal herself? Surely that was going too far.

Arlette rushed into speech. 'Grandpapa, I do dread Father becoming Count. And not only because it will mean you are gone—'

'My thanks, child,' Robert murmured dryly.

'Papa's bad enough now,' Arlette continued, 'and he's not even Count. What will he be like when he is?'

'He'll do his duty, I hope. As you'll do yours.'

'But, Grandpapa, what *is* my duty? I keep asking, and no one will tell me. I've learnt to read and write. I can ride as fast as any of the squires. I can hawk, and hunt. I can sew, keep accounts—'

'No need to vaunt your accomplishments to me, my girl,' Robert broke in, smiling. 'I'm well acquainted with them. I'm also well acquainted with your deficiencies.'

'My deficiencies? But I've taken great pains to learn everything Father Josse set out to teach me. I've—'

'Plainly he made some omissions.'

Arlette stared.

'Did Father Josse ever mention patience to you, my dear? Or humility? Or obedience? Or . . . ?'

'Oh, Grandpapa. I only want to know what Father has

planned for me. It is my life, after all.'

Count Robert sucked in a breath, and shook his head, and his blue eyes were for a moment full of pity. 'Your life? Oh, my dear, dear, girl. You might be as learned as a monk, and as wise as King Solomon, but you have failed to learn the most basic lesson of them all.'

'I don't understand.'

Robert smiled. 'You will, one day. But I can't teach you. I'm too old and worn. I can only pray that your understanding won't be bought with too much suffering.'

Arlette fiddled with one of her pawns. 'I hate riddles, Grandpapa. All I want to know is what Father has planned for me. Am I to be married?'

'Naturally, you'll marry. What else could you do?'

'Who? Have you chosen someone?'

'Negotiations are in hand.'

'Who is it? Tell me!'

'Not now, Arlette. I'm weary.'

'Tell me!'

The count lifted his head and fixed his granddaughter with a cold stare. 'Not now, Arlette. The game, if you please. I seem to recall it's your turn to start.'

'But, Grandpapa—'

'Your move, Arlette,' Robert said, sternly. Fond as he was of his passionate, red-headed granddaughter, he could not tolerate disobedience in her. And the sooner she learned that, the easier her life would be.

'Yes, Grandpapa.' Arlette picked up a pawn, and made her move.

Arlette lost the chess game. Her heart wasn't in it, but at least her grandfather had been pleased to win. Lately he'd been losing, and that made him bad-tempered.

Afterwards, Arlette wandered round Huelgastel bailey. It was well past the time that she should have retired but she was not sleepy. She could hear those men-at-arms who were not standing guard drawing out their pallets and settling down for the night in the hall where they slept communally.

The January sky was flecked with silver stars. At intervals along the castle walls, torches threw yellow streamers into the blackness, and braziers of coals glowed like giants' lanterns. Black shapes flitted in front of them as the castle guards took turns to warm hands that were pinched with cold.

And it *was* cold. The wind had shifted to the east, and nipped her toes. Arlette shrugged herself deeper into her cloak. Her hood was lined with squirrel, and the soft fur was warm against her cheek, like a gentle caress. It put her in mind of Gabriel, not that his coat had been as soft as a squirrel's; his had been coarse and scratchy, and smelt terribly of dog, especially when he had been out in the rain. Oh Gabriel. There must be some part of him left; he could not be entirely gone. That special spark that had been Gabriel, perhaps it was up there with those stars? Arlette knew that Father Josse would condemn that as a blasphemous thought. According to the castle priest, animals did not possess souls. Arlette disagreed. Overwhelmed with a rush of misery that twisted her insides, she turned blindly for the stable. She could not go to bed yet. She would not sleep. Perhaps, if Jehan was on duty at the gate, he might talk to her awhile.

The door of the smithy was closing as she passed it, and Arlette caught a glimpse of the forge shining like the baleful red eye of a dozing dragon. 'God give you a good night, Gradlon,' she called.

'And you also, my lady,' the smith returned. The dragon's eye closed with a click as Gradlon bolted the smithy door.

Her footsteps were loud on the flags in the yard.

Jehan was not at the gatehouse. Arlette retraced her steps and found herself in the stable, staring at the spot where Gabriel had breathed his last. Her throat constricted with unshed tears.

A hand fell on her shoulder.

'My lady? What are you doing here at this hour?'

It was Jehan. Arlette's heart lifted. Since Agata had been sent away both he and Aubrey had been instructed to address her with proper formality, but their friendship remained as firm as it had ever been. It transcended titles.

'Jehan! I . . . I was hoping to see you. I thought you were on guard.'

At sixteen, Jehan had shot up several inches, and towered over Arlette. He thrust back his mop of dark hair, and gave her an understanding look.

'I heard about Gabriel. I'm sorry,' Jehan said.

Arlette nodded. Jehan's sympathy choked her, and she couldn't speak.

A friendly arm went round her shoulders, and she turned her face towards the comfort of Jehan's brotherly breast. Thank God she had Jehan.

'Do you want to tell me about it?'

'No. I want to forget it, but how can I when it was Gabriel?'

'I know. Shall we go outside? This place can only remind you—'

'It's freezing out there.'

'Perhaps you should go back to the hall. Your father might be wondering where you are.'

'Let him wonder,' Arlette said. She was becoming bitter. She knew better than to speak to unguardedly, and she reserved most confidences for her friend and maidservant, Clemence, but Arlette trusted her old playmate. Jehan wouldn't dream of repeating what she said. 'My father doesn't care one whit about me,' she went on. 'I am only important to him in so far as I fit in with his grand schemes.'

'Something's happened,' Jehan said slowly, 'apart from Gabriel, I mean.'

'I'm to be married.'

Jehan drew Arlette to the doorway where the light from the walkway torches pooled on the frosty ground, and scrutinised her expression. 'And that surprises you?'

'No. Everyone's taken great pains to ensure I know my duty, but I loathe the idea of having to leave Huelgastel. I could be sent anywhere – it might not even be in Brittany. I hate not having any say in it.'

'Is the man not to your liking?'

'I don't know. No one will tell me who they have in mind, not even Grandpapa. And knowing my dear father, and how he delights to torment me, it will be someone twice my age with bad breath, a pot belly and—'

'You don't know that. He might be a prince among men . . .'

'I'd rather marry you, Jehan.'

'Me?' Shocked, Jehan snatched his arm from about her.

Arlette laughed. 'Don't look so disapproving, Jehan. I like you, you know that. And I know you like me.'

'Yes, but Arlette . . . my lady . . . be sensible. You're the granddaughter of a count, while I'm the grandson of a monk who broke Holy law and took a mistress . . .'

Footsteps crunched across the yard. Jehan took Arlette by the shoulders, and pulled her inside. 'Listen, my lady,' he said, earnestly. 'You must tread carefully. I've noticed how easily your father is roused these days. I was told that he's involved in some dispute over your lands—'

Arlette wrinkled her nose. 'A dispute? What dispute?'

'I don't know the details, something to do with distant kin of yours. At any rate, he's like a bear with a sore head. He had one man flogged within an inch of his life yesterday over a trifling matter of a blunted blade. Be clever. Don't anger him. Go along with his plans. He'll force you anyway, in the end. Save yourself the suffering.'

'I've tried to be a good daughter. I've tried to love him, and win his love. But whatever I do, it's either wrong or not enough. There's no pleasing him. He doesn't love me, Jehan.'

'I think he does, in his way.'

'Do you?' Arlette's laugh was unhappy. 'I can't see it. I'm beginning to hate him. Isn't that dreadful? I'm beginning to hate my own father.'

'You know that's a lie. Fall in with his plans with a good grace—'

'But, Jehan. I don't want to marry a stranger. I'd far rather stay here and marry you . . .'

The stable door creaked on its hinges, and François de Roncier was framed in the doorway, coppery hair a helmet of fire in the bailey torchlight.

Arlette groaned inwardly, and stepped hastily away from Jehan, though she instantly regretted the movement, for it made it look as though she and Jehan were guilty of some transgression.

'What's this?' her father demanded, voice like a saw.

'Jehan and I were talking, Papa—'

'Talking? Aye! Of marriage, and don't waste your breath denying it. I heard you. *And* he had his arm twined round you. I saw that too. Come here, girl.'

Arlette stepped forwards, and her father's hand closed round her arm like an iron band. With a sinking heart, Arlette realised what her father thought she and Jehan had been doing in the darkened stable. Noblemen often married their daughters at her age or younger, and her father thought she and Jehan were sweethearts. It was vitally important that Arlette convince her father of the truth, not for her sake, but for Jehan's. 'Papa, let me explain—'

But her father was not in a listening mood, and he hauled her to the door as though she were a sack of meal.

'Captain Malait!' he called. 'Captain Malait!'

'Mon seigneur?' A soldier's heavy boots clumped along the guards' walkway over the stable, and the ladder creaked as a large man descended to ground level. Otto Malait stood before them, a vast Viking, a blond bear of a man. He snatched up a flambeau and his smooth, horned helm glinted when he moved. 'You called, mon seigneur?'

'Aye. I want this one—' Arlette's father jerked his thumb at Jehan who was standing silently in the stable doorway, running his hand uneasily round his neck – 'putting under lock and key until I decide what to do with him.'

'No, Papa! Jehan's done nothing! He's a friend, nothing more!'

'I'll be the judge of that. Take him away, Malait.'

'Mon seigneur.'

Jehan looked stunned as Captain Malait approached him, meekly submitting when the Norseman took his arm in an armlock. 'I . . . I'll not run away, Captain,' Jehan said, wincing.

Captain Malait grinned. 'That you will not.' He led Jehan away.

For the first time in her life, Arlette knew real fear, as it dawned on her that by befriending Jehan she had put him at risk. She stared at her sire. 'You won't hurt Jehan, will you, Father? He did nothing. I was upset about Gabriel and he—'

'I saw him mauling you.'

'No, Papa. It wasn't like that.'

Lips firmly closed, her father dragged her across the icy flags towards the keep.

'Papa, please. Listen to me . . .'

Arlette was frog-marched through the hall, her father ignoring the startled stares and muttering of his sleepy retainers, and maintaining a steely silence.

'Papa? What are you going to do with Jehan?'

Without a word, Arlette's father dragged her up the winding stairs to the chamber she shared with Clemence at the top of the west turret.

'Please, Father. Jehan did nothing.' Arlette tried to pull her arm free so that she could turn and face him, but he tightened his grip. She moaned, partly from the pain and partly from frustration.

François had reached her bedchamber door. Kicking it open, he thrust Arlette inside. 'There you are, mademoiselle. And there you'll stay.'

'But Father, we were only talking . . .' They had awakened Clemence. Arlette could hear her moving about in their bed.

'It's appearances that matter, my girl. So far God has not blessed me with a son to uphold the family honour, so that duty falls on you. And you're staying in here until you learn that my daughter does nothing, *nothing* that might put her honour in question. Good God, girl, I'm negotiating with Count Etienne Favell on your behalf. If he hears so much as a murmur of gossip against you, he'll not take you. Clemence!'

François lit another candle.

'Mon seigneur?' Clemence blinked, not fully awake yet. She pushed a trailing lock of blonde hair out of her eyes, and clambered out of bed. Padding across the reed matting in her linen shift, she came to stand at Arlette's side.

Clemence's waist-length hair was the colour of ripe wheat. Her figure had developed in the years since she had come to Huelgastel. No longer a little girl, her bosom was full and her waist was slim. She was a lovely young woman, who took a sensuous pleasure in dressing to her advantage, and snared men's gazes wherever she went. Extraordinarily, her chief attraction was that she was quite without vanity. Blessed with a contented nature, it never occurred to Clemence that she might trade on her looks for her own gain. She dressed with care simply to please herself.

'You're to come with me, Clemence,' François said. 'I'm separating you two. Bring what you need.'

Clemence's blue-grey eyes blinked. 'Now, mon seigneur?'

'Now.'

'Yes, mon seigneur.' Clemence bundled up a couple of gowns, took her cloak from the peg on the back of the door, and slipped on her shoes. On her way out, she gave Arlette's hand an affectionate squeeze.

Arlette bit her lip. She was not afraid for herself so much as for Jehan. What *was* her father going to do with Jehan? She wrapped her arms about her middle. She could not think how she could help Jehan if her father would not listen to her.

'Now daughter, it's bread and water for you. Let's see if a week of it will teach you some sense.'

The bedchamber door slammed. The key grated in the lock. And Arlette was alone.

Arlette had always shared the round turret room with someone. First with Agata, whom she had loved, and then with Clemence, whom she had come to love too. She was not used to being alone.

Officially, Clemence was Arlette's personal maid-servant, but the girls' relationship had grown into something far deeper than that. They had become devoted to each other; Clemence had become Arlette's best friend. She would miss her. Wondering if she was to be denied the pleasures of Clemence's friendship on a permanent basis, Arlette sank on to her bed, and put her head in her hands.

She ached with fear for Jehan but, try as she might, could see no way to help him. Her father had said that it was appearances that he was concerned about; perhaps that was a hint to her that he knew she and Jehan had done no wrong. Her father was a stern man and a harsh master, but Arlette knew he had a deep respect for Jehan's father, Hamon le Moine. Count Robert's seneschal was a long-serving, diligent and trusted member of the household. That, and the fact that Jehan had never shirked his shifts, must weigh in his favour, surely? Arlette would pray for Jehan − little enough in all conscience − but at the moment that was all she could do.

She lifted her head, and sighed. 'Count Etienne Favell,' she murmured. Her father had let fall the name of the man he proposed to make an alliance with. The name meant nothing to Arlette, and she was unable to visualise its owner. 'Count Etienne Favell.' So her father had it in mind for her to be a countess? He would gift her with a large dowry and marry her to a count . . .

Arlette didn't want to be a countess, dowry or no. All she wanted was that Jehan should not be whipped and that Clemence should be returned to her bedchamber. Miserably, she kicked off her boots and unlaced her gown. Dropping it on to the matting, she rolled into bed, and curled herself up into a tight little ball.

'Please, God, don't make me into a countess. And let me keep my friends.'

Even as she uttered her prayer, Arlette knew that if duty decreed it she would accede to her father's wishes and marry this count. Her own desires could not come before her duty to her family.

Some fifteen miles away as the crow flies, Anna, a farmer's daughter, was waiting in a dolmen to meet a youth who was a distant cousin of Arlette de Roncier. The dolmen, or Old Ones' temple, was one of a handful of mysterious stone constructions which legend maintained had been ancient when Jesus first trod the Galilean lakeside. These monuments to a vanished era were clustered round the fishing village of Locmariaquer, which sat on the western arm of the land encircling the

Morbihan Gulf; and they attracted a host of colourful superstitions about forgotten pagan cults, and sun-worship and human sacrifice, and as a result were largely shunned by the native peasantry.

From the outside, the dolmen appeared to be a huge oval stone resting on the grass, but round to one side, steps ran deep into the earth. These led beneath the stone into a dank, murky cavern. It was an eerie, unlikely trysting place, and Anna had never ventured into the dolmen before, having a healthy peasant's dread of the unknown. However, in this instance, her feelings for the youth were strong and she had overcome her instinctive fears. She had brought her family's iron lantern, the one with the horn windows, with her. She set it on the earth floor.

The youth's name was Raymond Herevi. He was the same age as Anna, fourteen, and he lived all the way across the bay in the thriving port of Vannes. Anna had not known Raymond long, having met him on St Gildas' Day when her father had taken her to the fair held near the saint's monastery at Rhuys. Anna had been flattered by Raymond's interest, but did not know him well enough to be confident he would turn up. Tightening the strings of her woollen hood, and thrusting her hands inside her cloak, Anna decided to give him a little more time.

She had only waited a couple of moments when she heard a movement outside.

'Anna? Anna, are you in there?'

Recognising Raymond's voice — she liked his voice — Anna picked up the lantern and went to the bottom of the steps. She held up the lantern. 'Here. I'm in here.'

Raymond, muffled in a thick mantle, descended the steps. 'Hello, Anna.'

'Hello.' Now that Raymond was here, Anna felt awkward. 'I . . . I wasn't certain you'd come,' she began to babble, 'Vannes being such a great distance from here.

I've never been to Vannes. Father has only ever taken me to St Gildas' Fair. Apart from that I've never left Locmariaquer.'

Raymond flung back his capuchon. 'I sailed with a night-fisherman across the bay.' He moved towards her. 'It freezes you to your core in a boat on the bay, Anna . . .'

'Does it? I'm cold too,' Anna said innocently. She was trying to see Raymond's eyes, which she remembered as being green like the spring wheat when it first pushes its way through the soil. She liked Raymond's eyes. When he took her hand, she smiled shyly at him.

'You're sweet when you blush,' Raymond whispered.

'H . . . how do you know I'm blushing? It's too gloomy to see . . .'

'I can see well enough.' Raymond removed his cloak and dropped it on the ground. 'Come, Anna, of the dark eyes and night-black hair, let's sit and talk.'

'But your cloak . . . You said you were cold . . .'

'You can warm me.'

'Master Raymond . . .' With infinite gentleness, Raymond drew Anna on to his cloak, and Anna found her protests died on her lips. She could not be afraid of Raymond, not when he was so gentle with her. Keeping fast one hand, he put his other arm around her, leaned towards her, and nuzzled her cheek.

'Hold me, Anna. I want to be held.'

His lips were soft against Anna's cheek, his movements unhurried and not at all threatening, but when his hand strayed to cup one of Anna's full breasts, she gave a slight murmur of protest. Anna was very attracted to Raymond Herevi, but she was innocent, and this was progressing too rapidly for her. Immediately she demurred, Raymond released her and sat back.

'It's all right, Anna.' His voice was warm, and reassured her. 'Don't be afraid.'

'I'm not afraid, but . . .'

'I know. Don't worry, I'd never do anything you didn't want me to. Tell me about your family. Have you always lived here?'

Anna relaxed. 'Yes. My father's a tenant farmer and, as you know, our cottage is close by in the village. I have an older sister, but she fell in love with a mason. Sir Blundell – he's our lord – allowed my parents to pay the bride fine, and my sister married her mason. She accompanies him wherever he can find work. We haven't seen her in years. There's just Mother and Father and me now.'

'No brothers?'

'No. They tried, after me, but none came.'

'No faithful admirers?'

'No.'

Raymond's hand rose, and lightly he stroked Anna's earlobe. She felt it grow warm, glanced at his face, and caught Raymond's eyes. Then she found she could not look away – not that she wanted to . . .

'T . . . tell me about *your* family, Master Raymond.'

Raymond's hand moved carefully along her neck, and Anna found herself tilting towards his caress. He smiled at her. 'You like that, don't you?'

Anna gave an embarrassed little nod, and in one swift movement, Raymond leaned forward and planted a brief kiss full on her lips. Then he sat back, wrapped his hands round his knees, and fixed his eyes on the lantern, as though he had never touched her at all.

'My family,' he said, thoughtfully. 'You want to know about my family?'

'Aye.' Anna was wondering whether he would kiss her again.

'It might repel you . . .'

Nothing could repel her. Anna managed to laugh. 'I don't think so.'

'Very well. You asked. My mother's a concubine . . .'

'A concubine?'

'Aye. She's the mistress of Sir Jean St Clair, and I'm their eldest child. They're not married, so I'm illegitimate. I have two sisters, and we live near the cathedral in Vannes.' He turned his head towards her, and his green eyes seemed to challenge Anna. 'There. Now I've told you, I suppose you won't want to know me.'

There was bitterness in Raymond's voice, but Anna didn't listen to that. What Raymond had confessed was shocking, quite shocking, and Anna's parents would be horrified if they knew of her association with a knight's bastard. But Anna did not care. She sensed a deep hunger in Raymond Herevi, a deep hurt and a desperate need to be loved. Her soft heart was moved. 'Oh, Raymond,' she said and, reaching out her hand, she pulled him into the circle of her arms.

Chapter Five

On the south bank of the ice-edged River Dordogne in the Périgord region of the Aquitaine, Count Etienne Favell was hunting boar with his nephew and heir, Sir Louis Favell, and Louis' wife, the Lady Petronilla Favell. Sir Gilles Fitzhugh, the count's young castellan, and half a dozen squires were privileged to accompany them. All were warmly wrapped, as befitted the season, and their clothes proclaimed their status.

Count Etienne's cloak was of heavy imported rich red silk, and snugly lined with ermine. A thick green skull-cap was jammed on his head, and decorated with a gold brooch. The Count's hair was thinning on top, but he wore it long at the back by way of compensation, and thin wisps of greying hair protruded from behind the cap like a dirty fringe. The count's eyes, a cold green, were narrowed to slits against the wintry wind, and almost lost in rosy, corpulent cheeks. A pack of hounds, dicing with death, barked and bubbled around his black destrier's heavy, iron-shod hoofs, for they had not yet got wind of their quarry.

Sir Louis, Lady Petronilla and Sir Gilles wore woollen cloaks — soft brown, violet and grey respectively: not for them the crimson, which never came cheap. Their linings were of coney, while the squires made do with wool alone, worn over their padded gambesons. The nobles wore hats — Lady Petronilla's was of velvet, and a peacock's feather danced along behind her. The squires' headgear consisted of short hooded capes over their cloaks that had no ornamentation save for the scalloped edges.

Count Etienne was in an ill-humour, for he had no liking for his nephew's wife.

'How much of this land is yours, dear Count?' Petronilla asked for the second time, while she eyed the count's domain with predatory grey eyes.

Etienne, who was master of a broad sweep of territory which stretched further than even Petronilla Favell's greedy eyes could see, threw a glance of acute dislike at his nephew's wife, and spurred his mount, Snowstorm, into a gallop, away from both baying hounds and baying woman. The sooner he put a good distance between himself and Petronilla Favell, the better. The count did not consider his dislike to be merely a matter of prejudice. It wasn't simply that Petronilla − ridiculous name − had not been born into the knightly class; it was more personal than that. There was something about her nature that drove him into a frenzy.

The woman seemed utterly oblivious of the honour his nephew, Louis, had done her by marrying her. Louis had gallantly rescued her from life as a burgher's wife in nearby Domme, and his reward was that he was bullied and nagged from dawn till dusk. Fortunately for Etienne, the couple spent most of their time at their manor, but Etienne needed Louis' help over this matter of the marriage contract with de Roncier's daughter and, as luck would have it, Petronilla had been keen to pay Count Etienne a visit. And Etienne knew why that was. She couldn't pass up the chance to gloat over the domain that Louis would one day inherit if Etienne failed to get himself an heir.

At forty-seven, Etienne Favell had seen two wives into the grave, but he had no children, not even a girl. And until such time as he sired a child, Louis was his heir. And until Louis had married this burgher's daughter, Etienne had been content with that arrangement.

Sadly, marriage to Petronilla had revealed Louis Favell in an unflattering light. Etienne could not permit a man who could not withstand the nagging of his wife to become count in his stead. If Louis had proved he could stand up for himself, Etienne would have let matters rest; but alas, Louis had not. He suffered Petronilla's carping and nagging with a patience and humbleness that was most unseemly in a future count.

So Etienne was considering wedding for the third time. He must get an heir. He had summoned Louis and his dreadful wife to his castle, La Forteresse de Aigles. The reason for his summons was simple. Louis was to go to Brittany, and look the de Roncier girl over to ensure she looked a likely breeder. Louis was to negotiate his marriage contract. And while Louis was safely out of the way, Etienne had other, secret, business to attend to.

That night, in the guest bedchamber at La Forteresse, Petronilla started her campaign. Her husband was still undressing for bed. A strongly made, stocky man in his late twenties, Louis Favell was cursed with an amiable, peace-loving nature that was of little use to him as a knight, and gave him no defence against his determined, burgher wife.

'Pass me that wolf-skin, Louis. There's a draught whistling under the door,' Petronilla said, wrapping her loosely knotted brown hair about her neck to warm her, and shivering under the covers. 'And then you can tell me what the old weasel's up to. What does he want?'

The light in the chamber came from a mean fire in a tiny fireplace in one corner of the room, and from a tallow candle which had been set on Petronilla's leather travelling chest next to the bed.

Covering his wife with the soft fur, Louis climbed into

bed wearing his linen chainse for warmth. He slid his arm around Petronilla's waist and his dark head came to rest against her shoulder. 'I'm to go to Brittany as his emissary—'

'His emissary? You? Why do you have to go? Holy Mother, the man's got dozens of men answering to his nod, but he has to waste your time . . . When do you go?'

'End of the week.' Louis' hand slid over his wife's breast and down to the hem of her night-gown. He nuzzled her neck and, encouraged by a responsive kiss, he lifted her shift, his hand wandering up along Petronilla's slender calves, and over a soft thigh. His hand came to rest between her legs. He put his mouth on one dark, pointed nipple, and sucked experimentally.

Petronilla gave a soft, pleasurable sigh, and relaxed her thighs. 'Why? What's so important that it won't wait?'

Louis began moving his hand and fingers in the slow, gentle rhythm that transformed his wife from a calculating, distant woman into a warm, wild, sensual animal. Petronilla squirmed, and moaned beneath him. When Louis removed his mouth from her nipple, she moaned again, except that this time there was wanting in her moan. 'His marriage,' Louis said. 'He's considering marrying and I'm to negotiate the contract.'

A strained quiet fell over the bedchamber. Petronilla — both the draught and her pleasure forgotten — sat up. She put her hand over the one Louis had between her legs, and stilled the movement. 'His what?'

'His marriage. My uncle's toying with the idea of taking another wife.'

'But he can't!'

Louis smiled, a smile of resignation. 'But he can. He wants an heir.'

'You're his heir! What need has he of another?'

Louis gazed earnestly at Petronilla. 'He wants children of his own. Is that so unnatural? You should comprehend

100

that. You said last week you hoped that you—'

'If your uncle marries, we'll lose all this . . .' An expansive wave of Petronilla's arm took in the entire Favell county. She hadn't married Louis for a piddling manor which only brought in enough pence for a pauper. She hadn't married him for love, for though she enjoyed sharing the pleasures of the flesh with him, Petronilla Favell loved power more than she would ever love any man. She'd married Louis Favell for his prospects. She hoped Louis wasn't going to be reasonable about this matter of his uncle's marriage. She hated it when he was reasonable. If only Louis would show a bit of passion now and again . . .

'It is his right,' Louis said, easily.

'Right? Pah! Who's he after?'

'A child, Arlette de Roncier. She's eleven.'

'That's almost old enough for his purposes, the lustful old tup.'

'Petronilla! You seem to be forgetting who you're talking about.'

'My apologies,' came the sarcastic response. 'Honestly, Louis, you must do something about this. We can't have him getting another heir.'

Louis shrugged and tentatively moved his hand. Petronilla pushed it away. 'What can I do?' Louis said, helplessly. 'I don't see how I can prevent my uncle from marrying if he's a mind to.'

'You say you're to negotiate the marriage contract?'

'It's early stages, but aye.'

Petronilla fell silent for a space, thinking, and then a thoughtful smile spread slowly across her face. 'He got no children out of his first wives. The fault must be his, I'll swear his seed is weak, but in case it is not, I know what we must do . . .'

Louis regarded his wife with wary brown eyes. 'What? What must we do?'

Petronilla smiled and, replacing her husband's hand between her thighs, she drew his head to her breast. 'We'll talk about it afterwards, Louis.'

'Afterwards?' Louis smiled.

Petronilla tugged up her husband's chainse.

'Aye, Louis. Afterwards.'

In her tower room, Arlette was seated at the beechwood desk she used when studying with Father Josse. There was a knock at the door: an uncommon courtesy, given that she was locked in – and had been for five days – as the whole of Huelgastel knew. It was time for her to receive her daily ration.

'Come in.' Arlette put her psalter down. Her psalter was the one book her father had permitted her to keep during her incarceration. All Father Josse's other manuscripts and parchments had been summarily removed the morning after Gabriel's death. Would Clemence knock before bringing her her bread and water? Arlette thought it unlikely, but she was longing to see her friend, and hoped it was her. So far one of her father's dour-faced mercenaries had been sent up with her food. He had been uncommunicative, and Arlette had not even been able to winkle his name out of him. Arlette was desperate to see a friendly face, and to discover what Jehan's fate had been.

The key rattled in the lock, and a tousled flaxen head appeared round the door. Not Clemence, but another routier. Unconsciously, Arlette sighed. This one had pleasant blue eyes though, and he smiled across at her. Arlette knew this one's name. He was called Ned Fletcher, and he was English. He had been in her father's troop for two years. During that time, Arlette had never spoken to him, but she had always thought he looked kind. Would he give her news of Jehan? Arlette guessed that he was not much older than Jehan, so he must know him.

'Lady Arlette?'

'Come in, Fletcher.' Arlette took the tray containing a brown wheatloaf and jug of water from the English soldier. She tried not to appear too hungry, but the five days of fasting was having its effect on her young, growing body, and she was hard put not to snatch up the loaf and tear at it with her teeth. Holy Mother, but that loaf did smell good.

'It's warm yet, fresh from the oven,' Ned Fletcher said, having seen where her gaze was fixed.

'My thanks. I shall enjoy it. I had stale black rye before.'

'Only another two days to go, my lady,' Ned Fletcher said, sympathetically.

'Aye.' She paused. 'May I ask you a question?'

Ned Fletcher smiled. 'My lady?'

'Do you know what happened to Jehan?'

Ned Fletcher flushed to his ears. He stared at the rush matting at his feet. 'I . . . I'm sorry, my lady. I'm forbidden to talk to you about Jehan.' He began to close the door.

Arlette clutched desperately at his hand.

'My lady. Please, you must not.'

Sensing a softness in the young Englishman, Arlette ruthlessly pulled him back into her chamber. 'Tell me, I beg you. Is Jehan all right?'

'My lady . . .' Strong, blunt, fingers began to prise her fingers open, but Arlette could see he was unwilling to hurt her, and clung all the harder.

'Is Jehan alive? Tell me that, at least . . .'

Ned Fletcher freed himself and, swift as lightning, dodged round the door. The door swung shut.

'Ned, please!' Stumbling to the door, Arlette struck it so hard with her fists she grazed the skin on her knuckles. The key turned in the lock, and then Ned Fletcher's whisper came muffled and low through the oak.

'Jehan's well, my lady. He's not been beaten.'

Smiling with relief, Arlette sank to the floor and licked her bruised knuckles.

Two days later, in the family solar above Huelgastel hall, the Countess Marie de Roncier was engaged in conversation with her son.

'Tell me, François,' the countess was choosing fabric for another winter gown, and several bales of cloth were partially unrolled on the trestle in the middle of the solar, 'How long do you intend keeping your girl mewed up? Don't you think she's been alone long enough?'

Marie's forty-eight years lay heavily on her. Out of sight beneath her veil lay hair as white as her wimple. Her complexion was sallow and dry; and deep, bitter lines radiated outwards from her tightly compressed lips, legacy of her loveless marriage. Her large fleshless beak of nose was cold, her skin was stretched tautly across it. Thin as a lathe, the countess had bony and brittle-looking arms which protruded from the sleeves of her gown like dry sticks. Several rings — with claw settings and large gems — had been pushed over her painfully enlarged finger-joints. The backs of her hands were mottled with age-spots.

The serving woman, Lena, hovered anxiously at the countess's elbow. Whenever François de Roncier's hazel eyes travelled in her direction, Lena blushed rosily.

The countess fingered a section of blue open-weave wool and grimaced. 'Coarser than a hair shirt,' she pronounced. 'It would be a penance to wear it.' Reaching for the next roll of cloth, she drew it towards her.

Over her gown, the countess wore a three-quarter-length fur wrap. Fragile and delicate in appearance, Countess Marie de Roncier looked as though a puff of wind would snuff her out. But appearances were deceptive. Marie de Roncier was a tough old bird, as a close inspection of her hard, dark eyes would reveal. Almost as black as jet, and bright, nothing escaped their notice.

'François, about Arlette,' she prompted.

'I was going to let my daughter stew till this evening,' François responded, idly feeling the quality of the gaudier of two yellow cloths laid out for his mother's approval. 'I'd planned to visit her after evensong, to see if she were in a more compliant mood, but another night of solitary confinement may not go amiss. I'm expecting Count Favell's emissary any day, and I want to be certain we'll be spared any embarrassment.' He looked up from the material he had been inspecting, and winked at Lena. 'This stuff feels warm, ma mère,' he said.

Marie de Roncier lowered her hooked nose over her son's choice. 'Mustard? With my colouring? No, François, I think not.' She glanced at Lena, adding dryly, 'That's a younger woman's colour. This fern is more to my taste, though at my age perhaps I should choose grey . . .'

'No, Maman. Have the green if you like it.'

'François, about Arlette . . .'

'Maman?'

'Would you like me to speak to her? Perhaps as a woman, I might be able to influence her. Clemence and Eleanor have done well, but I am painfully aware that while Arlette has learnt stitchery from Clemence and Holy Writ from Eleanor and Father Josse, there are aspects of her education that appear to have been sadly neglected.'

Countess Marie realised that she herself had devoted little attention to the child. She was by nature a practical woman, who enjoyed running the household but — apart from with her husband, whom she adored unrequitedly — was economical with her affections. Besides, she had never seen what was to be gained by becoming too fond of a granddaughter who would one day be sent away in marriage. But now that day seemed to be drawing near,

the countess was beginning to feel a certain responsibility
for the girl's welfare, and a consciousness of how her
behaviour might reflect on the family as a whole.

François de Roncier's ruddy face creased in
puzzlement.

'Arlette's education neglected? Which aspects,
Maman?'

'I know you discovered her in the stables with Jehan le
Moine,' Marie said, 'but I'd wager it was perfectly
innocent.'

'I know that, ma mère, but Arlette must learn to protect
herself against gossip if she's to be Countess Favell . . .'

'François, you know your daughter only has room in
her heart for her animals. It would never have occurred to
her that people might misinterpret her meeting with
Hamon's boy.'

François scowled. 'It should have occurred to her.
Father Josse informs me my daughter has intelligence . . .'

Marie smiled thinly. 'She's naïve, but I agree it won't
do. Let me speak to her. I'll go up later when I've finished
with this.' She nodded at the maidservant. 'Lena, roll up
the stuffs, will you? All except that green, we shall be
cutting that this morning. And find my shears.'

'Countess,' Lena sprang to do her bidding and, as the
maidservant brushed past Marie's son, he ran his hand
swiftly, surreptitiously, over the girl's buttocks. Lena gave
a stifled giggle.

Marie de Roncier, noting both gesture and giggle,
pursed her lips, but otherwise gave no sign that she had
observed anything.

'Grandmère! I didn't expect to see you here,' Arlette
exclaimed, when her door next opened and the Countess
Marie stood on the threshold, panting slightly from the
climb to Arlette's turret room. This was the first time a

member of her family had approached her since her incarceration, and Arlette hoped that it heralded the end of her punishment. Running to her bed, Arlette smoothed the coverlet, for there was nowhere else that her grandmother could sit, apart from the stool at the desk, which had been brought in soon after Clemence's arrival at Huelgastel. The stool was too high and unstable for an elderly woman. 'Do sit, Grandmère.'

The countess acknowledged this courtesy with the slight smile which was the most her narrow lips ever managed. 'My thanks, child.' Walking across the matting, she sank on to the bed, while Arlette stood uncertainly in front of her, playing with her plaited silk girdle. 'Arlette, your father informed me of your behaviour—'

'I did nothing! Jehan—'

The countess fixed her granddaughter with stern black eyes. 'Arlette, you are intemperate. Be pleased to hold your tongue in check until I have done.'

'My pardon, Grandmère.'

'That's better. Listen, child, your father has great plans for you, and you should strive to be worthy of them. He is negotiating your marriage with Count Etienne Favell.'

The countess paused, and Arlette judged a response was called for. 'I know, Grandmère.'

'You sound displeased, child. Are you not sensible of the high honour that is being done you?'

'Yes, Grandmère, but—'

'Then you should know better than to consort in the stables with young men after curfew.'

Another pause. 'We did nothing,' Arlette insisted, adding bluntly, 'Jehan and I are not lovers, if that's what everyone is fussing about.'

Gently, Marie took her granddaughter's hand, noting the fresh, unblemished skin and the straight, supple fingers. 'The hand of a young girl,' she murmured.

'Grandmère?'

'Arlette, I know you and Jehan are innocent. And so does your father, and Eleanor. But your father is right to be concerned about your behaviour. You're grown up, old enough to wed, and you must consider your position.' The countess sighed. 'I blame myself. Your mother died when you were very young, and I should have overseen your upbringing. Instead I left you to your father and Eleanor, who relied too much on Agata before Clemence came to the castle. And lately you have spent much time with Father Josse. He has given you a clerk's education. I should have stopped it . . .'

'But, Grandmère, I *like* to learn. I *like* what Father Josse has taught me.'

The thin lips tightened. 'Arlette, you interrupt . . .'

'My apologies, Grandmère.'

'In the past you were permitted to run wild. You made unsuitable friends. I know you have changed, but your father fears a return of your former unruly behaviour. Count Favell's emissary will arrive any day, and I want you to swear to me that you will behave impeccably. Well, Arlette?'

Arlette had to ask. 'What happened to Jehan?'

'He's gone.'

'Gone? Where? Did father hurt him? Ned Fletcher told me he was not beaten . . .' No sooner had that last sentence fallen from Arlette's lips than she regretted it. She did not want to bring her father's anger down on the young Englishman's ears. Fortunately, her grandmother did not appear to have noticed her slip.

'Jehan has been sent to another household. Its precise location should not be of any interest to you. He will continue with his military service there. Well, child? Your promise, if you please.'

Arlette sent her grandmother an appealing look. 'Jehan wasn't beaten, was he?'

'He was not. Now put that young man out of your

108

head, child, and give your grandmother your promise. You will behave when Count Favell's emissary arrives?'

'I'll behave. I swear it, Grandmère. May I see Clemence?'

Marie de Roncier granted her granddaughter another of her thin smiles. 'You may. She's in the solar, sewing with Lena. Now that's an activity suited to a young countess . . .'

Arlette did not enjoy sewing; she had not the patience for it, and found it a trial to keep still for long, but if it meant she was to be allowed out of her room . . .

Stored in Arlette's heart were a number of questions, and Jehan's exact location was but one of them. Arlette burned to know more about Count Favell. Where did he live? How old was he? Was he kind like her grandfather? Or was he like her father? When would she marry him? For her grandmother's benefit Arlette forced a smile, and in case her grandmother should be irritated, and change her mind about releasing her, Arlette sealed her curiosity up inside her, and accompanied her grandmother down the winding stairs to the solar. Perhaps Clemence had managed to pick up some news concerning her suitor . . .

Heulgastel chapel, a slender, barrel-vaulted room whose ceiling was azure and spangled with silver stars, was of no great size. The chapel was reached via a long, gloomy passage which led from the family solar.

Lady Eleanor de Roncier, now almost twenty-two, spent much of her time in the chapel, watched by the saints whose painted images marched along the chapel walls. That afternoon, Lady Eleanor's private contemplations were interrupted by a loud footfall in the corridor. Someone entered the chapel. Lady Eleanor kept her neat head bowed over hands which were clenched hard on a coral rosary. Her elongated sleeves hung over the edge of her ornately carved prie-dieu, and her brown velvet skirt spread wide across the red-tiled floor. When the newcomer knelt at her side, Lady Eleanor did not glance up, not until she had completed her prayers. Then she lifted her head, fixed her light blue eyes on the great, bronze crucifix which hung over the altar, and crossed herself.

A wintry grey light shafted down through three narrow window slits behind the altar. Two beeswax candles burned in polished brass stands — both the costly candles and the stands being an offering from Lady Eleanor herself. The candles' fragrance filled the chapel, right up to the star-spangled ceiling. Lady Eleanor had embroidered the altar cloth. A vase of evergreens brightened a plain, whitewashed niche: that, too, had been placed there by her hands.

When she was ready, Lady Eleanor turned to her companion. 'Count Robert!'

'Praying for a son, Eleanor?' the count asked, looking at his daughter-in-law with kindly eyes.

Robert enjoyed watching Eleanor. She was beautiful in an ethereal, well-bred way. Her gentle, almond-shaped eyes looked at the world past curly light eyelashes. She had arched brows and light blonde hair, good bones, and skin like alabaster. She was slender, and her breasts were high. Her hands were long, and spoke of an aristocratic pedigree. Lady Eleanor's tragedy was that her lineage had not guaranteed her fruitfulness. Eleanor had been married to Count Robert's son for nigh on eight years, and had still not shown the slightest sign of quickening. And Count Robert could not lay the blame for that at his son's door, given that François had got Arlette and her poor, dead brother out of his first wife Joan, and that a number of his son's bastards littered the Duchy.

Today Eleanor's fair hair was twisted into a bun at the back of her neck and secured with gold netting. Not a strand out of place, as usual. A round jewelled cap perched on top of Eleanor's head, secured by a silk barbette under her chin. Her thick velvet gown was laced at the sides to reveal a cream silk under-gown.

'Eleanor?'

Eleanor blinked and, to Robert's astonishment, a faint flush brought some colour to the smooth, alabaster cheeks. Robert had never seen his daughter-in-law blush before.

'Aye,' she answered him softly, taking her time. 'I *was* praying for a son, mon seigneur. And this time . . . this time . . . I have hopes . . .'

The extraordinary flush deepened. Count Robert examined Eleanor's face with care. 'You think you might be with child?'

'It's early days, mon seigneur, but I have my hopes.'

Robert beamed, and patted one of the elegant white hands. 'Oh, my dear, I do hope so. I shall pray for a son for you.'

'Thank you, Count Robert.'

Gently, Eleanor withdrew her hand. Robert had noticed before how his daughter-in-law shunned physical contact with her fellows. Not for the first time he wondered how she survived as wife to a son as lusty as his. Gracefully, Eleanor rose to her feet. 'You're not leaving on my account, I hope,' Robert said.

Eleanor smiled. 'No, mon seigneur, I promised to help Countess Marie instruct Arlette in some dressmaking.'

'So my wife saw to it that François released her? Good. I hoped she would.' Robert paused. 'Eleanor, I should like you to keep counsel on your news for the time being . . .'

'I wasn't going to mention it to anyone, save you, not until I'm certain.'

'Good. If Count Favell gets to hear of it, he might think twice about allying himself with my granddaughter. It's one thing to want to marry an heiress, but if you give my son a boy . . . You understand, my dear?'

'Perfectly, mon seigneur.'

'And send Arlette to me, would you, Eleanor? When she's done with her needlework, naturally.'

'Of course, Count Robert.'

Sedately, Eleanor withdrew, her trailing hem sweeping the tiles. Robert heaved himself up from his prie-dieu. Along the north and south walls of the chapel ran two stone ledges covered with downy silk cushions. Stretching, the count wandered across and sat on one. He leaned his back against St Paul. He had much to consider . . .

If Eleanor was with child, he must get Arlette's marriage contract signed and sealed before the news came out. By reputation Count Favell was a wily, parsimonious old soul, who would bear watching.

An unexpected constriction in his chest called a halt to his musings. Robert gasped, grimaced, and massaged his breast. 'Sweet Jesus, not again.' There was nothing he could do, save hold himself still as a stone, and pray the spasm passed, as it usually did. In a moment the tightness eased, and Robert's breathing resumed its normal rhythm. He picked up the thread of his thoughts . . .

If Eleanor was with child, it would change the course of the lives of everyone in Huelgastel, probably for the better. But until she held a son in her arms, Arlette remained heiress. And Arlette should marry Count Favell.

And if Eleanor was not with child . . .

In that case, Robert was aware that any heir Arlette gave Count Favell would be likely to milk the de Roncier estates for all they were worth. His people would have to answer to an absentee landlord, for it was not likely that a Favell would favour Huelgastel over his county in the Périgord. Favell would visit them from time to time, to check up on the new steward he would be likely to install — Count Robert's own steward, Hamon, had best consider his future. Robert reminded himself to ensure

112

Hamon had somewhere to go. He'd not like to see an old friend cast out like a beggar.

None of these thoughts was fresh to Robert; he had turned them over in his mind many times before. But until François produced a boy, there was little he could do to ensure the security of his people. Marrying Arlette to Count Favell was the best course open to them, for Count Favell was powerful, and he would be bound to protect them. Robert had to ensure his granddaughter understood that.

Was Eleanor with child? She could be mistaken. What was it she had said? It was early days. And it could scarcely be safe to assume that a healthy heir would inevitably result, even if she were. Robert recalled the tragedy of Joan and little François well enough. No, he could not afford to alter his plans for Arlette, not at this stage. When Count Favell's emissary arrived, he would be treated with all due courtesy, and Arlette would be betrothed.

The unpleasant tightness was back in Robert's chest, squeezing the breath out of him. The tightness increased, and he felt a terrible coldness in his chest, as though a dead man were clinging to his heart. A dead man with hands that gripped like a vice . . .

Robert opened his mouth to cry out, but couldn't find the breath. He clutched at his breast, fighting for air. His lungs burned, his eyes bulged in their sockets. Staggering to his feet, he managed a couple of steps towards the door, croaking for help. At the end of the chapel passage his wife was sitting sewing with his granddaughter. They must hear him. They must.

He gave another, desperate, gasping cry. But knew it was not nearly loud enough. The chapel corridor was long, and the door at the other end shut to keep out the draughts . . .

As Count Robert fell he wondered whether a man who

113

died in God's house would already be half-way to Heaven.

Countess Marie could yet set large stitches in a broad canvas tapestry, but her fingers could no longer manage the finer ones that clothing required, which was why she had roped in Arlette, Eleanor, Clemence and Lena to sew her green worsted.

After three hours of painstaking sewing, Arlette found her afternoon of freedom was beginning to pall. And because her grandmother and her stepmother had not left her alone with Clemence for a single moment, she had been unable to wring any information from her friend about Jehan, or Count Favell, or her coming betrothal.

Thankfully, January afternoons were relatively short.

'Lena,' Countess Marie said when the light was beginning to fade, 'fetch us some tapers.'

'Countess.'

'And you, girls,' the countess fixed Clemence and Arlette with her dark eyes, 'you may put your work aside. You've done well.'

With a barely concealed sigh of relief, Arlette set aside the sleeve she had been sewing. 'I'd like to take a walk,' she said. 'Will you come with me, Clemence?'

Arlette's stepmother looked up. 'You will have to wait for your walk, Arlette. Your grandfather wants to see you.'

Arlette jumped up, smiling. 'Where is he? I'd not hoped to see him before supper . . .'

'Count Robert was in the chapel when I saw him,' Lady Eleanor's smooth brow clouded. 'But that was some hours ago. I wouldn't have thought he'd still be in there. Did anyone see him pass through here on his way out?'

'No. Don't worry, Belle-mère. He's dozing, most likely,' Arlette said. 'I'll go and see.'

Arlette entered the cool chapel passage, hoping she would find her grandfather in a good humour. She wanted

114

nothing better than a private conversation with her grandfather, for she had noticed how the old man was always more amenable to her wishes when they were alone. In the great hall he was unable to forget that he was the Count de Roncier, he was on show in front of his retainers, and though he always treated her fairly, he gave her no rein. But when Arlette and her grandfather met privately, his attitude towards her underwent a subtle change. He demonstrated his affection more openly, and allowed her to weedle him. If Arlette could talk to her grandfather in private, she was certain he would provide her with answers to some of her most pressing questions.

She pushed open the door. 'Grandpère?' But her grandfather's walnut prie-dieu was empty. 'Grandpère?' And then she saw him, lying on his back on the red tiles. At first Arlette did not appreciate the significance of what she was seeing. She moved towards him. 'Grandpère? You've fallen, let me help you.'

Count Robert was spread-eagled among a tumble of plump silk cushions; his strong, gnarled hand had clenched the delicate fabric of one of them so hard that his nails had ripped the cover. One or two feathers had escaped, and these created a cruel illusion of movement, for they drifted gently across the tiles at Arlette's approach.

'Grandpapa?'

Silence, save for the hissing of an altar candle as it burned off an impurity in the wax.

'Grandpapa?' Arlette dropped to her knees, and her heart began leaping about in her chest. Her grandfather was not moving. His eyes were open. Blue eyes staring at a star-spangled azure ceiling; beautiful blue eyes, which were misted over as Arlette had never seen them, so they were both heart-rendingly familiar and distressingly strange. Where was their sparkle? Their life? Count Robert's skin was pale as marble. And cold as marble?

Quivering, Arlette touched her grandfather's cheek. Cold as marble. Gone. Her grandfather had gone to the angels.

Kneeling at his side, it was some time before Arlette moved. She drew a deep breath and straightened the long limbs. She steeled herself to tug the rent cushion from her grandfather's clutch. She crossed his hands on his breast. She brushed off the feathers. Then she pulled the proud head on to her lap, flinching from the direct gaze of the sightless eyes. With a tight jaw, she closed them and began stroking his thick white hair. Gently, she rocked him from side to side, and crooned softly to herself.

Count Robert would have been proud of his granddaughter. She had not shed a single tear.

François de Roncier, oblivious of the fact that he was now count, was riding with Otto Malait as his escort through the outskirts of Vannes.

François and his Viking captain proceeded at a brisk trot past St Patern's church; their breath and that of their horses curling like white smoke through dank air that held the briny tang of the nearby sea. Their horses' hoofs rang on the frozen ground. The two riders were later than they had intended, and dusk was closing in. If they did not make haste, the town gates would be barred when they returned. They passed under the prison gate.

François addressed the gate-keeper, a surly, beetle-browed fellow, who was all but swallowed up in a moth-eaten brown capuchon that was acres too large for him. 'We'll be back within the hour.' François tossed the man a penny. 'I've another of these for you if you'll stay to let us out.'

'I'll stay.'

The horsemen's ultimate destination was a narrow thoroughfare south of St Peter's Cathedral, where Tomaz the goldsmith had his workshop. François had commissioned Tomaz to make a gift for his wife. He gave

Eleanor many gifts, but she remained cold and remote. And in bed, Eleanor had yet to warm to him. François lived in the hope that one day his wife would change.

François took what comfort he could from Lena, his mother's maid. Lena welcomed him, made François feel like a king; but for all her enthusiasm Lena was not his equal, and François longed to win Eleanor's affection. He was fond of his beautiful, high-bred wife and longed to touch her heart. Though cool, she was a good companion, and saw to it that his daily needs were met, though it was true she had yet to provide him with the son he so desperately required. On more than one occasion his mother had suggested that François should put Eleanor aside and marry a fertile woman. But François could not cast her aside. His liking for his wife might be a weakness, but it was one he could not stamp out.

Eleanor's simple tastes confounded François. Most of the gifts he had brought her were squirrelled away in a rosewood casket in their bedchamber, and never saw the light of day. But observing how his wife haunted the chapel, and her predilection for religious rite, François had been inspired to charge Tomaz with fashioning a gold reliquary cross for her. It was to be set with a few seed pearls, nothing too ornate, she did not appreciate elaborate jewellery. François planned to give it to her at Candlemas, a few days hence. And if he could but acquire a suitable relic to put inside it . . .

A few moments later, François de Roncier and Otto Malait drew rein outside the unpretentious wooden building which served as house and workshop for the goldsmith. At ground level, the workshop fronted the street. The shutters, both of the workshop and the living quarters above, were closed. The house appeared to be deserted.

Undeterred, François guided his horse up to the dwelling, stood in his stirrups, and rapped sharply on the

117

upper storey shutters with his crop. 'Tomaz! Open up! Tomaz!'

Some moments passed.

'Tomaz! *Tomaz!* Devil take the man, where can he be?'

'There's someone in there, mon seigneur, I can hear them . . .'

The bolt scraped back, the door opened a crack, and a clumsy, hairy hand appeared. It had always astounded François that such ugly, ungainly hands could produce such clever, dainty works of art. There wasn't a goldsmith with half Tomaz's talent in the whole of Brittany.

Tomaz peered out. His swarthy face was pale, there were dark circles under his eyes, and his eyelids were red. 'M . . . mon seigneur! I'm closed today, but for you I'll open. Fortunately I completed your cross early, or it wouldn't be ready.' He opened his door, and stood aside for François to enter.

Dismounting, François tossed his reins to the Norseman and went inside. 'Wouldn't be ready? That's unlike you, Tomaz. What's amiss?' He walked up to the goldsmith's workbench which was unnaturally empty except for a crucible and a bunch of dried herbs. Herbs? Idly François picked up the crucible. 'Your furnace is out, Tomaz. You've not been working.'

Tomaz didn't reply, but took a key from the cluster hanging from his belt and went to open one of the strongboxes which were, as François knew, bolted to the floor. He withdrew a package wrapped in velvet.

'Here you are, mon seigneur. I hope it pleases your lordship.'

'It's your wife Eveline, isn't it, Tomaz? Is she ill?' François asked. Before he had married Joan, François had known Eveline well. A pretty, fair girl, daughter of a wealthy merchant, she had initiated François into the delights of love and when his association with her had come to an end, they had parted on good terms. François had never forgotten her, and had been happy to hear of her marriage with Tomaz.

'Aye, mon seigneur. It is Eveline. She . . . she's taken sick . . .' The goldsmith blinked wearily, and rubbed his eyes. 'It was only a cold to start with,' he went on, 'but it got into her lungs; and though we tried every remedy and concoction in Pierre's herbal, nothing seemed to have any effect.' Tomaz swallowed. 'I've not worked for three days for nursing her. But I think she's on the mend now.'

'I'm glad,' François said.

Tomaz watched François closely as he unwrapped the cross. 'You like it, mon seigneur?' he asked anxiously.

François turned it carefully in his hands. Tomaz had edged it with loops of filigree wire, and set the seed pearls along the rim. The back of the cross was partly transparent, the door to the reliquary being made from rock crystal upon which Tomaz had engraved Eleanor's name.

'Who showed you how to do this?' François enquired. Tomaz could not read.

'Father Mark. You . . . you like it, mon seigneur?'

'It's exquisite,' François said. 'But then, your work always is.' He drew his purse from his belt, counted out what was owed and, as an afterthought, added more.

'My lord! You are generous . . .'

'For your children, Tomaz. It will help while your wife recovers.' And, stowing the precious cross securely in his wallet, François went out to his horse, leaving an astonished Tomaz stuttering his thanks.

Chapter Six

In the chapel, the Dowager Countess Marie, as she would be known from henceforth, stood stock-still beside the open bier which had been placed in front of the altar, jet-black eyes riveted to her husband's face. Her new green gown had been put aside: she was wearing the gloomy widows' attire that she would wear for the rest of her life.

Hunched over her walking stick, she ignored the comings and goings as the more senior members of the household filed into the chapel to pay their last respects to Count Robert. Marie de Roncier's cheeks had lost even their sallow look, seemed quite without colour, utterly bloodless. The shape of her skull was more visible than ever, the hooked nose more pronounced. The dowager countess had not spoken since Arlette had come to her with news of Count Robert's death.

The new count, her son, had not returned from Vannes and, until he did so, and had been told of his father's demise, Marie would watch in silence at her husband's side.

Countess Eleanor and the Lady Arlette shared the dowager's vigil; the countess at her prie-dieu, and Arlette on the stone bench which skirted the south wall.

After an hour, Arlette rose and went out, returning some moments later with a stool. 'Grandmama, you should sit down.'

No answer. Not so much as a flicker of the dark eyes.

When Arlette touched her grandmother's hand, the old woman started.

'Arlette?' Marie de Roncier spoke as though from a hundred miles away; her gaze never left the beloved face.

'You should sit down, Grandmama.'

'I'll sit when François has come, and not before.'

Arlette knew her grandmother could be as stubborn as a mule, and was not prepared to argue. 'Very well, Grandmama.'

The flow of mourners had ceased. Footsteps were scurrying along the passage.

A tall, handsome man, whose curly brown hair was tonsured, and who was wearing the habit of a priest, burst in. 'Ma dame, your son—'

François de Roncier's entry cut off Father Josse mid-sentence. 'Mama! I've only just been told . . .'

At the sound of her son's voice, a quiver ran through the dowager countess. Slowly, she lifted her eyes from her husband's face and held out a hand. 'François!'

The new count was across the Chapel in two swift, energetic strides. He took his mother's hand and raised it to his lips. 'Mama, I'm sorry,' he said, sincerely. He looked at his father and fell silent. Eventually he cleared his throat. 'When did it happen?'

His mother clung to his hand. 'This afternoon. It happened in here. Robert was on his own. Arlette found him . . .'

The Count glanced across at his pale-faced daughter, sitting by the wall, two long red plaits trailing down her breast. Arlette was watching him as though he were a demon sent to torment her. He saw her open her mouth, then apparently think better of it, and close it again.

'Daughter? You've something to say?' The look she gave him was startled, the look of a doe before the hounds gave chase, and it occurred to François for the first time that perhaps his treatment of her had been over-harsh.

Etienne Favell would not want her spirit broken. He would want a strong woman to mother his children.

'It's Grandmama, Papa. It must be two hours since she sat down. Can you make her rest?'

François glanced at his mother. Staring out of dark sockets, her eyes had been drawn back to his father's lifeless face, as though there were an invisible thread pulling them there.

'She just stands there, gazing at him . . .'

François ran a hand through his cropped copper hair. 'Arlette, send for Lena, would you? I noticed her in the solar.'

Arlette left the chapel.

The count attempted to lead his mother to the door.

'No, François . . .' The dowager countess resisted. 'Let me stay. I want to look at him while I may.'

'Mama, it's time the coffin was nailed down. Say your last farewell.'

Like a puppet, Marie stepped up to the bier to kiss her husband's cheek.

Arlette returned with Lena.

'Lena, escort my mother to her chamber, she needs to rest.'

Lena bobbed him a curtsey. 'Aye, mon seigneur.'

The dowager countess lifted her head and her haughty, beak of a nose pointed at the stars on the ceiling. 'I can manage, François. I can manage.' Stick tapping, she made her way to the door. 'Lena can see to it that I'm not disturbed.'

'Madame.'

The dowager countess tapped her way out and down the corridor followed by Lena.

François de Roncier, Count, turned to his wife. She was looking at Father Josse, listening religiously to some prayer the priest was mouthing. François wished that Eleanor would give him half the attention she gave the castle priest. 'Eleanor?' he spoke sharply.

His wife's pale eyes met his. 'Mon seigneur?'

François held out his hand. 'Come, Eleanor. It's time we showed the new count and countess to the people of Huelgastel.'

Eleanor bent her head in acknowledgement.

Louis Favell, emissary of Count Etienne Favell, arrived at Huelgastel in time for Count Robert de Roncier's funeral on Candlemas Eve.

He attended a simple ceremony which was held in the family chapel, before Count Robert's remains were carried out to the hallowed ground outside the curtain wall. The count would be placed in the family tomb. The granite slab covering the tomb had been levered off, and the grave-pit yawned wide to receive him. The de Roncier coat of arms – a cinquefoil in a circlet of briars – was carved deep into the stone. In the burial chamber, two of Count Robert's squires were waiting to receive the coffin and set it in its final resting place.

Standing with Count Robert's close kin around the grave, and with a suitably mournful expression pinned to his face, Louis was free to observe the de Roncier family.

'O, Almighty God,' the priest began to intone. The sound reminded Louis of a swarm of distant bees. He let the noise flow over him.

Nearest the graveside, the dowager countess was supported on one side by her granddaughter Arlette, and on the other by the new countess, Eleanor. The three women were sombrely clad, the two youngest in grey, the older woman in stark black. Louis could see nothing of the dowager countess's features, for she had covered her head with a black veil.

'We humbly commend the soul of this Thy servant . . .' The priest's droning continued, while Louis assessed Arlette de Roncier. She was a pretty child, if one liked that red hair. She was well-formed, though to judge by her hips and breasts, not quite fully grown. That drab grey suited her, it made the most of her exotic colouring. She looked too young for his uncle — far too young. Louis sighed. For all that grief had made Arlette de Roncier pale, and had put charcoal smudges under her eyes, she looked hale enough to produce a child or two.

It was fortunate for Louis that Petronilla had come to the conclusion that his uncle was incapable of siring a child, or his task here would be impossible. Petronilla had pointed out that Etienne Favell had had two wives already, and had not managed to provide one child. 'Consider, Louis,' Petronilla had said that night in his uncle's guest bedchamber, 'how likely is it that your uncle should have had the misfortune to marry *two* infertile women? No, I'd be prepared to take my oath that the fault is in him. Weak seed. That's his problem.'

But, in the unlikely event that the fault was not Etienne's, Petronilla had instructed Louis to do what he could to delay the marriage.

'Your uncle will never know that it was *you* who insisted the delay clause should be inserted,' she had insisted. 'He will not be there when you negotiate. You can tell him the child's father is fond of her — is not ready to lose his only child yet or some such excuse — that will remind Etienne that if he wants to marry an heiress, there's a price to pay. Or you could say her family want to wait until she has grown up a little — until she's fifteen, perhaps. I'm confident you'll come up with a suitable explanation.'

At that moment Arlette de Roncier looked across the grave-pit and exchanged glances with her father, and the look that father and daughter gave each other was far from fond. The girl looked fearful and nervous. Her father frowned, and quickly looked away. If Louis was to delay the marriage between Arlette de Roncier and

Etienne Favell, he would have to look for a reason other than family affection. There did not appear to be much love lost between those two.

'May he rest in peace,' the priest chanted.

'Amen,' Louis responded along with the rest of the funeral party.

Having dispatched his nephew Louis to Brittany to negotiate his marriage contract, Count Etienne's mind turned to his 'special business'. For this it was imperative that Petronilla Favell was well out of the way.

To this end, the count swallowed his distaste and, riding his great grey, Snowstorm, personally saw to it that his nephew's wife was escorted back to their manor. His loyal and trusted castellan, Sir Gilles Fitzhugh, rode behind them with a squire. Though Sir Gilles and Lady Petronilla had been friends once, these days they only ever spoke to each other when they had to, and Sir Gilles made no attempt to ride alongside her.

Sir Gilles was a tall, well-built man in his third decade, with dark blond hair and blue eyes. He looked his best on a horse, and when he was in full armour, he made an impressive figure. Blond brows bunched, Sir Gilles contented himself with frowning at Petronilla's back. His pride would only permit him to stare at her when she was not looking. He was confused. Lady Petronilla aroused emotions in him which ought to have died when she had married Louis. But the emotions had not died. Day and night they haunted him. Day and night he longed to be free of them.

As he rode, the castellan's heart twisted remembering the summer, it did not seem so long ago, when he had exchanged vows with the slant-eyed merchant's daughter. Her grey eyes had sparkled, apparently with happiness, and she had showered him with kisses and soft words. She had promised to marry him. Easy lies. Gilles had been living in a fool's paradise, for no sooner had he introduced Petronilla to Louis Favell, his friend and the count's heir, than she had transferred her affections to him. The transfer had been immediate and thorough. So thorough that even now, years after, Gilles felt bemused when he thought about it. He tried not to think about it too often. He was a knight, a fine catch for a pretty merchant's daughter, but she had loved him only until the count's newphew had entered her life.

He had been useful to Petronilla in as much as he had provided her with an introduction to Louis, and she had proved herself to be no better than a feckless whore with an eye on Count Etienne's title. Since she had spurned him, Sir Gilles had done his best to kill off all tender feelings for her. But he was afraid, very much afraid, that in this he had failed.

He glanced at Count Etienne, alongside Petronilla. The Count valued him for his cool head, for his logical approach to administration. If only Etienne knew, Gilles thought, of the grievous secret he nursed in his heart.

Unaware of the turmoil in his castellan's head, Count Etienne was happy to ride in silence, quite unembarrassed by the lack of conversation. By nature he was disinclined to talk simply for the sake of it. He would rather be left alone to pursue his own thoughts, and understood that his castellan felt the same. He had noticed how Sir Gilles avoided Petronilla and had long ago come to the conclusion that Sir Gilles must have developed almost as great an antipathy towards Petronilla as he felt himself. It was one of the reasons he trusted the man so much. Etienne and Gilles thought alike, and neither of them cherished any illusions as to the nature of Petronilla's character. If only Louis had half the intelligence of Gilles. If only Louis would remove his blinkers.

Favell Manor was huddled at the bottom of the cliff at the farming village of La Roque-Gageac. Not only was the manor built in stone — most of its neighbours were wooden constructions — but it was the largest at the end of a row of houses which clung to the riverbank, and was encircled by a sturdy stone wall the height of a man. The ice-encrusted River Dordogne flowed within feet of the Favell's front gate. It was a pleasant, well-built house, with a south-facing yard which trapped the sun in summer; and though it could not compare with Count Etienne's castle, most women would think it heaven to live there.

But as they rode up to the manor, the count could not miss the disparaging glance Petronilla flung at her home. Petronilla Favell, he reminded himself, was not most women. Petronilla Favell had her eyes on his domain, and that was one of the reasons the count was sending her away. The other reason concerned his 'special business'. It was vital that neither Louis nor his wife had an inkling of what Count Etienne was planning. The count knew that Louis was unable to keep anything from his meddling wife, and he wanted Petronilla Favell's long nose kept out of this.

'I don't know why you insisted on escorting me back, Count Etienne,' Petronilla said sweetly, and the plume in her hat danced in the frosty air. Petronilla's grey eyes belied her tone, for a moment they rested on Sir Gilles and they were, as usual, sharp as needles.

'I have the rounds of my estate to do, my dear, and with Louis being away, there would not have been anyone to entertain you . . .'

'I would have been happy on my own at La Forteresse, dear Count,' Petronilla declared. 'I love it so, I don't need anyone to entertain me when I'm there.'

Another dissatisfied glance at her home. She was implying, not very subtly, that she was bored at Favell Manor.

'I'm sure there's plenty to occupy you here, my dear.'

The count did his best to be polite, even to this woman. Never let it be said that Count Etienne Favell was anything but courteous. 'I prefer to think of you safely in your own bed while I am absent, dear Petronilla.'

The horses, growing impatient, side-stepped and champed on their bits. The count and his nephew's wife glared at each other.

'Won't you and Sir Gilles come in and get warm, and refresh yourselves?' Petronilla asked, and her lips shaped a passable smile.

'My thanks, but no . . .'

One of Petronilla's house-servants had run up to unlock the iron gates. Etienne waved at his squire to hand Petronilla's travelling chest over.

'I've several miles to cover, and I don't want to founder the horses. Daylight is rationed at this time of year, and I must make the most of it.'

'Where was it you said you were going?' Petronilla asked.

Etienne hadn't breathed a word of his destination to anyone, not even to Gilles Fitzhugh, and he wasn't about to reveal it to Petronilla. Busying himself with his reins, he affected not to have heard her. He had done this before, to good effect. If he continued to use that ploy, with any luck the woman would think he'd gone deaf, and would cease to address him altogether. Now that would be something . . . Etienne felt a grin surfacing and suppressed it.

'Fitzhugh, are you ready?' he asked.

'Aye, mon seigneur.'

Petronilla had dismounted, and her beady grey eyes were narrowed. She knew something important was being kept from her, and she loathed it.

Etienne gave her a cheery wave. 'Farewell, my dear.'

He saw Petronilla grind her pointed teeth, and was forced to hide his smile behind a gauntleted hand. The woman was burning to know his destination, but could not bring herself to pose another direct question.

'Farewell, Count,' she answered. 'Till we meet again.'

'Till we meet again.' Etienne squeezed his knees, and Snowstorm lurched forwards.

He managed to contain his laughter till he and Fitzhugh had come to the bend in the river where they forded it. He looked at his castellan. 'I enjoyed that, Gilles.'

Gilles Fitzhugh was one of the few men privileged to address the count by his baptismal name. 'You bait her too much, Etienne,' he grinned, more relaxed now Petronilla was out of sight. 'One day she'll tear your hand off.'

'You think so?' Etienne shook his head, and the brooch in his hat flashed in the sunlight. 'No, she won't. Not while she thinks her dear Louis has a chance of inheriting.'

Etienne was startled to see the sobering effect his statement had on his castellan. Fleetingly, the younger man's lips twisted contemptuously, but the expression was gone so swiftly that Etienne wondered if he had imagined it.

'True enough,' Gilles answered. 'But you could do worse than watch her, nonetheless.'

'We've shaken her off for now.' Etienne turned to his squire, who was riding at a discreet distance behind them, leading the packhorse which had carried Petronilla's travelling chest. 'Gervase?'

'Mon seigneur?'

'Sir Gilles and I will proceed alone. You're to take that animal back to La Forteresse.'

'Aye, my lord.'

'I'll be back in two days and, as Sir Gilles is accompanying me, Sir Robert has been given my authority.'

'Aye, my lord.'

Etienne turned Snowstorm's head northwards, and Gilles Fitzhugh followed suit.

Count Etienne had good reason for wanting his relatives out of his hair, for he was considering backing a rebellion against his overlord, Richard Plantagenet, Duke of Aquitaine.

The duke had been overlord of the Aquitaine since 1179 and, much to the chagrin of the local nobility, had been showing his teeth. In the north, in Limoges, rebellious citizens had been punished by being forced to pull down their own city walls, leaving them too vulnerable to defend themselves or turn against their duke ever again.

Generally, there was little respect for Angevin authority in the Aquitaine, and the duke was yet to establish a central administration there. Richard Plantagenet might have had some success subduing the lords in north Aquitaine, but here in the south, they were not so tractable. Count Etienne and his peers did not consider it an advantage to have to pay dues to Richard Plantagenet. They valued their independence, and would not surrender any part of it to anyone, not even to one of Eleanor of Aquitaine's sons.

'Etienne? Where are we bound? You'll tell me now, I take it?'

'Assuredly, my friend. We're heading for the City in the Rock.'

'La Roque St Christophe? I've heard of the place, though I've never been there,' Gilles said.

'Nor I. It's a naturally fortified town, built into a cliffside. Sounds intriguing.'

'What's this about, Etienne? Whom are we meeting?'

'You recall that last spring Count Périgord, fearing Duke Richard was causing a disastrous shift in the balance of power, came out openly against the duke?'

'Of course I remember. But the damn fool moved too soon, and had too little support, and he was forced to surrender Périgueux . . .'

Etienne nodded. 'That's it. Recently, Duke Richard has showed more signs of wanting to interfere with local government. He's imposed new dues, but what is worse he wants to inflict the Norman ruling on inheritance of land in the Aquitaine. Something has to be done. I won't brook any infringement on my rights . . .'

Gilles shook his head, and his fringe, which protruded from under his hat, waved in the breeze. 'The Angevins have all been restless since their Christmas court broke up in disarray. They've not stopped trying to outmanoeuvre one another ever since . . .'

Duke Richard had refused to pay homage to his older brother, the Young King Henry, and stormed off to fortify his castles. The Young King had followed Richard, ostensibly claiming to act as a peacemaker, but in reality he had been protecting his own interests.

'And they're still fighting, hammer and tongs,' Etienne smiled, 'both of them after the duchy.'

His friend's blue eyes twinkled. 'You don't seem unduly concerned, my lord, at the outbreak of hostilities within our duke's family?'

'No. This family squabble gives us the chance to pick another contender for the dukedom . . .'

'The Young King?'

'Exactly. He's hungry for land. Consider, Gilles; his two younger brothers have land. Richard holds the Aquitaine, and Geoffrey holds Brittany. But Henry, though he will be king of England one day, and suzerain over them all, has no land — he must wait for his father to die. And does he help his father rule his lands while he's waiting? No. Does he try to learn what kingship is all about? No. The Young King plays at being a king. He hires a mercenary army that he cannot afford. He does the round of the tournies. He's the perfect, handsome, chivalrous prince. He takes the pomp and the ceremony and the glitter, but he has not time for the mundane, day-to-day running of affairs. In short, my dear Gilles, he sounds exactly the sort of man we should have as our duke.'

'And he's at Roque St Christophe?'

'He is indeed. I shall pledge my support.'

'He'll want more than any pledge, Etienne. He'll want coin. Can you afford it?'

'Not at the moment,' Etienne replied frankly. 'But I will be able to soon. Why do you think I've chosen de Roncier's heiress to be my bride?'

Gilles laughed. 'And I thought it was an heir you were after . . .'

'God willing, she'll give me that too; but it's the girl's land and its revenues that is the chief attraction.'

Leaving the River Dordogne behind them, Count Etienne and Sir Gilles rode in a north-easterly direction through thinly wooded countryside. The count had taken care in choosing his road. Owing to the need for discretion, he and Gilles were travelling without the usual armed escort, and he did not want to ride into an outlaw's ambush. Their safety came first, and though the way was longer, the count had decided it would be safer if they got on to the pilgrim route as soon as possible. There were always pilgrims, mad enough or penitent enough to be travelling to Santiago de Compostela, even at this time of year. There was safety in numbers.

In places, trees' branches, stark and leafless and iced with frost, hung over the road. Frozen leaf mast crunched beneath their horses' hoofs. The path was clear, the way open, and every now and then the woods gave way to farming hamlets where it was possible to rest, and to refresh the horses.

They made good time, and reached the church at Tayac an hour or so after noon. Filtering weakly through the trees, the wintry sun fell on the west wall of the church, giving warmth to the pale ochre stone. As they rode past the west door, Gilles craned his head to cast a knowledgeable eye over the fortifications which topped the bell-tower.

Tayac was one of a series of fortified churches which had been built in the area in recent years. The times were uncertain, and nobles and lords were not the only ones who sought to protect their own. Churchmen and villagers craved security too, and the fortified churches met this need. Tayac church had a bell-tower at both the west and east end, each crowned with a soldiers' covered walkway, and each complete with slits for firing arrows.

'Looks solid enough, and each tower can fire from both sides. Small, but defendable.' Gilles approved.

'Not far now, Gilles,' Etienne said. 'Little more than an hour. The road follows this river north—'

'The Vézère, isn't it?'

'Aye.'

'The road's better here,' Gilles observed.

'Naturally.' Etienne's voice was cynical, and he waved a deerskin gauntlet at a group of travellers who were crowding through the west arch into the church. They all wore pilgrims' wide-brimmed hats, and carried staffs. They had cheap silver souvenirs, from the various shrines they had visited, pinned to their cloaks, and these glinted in the watery sunlight. 'Pilgrims pay for their mementoes. They need food and drink, and lodgings at night. They're good business. They fill church coffers. That's why the churches on the pilgrim route keep the roads clear. And that's why we're approaching La Roque St Christophe from this direction.'

It was dusk when they reached the fortress. From the bottom of the Vézère valley rose a great white cliff. Wattle and daub houses clustered around the base of the cliff, but that was not all: higher up, on two levels at least, more houses clung like barnacles.

'My God, Etienne, there's a whole city up there.'

'Aye. It's more impressive than I had imagined. How do you suppose we get up there?'

Etienne's question did not remain unanswered for long, for at their approach a bell pealed high above their heads, and when their horses reached the base of the cliff, two youths approached them.

'Can we help you, sirs?' asked one of the youths, who had lost a front tooth. Both he and his companion carried stout staves.

'I hope so. We've heard that a certain – ah – member of the duke's family is staying here. May we see him?'

'You're expected, I take it, messieurs?'

'We are.'

'Then if you'll entrust your horses to Jean, and will remove your swords, I'll take you up.'

Past the houses, a tented city had been struck at the foot of the cliff, and Etienne and Gilles were conducted through it. Camp-fires were being lit. Blackened, three-legged cooking pots were being balanced in the embers, and an assortment of smells, tempting and not so tempting, met their nostrils. Meats were being roasted on home-made spits, and to judge by the size of the cuts, much of it was small game, trapped locally. Raucous, uncontrolled male laughter floated out through the chill, evening air, punctuated occasionally with wild, female laughter. These must be the Young King's infamous Flemish mercenaries, used to living off the land. Etienne was glad they had not camped on his holding.

They were directed along a narrow path rising upwards from the valley floor. They climbed some steps: the wall of the cliff kissed one shoulder, empty space the other. The path rose steeply, the cooking fires shrank and the campsite noises fell away.

They and their escort reached a heavy, weathered door,

where they were challenged. The door opened, and to their astonishment, Etienne and Gilles saw the ledge had vanished. It began again a few yards further along the cliff-face, and a drawbridge of sorts had been lowered to permit them to cross. There was another weathered door to negotiate, and a long dark passage, and at last Etienne and Gilles found themselves standing on a broad stone shelf, high up the cliff.

The shelf was several dozen yards wide, wide enough for whole wattle houses to be built on it. Each house used the back of the cliff as a wall. A path skirted the front of the houses, and the Vézère valley spread out below them.

'Extraordinary!' Etienne exclaimed as they were ushered into a chamber in one of the houses. The room was plainly furnished with a rustic, unpolished table and two benches. Etienne availed himself of one of the benches.

A boy entered carrying a tray with an earthenware jug and four pottery goblets. 'Wine, mes seigneurs?' he asked.

'Thank you.'

The boy poured the wine, handed Etienne and Gilles a goblet, and left.

It was some time before the man they had come to see strode in, stripping off his riding gloves. Etienne made his bow.

Henry the Young King was tall and handsome and walked with a swagger, heels clicking on the smooth stone floor. His clothes were bright, and looked expensive despite being splashed liberally with mud. His elegant, knee-high boots were also mired. He wore his short riding cloak like a Roman, over one shoulder, and it was pinned with a round gold buckle the size of a hen's egg. He went straight for the wine on the table.

'Apologies for the delay, but I've been trying to

supplement my diet, and it was a hard chase. Favell, isn't it?'

'That is so.'

Henry Plantagenet took a long draught of his wine before saying, carefully, 'I've heard it said that the current captain of the ship displeases you?'

Etienne assented. 'Your Grace hears correctly. I am ill-content with the status quo.'

'And is yours a lonely voice crying in the wilderness? Or would you say that you have the support of the majority of the ship's crew?'

'A sizeable proportion of the crew think as I do, Your Grace. I fear a mutiny is in the offing.'

'Would a different captain solve your problem?'

Etienne hesitated. 'If it were the right captain, Your Grace. We would have to ensure that the new man had a clear understanding of local custom, and he would have to swear not to violate ancient privilege.'

'And if such a man existed, and was prepared to uphold your customs, you'd fight in the mutiny on his behalf?'

'Your Grace,' Etienne temporised, 'you can see for yourself I'm no longer young. I'm strong yet, but my fighting days are over. I can pledge you support—'

'Money? You mean you'll support me with money?' Henry the Young King had a charming smile. He waved a vague hand towards the clearing at the bottom of the cliff where his Flemish mercenaries were camped out. 'I've a few debts to settle, Favell.'

'So I observe, Your Grace. And I expect to be in a position to assist you quite soon.'

When he wanted to, Henry the Younger could make his smile dazzling. One of his elegant boots hooked out a bench from under the table. He sat, and gestured to Etienne to do the same. 'Be seated, Count Favell. You and I have much to discuss . . .'

* * *

137

March. Lady Day.

Arlette and Clemence woke at dawn, washed and dressed quickly, as was their habit, and crept down the twisting stairs, through the solar, and down another turn towards the great hall where, at about this time, the men-at-arms should be breaking their fast.

The torchlit hall was empty, save for a couple of scullions, Rojer and Dewi, who were sweeping the soiled rushes into the fire. They always changed the rushes at Huelgastel on Lady Day.

'That's odd,' Clemence voiced Arlette's thoughts. 'The men have breakfasted already. Look, you can see what's left of it. Was your father planning a hunt today, Arlette? Perhaps the men are acting as beaters.'

Dewi's broom had unearthed a terrier who had been dozing under a trestle, and the startled animal snapped, took hold of the broom, and shook it as though it were a rat. 'Leave it alone.' The hapless scullion tugged at his broom, but the terrier held on, snarling. 'Oh, for Christ's sake, the stupid cur. Rojer, lend a boot . . .'

Rojer strode up to the dog and administered an efficient kick to its rump. Arlette winced. The dog yelped and scuttled into the marsh − the least frequently changed area of rushes under the high table. The marsh stank. Arlette hoped Rojer and Dewi were going to renew the rushes there too.

'Arlette?' Clemence said, still waiting for her answer. 'Is there a hunt on?'

Arlette frowned. 'No. If Papa had been planning a hunt on as large a scale as that, we should have heard of it. And he's left the hounds. But it looks as though something unusual is happening. I wonder what?'

Clemence looked pointedly at what was left of that morning's bread. 'It looks like a battlefield. What they've not eaten, they've mangled. Do you think Marthe will have kept anything back for us?' Marthe, the cook's wife, still reigned over the bakehouse. She was responsible for producing the dozens of loaves that the castle devoured daily. Normally, the girls were among the first to creep into the bakehouse, and Marthe always had a fresh-baked loaf ready to pull out of her brick oven for Count François's daughter and her maidservant. But if the count and his men had got to the bread first . . .

Marthe was ensconced on her stool in the bakehouse, supervising her two big daughters who were kneading dough for another batch of bread. A motherly woman of ample proportions – she had no waist at all and was as round as a ball – Marthe's enormous girth was proof that she at least enjoyed the fruits of her labours. Her daughters, though large, were as yet no match for their mother.

When Arlette and Clemence entered, Marthe looked up. 'Good morning to you, Little Lady.' Marthe smiled, and a dimple flashed in each of her round, red cheeks. 'Though only the good Lord knows why I continue to call you "little" when you're growing so tall. Good morning, Mistress Clemence. You've been beaten to it today . . .'

'Oh, Marthe,' Arlette wailed, dramatically clasping both hands over her belly as though she were starving, 'don't tell us you've nothing left.'

'Not a crumb, Little Lady. They've eaten everything. You'll have to wait till the next batch is due to come out,' Marthe said, very straight-faced.

Arlette stared at Marthe, whose face was just a little too straight, and dropped her dramatic pose. Marthe had a loaf for them, she could tell. But Marthe loved to tease. 'And how long will that be?' she asked.

Marthe eyed the bread which her two daughters were pummelling furiously. 'When they've finished, the loaves will have to rise. Then they can go into my oven.' Marthe smiled. 'Come back in about an hour, my ladies.'

'Oh, Marthe,' Arlette feigned disappointment, 'not an

hour. We were hoping to go for a ride, and we'll be faint if we don't eat before. We were relying on you.'

Exchanging glances with Arlette, Clemence stepped forwards. 'Marthe? Marthe, you're not serious are you?'

A wide grin split Marthe's honest face. She could never keep it straight for long. Wiping her floury hands, Marthe tucked a stray strand of hair beneath her wimple, waddled over to the log basket and picked up a cloth. She opened the oven door. The bread peel — a long wooden paddle used for removing bread from the oven — was balanced on one side of the oven. Marthe took it up, and in a moment was wrapping a fresh, hot wheat loaf in the cloth. She tossed it to Arlette.

'There you are, Little Lady.' Marthe shut the oven, replaced the peel, and waddled back to her stool by her daughter's work bench. 'You didn't think old Marthe would forget you, did you?'

'My thanks, Marthe,' Arlette said, cuddling the warm loaf. 'Marthe?'

'Mmm?' Marthe was scowling at one of her daughters. 'Not like that, girl. Not as though you were afraid of it. Put some effort into it. That's better.'

'Marthe?' Arlette repeated. 'Do you know where Papa went so early? You didn't happen to hear . . . ?'

'No. I didn't.'

'Oh. Thanks for the bread, Marthe.'

They were in Huelgastel Chapel before noon, in plenty of time for Mass. Being Lady Day, it was the Feast of the Annunciation, when the Archangel Gabriel proclaimed to the Virgin Mary that she would bear God's son, and the celebratory Mass could not be missed.

Arlette tried not to think about the other Gabriel, her faithful hound. It was still too painful a memory.

Countess Eleanor was already in the chapel, reciting the Angelus. The girls went to kneel at their place. There was plenty of space on Arlette's hassock, so as a rule the girls knelt together. Clemence shared both Arlette's kneeler and prie-dieu, not having one of her own.

Arlette picked up the cedarwood casket she kept on the shelf of her prie-dieu. It had been brought back from the Lebanon as part of a crusader's booty, and her rosary rattled about inside it.

'Let me open it,' Clemence hissed in an undertone.

Arlette's rosary box was no ordinary casket. It was a puzzle box, and the heads of the Apostles were carved along its sides. There was no lock, and no sign of any hinges, and it only slid open when the haloes of three of the Saints were depressed in the correct combination. For months Clemence had been trying to discover the knack of it, and last week she had succeeded for the first time. The novelty was yet to wear off.

Arlette handed the box to Clemence, who set to work.

There was a stir in the doorway, and a black-garbed Marie de Roncier entered. Lena followed in her train, carrying a rug for the dowager countess who felt the cold.

'Done it!' Clemence whispered, triumphantly withdrawing Arlette's rosary.

'Hush, girls.' Countess Eleanor shook her head, gently reproving. 'Mass is about to begin.'

Arlette frowned. Her family seemed to be shrinking daily. What with her grandfather's prie-dieu being empty, and now her father's . . .

François de Roncier, though not as devoted to his religion as his second wife, usually attended Mass on the more important feast days.

'Where's Papa?' Arlette whispered. 'Is he not back yet? Father Josse won't begin without him.'

'Your father has business in Vannes, Arlette, and he will be attending a service at the Cathedral. Father Josse has been informed.'

'Oh.' During the morning, Arlette had discovered that

her father had taken not one of his mercenary troops with him, but two. The men under Captain Malait had gone, as were Captain le Bret's men. What could her father be doing in the port of Vannes that required so many routiers?

Father Josse entered, a ghostly white blur amid a swirl of incense. Arlette bent her head, and tried to give Our Lady's Mass the attention it merited.

After the service, Arlette took her cedarwood apostle casket into the solar and put it on the table. Its creator had probably intended that the box be a reliquary, but it was wasted on Arlette's rosary, which was made with cheap, imported glass beads, and which left it all but empty. It would make a much better trinket box. Later, when Arlette went upstairs, she would put it in her room.

Chapter Seven

A couple of nights after Lady Day, Arlette and Clemence were readying themselves for bed. They had been talking and it was well past midnight. They had much to talk about.

Louis Favell, having completed his errand and successfully negotiated a marriage contract for Arlette and his uncle, had departed for the Dordogne that evening. It had been agreed that Arlette would visit her betrothed in the summer, but that the couple would not wed until Arlette was fifteen.

Arlette saw the delay as a welcome reprieve. She had mixed feelings about her betrothal, and had feared she might be sent away immediately. By now a strong sense of duty had grown in her — she was honour-bound to marry; and she hoped that by the time the summer came, she would have become used to the idea of marrying Count Etienne Favell, who was, she had learnt, even older than her father.

She was perched on the edge of the bed while Clemence combed out her long red hair with an ivory, double-sided comb. The branched candlestick had been placed on Arlette's desk, and from time to time the candles in it flickered.

'At one point I thought I was safe,' Arlette admitted. 'I thought they'd never come to terms. Especially when Sir Louis insisted that he took part of my dowry back with him as a sign of good faith. Did you see Papa's face when that clause was read out?'

Clemence nodded. 'I did. He went puce. It's best to skip to one side when your father—' Clemence broke off, horrified at what she was saying. She was talking about Count François de Roncier. 'My apologies, Arlette. I'm being disrespectful.'

'You're being truthful. Oh, Clemence, I know my duty, but I'm not sure that I want to be Countess Favell. I can't imagine living anywhere but here. I was meant to live here; I belong here. I love this castle, and the people in it; I love paddling in the river when no one is watching; I love riding through the woods. In short, I don't want to leave. What is the Aquitaine like, I wonder?'

'The songs say it's beautiful. You'll soon get to know the people. And there are woods there to ride in, and a river—'

'I know,' Arlette cut Clemence off with a wave of her hand. 'But I won't *know* it. I won't be a part of it, because I've not grown up with it. I won't know which hollow tree the woodpecker likes to nest in; I won't know which ride is safe to gallop along full pelt without my horse Bluebell risking catching her leg in a tree root. Oh, Clemence, it may be wrong of me to say this but I wish I didn't have to leave. If only there was another way to please my father.'

For all that she understood Arlette's dilemma, Clemence was realistic. 'You have no choice, do you? Many would envy you—'

'Not if they knew Count Favell's age. Sweet Mother, Clemence, they told me the man's nigh on fifty!' Arlette paused, and chewed an almond-shaped nail. 'What do you suppose he looks like?'

Clemence had finished her combing, and deftly wound Arlette's hair into a loose braid which fell down her back. 'Sir Louis described him, Arlette.'

'Ah, aye. He said his uncle had a sharp intellect, and

144

appreciated the finer things in life — I didn't like the way he looked at me when he said that. He said Count Etienne has green eyes, and is tall and strong. In short, my aged suitor is a fine figure of a man. At fifty?' Arlette laughed, unhappily. 'Is it likely? He's about as old as Grandpapa was.'

Clemence's blue-grey eyes were round with sympathy. She put a hand on her friend's arm. 'Don't be sad, Arlette. You know your marriage is inevitable. Try to accept it. Your father has become count and he has set his mind on it. You should know by now that he won't let you win if you try and oppose him — you only hurt yourself. You would be better served by channelling your energy into making your marriage work—'

'Jehan said something very like that,' Arlette said, 'before he was sent away.'

'Jehan showed sense.' Clemence smiled, and handed Arlette the comb. 'Come on, mistress — ' such was the bond between the two girls that Clemence only named Arlette 'mistress' when she was teasing, or angry, or when Arlette's father was in earshot — 'it's time you untangled your maid's hair.'

Arlette took the comb and smiled back, albeit weakly. 'You are right. I shall accept my lot, even though it means bidding Huelgastel farewell. You must be the bossiest maidservant in Christendom. Why do I put up with you?'

Clemence laughed. 'That's easily answered. No one else would put up with *you*.'

Arlette tugged gently at a golden strand and Clemence yelped. 'Ow! Arlette, that hurt! Have a care. I want some hair left when you've finished.'

Arlette grinned suddenly, saying slyly, 'Aye. You think you'll snare Morgan le Bihan with it, don't you?'

The castle falconer had taken to bringing Clemence little gifts: a silver thimble, some cherry-coloured ribbons he had bought from a passing pedlar, a trinket box he had made from apple wood. Thinking of Clemence's trinket box reminded Arlette of her apostle casket, which she had yet to collect from the solar.

'You don't return Morgan's gifts, do you, Clemence?' Arlette said, peering over Clemence's shoulder to study the effect of her words.

Clemence's pink cheeks went as bright as a poppy. 'Why should I return them? If he likes giving me things—'

'You like him, don't you?'

'Morgan le Bihan? I don't know what you are talking about, Arlette. He's dour and shy. Besides, I'm taller than he is . . .'

Finishing Clemence's hair, Arlette put both hands on her friend's shoulders and turned her so that the two girls were facing each other. 'I'm serious, Clemence. I need to know whether you feel particularly attached to anyone at Huelgastel.'

Clemence wrinkled her pretty nose. 'Why?'

'Because, oh bossiest of maidservants, I want to ask my father for permission for you to accompany me when I leave to marry Count Etienne, and I wouldn't want to take you away from anyone you are especially fond of. Would you like to come with me? It's a long way off yet, but I would be easier in my mind if I thought you were coming with me.'

Clemence blinked, and for a moment her eyes were moist. She gripped the hands on her shoulders. 'Oh, Arlette. Do you need to ask? I'm fond of *you*. I do like Morgan, of course I do, but you come first in my life. You're like a sister, a soul-mate. There'll be other Morgans, and if there are not — ' Clemence gave the shrug of a girl whose affections had never been seriously engaged — 'I daresay I'll survive.'

Arlette looked at Clemence's shining sheaf of hair, her pure complexion and her soft, melting eyes. 'Oh, there'll be other Morgans, I promise you, Clemence.' She hugged her. 'I'm glad you want to come with me. I'll ask Father next time I see him.'

'You do.' And, clambering over to her side of the bed, Clemence crawled between the sheets, sighed, and shut her eyes. 'Sweet dreams, Arlette,' she murmured sleepily.

Clemence fell asleep as easily as the castle cats, and Arlette rather envied her that ability, for Arlette herself often lay awake for hours, thinking.

'Sweet dreams, Clemence,' Arlette responded, moving to the door.

A sleepy eye opened. 'Where are you going?'

'Only to the privy. And I left my apostle casket in the solar. I'll collect it on the way back. I won't be long.'

'Mmm. Goodnight, then.'

Owing to the lateness of the hour, many of the lights in the wall-sconces had been extinguished, and the castle passages were full of rustling shadows, queer midnight noises, and sinister dark nooks. But Arlette knew her way about Huelgastel blindfolded, and made her way swiftly down the turret stairs. At the bottom, she passed through a curtained doorway and entered the chapel passage. The door to the chapel was on her left and, as Arlette went past it, she caught her foot on something soft.

Her heart missed a beat, and for an instant she wished she had prevailed upon Clemence to go with her, but then she heard an indignant miaow, and smiled to herself.

'Oh, it's you, Minnow. No doubt hoping for a night on the cushions in the chapel, eh?' She bent and picked up the cat, who purred. 'You can come with me for the moment. I'll let you into the chapel later.'

Arlette proceeded down the chapel passage. Voices drifted to meet her. A strong yellow line of light was clearly visible at the base of the solar door. Arlette was clearly not the only person to be up and about in the family quarters.

With a yard to go before she reached the door, Arlette paused. If it was her father, and he was having a conference, she could not simply march in. The walls of the passage were plaster and lath, and in the dim and distant past one of Arlette's ancestors had had a squint made in the wall at that point. The squint was obscured by an ancient tapestry; Arlette had discovered it when she was five, while playing hide and seek with Jehan and Aubrey. She had shown it to Clemence when she had arrived: the two girls had kept it as their secret. They had learned much about castle life with the aid of the squint.

Hugging Minnow tightly to her chest, Arlette elbowed her way behind the tapestry and put an eye to the squint.

She saw her father — how fortunate that she had not charged in — in conversation with a tall, stately-looking man, with a polished dome of a head, and long, long, white hands. Her father's visitor wore the distinctive black robes of a Benedictine monk. A Benedictine monk? What could they be discussing that required such clandestine conduct?

Arlette knew she should not listen. Arlette knew she should turn immediately and go to bed. But her curiosity had been aroused, and she could not have turned and walked away for all the silver in the mint at Nantes.

' . . . It certainly stirred the hearts and consciences of the townsfolk,' the count was saying, 'and I for one will never forget it. Permit me to donate a small sum to your order in gratitude for your moving oratory in the cathedral on Lady Day.'

On the surface her father's words sounded perfectly innocuous. But this was not the sort of comment she expected from her father, and Arlette had not forgotten that Lady Day was the day her father and his troops had mysteriously absented themselves from Huelgastel. She strained to hear more, and saw a leather pouch pass from the count's clumsy, calloused, worldly hands to the monk's thin, white, spiritual ones; though Arlette observed that they were not so spiritual that they could not grip the pouch firmly, nor did they resist the temptation to weigh the pouch to assess the magnitude of her father's gift.

'You are generous, Count François,' the Black Monk said. His voice was high-pitched, and penetrated the squint better than the count's. 'And you are not the only one to have benefited. I rejoice to be able to tell you that Vannes is the better for being purged of its most notorious sinner. Yolande Herevi has gone.'

The monk's voice faded and while Arlette strained to hear more she wondered who Yolande Herevi was. Why should her father be interested in her leaving Vannes?

The monk's voice strengthened. 'Sadly, there was a fire the day she left . . .'

'Oh?'

Though she could not have said why, Arlette sensed her father knew this too.

'Aye. It whipped through the west quarter, reaching as far as the cathedral. The west end was completely burnt out, but it's an ill wind. That cathedral was a disgrace. The bishop had been intending to rebuild it in stone. The fire gives him the excuse to further his ambitions sooner.'

Minnow shifted in Arlette's arms and, fearful that the cat was about to make a noise that would betray her presence, Arlette turned her attention to him for a moment, stroking him into purring contentment. When she was confident she had lulled him into being quiet, she began to listen again.

'Injured?' the Black Monk said, presumably in response to a question from her father. 'No. We sustained no injuries. But Yolande Herevi's mother died. She was old but, unlike her daughter, she was no sinner. She was one of the faithful, God rest her.'

'God rest her,' Count François echoed, and Arlette

149

heard clearly the insincerity in his voice.

'I should take my leave, Count. I shall say a Mass for the soul of your father, and pray for your family.'

'My thanks, Father. Will you pray also that God grants me a son? Recently my wife had hopes but, alas, she was disappointed . . .'

'Such things rest in God's hands, Count. But assuredly, I will pray for you. Your generosity will not be forgotten. And should you require my services again, please ask, and you shall surely receive . . .'

'My thanks, Father Jerome. Permit me to show you out.'

The count and his midnight visitor moved out of Arlette's line of sight, and their voices dwindled.

Arlette emerged from behind the tapestry, her mind a-buzz with questions that would probably never be answered. 'Well, Minnow, what do you make of that? Has Father turned religious that he should be asking Benedictine monks to speak in the Cathedral?'

Minnow purred.

'And who is Yolande Herevi?'

Minnow purred.

'Oh, you're useless, Minnow, quite useless. Come on, let's fetch my apostle casket, and then I'll take you back to your cushion in the chapel.' Arlette spoke briskly, but it was with a thoughtful and puzzled air that she returned to her bedchamber that night.

Raymond Herevi and Anna had agreed to meet at their usual trysting place, a dolmen near Locmariaquer, at the tenth hour.

Anna arrived punctually, not wanting to miss a moment that might be spent with Raymond Herevi. She had thrown off her superstitious fear of the dolmen, and the dark, damp burrow which had so terrified her at their first assignation, now seemed to be a bower of bliss.

Anna had brought both her cloaks and a blanket, for she and Raymond had become lovers, and Anna was a practical girl. She wanted their union to be as sweet as possible. Raymond was a gentle, considerate lover; and though Anna knew her parents would brand her a fornicator should they find out her secret, their loving was more than precious to Anna. It had become her reason for being.

While Anna arranged the blanket and cloaks, she cursed herself as all kinds of a fool. She should not feel like this. What with the differences in their station, there could be no future for them together. Anna could see nothing ahead of her, nothing — except pain.

Raymond may be illegitimate, but he was a free man. He could go where he liked and marry whom he wished.

Anna was a villein. She was tied to the land her father worked. She was the property of the lord of the manor, Bertram Blundell, and could hardly stir a step without asking his leave. And Sir Bertram would never permit her to marry off his land, not unless her parents paid a huge fine, like the one they had had to pay when her sister had married her mason. Anna's parents could never afford to pay another such fine, the first had all but crippled them. Anna did not blame Sir Bertram, it was not his fault. If every lord let his villeins wed where they wanted, there would be no one left to work their lands.

Not that Raymond would ever ask for her in any case. Why should Raymond Herevi marry a serf when he could have a free woman? Anna *knew*, she *knew*, that the day would come when Raymond would get up and say goodbye and walk casually out of her life. However good their loving had become, Raymond would turn his back on Anna, the farmer's daughter, and he would find himself a free woman and marry her. Occasionally, in a quiet moment, he might remember Anna. He might even smile at a fond memory, but that would be all.

151

Anna sat on the makeshift bed she had made, and thought about the last time they had met, on Lady Day. He had told her a tale then that was more astonishing than any a travelling minstrel had composed.

Some of what Raymond had told her had been difficult to grasp, but the gist of it had been clear enough. Raymond had said that a black monk who had been preaching at the cathedral had been responsible for setting a mob on his sister. From Raymond's somewhat emotional account, Anna gathered that he had seen the poor girl being hounded through the streets, and had barely managed to get her safely inside their house. They had narrowly escaped being stoned to death by the townsfolk whom the monk had inflamed with his preaching.

'You see, sweet Anna,' Raymond had said, 'how my family are reviled. Not everyone is as tolerant as you. We are despised by respectable folk, and the new Count de Roncier wants to get rid of us, so all he has to do is pay a preacher to inflame the congregation, and they turn on us. My guess is that Mama will want to leave Vannes after what happened to Gwenn.'

Anna knew Gwenn was Raymond's sister, but the other name was strange to her. 'Count de Roncier? Who's he?'

Raymond gave an ugly laugh. 'He's a powerful landlord who has recently inherited a vast slice of Brittany east of Vannes.'

The old horn lantern gave a dim light, but Anna could see anger and worry were carving deep lines on Raymond's brow. Tenderly, she reached up and smoothed them away. 'Why should this great lord hate your family?'

'We're relations. His mother and my grandmother are sisters. My grandmother is the elder of the two sisters. It is she who should have inherited the de Wirce holding, not Marie de Roncier—'

152

'So this Count de Roncier is afraid of losing land to your family?'

'That's it in a nutshell.'

'When did you find this out, Raymond?'

'Today. The first I knew of our connection with the count was when I learned that he was the one behind what happened to Gwenn.'

'Why did the count strike today?'

'Eh?'

'Well, I know *you* didn't know about *him*, but presumably he has known about you for years. Why did he wait till now?'

'His father, Count Robert, prevented him, I expect,' Raymond said. 'The old count was once betrothed to Izabel — my grandmother. Count Robert was an honourable man, he will have stayed his son's hand. But his son is cast in a different mould. Now the old count has died, Count François is free of all restraints. And the swine started his campaign by frightening my sister, an innocent child who never hurt anyone . . .'

Anna shuddered. 'I don't understand all this, Raymond, but it frightens me, this talk of campaigns. Oh, Raymond,' Anna clutched his hands, 'I'm afraid for you. You will be careful, won't you?'

Raymond had promised to be careful. And he had drawn Anna to him, and kissed her till she forgot all about great lords, and mobs, and black monks.

Anna knew that Raymond liked her, and he had demonstrated that he trusted her by unburdening himself to her. Raymond Herevi was not like some of the young men Anna knew of whose hands would slide up any woman's skirt. But Raymond Herevi had within him a cool core of logic. When he looked at Anna she knew he saw Anna the villein. A pretty villein, perhaps, and one whose company he enjoyed, but a villein nonetheless. Raymond would never allow himself to become more than fond. He would never love her.

Knowing this should have brought Anna to her senses; but she could not help herself. It was rather like jumping off a high cliff: once she had gone over the edge, she could not stop herself falling.

Anna shook her head to clear her thoughts. Where was he? He was always late. Perhaps he was not coming today. Was he not coming because he no longer needed the comfort Anna was able to give him? Or had that Count de Roncier done something dreadful? Was he hurt?

Anna waited on.

As the hours passed, her anxiety gave way to fear, and tears, for herself and Raymond. Dear God, keep Raymond safe, she prayed. Let him love me. And let me not be pregnant. Dear God, keep Raymond safe. Let him love me . . . She knew she could not wait much longer. She had work to do on the strips in the fields next morning, hard physical work, work which broke her nails and made her hands black and grimed. She must be up with the dawn, ready and willing, or her father would want to know the reason why. Anna shuddered as she thought of the consequences if her father should discover that his daughter had lost her innocence to a man who would never wed her. Part of her longed for Raymond's child, so she could have a part of him to love for ever, but she knew that if she did so, her father would kill her.

'Oh, Raymond,' she sighed. Where was he?

Anna returned to the dolmen the next night with the blanket and her two cloaks, in case she had misremembered the day. But Raymond did not come that night either. She considered taking the extraordinary step of sending Raymond a message. She did not know exactly where Raymond lived; but she knew he lived near the cathedral in Vannes, and she knew his full name, so it should not be impossible. She had to know if he was well.

She couldn't send a letter. Anna could neither read nor write, and if she asked the village priest to act as her scribe he would surely become suspicious and might inform her parents that she had formed an unsuitable attachment. Perhaps she could send him something instead . . .

Anna went about her daily chores with a heavy heart. She would not send Raymond anything. If he wanted to see her, he would come. And if he did not, then all the messages in the world would not bring him to her. She wanted him willing, or not at all.

In the meantime, all Anna could do was try and get through each day as it came, and hide both her concern for Raymond, and her own profound misery, from her parents.

One fine day at the end of March, Anna was hoeing the family strips in the field north of the village. A blustery wind had scoured the sky of clouds, and shaken the rooks from their rookery. The wind swallowed the birds' scratchy voices, but Anna could see them, black specks tossed up against the blue, battling with the wind. They seemed to love it. Anna stole a moment to lean on her hoe and watch the birds as they hurled themselves into the wind, rising and falling, then circling over the copse.

There was a lull in the wind and, between gusts, Anna caught the sound of a horseman riding up the lane behind the hawthorn hedge. She turned back to her work, bending determinedly over her hoe as she loosened the damp soil.

'Anna? Anna?' A familiar, much loved voice spoke from behind her.

Anna dropped the hoe and whirled round. 'Raymond!' She had to brace herself to stop herself from flying into his arms. He was standing on one of the stones which marked the boundary between her family's strip and their neighbour's. His wavy brown hair was windswept, and in

155

daylight — it had been a long while since Anna had seen Raymond in daylight — she could see the chestnut lights in it. His eyes glittered bright as emeralds. Raymond was unharmed and, to Anna's mind, more handsome than ever. A bay horse was tethered to the hawthorn hedge. A dark flush stained Raymond's cheekbones: he was scowling, and his expression was angry, but to Anna he was the most beautiful thing in all Brittany.

She stooped for her hoe, trying to remember she was working on the north field in full view of everyone. She must hide her emotions. 'What is it, sir?' she said. It was a miracle her tone was so calm. Inside she was churning.

'I'm sorry I didn't meet you, Anna . . .' Raymond spoke quickly and quietly, glancing over his shoulder as he spoke.

Following his gaze, Anna saw that her father was stalking towards them with some young seedlings that Anna was to transplant.

' . . . But much has happened, and it slipped my mind. Can you meet me when you've finished here?'

Anna didn't hesitate. 'Where?'

'At the Anchor.' The Anchor was the only tavern in Locmariaquer, and was located on the quayside, facing the harbour.

'I'm not permitted inside . . .'

Anna's father was almost upon them.

'Outside, then,' Raymond muttered in that same rapid undertone. 'At the end of the quay by the blackthorn. In an hour?'

'Two. In two hours,' Anna said.

Raymond gaze a gruff grunt of assent, and marched stiffly back to his mount.

Anna's father had reached her and was thrusting the sacking-wrapped seedlings into her hand. 'There you are, all ready to plant. Who was that, Anna?' he asked, staring after Raymond.

Anna peeled back the sacking, made a show of examining the seedlings, and lied through her teeth. 'I've no idea. Just a townsman who'd lost his way.'

It was rather more than two hours later before Anna was free.

She walked down Church Lane and ducked into the domed, stone-built church backing on to the harbour, in order to dip her hands into the piscina and bless herself with holy water, for luck. Muttering a swift prayer — the same one she had been repeating to herself for days now — Anna emerged on to the quayside.

Here the wind was keener, and cut like a knife. Evening was drawing on, and while the feeble March sun had managed to warm the fields, here, by the shore, the breezes blew all the way from the Great Sea on the other side of their low, narrow spit of land, and snatched the heat away before one had time to benefit from it.

Anna shrank into her hood, and wished her cloak was thicker. The door to the Anchor was open, and through it Anna could see a welcoming fire. Several customers were huddled over the trestles nearest the blaze, cradling steaming mugs of mulled ale. Anna wished she could meet Raymond openly in the tavern, it looked so snug in there. But she knew she could not, and sailed past the Anchor, and as she did so, one of the customers nearest the door rose, tossed the landlord a coin, and left. It was Raymond.

He met her, as they had agreed, by the blackthorn bushes.

'Anna!' Raymond caught her hand and pulled her behind the thicket. It was too early in the season for there to be leaves on the blackthorn, but a froth of white flowers provided them with some cover from prying eyes. The wind wound its way determinedly through the thorny twigs, and nipped Anna's ears. 'Where have you been,

Anna? If you'd left it a moment longer, you'd have missed me.'

Anna stared at her lover in disbelief. 'You wouldn't have come all this way and then gone without seeing me?'

'I've been in the tavern an age. I thought you weren't coming. I thought . . .'

Anna gripped Raymond's hand fiercely, and caught his gaze, understanding that although Raymond was her superior, his illegitimate birth and his mother's notoriety made him feel as vulnerable as she did. 'I couldn't help being late, Raymond. My father held me back. He kept finding another task for me to do, and another, and I couldn't escape. You should have had faith. If I tell you I'm going to meet you, than I'll meet you,' Anna said firmly, quite forgetting that not so long ago it had been she who had lacked faith.

'I'm sorry, my Anna. I should have trusted you.'

'Oh, Raymond. What would I have done if you hadn't waited? I've been worried half to death wondering if that Count whatever-his-name is—'

'De Roncier.'

'—Wondering if Count de Roncier had harmed you.'

Raymond's green eyes were like ice.

'Raymond? What is it? The count *has* done something.'

Raymond nodded brusquely and, seeing Anna shiver, pulled her inside his cloak. Happily, Anna wrapped her arms about Raymond's slim waist, and buried her face in his tunic so she could breathe in the warm smell of him.

'Aye,' Raymond spoke over the top of her head, in a harsh, clipped voice that bore no resemblance to the voice Anna loved. 'Count François has been busy, or rather his friends have, for no one saw him at the fire. No, the count is too clever to be implicated himself. But one of his men was seen—'

Anna drew her head back so she could see Raymond's expression. He looked as fierce as he sounded, and the

158

hands on her shoulders felt like eagles' talons. 'Fire? What fire? Raymond, what *are* you talking about?'

He made a visible effort to control himself. The hands on her shoulders relaxed.

'It happened the day after I saw you. There was a fire in Vannes, Anna, and our house was burnt down—'

'Holy Mother! Was anyone hurt?'

'My grandmother, Izabel, was killed.'

Anna made the sign of the cross on her breast. 'The one who is — was — sister to Marie de Roncier?'

'Aye.'

'God rest her. Raymond, I'm so sorry.'

Raymond looked down at Anna, and his green eyes softened. He kissed her brow. 'You're a sweet girl, my Anna. I've been trying to piece together what happened that morning.

'I was on my way back from seeing you. Mama and Sir Jean had left Vannes for Sir Jean's manor: as I suspected, Mama was not prepared to live in Vannes, not after they tried to stone Gwenn. My grandmother and my two sisters were to follow my parents when I returned from seeing you. But I was late, Anna. Oh, God, that I should have been late that morning of all mornings. By the time I got there—'

Raymond broke off, and rubbed a face grown haggard with some grim memory. Anna waited for him to continue.

'It was not as though Sir Jean had not taken sensible precautions,' Raymond said, at last. 'He had provided us with an armed escort. We should have got to Kermaria quite safely—'

'Kermaria?' Anna could not suppress a tingle of excitement. Kermaria was a hamlet built in the marshlands to the north of Locmariaquer, closer to Anna's village than Vannes; perhaps after all Anna might be able to see more of him. 'You've moved to Kermaria?'

'Aye,' Raymond replied, distantly.

Her lover's thoughts were back in Vannes on the day of the fire. 'How do you think the blaze started?' Anna prompted, gently.

Raymond started. 'What? Oh, Gwenn saw one of de Roncier's routiers in our house. The brute had taken a torch to the place and attacked my grandmother. There's no doubt that he was a de Roncier man. Just as there's no doubt that it was the count who was responsible for the fire. The whole street went up like brushwood, but only my grandmother died. I got back too late to save her.'

'Oh, Raymond.'

The cold March wind whistled through the blackthorn.

Raymond rubbed his face against Anna's cheek. 'So you understand, my sweet, why I missed our meeting. There's been so much to do, what with moving to Kermaria, and Grandmother's funeral. I'm sorry if you've been worried.'

Anna smiled. 'I was worried, and I'm very sorry about your grandmother. But Raymond, I'm so relieved you still want to see me.'

'Want to see you? Of course I want to see you! You're my sweet Anna of the dark brown eyes. Come closer,' he murmured in his loving voice, 'and give me a kiss.'

Chapter Eight

The Bishop of Vannes was an energetic fund-raiser. As a result of the fire, he invited the local nobility to inspect the damage to his cathedral; whereupon he lectured them at length about the perils of storing up wealth on Earth, in the hope that they would be persuaded to reap their rewards in Heaven and that substantial bequests would be forthcoming.

Countess Eleanor, returning from the bishop's conference, rode up to Huelgastel gatehouse with her escort. A prudent young woman, the countess had not promised the bishop any funds, for she must have her husband's permission. She was, however, resolved to broach the subject with Count François as soon as she could.

She heard her husband's enraged bellow even as she and her escort were trotting through the mouth of the portcullis. Her stomach knotted, and she wondered which poor soul had been so imprudent as to incur her husband's wrath. Not Arlette, surely? Arlette had not done anything rash in an age, and Eleanor had hoped that her stepdaughter had learnt some sense at last.

The bellowing was coming from the stable. Aubrey le Moine, Jehan's younger brother, was standing outside, nursing an angry red weal on his cheek, a weal that could have been made by a riding crop. He was gazing through the stable door as though the Devil himself had taken up residence in there.

161

In the bailey, Eleanor dismounted, and relegated the bishop's fund to the back of her mind. She must deal with this first. Eleanor hated conflict of any sorts — loud words made her quake like a jelly — but though she quailed inside, she felt it her duty to try and temper her husband's wrath.

When Aubrey saw her, his anxious young eyes filled with hope and he broke into a shambling run.

'Countess! Come quickly!'

Just then, Arlette's voice rang out, clear as a bell. 'Stop it, Papa! Stop it! You'll kill him!'

Countess Eleanor had been taught it was beneath her dignity to run anywhere, but she could walk very quickly.

Inside the stable an extraordinary scene greeted her.

A man, Eleanor assumed it was Olier, the head groom, was lying curled up on the straw with his arms flung protectively about his head. Her husband stood aggressively over the groom, feet astride, a strong, freckled fist bunched around his crop. He was beating Olier, or rather attempting to beat him, for Count François was being hampered by his daughter. Arlette had attached herself to her father's arm, and was preventing him from doing more than tap the groom. Arlette's veil lay underfoot, and one of her plaits had unwound so that her hair flowed like a shining red stream over her shoulder. Her eyes were bright and hard as sapphires.

'How dare you, daughter!' With a violent movement, François flung Arlette off and, hair flying, Eleanor's step-daughter flew backwards, striking her head on a stall and sitting down, dazed.

Count François raised his right arm. Olier, seeing his shield had gone, whimpered with terror. Eleanor crossed her fingers and stepped forwards, heart pounding. She had intervened once before and saved a serving-wench a beating. Could she do it again? 'My lord?' she said, attempting to sound calm. 'What's amiss?'

On hearing her voice, the count froze mid-stroke, and turned. He looked like a demon. His ruddy cheeks were engorged with hot, angry blood; the whites of his eyes had gone pink; his coppery hair was untidy and slick with sweat. Not for the first time, Eleanor wondered whether hatred of her had inspired her father to marry her to François de Roncier. Or had he not been aware that François could at times be more monster than man? Eleanor kept her dislike from her face, and her head high, and regarded him steadily.

'My lord?'

'Ma dame!' The count stuffed his crop into his belt and smoothed down his hair.

As he walked towards her, the livid colour faded rapidly from his cheeks. Eleanor had noted that she had had that effect on the count before; perhaps the count was malleable, to a degree. It did not make Eleanor like him any the more, but it gave her something to think about. Perhaps she was not quite the impotent cipher she had thought . . .

Eleanor divined François was going to bow over her hand, so she kept her polite smile nailed to her face, and ignored the sudden cramping in her belly that proximity to her husband always caused.

Olier scrambled to his knees and crawled across the straw to where Arlette was sitting. Eleanor's step-daughter was groaning and holding her head but, other than that, blessedly quiet for once. Praying that the blow had knocked some sense into Arlette's head, or that at the least she was too stunned to intervene, Eleanor spoke again. 'What's amiss, my lord?'

The count kissed Eleanor's hand, and to her annoyance retained it. He glanced at Olier. 'That indolent oaf has continued to employ Aubrey in here without my leave—'

'But didn't young Aubrey take on his brother's guard duties?' Eleanor asked.

163

'Aye. And that's as it should be. He's growing up, and it's suitable work for a young man whose father is my seneschal. But this insolent churl − ' a dark glance at the man kneeling at his daughter's side − 'thinks he knows better. He has the gall to inform me that Aubrey has a love of horses, and no love for the fighting, and in his opinion Aubrey should be employed here permanently. *His* opinion indeed—'

'Maybe Olier is right,' Eleanor said softly.

François continued as though he had not heard her. 'That's what comes of employing freemen instead of villeins. Villeins may not have much between their ears, but they know to keep their opinions to themselves, if they have any. And furthermore, wife, Olier claims that a couple of grooms are not sufficient. He needs more help in here. Pah! His predecessor, what was his name . . . ?'

'Edgar.'

'That's it, Edgar. Edgar never complained. This fellow's a lazy dolt who uses others to cover up for his slothfulness.'

Olier had been working at the castle for a year. At the beginning he had struck Eleanor as a keen, friendly young man. But if she thought back, it occurred to her that lately Olier had not been so friendly, indeed at times his manner had been almost surly. Eleanor glanced about the stable, and noted the ramshackle temporary stalls which had been squeezed in to accommodate the additional horses her husband had purchased, as well as the mounts some of his mercenaries had brought with them. The routiers were meant to care for their animals themselves, but there was no denying that they, and the count's new stock, must create more work for Olier and his two assistants.

The stable was cramped and dilapidated: a half-wit could see that Olier had either lost heart or simply not had the time to maintain it properly. He had been a good groom when he had arrived at Huelgastel: it would be a nuisance if he was driven to seek employment elsewhere. Unlike villeins, freemen could up and walk off, a fact which her hot-tempered husband often seemed to forget.

The countess was relieved to see her step-daughter climb shakily to her feet, but she didn't trust her to keep her tongue between her teeth. Without giving Arlette time to marshall her thoughts, Eleanor steered her husband into the bailey. 'May I speak with you a moment, François?' she said, for all the world acting as though the distressing scene in the stable had not taken place at all. 'I'd like to discuss my plans for the herb garden.'

'Certainly, my dear.' The count followed her lead; there was no longer the slightest trace in his face of the demon that had possessed him in the stable.

Although Eleanor was resolved to try to help Olier and Aubrey, at this moment she was content to have stopped the beating. Countess Eleanor de Roncier had learned that sometimes one could achieve more if one bided one's time. Her rash step-daughter — while she could on occasion curb her wilder impulses — had yet to learn that lesson.

Count François knew where his wife was leading him.

On the other side of the keep, facing south, and within the confines of the curtain wall, was a paved courtyard. It had no official use, and had become a depository for broken or unwanted items. At that time it was home for a waggon with a broken axle, several barrels that needed the attention of the cooper, a cracked section of guttering that was awaiting re-casting, a half-rotted hen-coop, a rusty sieve, and a worn mill-stone awaiting the grindstone dresser who came three times a year.

Indulgently, François allowed Eleanor to lead him into the yard. He propped himself against a creaking waggon with a broken axle. 'You wished to talk to me, Eleanor?'

'Yes, mon seigneur,' Eleanor said softly, removing

her hand from the count's arm.

François noted the withdrawal with regret. His beautiful, fragile countess was not given to demonstrations of affection, but she had clung to him all the way across the bailey, and he had liked it. He wished his wife were not so aloof, and yet . . . He wondered if she was aware how much of a challenge he found her.

'I've told you before, Eleanor, you can call me François when we're on our own.'

'Thank you . . . François. This site would be ideal for the garden. If I can have your permission to have this debris cleared . . . ?'

François waved a hand agreeably. 'Granted.'

'. . . I thought perhaps . . . young Aubrey?'

'Aubrey le Moine?' François asked, sharply.

Eleanor responded with an abstracted smile. 'Mmm. He's a sweet, respectful lad.' She put a slender, white finger to her mouth, and frowned thoughtfully at the paving slabs.

'But I told you, I wanted Aubrey to step into Jehan's shoes. He's tall and strong for his years—'

'What?' Another vague smile, which had François's loins afire. 'Oh, yes, thank you, my dear. He does look strong. Just what I need.'

She had called him 'dear'. Eleanor had never called François 'dear' before. First the linking of arms in the bailey, and now this. François overrode his objections to Aubrey becoming his wife's assistant gardener.

'I thought,' his wife continued, apparently oblivious of her husband's trend of thoughts, 'we could clear these stones, save for a patch which would cut through the beds in the shape of a cross.'

'A cross?'

'It will make weeding easier. I should like four beds to start with, but I may divide them later. I thought lavender for the edging – lavender has so many uses, apart from its scent. I could plant a bay tree here,' Eleanor waved at the centre of one of her imaginary herb plots, 'and rosemary here. And over here . . .'

François listened with half an ear while his wife outlined her plans for the herb garden. There had been a herbarium in the Castle when his mother was younger, and everyone had benefited from the supply of fresh herbs. But as far as François was concerned, this was his wife's domain; his knowledge of the subject was patchy. It would be good to know that a plentiful supply of medicaments was available, though, and he was especially fond of sage stuffing in his poultry.

'Sage,' François interrupted Eleanor's catalogue, 'you must plant some sage.'

'But naturally we will have sage, red sage, it's the best cure I know of for a sore throat. I listed it just now, didn't you hear?'

'My apologies, Eleanor, my mind was wandering. But I've heard enough. Your herb garden will obviously flourish, and you may have young Aubrey to help you.'

'Thank you.' Eleanor smiled, and it seemed to François that her smile was not quite so distant as it had been. She drew closer, so François could smell the jasmine scent that she used. Her pale eyes lifted — at this distance he could see they were flecked with yellow. 'François, I can see that some large matter is preying on your mind.' She laid tapering fingers on his sleeve. 'I . . . I've been worried about you lately. You seem . . . preoccupied much of the time. Won't you share your troubles with me? It may ease you, and,' she gave a fluting laugh, 'I may be able to help.'

François frowned. His wife had never before encouraged his confidences, and he was uncertain of his ground. A wife was meant to run a man's household, and give him lusty sons. Eleanor had been well-trained, and was more than competent to fulfil the first part of the bargain, if only his mother would relinquish all authority to her.

And the second part of the agreement? François could not claim that Eleanor had yet repudiated him in bed, but he could wish she had been more responsive, and as yet his seed had fallen on barren ground.

But all at once she was not only giving physical demonstrations of affection, but also admitting concern. If he were to confide in Eleanor rather than his mother, perhaps his wife would gain confidence in *both* areas. The castle folk were bustling about their business all about them, but no one was within earshot, and no one was taking any notice of the count and his countess. The paved yard was as private a place as any for confidences.

'I *am* preoccupied, Eleanor,' he admitted.

'Will you share your cares with me? Is it Arlette? Are you worried about her marriage?'

François covered the hand on his sleeve with one of his own, and looked into his wife's remote, other-wordly eyes. 'It's not Arlette. It concerns a distant cousin of mine, Yolande Herevi—'

'Yolande Herevi? I've not heard the name before.'

The Count smiled. 'I wouldn't have expected you to know about a disreputable woman like that. Her infamy is confined to Vannes, I think.'

'Infamy?'

'She's a slut. She's the mistress of Sir Jean St Clair.'

'Now St Clair's a name I know. Doesn't he fight in the tourneys?'

'That's his younger brother, Waldin.'

'Oh. And Yolande Herevi's kin to you?'

'Aye.' Moving with Eleanor to the worn mill-stones, François seated himself, pulling her down beside him. 'Her late mother, Izabel Herevi – ' François saw no reason to explain that Izabel Herevi was his mother's elder sister – 'had a tenuous claim to some of Mama's dower lands and now the old woman is dead, I fear her daughter may resurrect the claim. But,' François struck his thigh with his fist, 'we have held the lands for years, and I'm damned if I'll release them. I need those lands and their revenues. I've had to provide a fat dowry for Arlette, and it won't stop there . . .'

Eleanor's pale eyes rested thoughtfully on a grey pigeon which had landed in the yard and was pecking at the cracks in the paving slabs. 'It must be a very tenuous claim to have lain dormant all these years, François. Are you sure you are not worrying needlessly? If the woman is a concubine, there won't be a lawcourt in Christendom that would support her over you. Surely your father would have acted if he had thought there was any real danger of the claim being successful?'

François saw no need to explain that Count Robert had once been betrothed to Izabel Herevi, and had continued to nourish tender feelings for her, which was why his father had never lifted a finger against the old woman. 'Events have moved on since Father's death,' he said. 'St Clair has taken the Herevi woman, and their three bastards—'

Eleanor flinched.

'I beg your pardon, my dear. St Clair has taken his mistress and their three children to his manor. St Clair is an ambitious charmer with an eye for easy pickings. He might marry her.'

'A knight, marry his mistress?' Eleanor drew her fine brows together. 'That's absurd.'

'You sound exactly like Mama,' François said, sourly. 'She does not think it likely either. But she doesn't know St Clair as I do. He's an ambitious schemer, and if he thinks he's anything to gain by marrying that woman, he'll do it, and to hell with the consequences.'

The pale eyes regarded him steadily. 'You are truly worried about this, aren't you, François?'

'I am very concerned. It's *my* land, and I won't permit a jumped-up knight to wrest it from me. De Ronciers protect their own.'

Eleanor gave him a cool smile. 'What do you propose to do about it?'

'Nothing much I can do, at the moment. St Clair's removed his whore—'

A pained expression again disturbed the unruffled calm of Eleanor's features.

'—the Herevi woman, I mean, to his manor. Short of razing the place to the ground, I can't see that I can *do* anything.'

'It's St Clair's move,' Eleanor said, slowly.

'Aye.'

'You'll have to be patient, then.' She lifted her narrow shoulders. 'He may do nothing. You have no proof he's after your mother's dower lands, have you?'

'Proof? No. I don't need proof. I *know* he covets it.'

'You mustn't let this make you ill, François. You must learn patience. You must wait—'

'Wait! That's the one thing I cannot do. I want this settled *now*.'

'I think, François,' the count's wife said softly, 'that in this instance, you have no choice.'

François could think of nothing to say. He looked gloomily at his wife, and for an instant he could have sworn a tiny smile of satisfaction flickered across her proud mouth. Irritably, he dismissed the thought, and set it down to too much spiced wine at noon.

June 1183, in the valley of the River Dordogne
In the spring of that year, Henry the Young King, having run short of funds to pay his Flemish foot-soldiers, had resorted – not for the first time – to plundering the treasuries of some of the provincial abbeys. The Prince had succeeded in drumming up some half-hearted support

170

for his cause, but most of the barons in the Aquitaine were cautious. They were wary of allying themselves with a prince who warred with his father and brother and held no real title to any land. Only a few had been prepared to back him with significant amounts of gold. And significant amounts of gold was what the Young King needed.

So the Young King had cast his net wide.

He had raided churches in Brittany. He had raided St Martial's at Limoges. But the Prince's final and most outrageous deed was a raid on the shrine at Rocamadour in the Aquitaine where, not content with stealing the famous sword which was reputed to have belonged to Roland, his men committed the sacrilege of profaning St Amadour's body.

The sword was sold for a reasonable sum, and some of the Prince's troops received their dues.

What happened next was viewed as God's judgement.

The Young King caught dysentery, and became very ill. When Henry arrived at Martel, his bed was set up in a house sympathetic to his cause on the corner of the market square.

His troops camped in the square and hoped the Young King would recover, because not all of them had yet had their money.

The citizens of Martel barred their windows and doors, and instructed their women, especially the young and pretty ones, to stay indoors. They, too, hoped the Young King would recover, for the citizens of Martel had heard alarming tales concerning the Young King's Flemish foot-soldiers.

In a chamber on the upper floor of the house overlooking the square, the Prince lay perilously sick with the fever. His squire sat cross-legged outside the door. The door was closed, but the sounds of the sickroom, of groaning and vomiting, carried to the landing. The squire had been waiting some time, but at last the Prince's chaplain, who was skilled in the healing arts, emerged from the chamber and joined him.

The squire, a well-made lad with straight, dark brown hair and eyes to match, jumped to his feet. 'Is he any better, Father?'

The Prince's chaplain shook his tonsured head. 'I'm afraid not, Guyon. His Grace is, if anything, more ill than when we arrived. Take these sheets downstairs, will you, and have them boiled?' He thrust some soiled and evil-smelling linen at the squire.

'Aye, Father.'

'And see if they've any more linen to spare. The least we can do is try to keep him clean. Then you can come in and lend me a hand.'

'Aye, Father.'

Sensing he was dying, Henry the Young King confessed of his crimes and sins, and sent a message to his father, begging forgiveness for fomenting revolt. So certain was he that death was approaching that he gave all his earthly possessions away.

He gave Guyon, his faithful squire — one of the few who had remained with him to the end — a heavy gold ring and a gold brooch.

When Henry Plantagenet's messenger arrived from Limoges with the English King's pardon, any fears he may have nourished that the Young King's repentance was insincere were dispelled as soon as he saw him. The Young Prince was doing heavy penance in the house overlooking Martel market square.

To symbolise his acknowledgement of his criminal acts, the Young King had had a noose placed about his neck; and, though he was in mortal agony, he was wearing a hair shirt under his crusader's cloak, and lying on a bed of cinders. A heavy wooden cross lay on his breast.

172

Henry the Young King heard the messenger deliver his royal father's pardon, and put on the sapphire ring his father had sent him as a tangible token of his forgiveness. He had given everything else away.

He died soon afterwards, in the bleak, grey hour before dawn.

Guyon, loyal by nature, was not stupid. It was likely the Flemish mercenaries would react badly when they learned of the Prince's death and realised that they would probably never get their money. He did not want his throat slit for the ring and the brooch. Accordingly, the Young King's squire bundled up his belongings, and crept out of the house overlooking the square.

He was in the saddle, and a mile out of Martel, by the time the first ray of sunlight slanted across the valley.

The rebellion the Young King had fostered died with him.

Chapter Nine

March 1186

Countess Eleanor's herb garden was now well established. As the first new shoots of the year appeared, she took Arlette out to discuss the spring planting.

Happy to be outside, even if it was within the inner bailey, Arlette looked at the awakening plants and listened attentively. She was fifteen, a woman full grown; she had reached the age at which it had been agreed she was to be married, and by the year's end she would be sent to Count Etienne. Despite the agreement her father had made with Louis Favell when they had signed her marriage agreement, she had not visited La Forteresse in the summer of 1183, and had yet to meet her fiancé. The reasons for this change of plan were given as political, and Arlette had not pressed to go, seeing the delay as something of a reprieve. She was yet to come to terms with her role as Countess Favell, but lately she had become aware that her attitude to her forthcoming marriage was undergoing subtle changes.

Most of her life Arlette had felt powerless, unable to bring her mother back, unable to make her father love her, unable to have much effect on the life going on around her. And one day, observing Eleanor, it had dawned on Arlette that if she were to become a countess that might change. Somehow, Eleanor managed to influence her father. Perhaps she

175

may learn to influence Count Etienne.

Over the past few years Arlette had come to respect her quiet, gentle stepmother. For Arlette, Eleanor had become a source of peace and calm. Eleanor was not an easy woman to love, she kept her thoughts and feelings very close, but she did have a soothing effect on Arlette's father.

In fact the gentle Countess Eleanor was a force to be reckoned with. She did not rush at things like a bull at a gate. No, she worked at problems in a quiet, roundabout way. But this approach, Arlette realised, was highly effective.

Take that affair over two years ago with Aubrey and Olier. Arlette, by interfering directly, had provoked her choleric father into a worse rage, while the countess had seemed to ignore the scene. At the time Arlette had despised Eleanor for her weakness. But by sunset Eleanor had succeeded in wresting Aubrey from his hated guard duties, setting the boy to work in her garden. A week later, the countess had enlisted Rojer and Dewi — two of the kitchen scullions — as additional helpers. And a week after that, the countess had declared Aubrey redundant, and had him deployed elsewhere. And where was he deployed? The stables. Not content with this coup, she had also ensured that Simon, one of the cook's grandsons, was installed in the stables too, and the three of them — Aubrey, Simon and Olier — had since transformed them.

Arlette could learn much, she decided, by watching Countess Eleanor's methods. In public, Eleanor was always distant with François; invariably polite, but aloof. Arlette could see her father liked that. He brought Eleanor many gifts, which she accepted with courteous indifference. Yet François appeared to adore his wife. Arlette had tried to ape her stepmother's manner with him, but she found she could not. She was too anxious to please him. Was the love that she felt for her father the very thing that drove him away?

Perhaps it was too late for Arlette and her father. But when she reached La Forteresse, she would follow Eleanor's example. Watching her stepmother as she snapped off a straggling lavender shoot and crushed the leaves to release the scent, Arlette vowed to have Count Etienne eating out of her hand.

Eleanor looked across the lavender at Arlette and smiled. 'I'd like to leave you in charge of the gardeners today, Arlette,' she said.

'I'd be delighted.'

'I'm going to the cathedral in Vannes. Get them to trim this lavender hedge, will you? And make sure they're ruthless with it; I need the space for more thyme. When they've done that, they can cut back the fennel, down to the roots, and the soapwort. I'm experimenting with the soapwort, and I'd like it divided. They can leave half where it is and put the rest in this bed over here. But first I'd like all the soil worked over, the dead wood removing . . .'

A relentless clanging was coming from the forge in the outer bailey, and it almost drowned the countess's soft voice. Gradlon had been working ceaselessly for days, ever since Arlette's father had stormed into the armoury and commanded his captains to give all the weapons a thorough overhaul. Arlette hoped that her father had not scented trouble. She hoped he was not *making* trouble . . . Ever since she had overheard that conversation with Father Jerome, the black monk, Arlette had kept her ears open for news of 'that Herevi woman', but she had heard nothing more. Surely this sudden spring cleaning of the armoury could have nothing to do with her? François de Roncier had irons in many fires. Arlette wondered what he was up to this time.

The countess raised her voice above the clamour. 'You understand what needs doing, don't you, Arlette?'

'I do.' Arlette pointed at the mint. 'Look at that, Belle-mère, its shoots are everywhere . . .' Arlette trailed off, for round the corner of the keep strode Nicholas Warr, the castle's master bowman, in the company of Captain Malait, her father's Viking mercenary captain. Malait's horned helmet glinted in the sun, and his padded military gambeson added extra inches to his chest, though he scarcely needed them. The archer, a long spindle of a man in comparison to his bear-like companion, wore a tight tunic and hose and close-fitting leather capuchon. His archer's arm-brace was in place, and his bow was slung over a bony shoulder. The two men headed what looked like half of Malait's troop. Three troopers were staggering under the weight of heavy straw butts, the others all carried bows. All were wearing quivers in addition to their swords. Arlette frowned. She had thought Captain Malait's troop relied on the sword. Why this unusual interest in archery? What *was* going on?

'Aye, mint's worse than ground-elder,' the countess said placidly. 'Given half a chance it would invade the whole herb garden. But we can't root it out completely. It's a useful herb.'

'We could build a little wall round it to contain it.'

Eleanor gave Arlette one of her dreamy smiles. 'That is a good idea. I see I can leave everything with you.' And calling for her maid to bring her riding gloves, the countess went into the keep.

Though Arlette was supposed to take the overseer's part, she enjoyed working in her stepmother's garden, and now she hitched her over-skirt up, tucking it into her belt, and began dirtying her hands, selecting the right sized stones to build a wall around the mint.

Rojer and Dewi hacked happily at the lavender bushes.

A clattering and shouting started in the outer bailey, as though someone was competing directly with Gradlon's clanging of hammer on anvil.

'What's going on, Rojer?' Arlette asked. It could not be the mercenaries drilling, though it sounded very much like it, for both her father's troops had gone through their routine twice the day before.

Rojer laid down his pruning shears and went to see. He was back in a moment. 'Captain Bond's knocking his men into shape, my lady.'

Captain le Bret had left her father's service three years earlier, taking his cousin, young Ned Fletcher, with him, and Alan Bond had replaced him as mercenary captain. Arlette had never found out why Alan le Bret and Ned had gone, but was certain the English mercenaries' departure was connected with the mysterious events on that Lady Day that had culminated in the cathedral being destroyed, and the mysterious concubine, Yolande Herevi, fleeing Vannes with her family. Had Arlette's father done something unpalatable that day, something that even two hardened mercenaries had been unable to stomach? It was becoming clearer by the day that this must be the case. Arlette wondered how her father squared this with his conscience. She had been imbued with a strong sense of honour, but her father's concept of honour, she was discovering, was more flexible than hers. Did he take the view that the end justified the means?

Arlette turned her thoughts back to the present.

'Knocking his men into shape?' she said. 'Are his troops simpletons? They've been hard at it for weeks, they must know their paces by now.'

Rojer grunted and pruned a straggling branch. 'Can't say, my lady,' he replied, without much interest. 'Maybe there's trouble brewing.'

Arlette leaned back on her heels and thrust back a stray lock of hair with the heel of her hand, unaware that her palms were as dirty as her fingers, and she had streaked her cheek with soil. 'Trouble? I hope not. I've not heard of any trouble.'

Arlette knew her father disliked the idea of paying homage to Duke Geoffrey, and she knew that more than once letters had been exchanged between her father and the French king, Philip. But she knew nothing of the contents and, as her father would be likely to choose death rather than discuss politics with his daughter, she could only suspect that her father favoured the King of France over the Angevin duke.

'I don't think my father would rebel openly against the duke,' Arlette murmured.

'My lady?'

Arlette pulled herself together. Whatever the cause of the sudden increase in military activity, she could not be discussing her father's affairs with the gardener. 'Rojer, let Dewi finish that hedge. You can move on to the rosemary . . .'

'Aye, ma dame.' Rojer went over to the bay tree and began attacking it with his pruning shears.

'Not that one, Rojer! That's bay. *This* is rosemary.'

One month later, Arlette lay cosy in her bed, listening to the soothing rise and fall of Clemence's breathing. The girls' candle had blown out, and the room was dark as black velvet. It was past midnight, and something had awakened Arlette, but though she strained her ears she could hear nothing out of the way. Then Arlette caught the sound again, as the April night breezes lifted a murmur from the courtyard below and tossed it through their narrow window slit; she also heard the neighing of a horse, the stamping of a hoof, and a low, muttered command. It sounded very much as if her father's mercenary horse-soldiers were mustering. At midnight?

Arlette lay still and silent as a stone, listening. There — she heard it again — more muffled commands, and the chinking of bits. What was happening?

Though Arlette was never consulted on matters of

policy, she had discovered that politically her father was in a tricky position. He owed allegiance to Duke Geoffrey for the lands he held in Brittany, but in addition to his Breton holding, the count had interests on the border between Philip of France's small kingdom and the duchy of Aquitaine. For these lands he owed allegiance to the King of France. Since Henry of England had lost his eldest son, Richard Plantagenet had held the Aquitaine uncontested. But, in 1185, Henry Plantagenet had lost patience with Richard and, seeking to shore up his power, the English King had forced his rebellious son to hand the Aquitaine back to Queen Eleanor.

There was a long-standing dispute over the precise location of the boundaries of Count François' lands on the border of the Aquitaine, and this dispute put her father into direct conflict with Queen Eleanor, mother of his Breton overlord. But the count had not mentioned the boundary dispute for months; he seemed more concerned over the fact that King Philip of France was unmovable on the question of his sister Alice marrying Richard Plantagenet. This Arlette's father was set against. An alliance between France and Richard Plantagenet, the potential Duke of Aquitaine, would make his holding just north of the Aquitaine even more untenable.

Reaching for her woollen wrap, for the spring night air raised goosebumps on her arms, Arlette swung out of bed, groped for her sheepskin slippers, and padded to the door. She had known for the past month that this feverish preparation was more than 'spring cleaning': her father was obviously working on some secret campaign. Now was Arlette's chance to find out what that was. She was frightened of the outcome, for should her father take exception to her interest in his affairs, it might mean a beating. But curiosity was strong in her.

Quietly, Arlette lifted the door-latch and padded up the twisting turret stairs. She would have a good view of the

181

bailey from her turret. It was fortunate that Pierre was on watch on top of the turret that night. He was eight years old, another grandson of the cook, and he adored her. Pierre would let Arlette observe the goings-on in the courtyard below without betraying her interest.

'Who's there?' Pierre called the instant she stepped through the doorway. The boy had been sitting in a crenellation watching the activity below. Snatching up a lighted torch he waved it under her nose. 'Oh! Lady Arlette, it's you!'

'I heard the noises,' Arlette said, 'and I wanted to know what was happening.'

Pierre thrust the flambeau back in its bracket. 'Everything, my lady. Look, both troops are down there, all mounted up. Why there's even a cart for the archers. Look at them all clutching their bows.'

Arlette didn't move. 'Pierre, please move that light.'

'My lady?'

'It shines on your face when you look down. Anyone down there can look up and see you. I don't want to be seen.'

As the boy leapt to do her bidding, Arlette peered through a crenellation on to the scene below. The inner bailey was awash with the yellow flaring light of a hundred torches. At first glance it looked as though Huelgastel had been invaded by an army. The courtyard was a seething mass of prancing, curvetting horses; of sweating grooms, and stone-faced mercenaries.

'They make quite a show, don't they, my lady?' Pierre murmured. 'Don't you think they look terrifying?' he added, a blend of awe and pride in his tone.

'Terrifying,' Arlette agreed.

Upon closer inspection, Arlette realised that the throng below was not the disorganised rabble it had first seemed. She could make out some individuals. There was her father, mounted on his big-boned brown charger, the

182

vicious one which took heed of no one and nothing, and had even kicked Aubrey in the head and left him dizzy for a week. The count was wearing his new mail coat; its links gleamed like silver fishscales in the torchlight. And that other mounted soldier with the horned helmet and the sleeveless gambeson could only be Captain Malait. Mounted on a restive, ugly grey, the Viking was in conference with the other captain, Alan Bond. Bond nodded at something the Norseman had said, and rode to the head of his troop.

'Look, my lady.' Pierre interrupted Arlette's train of thought. 'They're leaving. The count's waving them out.'

Arlette watched as the first of her father's mounted troops poured under the portcullis and over the bridge.

'The archers are going too,' Pierre said.

The archers' waggon, bristling with bows, rumbled out of the bailey, a gigantic, wheeled hedgehog.

'There are so many lights, it's bright as noon down there,' Arlette said.

Even from their perch in the turret it was not difficult to make out Nicholas Warr, the master bowman, bouncing along with his fellow archers in the cart. Each man had a full quiver, and Arlette could see bundles of spare arrows tied to the side of the waggon. She bit her lip, and regarded the stick-like form of Nicholas Warr thoughtfully. Nicholas Warr had been at Huelgastel since May the previous year; was the frenetic activity since his arrival a coincidence?

'Who did Nicholas Warr work for before he came here, Pierre?' she asked the boy-sentry.

Pierre shrugged. 'Don't know, my lady.'

'Has he always been an archer?'

'I think so. I heard he'd saved Captain Malait some years back.'

'And that's all you know about him?'

'Yes. Except that I heard someone teasing him about

hiding away in a bog for years.'

'A bog? What do you mean? What bog?'

Pierre grinned. 'Wasn't a bog really, but the manor at Kermaria by the marshes.'

'Kermaria? You're sure?'

'Positive.' Pierre leaned out over the crenellations. 'That's odd, my lady, have you noticed? The troops are handing in their torches at the gatehouse as they leave. They're riding out in darkness. Why should they do that – one of the horses might stumble and break a leg . . . Does that strike you as odd, my lady?'

But Arlette was not altogether surprised; for by now she was convinced that her father's business that night was far from honest. She made a noncommittal noise in her throat, and stood with Pierre until the waggon had disappeared into the night, and the last rumble of wheels had faded away.

Then she turned and went back to bed, feeling pity for the inhabitants of wherever it was her father was bound.

The next night was another calm one, and Arlette was wakened from her slumbers once more by noises floating up from the bailey. Without hesitating she slipped from her bed. Clemence, as ever, slept like a log. Her friend's cheeks were flushed, and a faint smile played across her lips. Clemence was dreaming of Morgan, no doubt.

Running up the stairs, Arlette pushed open the door which led to the turret roof before hesitating. She had been lucky to find Pierre on duty here yesterday, but the boys rarely did the same stint twice. Whoever was on guard today might not be so sympathetic.

'My lady!'

It was Pierre again, all smiles on seeing her. Arlette breathed a sigh of relief and stepped forwards. As soon as he saw her he whirled to snatch the flambeau from its iron rest and moved it safely across the parapet.

'I prayed it would be you on duty, Pierre,' she said. 'But as you were here yesterday, I couldn't be sure.'

'When your father rode out he took most of the garrison with him, my lady. Those left behind have to do double duty.'

Moving to a crenellation, Arlette peered out. The drawbridge was raised, and a troop of men had ridden in, her father and another in the advance guard. The archers' waggon brought up the rear.

'So they're back.'

'Aye, my lady. But not all of them. I've not seen Captain Malait's troop.'

'Who's that, riding beside my father? His helmet obscures his face.'

'Alan Bond, my lady.'

Arlette's father and Alan Bond dismounted. Her father's companion removed his helmet, and his clear-cut, handsome features were visible even from their eyrie. He took the count's reins, and limped with both his and the count's destrier to the stable, where a sleepy Aubrey waited, knuckling his eyes, in the doorway.

Arlette noticed a bandage tied round the captain's thigh. 'Captain Bond's been hurt,' she said.

Her eyes flew back to her father. She could not help but be concerned for him, though he looked hale enough, striding towards the hall with his usual vigour. 'Is my father all right, do you suppose?'

'The count seems to be unharmed, my lady, but look at those poor beggars in the waggon. I think Countess Eleanor's healing hands will be needed.'

The waggon was being driven right up to the keep, the entrance to which was almost directly below them, to the right. Arlette craned her neck to get a better view of the horses and cart directly below them. This was not the archers' waggon, which was of plain, unpainted wood, but another, longer cart, painted green. It was full of

185

wounded men, men whose hurts looked infinitely worse than the wound which Alan Bond appeared to have sustained. One or two of the men were sitting; one held his roughly bandaged head between his hands, groaning repeatedly. A trooper held his upper arm and rocked back and forth, back and forth. Their eyes were hollow and their faces glazed.

'Dear God!' Arlette crossed herself, and steeled herself to look at the other men in the cart — those who were supine. One had a white cloth pressed to his chest, a dark stain seeping out from the centre. Another — her mind froze at the sight — had lost an arm. Another . . .

Fighting down a rising sense of nausea, Arlette turned blindly for the door.

Pierre's brown eyes were round and interested; he was absorbing the grisly scene with childish callousness. 'Are you going back to bed, my lady?' he inquired innocently.

'No. I must go and help them. Pierre, I should like you to do me a favour.'

The boy's eyes were fixed greedily on the scene below. 'My lady?'

'It's a secret.'

His dark child's eyes turned to meet hers. 'My lady?'

'I'd like you to make some discreet inquiries for me—'

A frown puckered his brow. 'D . . . discreet?'

'Yes. I'd like you to find something out for me, and I don't want anyone to know what you're about. Pretend you're just curious. Do you think you can do that?'

Pierre's small chest swelled. 'Of course, my lady. I'll do anything for you.'

'Good. See if you can find out where my father and his men went when they left last night, and what they have been doing. But be careful. My father obviously wants as few people as possible to know about this.'

Pierre nodded, pleased and proud to have been taken into Arlette's confidence.

186

'My thanks, Pierre,' Arlette said seriously. 'You're a true friend.'

Arlette dragged a decent gown over her shift and awoke Clemence. In this emergency they would need as many hands as possible. Together the girls made their way to the hall.

Arlette paused for a moment with her hand on the latch to take in the scene. All the flambeaux had been lit, and the great iron candlestand had been dragged to one side of the fire. Rojer was jamming a couple of dozen candlesticks into the prickets and lighting them with shaking hands. Arlette's heart sank. She knew what that extra light meant, so close to the fire: there would be much bloody surgery in Huelgastel hall that night.

The wounded men were being helped – or carried, according to their needs – to pallets ranged round the hearth.

Any hopes that Arlette cherished that she might make inquiries of her own were immediately dispelled, for her father, talking energetically with Captain Bond, had seen her. His russet brows drew together, but he did not pause in his conversation, throwing his head back in amusement as he spoke.

Arlette caught the words 'necessary losses . . . but I'm pleased with the outcome'; thus encouraged to believe her father was not angry, she disregarded his initial frown and ran towards him.

'Papa! What has happened? Are you all right?'

The count sighed. 'Get me some wine, Bond, and mull it if you please.'

'Aye, mon seigneur.' Captain Bond saluted and headed for the wine-vault.

'Papa? You're not hurt?'

Dark shadows under her father's eyes betrayed a lack of sleep, but despite these and the frown gathering again in

187

his brows, there was a brightness, an excitement in his eyes that Arlette could not miss. His cheeks were flushed.

'I'm well enough, daughter, a little saddle-weary, but well enough.' The count stretched, and Arlette could have sworn the twisted smile on his face was one of triumph. A groan from one of his men attracted his attention. 'However, some of my men are a little worse for wear.'

Arlette remembered the man in the cart who had lost an arm, and shuddered.

Bored with her company already, her father was turning away. 'Go and waken your stepmother, there's a good girl. One of the troopers took an arrow in his thigh, and it seems to have smashed the bone. He was bleating like a motherless lamb all the way back.'

'Sweet mother! When was he hurt?'

The count's eyes became vague. 'When?'

'Did it happen today? Was the man wounded today?'

The count shook his head. 'Today? Yesterday? What difference does it make when the man took the arrow?'

'It could make quite a difference to the trooper, Papa,' Arlette explained, though her father must realise this as well as she. 'If he was wounded recently, there's a chance Belle-mère and I might save his leg. If not, infection will have set in and . . .'

Her father shrugged, and glanced at the iron candlestand, which was throwing a bright ring of light over one of the pallets. Clemence knelt by it, mopping the brow of its occupant, a groaning, pasty-faced trooper. Arlette knew without being told that this was the man who had taken the arrow, and that not even a surgeon from Salerno could save that man's leg, because the poor wretch had been wounded the night before.

'Do your best,' her father said briskly. 'You know who to ask if you need assistance.'

'Yes, Father.' Arlette turned to the fire, bracing herself

for what would probably be the worst night of her life. If it came to an amputation, who would wield the knife? One of the mercenaries? Arlette would be glad of her stepmother's cool, calming presence.

It was dawn before Arlette and Clemence were free to climb the turret stairs and rest.

Pierre intercepted them on the stairs. 'My lady!'

Arlette blinked, trying to focus her aching eyes on the boy. She was exhausted, worn out with watching other people's pain, worn out with feeling impotent. Though she had worked as hard as she knew how, she had not been able to save many of the severely wounded. She felt utterly helpless.

Clutching the broad rope that was pegged at intervals up the outside wall of the stairwell, Clemence went on ahead of her up to their chamber.

Wearily, Arlette rested her back against the cold stone wall and looked at the boy.

'I found out what you wanted to know, my lady!'

'Pierre?' For a moment Arlette could not think what he meant.

'You know, my lady. I've learnt where the men have been. There's been a great battle!'

'I gathered that,' she responded dryly. Then, seeing disappointment creep into the child's eyes, Arlette fought back her tiredness and forced an expression of interest on to her face. 'What did you learn?' she asked. She had been too busy nursing to have time to glean any information from the men, even if they had been in a fit state to tell her anything.

'The battle took place at Kermaria. You remember, my lady? That's the place that Nicholas Warr came from before he came here.'

'Kermaria? Are you sure?'

Pierre nodded energetically. 'I learned more, my lady.'

189

Arlette's interest had quickened. 'What?' she asked urgently.

'I heard the names Herevi and St Clair,' Pierre said.

'Herevi? My father has mentioned that name, but St Clair . . . ? What's the connection, I wonder?' Arlette tried to order her muddled thoughts, but she was so tired that her mind wasn't focusing any better than her eyes.

'Do you want me to probe around a bit more, my lady?'

'If you would.' Arlette wished she and her father were on better terms, so she could ask him directly what all this was about. But she knew him well enough to understand he would resent her interest as interference.

They had reached Arlette's door. Pierre sprang to open it for her and, blindly, Arlette stumbled through. Clemence was already tucked up. Arlette fell in beside her, still clothed, and drew the covers over her head. She must think, make sense of Pierre's words but, even as she tried, her eyes were closing and she was drifting into a deep, exhausted sleep.

Raymond had been lying in a ditch near Kermaria for almost a day when he recovered consciousness and came back to pain.

He groaned, and at once suppressed the sound, for with returning consciousness came memory. Count François had crept up on Kermaria in the dead of night, and had attacked them at dawn. It had been a dawn that Raymond would never forget, though he could not recall much about the battle itself, having been forced out of the action early on when he had taken a glancing blow to his head. He had come round soon afterwards, though, while one of de Roncier's routiers had been dragging him out of the hall and into the yard. The filthy cut-throat had pinched his boots, and slung him atop a body. Somehow Raymond had managed to keep still, somehow he had kept his nerve. But it had not been easy, because

Raymond had known and liked the soul that had once inhabited the body he was lying on. It was Denis the Red, his father's merry sergeant, and they had drunk away many an evening together. Not any more. Damn de Roncier. Damn that devil's whole family. One day, Raymond vowed, he would see to it that the de Ronciers were made to pay for the count's sins.

Warily, Raymond lifted his head and peered into the early morning sun, over the nodding tops of the reeds which grew so abundantly near the estuary. His head felt heavy, the marshland tilted sickeningly. He had to move slowly.

A straggle of geese were moving sedately across a cloudless sky. Raymond sought out his father's manor, a small stone tower which peered over a moss-encrusted wall. Someone was on look-out on top of the tower, watching both the marshes and the approach road from Vannes. A de Roncier man, he had to be. Hastily, Raymond withdrew his head, and the painful pounding this movement engendered reminded him to move with care.

He sank back into the reeds, careless of the damp. Every muscle in his body shrieked with his slightest movement. How long had he been lying in the ditch? One day, two? As consciousness returned gradually, it brought with it more discomforts. Raymond had a raging thirst. His face felt stiff and battered. When he moved his mouth, a sharp pain shot along his cheek from chin to temple. Gently, Raymond probed the painful area.

'Holy Christ!'

He could not see the extent of the wound to his face, but it felt as though someone had tried to slice his head in two. The gash felt deep, he thought it might be healing, he could feel dried blood running along its length. The front of his tunic was stiff with the stuff. Raymond began to shiver, and raised his head to peer at Kermaria manor.

He wondered whether his father was dead, and his

uncle, Waldin St Clair, the great tourney champion. He had not seen their bodies, but what he had seen had convinced him that de Roncier had been ruthlessly efficient. And what had happened to Raymond's baby brother, Philippe? Would de Roncier harm a babe? Raymond thought it likely, for brother Philippe, as his father's legitimate heir, had a claim to some of de Roncier's lands. Undoubtedly that was what this massacre had been all about. De Roncier had cold-bloodedly sought to eliminate his rival.

And what about his sisters, Gwenn and Katarin? The girls posed no threat to the count, but Raymond was not reassured that this would guarantee their safety.

The sentry was standing at his post. Baby Philippe's legitimacy gave Raymond no cause to love his brother, for it gave him precedence, robbed him of his birthright. Nonetheless, Raymond couldn't stomach the thought of an innocent falling under that butcher's knife. Raymond spotted a brace of guards walking the length of Kermaria's fortified wall. However urgent the questions that whirled in Raymond's head, he could see it would be insane to return to find answers. If he came within a hair's breadth of the manor, he would be done for. If his brother and sisters were living, Raymond could best help them by biding his time. He would heal himself, and while he was recovering he would plan his revenge. By the time Raymond was finished de Roncier would rue the day he had first seen daylight.

'Damn Count François,' Raymond muttered. 'Damn him to hell.'

He swallowed. Before Raymond did anything, he had to find fresh water. He struggled to all fours and, keeping his head below the level of the reeds, began working his way south, following the line of the river. His muscles ached, his head throbbed with every step he took, but he moved at a steady pace. There was only one place

Raymond could go where he thought he would be safe, and before he went much further he would have to find some boots, and some money. With what he planned to do, he would need money.

Chapter Ten

Madalen, one of St Clair's tenants, whose cottage was built in the shadow of Kermaria manor walls, was cutting reeds downstream. In the fighting, the thatch of Madalen's cottage had been damaged, and she intended to make her repairs as soon as possible. Madalen could not afford to let the events of the previous day steal any more of her time. She and the rest of the villagers had been shocked by what had occurred at their village, but they had wasted a day mourning, and a day was all they could afford. It was not that they lacked respect for Jean St Clair. As masters went, he was a good, fair one. But now Jean St Clair lay stiff and cold; they could do no more for him, and there was work to be done. Gripping her scythe with work-reddened, reed-scarred hands, Madalen sliced through the thick grasses with easy, confident strokes.

A woman of solid bones and no little strength, Madalen was not afraid of working alone on the marsh. When she first heard the rustling she ignored it, taking it for a duck or a coot returning to its nesting place. She glanced up, reminding herself that she must remember to check the hidden nets she had set out for catching wildfowl, and resumed her scything.

The short scarf which kept Madalen's greying hair out of her way had slipped as she worked. Not three yards away, the rushes rattled. Madalen lifted her head, hooked the scythe over her arm, and re-tied her scarf.

195

'Is anyone there?' she asked, not really expecting any response.

'Madalen!'

The rasping whisper had Madalen's capable fingers grabbing for her scythe. 'Who's there? Who is it?' She held her scythe before her, a curved moon of a blade that glinted in the morning sun.

'Help me, Madalen!'

The reeds parted, and a *thing* that might once have been a man crawled out. Madalen found herself gazing down at a bloody, mutilated, gargoyle of a face. 'Mother of God!' Madalen backed, caught a foot on her bundle of cut reeds, and stumbled. Righting herself, she searched for an avenue of escape.

'Madalen! Help me! Don't you know me?'

The thing crouching like a demon in the reeds had green eyes, the most beautiful green eyes. Madalen knew those eyes. Every maid in Kermaria had fallen under their spell at one time or another.

'Master Raymond!' Madalen dropped the scythe and fell on her knees before the son of her former master.

'Thank, God,' Raymond said. 'You know me. For a moment I thought you were going to finish me off with that scythe—'

'Master Raymond, your poor face . . .'

'Never mind that. Madalen, have you any water?'

'Of course, sir. Here.'

Madalen thrust a worn leather bottle into Raymond's hands and watched St Clair's once-handsome bastard son drink her bottle dry. 'What will you do, sir?' she asked, still gazing in disbelief at what had been done to Raymond Herevi's face. Master Raymond would find the girls a mite shy from now on, though the worst scar would be confined to one side of his face. If he got that wound cleaned, the rest of his hurts looked superficial. Caked blood, mostly.

'Madalen, you must tell me what you know. What's happening at Kermaria? Is de Roncier still at my father's manor?'

'No, sir. He left in the night, but he's left some of his men . . .'

Raymond nodded, flinching at the pain which shot through his brain. His head felt as though it had swollen to twice its normal size, and he was experiencing great difficulty concentrating. If it were not that it were so important, he would lie down where he was – damp marshland and all – and sleep. The reeds in front of his eyes blurred. His head lolled.

'Sir, you're very pale . . .'

Raymond lifted his head. 'Go on, Madalen. What happened to my father? Did the count take him prisoner?'

Madalen's broad, homely face reflected her distress. One of her strong, work-worn hands came out and gently touched Raymond's knee. And though she did not speak, the gesture said it all. 'I . . . I'm sorry, sir . . .'

Raymond buried his battered head in his hands. 'Oh, dear God. Why? *Why?*'

Madalen watched the downbent head, and said nothing. She was twice Raymond Herevi's age. Raymond was the son of a knight while Madalen was a tenant farmer, but rather to her astonishment Madalen found she could sympathise with him. In one sense, Raymond Herevi's illegitimacy made him an outsider, but Jean St Clair had loved his firstborn, and had always ensured he had a place in the running of the manor. Raymond Herevi was used to the good things of life; he was used to being protected. And now, in one stroke, all that had changed. Not only had the boy lost his father, but he had lost his place in the world. He was on his own.

Guided by intuition Madalen moved closer. Wrapping her capable, motherly arms about Raymond Herevi, she

197

held him. He was trembling. She rocked him gently, until the trembling ceased.

Moving back to a proper, respectful distance, she swallowed, and wiped her eyes with her skirt. 'There's more, I'm afraid, sir. If you're ready to hear it . . .'

'I'm ready.'

'Your uncle is dead, too.'

'How?'

'Fighting. I'm told he died at your father's side. He died bravely — they both died bravely.'

'And the girls?' The green eyes were fever-bright. 'What did the butcher do to them?'

'I don't know, sir. The only member of your father's household I've seen since the raid was Mary Brice. They took her away under armed guard. But your sisters I've not seen. I don't know what's happened to them.'

Raymond leaned forwards and gripped Madalen's arm. 'What do you mean, you don't know? Someone must know.'

Madalen shook her head and her scarf slipped again. 'No. It's a mystery, Master Raymond. No one's seen a sign of either of your sisters, or your baby brother since the attack began. Of course, while the fighting was going on we villagers were not in a position to see anything—'

'You mean you were hiding,' Raymond said, caustically.

Madalen's chin lifted. 'Yes. I admit it. I hid. But what do you expect? It's not my land that I should lay down my life for it. We're not all taught to fight, or issued with swords and armour—'

'Some of you might have helped—'

'Some of them did. And what was their reward? They're lying out there in the yard like dead meat. Leaving widows and children to mourn them. So those of us with sense learn early on in life to keep our heads down. I'm sorry your father is dead, and I'm sorry about your uncle

198

too. They were good men. But . . .' Madalen tailed off. Raymond's pallor was growing more marked by the minute. 'I'm sorry, Master Raymond, but that's how it is.'

Raymond linked his hands round his knees and stared moodily over the marsh. 'I understand, Madalen. What will you villagers do?'

'We will carry on the best we can. We'll wait for someone to tell us who our new master is to be.'

A beam of sunlight reached over the reeds and danced on Raymond's tangled hair, burnishing the parts that were not streaked with dried blood to a bright, coppery brown. His head sank lower.

'Master Raymond? You can't sleep here.'

'Too tired to move.' Raymond began slurring his words. 'Can't move.'

'You have to. Look, I know every rush and willow in these marshes. I can keep you safe here. If the count sends every man he's got, he'll not find you. Listen, Master Raymond – ' seeing that he was sliding into unconsciousness, Madalen shook him – 'it's plain you can't go back to your father's manor. Can you think of anywhere safe we can take you?'

'Locmariaquer,' Raymond mumbled.

He was slipping fast.

'Locmariaquer?'

'Find Anna. She'll help. Hide me in dolmen . . .'

Raymond keeled sideways and fell into Madalen's waiting arms.

Madalen enlisted the help of her brother, Joel, and between them they wrapped Raymond in a blanket and staggered with him to a boat which took him away from Kermaria. Once safely out of the count's reach, the still-unconscious youth was transferred to a willow litter and, with the help of a donkey, dragged to Locmariaquer.

199

Madalen and Joel found the dolmen and, taking the precaution of muttering the paternoster and crossing themselves at least a dozen times to guard against any evil spirits that might live therein, they carried the wounded young man into it and left him there.

Next, Raymond's benefactors made their way to the Anchor, where they knew they would find some well-earned sustenance, and where they hoped they would discover Anna's exact location so they could get a message to her. Fortunately, Madalen and Joel encountered Father Yann, the village priest, in Church Lane. This was fortunate not only because Father Yann knew who Anna was and where she lived – there was only one Anna in Locmariaquer – but because Father Yann was probably the only person in the village who could take a message to Anna and not arouse suspicions.

Until Raymond was fit enough to defend himself, his presence in the dolmen would have to be kept secret.

Night had fallen when Anna received Father Yann's message. As soon as she dared, she crept out of her father's cottage and ran to the dolmen. Being afraid of discovery, she had not dared to light her lantern, and had tripped twice on the way, spilling the precious contents of her basket of bandages and food and being forced to stop and retrieve them. When she finally reached the dolmen, she found two figures sitting like carved sentries on either side of the entrance. They rose at her approach.

'Are you Anna?' The man barred her way.

'Yes. Where is he? Is he all right?'

The man stood aside and jerked his head down the steps cut deep into the turf. 'He's down there. He's not spoken since this morning.'

'Holy Mother, no. I must light my lantern. Here, hold this for me. Thank you.'

As the wick flared Anna and the man took stock of each other.

'I'm Joel,' he smiled, 'and this is Madalen,' indicating his sister.

'I . . . I must go to him.' Anna started down the steps, hesitated, and looked back. 'Bless you both for bringing him here. I'm sorry I've nothing I can give you.'

'That's all right, girl. I can see you're no great dame to hand out largesse.'

'No.'

'You love him.'

'Yes.'

Joel sighed. 'There's one thing I ought to warn you about, girl.'

'Yes?'

'He's . . . he's not the handsome lad he was. His face . . . is badly cut . . .'

The lantern jumped.

' . . . But as you love him, it won't make any difference, will it?'

There was a short, stunned silence, before Anna's quiet answer. 'No.'

'I just thought I should warn you, girl,' Joel said, gruffly. 'Because he doesn't look pretty.'

Anna descended the steps. 'Raymond? Raymond? Can you hear me?' she whispered.

He was lying at the other side of the cavern, with the right side of his face turned to the wall.

Anna set her lantern and basket down on the cool, beaten-earth floor and went down on her haunches beside her lover. From this angle his face looked no more than battered and bruised, and it wore a peculiarly innocent, boyish look.

'Raymond?' Anna laid a tender hand on Raymond's shoulder, and shook it.

The unconscious Raymond gave no indication that he

could hear her; his eyelids didn't so much as flicker. Anna grasped him by the chin and turned his face towards her. Though Joel had given her due warning, Anna was thankful that Raymond was deep in a faint, for she was unable to suppress a gasp of horror at what she saw.

'Sweet Christ!'

She drew the lantern towards her and bent to examine the wound. As Joel had indicated, it was a deep cut: it must have been made by a sword. It looked as though it was beginning to heal but, however well it healed, the right side of Raymond's face would never be handsome again. Peeling the blanket away, Anna inspected him for more damage but, to her relief, found none. She felt confident that with God's help she could save him. Her examination finished, Anna wrapped Raymond safely in his blanket – it was damp and chilly in the dolmen – and carefully set about cleaning his face. She had not found time to ask Joel what had happened at Kermaria, but Raymond's confidences led her to suspect that this Count de Roncier must somehow be implicated. When Raymond was recovered he would explain it to her.

May arrived, bringing with it warmer winds, and the spring flowers bloomed all over the peninsular. The hawthorn hedge, which fenced in the villagers' strips by the road to the dolmen, was starred with pink and white blossom. The gnarled branches of the old wild pear tree hung like snowy garlands over the road. The grass around the dolmen was dotted with daisies and buttercups.

Raymond was yet to set foot outside his pagan sanctuary and, protected by the superstitious fears that kept most folk well away from the Old Ones' temples, none of the villagers save Father Yann had any idea he was hiding there.

Over the past couple of weeks Anna had devoted every spare moment to tending him. He had lost much blood, and his recovery was slow, but Raymond was blessed with a strong, healthy body, and a will to recover. He had a good appetite, and Anna grew quite adept at sneaking food from the cottage. Raymond ate so much that she even considered begging left-overs from the inn, but decided against that for fear of discovery.

After learning from Raymond that Count François de Roncier was responsible for his change of fortune, Anna refrained from questioning him further, partly for fear of upsetting him while he convalesced, but partly because she feared he was nursing revenge in his heart. She could see it in his eyes, they were quite shuttered sometimes, and at such times she could not reach him. Fearing this revenge would take Raymond away from her, she avoided reminding him of it.

One evening, when Anna was bringing him some bread and cheese, she was horrified to find him sitting out on one of the flat stones by the dolmen's entrance, scarred face turned towards the westering sun. Anna did not look at the scar on the right side of Raymond's face, never really focusing on it, except when she needed to assure herself that it was healing well. The scar was red and puckered and angry; it ran from temple to chin, dividing the right side of his face into two.

At that moment fear of discovery was uppermost in Anna's mind. If anyone should chance to walk that way, they would be bound to see him.

She hurried over. 'Raymond? Are you run mad? You're in full view!'

Raymond's green eyes met hers, coolly. 'I wanted to see daylight, Anna. I can't stay cooped up in that pit for the rest of my life. I have to come out some time.'

So they had come to it at last. 'Yes, I know, but—'

'It's time I made plans.'

Anna's heart sank. She had been dreading this day, though deep down she had known that these few weeks had been stolen ones. Raymond had come to her in his time of trial, but she could not expect to keep him for ever. Anna stared, agonised, into the beautiful green eyes. Raymond Herevi would always be the most beautiful thing in her world.

'You're leaving,' she said.

Raymond stood up, and stretched. 'Don't look at me like that, Anna. You know I can't stay for ever—'

'Yes, but I hoped—'

The green eyes were remote. He had already left her, she could see that.

'Don't be silly, Anna,' he said, not ungently. 'I have obligations. I have . . . had a family. I can't pretend they never existed. I must find out what has happened to my brother and two sisters. They may be alive. For all I know de Roncier might have them festering in some dark dungeon. I have to know what their fate was. I couldn't live with myself if I thought they might be imprisoned somewhere, at the mercy of the count.' Raymond took Anna gently by the shoulders and kissed her on the forehead. 'Say you understand, Anna. Say that you forgive me.'

'I understand.' Anna gave him a watery smile, the best that she could produce at that moment.

'My Anna. Have I ever told you how pretty you are? My loving Anna of the dark brown eyes.' Raymond pulled Anna close, so that their bodies were pressed together with not an inch between them.

Anna managed a giggle. 'You are feeling better, Raymond, aren't you?'

'Come inside, and I'll show you exactly how much better I'm feeling . . .'

The main well in Huelgastel was located in the inner bailey. Clemence, staggering under the weight of a heavy bucket of water, picked her way past a pile of fresh horse-dung and went into the hall. The dowager countess had had a bad fall the previous spring and from time to time her failing health caused her to retire to her room. Clemence had volunteered to help Lena fetch water for her. The countess had requested a bath and, because of her current state of health, her maid would have to baby her. Until the job was done the family quarters adjoining the solar would be in an uproar. The countess was a difficult woman at the best of times, and since she had been laid up in her bed, she had been impossible. Clemence had felt sorry for Lena, always at the receiving end of the countess's ill-temper, and had offered to help.

Head down, puffing with the exertion, and gripping the wood-bound handle of the pail for all it was worth, Clemence huffed her way down the hall. She was half-way to the stair-well when she collided with someone.

'Whoa, there! Not so fast, young lady! May I carry that for you?'

Startled, Clemence released the bucket with a thump, and looked up. She had to tip her head back a long way, for the young man with whom she had collided was exceptionally tall. She did not know him well, for he had but lately joined the count's household. It was Walter Venner, a newly dubbed knight whose gilded spurs sparkled brightly; he was smiling at her. Though the knight had been part of the count's household since the beginning of May, this was the first time Clemence had seen him smile. She had him set down as self-contained and unfriendly, even with his peers.

'You, sir? Help me?' Clemence asked, startled and a little alarmed at this attention from a knight, even if he was the lowest ranking knight in the household. Had Morgan been in the hall – Clemence knew he was not, for she had exchanged a couple of secret kisses with the falconer in the mews not half an hour since – she might have expected an offer of help, but not from this stranger.

'I'm not going to bite you, girl. I want to help you, that's all. You're the prettiest girl in the castle, and you shouldn't be lugging great pails of water about.'

Clemence stared suspiciously into Sir Walter's hazel eyes, certain he was mocking her, but they seemed quite guileless.

'Oh! Thank you, sir. I was taking it to the solar to heat on the fire.' Tossing her blonde plait over her shoulder, Clemence led the way, throwing the knight a puzzled glance over her shoulder as she went.

Sir Walter was straight of limb and strongly made. He wore his dark, curly hair short. His eyes were a muddy hazel, his features were pleasant enough when he smiled, but when his face was in repose they were unremarkable. An uncommunicative man until now, Clemence had noticed that Sir Walter usually sat at the bottom end of the high table with the de Roncier family, but he invariably kept himself to himself. Though Clemence had seen him drinking with the rest of the men, she had not seen him drunk. He seemed to have a sober disposition in every way: she did not think he would be much fun.

They reached the solar. Sir Walter deposited the bucket by the fire.

'Here all right for you?' he said.

'Yes, thank you.' Clemence smiled.

'My pleasure.' Sir Walter turned and tramped down the twisting stairs.

Clemence filled the large cauldron she had brought up from the cook-house, picked up a cloth and swung the creaking chimney crane out into the room. The solar crane was not often used, and was in need of some grease. Next Clemence hooked the pot on to the crane and swung it back over the fire. Sitting herself on a stool close by, she waited for the pot to boil, and smiled to herself as she waited.

As far as most members of the household went,

Clemence was insignificant. She was Arlette's maid-servant, and however well Arlette might treat her, however well the girls got on privately, she would always be only a serving-girl. But it was beginning to dawn on Clemence that she was not entirely insignificant, and that it was not only Morgan who found her attractive. What was it Sir Walter had said? That she was the prettiest girl in the castle.

The door leading to the chapel corridor opened and Countess Eleanor emerged with her new maid, Mary Brice. Mary had a long sad face, lugubrious topaz-coloured eyes, and a pious expression which had immediately recommended her to the countess. Like Sir Walter, Mary was a relative newcomer to the castle. The maid had ridden in one afternoon with Nicholas Warr as her escort. The archer had claimed that Mary was recovering from some bereavement – she certainly had seemed weepy and distressed, and had refused to talk to anyone. Countess Eleanor had taken her under her wing, and when the countess had discovered that Mary's faith was all-important to her, Countess Eleanor had insisted that Mary become her personal maidservant. Kindred spirits, they were well suited. Clemence had only ever seen Mary in conversation with the countess. Nicholas Warr had from time to time attempted to speak with the woman, but each time Clemence had seen them, Mary had rebuffed him.

Countess Eleanor's brown velvet skirts swished across the boards, her calf-bound prayer book clutched in one long-fingered hand.

'Is that water for my mother-in-law, Clemence?' the countess enquired as she moved over to the coffer where she kept her needlework.

Clemence rose and gave a little curtsey. 'Yes, Countess.'

'You're helping Lena?'

'Yes, my lady.'

'Good girl. Don't forget to damp down that fire and replace the fire-guard when the water is hot enough. That fireplace was not designed to hold such a blaze. The surround is made of granite, but as you can see the rest of the floor is wood. We must be careful to keep the fire contained.'

'I understand, Countess,' Clemence said.

Satisfied, the countess nodded and turned away, drawing a bundle of folded linen from the chest. 'Come, Mary. Here are the vestments I'm working on,' she said. 'Would you care to assist?'

'I'd be honoured to be entrusted with praising the Lord in such a way, Countess,' Mary answered softly. 'They look beautiful.'

Countess Eleanor and Mary Brice bent their heads over the stitchery, and began an involved discussion on whether to use gold thread or red silk for the fringing on the chasuble. Clemence reseated herself and stared once more into the dancing flames.

Each morning, the dawn light filtered slowly and shyly into the dolmen, so shyly that, even at noon, the chamber under the earth was barely twilit.

Raymond and Anna lay entwined in their blankets, and watched the shadows shift. Today was the day that Raymond had decided he would make his first move.

Anna sighed, wrapped her arms more tightly around Raymond's naked chest, and prayed that God should grant her the strength to keep her secret from Raymond.

Her courses being very late, Anna suspected she was pregnant, but she was determined not to tell her lover.

She did not want to use her pregnancy to compel him into staying with her. She loved him too much. Agonising though this was, Anna wanted him willing. Though now, despite her noble resolutions, she heard herself say, 'I wish you didn't have to go.'

Raymond gave a contented yawn, and his hand came out to ruffle Anna's hair. 'Mmm.' He kissed her nose, and threw back the blankets with a decisive movement. 'So do I. But I have work to do. I have to search for Philippe, and my sisters.'

'You might not like what you find,' Anna said.

Raymond stood up and reached for the homespun chainse that Anna had made for him. 'I know. Don't you think I haven't thought of that? Lying here so long, I've thought of little else. But even if all I find is a pile of bones, I have to go. Damn it all, Anna, I have to *know*.'

Raymond's cheeks were dark with passion. 'You want revenge,' Anna said softly.

In the midst of stepping into his breeches, Raymond paused, and shot her a shrewd look. 'I admit it. I do want revenge. I hate de Roncier, and everything that's his. I won't rest till I've done my best to bring him and his entire family to destruction.'

'Raymond!' Though Anna had guessed that thoughts of revenge had sustained Raymond in his darkest hours, the bitter vehemence in his voice alarmed her.

He met her gaze, unabashed. 'I'm sure you'd feel the same in similar circumstances.'

Anna bit her lip; she did not agree. 'I hope it makes you happy, Raymond. But . . .' For all that she blinked them away, tears welled in her eyes and began to spill over. 'But I fear it will only lead to more pain and suffering. Oh, Raymond, can't you stay here? I'll love you for ever, you know that. Why do you have to go? The count will most likely kill you. And what use would that be to anyone?'

Raymond sat down on their makeshift bed and took Anna's hand. 'Oh, God, Anna, we've been through this a hundred times. You're very sweet, and I am fond of you – you mean more to me than any woman . . .'

'I do? Truly?'

'Truly. You must believe me. You are sweetness itself. My own, lovely Anna.' He stroked her hair. 'I wish I could ensure your safety until I come back but, as you know, the only money I will have will be what I can beg from Father Yann.'

Anna felt her face stiffen. 'I understand. And I don't want any money from you, I love you.'

Raymond brought his face close to Anna's and leaned his cheek against hers. 'I know you don't want money, sweet. But you might need it. What if . . .' He hesitated, and laid a gentle hand on her belly. 'What if there's a child? Had you considered that?'

Hoping he had not noticed her sudden intake of breath, Anna looked down at her hands. 'If we have a child I shall love it,' she declared, fiercely.

Raymond raised her face and rubbed his nose gently against hers. 'Anna, though I have to go, I'm not finding it easy. Will you wait for me?'

'You know I will.'

He hugged her. 'Sweet Anna. You're all I've got. You're my jewel. Anna, there's something I want to ask you.'

'Yes?'

His fingers played with her ear. 'Would you marry me, Anna?' His voice was oddly hesitant. 'Please?'

Anna sat very still. She couldn't believe he meant it. 'M . . . marry you? You don't have to marry me, Raymond. I'll wait for you. I know I'm only a peasant, but you can trust me. I love you. I've said I'll wait for you, and I will wait for you.'

'I know that, Anna. I'm not insulting you. I'm asking you to marry me because I love you.'

For a moment all she could do was stare at him. 'But Raymond, you can't. I'm a peasant.'

Raymond carried one of Anna's calloused, work-worn hands to his lips and kissed each of her broken nails in turn. 'I'm serious, Anna. Please give me your answer.'

Still staring at her love in disbelief, Anna heard a voice tell her this was madness. She could not marry Raymond Herevi. In the ordinary course of events a knight's son could hope to become a knight himself one day. Besides, she was owned body and soul by Sir Blundell, and neither her parents nor Raymond could afford the merchet – the marriage fine.

But even as these qualms surfaced, she heard her own voice saying, 'Yes! Yes, of course I'll marry you! But when? And how?'

'Father Yann can see to it. Today. But you won't be able to tell anyone that we have married – not even your parents. De Roncier's a madman, he believes me dead and that's how I want it to stay. If he hears so much as a whisper that I am alive, and have married you, it could put us both in danger. You must promise me, Anna, not a word to anyone.'

'I promise.'

Overwhelmed by a rush of conflicting emotions that had her laughing and crying together, Anna covered his face with kisses. 'Oh, Raymond. You've made me so happy.' She drew back, for her heart was filled with a piercing sadness too. 'If only you didn't have to go.'

'My feelings for you cannot turn me from the path I have chosen.' Raymond stroked her hair. 'I'm going to Huelgastel—'

'He'll kill you!'

'He will not. Remember, de Roncier doesn't know me from Adam.' Wryly, Raymond ran his fingers over the long scar on the right side of his face. 'And even if he did, he wouldn't recognise me with this new mask of mine. I'm leaving my old life behind me. From now on I'm Gwionn Leclerc, a scribe who had the misfortune to be set upon by outlaws on the road from Rennes. Now, dry your tears and get dressed.' He grinned. 'We have two reasons to see

211

Father Yann now. We can ask him to marry us, and I must persuade him to trust me with some money.'

'He will be pleased to marry us,' Anna told him. 'He knows we are lovers. The only reason he consented to me caring for you here was because he feared for your life.'

'Then come on, Anna. Father Yann and our wedding awaits.'

Mary Brice walked briskly out of the hall and into the inner bailey. Summoning up all her courage, she kept her head high and her shoulders back, and marched under the arch to stand for a moment in the outer bailey. She intended to discover whether she was being held prisoner in Huelgastel, or whether she was free to leave when she wished.

The portcullis was open, and two guards with spears were stationed inside the curtain wall. Two more lounged at the other end of the bridge.

Drawing in a deep breath, Mary made as if to pass through the gate.

One of the sentries levelled his spear at her breast.

Mary stopped. 'What do you think you're doing?' she demanded, in as haughty a voice as she could manage.

'You're Mary Brice, aren't you?'

'And what if I am?' Mary glared at the sentry, an elderly fellow with a drooping grey moustache and kindly brown eyes.

'Does the countess know you're here, Mistress Brice?'

Mary pursed her lips, and scowled at the point of the spear, which withdrew a fraction. 'Are you telling me I cannot leave?'

'Go back to the countess, Mistress Brice. She'll look after you.'

After glaring at the man for a few moments more, Mary realised her question had been answered: she was going

nowhere. She swung on her heel and went to look for
Countess Eleanor.

Mary and her mistress were sitting in the window alcove of
the solar where the light was best, embroidering white
lilies on a chasuble destined for Father Josse. The window
overlooked the inner courtyard − of a new design, and
glassed, it was the castle's pride. A large window, with
three paned lights, it was set in a recess high in the thick
solar walls. The seat was reached by clambering up a
couple of steps, and like the stone benches in the chapel,
the seat was scattered with cushions. It was rather like
being in a small private room, high up and out of the way
of the solar at large. Mary had been sewing placidly for a
while when she decided to pose the question that had been
uppermost in her mind since her clash with the sentry. She
fastened off the thread that she was working on and said,
'Am I a prisoner here, Countess? I tried to go for a walk
this morning, but the men at the gatehouse wouldn't let
me beyond the portcullis.'

The countess looked up, slim brows raised in surprise.
'A prisoner, Mary? Is that how you feel? Have I not made
you welcome? Do you not feel comfortable with me?'

Mary's large bosom rose and fell. The countess had
evaded her question. 'No, Countess. *You* have made me
very welcome. *You* don't make me feel as though I'm a
prisoner at all. I like working for you. In fact,' she
admitted, 'I'm happier working for you than I ever was
before.'

The countess bent over a lily. 'So why this talk of being
a prisoner, Mary?'

Mary hesitated, uncertain as to how much the countess
knew of her husband's affairs. She selected a new strand
of silk and threaded her needle.

'Do you know where I came from, Countess?' she
asked.

213

'Kermaria. You worked for Jean St Clair.' Countess Eleanor lifted her head, and gave Mary a reassuring smile. 'Did you think I didn't know what my husband has done, my dear?'

'I . . . I didn't know what to think, Countess.'

Eleanor leaned forwards and patted Mary's knee. 'That day you were brought here—'

'I was brought here so I wouldn't have a chance to reveal what the count did,' Mary blurted.

'Most likely,' the countess nodded serenely.

'And I've no idea why I submitted so tamely. I don't know why I didn't make more of a fuss.'

The countess shook her head, and her veil swung gently about her face. 'Yes, you do, my dear. You know perfectly well. You didn't make a fuss because you were stunned by what had happened; and moreover, you knew that if you did make a fuss, your life would be at stake.'

Mary's head dropped, and her pale brown hair, which was escaping her headdress, hung in ringlets by her ears. 'I was a coward, my lady.'

'No. You took the only road you could.'

'I don't want you to think I'm ungrateful, Countess. I'm delighted that you want me for your maid. You're a good, Christian mistress. But I need to know. Am I to be kept prisoner here for ever?'

Eleanor bit her lip. 'Don't ask me that, Mary. Please.'

'I am to be kept prisoner then. I thought as much. I may not be noble, my lady, but my family have been freemen for as long as anyone can remember. The count has no right to keep me here against my will!'

'Hush, Mary.' The countess leaned forwards again, and lowered her voice. 'Be thankful you're not lodged in the dungeons. Be thankful I needed another maid, and took a liking to you. But don't despair. Be patient. Remember what Our Lord said about the meek inheriting the earth. In time, if you prove your loyalty, I'm sure the guards at

the gate will receive different orders. And then you will
have your freedom again.'

Mary nodded, resignedly. 'You speak much sense, my
lady. Besides, I've nowhere to go. My old master is dead,
and his children—'

'Yes?' The countess lifted soft blue eyes to Mary's.
'What about Jean St Clair's children?' she inquired in her
mild voice.

Mary raised plump shoulders. She liked the countess,
and the countess shared her passion for religion, but Mary
could not forget that the countess was married to the man
who had murdered Jean St Clair and devastated his land.
She must stick to her story in order to protect his tiny son
and heir. 'I showed your Viking captain the babe's grave,'
she said. 'As to St Clair's girls, who knows where they
are?' Mary noticed the countess's pale eyes were sad, and
remembered that the countess wanted children of her
own. 'I hope they got away,' she added. 'They were lovely
girls.'

Bored with always taking the air in the countess's herb
garden, Mary decided to stretch her legs and walk round
the two courtyards, the inner bailey and the outer. If she
was not to be trusted with walking beyond the confines of
the castle, she could at least look out over the bridge. They
couldn't stop her looking, surely? Perhaps the guards
would permit her to walk along their walkway on top of
the curtain wall. She would be able to see the forest from
there. The trees would be in full leaf. The wild hyacinths
would be dead and gone. Mary had a yearning to walk in
quiet shade.

The screeching of the swallows which flew over the
castle was clearly audible over the hum of a busy bailey.
The swallows nested beneath the machicolations on the
west side of Huelgastel keep; their babies must have
hatched, because the parent-birds were desperately arcing

to and fro across a forget-me-not blue sky. Mary guessed that Morgan le Bihan's hawks must all be safely in their mews for the swallows to be so active. Gradlon's hammer punctuated the swallows' high screams.

Mary drifted towards the outer bailey, resigned to the fact that her yearning for a walk in the wood would not be satisfied. If it were not for that fact that she did not have her freedom, she could be happy here.

She would never like Count François de Roncier: he was a black-hearted felon who deserved God's punishment. It was not right that his sins should go unpunished, and if Mary ever found a way to punish the count, she would take it. But she liked the countess, and was coming to admire her. Mary prided herself in being a just woman, and it would be unjust to condemn the countess for sins committed by her husband. After working for Eleanor for some weeks, Mary appreciated the difficulties of the countess's position. It was plain as a pikestaff that Countess Eleanor disliked her vitriolic, boorish husband as much as anyone else. Yet Mary had never heard a single word of complaint fall from her lips, not even so much as a hint.

Ostensibly, the count ruled Huelgastel with an iron hand. But he was not invincible. Mary had seen how he took note of his countess's wishes, and how, on occasion, the countess had intervened to save some poor wretch from a beating. Mary's countess was a God-fearing woman, and Mary would give her her undivided loyalty.

She paused at the bottom of the walkway ladder, and hailed the sentry who was leaning against a merlon, idly watching and listening to a heated argument in progress by the gatehouse. Mary closed her ears to the foul language one of the participants in the confrontation – a man – was using. The way some people took the Lord's name in vain – really, they were little better than heathens.

'Excuse me? Guard?' She called up the steps.

It was the elderly guard with the luxuriant moustache. When he saw Mary, he flashed her an impudent grin which would have looked more appropriate on a man ten years his junior.

'Ma dame.' He bowed.

Mary gritted her teeth and ignored his impudent gallantry. 'I've a mind to walk the wall,' she said, loftily. 'Is it permitted?'

Another bow, which again Mary ignored. He leaned his spear against the wall, and came over. 'Naturally, ma dame. Would you like some assistance?'

More furious swearing emanated from the bridge by the gatehouse.

Mary started up the ladder. 'I can manage, thank you.' She brushed aside the hand outstretched to help her.

'Please yourself, mistress,' the guard shrugged. He moved back to the merlon and continued his eaves-dropping.

'Blood of Christ, man! You *must* let me in!' The angry man's voice rose clearly to the walkway.

Mary suddenly felt cold all over; and found her feet refused to move. That voice. It was uncanny, a young man's voice, it was an exact replica of one she had never thought to hear again. But it could not be: Mary knew Raymond Herevi was dead. She had seen his body for herself, face slashed almost in two, lying amidst a pool of blood in the rushes of his father's hall.

Her frozen posture elicited a chuckle from the moustachioed guard. 'Terrible, isn't it, mistress, the way some people curse and swear? You'd think the Lord would shrivel their tongues as a penance, wouldn't you?'

'Can you see the bridge from there?' Mary asked.

'Yes.'

'May I?' And before the astonished sentry had time to respond, Mary elbowed him aside. A man in a hooded

217

cape stood on the wooden bridge, arms crossed at his breast, legs planted boldly apart, apparently staring at the gatekeeper who was peering short-sightedly at a vellum scroll.

'My name is Gwionn Leclerc. Can you read?' the hooded man demanded.

Mary's breath caught in her throat, and she drew the sign of the cross on her breast. The name was wrong, but that voice . . . that young man's voice. Was it Judgement Day that the dead should rise? Mary pushed her head and shoulders through the crenellation in order to catch a glimpse of the man's face, but his features were masked by his hood. If only he would look up.

'Steady, mistress.' Mary felt the guard's hands on her waist. 'It's a fair drop into the ditch.'

She straightened, and batted the guard's hands away. 'Take your hands off me.'

'My apologies, mistress, but it *is* a long drop.'

'I can see that,' Mary responded, and thrust her head back into the gap.

Behind her, the guard sighed, picked up his spear, and stumped off up the walkway. 'Women!'

The man on the bridge seemed to have grown roots.

'If you can't read,' he was saying, in exasperated tones which sent another shiver of recognition down Mary's spine, 'you could gawp at that till the moon turned blue, and you'd be none the wiser.'

The sentry at the gate, offended no doubt by the man's tone, lifted his eyes from the scroll. 'Be off with you. What need has Count de Roncier of a scribe, when he has Father Josse?'

Mary stood transfixed. It was not just the hooded man's voice, it was his stance, his manner, and that flaring temper. Master Raymond always had a temper. She was sure it was him.

'Listen, man, couldn't you at least take my scroll to this

Father Josse of yours. That letter proves my skill . . .'

'Be off with you. If Father Josse wanted an assistant, he'd take one in Holy Orders.'

'Please! Listen to me . . . !'

'Away with you.'

The hooded man shouted in desperation. 'I'll be staying at the Duke's in Vannes, if you should—' but the guard had turned away, and the man was left standing on the bridge, muttering to himself, scroll clenched in his fist. After staring at the ground for some moments, he flung the scroll into the ditch.

Narrowing her eyes with intense concentration, Mary watched him walk slowly back across the bridge. On the other side of the ditch, he turned and glared back at the Huelgastel, and Mary at last got a full view of his face. Dark brows arched over glittering green eyes which were set in a face that, once seen, would never be forgotten. It had been a handsome face once, but now – Mary crossed herself – now it was marred beyond repair by a disfiguring scar.

'Raymond!' Mary tried to call out, but shock held her mute. 'Raymond!' This time she managed a croak, but she was not loud enough. Raymond Herevi had turned his back, and already he was walking down the rutted road to Vannes.

Chapter Eleven

Sir Walter Venner knocked on the solar door.

'Come in,' Arlette answered.

The daughter of the house was curled up in the window seat with her maid, reading aloud from a leather-bound book. When Sir Walter came in, she snapped the book shut.

'Sir Walter?'

Clemence blushed.

'Excuse me for disturbing you, my lady,' the knight said. 'I'm looking for Mary Brice. Have you seen her?'

'Mary? Who wants her? The countess, I suppose. Isn't she downstairs?'

'No, my lady.'

Arlette waved at the other solar door. 'Try the chapel.'

'Thank you, my lady.' Sir Walter bowed himself out.

Mary was kneeling to the left of the altar, industriously polishing a brass candlestick as tall as a man. She made no sign that she had heard the knight.

'Excuse me, mistress.'

The countess's maid climbed ponderously to her feet. 'Sir Walter, isn't it?'

'That's right. I would like a word with you.'

Mary tucked her polishing cloth into her belt. 'Sir?'

'It's about Kermaria, Mary,' Walter said in a low voice.

Instantly, suspicion fired in the maid's eyes. 'Kermaria? I . . . I don't know what you're talking about.'

The countess had warned Mary that it might be dangerous for her to mention Kermaria, and Mary accepted that in her position that was sound advice. It was being put about that pirates were the cause of the trouble at Kermaria. Mary decided to stick to the approved version of the massacre.

'Isn't Kermaria that place devastated by pirates a month or so ago?' she said, widening her eyes. 'I heard they came up the river and destroyed everything in sight. Dreadful business, quite dreadful.'

The knight gave her a faint smile, and shook his head. 'I'd hoped for better from you, Mary. I'd heard that you are a devout Christian – but to lie, and in God's house . . .'

A muscle jumped in Mary's sturdy jaw, and she clamped her mouth shut.

'I think you know the truth, Mary. Yesterday evening Sir Ralph and I went carousing in the company of some of de Roncier's hired men – Nicholas Warr among them. Sir Ralph needs a squire, and he had an eye on one of Warr's archers. Ralph saw to it that Warr was well oiled. He wanted to see if Warr could be persuaded to part with the lad.'

Mary's topaz-coloured eyes were blank. 'Should this mean something to me, sir?' She could not see why the knight was confiding in her.

Sir Walter continued, gentle but inexorable. 'Warr wouldn't give Ralph his archer, and Ralph left. After he had gone, the wine he had bought seemed to take effect. Warr told me about you and Kermaria—'

Whipping her cloth from her belt, Mary turned back to the candlestick and began rubbing furiously. 'I don't think you should be taking any notice of what a drunken archer says, sir. He's only a common man, not of the knightly blood. He knows nothing of honour. Why, that one would lie and think nothing of it.'

222

'Warr maintains he brought you from Kermaria after a fight — a fight that to all intents and purposes sounds to have been a massacre.'

Mary polished for all she was worth. 'You shouldn't pay no mind to drunken archers.'

'I think I know what really happened at Kermaria, Mary,' Sir Walter said, in his quiet, insistent way. 'And I think you do too. It had nothing to do with pirates . . . I believe you know what happened to my brother.'

The busy cloth stilled. 'Your brother?'

Sir Walter moved to Mary's shoulder. 'Yes. My brother—'

'I don't know nothing about no brother of yours!' Mary cried.

'Mary, I appreciate you're afraid. I appreciate that you've a great deal to lose by trusting me . . .' Sir Walter paused, hazel eyes fixed on Mary's face. Though she had not admitted anything, the countess's maid looked the picture of confusion. She gnawed wildly at her lower lip.

' . . . I see I shall have to prove myself. I shall have to put my trust in you. My brother is Roger de Herion—'

'De Herion!'

Mary's eyes dilated, and a spasm — of pity? — flashed across her plump features.

'How do I know you speak the truth?' she cried anxiously.

'Roger is my half-brother. After my father died, my mother remarried. Josselin de Herion is my step-father. Now do you believe me? On my mother's life, I swear I won't repeat what you tell me to a living soul.'

In an agony of indecision, Mary twisted the cloth in her hands. 'Oh, God.'

'Tell me where Roger is. My poor mother is desperate.'

The maid was visibly moved. Her unusual eyes glistened with tears. 'Roger was Jean St Clair's squire,' she said, at length. 'But you would know that.'

'Yes.' Walter did not miss the maid's use of the past tense. It looked as though his worst fears were about to be confirmed.

'When the count attacked,' Mary continued, 'your brother took part in the fighting. Sir Waldin — he was Sir Jean's brother, the champion-at-arms . . .'

'Yes, I know of him.' There it was, that past tense again . . .

'Sir Waldin had been giving your brother lessons in swordsmanship but, despite the lessons, your brother was young and untried. He didn't stand a chance. None of them did.'

'He's dead?' Sir Walter asked, in a voice empty of emotion. He had expected as much, ever since news of the massacre at Kermaria had begun to filter through. Sir Walter had ridden to Kermaria to see the damage for himself, before he'd come to Huelgastel; but all he had found was a couple of burned-out buildings and a dozen ragged peasants who had been too terrified to tell him anything. The tales of pirates sailing up-river had been a little too glib to be convincing.

'You saw my brother's body?' Walter had to be certain, for his mother's sake.

'Yes, sir.' Mary shuddered as a hideous memory that she had tried to suppress leapt into her consciousness; once more she saw young de Herion lying in Sir Jean's hall with his insides spilling out across the floor.

'Thank you, Mary,' Sir Walter acknowledged softly. He bowed his head and went to kneel at a prie-dieu in front of the altar. Covering his face with his hands, he began to pray.

While the knight prayed, Mary watched him compassionately, wondering what he would do now he had confirmation that the lord he had sworn to serve *had* been responsible for his brother's death. Mary went on polishing the large brass candlestand and, while she

224

worked, offered up a prayer of her own. She had seen a great wrong done, and so far had been unable to discover how she could put it right. Mary should not question God's judgement, but deep in her heart she felt that it could not be part of God's plan for Raymond Herevi to be left wandering Brittany, while his two sisters fled with Sir Jean's heir to an uncertain future in the dubious company of an English mercenary.

But God, in His infinite wisdom, had sent this devout knight to her. God knew that on her own, Mary could do nothing, and so he had sent Sir Walter to meet her in His house for a reason. There was a message in this for Mary, a message from God. She would not ignore it.

An idea took shape in Mary's mind, a brilliant, God-given idea that would solve two problems at once; but she would have to go carefully. She did not want to frighten her new ally off before she was sure of him. Mary waited until Sir Walter rose from the prie-dieu.

'Sir Walter?'

The knight looked at her as though from a long distance. 'Mmm?'

'What do you plan to do?'

Sir Walter rubbed his chin and heaved a sigh. 'God knows. It's one thing to have one's suspicions about the count — but to have them confirmed . . .' His hazel eyes met Mary's directly. 'Quite honestly, Mary, I don't think there's much I can do. Without you testifying as to what you saw—'

'Testify?' she squeaked. 'I don't want to testify!'

'I know that, Mary. Don't worry, I gave you my sworn oath. No one will ask you to testify. In any case, who would take your word against that of Count François de Roncier?'

Mary decided to sow her seed. If it took root there would soon be three of them in Huelgastel with an interest in seeing justice done. 'Sir Walter, I have a favour to ask you – it won't cost you anything. Indeed you might benefit by it.'

'Name it. You have helped me by telling me the truth.'

'You mentioned that Sir Ralph was looking for a squire. I know someone who would be ideal for him. He's a relative of mine, name of Gwionn Leclerc . . .'

'Leclerc? That's a scribbler's name. Ralph won't want a damned scribbler. He wants a squire.'

Mary ignored the blasphemy, and tried to think which of Raymond Herevi's skills would best recommend him to Sir Walter. 'It's true my young cousin can write, sir,' she said. 'I've heard he's got a tidy hand, but he's not a scribe by temperament. He's one of the best horsemen I've seen. Keeps his seat as though he's stitched to his mount.'

'What's he like with a sword?'

Mary grimaced. Raymond's swordplay left much to be desired. 'He . . . he's not had much opportunity to practise, sir,' she said. 'But he would sell his soul to become a squire. He'd work at it.' Especially if it meant he would gain admittance to Huelgastel, Mary thought. She was beginning to perceive that Sir Walter might not be the strong ally she had hoped for, but if he was instrumental in bringing Raymond Herevi into Huelgastel, then Sir Walter would have served her – and God's – purpose. Raymond Herevi was strong. He would see that the wrongdoers were punished.

'Gwionn Leclerc, your cousin's name is?'

Mary assented.

'I'll look him over for you, Mary, but I'll only recommend him to Ralph if he shows promise. Where's he to be found?'

She remembered Raymond's last desperate shout to the guard. 'He's lodged in Vannes, at Duke's Tavern,' Mary said.

'The one near the cathedral?'

'That's the one.'

'I know of it.'

As Sir Walter left the chapel, Mary turned and faced the altar. She had done what she could. It was up to Raymond Herevi, posing as Gwionn Leclerc, to play his part. God would help him, Mary was sure of that. Soon there would be three of them. Three.

Not two days after his conversation with Mary, Walter Venner rode into Vannes alone. Raymond Herevi must have played his part to the hilt, because when Sir Walter rode back into the bailey, Gwionn Leclerc was walking at his stirrup. The guard posted at the gate was the same man who had refused Gionn Leclerc entrance before. He gawped and spluttered, but at Sir Walter's nod could do nothing but let him pass. So Gwionn Leclerc marched into Huelgastel, scarred face impassive.

Once accepted as Sir Ralph's squire, Gwionn wasted no time in seeking Mary out. She had put it about that she and Sir Ralph's squire were cousins, so no one should question their right to talk with each other. Mary had not considered that when she had concocted her hasty plan in the chapel, but she realised now that God must have been guiding her. She was taking air in the herbarium when Raymond approached her.

'Mary? Mary Brice?'

'Master Raymond! I'm so glad you're alive.'

'Hush, Mary. You mustn't forget the role you assigned me. I'm your cousin. Call me Gwionn.'

'I'll remember, Gwionn. Oh, dear lord! Your face—'

'Forget my face. How did you end up here, Mary?'

'That Viking lout had Nicholas Warr bring me here—'

'Warr? Here? Jesu, Mary, if he's signed with de Roncier he's bound to betray me! Thank Christ I've not run into him yet.'

Wincing at her 'cousin's' language, Mary's jaw dropped. In not taking that into account she had made a

227

grave error. Nicholas Warr had worked for Sir Jean, and he had not hesitated to betray details of Sir Jean's manor to the count when it suited him. He would recognise Raymond at once. Why should he spare Sir Jean's son?

Gwionn said, 'I never saw Warr in the fight at Kermaria . . .'

Mary snorted. 'That snivelling coward only came in when the fight was all but done.'

'I shall have to do something about him. My face may have changed, Mary, but he'll know me.'

Mary nodded, eager to make amends for her stupidity in not taking Nicholas Warr into her calculations. 'Yes. He will. I knew you by your voice alone.'

'My voice?'

'I heard you at the gatehouse—'

'So that's how you knew I was trying to get in. I wondered. Mary, I'm forever in your debt for getting Sir Walter to recommend me.'

'He was half-brother to your father's squire.'

Gwionn stared. 'God, was he? And does he know who I am?'

'No. I thought I'd leave it to you to tell him.'

The green eyes narrowed. 'I'll be frank, Mary. I want to see justice done. I want to see de Roncier pay for what he has done to my family.'

'So do I,' Mary whispered.

'I'm glad you feel as I do, Mary, because I'm not going to let anything stand in my way. Do you think we have an ally in Sir Walter?'

Mary hesitated. 'I couldn't say. Sir Walter had his suspicions that de Roncier was involved and not the pirates, and when I confirmed that his brother had died, he *was* upset. But I don't think he burns to see justice done.'

Gwionn's lips curled. 'Another coward.'

'If he is, Sir Walter's not cowardly in the physical sense.

228

He's the reputation for being tenacious in a fight, takes risks that others wouldn't consider—'

'You're saying he's stupid,' Gwionn sighed. 'I think it might be best if I leave Sir Walter out of my calculations for the time being, though he might come in useful later on . . . Tell me, are Philippe and my sisters here? Has de Roncier imprisoned them?'

'No, Mast . . . Gwionn. Gwenn and Captain Fletcher escaped with the little ones.'

'Impossible, Mary. No one escaped.'

At that moment Arlette and Clemence danced out of the keep, giggling.

Mary lowered her voice. 'They did escape. Johanna and I helped them. They slid down that half-finished privy and ran into the wood with Ned Fletcher. I've no idea where they were going, only that they got away. De Roncier sent out search parties, but they came back empty handed.'

Gwionn watched Arlette and Clemence walk across the inner court. 'What makes you so sure they weren't caught?' he asked. 'They could have murdered them and left them lying in unmarked graves.'

'No, I'm sure they're alive. It was something Johanna dreamed up. She told the Viking that baby Philippe had died of the marsh fever. They locked us up in the vaults and scoured the woods for Gwenn and the children. When they returned, they asked me to show them the infant's grave. Now why should they do that, if they had caught your brother?'

'What did you do?'

'I showed them the grave of that peasant's baby. They took it for your brother's and gave up the search.'

'Bless you, Mary, you've lifted a weight from my mind. I've been afraid that what's left of my family has been festering in some dark dungeon.'

'They escaped.'

Gwionn pointed at Arlette and Clemence. 'Who are those girls?'

'That's Lady Arlette in the green bliaud, and Clemence, her maid, in the blue one.'

'Lady Arlette?'

'The count's daughter.'

'She's prettier than I imagined her to be,' Gwionn said. 'Perhaps there might be some joy in what I'm going to do, after all.'

'And what may that be?'

Seeing Sir Ralph approaching, Gwionn Leclerc chucked Mary on the chin. 'First things first, cousin. I have to deal with Warr. The rest will keep. I'm in no hurry. I intend to pay a few debts, and I intend to enjoy myself while I do it. I only wish I knew where Gwenn took Philippe and Katarin. We have kin in the north, at Ploumanach. Perhaps she took them there.'

Gwionn soon discovered that Sir Ralph's liege lord, de Roncier, was visiting his land on the border between France and the Aquitaine. He was expected back at any time. Gwionn would have to act before the evening meal, when everyone gathered in the hall, for then Warr would be bound to see him. Waiting till the stable-hand, Aubrey, had left the stable, Gwionn sent the archer a message to the effect that the count had returned and wanted a word with Warr in the stable.

Then Gwionn pulled his capuchon over his head and sat down on a bale of hay in the shadows.

It was not long before the stick-like figure of the archer stood in the doorway.

'My lord?'

'Close that door.'

Warr obeyed without hesitation, and all was gloom — save for a golden stream of evening light pouring through an open stall at the other end of the stable.

230

'My lord?'

The only sound was the gentle breathing of the horses, and the soft rustle of straw beneath their hoofs.

Gwionn rose and stepped forwards, features still enveloped in his hood.

'Who are you?' Warr demanded. 'I was told my lord had returned.'

Gwionn stood before the archer, and flung back his hood. He made no attempt to keep the hatred from his eyes.

'Christ Aid!' Warr said. 'Master Raymond!'

'Oh no, Warr,' Gwionn corrected him, voice soft with menace as he fingered the hilt of the dagger that Venner had issued him with. 'You must be mistaken. My name is Gwionn Leclerc.'

Warr had his own dagger out in an instant.

'M . . . Master Raymond, I beg you.' Defensively, he brandished his weapon in front of him.

Gwionn Leclerc leapt back like a cat, his hands were yet empty. 'Tsk, tsk, Warr. You should be careful with that knife of yours. You always were somewhat clumsy when face to face with an enemy—'

Warr's face was grey. 'You've come for revenge.'

Gwionn did not deny this, but neither did he make any move to draw his own dagger.

Warr's fist clenched white on his dagger-hilt. 'You aim to kill me!'

'Do I?' Gwionn smiled. 'Do you think you deserve it, Warr? An eye for an eye, as the Good Book says. My father's dead, because you betrayed him. Do you think that your life should be forfeit too?'

'M . . . Master Raymond,' Warr began to babble. 'I never meant to betray your father. When I left his service my luck turned. I ran out of money—'

'So you came crawling to de Roncier, hoping he'd give you your thirty pieces of silver.'

231

'It . . . it didn't seem like that. I never thought he'd go as far as he did. Please, Master Raymond, have pity. Master Raymond . . .'

Gwionn's sensual lips curled in distaste. 'You're despicable, Warr. You always had a strong yellow streak. That's why you're an archer. You've not the stomach for hand-to-hand combat, have you?' Gwionn withdrew his dagger from its sheath, and made a show of examining the blade. 'Look, Warr. Sir Ralph has issued me with a shiny, new dagger. It's quite a good one, not as good as the one I had in Kermaria, of course, but good enough.'

Warr made a moaning sound in his throat.

'Aren't I lucky?' Gwionn went on. 'It's not been blooded yet . . .'

'No, Master Raymond. No!'

As Gwionn Leclerc moved towards the archer, his eyes were bright as green flames.

Aubrey found the archer, hanging from a roof beam, when he came back to the stable after dinner.

Bellowing for help, Aubrey righted the bucket which lay on its side just out of reach of the archer's feet, and dragged Warr down. The archer was quite dead. Apart from the bruising on his neck, there was not a mark on him.

Sir Hamon was not only the count's seneschal, representing the count in his absence in every respect, but he was also Aubrey's father. It was Sir Hamon's duty to inquire into the circumstances of the archer's death.

Outside, Gwionn Leclerc sidled up to the stable door, and stretched his ears to hear what was being said.

Kneeling by the body, Sir Hamon ran a hand through his thinning white hair and squinted up at the bridle. 'That's as you found it?'

'Yes, Father.'

'And the bucket was near by?'

'Yes, Father. It was lying on its side—'

'As though he had kicked it away?'

'Yes, Father. He must have looped the bridle over that hook, and—'

'Yes, yes, I can see that for myself,' Sir Hamon said testily. So far nothing untoward had occurred while the count had been away, but this suicide would reflect badly on him. If the count could find fault with the way the castle was run in his absence, the count would replace him. Sir Hamon already had a sneaking suspicion that François did not value him as his father had done – thought he was too old for the job. 'I may have the odd silver hair, Aubrey, but my mind's as clear as ever. There's no question but that it's suicide. Who could possibly gain by this fellow's death? It's a pity he chose your stable to do it in though, Aubrey.'

'Yes, Father. I wonder why he did it?'

'God knows. Perhaps he was in debt.' Sir Hamon climbed warily to his feet. 'It's damned inconvenient of the man. To my mind, it's a pity he didn't wait till the count got back.'

Outside, Gwionn Leclerc smiled and moved away.

One afternoon in June, when Count François had finished dispensing justice from his large seat in front of the hall fire, he summoned his daughter.

'I need to secure my position in the Aquitaine,' the count opened. 'It's time you left to begin your life with Count Etienne, as agreed. The count's nephew, Louis Favell, will be here soon. He is honouring you by offering to act as part of your escort. As is the custom, you will stay with the count as his fiancée, and you will sew your bride clothes, and generally prepare yourself for your new status. It has been agreed that the wedding will be next summer.'

'Yes, Papa,' Arlette said meekly, outwardly acting like

233

the dutiful daughter she knew he wanted her to be.

For the past eight years Arlette's life had been leading up to this moment. She had long ago come to terms with the fact that she would at some time have to leave Huelgastel and everything she held dear. Now that the moment of parting was finally approaching, her emotions were difficult to analyse. There was an empty feeling in the pit of her stomach, rather similar to the feeling she got when her father was angry with her. It was a poignant blend of hope and fear, but there was excitement there too. Not for the first time she wondered what her life as Countess Favell would be like. She hoped she would like the count. She hoped the count would like her, and that he would grant her privileges and power. But more to the point, she hoped her marriage would be successful so that it would reflect well on her family and make her father proud of her. De Roncier may be hiding secrets that did not bear examining in the light — Arlette knew her father was no shining white knight — but he was her father, and Arlette could not help but love him and pray for his approval.

She gazed earnestly into the red-rimmed hazel eyes. 'Will you miss me, Papa?'

The count's freckled fingers drummed on the trestle. 'How soon can you be ready to go?'

'In a couple of days.'

'Good. Favell won't be here till the end of the month. You'll need an escort from Huelgastel, I can't have you turning up like a beggar on Favell's doorstep. I'll see if any of my knights will volunteer to travel with you. If they're agreeable, they can stay on as your men when you get to La Forteresse des Aigles.'

Arlette gaped. 'Me, Papa? Have my personal bodyguard?'

'It will look well for you to have your own guard. As the future Countess Favell, you will need a personal escort. Are you agreeable, daughter?'

Arlette was so astonished that she lost her tongue for a full minute. This was the first time her father had asked for her agreement to anything. Was it because she was shortly to be Countess Favell? Was this a taste of the power that would be hers when she married? She had seen the influence Eleanor had over her father, and now here was her father actually asking for her consent. Perhaps the power Arlette dreamed of possessing was close to becoming a reality.

'Why, thank you, Papa.'

'Your party will leave next month, and you can travel by boat as far as Bordeaux.'

'By boat?' Arlette had never travelled far from Huelgastel, and she had certainly never been on a boat. She knew her father had a couple of ships moored at the port in Vannes. He had the nobility's scorn of trade, and hardly ever used his ships. Arlette suspected the ships were kept on simply as a means of demonstrating to the townsfolk that de Roncier was a force in the area.

'I've a consignment of wine awaiting collection in Bordeaux, and one of my ships will be sailing south for it. If Favell is agreeable, you can travel to Bordeaux by boat, and ride the rest of the way.'

'I'd like a sea voyage, Papa.'

'Good. See that you're ready when Favell gets here.'

'Yes, Papa. May Clemence come with me? I'll need a maid.'

'Clemence? Yes, Clemence may go with you.'

'Thank you, Papa.'

François waved his daughter away.

'Papa? Will you miss me?' Arlette asked again.

'Get out of here, girl.'

Anna's family had a small hand-mill. This was illegal, for by using the mill to grind their own meal, they avoided

235

paying Sir Blundell's miller to grind it for them, and thereby deprived their master of what he would consider his dues.

It was customary for Anna to grind the flour in the evening, using it to make the dough for the next day's bread. The dough would be left under a damp cloth and allowed to rise overnight.

The family's fire sat in the middle of the simple, one-roomed cottage; in the morning Anna's mother, Marharid, would blow the fire into life, and cook the bread in small clay pots which she embedded in the ashes.

For a couple of months Marharid had been watching her daughter with some concern. One morning, waiting until her husband Huberz was safely off on the lord's work, she spoke up.

Anna had just returned from washing herself in the water-butt outside. She took the honey-crock down from its shelf and, taking her eating-knife from her girdle, drew up a three-legged stool next to her mother.

'Mmm, that bread smells good!' Anna said. 'I'm so hungry!'

'I'm glad you got your appretite back, child,' Marharid said and, knocking a second loaf from its pot, she set it aside. That would be for Huberz when he returned.

Anna flushed, and turned her head away from the light.

Marharid sighed. 'It's no use hiding it from me, Anna. I know.'

Anna's head jerked round. 'Know? What are you talking about?'

'Anna, Anna. I'm your mother. I love you. I know you're with child.'

Anna's hands began to tremble so badly that she was forced to put the honey-crock on to the ground. She closed her eyes. 'I . . . I thought it didn't show,' she whispered.

Marharid squeezed her daughter's arm. 'Come, child.

236

You've been sick most mornings for two months now, and off your food—'

'I wasn't sick this morning, or yesterday—'

'No. That stage passes. When do you calculate the babe will come?' Marharid asked, easily.

Anna's brown eyes were wide with wonder. 'You're not angry Mother?' she asked.

'It had to happen, sooner or later. When do you expect the child?'

'November, Mother, at St Andrew's tide.'

'St Andrew's tide. That will give us plenty of time to arrange things. Don't look so tragic, Anna. I'll send your father to speak to Samzun—'

'No!'

'I beg your pardon?'

Anna burst into noisy tears. 'Don't tell Father, please don't. He'll have the hide off me!'

Marharid frowned. 'Are you trying to tell me that Samzun is not the father of your child, Anna? Who is the father?'

'Not Samzun.' Anna sobbed noisily. 'Not Samzun.'

'Who, then?'

Anna shook her head and sobbed all the louder. 'I can't tell you.'

'Come, Anna, be sensible.'

'I can't tell you! I promised! You can cajole me, and Father can beat me, but I won't tell you.'

'He won't marry you,' Marharid surmised. 'The bastard.'

More sobbing.

'Samzun is a soft-hearted boy,' Marharid persisted. 'He likes you. I'm sure that we will be able to persuade him to marry you.'

'I won't marry Samzun! I can't!'

'Be reasonable, Anna. What will your father say? You know his views. You know he won't keep you if you've got a man's babe in your belly.'

Anna looked hunted. 'Mother, you won't tell him, will you?'

Marharid looked at her daughter's stomach. 'You won't be able to conceal it for ever. It'll start showing soon.'

'Please, don't tell him.'

'I won't say a word, not yet, at least. But I think you should ponder long and hard, my girl. I urge you to consider Samzun—'

'I can't marry Samzun!'

'We'll see,' Marharid said, grimly. 'You may change your mind, given time.'

'Never! I'll never change my mind,' Anna cried.

She was still sobbing some minutes later when her mother stalked, stiff with anger, out of the cottage.

As Anna's tears subsided, she began to realise that she had been wilfully blind, thinking she could cope on her own. When her father found out things would only get worse. By hook or by crook, she must get a message to Raymond in Huelgastel.

Part Two

The Dark Tower

Thou hast set thine house of defence very high.
There shall no evil happen unto thee:
neither shall any plague come nigh thy dwelling.

Psalm 91

Part Two

The Dark Tower

Chapter Twelve

One glorious July morning in that same year of 1186, a couple of days after Louis Favell's arrival at Huelgastel, Gwionn Leclerc and Sir Ralph Verdun rode into the bailey to find Count François waiting for them to return.

Sir Ralph's destrier was a bay, Ares, while Gwionn, who had persuaded Aubrey to trust him with the best the stables had to offer, rode one of de Roncier's handsome black geldings.

The swallows were flying high. Swifts screeched as they darted to and fro in a cloudless sky, and above the swifts and swallows − a mere speck in the wide expanse of blue − a hobby circled lazily on a warm current of air, waiting.

'Where the devil have you been, Verdun?' the count demanded, striding up. 'I wanted to speak to you.'

'My apologies, mon seigneur,' Ralph swung out of the saddle and flung his destrier's reins to Gwionn. 'I had no idea you were looking for me. Ares needed exercising, and Aubrey suggested that Leclerc should take Star.'

Aubrey had rather unimaginatively christened the black gelding Star because of the white splash on his forehead. Gwionn would have preferred to have been mounted on a stallion, since riding was something he excelled at, and he had been keen to impress Sir Ralph with his horsemanship. However, in the event Gwionn had not been displeased with Star. A skittish horse, of a nervous disposition, he had taken to Gwionn, and Gwionn had found him a very responsive ride. Sir Ralph had noticed the gelding's unusual docility in Gwionn's hands, and had remarked on it. Reflecting that Rome hadn't been built in a day, Gwionn decided he hadn't made a bad start.

Pinning a blank expression on his face, Gwionn made a show of loosening the horses' girths while he listened to the knight and his lord. Whenever Count François came near him, he had to battle with an overwhelming impulse to snatch out his dagger and sink it deep into the count's broad chest. He had to tell himself that his time would come. His revenge was going to be a thorough revenge – a quick death at the end of a blade was not what he had planned for de Roncier. Gwionn wanted to see de Roncier squirm. He wanted to ruin his life as de Roncier had ruined his father's.

'Hmm.' De Roncier rubbed the copper bristles on his chin. 'It's about my daughter, Verdun.'

Gwionn sharpened his ears.

'You're aware no doubt that she'll be leaving with Favell in a day or so . . . ?'

'Yes, my lord.'

'I'm looking for a volunteer who will act as her escort, preferably a knight. It will look better if I send a knight. I've asked Venner, but he prefers to stay here. How about you? Would you care to escort my daughter into the Aquitaine?'

Gwionn tensed, and kept his face averted from the count. No. *No!* That must not happen. If Verdun volunteered to escort de Roncier's red-headed brat to the south, all his carefully laid plans would come to nothing, for he, as Verdun's squire, would be bound to go with them. He sent up a swift prayer for his knight to reject the idea.

A thoughtful expression entered Sir Ralph's blue eyes.

Gwionn's heart sank. Sir Ralph was considering the idea.

'I realise I can't compel you, Verdun,' de Roncier said persuasively. 'You're a free man, and you always were my father's vassal, not mine. But I'd be grateful if you would consider the commission.'

'Once Lady Arlette is safely delivered to her destination, what then? Would the escort return to Huelgastel?'

'Not necessarily. If they wished, and my daughter was agreeable, her escort could remain with her at La Forteresse as her personal guard.'

'I've always had a mind to see more of the world than Normandy and Brittany,' Sir Ralph said. 'May I have today to think this over?'

Count François smiled. 'Naturally. Give me your answer at dinner.'

In the sky above Huelgastel bailey, the hobby's sickle-shaped wings folded, and the bird swooped, swift as an arrow. There was a short cry, and the hobby soared away victorious on a current of air, with its yellow talons sunk deep in the blood-flecked white breast of a swallow which would fly no more.

Anna was up and dressed and walking briskly along Church Lane when dawn was a smudge of grey light in the east. She could think of only one person who might be able to help her, only one person who would truly understand her plight, and she prayed he would be sympathetic.

The wind from the sea was cool that morning, and Anna kept the edges of her cloak pulled tightly together, not so much to ward off the chill, but to hide her growing belly. A well-covered girl with a sturdy frame, Anna could in fact carry a deal more weight before her pregnancy became noticeable, but she was sensitive to her condition, and was certain everyone else could see what she felt to be obvious.

At this early hour, the fishermen's quarter of Locmariaquer was deserted, for the night fishermen had returned and retired to their cots, while the other villagers were yet to rise.

Father Yann's cottage was Anna's destination — a humble, tumbledown wattle-and-daub affair, which the villagers had thrown up for him on the eastern edge of the glebeland, with its back to the sea. In winter vicious blasts of wind would roar in from the Small Sea, threatening to shake the cottage apart. Father Yann's lack of practical skills had done nothing to improve his home over several decades. The villagers had long ago come to the conclusion that Father Yann's cottage held together due to the strength of their priest's faith, for the fact that it was standing at all certainly seemed to defy the laws of nature.

Anna strode up to the priest's door. Worm-eaten and decaying at top and bottom, it hung crookedly from a couple of sheepskin hinges which were worn to threads. Anna rapped as sharply as she dared on the door, and got a splinter in her knuckle for her pains.

She did not have to wait long before the door opened and Father Yann's sun-wrinkled face appeared in the gap.

'Why, Anna!' he said, smiling. 'What brings you here at this hour?'

'I need a friend, Father, and could think of no one else to ask. Only you will understand. Only you can help me. Will you?'

'If it lies within my powers, my child. Wait a moment. Let us discuss this in God's house.'

In the peaceful cool of the church, Anna blessed herself with holy water, and waited by the piscina, fingers absently outlining the large petalled flowers carved into the stone. Father Yann struck a light.

'This way, Anna, my child.'

Candle aloft, Father Yann led Anna into the womb of

his church to a polished bench at the side of the apse near the altar. Two bolted wall safes with wooden doors decorated with carved crosses, were cut into the stone walls.

'Sit down, Anna,' he said gently, 'and tell me what the problem is.'

A quarter of an hour later, when the altar was lit by a rosy shaft of light from the east window, Anna had finished her story. She rested her back against the painted plaster, dried her tear-stained cheeks, and smiled a watery smile.

'So you'll send a message for me to Huelgastel, Father?'

Father Yann patted her reassuringly on the hand. 'I'll do better than that. I'll deliver your message myself.'

Anna's eyes shone. 'Would you, Father? I don't want to put you to any trouble.'

'It's no trouble. I'd planned to go into Vannes next week, I've a petition to put before the bishop. I can take your message then. But I can't do it before that.'

'Next week will be fine, Father. Thank you.'

Father Yann rose, and went to the nearest wall safe where he kept inkhorn and quill and parchment. Unbolting it, he selected a small strip of vellum — vellum was costly, and Father Yann was no wastrel.

'Now, my dear, what exactly do you want me to say to your husband? Do you want to tell him about the babe, or the difficulties you are having with your parents over your status?'

'Both, Father. He must be told everything.'

To Gwionn's horror, Sir Ralph decided he would be pleased to act as Lady Arlette's escort. They were to leave that Friday. Gwionn's own impotence in the face of Sir Ralph's agreeing to leave Huelgastel infuriated him, but he had been unable to think of any way of persuading Sir

Ralph to stay. The blow that fate had struck him was cruel. After all his and Mary's careful scheming to get him inside Huelgastel, it had been his bitter misfortune to be taken on by the very knight who had volunteered to act as Lady Arlette's escort.

Inwardly seething, but unable to do anything to change his knight's mind, Gwionn stood at Sir Ralph's side and watched de Roncier's daughter take her leave of her grandmother in Huelgastel hall. The old woman had been carried down from her sickroom, draped in rugs, especially for this leave-taking. It was the first time that Gwionn had set eyes on the woman who had once been sister to his grandmother. Gwionn had clear and fond memories of his grandmother, who had been a pious, gentle soul. He could see little resemblance to her in the gaunt stick of a woman who had grown so thin that the bones of her skull were clearly visible beneath her taut, dry skin. Gwionn's grandmother had had a soft, quiet voice, while Marie de Roncier's tones and manner alike were abrasive.

She held her skeletal arms out to embrace Arlette. 'Farewell, my dear,' Marie de Roncier said. 'May God go with you, and may He bless you with many children.' At this point the dowager countess's hard black eyes glanced archly at Eleanor. The young countess lifted her chin and stared fixedly at one of the pikes displayed on the whitewashed walls.

Gwionn was startled to feel a pang of sympathy for de Roncier's barren wife. The count seemed genuinely fond of her, which had surprised him, for it had never entered his head that a man who could be so ruthless would be capable of feeling love. But even though the count was fond of Eleanor, Gwionn wouldn't mind wagering that her days as his wife were numbered. Witness that withering scorn in the dowager countess's eyes. If the Countess Eleanor didn't produce a child soon, and a boy at that, the count would find himself under pressure to have their marriage annulled. And then a fruitful wife would be found for him.

'Farewell, Grandmama,' Arlette said, and Gwionn saw a tear sparkle on one of the girl's light lashes.

'No, no, my dear. No tears,' the old woman said, gruffly. 'Remember, you go to fulfil the purpose for which you were born. Remember that you are a de Roncier. I shall pray for you.'

'Thank you, Grandmama.'

De Roncier's daughter straightened and turned. Her maid stepped forward with a light travelling cloak. While the maid fastened the cloak about her mistress's neck, Gwionn became aware that Arlette's gaze rested curiously on him. Her eyes ran swiftly over the scar on his face — every person he had run across since the battle had looked at his scar before looking at his eyes. As their eyes met, it was borne in on Gwionn once again that Arlette de Roncier was uncommonly pretty. She gave him a slight smile, and at first Gwionn did not respond. Then it occurred to him that perhaps all was not lost.

Arlette de Roncier was currently the count's only child. Until such time as the count produced a son, she was his heiress. And he was to accompany her all the way to the Aquitaine. He looked her up and down. He had noticed her prettiness before. But now he was disturbed to discover he found her prettiness attractive to him. Her breasts were high and small, smaller than Anna's, but well shaped. Her waist he could span with two hands. The girl's skin was as white as alabaster.

Perhaps God was pointing him in an alternative direction. Perhaps God was showing him a more indirect route to revenge, and perhaps — as Gwionn looked at the count's daughter his heart beat faster — perhaps the indirect route was the surest one. When he had first seen Arlette de Roncier, it had occurred to him that it might be a pleasant revenge to seduce her. But now a shocking thought took shape in his mind. Gwionn realised that he would enjoy having Arlette de Roncier – and not simply because he was out for revenge. He found her body desirable.

In the castle, Arlette de Roncier had always been hedged about with her father's retainers. Always she had someone with her, and Gwionn had soon abandoned his idea of seducing her as impractical and foolhardy. But if he was to travel with her to the Aquitaine . . . It might be possible for him to ensure de Roncier's brat was disgraced before she reached her husband. Now that was an idea worth considering. Gwionn didn't want to do anything precipitate, but he could sense new avenues opening up before him.

Accordingly, he tried to give the heiress a friendly smile. He only managed a stiff nod, but it seemed to satisfy her, for her smile widened.

All was definitely not lost.

Despite her mixed feelings at leaving Huelgastel, Arlette was able to enjoy the five-mile ride to the port of Vannes where her father's vessel was moored. It was a beautiful July day, and the air was pleasantly warm. The heavens were the colour of cornflowers, and every now and then a fluffy white cloud floated slowly across them.

Arlette's little cavalcade was headed by her father, Louis Favell, and Sir Walter. Her father's black mastiffs ranged alongside the riders, while the baggage mules brought up the rear. Louis and the count rode side by side, talking. Sir Walter, strangely silent of late, sat morosely on his destrier. Sir Walter was the only one to be riding a warhorse. Warhorses were not usually ridden through towns, and Count François and Sir Louis were astride showy, high-stepping Arabs, but Sir Walter could only afford one horse. Those in the escort who were journeying on to the Aquitaine, would part company with the count and Sir Walter at the quayside.

The two girls followed the count, while Sir Ralph and his squire rode a couple of horse-lengths behind them. A Sergeant Gautier from La Forteresse and two troopers, Selier and Clore, followed with the pack animals.

As a parting gift, the dowager countess had presented Arlette with Yseult, a delicately boned grey palfrey with Spanish blood in her veins. Arlette was delighted with her. Years ago Arlette had outgrown Honey. Honey had been replaced with Bluebell and now she had outgrown Bluebell. Bluebell had been passed on to Clemence who, though plumper than Arlette, had stopped growing when only a couple of inches over five foot. Clemence had never lost her awkwardness with horses, and still found even the placid Bluebell hard to handle.

The church of St Patern's lay on the outskirts of Vannes, outside the wooden palisade which protected the town's heart. As they passed it, Bluebell veered to the side of the road, dug in her heels and lazily began cropping grass.

'Get her head up, Clemence,' Arlette advised.

Clemence hauled on the reins. 'I'm trying, but she won't shift. Dear God, she's greedy. Wasn't she fed this morning?'

Arlette guided Yseult over to Clemence, and reached for her friend's reins. As Bluebell's head came up, Arlette noticed that Clemence's eyelids were puffy and swollen, her cheeks splotchy and red. Arlette felt a pang of guilt. Had she been right to ask Clemence to accompany her? Clemence had insisted that she wanted to come, but it looked as though she was missing Morgan already, and they had not even boarded ship.

'What is your secret?' Clemence asked with a brave smile. 'Why wouldn't she obey me?'

'You have to be firm, show her you're in charge.'

249

'Riding's an exhausting business,' Clemence said and, clinging to her saddle-horn with one hand, she pushed a blonde strand of hair from her face with the other.

Correctly interpreting her friend's comment as a request for help, Arlette looped Bluebell's reins round her saddle-horn and attempted to cheer Clemence a little. 'It's fortunate for you we won't be riding all the way to La Forteresse!'

Clemence smiled ruefully in agreement, before her mouth dropped again in a sad curve.

Sir Ralph and his squire had caught up and were waiting for them to proceed. Arlette smiled an apology at them. 'Bluebell seems to know this will be the last grass she sees today,' she said.

Sir Ralph, who liked Lady Arlette, smiled. Gwionn Leclerc, who hated Lady Arlette, but felt lustful whenever he looked at her, smiled too.

Their calvalcade trotted through the east gate and past St Peter's. The growing stone cathedral was all but lost under a complicated web of scaffolding, and masons were balanced precariously on the roofline, heavy hods stacked with roof tiles. Arlette caught her breath when she saw them stalking along so narrow a ledge, but the masons seemed unmindful of the danger as they went, singing and chattering about their task.

They rode past the market, a noisy blur of colour known as La Cohue, or The Crowd. Fish and oysters were a staple food of the townsfolk, and a pungent odour hung over everything. Reaching la rue de la Monnaie, Arlette looked about her with particular interest. This was the quarter which had burned to the ground three years ago, the day after the Benedictine monk, Father Jerome, had given his Lady Day sermon.

The mysterious Yolande Herevi had lived here.

Ever since Arlette had witnessed that clandestine meeting between Father Jerome and the count, in the solar, she had suspected her father had had a hand in the fire, but knew better than to broach the subject with him. If the count had done wrong, he would not thank her for pointing out the error of his ways. For all that she had tried, she and her father had never become close enough to confide in each other.

There was another matter she had never managed to discuss with him – the fight at Kermaria. Wisdom had made her keep her tongue still on that matter too, though she would not have hesitated to speak out if she thought she could have helped the poor wretches that had inhabited Kermaria. Rather reluctantly, Arlette had come to the horrifying conclusion that her father may have killed to keep tenure of his land. And this had been done to maintain the de Roncier honour? She would probably never know the full truth.

If ever she was in a position to fight for her family's honour, Arlette vowed she would not stoop to underhand means. She flung a glance at her father to see if he had noticed their whereabouts, but he was lost in conversation with Sir Louis, and if he had noticed anything, his manner did not betray it.

The street was narrow, this was no broad highway where several knights could ride abreast. It was sufficiently wide for Arlette's father and his companions to proceed, as long as any passers-by were prepared to press themselves against the houses – which, after one look at Count François and his companions, they were. Dogs nosed about among discarded chicken bones and slops, dumped directly from surrounding houses into the street. The smell was very ripe. Hens pecked and scurried, squawking, from under feet and hoofs. There was even a pig, tethered to a ring in one of the walls.

The houses were wooden, thatched, and cramped; and, despite having been recently rebuilt, were squashed together cheek by jowl. After the fire it would have been

251

sensible to leave gaps between the houses to form a natural break in the event of another blaze, but no doubt no one had been prepared to give up an inch of their precious land in order to allow the new houses the extra space. La rue de la Monnaie looked as it must have done when Nominoé had been made Count of Vannes by Charlemagne three centuries earlier.

A colony of house-martins' round brown nests clustered under the west-facing eaves. White droppings trailed down the walls from the mouth of the nests — they too looked as though they had been there for ever. The baby birds' ceaseless cries goaded their parents into flicking back and forth across the sky, faster than a weaver's shuttle.

A gaunt yellow mongrel was sprawled across one of the doorsteps, a cloud of black flies hovering around its head. When the animal became aware of the count's mastiffs, its ears pricked up and it shot to its feet, hackles rising. At that moment, the door behind the yellow cur opened, and its owner, a wimpled, dimpled townswoman appeared. She had a bowl of fish entrails in her hand. The woman glanced without interest at the count and his entourage before casually tossing the scarlet offal under the hoofs of Sir Walter's destrier. Arlette could have sworn she saw the woman smile as she leaned back on her doorjamb to watch them ride by.

The yellow dog streaked through the legs of Sir Walter's destrier. So did de Roncier's mastiffs. They clashed in the middle, a growling whirlwind of snapping teeth, and flying fur. Sir Walter gathered his reins more tightly in his hand and his battle-hardened warhorse stepped placidly over the fighting dogs.

Arlette frowned. 'Did you see that, Clemence?'

'I'm glad she didn't chuck that lot under Bluebell,' Clemence answered fervently. 'She would have jumped to the moon with that fight exploding beneath her.'

252

'Quite. I'll swear that woman did that deliberately—'

The offal had vanished into the dogs. The fight was over as quickly as it had begun. De Roncier called his mastiffs to heel, and proceeded as though nothing had happened. The yellow mongrel returned to its step, and began licking at the spots of drying blood.

As Arlette and Clemence passed the woman and her dog, the woman's eyes washed dispassionately over the girls before moving on to their rearguard.

Arlette shivered.

All at once the woman's manner changed. Her eyes bulged, her plump pink cheeks paled. She was staring disbelievingly at something behind Arlette. Arlette turned in her saddle. The woman was staring very oddly at Gwionn Leclerc.

Gwionn Leclerc looked queer, too. Like the woman, his face had emptied of colour. His face was strained, pinched and grey as though he had just seen a ghost. His scar was a livid red slash across the pallor. He stared straight ahead, green eyes glittering bright as emeralds, apparently oblivious to the woman, though Arlette's instinct told her that Sir Ralph's squire was acutely aware of her presence.

What was the matter with him? As Gwionn Leclerc drew level with the woman, a muscle twitched in his scarred right cheek. He sat easily enough but the hand controlling Star's reins was gripping so hard that his bones gleamed white through his skin. The yellow dog shook the flies from its eyes and stood. Its tail began to wag. It would have run into the street if the woman had not stayed it.

Arlette turned to Clemence. There was something very peculiar about Sir Ralph's squire, and she wondered if Clemence had noticed it. 'Clemence . . . ?'

Several large tears were trailing slowly down Clemence's cheeks.

'Oh, Clemence, please don't cry,' Arlette said. And on seeing her friend's distress, Arlette forgot all about Sir Ralph's strange squire. 'Don't be sad. You don't have to come with me if you hate the idea.'

Clemence sniffed. 'Of course I must go with you. It's too late to change my mind. Besides, you're going to a houseful of strangers. You need me to come with you.'

'Not if it's going to make you miserable, I don't. You go back to your Morgan. My father will take you. He won't mind. I was wrong to ask you to come with me.'

Clemence sleeved away a tear. 'No. I do want to go. I . . . I just − ' a sob − 'just didn't realise how much I would miss him.'

On the quayside, Gwionn had been left in charge of Ares and Star while de Roncier saw his daughter safely stowed. He secured the horses' reins to a ring in the wall of the Ship Inn, keeping his head down. His hands were shaking. He knew people who lived in this quarter, and he was praying he would not be recognised. This was not the time to reacquaint himself with them.

'Bring our horses on last,' Sir Ralph flung over his shoulder as he marched on to the wooden jetty.

'Very good, sir.'

De Roncier's clinker-built ship, *Fire Dragon*, was built to a design first developed by the Vikings. Gwionn knew the longship style of vessel was still deemed the best for crossing the Great Sea and most merchants' cobs followed that design. That much and more he had picked up from his old friends when he had lived in Vannes. Long and slender, *Fire Dragon* had a curved prow which terminated in a carved dragon's head The prow was painted. The dragon's eyes were monstrous, and red, and seemed to whirl balefully in the midday sun, as the ship rose and fell gently on the swell. De Roncier's ship was easily the longest at anchor that day. His colours − the hated gold cinquefoil, on silver in a circlet of black thorns — were flying from the top of the mast. The ship's square sail was furled.

Discarded nets lay in heaps along the quay, and here and there a fish's white skeleton had been picked clean by herring gulls. There was none of that cloying stench of the town here, only the fresh, briny tang of the ocean.

Gwionn watched the troopers who had escorted Sir Louis from the Aquitaine unload the pack animals, and heave Lady Arlette's trunks into a sling-hoist to be lifted on to the ship. The baggage mules would not be accompanying them. As space was limited on *Fire Dragon*, Sir Louis had undertaken to provide more mules at Bordeaux.

From under his brows, Gwionn shot a furtive glance at Count François who was standing with his daughter and her maid by the gangplank. They seemed to be disagreeing over something. He strained his ears to hear.

'No, my lord, your daughter is wrong,' the maid said, wringing her hands. 'I don't want to stay. I want to go with her. I was merely sad for a moment, but it has passed.'

'Are you sure, Clemence?' De Roncier's red-haired daughter asked.

Gwionn lost interest in what was obviously some petty woman's problem, and covertly studied the count. What had possessed de Roncier to choose that particular route to the port? Had the count discovered his identity? Or had he been gloating over past crimes? Gwionn realised his palms were sweating. He wiped them on his tunic. The woman with the yellow dog — Beatriz — had once been a neighbour of his, before the count's men had set the fire and forced his family to fly from Vannes. Beatriz and her dog had recognised him, scars notwithstanding, and for one spine-chilling moment, Gwionn had feared that they would betray his true identity. If that had happened he

255

was in no doubt that de Roncier would have tied his guts to a windlass.

'Leclerc! Leclerc! Wake up, man!'

The disagreement between Arlette and her maid had been settled. Both girls had boarded *Fire Dragon*, and Verdun was gesticulating wildly at him over the railing. Gwionn jumped to attention.

'Have you grown roots, Leclerc? All the other horses are aboard.'

Gwionn untied Ares and Star, and led them as quickly as he could to the gangplank. Thank God. There had been no old friends in the port that day. He was no sailor, but he would be glad when *Fire Dragon* was under way.

Three days later, when the sun was sinking below the level of the trees, Father Yann, riding a mule he had borrowed from the Bishop of Vannes, heaved himself out of the saddle by Huelgastel gatehouse. His eyes were sore. He was stiff as a board, and resigned to feeling worse later on. Sweat was running down his armpits, his face was sticky, and his grey cassock (it had once been black but several summer suns had faded it) was stiff with dust blown up from the road. Father Yann gave a heartfelt groan of relief as his feet touched the ground.

The sooner he delivered Anna's message, the better. He shook the worst of the grit from his cassock, and bent to wipe the sweat from his face with the skirt. He adjusted his girdle and, these offices done, turned to the guard on the gate.

The guard — a robust fellow with twinkling grey eyes and thick white hair which curled out from under his helmet — grinned. 'Ridden a long way, Father?'

'Further than I've ridden in many a long year, aye. This animal does not have the most comfortable of gaits: I ache from head to toe.'

'Have you come to see Father Josse?' the guard asked

helpfully. He was always helpful to men of the cloth. 'He'll be in the chapel, I expect. I heard the bell chime out the hour.'

Father Yann surreptitiously rubbed a bruised buttock. 'No, my son. I've not come to see Father Josse. My mission is to deliver a message to a young man who I believe has taken up employment here.'

'Oh?'

'Name of Gwionn Leclerc. Do you know of him?'

'Gwionn Leclerc? You must mean the lad Sir Ralph Verdun took on as his squire. Is he about eighteen, with brown hair and a badly scarred face?'

Some of the fatigue left Father Yann's expression. 'That's him. Where can I find him?'

The guard shook his head. 'You're too late, I'm afraid. He's gone.'

The priest went still as a menhir.

'Gone? But he can't have gone. I have a very important message for him. It's vital I speak to him.'

'Then you'd best hop back on that mule, Father. It's a long ride to where he's gone.'

Father Yann blinked into the guard's grey eyes. 'And where might that be?'

'He's gone with the count's daughter to the Aquitaine.'

'But he's coming back?'

The guard's mailed shoulders rose. 'As to that, I can't say. But you could inquire in the hall.' An expansive wave indicated that the priest could enter the bailey. 'If you take your mule to the stables, young Aubrey will see it cared for while you're here.'

'Thank you. I shall need a place for the night.'

'Ask for Sergeant le Goff. He'll fix you up. You'll find the well in the inner bailey, if you need it.'

Disconsolately, Father Yann led his mule under the jaws of the portcullis, and hoped that God would show him how he could best help young Anna now.

257

Four days into the voyage, Gwionn sat on the helmsman's bench in *Fire Dragon*'s stern, twiddling his thumbs while the wind whistled through his hair.

He was restless, and felt faintly sick. He had expected that a sea voyage would be exhilarating and exciting, but it was no such thing. Gwionn had been seasick before, in that other life when he had been Raymond Herevi. He had been on his way to see Anna. As Anna's image flashed across his mind, Gwionn's heart lightened. He had been sailing across the Small Sea in a fisherman's boat to visit her. He had felt sick then. But he had not expected to feel sick out here on the Great Sea.

It had been worse at the beginning. The first two days had been sheer hell. They had not even sailed on to the ocean proper before he was vomiting over the gunwale.

Sir Ralph had seen his squire was ill, and in his rough and ready way had said, 'Sick? Bad luck. You'll get used to the motion soon.' And Sir Ralph had left him to it, and stalked off to the ship's prow to stand by the carved dragon's head with Louis Favell.

But the most shaming thing of all had been that *she* had noticed his plight, and had come straight across, and fixed him with sympathetic eyes that were bluer than a June sky. She was a witch. She had even attempted to hold his hair back from his face while he spewed, but he had soon put a stop to that by batting her hand away.

'I'm all right, my lady,' he had gasped, as soon as he could. He had clutched the gunwale, barely managing to stand.

'No, you're not.' Deftly de Roncier's brat had reached up and unclasped his cloak, which was flapping uncontrollably and likely to become soiled.

Feebly, Gwionn had tried to fend her off once more, but *Fire Dragon* had lifted on another steep Atlantic roller. He had groaned and, as he put his head over the railing, had felt gentle hands lift his cloak from him.

She had stood by him until he finished. He had sunk on to the deck, resting his head on his knees, feeling as though he'd been turned inside out.

'Take slow deep breaths,' she'd advised, and had gone down on her haunches beside him, 'and hold them in your lungs. Shall I fetch you some water?'

Startled he had lifted his head and stared at her. This was the first time he had seen her at close quarters and, sick as he felt, he was conscious of a dangerous pull of attraction. He had almost laughed aloud. Back in Huelgastel he had had visions of seducing her, and here he was, vomiting his heart out, while she offered to fetch him water!

Owing to the strong winds, Arlette had removed her veil, and her extraordinary hair was escaping its coils to form a coppery cloud about her face. Her lashes were light, and matched her hair, but they were long and thick. Her nose was straight and spattered with freckles, and when she was smiling, as now, Gwionn could see perfect rows of even white teeth. She was prettier than Anna. If he had not known who she was, he could have found it in himself to like her. But he did know who she was, or rather who her father was, and any liking he felt for Arlette de Roncier must be firmly locked away. He would permit himself to feel lust for this girl — but liking? Never. And he had felt shamed that his enemy should see him sick and vulnerable.

'You would fetch a mere squire water, my lady?' he had asked, raising a brow incredulously.

Her smile had vanished, and quick red colour had run up her neck. But she had given him a cup of water, and handed him back his cloak, and mercifully since then she had left him alone; at least as much as possible on the only deck of a seventy-five-foot ship, most of which was taken up with horses or cargo or sailors' tackle.

Since then *Fire Dragon* had crawled past the salt marshes on the borders of Brittany; past the Loire estuary, teeming with traders and vessels from the shipyards; and now past the coast of Poitou, but at such a distance that all Gwionn could see was a dark blur lying on the horizon over the port gunwale.

'You're a better colour today, lad,' the helmsman observed.

'Yes. I feel much better.'

'I used to be like you when I first went to sea.'

Gwionn wasn't up to a conversation with the helmsman – he had some thinking to do – but it would do no harm to let the man rabbit on. 'Oh, aye?'

'Aye. Terrible it were. I remember my first run to London. The swell was worse than this. Ten, no, a hundred times worse . . .'

Listening to the helmsman with half an ear, Gwionn scanned the deck, careful to keep his eyes from straying towards the de Roncier witch and her maid who were seated with their backs to him on one of the benches fixed half-way along the ship.

A one-masted vessel, *Fire Dragon* was powered by a single square sail, though it looked as though provision had been made for some oarsmen, for there was a series of small sliding doors beneath the gunwales.

'Are those oar holes?' Gwionn interrupted a lurid description of green crested waves twice as tall as a cathedral tower.

'Those? Yes. She can take fourteen oarsmen if needs be.'

Gwionn indicated the benches. 'And they sit there?'

'Yes.'

At that moment Clemence, sitting beside her mistress, looked back. Seeing the helmsman and Gwionn gazing in their direction, the maid bent and whispered in her mistress's ear.

260

Arlette did not turn her head, but her shoulders stiffened, and her bright head inched up.

The helmsman chuckled. 'I think she likes you, lad,' he said.

'The maid?'

'No. I'm talking about the Little Lady. She was quick enough to trot over when you were ill.' He sighed. 'What a waste.'

'Waste?'

'Her being sent to be a countess to old Etienne Favell.'

'He's old, is he?' It hadn't occurred to Gwionn to wonder what Arlette's fiancé might be like.

'A regular greybeard.' The helmsman gave another sigh. 'Favell will only take her if she's a virgin. Counts are pickier than most. Have to be, I suppose, to keep their precious bloodlines pure. What a waste.'

The helmsman lapsed into a gloomy silence, and Gwionn stared at the sea. From time to time he found his eyes drawn to the girls on the bench. If the helmsman was correct and Arlette de Roncier did have a liking for him, his idea about seducing her might perhaps not be as insane as he had first thought it.

There were no facilities for sleeping on board *Fire Dragon*: this was only done in an emergency. Every night *Fire Dragon* crept into port, paid her dues to the harbour master, and tied up for the night. Leaving a couple of sailors on watch, *Fire Dragon*'s passengers and crew had taken lodgings in taverns.

Tonight, when they made landfall, Gwionn would try and speak with her. When they were at supper might be a good time. He would start by seeking Lady Arlette out. He would hide his hatred. He would be gentle and considerate. He would try and discover if Arlette de Roncier did have a liking for him. He would *make* her like him. Before he acquired his scar girls had found him attractive, and since then . . . since then there had only

261

been Anna. But Anna loved him. Was he still attractive to other girls?

If so, he would embark on his new phase of revenge, one which involved Arlette de Roncier more nearly than her father. He would strangle at birth any liking that he might feel for Arlette de Roncier.

As Gwionn was wondering if his plan had any chance of success, Anna's laughing face leaped into his consciousness. Firmly, Gwionn pushed it away. He would have to forget about Anna. He had business with Lady Arlette de Roncier before he could go back to his wife.

Chapter Thirteen

'I'm going to the harbour for a while, Mother,' Anna said as they walked back together to their cottage. They had been weeding the strips in the top field by the hawthorn hedge, and Anna held a willow basket containing freshly picked cabbage and onions for their supper, while Marharid carried the family hoe. 'I'll grind the wheat afterwards.'

A speculative light kindled in Marharid's brown eyes. She hefted the hoe on to her shoulder. 'But you were there only this morning. Why do you wish to go again?' Marharid's grey-flecked brows lowered. 'You're not going to see Padrig, are you?'

Padrig was son-in-law to the innkeeper of the Anchor, and he had a poor reputation with the girls in the village. Marharid jabbed a work-worn finger at her daughter's belly. 'Don't tell me that's the philanderer who's responsible for the child in your belly? I did warn you to give him a wide berth. He's a silver-tongued good-for-nothing wastrel, and you should have closed your ears to his pretty phrases.'

'No, mother, you're mistaken. It's not Padrig—'

'Who, then?'

Anna folded her lips tightly together.

'For the love of God, Anna, I'd never have thought you had it in you to be so mealy-mouthed. Tell me. Who is the father of your child?'

Anna's lips remained sealed.

'Anna, please. I'm trying to help you. Your father is bound to tumble to the truth soon. Why, yesterday he commented that you're filling out, growing into a real woman. You've only to increase a little more, and he'll realise his mistake. It's becoming obvious you're with child.'

'Mother, I'm sorry. I can't tell you. I swore an oath, you see.'

'An oath? Anna, dear girl, what kind of a man would bind you to a lover's oath, and then abandon you like this? Who is he? Holy Mother, if I discover you're lying to protect that swine . . . if I find out that it is Padrig, I'll do worse than see him in the stocks, I'll have him boiled in oil.'

Anna didn't want her mother making trouble for Padrig and his poor wife who suffered enough with her husband's real philanderings. 'No, Mother. It's not Padrig, I swear.'

'Who then?'

'You'll get no more out of me, Mother. I'm sorry.'

'But the bastard *is* married, isn't he?'

Anna looked away from her mother's too-penetrating gaze, and fixed her gaze on a pebble on the dusty track.

Marharid's voice rose. 'That's it, isn't it? Anna, I know you. You look away because I'm stumbling close to the truth. You've had an affair with a man who is married to someone else—'

Anna sighed, and lifted her eyes from the road. 'Mother, I have not.'

'Then why won't you tell me who it is?'

'I can't. I swore—'

'Whoever it is, he won't come back, you know. He's deserted you.'

'He will come back. I know he loves me.'

Marharid flung a distraught glance at the heavens, and

264

her brow was more furrowed than the strips in the top field. 'God help me. What should I do with her?' With visible effort she brought her voice under control. 'Samzun will have you, notwithstanding. I have spoken with him.'

'You haven't! Mother, I told you, I can't marry Samzun.'

They had reached their cottage. Still frowning Marharid leaned her hoe against the wall and unlatched the door.

'You will, you know, in the end.'

'I will not.'

Mother and daughter glared at each other for some moments before Anna went inside and deposited the basket of vegetables on the table.

'I'm going to the harbour. I won't be long. I'll cook supper afterwards.'

Marharid caught her daughter's sleeve. 'Who is it you're going to see at the harbour? Will you tell me that at least?'

Anna smiled. 'I'm going to see Father Yann. He's due to return from Vannes some time today, and Edouarz is bringing him back on his boat.'

Marharid's brow cleared. 'Father Yann? Does he know then, of your . . . your state?'

'Yes, Mother. Father Yann knows it all, and I've asked for his help.'

'Thank God. I was beginning to think you'd turned simple on us.' Marharid paused. 'Father Yann will recommend marriage to Samzun, you know.'

Anna gave her mother an unfathomable look. 'As to that, Mother, we shall have to wait and see, won't we?'

The Locmariaquer market cross stood on the quayside where the fishermen unloaded their catch in front of the Anchor. Anna sat on the steps of the cross, while white clouds scurried overhead. A pair of terns were flying out over the calm waters of the bay, hovering, beaks down, while they searched for fish. Because Anna wanted to discuss her business in private, she had taken the liberty of obtaining the great iron key to the church door from Father Yann's ramshackle cottage. She swung it to and fro in her hand, trying to conceal her impatience while Father Yann disembarked and made his thanks to Edouarz.

She managed to contain herself until the priest reached the cross, whereupon she leaped to her feet. 'Did you see him, Father? Is he well?'

Father Yann put his hand on her shoulder, and regarded her with soft, sympathetic eyes. 'It's best we talk in the church, my child.'

'Yes. Yes. I know.' Anna caught the priest's hand and pulled him towards the church gate, practically hopping from foot to foot. 'I took the key from your house. I didn't think you'd mind.'

'I don't mind.'

They walked to the church door.

'Is he well? How did he look?'

'Wait till we're inside, Anna.'

Something in Father Yann's tone brought Anna to a standstill. Her hands crept to cover her stomach. The key felt cold through her homespun bliaud. 'There's something wrong, isn't there?'

Father Yann swallowed, and Anna came to the dreadful realisation that it was not sympathy that softened Father Yann's eyes that afternoon, but pity.

'Father?'

Gently, the village priest relieved Anna of the key.

When they were seated on the long knotted bench by the wall in the apse, Father Yann took Anna by the hand.

'Anna, I took your message to Huelgastel, but I was unable to deliver it. Your Raymond — or Gwionn if you prefer — was not at the castle.'

'Not there? He's not ill?' Anna paled, and the fingers in Father Yann's hand tightened convulsively. 'He's . . . he's not dead, is he? That count hasn't killed him, has he?'

'Merciful Heavens, no. He's in the best of health, as far as I could make out. He's managed to find a place as a knight's squire, but his knight – Sir Ralph Verdun – has chosen to accompany Count de Roncier's daughter to her fiancé's castle in the Aquitaine. Gwionn Leclerc has had to accompany him.'

'The knight will return though, when the count's daughter reaches her betrothed,' Anna said, though she suspected from Father Yann's expression that this was not the case. She was clutching at straws.

Father Yann shook his head. 'No. Sir Ralph is likely to be away some time. De Roncier's daughter won't be marrying until next year, and apparently Sir Ralph has elected to remain in the Aquitaine as Arlette de Roncier's personal guard. He may stay even when she becomes Countess Favell. And Gwionn Leclerc will stay with him. He must. Anna, I know this won't help your most pressing problem, but I cannot help feeling that this is for the best. I never liked the idea of your Raymond going to Huelgastel. He was a good lad, but his grievances were eating away at him. Perhaps God in His wisdom has sent him away to give him time for his anger to cool and his inner wounds to heal. I shudder to think what might have happened if he had stayed close to Count François. It's better for his soul that he has gone to the Aquitaine.'

Dazed, Anna looked at Father Yann without really seeing him. Tied to the land she worked alongside her parents, she had the peasant's restricted view of the world, and as far as she was concerned Vannes and Huelgastel lay at the far side of that world. The Aquitaine might as well be on the moon.

'Where is the Aquitaine?' she asked.

Father Yann's knowledge of geography was almost as

limited as Anna's, but he had some knowledge of politics and was keen to share what he did know with Anna. 'The Aquitaine is a rich Plantagenet province which was under the rule of Duke Richard. I believe it lies many days' journey from here, far in the south-west. Richard Plantagenet displeased his father, so the reins of government were passed to his mother, Queen Eleanor. As I understand it, the Queen and her son work hand in glove, and it makes little difference to Duke Richard whether his mother or he hold title to the land. It hasn't stopped his quarrels with his brother, our own Duke Geoffrey. Why, only a few months ago, Duke Richard raided Brittany.'

The politics went over Anna's head. Queen Eleanor, Duke Richard — such names meant nothing to her, but she did grasp that the Aquitaine was far from Locmariaquer.

'And Raymond has gone to the Aquitaine? With this knight, Sir Ralph Verdun?'

'Yes. I couldn't deliver your message.'

'There must be some way of contacting Raymond. This Count de Roncier must write to his daughter.'

Father Yann's brows met in a worried frown. 'I thought of that. But think, Anna, what if someone reads your letter? We risk revealing that Gwionn Leclerc is not Gwionn Leclerc but Raymond Herevi. And that, as Raymond took great pains to stress, would be disastrous.'

'I see.'

'I'm sorry, Anna.'

'Where does this leave me? It's all very well for you to talk about Raymond's soul, but what can I do? My mother is badgering me to marry Samzun.'

Father Yann made a quiet clucking sound with his tongue. 'I've been expecting her to come up with that idea. And what does your father have to say?'

'He doesn't know yet. But I can't keep it from him for

268

much longer. Father, I won't marry Samzun, and you can't force me.'

'My child, you are married already. No one is going to force you to do anything.'

'But what shall I do? I'm at the end of my tether.'

'Let me consider your problem. I shall pray for guidance.'

Anna rose and, shaking out her skirts, folded her hands protectively over her growing belly. 'Very well, Father Yann. But I hope God gives you some guidance soon, because I can't keep my secret from my father for much longer.'

It was just before supper a few evenings later when Huberz revealed that he knew his daughter was pregnant. Anna was ladling rabbit stew from a soot-blackened pot dangling from a chain over the fire. Her parents were already seated.

Like her mother, Huberz took the news that he was to be a grandfather calmly – at first.

'Anna, my girl, you've been holding out on me. Haven't you something to tell your father?'

The hand holding the ladle jerked, and some of the stew fell hissing into the flames.

'F . . . Father?' Anna could feel her cheeks burning, and it wasn't the heat from the fire.

'Now, don't you go all coy on me,' Huberz said, cutting himself a generous hunk of bread. 'I've been watching you. You've been gaining weight lately, but it's more that that, isn't it? You're starting to waddle like a duck. And I may only be a man, but I know what's what, and when a woman starts to waddle, you can bet your last farthing a babe's in the offing.'

Thanking God that her mother had had the forethought to send her to the Anchor for a jug of cider that evening, which her father had already been supping – cider always mellowed him — Anna exchanged glances with her mother and took a deep breath. It was time for her to confess. It would not serve her to lie.

'Yes, Father. I'm having a baby. It will be born in November.'

'November, eh?' Huberz bit a piece from his bread and chewed thoughtfully.

Anna put a steaming bowl of stew before him, and received a preoccupied grunt of acknowledgement. Her father picked up his spoon. Anna served her mother and herself, and Huberz — who was partial to rabbit stew, and liked to do justice to his food — did not speak till his earthenware bowl was empty. Anna knew better than to congratulate herself on coming through the crisis unscathed. Her mother had not been angry until she had refused to marry Samzun, and her father was likely to react in the same way.

His stew finished, Huberz dropped his spoon on the table, and wiped the bowl with his bread to mop up the gravy. 'Don't keep me in suspense, daughter,' he said. 'Tell me who's going to be my son-in-law. Samzun?'

'No, Father.'

'Not Samzun, eh? I own you've surprised me. Ralph?'

'No, Father.'

Marharid leaned forward, brown eyes anxious. 'It's no use, Huberz. She'll play that game all day. I've tried, but she'll not let on. She won't tell you who the father is.'

Huberz's heavy face darkened. 'What?'

Anna hung her head.

'Now look here, my girl.' Huberz waved a big finger under Anna's nose. 'I'll not stand for this. You'll tell me now, and you'll tell me plain, the name of the father of your child.'

'I'm sorry, Father,' Anna said quietly. 'I can't tell you.'

Huberz brought his fist crashing on to the table. The soup bowls jumped. 'You'll tell me this minute, or I

270

swear, pregnant or no, I'll whip you into next week—'

'No, Huberz,' Marharid said, paling. She looked pleadingly at Anna. 'Please, Anna. Won't you tell us?'

Anna shook her head.

Huberz glared at his daughter for a moment or two, then shrugged. 'I won't force you to reveal your secret, Anna . . .'

'Thank you, Father.'

' . . . As long as you marry. I think Samzun will still have you.' Huberz looked to his wife for confirmation. 'He will, won't he, Marharid? God knows why, but that lad has always been besotted with Anna.'

'He'll have her, but she won't have him,' Marharid said. 'She won't have anyone.'

Huberz put his hands on his hips. 'Won't?'

From the expression on her father's face, Anna thought it wise to stand up and put a couple of feet between him and her.

'Won't?' he repeated.

'Father, don't force me. Please. You don't understand.'

A big man, Huberz lumbered to his feet. Anna braced herself.

'Listen, my girl, I'll say this once, and once only. You're pregnant and unwed, and that's your shame. But I know what it is to be young and in love. I'm willing to forgive, and forget – provided you marry, and give that child of yours a respectable name.'

'I'm sorry, Father, I can't.'

'And that's your final word?'

'Yes, Father.'

A stony expression settled on Huberz's wind-beaten features. He removed his gaze from Anna, sank back on to his bench, and spoke into his bowl. 'In that case, girl, you can pack up your things and leave—'

'No, Huberz!' Marharid objected, half rising from her place.

'Sit down, wife,' Huberz said, in inflexible tones that Anna could not recognise as belonging to her father.

'But, Huberz—'

'Marharid, sit down.'

Marharid sat down.

Huberz lifted his head and met Anna's gaze. He looked a different man to her; she could scarcely believe this was happening. 'So it's stay and marry Samzun, or go?' she asked.

'That's the size of it,' Huberz answered, coldly.

Still unable to believe that it had come to this, Anna swung on her heel and went to her bedbox. She packed mechanically, rolling her spare bliaud and tunic into her cloak. She had a bone comb of her own, a red ribbon, and a string of green beads that Raymond had given her, but little else.

While Anna gathered up her belongings, she could hear, as though from a long distance, her mother pleading with her father.

'Huberz, you can't do this.'

'I can.'

'Huberz, it's wrong.'

'It's wrong to bring bastards into this world.'

'Huberz, please reconsider. You'll regret this.'

'No.'

Anna was ready. Her cloak was a neat bundle under her arm. She went to the door and glanced at her father.

'Good bye, Father.'

Her father wouldn't even look at her.

'Mother?'

With a sob, Marharid rose from her bench. 'I'm not letting her leave us with no more that the clothes on her back,' Marharid declared. She ran to the basket that Anna had filled with vegetables that afternoon, and threw in a clutch of apples, a small loaf, and a soft white cheese. Running to Anna's bedbox, Marharid stripped the blanket from the mattress, and bundled that on top. Her hands were shaking as though she had the ague.

While Anna waited on the threshold, Huberz stared stolidly into his empty bowl.

Basket in hand, at last Marharid came to embrace her daughter. Tears glistened in her eyes. Anna could feel her own tears rising, but she held them down with a will she did not know she possessed.

'Farewell, Mother.'

'Oh, Anna. Please just tell us the truth or agree to marry Samzun.'

'He thinks to make me relent, but I won't. I can't marry Samzun.'

Marharid dashed away a tear, and mother and daughter moved out into the velvety evening air. 'No. I see that. And he won't change his mind.' Her voice cracked. 'God speed. I've put a few pennies at the bottom of the basket, don't lose them. Anna, I love you.'

Anna managed to smile. 'And I love you.' She raised her voice and directed it through the door. 'And I love you too, Father,' she said.

And relieving her mother of the basket, Anna walked off towards Church Lane, in search of Father Yann.

As Anna came down the lane, burdened by her bundle of clothes and the basket her mother had given her, dusk was settling over Locmariaquer like a soft grey cloak. The wind had dropped, and a feeling of calm embraced the harbour. Even the gulls in the bay had fallen silent. The sea was their cradle; it had rocked them to sleep.

The church door was ajar, so Anna went inside. Two candles burned on the altar, and a tall, shadowy figure knelt before it. A low murmuring like the buzzing of a distant swarm of bees reverberated around the stones. Father Yann was chanting the Compline psalms.

Anna deposited her belongings by the piscina, blessed

herself with the Holy Water, and waited for the priest to finish his office.

She had feared her father would be angry with her. She had feared a beating, but she had never really believed that he would throw her out of her home. Where would she sleep that night? And what of tomorrow night? And all the other tomorrows? How was she to survive? It was summer now, a kind season, and if the worst came to the worst Anna knew she could sleep in the hedgerows. It couldn't be much different from sleeping in the dolmen with Raymond. But what would happen when the baby was born? It would be winter then, and the weather would be cruel. What was she to do?

As Anna's worries multiplied and grew, she found herself focusing on Father Yann's voice. At first an unintelligible drone, all at once she found she was understanding the words. Father Yann was reciting one of the psalms in Breton, instead of the incomprehensible Latin the priests normally used. Because it was easier for Anna to listen to the words of the psalm than resolve her problems, she listened.

'He shall defend thee under His wings, and thou shalt be safe under His feathers: His faithfulness and truth shall be thy shield and buckler.

'Thou shalt not be afraid for any terror by night: nor for the arrow that flieth by day.

'For the pestilence that walketh in darkness: nor for the sickness that destroyeth in the noon-day.

'A thousand shall fall beside thee, and ten thousand at thy right hand: but it shall not come nigh thee.'

Beautiful words, comforting words. Words which spoke directly to Anna's soul. She sank down on to the cold stone flags, eager for more.

'For Thou, Lord, art my hope: Thou had set Thine house of defence very high.

'There shall no evil happen unto thee: neither shall any

274

plague come nigh thy dwelling.'

All at once Anna's being was filled with a sense of peace, and it was so complete, so all-encompassing, that in that instant she knew that everything was going to be all right. It looked impossible, but everything was going to be all right. She did not know how, because if she picked up her problems and examined them one by one, she could get lost in them and never find her way out. She knew it would not be easy. But suddenly, impossibly, Anna knew beyond a shadow of all doubt that, in the end, everything was going to work out right for her, and her baby, and for Raymond too.

His office said, Father Yann lifted his head and, without turning round, asked, 'Anna, is that you?'

'Yes, Father.'

'I've been praying for you, child. Come and sit beside me.'

Anna walked to the bench in the east end. 'My father has thrown me out because I won't marry Samzun,' she said.

Father Yann shook his head in mild reproof.

'You don't seem shocked, Father.'

'No, I expected as much.'

'What shall I do? I have nowhere to go. Mother gave me some pennies, but they won't last long. Do you think we could use the money to get a message delivered to the Aquitaine?'

'No. Save your money. You may need it. As I said, a written message to Raymond, unless delivered personally by me, or someone completely trustworthy, could fall into the wrong hands and betray him. It would cost more that a couple of silver pennies to buy a trustworthy messenger. And if Raymond's safety cannot be guaranteed—'

'I won't put Raymond at risk.'

'Then you must wait for him to return to you. Are you certain he will?'

'Yes, Father.'

'And are you content to have his child and wait for that time?'

'Yes, Father.'

'I've been meditating on your troubles, child,' Father Yann went on. 'You cannot marry Samzun, but I wouldn't be able to sleep at night if I didn't know I had found you a safe haven. I believe I have been given divine inspiration. I have thought of the very place where you can go, and have your child in safety, and wait for your Raymond.'

Anna clasped her hands under her breast. 'You have? Where?'

'Kermaria.'

Anna wrinkled her brow. 'But, Father, Count de Roncier sacked Kermaria. And Raymond told me the count's men were still crawling all over it when he escaped.'

Father Yann nodded. 'They were. But they were not stationed there long. Shortly after Madalen and Joel brought Raymond to you, the count's troopers left. The manor is derelict, and until someone proves they have title to it, or the duke reassigns it, it will remain so. Oh, the village still exists, the villagers have not left, but Sir Jean's manor is an empty shell. No one has any reason to go there.'

Anna stared blindly at the broad granite flags. 'You mean I can wait for him there? At his old home?'

'Precisely. The villagers will look after you when your time comes. The people of Kermaria were loyal to Jean St Clair, and it's in my mind that they would deal kindly with his grandchild's mother.'

'I can't tell them I'm married to Raymond. I promised I would keep that secret till he returns. Won't the villagers hold that against me?'

The priest shook his head. 'It is unlikely. Raymond

276

himself is base-born, if you recall. His parents did not marry till years later. Madalen and Joel proved their loyalty to Raymond by bringing him to you. My dear, I am sure that the villagers at Kermaria will accept you. And if,' hastily Father Yann corrected himself, '*when* Raymond returns, he will come to me and I will tell him where you are.'

Anna was coming round to the idea. 'I wouldn't be so far from my mother, either. I might be able to see her from time to time.'

'There is that. Well, child, what do you say? Do I take you to Kermaria at dawn, or do I pray for more divine guidance?'

Anna smiled. 'I should like to go to Kermaria tomorrow, Father. Thank you.'

Standing in *Fire Dragon*'s shifting prow with Clemence, Arlette glanced at her friend. They were now five days into voyage, and Clemence's blue-grey eyes were still red-rimmed with weeping for Morgan le Bihan.

Arlette grieved for her, remembering all the years when she had strived to win her father's affection. She could have filled a well with all the tears she had shed then. But her father had always kept her at a distance; her grandmother too. At last Arlette could see some sense in their attitude. It had made it easier for her to leave. Whilst she had watched Clemence's eyes fill with tears as the Small Sea was left far behind them, Arlette had been able to bid her father goodbye at the quayside without a qualm. It might have been different had her grandfather still been alive but, as it was, Arlette was lucky enough to keep the companionship of the only person she really cared for. Unlike Clemence, Arlette was not leaving her heart behind her. Arlette's heart was still intact; and God willing she would be able to gift it to the man who was to become her husband. Perhaps, after all, her father had taught her well. Perhaps, at last, Arlette should learn the lesson that if one remained detached, one would keep free of sorrows. Arlette had tried to adhere to this philosophy of detachment – her childhood had taught her that dependency was foolish – but sometimes she felt something vital was missing. Was her world greyer, and drabber than everyone else's? she wondered.

She squared her shoulders. This was nonsense. She was going to marry a count. She would surely feel as though she belonged when she reached Count Etienne.

Clemence gave a tiny, muted sob. Hearing it, Arlette put her arm about her friend's shoulders and hugged her. Her father and grandmother had been right. Better not to have a heart than suffer like this. Far better to live in a grey world than a bright, shining one, and suddenly have the colour snatched away.

Arlette glanced at Louis Favell. He was sitting astride a bench amidships playing nine men's morris with Sir Ralph. Did he resemble his uncle? she wondered.

'I hope he's kind,' she murmured under her breath.

'What?'

Clemence had heard her. 'Oh, nothing. I was thinking about Count Etienne.'

'We'll know soon enough,' Clemence said. 'Captain Potvin told me that this is our last day on the open sea. We'll be heading into the estuary tonight. I should think he will be relieved.' Clemence pointed at the stern where Gwionn Leclerc slumped, resting the back of his head gainst the gunwale. His skin was faintly tinged with green. 'I've never known anyone be so sick, and it's not even rough.'

'No.' Arlette looked about her. 'It is windy though, the ship is being buffeted about more than usual. And it's getting worse. It wasn't like this earlier. Look at that boat over there.'

Arlette pointed over the port bow, and the two girls

stared at a three man fishing cob which appeared to be fighting wind and waves to get back to the shore. It seemed to be losing headway.

'How strange,' Clemence murmured. 'There are no gulls. Where are the seagulls, Arlette?'

Arlette squinted at the sky, which was overhung with ominous, louring clouds. For most of the voyage *Fire Dragon* had skirted the coast, and screaming gulls had kept them company. The gulls had vanished, there was not even a distant speck on the landward side.

'I don't know,' Arlette answered. 'Yesterday at noon one of them landed at Gwionn Leclerc's feet, and ate his bread when he couldn't stomach it.'

'Maybe they think a storm's in the offing. Maybe they've flown back to land.'

The wind filled *Fire Dragon*'s sail, and whistled through the rigging. The ship surged forwards, lifting and falling on a series of larger and larger waves. In the stern, Gwionn Leclerc put his head in his hands.

'Excuse me, ladies.' It was the ship's captain, a bow-legged man of medium height who had a bald, sun-burned head which shone like polished mahogany. 'I think we're in for a bit of a blow. It might be better if you went amidships. You'll notice the swell less there.'

Clemence paled. 'Holy Mother. It *is* a storm. But it was clear and calm this morning, how can it change so quickly?'

Captain Potvin's weather-beaten face crinkled into a reassuring smile. 'We're sailing in unpredictable waters, mistress. The weather can turn here quicker than you can blink.'

Clemence crossed herself.

'There's no need for concern on our account,' Captain Potvin went on. 'This little squall should be over almost as soon as it's begun. *Fire Dragon* has enough ballast to weather it. We've been lucky with weather so far, the wind's been with us all the way. I had a feeling our luck must break.'

'We'll make port tonight?' Arlette asked.

'If this blows out soon, which I think it will. We're coming up to the Gironde estuary, on the final stage before Bordeaux.' The captain cast an experienced eye over the grey, wind-tossed waves.

Just then, a Jacob's ladder split the dark clouds apart, and for an instant the golden column of light illuminated the fishermen's cob, and the occupants struggling valiantly within it.

Captain Potvin raised an eyebrow at Clemence. 'If you want to pray for anyone, mistress, spare a prayer for those poor beggars. They're shipping water fast. Ho, there!' He hailed a crewman. 'Make sure our rowboat's secure at the stern.' *Fire Dragon*'s skiff was drawn along behind her, and Captain Potvin did not want to lose it.

'Come on, Clemence. We'd best get out of the way.' Arlette led her friend amidships and they chose a bench near the mast. She nodded at Sir Louis and Sir Ralph, who had finished their game and thrown the board in a box. The horses were tethered together nearer the stern, and from where Arlette was sitting, they blocked her view of Gwionn Leclerc, whom she knew lay suffering at the helmsman's feet.

The strengthening wind made the tall mast creak. A stray wave washed over the gunwale, spraying icy droplets on Arlette's cheeks.

A sailor was bailing steadily from under the horses' feet. Bluebell whinnied and tossed her head. Star answered, jerking hard at his bridle. As *Fire Dragon* rocked, one of the black gelding's iron-shod hoofs slipped and caught the sailor's hand. The sailor yelped. Star stamped another hoof and, with another yelp, the sailor rolled clear.

'I think I'll try and calm the horses,' Sir Ralph

announced. 'If their tethers break while we're going through this lot, we might lose one.'

'Your squire should do that,' Louis Favell was quick to point out.

Sir Ralph sighed, but answered without rancour, 'He's seasick, poor lad. Come along, Favell, make yourself useful.'

Louis Favell rose reluctantly. 'Next time, Verdun, you should pick a squire with a stronger stomach. Then you won't have to play his part.'

'Sound advice,' Sir Ralph said, easily. 'But I like the lad. He rides well, and generally he's keen to learn. That's why I took him on. My squire doesn't have to be a good sailor.'

The two knights lurched across the pitching boards to the horses.

The downdraught from the sail felt like icy fingers on Arlette's neck. Shivering, she glanced up. The canvas was bellied out by the wind; so much wind that she feared its seams would burst at any moment.

From the prow the captain was bellowing through cupped hands, but at first the wind snatched his words away. Eventually his voice reached them. 'Take in some sail!'

The crewman who had been bailing, dropped his bucket and sprang to the mast.

The gunwales were awash. The captain sloshed his way to the mast, clapped the sailor on the back, and continued astern to bellow instructions at the helmsman.

'I can't see that fishing boat any more, Arlette,' Clemence shouted, over the wind. 'Do you think they're all right?'

'I pray so.'

Clemence caught at Arlette's hand. Her fingers were slippery with spray, and cold. 'Look!'

Arlette looked. Gwionn Leclerc must have made a

miraculous recovery, for he was running to the side of the ship, feet splashing through the wash. He gripped the gunwale, scarred face chalk white, and peered into the churning sea.

'Man overboard!' he cried.

Arlette stood up. Not the helmsman, surely? No. Now that she was standing she could see the helmsman over the horses' heads, conferring with the captain.

'Man overboard!' Gwionn Leclerc repeated hoarsely, face straining desperately towards the ship's captain.

But the wind was too loud, the waves as high as houses, and at that moment a wall of rain hit them. The captain's mind was fully occupied.

Sir Ralph and Louis had their hands full with the horses.

A line had parted under the extra strain, and snaked about in the wind. The nearest sailor was frantically trying to secure it.

Arlette waded as quickly as she could across the unsteady boards to Sir Ralph's squire. 'Where? Where is this man?' she asked.

Gwionn pointed to a trough in the waves just slightly ahead of them. 'There. Not one of ours. A fisherman.'

Gripping the slippery gunwale, Arlette could see the man's head and hands. He had seen the *Fire Dragon*, had known the ship was approaching, and his arms were straining up through wind-whipped waves at his only hope of salvation. His head sank briefly underwater, but bobbed up again like a cork. He had dark hair, which wind and sea had plastered to his skull like a tight black cap. His eyes were dark pits, his face a mask of terror.

The rain stung Arlette's eyes. The wind howled. The sea boiled like a witch's cauldron.

'We must help him!' she cried.

'We need a rope . . .'

As Gwionn Leclerc and Arlette de Roncier cast about for a rope, the man's head was swallowed up by the waves. He popped up again, hands stretched desperately towards them. *Fire Dragon* was almost level with him, in a moment they would be past him, and in this sea it was all their helmsman could do to keep *Fire Dragon* steady. Arlette knew that if they did not reach the man in time, there would be no stopping to go back for him.

'Hurry! Please, hurry!'

'No rope,' Gwionn Leclerc shouted back. 'Hell.' His eyes lit on an oar, stowed under Clemence's bench.

'Mistress?'

Clemence hopped nimbly aside. Leclerc grabbed the oar and staggered back to Arlette.

She helped him lever the oar over the gunwale. Her dress was soaked and stuck to her like a second skin.

Fire Dragon rocked and bucked like an unbroken colt.

'I hope it's long enough,' Arlette said as they took a hard hold of the oar. The fisherman had seen them, and realised that they were offering him a lifeline. He began swimming towards the oar, but Arlette did not think he was going to reach it before *Fire Dragon* had sailed past him.

Gwionn Leclerc flashed her an impenetrable look. His eyes were bright as jewels, and his face was pale, all but for the livid scar which ran like a red weal across it. He looked both unguarded and vulnerable; but in that moment Arlette received the distinct impression that he disliked her. No, it was stronger that that. He despised her. Why should that be? she wondered in confusion. Recovering from her surprise, she returned to the task in hand. 'Can he reach it?' she asked.

'He'll have to,' came the grim answer.

Blinking into the teeth of the wind, Arlette could see the fisherman fighting the sea for his life. Nearer. He was slowly getting there.

'He's almost made it!'

Arlette and Gwionn's fingers were white on the oar.

Paddling furiously, the fisherman broke his stroke to reach for the oar, but he had not swum far enough, and snatched at thin air.

'Come on, man!' Gwionn urged. 'A few strokes more.'

The fisherman laboured on, but he was flagging. A hopeless look entered his eyes.

'Come on!' Gwionn shrieked like a demon. 'You can do it! *Now!* Reach *now!*'

The fisherman lifted his hand. He caught the oar. It slipped free.

Arlette groaned. A crew member ran up to help them.

'Come on!' Gwionn repeated. 'Try again!'

The hand rose and, this time, held.

'That's it!'

For a moment all the fisherman could do was hang over the oar, gulping in great mouthfuls of air, and sea. He coughed, looked up, and his unshaven face broke into an exhausted smile.

'You've got the oar?' Gwionn asked of the crewman.

'Aye, sir.'

Gwionn climbed half astride the gunwale to help the fisherman aboard.

Fire Dragon lifted on a high, rolling wave. A blast of wind hit the sail. Another stay parted, and lashed out, slashing Gwionn across the eyes. Gwionn's hands flew belatedly to protect his face. *Fire Dragon* skewed sideways, and Gwionn Leclerc pitched headfirst over the rail.

His head hit the oar before it hit water.

The fisherman grabbed for Gwionn's tunic, but his swim had robbed him of his speed, and he missed.

Gwionn sank out of sight in the grey, heaving water.

'God, no!' Arlette looked at the sailor. 'Can he swim?'

'Won't do him any good if he could,' the crewman

replied with a callous indifference that chilled Arlette to the core.

'How so?'

The crewman had been joined by a shipmate, who had a rope coiled about his middle. Unravelling it, he tossed it over the side to help the fisherman climb aboard. The fisherman would live to see another dawn, but what about Gwionn Leclerc?

'Squire's out cold, that's why.' The sailor shrugged. 'We can't go about in this squall. He's a dead man.'

Dumb with horror, Arlette peered over the side.

Gwionn Leclerc had surfaced, and his inert body lay face down on the angry sea, rising and falling, rising and falling.

'We can't just leave him! Can you swim?'

'Yes, but I'm no hero. I value my skin. I've a wife and four children.'

Arlette thought quickly. Jehan and Aubrey had taught her to swim in the river by Huelgastel. She had no husband yet, and no children to mourn her. Gwionn Leclerc had gone to such lengths to save the fisherman, and for him to drown because of it was a great injustice. Could Arlette stand by while that happened?

She made a decision. Swiftly kicking off her shoes, she unclasped her belt and stripped off her bliaud, so she was standing on the slippery wooden hull clad only in her linen shift.

The crewman's jaw dropped.

'M . . . My lady?'

The fisherman had his hand on the rail, and was almost aboard.

Arlette turned and ran sternwards. She loosed the rope of *Fire Dragon*'s skiff, and tossed it into the sea.

'My lady!' The helmsman goggled. Captain Potvin was back at the prow: he had seen the fisherman, but had not yet noticed that Arlette had set his skiff adrift.

Hanging on to his tiller like a whelk to its rock, the helmsman had been unable to lift a hand to stop her, and now he guessed her intention.

'No, my lady! It's madness!'

One of the crewmen had read her mind too. He began racing towards her. A determined terrier of a man, Arlette could tell at a glance that he would stop her if he could.

She swung a leg over the gunwale.

When the sailor by the fisherman's oar realised what Arlette de Roncier was about, shock loosed his hold, and the oar fell into the sea at the precise moment the fisherman tumbled on to the deck. 'Christ Jesus, Ivar, stop her!' the sailor yelled.

'My lady!'

'Arlette, no!'

The rain was a thousand pinpricks on Arlette's cheeks, the wind tugged her hair, and Gwionn Leclerc's inert form lay in the water drifting up and down, up and down. Already *Fire Dragon* was surging past him.

Arlette gulped in a lungful of cold Atlantic air, and dived. Before the sea closed over her head she heard the wind wailing in the rigging. Or was it Clemence, screaming for help?

Chapter Fourteen

Sir Hamon le Moine, seneschal of Huelgastel, galloped across the castle drawbridge and into the outer bailey at a cracking pace that was ill-suited to his high position and his silver hairs. He drew rein so sharply his destrier skidded to a standstill, almost catapulting him over his head.

Sir Hamon had ridden out that morning without a care in the world. He had been visiting the law-courts in Vannes for a judgement on a trivial boundary dispute which the count had been unable to resolve with a neighbour.

Aubrey had felt proud of his father. Casual and relaxed in his light wool tunic — the blue one with the silver borders that matched his hair — and a dark red cap, he cut a handsome figure. He looked distinguished and confident.

It was immediately clear to Aubrey that Sir Hamon was returning in a very altered mood. Aubrey took one look at his father's face and, without a word, stepped forwards to receive the horse into his care.

'My thanks, Aubrey,' Sir Hamon said.

Aubrey stared curiously at his father, wondering what had prompted the change in him. Despite the breakneck pace at which he had been riding, Sir Hamon's skin had a grey tinge to it. He should have been flushed and exhilarated. If Aubrey had not known it was ridiculous, he would have thought his father looked afraid.

'What's the matter, Father?'

'I've bad news for the count, and I fear how he'll take it.'

'Bad news, Father?'

But Aubrey was talking to empty space, for Sir Hamon had dismounted and was stalking through the arch into the inner bailey before Aubrey had time to blink.

Sir Hamon found Count François in the mews, feeding his peregrine while he talked to his falconer. The birds were in moult, and the count was itching to hunt.

'How much longer before I can use her, le Bihan? It seems I've been waiting for ever,' the count complained, holding a strip of raw liver up for the bird perched on his glove.

The hawk snatched the meat from his fingers, transferred it to its talons, and began ripping it with her beak.

'She's coming along nicely, mon seigneur. As you see, the tail feathers have grown, but the wing pinions have a little way to go. I think you should wait a while yet.'

'How long, man? How long?'

'At least two weeks, my lord. It would be better if you could leave her for a month, but—'

'Two weeks then,' the count said. 'Good.'

Morgan le Bihan caught Sir Hamon's eyes and shrugged. 'As you wish, my lord,' he said. 'But if she were my bird—'

At that the count met his falconer's eyes coldly. 'Your bird, le Bihan?'

Morgan took a step backwards, but kept his head up. 'I'm sorry, lord. You asked for my opinion, and I gave it.'

'My lord?' Sir Hamon intervened. 'If you have finished here, I need to speak with you.'

Count François threw a frown at his seneschal. 'Business, eh?'

'Yes.'

The count sighed. 'Here, le Bihan, you take her.'

The peregrine was transferred to the falconer's wrist, and the count and his seneschal strode to the north end of the mews.

'You went to the law-courts, and lodged my claim against Foucard?'

'Yes, my lord.'

The count stared at Sir Hamon, and Sir Hamon was aware of a knot of tension tightening in his stomach. The count's hazel eyes could be very penetrating. Even Sir Hamon, who had served this count's father for years felt like squirming under their gaze.

'They move at a snail's pace,' the count said, so gently that Hamon felt his stomach relax a little. 'They won't have come to a judgement on that today. You've heard something else.'

'Yes, my lord.' Sir Hamon hesitated. Even in a mild mood, his lord was a hard man to tell evil news to.

'Out with it, Hamon.'

Hamon put his hand in his tunic and pulled out a scroll. He was careful to keep his voice as neutral as he could. 'Someone has lodged a claim against *you*, my lord,' he said.

De Roncier stopped walking mid-stride, and glanced scornfully at the parchment. 'Someone's lodged a claim against me?' He flung his bright head back, and laughed. 'What claim? Who would dare?'

'If you read this, lord, you'll see.'

The count brushed the scroll aside. 'You've read it, doubtless. Summarise it for me.'

Sir Hamon complied, knowing full well that while the count could read and write, it was a task he found difficult. He always delegated it to others if he could. 'Put

289

simply, my lord, a knight by the name of Sir Gregor Wymark claims to be the legal guardian of one Philippe St Clair, who is at present an infant.'

At mention of the name St Clair, a quiver ran through the count, but since he did not interrupt, Hamon continued.

'He holds that this Philippe St Clair is the legitimate son of Jean St Clair, knight, and Yolande St Claire, née Herevi. He says that, as such, Philippe St Clair should have full rights and possession of the de Wirce dower lands.'

The count's cheeks flooded with angry colour. He had thought St Clair's baby son was dead and buried: Captain Malait had informed him that he had found the infant's grave. Malait claimed to have examined the body, and seen it for himself. 'Those lands were my mother's!' he exclaimed.

'Aye, my lord,' Sir Hamon agreed, irritated to hear that his voice was trembling. 'Everyone knows they were her dowry to your father, God rest him.'

'On what grounds does this knight base his claim, Hamon?'

'Sir Gregor maintains that your mother's dower lands really belonged to Izabel Herevi – she was Izabel de Wirce before she married, and your mother's *older* sister—'

'Damn it, Hamon, I know that. Christ, I thought I'd settled this once and for all at Kermaria.'

Sir Hamon thought for a moment. He had heard the rumours concerning Count François' night foray into Kermaria, but had never investigated the matter, only being thankful that he had not been involved. It sounded to have been a filthy business. If only Count Robert were still alive. A man of honour, one knew where one was when dealing with him, but his son was more slippery than an eel.

'My lord, Sir Gregor has requested that the justiciary take his claim to the highest authority—'

'To Duke Geoffrey?' The count's colour receded. 'Then we have nothing to fear, Hamon, old friend. The duke has other priorities. He takes an interest in his lands only in as much as they bring him revenues. It matters little to him which lord has title where. As long as he has his coffers filled from them, or he gets his knights' service in full, he's happy. Duke Geoffrey shows more passion for the tourneys than he does for his lands.'

Shaking his head, Hamon sucked in a breath. 'I fear you are misled, my lord. Last year the duke had a new assize written into the statute book. It concerned primogeniture.'

The count's cheeks went purple and, rather to his astonishment, Hamon found that he was beginning to derive some enjoyment from his lord's discomfiture.

'You mean the duke has established that rights of succession belong to the eldest?' François finally got out.

Hamon nodded.

'But that's a Norman ruling! Here it is the strongest man who wins. Geoffrey Plantagenet can't bring Norman rulings into Brittany.'

'But he has, my lord. Last year.'

'*Merde*.' The count narrowed his hazel eyes. 'This Sir Gregor is obviously begging for a visit,' he said, and his tone went dangerously soft. 'Where's his holding? Near by?'

'I'm afraid not, my lord. Wymark Manor is in Ploumanach, on the coast in the north of the duchy.'

The count's mouth worked but no more sound came out. Hamon peered over his shoulder to see the falconer watching them curiously, but when his glance crossed with Sir Hamon's, he looked quickly away. Hamon wondered how much of this conversation the falconer had heard. If the count was going to fall into one of his rages, it might be better for Morgan le Bihan if he pretended to have heard nothing.

The count's breath was coming in short, fast gasps. He put a hand to his temple and rubbed.

'Jesu, there's a drum in my head,' he said in a queer, breathless voice. 'That land is mine, Hamon. It's mine, do you hear?'

'I hear you, my lord. But I fear the duke may rule otherwise. If Izabel Herevi was in fact your mother's eldest sister—'

Count François uttered a grunt and clutched at his chest with a freckled hand. He paled, so much and so suddenly that the thread veins in his face vanished. Great droplets of sweat sprang on to his brow. His breath became ragged.

'My lord? Are you ill?'

'It's nothing,' the count gasped. 'A twinge. A moment of nausea. It will pass.'

Hamon laid a solicitous hand on the count's arm. 'Perhaps you should sit down, my lord. You're white as whey.'

'Christ, I'm not ill!' the count snapped, shaking off Hamon's hand. He gritted his teeth and continued with obvious difficulty. 'I'm angry! That land is part of my birthright, and no whelp of St Clair's is going to get it.' He cut short his tirade for a brief moment and struggled for air. The freckled hand that clutched at his chest opened and shut. 'If any man – *any* man, be he high or low – dares gainsay me, I'll fillet him and hang him up to dry.'

In the face of such fury, Hamon could only blink. 'Even the Duke Geoffrey?'

'Especially Duke Geoffrey.'

And before Hamon had time to absorb the astonishing threat that had fallen from his lord's lips, Count François dropped like a stone at his seneschal's feet.

Sir Hamon knelt, and shook the count's motionless body. 'My lord count? Count François, can you hear me?'

Arlette surfaced and spat out a mouthful of brine. The water was cold as death; so icy that it had stolen the air from her lungs. She shook the worst of the water from her eyes, hauled in some air, and scanned the sea for Gwionn Leclerc.

Miraculously, she spotted him straightaway, a few yards away. Her mad scramble to the stern of the *Fire Dragon* had not been in vain. But she lost sight of him almost at once, for the wind whipped the tip of a wave into foam and flung it in her eyes. The rain came down in steady sheets. Her world was all water and she must swim like a fish. Arlette struck out towards Gwionn Leclerc, with no thought in her head except her desire to reach him.

The water was grey, the sky was grey, but a faint yellow glowed behind the clouds — her watery world was a twilight world. Another wave rolled past her, overtaking Gwionn, and Sir Ralph's squire vanished again into the valley between waves.

Sea-spume or rain, or both, blinded her. She swam on, praying she would reach him in time. How long had he been face down in the sea? It could not have been above a few minutes, she had moved as quickly as she was able. Had she been quick enough?

God, or her guardian angel must have heard her prayer, for Arlette found herself lifted on the crest of another wave, and her hand closed about his ankle. The oar the crewman had dropped into the sea floated past them.

Panting, choking on salt water, she managed to turn Gwionn Leclerc over. His face — he would have been handsome before he was scarred — was waxen, but the scar glowed lividly in the weird yellow light. Taking comfort from this, Arlette fought to keep his head above water. In the struggle she pushed herself under before she got the grip right. More surf blinded her, got into her lungs.

Arlette coughed it out. The cold was penetrating the marrow of her bones. She was blinded by wind and spray, unable to stop to see he was breathing. God had helped her get so far. She would have to rely on Him to ensure that Gwionn Leclerc breathed.

Hands grasping under his shoulders, Arlette strained to see the rowing boat. *Fire Dragon*'s half-sail was frighteningly small now, receding into the distance, swallowed up by the storm and being driven heaven-knew-how-many leagues down the coast.

Unlike her father's ship, the skiff had no sail. It was drifting on the grey, white-flecked waves a few yards behind them.

Gwionn came round to consciousness to find his chest was one tight mass of pain. He could neither breathe nor see. He had little idea of his whereabouts. He choked, gulped in some air, and choked again. His vision cleared. He was damnably cold. There was salt on his tongue . . .

Suddenly, memory returned. He had fallen off the gunwale and into the sea. He was drowning. With that thought Gwionn made an effort to move his limbs, but he had been without air for too long and the movement was feeble. The movement, however, slight though it had been, was enough to duck him under the heaving surface of the water.

Something, or someone, dragged him back to the air. He coughed.

'Lie still.' A voice that he was unable to identify because of the storm, spoke urgently in his ear.

His lungs ached, and his vision was not yet clear. While he struggled to regain mastery of his senses, Gwionn had no option but to surrender to the care of whoever was dragging him along.

After some minutes, his hip banged against something hard. He blinked, and made out the side of a cob. He grappled for it.

'You all right now?' the breathless voice asked.

'Yes.' Gwionn clung like a leech to the boat.

The hands released him, and then they came up to rest beside his on the side of the skiff. Small hands; too small, surely, for a crewman's hands?

He turned his head to stare in astonishment at his rescuer.

'You!'

Her eyes were huge in her pale, freckle-spattered face. Her lips were blue, and her red hair trailed and curled like dark water-weed down her back. Arlette de Roncier!

'Can,' she was panting hard, 'can you get in? I'm spent.' Her head lolled against those delicate, aristocratic hands, those hands which he hated, those hands that had saved him.

A wave doused them.

Gwionn forced his numb limbs to respond, and heaved himself up and into the boat. The boat rocked, and he lay on the boards gasping like a fish in a net. From where he lay, sprawled across a pair of oars, he could see her fingertips over the rim of the boat.

Gwionn sat up. His brain cleared as he looked at her. This was the only daughter of his sworn enemy. This was Count François' heiress. He could take his revenge now, and no one would know. He peered through the slanting rain and driving wind. *Fire Dragon* was lost to sight.

No one would know.

He looked at the slender fingertips, the bowed head. She had said she was spent. All he had to do was to prise her fingers away from the side of the boat, pick up the oars, and head for some cove . . .

No one would ever know.

Christ! Why did it have to be her of all people? Arlette

de Roncier, whose destiny was to be countess, had put her aristocratic neck at risk by jumping into a sea that bubbled and frothed like a yeast tub. She had done that to save him, an unknown squire whom she barely knew. Why?

In an agony of indecision, Gwionn stared at what he could see of her hands. He could see her neatly manicured nails. One was broken. Had she broken it, saving him?

One hand slipped from view. And, cursing himself for being a sentimental fool, Gwionn lunged towards her. Kneeling up in the belly of the boat, he took her firmly by the wrist and pulled.

He was full of resentment at the predicament he found himself in. He was only saving her because she had saved him. He was setting the tally straight. This would not affect the settling of other scores. This would not stop him taking revenge for the wrongs that the count had done his family. That was a matter of family honour. He had sworn to avenge himself, and this debt between him and Arlette de Roncier would not be allowed to stand in his way. It was an unfortunate complication, but one he could deal with. This would not affect his plans.

He laid her beside the oars and looked at her. She had fainted. He put his cheek close to her mouth. She breathed. Oddly relieved, he took time to observe her.

She must have stripped off her finery before she had leaped into the sea, for she was clad only in a simple linen shift. The water had made the fabric translucent, and it clung to her breasts. She may as well have been naked before him. He stared for a moment at the twin points of her nipples, before his gaze shifted lower. Her hips were slender. He stared at the dark triangle between her legs which her wet shift did not conceal, before dragging his gaze away.

He wouldn't really want to cuddle her, as he had wanted to cuddle Anna. When stripped, Arlette de

Roncier would not be that special. She was just a bony wench, like any other. But she did have a pretty face, and he would be interested to try her out. Too skinny for his taste, Arlette de Roncier could still arouse his baser instincts, even when lying like a drowned rat in the bottom of the skiff.

But she had saved him and for that reason he had saved her. It would not stop him taking revenge on her if the opportunity arose.

Gwionn reached for the oars, and started to row towards land. It was then that he noticed that he did not feel sea-sick at all.

François awoke to find himself in bed. The first thing he focused on was the great, gory crucifix hanging on the wall opposite. He groaned and closed his eyes.

A cool hand flitted across his brow. 'My lord? My lord? Are you awake?'

Recognising his wife's voice, François reopened his eyes. 'Eleanor?'

Demure as a nun, his wife's fair hair was tucked well out of sight behind a snowy linen wimple. The pupils of her eyes were large in the perpetual twilight of the chamber. A thin sliver of light was slanting down through the window slit, and he estimated it to be after noon.

'How do you feel, my lord? Better?'

François could feel a slight tightness, a tension in his chest, but it was not distressing. Otherwise he felt perfectly normal. 'I'm fine, Eleanor.' He sat up. 'What happened?'

Eleanor gave him one of her gentle smiles. 'I was going to ask *you* that, my lord. Sir Hamon and your falconer carried you in on a hurdle. Sir Hamon said it happened in the mews.'

François grunted and flung back the covers. 'Sir Hamon brought me news concerning an affair I thought I had settled. I remember being angry. And after that . . . nothing.'

A slender hand came up to push the count back against his pillows. 'You should lie quietly for the rest of the day, my lord. I think you have inherited your father's weak heart.'

'Weak heart? Me? Nonsense. Eleanor, let me up.'

But Eleanor could be very insistent in her quiet way. 'No, my lord. This upset has made you ill, and you need time to recover. You will remain here. I will order your dinner brought here.'

'Jesu, Eleanor, don't invalid me.'

'You must rest, my lord—'

'François,' he corrected her.

Another slight smile. 'Very well, François, if you will take your nurse's advice and rest.'

François yawned. He did feel fatigued, and he could use the time to think. He allowed the covers to be drawn over him.

It had been a blow to discover that Jean St Clair's legitimate heir must be alive after all, and even more of a blow to find the infant had an ally in this Sir Gregor Wymark, and that they were taking their claim to the duke. Absently he rubbed at his chest.

'Two can play at that game,' he muttered.

'My lord?'

He looked at his wife. 'Eleanor, did I hear young Venner prattling about some grand tourney the King of France was holding next month?'

'I believe so, my lord. It's to be held near Paris.'

'Do you recall him mentioning that Duke Geoffrey will be attending?'

'Yes, the duke is going.'

François gave a satisfied smile. 'I've a mind to go myself. I'll take Venner, and a handful of men. It would be something of a holiday.'

298

'That sounds a good idea, my lord. You concern yourself too much with matters of estate. It is doubtless that which has made you ill.'

The count nodded, and sank deeper into his pillows. He had never liked the fact that he owed allegiance to Geoffrey Plantagenet. It might be a good idea to send a message to the duke concerning Philippe St Clair's bogus claim to the de Wirce lands. If Brittany saw reason, all would be well. But if not . . . If not, François could seek the French king out at the tourney. If he pledged allegiance to Philip of France, Philip of France would undoubtedly want to reward him. And a suitable reward might be to grant him support over the disputed lands.

And if Duke Geoffrey proved immovable over the question of primogeniture? 'There's more than one way of skinning a cat,' he said, thinking aloud.

Eleanor's fine brows came down. 'François, you have a very unsettling look in your eyes,' she observed. 'What do you mean, "there's more than one way of skinning a cat"?'

One of his wife's long white hands rested on the coverlet. François patted it. 'I've been inspired, wife.'

'You've thought how to resolve this matter that's been plaguing you?'

'Yes, Eleanor. I know exactly how to resolve it.'

In his own mind, the dispute over the de Wirce lands was already settled in his favour. And what he now planned for King Philip's grand tourney would merely set the seal on it, once and for all.

A combination of wind and strong tides had carried the skiff from the *Fire Dragon* down the coast and into the Gironde estuary.

Struggling to bring the little boat safely ashore, Gwionn battled against the storm for what seemed like hours, until the muscles in his arms and shoulders screamed for rest.

They made headway painfully slowly, for he had to fight his way across wave after wave of heaving grey water which seemed to be resisting him every inch of the way.

The boat was filling with water.

Arlette came out of her faint. She moaned, coughed, and sat up. Her features were pinched with cold, but she rallied at once.

'Can I help?' she asked.

'Only one set of oars,' Gwionn answered brusquely. 'Try to bale out the water.'

She did not waste time, and without a word grabbed the bucket tied to the stern of the skiff, and set to work, long hair trailing dark and damp across the linen of her shift.

They struggled past the foot of some limestone cliffs.

'Look!' Arlette pointed. 'At the top of the cliff — I can see the cross of a church, and some other buildings! If we can make landfall there, we will find someone to help us.'

Gwionn grunted, and struggled to bring the row-boat closer to land. The cliff-top was inaccessible from the sea, but farther along to the east he was finally able to make out a rocky beach.

'Keep baling,' he said.

Arlette complied and a little later the bottom of the boat scraped on shingle.

With a grimace of relief Gwionn dropped the oars, and jumped into the shallows. Steadying the boat, he helped Arlette out. They clung to each other for support, and staggered ashore where they collapsed onto the beach.

Arlette regained her breath first, blinking the rain out of her eyes, and thrust back her hair.

'We've been seen. Someone's running towards us,' she announced.

'What?' Gwionn frowned into the gusting wind, and his frown turned into a scowl as he saw a monk clad in the black habit and cloak of the Benedictine order clattering crab-wise across the shale. He had no liking for Black Monks. 'Oh, Christ.'

'What's the matter?' Arlette asked. 'Are you all right?'

'It's nothing,' Gwionn said, as he reminded himself that not all these monks were evil. Just because one of them had taken a bribe from Count François did not mean they were all tarred with the same brush. 'A momentary faintness. It will pass.'

The monk slithered to a halt and knelt beside them, cloak and robes plastered to his body by the wind and wet, tonsured skull glistening with raindrops.

'Praise be to God,' the monk said, crossing himself. He looked at Arlette, and blushed at the near-transparency of her sodden shift. Glancing away, he unfastened his cloak, and threw it around her shoulders. 'Praise God, you're both alive!'

'Barely,' came Gwionn's unsmiling reply. He flexed his shoulders, and groaned.

'I saw you from our church,' the monk went on. 'I prayed that the blessed Saint Radegonde would see your boat safely ashore.'

'Where are we?' Arlette asked.

'Talmont.' The Benedictine pointed in the direction of the monastic buildings huddled on the top of the cliff. 'Our church is dedicated to Saint Radegonde — patron of those in need of an anchor when in peril at sea. I came to offer you sanctuary from the storm. I am Brother Godfrey. And you are . . . ?'

Arlette felt very conscious of her bedraggled appearance, and the fact that under the Benedictine's cloak she was wearing only a shift. She gripped the edges of the cloak together and held her head high. 'I am Lady Arlette de Roncier, and this is Gwionn Leclerc, a squire. We were in my father's ship en route to meet my fiancé when we met with an accident.'

Brother Godfrey frowned. 'Your father's ship? Would

301

that be a square-rigged trading ship?

Arlette nodded.

'I saw such a ship long before I saw your little boat,' Brother Godfrey said. 'It was blown farther down the estuary.'

Arlette climbed to her feet. 'They will be looking for us when they come into port. We must send word that we are safe.'

'Rest assured, my lady, we will do all that we can to help you. But first I think we should find you and your squire some dry clothing.'

'Bless you, brother,' Arlette said, smiling, as they leaned into the wind, and made their way towards the monastery.

Later that afternoon, Gwionn found himself sitting by Saint Radegonde's church high on its cliff above the sea. He stared gloomily into the distance. The storm had died down as suddenly as it had appeared, and the clouds were breaking up. Behind him, ranged around a square, lay the stone built monastery buildings – the guest house, gatehouse, dormitory, cookhouse and refectory.

Gwionn had not seen Arlette for a couple of hours and, despite the fact that he had eaten a substantial meal of fish and lentil potage, with fresh bread lavishly spread with golden butter, he was cursing the fact that they should have been found and taken in by these monks. Had some of the fisher-folk who lived near by found them and taken them to a hostelry, they would doubtless be sharing the inn's common chamber that night, and he would – very circumspectly of course – have begun his seduction of de Roncier's daughter. She had saved his life, and for that he had pulled her into the skiff, but it would not stop him visiting his revenge upon her. Gwionn still wanted her disgraced.

But as matters stood, the monks – it had not taken

more than a few moments at Talmont for Gwionn to realise that these monks were unlike the Black Monks at Vannes – had put paid to this idea. These were good men, dedicated to following God's law. Their guest-house kept male and female visitors carefully segregated. Of course, it was extremely unlikely that his seduction would have succeeded even if he had been able to spend the night with Arlette de Roncier in the chamber of an inn. De Roncier had brought his daughter up to marry Count Etienne. She knew Count Etienne expected her to be a virgin. She would have to be mad to risk losing her position in society for the sake of a tumble in the hay with her knight's squire.

Gwionn sighed. Notwithstanding the likely failure of his plan, Gwionn should have liked to attempt to seduce Arlette. He wanted to *do something*. He must avenge his father, and he did not want to wait for ever to do it.

He had not moved from his spot on the wall, and was still staring out across the estuary trying to see the point at the other side, when the light began to fail.

Suddenly a clattering of horses' hoofs came to his ears, and he turned his head to see Sir Ralph Verdun trot through the gatehouse archway and into the courtyard in front of the church. Trooper Clore, who had Yseult and Star on leading reins, followed him.

Verdun saw Gwionn at once and, dismounting, strode across.

'Leclerc! Thank God you're safe,' the knight said, clapping his squire on the back. 'I never thought to see you again.' He looked anxiously about the courtyard. 'Where's the Little Lady? She is well? We were on the road, combing through the coastal villages in the hope that you had survived, when we ran into a monk from here who had been sent to look for us. He swore you were both well, but until I see her with my own eyes . . .'

Gwionn nodded. 'Relax. She's well. She's resting in the

women's lodgings. I take it *Fire Dragon* made port further down the estuary? Brother Godfrey — the monk who found us on the shore — said he had seen the ship being blown down the coast.'

'That's right. My God, Leclerc, you're a lucky man. I thought you were finished when you went over. And my heart nearly stopped when she went after you. You're sure she's all right? No ill-effects?'

'None, by the look of her. She's a strong girl.'

'We couldn't stop for you, you know,' Verdun said. 'Captain Potvin said it was pointless even trying to turn *Fire Dragon* round. We'd blown half way to Mirambeau before we knew where we were. And as soon as we'd landed we split up into search parties, hoping you had somehow survived and made land.' He beamed. 'Though I'm staring right at you I'm still finding it difficult to believe you're both alive. It's nothing less than miraculous.'

A door clicked shut behind them, and both men turned to find Arlette, humbly attired in a simple brown homespun, emerging from the guesthouse. Seeing Sir Ralph, she came across.

'Sir Ralph! How lovely to see you so soon! I thought it would be days before we managed to make contact with the ship again.'

Shaking his head, Sir Ralph bowed over Arlette's hand. 'No my lady. We were most fortunate. As soon as we put into port, we began inquiring for you along the coast, and we ran into the Benedictine almost at once. Clemence gave me some of your clothes, my lady, and I have brought them with me.'

'That was thoughtful.'

'You are very brave, my lady, to have dived into the sea after my squire,' Sir Ralph said.

'No.' Arlette laughed. 'I'm not brave. I didn't even think about it. If I had I probably wouldn't have done it.'

'You were courageous,' Sir Ralph insisted. 'Not many would have done so, whether they thought about it or not. But you must be tired. Do you think you should be up and about? After such an ordeal, shouldn't you be resting?'

'I've been resting for a couple of hours, but I felt the need to stretch my legs,' Arlette said. The truth was Arlette did feel worn, but lying on the spartan cot she couldn't help reflecting on how narrow an escape she and Gwionn had had. It frightened her to think about it, and she had decided that company would distract her from unpleasant thoughts.

'What do you recommend we do, Sir Ralph?' she asked. 'Ride back to *Fire Dragon* tonight?'

'No. You have taken your share of exercise for today, my lady. I'll warrant you'll be exhausted enough tomorrow without us rejoining the ship today. We'll get a peaceful night's sleep here, and I'll send word to Captain Potvin that we'll leave to join *Fire Dragon* at first light.'

'Very well. I shall take your advice.'

'You're going to rest?'

Arlette smiled. 'Yes, I'll rest. But first I've a mind to take a walk. Would you and Master Leclerc care to explore Talmont with me?'

Some days later, Louis Favell was leading the way along the bank of the Dordogne. He reined in to allow Arlette and Clemence to draw level with him. Poplars and willows in full leaf lined the river, and Arlette's party rode along a well-beaten track which snaked along the northernmost side. It was pleasantly cool in the shifting shade, and Arlette was grateful for the living green canopy which protected them from a glaring sun. The sun was at its zenith, the skies clear. Had they been riding in the open they would have been boiled alive. As it was, Arlette had elected to disregard protocol, and rode without her cloak.

The river flowed west, slow and lazy as a summer

dream. It was a Sabbath, and the river was quiet. Louis had explained to Arlette that on working days the Dordogne would be full of craft — the usual kind being the long, flat-bottomed gabares, or barges, which rowed up- and down-river. The gabares took local oak to Bordeaux, cut into staves ready for making into wine barrels. They returned with Bordeaux or Libourne wine, and salt to season and preserve their food — this last being rare so far inland. Without salt, none of them would survive the winter. The boatmen had to use draught animals — oxen usually — to come up-river, in order to render the Dordogne navigable in both directions. For the few miles where the river was not navigable, the boatmen would unload their cargoes on to pack animals, and proceed to the next stretch of easy water, where they would hire another gabare to complete their journey.

Looking at the peaceful river winding like a shiny grey ribbon along the valley floor, Arlette found it hard to imagine it full of craft and bustle and noise.

A water vole, surprised from a rock in the shallows, whisked into its hole. The fish were swimming near the surface, forming little eddies and ripples on the water which flashed silver in the sun. Here and there, turquoise dragonflies hovered and glimmered, iridescent, impossibly large, like jewels stolen from an emperor's regalia. Flies hung over the water. Swallows swooped to catch them. Arlette wished the swallows good hunting, for although there was shade by the river, there were too many flies. For the dozenth time Arlette brushed some from her face. Poor Yseult was plagued with them. Above the trees, swifts were screeching. Somewhere a goat bleated. A magpie screamed, and flew across their path.

Clemence crossed herself, and Arlette smiled to see her friend scanning the trees to see if she could spot another. One of the sisters at St Anne's had told Clemence that it was unlucky to see one magpie.

'Look, my lady,' Louis pointed across the river.

A rocky white crag soared skywards, high above the poplars. Grasses and shrubs grew in the cracks and ledges, and a couple of stunted oaks had managed to find a hold half-way up, leaning over the river at an odd angle. Most of the cliff was thick with shadows owing to the position of the sun.

'We're almost there,' Louis said. 'In a moment you'll be able to see La Forteresse des Aigles through the trees.'

Nervous now that she was within sight of her new home, Arlette looked again. The crag reared higher and higher, nearer and nearer, until Arlette was seized with the irrational thought that any moment it would fall and crush them all. It made her feel no bigger than an ant.

The trees cleared. And then she saw it. Her fiancé's chateau, commonly referred as La Forteresse, was made from yellow limestone; a sturdy, square-looking edifice which some master builder had managed to throw up on the peak of the crag. Like the cliff-face, the castle's walls were in shade, but even so they formed a solid mass along the top of the cliff. The lower courses looked smooth as butter, offering nothing in the way of grip for a climber. At the top, crenellated ivory teeth gnawed angrily at the sky. Look-outs were posted along the walls, their round helmets were tiny grey blobs against the backdrop of the sky. The middle section of wall rose higher than the rest. Indomitable, that section must be the donjon, or keep, though in Arlette's experience a castle's donjon was usually found at the heart of one or more encircling walls, in the inner bailey.

La Forteresse des Aigles bore no resemblance to Huelgastel; nor for that matter to any other castle Arlette had seen. There were four rows of windows in the blank yellow walls. The bottom two were huge; generous, wide windows, which did not seem to have shutters, and which must flood the chambers with northern light. The windows of the two upper floors were wide too, not as wide as the lower ones, but broader than was common. None of them looked in the least bit secure. But then a man would have to have wings to attack La Forteresse from the north. First he would have to cross the river, then scale the cliff and that sheer wall . . . The windows did not have to be secure, their position ensured their safety. On each level, to the side of the windows, four outlets had left stains on the yellow stone and betrayed the position of the privies. There was no sign of the eagles which gave the castle its name.

In reply to Arlette's question, Louis confirmed that the middle section was the keep.

'And that isolated-looking tower, further along, on its own at the end of the wall?' Arlette asked. 'What's that? It's taller than a cathedral.'

'That's La Tour Brune, the Brown Tower. It overlooks the road from the river. The lower half is used for storage. The top has not been used in years.'

Conscious of a sudden drop in temperature, and an illogical feeling of fear that she could not pin down to any cause, Arlette shivered.

Louis Favell's brown eyes were watching her. 'Are you all right, my lady? You have not caught a chill after your adventure at sea?'

'No, I feel very well, thank you.' Arlette thrust aside her sense of misgiving, and smiled. 'How do we get up there?'

Louis indicated the path in front of them. 'There's a ford ahead. From there, we have to double back before we can climb up to La Forteresse.'

'Good. I am looking forward to meeting your uncle,' Arlette said courteously. She wasn't looking forward to it at all; in fact she had never felt more terrified in all her life. What if Count Etienne didn't like her? What if she didn't like him? Her stomach had turned to water and, despite the warmth of the day, goosebumps were forming on her arms.

'By now the guard will have told him of our arrival,' Louis said. 'He'll be waiting at the gates to greet you when you arrive.'

Arlette swallowed, and urged Yseult towards the ford.

After fording the river, Arlette asked for a moment to tidy herself. She did not want to meet Count Etienne with the dust of the road in her hair. She must look her best, and must not disgrace her family. Louis Favell was agreeable.

While the men squeezed the last of the wine from their wine-skins, Arlette splashed her face with river water. Clemence re-braided her hair, and pulled out Arlette's blue silk veil and golden circlet from her saddlebag.

'Are you going to wear your velvet cloak, my lady, the indigo one?' Clemence asked. Lately Clemence had taken to addressing Arlette more formally, and when Arlette had questioned this, Clemence had insisted that it was fitting for her elevated status. As long as the girls remained close, Arlette did not mind how she was addressed.

'Thank you, Clemence. I shall most likely suffocate in it, but I have to put on a good show.' A sudden doubt assailed her. 'Do you think I should have had a red one made?'

Red, while it would have clashed most vilely with Arlette's hair, was one of the most costly dyes. It was only ever worn by high-ranking nobles or princes.

Clemence regarded her mistress's hair in unfeigned horror. 'Red, my lady? I should think not. You don't need a red cloak to convey your status. Your hair does that for you.'

Arlette grinned and, as she took the indigo cloak, she gave Clemence a swift hug. 'Oh Clemence, I am glad you came with me.'

309

When Arlette was sufficiently composed, she gave the signal for them to continue, and the weary horses toiled up the winding path to the top of the crag.

On the summit, the road forked: one way led to the castle; the other curled left into a thicket of oaks. Here, there was naturally no cliff to protect La Forteresse; instead a deep fissure split the rock on which the castle was founded. This natural chasm was spanned by a drawbridge which led to the gatehouse – two short, round towers, complete with arrow loops and a portcullised archway which gaped like an open wound between the two round gate-towers. La Tour Brune, which Arlette had noticed earlier, was on their right hand, at the far corner of the curtain wall. Square, it was perched on the white rock with the cliff falling away on one side, and the ravine on the other. Three times the height of the gatehouse towers, La Tour Brune cast a long shadow.

Sensing a cool stable, and fresh buckets of water, the horses trotted briskly across the bridge.

The ravine was dark and deep. Its sides were lined with jagged rocks, and ferns grew in the crevices. Arlette could not see the bottom from where she was on the bridge. Another good defence. Arlette wondered if the split in the rock extended along the south and west walls of La Forteresse. If so, it must be the best sited castle in Christendom.

A cluster of people was waiting in the courtyard. Arlette had been told the count was fifty. There was only one old man in the reception party by the gate. He was wearing crimson.

'My uncle,' Louis said.

Heart thumping, Arlette gripped Yseult's reins. Her face felt stiff, but she tried to keep her smile in place. Resplendent in his long tunic, and wearing his sword and polished brown boots, no doubt Count Etienne thought to do her honour. He wore a skull cap which matched his tunic.

Arlette exchanged glances with Clemence. 'Red,' she mouthed.

Clemence gave a little shudder. 'Not for you, my lady.'

Arlette guided Yseult towards him.

The count stepped to Yseult's head. He had a slight limp. Close to, he looked older. His face was very lined, the skin dry and marked with liver spots. Count Etienne's hair was grey, and fine, and when he turned his head to gesture to a tall woman standing behind him to come forwards, Arlette could see he wore it long at the back.

He looked up, smiling, to offer Arlette his hand to help her down. He had lost two of his teeth, one from the top and one from the bottom. His eyes were green, and struck a faint chord of recognition. Arlette gave the count her hand. It was a pity about the teeth, she thought, for he had a pleasant smile.

Rising to the occasion, Louis Favell spoke formally. 'My lord Count, may I present the Lady Arlette de Roncier? My lady, Count Etienne Favell.'

'Lady Arlette,' the count's eyes crinkled up at the corners when he smiled. 'Welcome to La Forteresse des Aigles.'

'Thank you, Count Etienne.'

When Arlette dismounted, she found the count was of average height, though his shoulders were stooped. In his prime he would have stood a little under six feet. She wondered if he had been handsome, before he had grown old.

Thank God for that kind smile, Arlette thought, as she allowed her betrothed to lead her towards the other people standing in the centre of the courtyard.

Like Huelgastel, the curtain wall had a soldier's walkway running around the inside, the several men-at-arms were at their posts, curiously eyeing the group in the centre of the yard. The stables and other outbuildings were built under the walkway; again this arrangement was familiar to Arlette from Huelgastel. Some stable hands ran up to lead the horses away.

'My dear, allow me to present Sir Gilles Fitzhugh.'

Arlette inclined her head at a tall, good-looking knight. He had blond hair, and eyes as blue as her own. 'Sir Gilles.'

'Sir Gilles is my castellan. And this,' the count gestured impatiently at the tall woman, 'is my nephew's wife, Lady Petronilla.'

Arlette was hard-put not to gape like a peasant, for Lady Petronilla was gowned like a Byzantine princess in the Favell colours, murrey and gold. She wore a stiff burgundy brocade bliaud, with a heavy gold floral motif painted on to the cloth. It fastened at the side with gold laces. The neckline was round and encrusted with embroidery — again in gold thread. Even Lady Favell's jewellery matched the Favell colours, for a garnet necklace glimmered on her white throat, and her fingers were weighed down by several heavy garnet rings.

Her brown hair was coiled up in a bun, and her headdress and barbette had been fashioned from gold cloth and was shaped like a crown. Large pearls — surely they could not be genuine — had been sewn at intervals around the headdress.

Arlette felt conscious of her own thin circlet holding her veil in place. She tilted her chin up. Seized with an impulse to laugh out loud, Arlette was careful to avoid Clemence's eyes. There was a message here for her from Lady Petronilla, but Lady Petronilla was suffering in order to deliver it. There were unsightly sweatmarks under her arms, and moisture on her upper lip. In this heat, Lady Petronilla must almost be fainting.

Lady Petronilla showed two rows of small, perfect teeth. 'My lady. We are so honoured to meet you.'

Lady Petronilla's eyes were grey, and hard as pebbles, and looking into them Arlette was left in no doubt that the smile on Lady Petronilla's lips was as fake as the pearls on her headdress.

She would pay Lady Petronilla back in her own coin. 'My lady,' Arlette murmured. 'What a magnificent gown. You do me too much honour.'

The Byzantine crown jerked back, and the pearls glinted in the sun.

Count Etienne, manlike, did not appear to have noticed anything amiss.

'Lady Petronilla,' he said. 'Would you be so good as to escort Lady Arlette and her maid to their chamber?'

Petronilla Favell stretched her lips in another counterfeit smile. 'It would be my pleasure, Count.' She bowed her head. 'Come this way, Lady Arlette.'

Chapter Fifteen

That evening, Count Etienne held a feast in Arlette's honour.

Head whirling with the noise and her own nervousness, Arlette sat at the head of the top table in a cushioned chair with carved arm-rests that was grander than her father's chair in Brittany. Count Etienne sat beside her in a chair the twin of hers.

Scanning the hall for a friendly face, Arlette caught sight of Clemence on the next table. She had been seated with Gwionn Leclerc, a small kindness which Arlette knew she had Sir Ralph to thank for. Clemence was as much a fish out of water as she was in La Forteresse, and Clemence would feel more relaxed with Gwionn Leclerc – someone she knew, if only a little.

The hall of La Forteresse was square and held almost twice as many people as did Huelgastel's. The din was appalling, and they had not even broken the meats yet. Dogs barked, dishes clattered, voices rose and fell and people shrieked with laughter. The fireplace was as large as Huelgastel's, but this fire did not smoke. The rushes had been sweetened with thyme and lavender. The hall walls were whitewashed, and hung on two sides with large tapestries. One of them was a magnificent picture of King Arthur with his knights of the round table, larger than life, while the other captured a hunting scene.

The count's colours, the burgundy and gold that Lady

Petronilla was wearing, were emblazoned upon gonfanons which swayed gently from poles spaced two yards apart around the walls. Beneath the gonfanons, liveried stewards stood to attention. Some had napkins over their arms, indicating that they would serve the high table. One grasped a wooden staff.

The ceiling was so lofty that the beams were almost lost to sight. On the wall facing Arlette was a minstrels' gallery. It was currently occupied by three men and a girl. The men all had instruments: one had a lute, one had a flute, and one a harp.

'You would like to hear them?' the count asked, having seen where her gaze rested.

'Please.'

Count Etienne raised a languid hand. The steward with the staff thumped it on the floor, and the din lessened.

Immediately Arlette felt some of the tension drain out of her.

'Better, eh?' the count smiled.

Arlette nodded and tasted her wine. It was rich and sweet, and she liked it.

The minstrels played a plaintive air while the dishes were brought round by the liveried stewards. The girl sang.

Fingers clasped round her silver goblet, Arlette stared at the girl, feeling faintly envious of her freedom.

'You like Michelle's song?' the count wondered.

'Very much, but . . .' Arlette hesitated. One of the packmen who brought ribbons to Huelgastel had told her about the trouvères, as the female troubadours were called, but this was the first time Arlette had seen one. The packman had made them sound vaguely disreputable. 'Does she travel all over the Aquitaine singing her songs?'

The count smiled his kindly smile, and his eyes twinkled. His eyes were as kind as his smile, Arlette thought. She was beginning to feel more relaxed in his

316

company. Count Etienne reminded her strongly of someone, but Arlette could not place the resemblance.

'She does. With her father, that's the lute-player, and her brother, the flautist. I've hired them for a month or so. Do you like music?'

Arlette nodded. 'Indeed. My father doesn't have an ear and, after my mother died, he always said he'd lost interest in music. It's a long time since I've heard anything other than the Ave Maria being chanted in chapel.'

'If you like them, I'll set them on permanently. But don't judge them on one song alone. Listen to their repertoire.'

'Thank you, Count Etienne.'

Louis Favell sat between Arlette de Roncier and his wife. Petronilla, who was sharing a trencher with her husband, picked at her food. She regarded the count's fiancée with baleful eyes. Louis hoped she was not going to make trouble, for Petronilla had a sharp tongue when she had a mind, and by the sound of it, Arlette de Roncier was not one to take an insult lying down.

Petronilla watched the newcomer ceaselessly. Arlette's head was turned towards her betrothed. The chit was pretending to listen to him, clasping her wine cup with fingers that trembled. Something sparkled in the light from the flambeaux, and Petronilla's eyes narrowed. A gold ring with a large, dark red stone hung slack on the de Roncier girl's narrow, shaking fingers. No semi-precious garnets for her: the Favell betrothal ring had a blood red ruby in a claw setting. It needed to be made a great deal smaller before it would fit her properly. It would have fitted Petronilla without needing to be altered at all.

Lady Petronilla thinned her full lips and tried not to stare at the ring. She had always liked that ring. She had hoped that one day it would come to her, and seeing it on that red-haired chit was enough to put her off her meat. It clashed odiously with her vulgar hair.

Petronilla waited until the feast was well under way before speaking to her husband. She was careful not to mention the ring. 'How old's the girl meant to be, Louis?'

'Fifteen.'

Petronilla tossed back her veil, and her keen grey eyes narrowed. 'She doesn't look it. Look at them, Louis. Do you think it's disgusting?'

'Disgusting?'

'Spring wedding winter. And spring looks terrified out of her wits: look at her, she's pale as porphyry—'

'That's her natural colour. Besides, it's the way of things, Petronilla. She's an heiress, and my uncle will have her. She brings him more than the de Roncier lands. She brings him hope. He will try for an heir.'

'And you? Will you simply accept it?'

Louis sighed. 'We must accept it. If God wills it that I shall be my uncle's heir, so be it. But if He wills that the count fathers children on Lady Arlette, then we must accept that too.'

Never! Petronilla thought. She hadn't married Louis for his manor. She had been considering paying a visit to the village wise-woman, Lisette, but she had thought it best to delay until she had seen the girl for herself. She would delay no longer. If Louis refused to look after his interests, she would do it for him, and she knew Lisette's stock of herbs was comprehensive enough to answer every need.

'She hangs like a dog on his every word,' Petronilla said. 'She's desperate to please. It's not very dignified.'

'I disagree. She shows respect for my uncle. That, too, is as it should be.'

Petronilla's pointed elbow dug her husband in the ribs. 'Would you like it if I were like that, Louis?'

Louis grinned, and under the table his hand slid to caress his wife's thigh. 'I like you just as you are. I wouldn't change you for the world.'

Briefly, Petronilla's lips curved. 'Sometimes, Louis, you're almost romantic.'

Again Lady Favell's grey eyes swept the board and, as they came to rest on Arlette de Roncier once more, the smile faded. A calculating look entered her eyes. Her maid had told her an interesting snippet. Perhaps there would be no need to visit Lisette, if there was a grain of truth in what she had heard.

'Louis?'

'Mmm?'

'My maid brought me some gossip concerning Lady Arlette. Of course, I told her that it couldn't be true, but it did worry me. She said the girl had passed the night, alone, with Sir Ralph's squire.'

'That gossip is pure myth.'

One of Lady Petronilla's plucked brows made a hook.

'A storm blew up,' Louis explained. 'There was an accident and Lady Arlette and the squire went overboard. They saved themselves by climbing aboard the ship's rowboat. Somehow they got ashore on their own. The wind blew the main vessel south. When we landed we didn't hold out much hope that either of them had survived, but we sent out search parties. Sir Ralph discovered that they had taken refuge in a Benedictine monastery.'

'So they were not alone together?'

'In a monastery? With scores of monks to chaperone them? Is it likely?'

Gwionn Leclerc was sat on the next table, below the dais. Petronilla looked him over. 'He's very handsome,' she commented, 'for all that he's blemished. You are sure that nothing, er, untoward went on between them, before the monks found them?'

Louis rubbed the bridge of his nose. 'It's no use stirring that pot, my girl.'

Petronilla spluttered. 'Stirring which pot? I'm sure I don't know what you mean.'

'Yes, you do. You're implying that Lady Arlette and Gwionn Leclerc . . . It's unthinkable, Petronilla. She's a count's daughter. And if you care to observe them, you'll see that, when she's not looking, he often scowls at her. It's my belief he dislikes her.'

'Perhaps he's jealous that she's to wed.'

Louis shook his head. 'Leave it, Petronilla. Arlette de Roncier is as pure as the driven snow. And now that she is to be lodged here, we can ensure that she stays so.'

'It's a long time until the wedding, Louis,' Petronilla said lightly. 'Anything could happen between now and the spring.'

Louis Favell's brown eyes became shadowed. 'Petronilla, you won't interfere, will you?'

'Interfere, Louis?'

'You won't do anything foolish to stop this marriage?'

Petronilla laughed, a high tinkling sound, which drew Lady Arlette's gaze. 'Be serious, Louis, what could I do? I'm only a woman. I have no power whatsoever.'

Favell looked unconvinced.

'Louis, how long are we staying at La Forteresse?'

He shrugged. 'I haven't broached that subject with my uncle. Why?'

'One look at that poor child should tell you why I'd like to stay. She needs a friend, someone in the family to help ease her into her new position. If we were to stay here, I could be that friend. It could only be to our advantage to befriend her. I could show her around.'

The anxiety failed to leave Louis' eyes. He knew his wife well. 'You would?' he said doubtfully. 'I'm sure she could do with some help. But you promise to behave yourself. Can I trust you not to meddle?'

'Of course, Louis,' his wife assured him, as a small smile crept across her lips.

Towards the end of August, a bow-backed sentry, Gosvin,

stood at his ease with his helmet pushed to the back of his head. He was posted by La Forteresse portcullis, and was idly listening to the incessant whirring of the crickets, when he heard a single set of hoofbeats coming slowly up the rise from the river. His co-sentry Fulbert, whose turn it was to take an unofficial catnap, was slumped against the base of La Forteresse walls, prudently tucked out of sight, snoring.

Gosvin straightened his stooping spine, adjusted his helmet, went to stand directly under the portcullis, and stood to attention.

A knight rode into view. He was wearing his mail coat, but his head was bare, and his dark curly hair lifted gently in the warm afternoon breeze. Although the knight travelled alone, and there were so many saddlebags stowed about his horse that he could not possibly be contemplating taking any military action against La Forteresse, Gosvin knew his duty.

'Hola, Fulbert,' he roused his companion.

Fulbert was on his feet before he had rubbed the sleep from his eyes. He took his place at Gosvin's shoulder.

The knight's horse, a black gelding, clattered on to the drawbridge. The crickets faltered, then ceased.

'Is this La Forteresse des Aigles?' the knight asked, casting a weary eye over the castle. His horse's dark flanks were foamy and glossy with sweat. They had had a long ride.

'It is. Your name, sir?'

'Venner. Walter Venner. I've brought a letter for Lady Arlette from her stepmother, and grave news for Count Etienne.'

'Any proof of identity, sir?' Gosvin asked.

'Do you know the de Roncier seal?'

Gosvin nodded.

The knight drew a scroll from one of the saddlebags.

321

Gosvin blinked at the seal, stood aside, and waved the knight through.

'In you go, sir. Fulbert will show you where to go.'

'My thanks.' The knight hesitated, a crease in his brow. 'You wouldn't happen to know if Sir Ralph Verdun has remained here, would you?'

'You mean the knight that keeps watch on Lady Arlette?'

'That's the one.'

'He's here,' Gosvin answered.

'And his squire, Leclerc?'

'He's here too.'

The crease on the knight's forehead vanished, and he spurred the black gelding into the bailey.

There was a moment's silence before the crickets resumed their song.

In the solar, Arlette was sewing seed pearls on a pair of kid gauntlets she was making for her betrothed. Lady Petronilla and Clemence were with her. One of the servants came in with the letter.

'It's for Lady Arlette,' the servant said, in response to Petronilla's inquiry. 'From Huelgastel.'

'A letter from home? For me?' Arlette snatched the scroll eagerly from the servant's hands. 'Who brought it?'

'A knight, my lady. He's speaking with Count Etienne now.'

Arlette hoped the letter was from her father, but one glance at the easy flowing script on the scroll disabused her of that idea. Her father's handwriting was never so neat. The eagerness faded from her eyes.

'Not bad news, I hope,' Petronilla asked, grey eyes frankly curious.

'I pray not. The letter's in my stepmother Eleanor's hand,' Arlette told her. 'I'll read it upstairs. Would you excuse me, Lady Petronilla?'

'But of course.'

Arlette rose. 'Clemence, will you accompany me?'

Clemence set her sewing aside.

Petronilla sat thoughtfully, listening to the two girls' voices as they climbed the stairs. When she could hear them no longer, she thrust the muslin veil she had been working on into her workbasket and marched off to find Count Etienne. If de Roncier had sent a knight with news from Huelgastel, she was not going to be the only one left in the dark.

Lying on her bed with Clemence, Arlette broke the seal and began to read.

The Feast of St Augustine, 1186.

Daughter, I greet you well with God's blessing
and mine, and trust you have settled in at La
Forteresse des Aigles.

Your father has bid me put quill to parchment
and wishes me to send you his fond regards.

Let me tell you our news. Not long after you
left us, your father took sick. He was angered
and fell down in a fit. I feared he may have
your grandfather's affliction, a weak heart. But
I think that my diagnosis must have been wrong,
so there is no need for you to worry unduly
over him. Your father made a miraculous
recovery, so miraculous that he was able to
insist on travelling to Paris to attend King
Philip's tourney. He seems to have enjoyed his
holiday, despite the black shadow that was cast
over it by the tragic deaths that took place
there.

Have the sad tidings reached the Aquitaine?
I feel sure they must have. In case they have

323

not, Walter has been charged with informing
Count Etienne.

No one knows how it happened, but our Duke
Geoffrey, brother to Duke Richard who holds the
Aquitaine, was unhorsed in the mêlée and
trampled on. He died. Your father took part,
though he refused to describe the mêlée to me.
But I had it from Venner, who also participated,
that it was a veritable bloodbath. I shudder to
think that it could just as easily have been your
father who was unhorsed. We should both be glad
that Count François does not usually spare the
time to attend the tourneys. I agree with the
bishops, they should be banned. King Henry
Plantagenet does not permit them in England.
What a terrible irony that his third son should die
at one in France.

Duke Geoffrey's widow, Constance, is
rumoured to be with child. Now that your future
is assured, I know I can confess to you, dear
daughter, that the sin of envy grips me when I
think of her state. I envy her for the child she
carries, though I do not envy the duchess her
future. She has no son and, if this child is male,
she will have to fight off the wolves in order to
keep the inheritance in one piece. She will have to
be both father and mother to it. Poor woman.
She deserves your prayers and mine.

So, we in Brittany have no Duke. What's to do?

I worried at first that these events might have a
bad effect on your father's health. But,
astonishingly, your father is unruffled by all this.
He is quite recovered from that strange fit he fell
into. In fact, he is in fine spirits, the best that I
have seen him in since we were wed. I would that
you could see him.

There, you have the main substance of my
tidings. Little else of note has occurred.

Your father's wolfhound bitch has had a litter
of four pups. She had them in our bedchamber
and they chew everything, including the bed legs.
You would like them. I cannot say I dislike them,
but one of them got hold of my missal. There was
not much left when I found it. I have asked your
father if the pups may be moved to the stables.
He has agreed.

May Almighty Jesu preserve and keep you till I
write next.

Your affectionate belle-mère,
Eleanor, Countess de Roncier.

When Arlette had finished, she glanced at Clemence.
'Would you like me to read it to you?'

'Please. But first . . . is . . . is there any mention of
Morgan?'

Arlette made her voice soft. 'No. I'm sorry, Clemence.
But if you like, I'll ask news of him from my stepmother
when I reply. Would you like that?'

Clemence bit her lip, and Arlette saw her swallow. It
was some moments before she answered. 'No. No. I think
it would only prolong the agony, don't you?'

Arlette had no answer to that, so she picked up her
letter and began to read it aloud.

Count Etienne told Petronilla that a room had been found
for Sir Walter Venner adjoining the solar. Sir Walter had
gone to collect his belongings.

On the pretext of checking the knight had enough linen
for his needs, Petronilla peeped into the chamber. It was
empty. She hovered on the stairs outside. Chamber was
something of a misnomer for Sir Walter's quarters,

because they only measured four foot by six, and the truckle bed took up most of the space. There was one slender window slit and, even at noon, the room remained gloomy. In recent years it had only been used for storage, but someone had entered it recently and left a torch burning. The whitewash was coming off in flakes. Sir Walter's chamber was more spartan than an anchorite's cell.

She did not have to wait long. A brown, tousled head came into view, and a pair of hooded hazel eyes. Sir Walter's head was immediately followed by the rest of him. He had roped in Gwionn Leclerc to assist him, and the two were talking about Count François.

Their conversation cut off abruptly when they noticed Petronilla, and something about their manner set her spine tingling. It was not that they were being furtive exactly, but she formed the clear impression that her presence on the stairs was unwelcome.

She moved quickly forward, all smiles, and offered Sir Walter her hand. 'I heard there was a handsome new knight in the castle. You must be he,' she said effusively. 'Welcome. I am Petronilla Favell.'

Sir Walter's cheeks went bright pink. Dropping his saddlebags, he bowed awkwardly over Petronilla's hands. 'Sir Walter Venner, at your service, my lady.'

Murmuring an appropriate reply, Petronilla stepped over the threshold into Sir Walter's room. 'I've come to see that you've everything you need. Linen, and so forth.'

Sir Walter hesitated in the doorway, with such an embarrassed expression on his face that Petronilla could have laughed out loud. This prim knight was afraid of flouting convention. He was reluctant to enter the chamber in her company.

'You are kindness itself, my lady,' Sir Walter said stiffly. 'But Count Etienne has already asked a man-servant to prepare the room.'

The very subtle stress Sir Walter put on the word 'manservant' managed to convey to Petronilla his disapproval of her entering his room.

Petronilla walked towards him, and gave a soft sigh. She lifted a hand and let it rest very lightly on Sir Walter's chest. Looking as frightened as a startled rabbit, Sir Walter took a hasty step backwards. Because she was enjoying herself, Petronilla ignored this slight. She did so love to tease a man, especially when he had not the first idea how to respond. She loved to see a man discomposed. Louis had been like that, until he had grown used to her.

'And you're quite sure I can't help you in any way?' she asked in her most seductive tones.

Sir Walter backed on to the landing, and trod on Gwionn Leclerc's toes. 'N . . . no, my lady. I have everything I need, thank you.'

Petronilla gave him one of her best siren smiles. 'I am so glad,' she murmured. 'But do let me know if you think of anything, anything, that you might want.'

'I . . . I will.'

Head up, Petronilla sailed down the stairs.

Walter Venner rolled his eyes, and hefted his saddlebag into his room. 'Bring those things in, Gwionn, for Christ's sake, and shut the door after you. Who is that woman?'

'Lady Petronilla. Louis Favell's wife.' Gwionn closed the door.

'What a ghastly creature. Is she always like that?'

Gwion grinned. 'Not always. You must have taken her fancy.'

'God's bones! I hope not.' He sat on the bed, shaking his head. 'A ghastly woman. Quite ghastly.'

'I gather you've something to tell me concerning our mutual enemy?' Gwionn asked.

Walter's head came up. The hazel eyes were full of concern, and not a little fear. 'H . . . how did you know?'

Gwionn laughed. 'I can't believe a knight would

volunteer to act as de Roncier's message-boy unless he had some ulterior motive. You've something to tell me.'

Just then, Petronilla, who had been waiting on the lower landing until she heard the door latch fast, glided quietly up the stairs. Positioning herself so she could see anyone else who might chance to pass that way, she put her ear to the door.

On the other side of that door, Sir Walter made room for Gwionn on the bed.

'Sit down, man,' he advised. 'This tale is tangled, it will most likely take some time for you to unravel it.'

Gwionn sat down.

Pulling gently at one of his ear-lobes, the knight began. 'Now the first part of the tale is no secret. I told it to Count Etienne, and you will no doubt have to suffer hearing it all over again when you go downstairs. It concerns Duke Geoffrey of Brittany, and a tournament held near Paris in the middle of August.'

Unable to see any possible link between his affairs and those of Duke Geoffrey's, Gwionn frowned. 'But Walter—'

Walter held up a hand. 'Hear what I have to say, all of it, before you make any judgements.'

'My apologies.'

'The tournament was a grand one, everything was done on a lavish scale. Half the nobility of Christendom went to it. De Roncier attended, and I accompanied him. It went well at the beginning: there were few casualties, but most of them were minor injuries, broken legs or collarbones and the like.'

Gwionn nodded, visualising the scene. His uncle, Waldin St Clair, had been a tourney champion, and he had described the destriers thundering up the lists, great hoofs throwing up clouds of sand and sawdust. Gwionn could imagine the screams of encouragement from the crowds in the stands, the hoots of derision as a knight was

328

unhorsed, and the splintering of wood as lances flew apart. He could see the fluttering pennants, the brightly caparisoned horses.

The knight continued. 'Yes, all went well up to the mêlée. I took part, as did Duke Geoffrey, de Roncier and many others. As with all mêlées, it was chaos from start to end, every man for himself. But the trumpets were sounded early this time, because Duke Geoffrey fell from his horse and was trampled to death.'

'Holy Mother! The duke died?'

Walter nodded soberly. 'Aye, and as luck would have it, I was quite close to him at the time. I saw what happened.' He lowered his voice. 'It was de Roncier.'

Gwionn clutched at Walter's arm, eyes very bright. 'What do you mean it was de Roncier? Are you telling me de Roncier killed Duke Geoffrey?'

Walter met the intense gaze steadily. 'The duke was riding a coal-black monster that most of the other destriers would not go near. But de Roncier rode a terror to equal the duke's.'

Gwionn nodded. 'I remember that horse in Huelgastel stable. He's half-devil.'

'Quite. To continue. De Roncier chose his moment well. Everyone was distracted because one of the squires had taken it into his head that his knight was being victimised. A noble fool, the squire broke the rules and ran on to the field. He paid for his foolhardiness with his life. He took a spear in his chest, and toppled like a tree. God knows how he thought his intervention would have helped his knight. He wasn't even mailed. Then up runs someone else, one of the stewards, I suppose, to drag him away. This distraction caused a momentary lull, and drew all eyes. You can imagine it, Gwionn, everyone was put off their stroke. I would have been distracted too, if it hadn't been for the duke's black.'

Totally absorbed in the knight's tale, Gwionn frowned. 'The duke's destrier?'

'That's it. The brute bit my gelding, who did not take kindly to such treatment. That was when I noticed how close I was to the duke. He hadn't seen me, he was watching the wretched squire writhing about in the sand. I pulled back, and as I did so de Roncier took advantage of the lull and spurred up to the duke, ostensibly to take a look at the lad. De Roncier had his sword out. I saw it catch the sunlight, and I don't know how he did it, he timed it to perfection, but as we re-engaged and the clanging started up all around, I'll swear he cut the duke's girth. It was so nimbly done, I hardly realised what I was seeing. Then the fight swirled on, and de Roncier disappeared into the mill.'

'Surely someone else saw de Roncier cut that girth?'

'No. Only me.'

'Did you see his face?'

'No. He had his visor down. We all did.'

'But you'd swear it was him?'

'I know that terror he rides. And his colours. It was de Roncier. There was nothing I could do. I tried to warn the duke, but someone came between us, and moments later it was all over. The duke had his destrier rear up, to avoid a charge from a group of Burgundians who had banded together. His saddle slipped, he fell, and by that time the Burgundians were upon him. They tried to draw back, but they could not. The mess they pulled out of his armour afterwards was scarcely recognisable as a man.'

'And the saddle?' Gwionn asked, leaning forward. 'Surely someone must have noticed that cut girth?'

'Not at first. There was too much weeping and wailing for anyone to think of examining the saddle. I did though.' Walter shook his head. 'But to no avail. It had been trampled almost to a pulp. And the girth was missing. No trace of it anywhere. He covered his tracks well.'

Gwionn let out a slow whistle. 'By Christ, Walter. I don't know what to say. I shall have to think. But I'm eternally grateful to you for bringing me this information.'

Walter lifted his broad shoulders, and gave a wry smile. 'I could hardly have put this in writing.'

'Hardly. But you didn't have to come all this way to tell me. I thank you, with all my heart.'

'You're not the only one to suffer at de Roncier's hands. He killed my brother,' Walter said simply.

Gwionn rubbed the back of his neck. 'It doesn't make sense, Walter. There's something missing, something we don't know about. De Roncier never does anything unless there's profit in it. How does he benefit from Duke Geoffrey's death?'

'I can answer that.'

Green eyes met hazel. 'Go on.'

'This touches on your family. Someone had brought a case against de Roncier to court. They claim to hold title to the de Wirce lands – you know, the lands that Marie de Wirce brought Count Robert de Roncier when they married—'

'I know.' Gwionn's mouth was grim. 'That she-wolf stole those lands from my grandmother, Izabel. She stole from her own sister.'

'I surmised as much. When Count François heard that this case was being brought, he was so enraged that he had a seizure. I was curious as to what would affect him so strongly. I made inquiries. Sir Gregor Wymark is bringing the case on behalf of his ward, Philippe St Clair—'

'Philippe! Alive! My little brother – alive!'

Walter smiled. 'Good news, eh? Makes something of a change for you, I think.'

'It does indeed.'

331

There had been a time when Gwionn had been jealous of his baby brother, well aware that, as his father's legitimate son, it was Philippe and not he who would stand to inherit his father's lands. But his jealousy had been burned away on the day that de Roncier had attacked Kermaria. It seemed petty now, that old jealousy of his. It warmed his heart to hear that Philippe was alive. Other heart-warming thoughts rushed in on him.

'The only way my brother could have reached Sir Gregor's manor in Ploumanach,' he said, face alight, 'is if my sister Gwenn reached there safely. Mary was right!' Gwionn grinned at Walter, and gripped his shoulder. 'Both my sisters and my brother must have survived their flight.'

'I am glad, for your sake, Leclerc.'

'Everything slots into place.'

Walter nodded. 'Even down to de Roncier's cutting the duke's girth.'

'You run ahead of me. Explain.'

'Last year, the duke held an assize, and the laws of succession in Brittany were brought in line with those of Normandy. When there is a question over the matter of succession, preference is now given to the eldest child.'

Gwionn gave a shout of delighted laughter. 'Primogeniture! By Christ, I would have given my last penny to have seen de Roncier's face when he discovered that!'

'Hush man,' Walter glancing obliquely at the door.

'My apologies,' Gwionn said, lowering his voice. 'Listen, Walter. Of the two de Wirce sisters, my grandmother was the eldest. The courts would have decided in her favour.'

'Precisely. And that, I suspect, is why the duke was killed. Count François hopes to have the assize overturned now the duke is dead. Frankly, having seen the duke's lady, I doubt that he'll be successful. The Duchess

Constance is a formidable woman, and I think she'll enforce her late husband's laws.'

There was a thoughtful silence, then Gwionn said quietly. 'The de Wirce lands are not great, Walter. Not when you consider the rest of de Roncier's holdings. I find it hard to believe he sets so much store by them.'

'It's pride, I think. He won't let go of what he believes is his.'

'How many people has he killed to uphold that pride?' Gwionn asked. 'And the latest, by your account, a royal prince? Walter, that man has to be stopped.'

'I agree. But how?'

The door latch rattled, and lifted, and the two men on the bed exchanged glances.

'My God,' Walter said in a frantic whisper. 'If de Roncier learns one word of our conversation, we're dead.'

As the door swung open, Walter snatched out his dagger and sprang behind the door.

A woman entered. Walter had only met her once but he knew her immediately. It was Petronilla Favell.

She stood in the confined space in front of Gwionn, and spoke without turning round. 'Sir Walter? Do take that blade from the back of my neck and come out of there. You know you're not going to kill me. You're far too chivalrous to harm a helpless woman.'

Helpless? This woman was about as helpless as the Medusa. But she was right. Walter could not kill a woman in cold blood, even if he put his own neck at risk by letting her live. Sheathing his dagger, he emerged.

'How much did you hear?' he asked bluntly.

Petronilla Favell's hand came to rest on his chest. 'Everything.' Her smile was wide and predatory.

'Oh, Jesu,' Gwionn said, hand inching to his dagger hilt.

With a sick lurching in the pit of his stomach, Walter recognised that Gwionn did not have any chivalrous scruples. Gwionn was more than ready to kill to save his skin.

'No, Gwionn,' he said urgently. 'That is not the answer.'

'But she heard everything! She admits it! What else can we do?'

'You can think, for a start,' Lady Petronilla intervened sharply. 'Gentlemen, you and I have much in common. We should be allies, not enemies.'

Gwionn Leclerc's green eyes narrowed. 'How so, my lady?'

Lady Petronilla smiled winningly at Walter, whose face felt as hot as a furnace. 'If you would be so good as to shut the door, Sir Walter, I'll explain why.'

Chapter Sixteen

St Andrew's day dawned at Kermaria, and brought with it a sharp frost.

The reeds and rushes, half frozen, stood stiff and brittle on the flats, unmoving in the light wind which had dropped considerably since the night. Then it had blown steadily, a cold north-easterly, and its freezing breath had left a thin skin of ice on the wetlands.

Nimble as a goat despite her expanded belly, Anna trod the narrow trackway between the boggy patches with the sure-footed confidence of one who had been born and bred on the marsh. She was looking for an eel-trap. Since Father Yann had brought her to Kermaria she had explored every inch of its terrain, for this was Raymond's home, and while she familiarised herself with all Kermaria's aspects, Anna felt closer to her husband. While the child within her grew, it had been her way of keeping faith with him.

Father Yann had taken her directly to Madalen's cot, a humble, much patched dwelling; one of a number of villagers' cottages which clustered untidily around the manor's perimeter wall. If it were not for the fact that Kermaria's stone curtain wall formed the fourth side of these houses, she doubted they would have stood for long. As it was they looked as if they had been trampled on by some vengeful giant. Anna knew all about Count François' dawn raid on Kermaria, and the damage he had done and, like most of the other cottages, Madalen's — which must have stood near the heart of a battle — still bore the scars. The door frame was cracked, so the door no longer shut close, but worse than that Anna could see fire damage to one of the walls abutting the manor wall. It was nothing that a man who was good at carpentry could not mend, the blackened timbers could easily have been cut away and replaced. But they had been allowed first to crumble and then to rot, until a gap as wide as the blade of a sword had formed between the curtain wall and the cottage wall, and rain and wind and snow could ease their way into the room. High up the stone wall, near the crack, a thick carpet of green moss had established itself. It would be very cold in winter.

It had been a warm spring evening, though, the day Anna had arrived at Kermaria. Madalen had been eating a light supper of the hard black bread that was the peasants' staple food, and a broth with a pungent fishy aroma, overlaid with the smell of turnips and onions. Madalen must be using up the last of the winter's store of vegetables, as fresh cabbage and leeks and peas would be available soon. Her brother Joel, who shared her cottage, was with her. A long-handled reed scythe leant up against an upright bundle of reeds, and Anna decided these must have been cut some months since and not dried properly, for she could see, and smell, mildew.

Recognising both Madalen and Joel, Anna had clutched her basket and belongings and smiled nervously. When brother and sister regarded her with cold, unresponsive brown eyes, her smile faded. Their clothes were more threadbare than she remembered, more dirty, and Madalen's homely face was thinner, etched with new, deep lines.

'Here's Anna, Madalen,' Father Yann said brightly. 'She needs your help.'

Madalen looked up from her potage, glanced

assessingly at Anna's belly, and said flatly, 'I doubt *I* can help, Father.' The hard gaze shifted to Anna's face. 'Are you carrying his baby?'

She did not seem in the least surprised, but her bluntness embarrassed Anna, who flushed. 'Yes.' No need to say who 'he' was.

'Wouldn't he marry you?'

Feeling her flush deepen, but unwilling to break her promise of secrecy to Raymond, Anna hesitated.

Father Yann stepped up to Madalen's table. 'The lad loves her, and has pledged himself to her before me, but he went away before he knew of her condition.'

Madalen's brown eyes regarded the priest steadily. Anna thought she saw the ghost of a smile flicker across Madalen's mouth, but was not reassured. It was an amused smile rather than a warm one. One corner of the house was crammed with half-finished wickerwork — among them a duck's nesting basket, an egg basket with no handle, and a bird cage with the roof half complete.

'Raymond Herevi's gone to Huelgastel?' Joel inquired.

'Yes,' Father Yann said. 'He's searching for his siblings.'

Madalen's laugh was incredulous. She shook her head. 'He won't find them there.'

Anna forgot her awkwardness. 'Why not? What do you know? You told Raymond you had no idea what had happened to them.'

Madalen spooned in another mouthful of broth and, chewing vigorously, shrugged. 'I didn't, at the time. But later, when he'd gone, I had words with Klara, who had worked as a maid in the manor. She told me that Raymond's sister escaped with the children.' Amusement lit Madalen's brown eyes for a second. 'Went down the privy, they did, and ran into the forest. So you see, Raymond won't find them at Huelgastel.'

Anna turned to Father Yann and gripped his arm. 'Did

you hear that, Father? His family got away safely. Do you think he found that out before he went to the Aquitaine? He can come back now, surely. There's no need for him to stay if his brother and sisters are not held by the count.'

'Use your head, girl,' Madalen sounded impatient. 'You can't believe the only reason he went to Huelgastel was to find his family. Master Raymond is out for revenge.'

'He'll come back soon. I know it,' Anna said with conviction.

Madalen opened her mouth and her hard brown eyes looked at Anna for a long moment then, abruptly, the reed-cutter's broad face softened and she shut it again.

'What do you want us to do, Father?' Joel asked.

'Look after Anna. Since learning of her condition, her father has washed his hands of her, and I cannot see her reduced to wandering the countryside like a beggar. She loves Raymond Herevi. She is carrying the grandchild of Jean St Clair, and it's right that she should be sheltered at Kermaria. I know the villagers think highly of you. If you accept her, the others will too. Will you help?'

'I can work,' Anna put in. 'I'm used to field work—'

'Not many fields round here. We work the marshes, and trade for our provisions.'

'I'm willing to learn. I'm strong and—'

'Pregnant?'

The flush was back, burning her cheeks. Anna lowered her head. 'I'll do my best. I'll not be a burden.' She raised her head and stared at Madalen. 'Please help me, Madalen. I've nowhere else to go.'

Madalen leaned her elbow on the table and rested her chin on her reed-scarred hand. 'Do you honestly believe Raymond will come back for you?'

'Of course! He promised.'

Madalen sighed. 'Raymond Herevi always talked very prettily, Anna. You wouldn't be the first girl he's

338

broken promises too, you know.'

'It's different with me,' Anna said, and folded her lips together.

The brown eyes regarded her steadily. 'Yes,' Madalen said, slowly. 'I think that it is. You've committed the sin of fornication, and yet you've managed to get a priest on your side, one who has witnessed Raymond pledge himself to you. Marriage is a pledge of sorts, isn't it?'

Struck dumb, Anna thought of her promise to keep silent and didn't reply.

Neither did Father Yann. His hand went to his cross, and his long fingers caressed it, as though he were seeking guidance.

Joel shifted uneasily on his bench. 'Madalen,' he began uncomfortably.

His sister ignored him. 'You're more than pledged to Raymond Herevi, aren't you, Anna?' the reed-cutter pressed. 'You're married, and Father Yann married you.'

'I'm not!'

'No?' Madalen laughed. 'If you two could see your faces. Neither of you are good liars.'

Anna could see it was hopeless. There was no keeping the truth from Madalen.

'It's true,' Anna admitted, after a pause. 'But Raymond made me swear to keep our marriage a secret.'

Now that he was not being put in a position where he was being forced to lie, Father Yann's tongue loosened again. 'It's in my mind that the lad sought to protect Anna and any child she might have from de Roncier. As I said, he went away ignorant of her condition, but the possibility of there being a child must have crossed his mind.'

'You must not tell anyone,' Anna said. 'For his sake, the son of your dead master, you must promise.'

Joel and Madalen exchanged glances, and nodded.

'We promise, girl,' Joel said, reassuringly. 'Your secret's safe with us.'

'And Anna may stay here? You'll put a roof over her head?'

Madalen's broad face was split by a slow smile. 'Aye. She can rest here.'

Joel rose and, taking Anna's basket from her, set it by the bundle of mouldering reeds. 'Welcome to Kermaria, girl. We'll not turn the mother of Jean St Clair's grandchild out of her home.'

'Bless you both,' Father Yann said as he left.

Anna was given a large bowl of broth.

'She could live in the manor,' Joel said thoughtfully while Anna ate. 'With Klara, and some of the other women.'

'The manor! It's wrecked. De Roncier made sure of that.'

'We could clean it up.' Joel's face brightened. He had been the cook for the household when Jean St Clair and his family had occupied the manor. Joel had been taught by Raymond's mother, Yolande, and had enjoyed his work. His life had seemed empty since he had not had a household to cater for. 'Kermaria's never recovered since de Roncier attacked it. The whole village has suffered, we've all lost heart. Perhaps if Anna moves in – and she is carrying St Clair's grandchild – the place will come to life again. St Clair brought it back to life before. Maybe this is what we need, Madalen.'

And so it had been.

The villagers had accepted Anna easily. Kermaria was an out-of-the-way place, with no resident priest to prick the villager's consciences. There were some monks from a nearby cell in the forest – St Félix-in-the-Wood – but their visits to the chapel were infrequent, so Anna had not had to run the gauntlet of righteous indignation at her apparently unblessed state.

The manor itself was a mysterious place: tower-like, it had cellars and vaults for storage, and over this a knight's hall, whose lime-washed walls were scuffed and marked and bare of wall-hangings. Above the hall, reached by a twisting stair, was a solar, and topping that a guard's walkway and guardhouse. This latter was unmanned, and had been for some time. A small chapel stood next to the house; in the yard in front stood a well. There was a moat, but it was full of weeds and dead grasses, and a couple of raggedy hens pecking for seeds. The place looked virtually derelict.

Anna had helped shift the broken and smashed furniture out of the manor house, into the yard and on to a bonfire. She had helped sweep the floors clear of leaves and dust. Jafrez, the village carpenter who had taken to the bottle since the massacre at which his lord had been killed, had been prised away from his bottle, and the empty shell of a building had rung with hammering from dawn till dusk. The doors, some of which had been knocked off their hinges and lay where they had fallen, had been rehung. Other doors, battered almost to kindling, had been patched where possible, or renewed. Charred and mouldering wall-hangings were dragged from the walls, and they too were flung on the fire.

The shutters on the windows were repaired, and scraped and oiled sheepskin − poor man's glass − was stretched across the narrow window frames.

Anna and the St Clairs' maid, Klara, made a straw mattress − large enough for them to share until Raymond Herevi came home − and moved into the solar above the hall.

The months passed.

Anna had come to enjoy her life at Kermaria − as much as she could enjoy a life that was empty of Raymond. But it was a queer life, rattling around the huge, empty manor house with Klara, like two peas in an otherwise empty pod. There was hardly a stick of furniture, though Jafrez did knock a table up for the girls

— St Clair's trestles had apparently all been burnt by de Roncier. The villagers spoiled her, bringing her gifts of eggs, and game or fish from the marsh. And although Anna trusted Madalen and Joel to keep news of her marriage to Raymond secret, the mere fact that she was carrying Jean St Clair's grandchild was enough to ensure that she was treated as though she was lady of the manor.

Klara acted as her maid and after Jafrez had finished work on the manor, Joel and he started work on the cookhouse. Joel started cooking again. Madalen told Anna he had lost heart after the massacre, but now that Anna was here he came to life. He cooked for Anna and Klara, for himself and Madalen. The villagers brought him their dough, and he baked it for them in the manor's round brick oven.

Anna, used to a life of hard physical toil, became restless, so Madalen who, now that Joel had broken free of his depression, had more time on her hands, taught her how to cut reeds. She took Anna up the estuary to where the withy beds were, and demonstrated how to cull the bendy green willow shoots, though she did not permit Anna to do that work, because of her pregnancy. Anna was shown how to strip the willow, which she did till her fingers bled and did not mind it, for she felt happy at Kermaria and wanted to repay Madalen for her kindness in persuading the villagers to take her in. She learned how to weave baskets, and eel traps, and lobster pots for sale to fishermen at Locmariaquer. She made a pair of wicker stools for her and Klara to use at the manor.

Her pregnancy advanced. Her body became very ungainly. Klara cosseted her. And now, St Andrew's tide was upon them. The babe would come any day.

Anna had been forbidden to work which was why she was walking on the marsh. As she picked her way along the path, the wind died away completely and Anna wondered if any lady had ever been so pampered as she had been in recent months. No work. It was unthinkable that her hands should be idle. She had always had something to do. Even a real lady would have had work, for a real lady would have had linen to mend and shiny satin wall-hangings to make, but Anna had no knowledge of such things, only having been taught to cobble together the coarse wool weaves to make simple, workaday garments for herself and her family.

She had made the baby's clothes weeks earlier from a gift of linen sent from her mother via Father Yann.

The ground, normally spongy, was slightly frozen, and crunched under Anna's feet before it gave way. The cold made her breath hang about her like smoke from the smokehouse that Joel had constructed in the manor yard. A line of geese trailed untidily across the sky, where a grey mass of clouds hung low on the horizon. Anna thought of snow, but she did not think the clouds were dark enough for that, nor was it so cold, though her fingers, poking out of the woollen bandages that she had wrapped like fingerless gloves round the palms of her hands, were blue. Her toes felt like tiny blocks of ice, for all that she had stuffed straw into her boots to keep them warm.

A clump of silver birch trees lay to Anna's right. Their bark was sloughing off in large silver flakes, and their leafless branches formed a delicate black trellis through which she could see the sky. When Anna reached the tallest tree, she stepped off the path. This was where she had left the eel-trap. Madalen had assured her that this was a good time of year to catch eels, and the best time to eat them.

Squatting down on the edge of the marsh – she could no longer bend so great was her belly – Anna drew out her trap. It was heavy, and full, with two – no – three wriggling black eels. They were fat ones, so there would be more than enough for Joel and Madalen as well as Klara and herself to have baked eel for supper. If there was any over, Joel could try smoking it; smoked eel would make a welcome addition to their diet in the cold winter months ahead.

Holding the eel-trap firmly in one hand, for Anna was feeling squeamish today and had decided to ask Joel to kill her eels, she began retracing her steps. It was then that she heard the sound. It was scarcely audible at first, so faint that she dismissed it as her imagination, a mere trickle of notes which hung for a second on the dank November air.

Then she heard it again. Another shimmer of sound, like ripples on a river in summer when the water leaps and dances over the stones on the river bed.

Anna looked about her. Ahead stood a clump of alder. Next to the trees a squat cluster of buckthorn reached their spiky fingers to the sky. The reeds whispered, and a mallard paddled out across a stretch of water that was smooth as silk. Anna's eyes, for no reason that she could put her finger on, were drawn back to the alders. At their base lay a dark shadow.

The sound floated out across the wetlands. Being all lightness and sunshine, it did not match the chill heaviness of the day. Anna walked toward the alders. She could see the dark shadow clearly now: it was a length of patched brown canvas stretched out over two poles to form a basic tent; a young man was sitting cross-legged on a blanket in the shelter, playing a small harp. A grey wisp of smoke trailed upwards from his camp-fire.

The sound drew her, so she forgot all caution and her feet did not stop until she was two yards from the harpist, who was lost in his tune, and did not hear her.

He had wiry brown hair, and long fingers which moved up and down the harp as though he were caressing it. His harp was painted red. His eyes were focused on infinity.

'Good day,' Anna said, and half of her mind wondered why she was being so incautious. She did not usually address strangers. But a harper would not harm her surely? And from where she was standing she could see the top of Kermaria tower. If it became necessary, all she would have to do would be to shout and Joel or Jafrez would come running.

The harper looked up, and his gaze slid briefly over Anna's belly which protruded from her cloak. She drew it closer about her and he smiled. His eyes were blue like a summer sky — but then with his music that only seemed natural. He was wearing a sheepskin jerkin, and bound leather trousers, and a moth-eaten velvet skullcap.

'Good day.' His voice was pleasant and friendly, and his hands flowed over the harp, so the music streamed on as he spoke. 'Where are you from?'

Anna waved down the track towards the manor. 'Not far. I live at the manor at Kermaria. What lovely music you make.'

'You're from the manor? Are you its lady then?'

Anna laughed. 'I wish I was.'

The harper sighed, and lifted warm blue eyes to Anna's. His fingers continued to draw glorious chord after glorious chord from his harp. 'I wish you were too, pretty lady. Then I could ask you a boon, and you in your generosity could grant it to me and I would be happy all winter.'

He stopped playing abruptly, and set the harp aside. With a theatrical gesture he indicated that Anna could sit down beside him. 'Pray be seated, sweet lady.'

'Thank you.' Anna warmed to the harper's flattery, and his half-joking manner, and grimaced ruefully. 'There is more of me than I'm used to, and I do get tired.'

He gazed at the trap she held. 'What have you got in there? Eels?'

Anna nodded, and looking curiously at the harp, leaned forwards to touch the strings. 'Tell me, sir, what boon would you ask me, if I was lady of the manor?'

'I'd ask you if there was a minstrel at your manor. I'd ask you if you needed a jester. Why, for a lady as beautiful as you — ' he inclined his head at Anna, and she saw that one of his teeth was cracked — 'for someone like you, I'd be prepared to be a slave — your devoted slave. But I'm sure that a lady like you would have slaves enough, and no doubt you don't need another.'

'What's your name?'

'Barthélemy, Barthélemy le Harpour, at your service.' Another little bow of the head. 'And you?'

'I'm Anna.'

'Anna . . . ?'

Anna tried not to flush. 'Just Anna.'

Barthélemy winked. 'Well, just Anna, do you think your lady would give a warm welcome to a minstrel if I escorted you back to your manor?'

'It . . . it's not like that.' Just then a severe pain tugged the muscles of Anna's womb. She gasped, and clutched her belly.

'What's the matter?'

'I . . . I . . . it's nothing. I'm sure it will go away again.' Anna struggled to rise. The pain eased. She picked up her eel-trap. 'I think I'd best be going back now, Barthélemy le Harpour.'

'It's the baby isn't it?' he asked, frowning. 'Your baby's coming.'

'I think so. But babies don't come quickly, so it can't be for a while yet. That was the first pain. All the same, I think I'd better take my leave—'

Anna gasped, went grey, and dropped instinctively into a crouch.

'Ah, God! Barthélemy! It hurts!'

'Jesu, lady. I'd best help you get back to the manor. You won't get far on your own if it hurts that badly already.'

The contraction went quickly, and with his help Anna

346

hauled herself to her feet. 'Thank you. Yes. We'd best be quick. I didn't know the pains came so quickly at the beginning . . . Oh, no! Not again. Barthélemy! Help me!' She dropped into the squatting position again.

Barthélemy felt a nervous sweat break out on his brow. A sinking sensation in the pit of his stomach told him that there was no way that he could get this girl back to her manor in time. Her baby was going to be born in his tent, and there was nothing he could do to prevent it. Barthélemy was not sure that he could cope with this situation, it was certainly not one he would have chosen to find himself in, but he had three sisters − all older than him − and he had listened to their chatter often enough to have grasped the rudiments of childbirth. Was that enough to see him through this?

He noticed the sweat had broken on Anna's brow, and a glassy, other-wordly expression had come over her eyes. He came to a decision. He would have to do his best.

He went down on his haunches and took her hands in his. 'Anna? Anna, can you hear me?'

'What?'

Dazed, pain-filled eyes looked up at him.

'Your baby's coming. You'll have to trust me. Can you trust me?'

She gave him a valiant smile. Her hands shifted and gripped his like a vice. Anna was fitter and looked healthier than any of his sisters. Barthélemy hoped that this would make it easier for her, and him.

'Yes.' Anna groaned. 'I'll trust you. I'm not quite ignorant. I've seen a babe being born at home. Between us we should know what to do. Oh, Barthélemy. It's like a knife.'

'I think that's a good sign,' he said, crossing his fingers. 'I think it's fierce because you're strong.'

'I should have had some warning,' she gasped. 'I could have got back.'

'It's happening swiftly, because you're fit.'

'I'm afraid.'

'Don't be. I can go to the manor for help.'

Her grip became agonising. Barthélemy bore it without a murmur.

'Don't leave me! Stay with me. Go for help later.'

'I'm here. Try to relax. Here, let go of my hand for a moment, I'll make a place for you to lie down.'

Anna gritted her teeth against a contraction, and nodded. 'And put some . . . water on to boil.'

The harper ducked into his tent and, after a few moments' flurried activity, Barthélemy led her under the canvas. He had piled up his spare set of clothes to form a pillow for her. He removed Anna's cloak, and added that to the pillow. Anna sat down, and tried to lie back.

Another contraction tightened Anna's belly. She bit her lip in an attempt to prevent herself from crying out, but this pain was worse, it felt as though her insides were being torn apart.

Barthélemy set a pot of water on his fire.

An agonised groan slid from between Anna's lips. 'Barthélemy!' she panted. 'It's like rats are eating my entrails!' She struggled to get up.

He was at her side at once, a gentle, long-fingered hand pushing at her shoulders. A hand that reminded Anna very much of Raymond's hand, being soft and white, and not calloused by hoe or spade or reed-scythe.

'Lie back, Anna. Don't fight it. It must be coming soon. Will you let me look?'

One part of Anna felt shy and shamed by Barthélemy's suggestion, but another part – the part of her that had taken over while her labour was upon her – could see the sense in his suggestion. Nevertheless she shook her head.

'No. You don't understand. I'm not fighting it. It's the lying back that's fighting it. It's slowing it down, and that makes it worse. 'Let me up . . . ah, Jesu!'

He didn't try to stop her, for which she was thankful, for Anna was in no condition to fight for what her instinct told her she needed. Panting, in between pains, she glanced at her companion. His high cheekbones jutted out of cheeks that had gone pale as marble, his brown brows had formed a worried line, and his hands were shaking.

'What do you want, Anna?'

'Out, out. I have to get outside.'

Between them they levered Anna out of the tent, where she squatted on her haunches and hugged her belly. At her side, Barthélemy supported her.

'Christ, Anna. Will it work like this?' His voice trembled. As far as he knew, women gave birth in bed, lying down, not squatting as though they were relieving themselves on a privy.

'Yes.' Anna was flooded with a sense of relief. As soon as she had gone down on her haunches, the pains had stopped being pains and become just sensation — extremely powerful sensation, sensations that she would not like to feel every day, but sensations that she could cope with. Having neither the words nor the energy to explain this to Barthélemy, Anna said simply, 'It feels right.'

She hitched up her skirts, and began pulling off her close-fitting hose.

Still supporting her, Barthélemy glanced at the ground. Coarse marsh grasses and dead fern, no fit cradle for a babe.

'Anna . . .'

Panting all the time now, she saw where his eyes were fixed. 'My cloak. Get my cloak,' she gasped.

Swift as lightning, he obeyed her, and between them they folded the cloak and spread it over the damp ground.

Anna smiled her thanks at Barthélemy, and gave a

strangled groaning sound that the musician in Barthélemy noted had a different tone to all the other moans she had made. 'Hold me from behind,' she gasped. 'For as long as it takes.'

Her voice had changed too. There was an urgency to it that brooked no contradictions. Barthélemy did as he was told.

'Hold my skirts out of the way if you can. I can't—'

And then Anna gave another of those strange, strangled sounds that seemed to come from within her core, and after that she spoke no more with words.

Barthélemy knelt up behind her, holding her under her arms. From time to time he felt her body shudder and shake with the effort of giving birth. He was terrified. He was exhilarated. It was very animal, very exciting. The sounds were extraordinary, but natural, and he marked them all. Occasionally Anna gave vent to a grunt or groan, and these sounds were entirely bestial. He wondered why it did not revolt him. As he grasped Anna's skirts, and braced her body, he could feel her perspiration running down his hands. He prayed the babe would be hale and whole.

Anna's thigh muscles juddered, and she seemed to thrust her body against him. Barthélemy tightened his grip. Suddenly she gave a clear, high cry, and drew in a breath. Her body sagged.

And then Barthélemy heard a note from a new set of lungs; a cough, a choke, followed by a thin mewling like a day-old kitten. The mewling gathered strength, until it was fully fledged. Anna's baby was crying. Her labour was done.

Barthélemy craned his neck to see. And there, in the nest they had made of Anna's cloak, lay her baby. The cord was still attached, the baby was covered in a film of blood and mess, but it was alive.

'We did it!' Barthélemy gasped triumphantly, and eased

Anna on to her side on the cloak. 'We did it!'

Anna smiled gratefully at Barthélemy, and reached for her baby. It was a boy.

'Jean,' she said, picking him up and lifting him to her breast. 'His name is Jean.' Exhausted, but happily cradling Raymond's son, she closed her eyes as Barthélemy dealt with the cord. 'Barthélemy, have you anything to drink?' she asked sleepily. 'I'm parched.'

Anna's stamina amazed him. She slept for an hour, wrapped in Barthélemy's cloak, and then got up. The baby was swaddled in one of Barthélemy's tunics.

'What are you doing?' Barthélemy asked, thinking of his Norman sisters. His sisters would surely have seized their chance to lie in bed for a week after having given birth. But his sisters were daughters of an impoverished knight who had too many children and could not afford to clothe them all. Barthélemy's father had been only too relieved when his youngest son had announced he was going off to make his fortune as a minstrel. Anna was not the daughter of a knight. She was a peasant girl, but Barthélemy admired her more than he had ever admired his sisters.

'Going home.'

'Shouldn't you rest?'

'I'll rest at home.'

'Sit down, woman. You might faint and fall in a bog.'

'I never faint.'

He smiled, a charming, practised, troubadour's smile. 'You've never given birth before, have you?'

'No.'

'Sit down then, while I pack my things.' He hesitated. 'Or is it that you're ashamed of me?'

'Ashamed? Why should I be ashamed of you? I've only just met you, and already you've proved yourself a true friend.'

351

'Your lady won't beat you for bringing a stranger to the gates?'

Anna's lips curved, and her brown eyes danced. 'I won't be beaten. And you're welcome to stay for as long as you like.'

Barthélemy had not been looking forward to the idea of sleeping in the open now that winter was drawing on. Anna's invitation was exactly what he had been praying for. Unable to believe his luck, Barthélemy stared at her to ensure she was not teasing him. 'Careful, sweet lady, lest I take you up on that. It's a cheerless bed I have under the stars in winter.'

'My manor is no palace,' Anna warned him.

'Your manor? I thought you denied being its lady?'

'So I did.'

Anna bent a loving gaze upon her sleeping baby's face and, seeing that he was forgotten for the moment, Barthélemy shovelled his belongings into his pack, and struck camp.

Barthélemy found that Anna had not lied to him about there being no lady at the manor, although the inhabitants of the village treated Anna for all the world as though she were its mistress. It took some while for Barthélemy to fathom out the reasons for this, for Anna made no bones about her humble background as daughter of a peasant farmer from Locmariaquer.

Barthélemy was given a straw pallet in the hall, and he slept there in splendid isolation, while Anna and her 'maid', Klara, slept in the solar. Anna told him she felt much safer knowing he was sleeping downstairs. Barthélemy felt lonely, but they had rooted out a couple of moth-eaten blankets, and he was warm at least. All in all, he reckoned himself lucky to have found a haven for the winter.

Klara was a buxom wench with a thick hank of honey

brown hair hanging down her back. She liked the sound of her own voice, and so Barthélemy had no difficulty worming information out of her. It was she who told him that there had been an ancient feud between the lord of the manor, Jean St Clair, and a powerful Breton baron. This feud had ended badly for Jean St Clair, who had been killed. His family had fled, seeking sanctuary. But Barthélemy also discovered it would take him some time to plumb all of Kermaria's mysteries, for even when he had winkled as much out of Klara as he could, he sensed there were more dark secrets.

The villagers were quite soppy about Anna's baby, and Barthélemy learned that the infant was Jean St Clair's grandson – hence her choice of name for the child. But where was the baby's father? Where was St Clair's son? Had he abandoned Anna whom the villagers were treating with all honour? Or would the day dawn when he would march across the bridge and acknowledge his son, as Anna clearly believed? Barthélemy wondered at his interest in the matter, but found that he cared about Anna's future. He wanted her to be happy. It must be because he had been there the day her child was born.

Still, Barthélemy had all winter, and fathoming out Kermaria's secrets would speed the passing of the gloomy, tedious winter nights.

Come spring, he would be back on the road, but in the meantime, it amused him to wonder. All in all, he was glad his harp had drawn Anna to him.

Barthélemy stayed at Kermaria until the warmer weather came. He had grown fond of Anna, and felt more of a pang than he liked to admit at their parting.

Anna walked with him as far as the bridge over the weed-filled moat, a sleepy baby Jean draped over her shoulder. She sat on the low bridge wall.

'Farewell, Anna, and thank you for your hospitality.'

'It was a pleasure. Besides, you have repaid us in full by sharing your music and teaching us all your songs. Everyone enjoyed it. Your visit has been something of an event.'

'It was the least I could do.' Barthélemy hesitated, and a slight flush stained his cheeks, which Anna, whose attention was on her baby, did not see. 'And if you ever find that you develop the wanderlust, Anna, I'd be glad for you to come with me. You have a sharp ear, a clear voice, and you're a good mimic. You could do worse than become a trobiaritz.'

'A trobiaritz? Me?' Anna's laugh was disbelieving. 'I don't have that sort of a voice. Only aristocratic ladies become trobiaritz. I'm too common.'

'With your ear, it would only take you a couple of heartbeats to copy their tones,' Barthélemy told her, adjusting the straps which held his back-pack and harp in place.

Anna shook her head, rocking herself ever so gently so that her baby would stay quiet. A sparrow landed on the bridge, picked up a piece of straw and flew off with it. Her eyes followed the bird's flight. 'Next winter, if you find yourself short of lodgings, we'd be delighted to have you here.'

'You're very kind,' Barthélemy replied. 'I might take you up on that.'

'Where will you go first?'

'South. I shall go to Nantes, and then I'll make my way to Poitiers and then—'

Anna stopped rocking Jean, and snatched at Barthélemy's arm. 'You go to the Aquitaine?'

A queer, knowing smile twisted Barthélemy's lips. 'Yes. I've not been there, but the Aquitaine is the place where musicians are valued above all else.'

'You might see him,' Anna murmured.

Barthélemy affected not to have heard her. 'Hmm?'

'You might see Raymond.'

'Come with me, Anna. And then you might see him for yourself.'

Barthélemy had learnt that Raymond was the father of Anna's child, but he had no idea that they were married. He thought it likely that Anna's lover had discovered her pregnancy before abandoning her.

One hand stroking her baby's back, Anna hesitated. 'Would that I could . . .'

Catching the wistfulness in her tone, Barthélemy pressed her. 'Anna, you could come with me. What's to stop you? I'd look after you. I'd be pleased if you came.'

'I'd be a nuisance.'

'Oh, I wouldn't let you be idle. You'd be another act in my repertoire. They'd love you.'

Firmly, Anna shook her head. 'No, Barthélemy, you're very kind. But I cannot leave here. Jean is too young and too precious to hazard with a pedlar's life. And I should stay here in case Raymond returns.'

'Very well. I'll say goodbye.'

'God be with you, Barthélemy. Barthélemy?'

'Aye?'

'If . . . if you do run across Raymond, will you give him a message for me?'

'You know I will.'

'Tell him Anna loves him, and tell him about Jean. Ask him to come home.'

Barthélemy leaned to press a chaste kiss on Anna's cheek, and made as if to move off. 'I will.'

'And Barthélemy . . . ?'

'Aye?'

'You remember he's calling himself Gwionn Leclerc?'

Barthélemy bit down a bitter smile. Anna had spent the winter singing eulogies about Raymond Herevi, and Barthélemy remembered every word of them. 'I remember.'

'If there's some reason he can't come home, and you do come back to winter here, perhaps you could take me to him — next spring, that is, when you set out again.'

Barthélemy's face lightened. 'Are you saying that if I find your Raymond, next spring you'd be willing to come with me as my trobiaritz?'

Gazing fondly at the infant dozing over her shoulder, Anna nodded. 'Certainly. At least till we reach Raymond. Jean will be bigger then, and more able to adapt to the wanderer's life.'

Solemnly, Barthélemy turned Anna's face to his, and his blue eyes gazed for a long moment into hers. 'Very well, Anna. Since you ask me, I'll find your lover and come back to take you to him. And you'll be my trobiaritz. Agreed?'

'Agreed.'

'I'll seal our bargain with a kiss.'

Barthélemy le Harpour leaned forward and kissed Anna full on the lips. He was gentle, but insistent, and he took his time about it. Then he pulled himself away, and walked jauntily down the road, whistling a love song as he went.

Confused, Anna lifted a forefinger to touch her lips where he had kissed her.

She stared after the harper long after he had vanished behind the hawthorn hedge that screened the bend in the road.

Chapter Seventeen

Spring 1187
*Duchess Constance of Brittany, whose husband Geoffrey
had been killed at the tournament the previous summer,
gave birth to a son, Arthur. The Breton people rejoiced,
and all over the duchy the church bells pealed.*

Capuchon up, for the sky was grey and rain was
imminent, Gwionn rode through La Porte des Tours in
Domme, and turned his horse's head towards the market
square. He was looking for Arlette de Roncier, who had
apparently ridden into the town with her maid and Sir
Walter as company. The priest from Huelgastel had
arrived with another letter for Arlette from her
stepmother, and Gwionn, in a sweat to know its contents,
had offered to find her and deliver it.

Since the end of the summer, Sir Walter had been
unwilling to return to Huelgastel. Instead, the knight had
pledged his allegiance to Count Etienne, and had made La
Forteresse his home.

It was several months since Gwionn and Lady
Petronilla had persuaded Sir Walter to send a signed
declaration to the law-courts revealing what he had seen
de Roncier do on that fateful day in August. The courts
were notorious for dragging their feet, but surely on a
matter that touched on treason, they would move quickly?
Gwionn was certain that the game would be up for de

Roncier, and he hoped Arlette's letter from Brittany might confirm this.

He had spent the past few months amusing himself by conducting a mild flirtation with de Roncier's daughter. He had not made any attempt to seduce her. Yet. It was not the right time for that. If Gwionn was to be the instrument of Arlette de Roncier's downfall, he wanted to pick the right moment. If he rushed it, he'd spoil his chances. But if he waited . . . Gwionn felt confident of his ultimate success, for he could not help but notice that he brought more blushes to Arlette de Roncier's cheeks than the old count did. So he had begun his pretence of being under her spell. He enjoyed dallying with the daughter of the man who he soon hoped to see toppled from his perch.

Arlette and her companions were not to be found in the market, but Gwionn tracked them down on the cliff walk high above the river.

At the base of the cliff the Dordogne flowed inexorably by, a silvery pathway winding eventually to the Great Sea, carrying the gabares with the same relentless impartiality as it must have carried barges since the time of the Romans. The river moved slowly by, quietly oblivious of the men who traded busy as ants along its banks. The barges sat low in the shining water, being stacked high with oak staves which were destined for vintners' coopers in Bordeaux. Beyond the river the Dordogne valley rolled gently to the horizon, a fertile carpet of trees and fields, rich with every shade of green, burgeoning with new life.

'Lady Arlette!' He strode towards them.

De Roncier's daughter looked up from her contemplation of the river, and threw back her hood. Her face lit up when she saw him.

Sir Walter, earnestly conversing with Clemence, glanced up, but on seeing it was Gwionn, continued with his conversation.

A fair-minded man, Walter did not extend the grievance

he felt against de Roncier to his daughter. Arlette's father may well owe him for the death of his brother but, unlike Gwionn Leclerc, Walter had never thought to continue the quarrel with Arlette. She was a pleasant enough girl as far as he could see, and he was happy to serve her. Walter's duty that morning was to protect Count Etienne's betrothed from strangers. Gwionn Leclerc was no stranger.

'Master Leclerc!' Arlette smiled. 'You didn't tell me you were coming to the market.'

Oh, yes, Gwionn thought, looking deep into limpid blue eyes. It was almost time, this pigeon was almost ripe for the plucking.

'A letter came for you,' he said.

She took it eagerly. 'My thanks. But you didn't have to ride out especially. You could have given it to me on my return.'

'True.' He made his lips smile. 'But then I would have been denied the opportunity of talking to you outside the castle.' There, that had done it, Gwionn thought, triumphant, watching a faint flush colour those pale cheeks.

'Outside the castle?' she asked, looking directly into his eyes, before pinning her gaze firmly on her letter, which she had not yet opened.

'There are too many flapping ears in La Forteresse,' Gwionn said. 'And I find I have things to say to you that I do not want anyone to overhear.'

'I . . . I do not think you should be talking to me like this, Master Leclerc.'

She turned her back and walked down the cliff path, breaking the seal on the letter. The path was wide enough for two and, after a moment's hesitation, Gwionn kept pace beside her. She made no objection, but she was conscious of him, he knew, for the cheek that faced him was bright as a poppy.

359

A few yards down the path was a bench, carefully sited so that anyone seated on it had a clear view of the river and the wooded valley stretched out below them.

'Why don't you sit down to read your letter?' Gwionn suggested. 'This seat must have been put here by some good burgher of Domme who likes to watch his cargoes floating up- and down-stream.'

Arlette murmured agreement, sank on to the bench, and began to read.

'May I join you?' Gwionn sat down, close, attempting to read the letter over her shoulder. His thigh brushed hers, but she did not notice: Arlette was transfixed by what she read.

Palm Sunday 1187

Dearest Daughter, before God I am your loving stepmother. I greet you with a heart full of sorrows, but firm in the knowledge that God will give you strength to bear the ill tidings that I have to disclose to you.

I am writing to you because your father cannot, and as his heiress you have a right to know what has happened. I shall try and relate the whole substance to you, without any omissions, but with your father in his present sorry state of health, that is difficult. Your father has always liked to govern for himself, and was not much in the habit of conferring with me, although he did on occasion. I do not know the whole story, but here follows my best interpretation of what has happened.

This week last came riders with news from the law-courts in Vannes. A claim had been made against your father with regard to the de Wirce lands. I am sorry to say that the claim went

360

against your father. Your father was so incensed
at the court's ruling that he was taken ill again,
and fell down in another fit. This one was worse.
Ever since his attack your father has been unable
to move or speak. I detected some spark of
intelligence in his eyes and, noticing that your
father was able to blink, have developed a very
rudimentary method of communication with him,
but it is woefully inadequate.

Concerning the de Wirce lands, I am told that a
Philippe St Clair claims descent from your great-
aunt Izabel who was sister to your grandmother.
Phillipe St Clair is little more than a babe, but he
has a guardian, one Sir Gregor Wymark, who
speaks for him. It is this Sir Gregor who has put
forwards the child's claim. The court has placed
all the de Wirce lands into Sir Gregor's care. They
no longer form a part of your inheritance.

As you know, the de Wirce lands are but a
small portion of the de Roncier patrimony, and
you may well be wondering why the loss of them
came as so great a blow to your father. Sadly, I
have to tell you that there were more blows.

At the same time that your father received
notification concerning the court's judgement in
the Phillipe St Clair case, he received word that
someone has laid a very serious allegation against
him.

Your father has been accused of treason.

A document has been lodged in the bishop's
care, and this document alleges that your father
was directly involved in the death of Duke
Geoffrey last year. I am in a fog as to the exact
nature of the accusation, but there is a witness
who was present at the mêlée. I do not know the
name of this witness. The bishops will not reveal

it. The allegation is being taken very seriously.
There is to be an investigation, and the duchess is
involved.

Your father is in no fit state to defend himself.

Dear daughter, you and I both have cause to
know that your father is not a temperate man. We
both know the rages that he can fall into. But
your father's rages have always blown over, like
summer storms, and I cannot believe that these
allegations can be founded on truth.

The ducal court will investigate, and in the
meantime, your father's title and his lands have
been confiscated. Your grandmother, your father
and I have been forced to take up residence in the
guest house at St Anne's Priory. It was that or
live on the charity of our neighbours, and I think
to live on a neighbour's charity would kill both
your father and your grandmother.

Dear daughter, none of these events bode well
for your future relations with Count Etienne. The
count will not be pleased that his bride is daughter
of a man suspected of murdering one of the
Angevin princes. He will not be pleased at losing
the rest of your dowry, not to mention the de
Roncier lands which would eventually be yours if
(as now looks extremely likely) I am fated never
to give your father his male heir.

I have little comfort to offer you.

In your letter to me, you said that Count
Etienne seems a pious man. I pray that this is so,
and that he will not take his disappointment out
on you. I do not envy you the position you are
in.

I shall write separately to Count Etienne,
explaining our new circumstances to him. Father
Josse has undertaken to deliver the letters. When

he has delivered them, he is to return to
Huelgastel where he and Sir Hamon are to ensure
that the day-to-day running of the castle continues
as normal. All our old retainers are to be
permitted to stay there. Duchess Constance wants
Huelgastel in good working order — she does not
want to lose her revenues. I trust that one day the
de Roncier name will be cleared and we will be
able to return with our heads high.

Dear daughter, you have my deepest sympathy.
I have no suggestions for you, except that I think
you should prepare yourself for the possibility
that the count may no longer want alliance with
our family.

I pray for you daily.
Pray for your father. He suffers much.

Your loving belle-mère.
Eleanor de Roncier.

Arlette set the letter on her knee. The poppy-bright colour
in her cheeks had drained away, leaving her as pale as
marble. With shaking hands she re-rolled the scroll,
thrusting it in the drawstring purse that hung from her
belt.

'Lady Arlette? Is something wrong?' Gwionn put a
light hand on her arm.

She did not answer at first, and when finally she turned
towards him her eyes were huge and bright with emotion.

'It's my father,' she said. 'He's taken very ill. He had
one of his fits, and this time my stepmother fears that he
will not recover. He cannot move any of his limbs.' She
gave a slight sob. 'He's lost his speech too, but Eleanor
writes there's intelligence in his eyes. I find I can take no
comfort in that.'

Gwionn could take comfort from that. If it was true

363

and de Roncier was made prisoner in his own body, then that was justice of sorts.

'It must be hell for him, Master Leclerc.'

'It must.'

'Poor Papa. Eleanor tells me they're caring for him in St Anne's Priory.'

'St Anne's Priory? Why St Anne's?' None of this was precisely the news that Gwionn had been expecting, but it was, nevertheless, music to his ears. De Roncier was suffering, and he rejoiced in it. He strove to keep his elation from showing in his eyes.

'My father's sister is prioress at St Anne's,' she said.

'Is there any other news?'

Arlette rose from the bench. 'There is.' Coolly, she gathered her skirts and drew away as though distancing herself from him. 'But I need to discuss that with Count Etienne. Do you wish to ride back with us, Master Leclerc?'

Gwionn put his hand on his heart. 'How could you doubt it, my lady?'

This sally brought some of the colour back to her cheeks, but her eyes were no longer warm and limpid as they had been a few minutes ago. All at once Gwionn found himself wondering whether he had misjudged her. Perhaps his pigeon was not quite as ready for plucking as he had hoped.

They rode swiftly back. Arlette would not permit any detours.

Count Etienne was in the stables when they clattered into the bailey. He emerged so quickly, it was as though he had been waiting for them to return. He fixed his eyes on Arlette; his expression was sombre.

Arlette, who had been praying for a favourable reception from her betrothed, felt her heart sink to her toes. She dismounted.

'Mistress Arlette, would you be so good as to step up to the solar?' the count asked.

Without his usual reassuring smile, the count looked a different man. His mode of address did not escape Arlette either. She had lost her title along with her father. This did not look good. It looked as though the count *was* going to penalise her for her father's ill-fortune. She must do her best to put things right.

In the solar above the hall, Count Etienne dismissed Clemence with a brusque wave of his hand.

'Your mistress and I need to converse privately,' he said.

Clemence glanced at Arlette, who nodded, and she left the room.

'Well madam? Did you receive your stepmother's letter?'

'I did, my lord.' His green eyes were cold now, quite calculating. They made Arlette's spine prickle, and brought back that faint remembrance of someone else that always eluded her. All at once she had it. Gwionn Leclerc. Her mind raced. It was a coincidence, of course, and Gwionn Leclerc had never looked so angrily at Arlette, but the resemblance, once noted, was unmistakable.

Count Etienne and the Breton squire shared many physical characteristics. Several decades separated them, which was why the similarities must have escaped her for so long. Count Etienne was well past his prime, Gwionn Leclerc had yet to come into his. Count Etienne's hair was lifeless and thin and touched with silver, while Gwionn Leclerc's was thick and springy. But if she tried to imagine Count Etienne in his youth . . . They had the same build, and Count Etienne would have been much the same in height as Gwionn Leclerc, though Gwionn did not have the count's limp. Both count and squire held their heads proudly. And as for their eyes — even now they were remarkably similar. It was a freak of nature, a fluke, but

Gwionn Leclerc resembled the count so nearly he could have been his son. Now the likeness was borne in upon her, Arlette wondered why she had been so slow to notice it.

'And you understand the contents of the letter?' the count pressed.

'I do.'

'So you will also understand when I say that our marriage contract is invalid.'

Arlette gulped. He was very blunt. 'Invalid, my lord?'

'Invalid.' Count Etienne tapped the toe of his knee-high polished boot against the trestle. 'I'll make no marriage alliance with a dowerless wench whose sire is accused of treason.'

Arlette found herself staring at the rushes at her feet, unwilling to take in what the count was saying. Someone had spilt candlewax on the rushes and several of them were glued together with the stuff.

Practically all her life, for as far back as she could remember, had been spent in preparation for marrige to this man. It was not a marriage she would have chosen, but this was the marriage she had been bred to and this was the marriage she would make. Her father may be ill, and under a temporary cloud, but she refused to be cowed by his disgrace. She was Arlette de Roncier, and it was her firm intention to become Countess Favell, if it was the last thing she did. She had worked for it. He could not cut her off as though she were of no account. He had signed a contract with her father, and if her father was not able to see him honour it, she would. It was her right. It was her duty.

She lifted her head, and studied the count's face. For all that flesh sagged with age, his expression was stony, implacable. Here was a man who, like her father, was used to his word being law. He was not used to being crossed. But cross him she must, if she were to fulfil the role for which her father had prepared her.

Anger would not serve her. She did not want to rouse Count Etienne's dislike, what use would that be when they did finally marry? She did not want her future husband to hate her. She decided to try pricking the count's conscience.

'But, my lord, you have already had part of my dowry,' she said.

'You can have it back,' came the swift answer. 'Use it to buy yourself a place in a nunnery, for no one will take you now. Our contract is terminated.'

So much for conscience, she thought. 'But you cannot so lightly break your word!'

'No? Don't be naîve. The terms of the contract I signed with your father specifically stated that his lands would come to me via you. As an heiress you were desirable as a bride. As a dowerless girl whose father stands accused of treason, you are worthless.'

'Worthless?' A bitter rage engulfed Arlette, but she strove to hide it.

'Aye. The contract was based on the lands you would bring me. But now your father is on trial there is no guarantee the de Roncier lands will come to me. I consider the contract invalid.'

Arlette dredged up a smile. 'My lord, I think you are making a mistake. My father only stands accused, nothing has been proven. I feel sure he will be vindicated, and Huelgastel will be restored to him.'

'By your stepmother's admission, your father doesn't *stand* at all,' the count said, voice edged with impatience. Then he gentled his tone, and his expression became almost kindly again. 'Your father's a cripple. Accept your change of circumstances with a good grace, girl. It's the best you can do. Be assured, you and I will not wed.'

A draught on the back of her neck informed Arlette that someone had opened the door from the family apartments. She did not turn round to see who had entered.

She lifted her chin. 'And the heir that you need, my lord? It will take time to negotiate another marriage contract. How much time do you have left, my lord?'

The green eyes – so very like Gwionn Leclerc's – flashed. 'You are impertinent.'

'No. Practical. You are not as young as you would like to think, my lord.'

Count Etienne drew himself up to his full height. 'Use what weapon you will, girl, but there will be no wedding between you and me. I've no use for you. I'll give you a day to pack your belongings. You can take your entourage back to Brittany.'

'I shall not go.'

'Indeed you *will*.'

The count's face suffused, just like her father's did when he was angered. It made Arlette's heart quail.

'No, I won't,' she stood firm. She was used to standing firm in the face of a man's fury. 'And I don't think that you can force me. Years ago my father signed a contract with you in good faith. He brought me up to be your wife. I left my home and came here in good faith. I will not be driven from La Forteresse like a rabid dog, just because someone has made unfounded allegations against my father. I *will* be your wife. I *will* become Countess Favell. You have made a legal contract with me and, God help me, I'll make you honour it.'

Count Etienne stared blankly at Arlette. Then he threw back his head and released a guffaw loud enough to rattle the rafters.

'Madam, you're all bark and no bite. If you don't go gracefully, I'll kick you through my gates myself. Be ready to leave at noon tomorrow. Till then, adieu.'

He turned on his heel and strode down to the hall.

Arlette stood like a graven image in the middle of the

solar, hands clenched at her sides. She felt as though she'd been run over by a cart. Her heart was thumping, and she was seized with the most unladylike desire to break something. She controlled the impulse, but barely. She had never felt so humiliated in her life.

Behind her a skirt rustled.

'Clemence?' she asked, without turning.

'No, my dear. It's Petronilla. I am so sorry—'

'Are you?' For all that she fought it, she knew she sounded bitter. 'It occurs to me that you should be jumping for joy.'

White nostrils flared as Lady Petronilla drew in a sharp breath. 'How so?'

'If I am to be shipped back to Brittany, Count Etienne will not be marrying in the summer. Your husband will be his heir again. And most likely he will remain his heir. Does that thought not please you, Lady Petronilla?'

Without waiting for a reply, Arlette stalked out of the solar, and went to bring Clemence up to date with events.

'Holy Mother, what will you do?' Clemence asked, round-eyed.

'God knows,' Arlette said, pacing around the confined space of her chamber. She glanced at the heavy betrothal ring still weighing down her finger, and sent Clemence a rueful grin. 'It's queer, I'm sorry that my father is ill, and I know I should feel most for him, but the emotion that grips me most strongly is fury. Clemence, I'm so angry, it frightens me.'

'Angry? With Count Etienne?'

'Yes. If he walked into this room this second, and if you put my dagger in my hand, I think I'd kill him.'

'You wouldn't. That's your pride talking,' Clemence said.

Rising, Clemence cheerfully began removing Arlette's gowns from the wardrobe. She would be glad to return to

369

Brittany, Arlette realised, for then she could be reunited with Morgan le Bihan.

Clemence continued, 'You'll feel better when we've put some miles between us and the Aquitaine. Then you can forget Count Etienne. If you ask me you're better off without him. Why waste time over a man who is so concerned with politics that he values you only for the lands that you bring him? My advice is that we do exactly as he says. We should pack, take back the half of the dowry that your father gave him, and go. We could be ready by this afternoon if you wish.'

'Clemence, you don't understand,' Arlette said with a sad smile. 'I must marry the count. He signed a contract with my father. My father is ill and cannot see him honour it, but I will.'

'Honour?' Clemence snorted. 'Honour won't give you a happy marriage.'

'I don't believe in happiness,' Arlette said. 'But I do believe in power. Power, or the lack of it, can transform people's lives. Can you imagine my father, now he has had his vigour and power stripped from him?'

Clemence shook her head.

'Neither can I. One moment he's a count who only has to crook his little finger and dozens of people run to see to his every whim, and the next he's a helpless invalid, reduced to relying on nuns' charity. God doesn't give us many chances to take what we want from life. I have watched, and seen how men have all the power.'

'There's Queen Eleanor,' Clemence pointed out. 'The Queen always took a keen interest in politics—'

'Queen Eleanor is the exception that proves the rule. Besides, you merely confirm what I was going to say. The only women that I have ever seen wield any kind of power are those married to powerful men. Queen Eleanor is a good example. Duchess Constance is another. Despite having recently given birth to a baby son, she is directly

370

involved in this affair with my father—'

'You can hardly blame the duchess for that,' Clemence said, 'since it touches on her husband's death.'

Arlette was not to be sidetracked. 'My grandmother had power when my grandfather was alive. And after he died, my father came to rely on her counsel. As I said, women only ever have power if they marry powerful men. Count Etienne is a powerful man. He swore to marry me, and marry me he will. You can put those clothes back in the press, Clemence.'

'Queen Eleanor angered her husband and got shut up in a tower,' Clemence reminded her.

Arlette laughed. 'I never said it was easy, Clemence. I shall be very careful not to anger—' She broke off abruptly, a pensive expresssion entering her eyes.

'Arlette, what's the matter?'

'You've given me an idea, an extraordinary idea!' Arlette cried, flinging Clemence a brilliant smile. 'Clemence, pack my things, if you please.'

Dizzy with her mistress's lightning changes of direction, Clemence dipped her head in agreement. 'We're going home, after all?'

'No, Clemence. But I'm moving out of this chamber. I'm going to lock myself in the Brown Tower.'

Clemence blinked. 'I beg your pardon, my lady?'

'La Tour Brune. It's disused, remember?'

'Yes, but—'

'I shall move in tonight.'

'But, my lady—!'

Arlette's eyes were bright as lamps. 'Fetch me parchment and ink.'

'What, now?'

'At once. There is not a moment to lose. I shall write to Queen Eleanor. Tonight. And I shall write to Duke Richard – he is reputed to be a man of honour. I shall write to my stepmother and the bishops, not forgetting

Count Etienne's friend, the Bishop of Cahors.'

Clemence frowned. 'But what will you say?'

'I shall put my case. I shall inform the bishops that the betrothal agreement was between our two families. I cannot remember the exact wording of the contract, Clemence, but as far as I recall the disposal of my father's lands was a secondary point, and the marriage itself was in no way dependent upon it. Remember, at that time my father still hoped for a male heir. He was very careful with the wording.'

'Where is this agreement?'

'There are two copies. Count Etienne has one, and my father the other. I shall ask Eleanor to send our copy to the Bishop of Vannes. She is a pious woman, and has the bishop's ear, and although my father is being investigated I am sure he will see I get a fair hearing. When he sees the wording of the agreement, he will understand that Count Etienne cannot simply walk away from his obligations. The Church will take my part, and Count Etienne will have to marry me. He can't afford to alienate the Church. No great lord can.'

Clemence chewed on a fingernail. 'Arlette, are you sure you want to do this? The count won't submit easily.'

Arlette's chin went up. 'I am set on it. I shall write to His Holiness the Pope if necessary. My father may be under a cloud, but I refuse to live in its shadow. I know my rights. The letters will have to be sent out tonight.'

'Count Etienne will not allow it.'

'He won't know about it. I'll send them to my stepmother with Father Josse. He'll return to Brittany tonight if I ask him. And when the letters are safely on their way we'll go the tower. And I swear to you, Clemence, I shall not stir one foot from that tower, until I have shamed Count Etienne into honouring our marriage contract. Even though my father is believed dishonourable, I will show the count I am not.'

Arlette and Clemence did not eat in the hall that night. Instead, Clemence brought a tray up to their room while Arlette scribbled furiously. No one objected to their absence from the hall. No doubt the count was thankful that he was spared the discomfiture of dining with his unwanted fiancée. No doubt he thought she was too shamed to come down and eat with him. He would be thinking that he had got his way, and that she was going to leave quietly.

The letters written, Arlette wrapped them all in one large piece of vellum which she addressed to her stepmother and sealed with red sealing wax.

'Would you go and fetch Father Josse please, Clemence?'

Father Josse had taken the letters as requested, and without demur.

They waited until after dark and began to move in to the tower when the household had retired, crossing and re-crossing the bailey several times. The bottom section of La Tour Brune was filled with bales of hay and sacks of oatmeal destined for the stables.

The groom, Jacob, was talking to some of the men-at-arms on the walkway, and none of them could fail to see Clemence and Arlette as they trudged solemnly back and forth across the yard with Arlette's trunks and belongings. They attracted a curious audience, who were clearly nonplussed by the proceedings, and while they felt that they should do something, they did not know what.

After a hasty consultation with one of the guards, Jacob moved to intercept them. 'My lady? Can I help you?'

Arlette smiled at the groom, whom she liked. He took good care of the horses, as Aubrey had done at Huelgastel. He would care for Yseult for as long as it took. 'You will have heard that I'm supposed to be leaving tomorrow, Jacob?'

Jacob grunted, and looked at his feet.

'These are some of my belongings,' Arlette said pleasantly. 'I thought it would save time if my maid and I brought them over tonight, and stored them temporarily in the tower. Then we can leave quickly and quietly in the morning. The less fuss there is, the less of an ordeal it will be for everyone, don't you agree?'

'You'll need more light, my lady,' Jacob said, reaching a flambeau down from the wall, and lighting the girls' way for them. 'And would you like some help shifting those travelling chests?'

'Thank you, that would be kind.'

Half an hour later, Jacob had finished heaving the last of Lady Arlette's boxes through the door of the tower, and was able to resume his conversation with the guards, Gosvin and Fulbert, on the walkway.

'Beats me why you offered to help them,' Fulbert observed, yawning. 'It was a rare treat for me to see a lady yoked in the same harness as her maid. What are they up to? Preparing for a siege?'

Jacob laughed. 'You heard the gossip. She's not turned out to be quite the lady that the count was expecting. She's being packed off to Brittany tomorrow, and wants the boxes handy for an early departure.' Jacob stooped to rub one of his knees. Lately they had begun to ache, a sure sign that age was creeping up on him, and lifting Arlette de Roncier's boxes had done them no good. 'Poor girl. She must feel very shamed.'

Gosvin made an impatient noise. 'You're soft, Jacob. Don't waste any sympathy on her. Tough as old boots, that one.'

'I'm not so sure—'

'She may have been pushed off her pedestal,' Gosvin

said, 'but she was brought up as a lady, wasn't she? They have airs and graces, I'll grant you, but they breed them hardy too. Look at Lady Petronilla.'

'That one! She was never brought up as a lady. She's tough because she's a merchant's daughter. Her airs and graces are assumed.'

'Jacob?' Fulbert interrupted, eyes trained on the tower. 'Why haven't they come out? Are they bedding down in there?'

The tower door had been closed. And through a window slit on one of the upper floors, light was flickering. A moment later more light flared from the floor above that. Arlette de Roncier and her maid appeared to be exploring.

'What the devil?'

In a moment Jacob was across the bailey, trying to open the tower door. It resisted all his efforts.

He returned to the walkway.

'Well?' Gosvin demanded.

'I don't understand it. It's bolted from the inside. Lady Arlette and her maid have locked themselves in.'

Fulbert gave a short bark of laughter. 'Told you. It is a seige. She's not going to go easily.'

'No. Tough as old boots,' Gosvin murmured agreement. 'Tell you what, Fulbert. If it's a siege, I'll lay you odds as to how long she'll hold out.'

'If you're right, which I doubt,' Jacob said, 'she'll not last a day.'

Fulbert spoke up. 'A week. I'll give her a week.'

Gosvin rubbed his chin thoughtfully. 'No. I reckon she'll last longer. I'll give her a month.'

'Done.' Fulbert grinned. 'Gosvin, you'll lose you know. It's like taking money from a babe.'

Gosvin punched Fulbert playfully on the arm. 'Lose? You'll be the one with the light pouch when this is done.'

Jacob peered across the yard, where the light from the

upper window had steadied. 'It looks at though they've settled up at the top.' He frowned. 'Shouldn't you inform your captain about this?'

Gosvin grinned. 'No, man. It will be more interesting if we let them get well entrenched, and wait for the morning. I think I'm going to enjoy this.'

An uneasy expression flitted across Fulbert's face. 'Perhaps we should tell the captain?' he said.

'No. Everything's peaceful tonight, isn't it?'

'Yes.'

'Right you are then. I'll have a word with the captain tomorrow.'

Early the next morning, Petronilla's maid brought the news to her mistress who was dictating a letter to Father Theobald in the solar.

'My lady,' she panted, having run all the way from the bailey to the solar. 'You must come, and quickly!'

'Calm yourself, Rose. What's happened?'

'It's Lady Arlette and her maidservant! They've barricaded themselves in La Tour Brune, and they refuse to come down. They say they're not going to leave.'

Petronilla stood up. 'Ridiculous. They must leave. Does Count Favell know of this?'

'Yes, my lady. He's down there, trying to lure them out.'

'I shall come at once. Father, if you'll excuse me. We'll finish this later.'

'Of course, my lady.' Father Theobald bowed his tonsured head, and sprinkled sand on to the parchment with a hand that an untreatable combination of age and infirmity caused to shake like a poplar leaf.

Outside, a small crowd had gathered at the base of the tower. Petronilla went to her husband.

'Won't she come out?'

Louis shook his head. 'The girl must have run mad. She

thinks to force my uncle to marry her.'

Petronilla eyed the studded tower door, which was firmly closed. 'There's no chance of that, thank the Lord,' she whispered, smiling with quiet satisfaction at her husband. 'Etienne has made up his mind. You're his heir again.'

Louis lifted a finger to his lips. 'Hush. My uncle is speaking.'

Count Etienne stood with his comely castellan, Sir Gilles, before La Tour Brune, cupped his hand around his mouth and threw his voice up to the middle window.

'Madam, you'll come to rue this day. I will not countenance such behaviour. However, if you come out at once, I am prepared to forget this unfortunate incident. No one outside these walls need ever hear of it.'

Arlette de Roncier's reply came clearly to all ears. It was brief and succinct.

'I seek justice, my lord. You swore before witnesses to marry me. I will not be set aside.'

Count Etienne's green eyes glowed like fire. 'Madam, you must reconsider. You force me to actions I would prefer to avoid.'

The girl's voice floated down. 'What, will you starve me out, my lord?'

Count Etienne ground his teeth. 'Come down at once and put an end to this nonsense.'

'I will not.'

The count shrugged. 'Very well. Stay there till you rot, you'll not sway me.' He jerked his head at Sir Gilles, and lowered his voice. 'She'll come out soon enough, I'll warrant. When she gets bored. Then we can pack her off home.'

Blond brows knotted, Sir Gilles nodded.

Count Etienne swung on his heel, and marched into the keep.

Up on the walkway, Troopers Clore and Selier, who

had heard the tale from Gosvin and Fulbert and disbelieved it, looked at each other in slack-jawed astonishment.

'Holy Christ and all his angels, I never thought I'd live to see so small a wench throw down so large a challenge,' said Clore, admiringly.

'No. Do you suppose he will starve her?'

'Not entirely, but I expect she'll be put on half rations.'

Smiling, Lady Petronilla drifted off on her husband's arm. She averted her gaze from Sir Gilles as she passed him.

Sir Gilles, whose blond brows had remained bunched, found himself staring angrily at Petronilla Favell's retreating back.

'Worthless,' the castellan muttered to himself, as Lady Petronilla was swallowed up by the keep. 'And heartless.'

He resented the fact that Petronilla Favell still meant something to him. She must. Why else should the blood tingle in his veins when she was near, and all thoughts but thoughts of her fly from his mind? She made a madman of him. He had loved her. Could she not see that he would have loved her till Judgement Day? Did that mean nothing to her? Gilles was becoming obsessed, and he hated it.

The feelings that Petronilla the merchant's daughter had aroused were as powerful now as they had been when he had made his first declaration of love on the Cliff Walk overlooking the river at Domme, except that Gilles was no longer sure what it was she made him feel. He only knew that he wished it would stop. He wanted to be free of it. It could not be love, this pain that made him want to cry like a baby.

Was it hate? Had his love turned to hate? The door of the keep slammed, and Gilles tore his gaze away. She was beautiful today. Happiness always made her look especially beautiful. So she had looked when she had told

378

him that Louis had asked her to marry him. Triumphant. Transfigured.

Her face had that same bright glow today. And if he judged her aright, he knew what had caused it.

Chapter Eighteen

After Count Etienne and his gawping retainers had left the bailey, Arlette left her tower window and wandered down the turning stairs to look over her prison with new eyes. It was one thing to have bolted herself in the tower, in the white heat of rage, but it was quite another to know she must stay there until she had had some response from the letters she had written.

A few moments ago, while Count Etienne had been trying to persuade her to come out, Arlette had been tempted to inform him about the letters. She had not done so because it occurred to her that Count Etienne might still have time to send a couple of knights chasing after Father Josse. If they caught up with the priest, they could simply confiscate her letters and prevent them reaching her stepmother. That must not happen. Until she heard that the letters had reached their destination she would keep silent.

Yesterday, the count had called Arlette naïve, and that had rankled, but she was not so naïve that she did not realise that the count would be far more likely to treat her justly if he knew she had won the Church over to her point of view. Count Etienne was a God-fearing man. He could not afford to alienate the Church. The Church — assuming that their interpretation of the wording of her betrothal agreement coincided with her own — was Arlette's only hope. The Church's influence was felt in every level of society, and a count who wanted his own authority to be respected could not afford to flout Church ruling. On matters of marriage the Church's ruling was sacrosanct.

Count Etienne thought she would give in soon. He thought her will was not equal to the task before her. Arlette knew he was wrong. She would stay in this tower until Count Etienne honoured his marriage contract.

During their first night in La Tour Brune, Arlette and Clemence had explored thoroughly – not that there was much to explore. The tower only had three floors. The door was on the ground or lower level, and led into the bailey. The light was weakest at ground floor level, there being only one window overlooking the bailey. The stone-flagged floor was strewn with hay which had escaped from several musty bales. The plaster walls were grimy and grey. To one side there was a platform made with slats of wood, and raised off the ground on mushroom-shaped stones to keep the rats away. Half a dozen sacks of meal stood on this platform. A couple of broken pitchforks lay in the corner furthest from the door. One of the grooms had left a lantern hanging on a hook. Close inspection of this revealed that the candle had burned down and had not been replaced. The lantern's horn door was cracked and dirty.

'I'll clean it,' Clemence offered.

Arlette smiled. 'Let's wait and see if we're going to be allowed candles first, eh?'

Silently, Arlette wandered back up the narrow stairs to the first floor, pondering on the enormity of what she had done. She felt excited, nervous rather than frightened. She had no explanation fo her lack of fear, and could only put it down to the fact that she knew she was in the right. Perhaps all the implications of her self-imposed incarceration had not sunk in yet.

She would not change her mind.

On the second floor, there was another unglazed window slit; this too overlooked the yard, and it was through this one that Arlette had called down her defiance of the count. Thinking about it, she felt uneasy, and acknowledged that she had perhaps been rather hasty in making their quarrel so public. In doing so she had attacked his pride, and made it difficult for him to back down. She could see that, now it was done, but at the time the only thought in her head had been to get her sense of injustice across to him.

Admittedly, Count Etienne was all but a stranger to her, but if his reactions were anything like her father's would have been under similar circumstances, he might never forgive her. All at once, it was borne in on Arlette that she might find herself in her prison for a long, long time.

Noblemen like her father and Count Etienne could not afford to let it be seen that they were being bullied by a slip of a girl, even if that slip of a girl was to have been their future wife.

Sighing, she looked round the second room. Save for a scattering of birds' droppings on the dusty floorboards, indicating that perhaps pigeons had once taken roost there, it was quite empty. The plaster skin on the walls was yellow as opposed to the grey downstairs, and patches had fallen off revealing the limestone beneath.

The upper floor was the cleanest, which was why they had slept there the previous night. Arlette trailed on upstairs, Clemence as ever in her wake.

The top room was full of light, having wider arched windows on two sides and an arrow loop on the eastern side. If Arlette stood by the arrow loop and craned her neck, she had a good sight of the approach road which climbed the cliff to La Forteresse. Both windows and arrow-loop had wooden shutters, which worked.

'We should be grateful for these,' Arlette murmured as

she moved round, testing each shutter in turn. 'Else the wind would howl about our heads, and bring with it rain and snow and Lord knows what else.'

'Do you think we'll still be here in the winter?' Clemence asked.

'God knows, but I tell you this, Clemence, it won't be me that gives way.'

Clemence looked at the stubborn set of Arlette's jaw, bit her lip, and changed the subject. 'Saints, but it's dusty!' she exclaimed, running her finger along a shelf on the wall.

'It's cleaner and dryer than the other rooms,' Arlette said, eyeing the floor. She and Clemence had slept on two pieces of sacking foraged from the ground floor. Broad day revealed them to be none too clean. Arlette shuddered. 'Did you see a broom in the storage area?'

'No.'

'We should be able to make one from something,' Arlette went on. 'So we can clean the top two floors at least. I think we should continue to sleep up here. It won't be that bad. We can use the floor below as our solar.'

Clemence smiled.

On impulse, Arlette went over and hugged her.

'What's that for?' Clemence asked.

'For being my friend. For accepting what I do without judging me. For standing by without complaining.'

'What else should I do?' Clemence asked, wondering.

Arlette laughed. 'You could leave me for a start. There's no earthly reason for you to stay in this dusty old tower. I wouldn't force you to stay at La Forteresse, Clemence, and I'm sure Count Etienne would release you if I ask him. His quarrel is with me, not you. In fact, he'd probably be delighted to see you go. I should think he would find the idea of me being left in solitary confinement most appealing.'

384

Clemence shook her head. 'My place is with you, Arlette.'

'I may be here some time.'

'I'll take that risk.' Clemence wrinkled her nose. 'What's worst is that musty smell downstairs. You won't want your things left there. Shall I bring your clothes up?'

'If you would. But there's no rush.' Arlette sent her friend and ally a twisted smile. 'As I won't be giving in, we've all the time in the world.' She moved to the stairwell which wound up past the third level, and peered towards the top. 'I wonder if we can get onto the tower roof. I can see a door. Do you think it leads there?'

And so began Arlette's lengthy incarceration in La Tour Brune.

Twice a day they were brought plain but nutritious food. Some days their diet was more spartan than others, and they lived simply off bread and goat's cheese.

Two weeks after Arlette and Clemence had barricaded themselves in the tower, Count Etienne and Sir Gilles came to stand in the yard below the tower. Six troopers accompanied them, carrying a small battering ram hewn from an oak tree.

'I've had enough, Gilles,' Etienne said, head tipped back as he looked at the tower. 'This business has gone on long enough. I want her out.'

Sir Gilles eyed the black studded door, and the four troopers waiting on one side. 'You're planning on using the battering ram, my lord?'

'Yes, if she won't come out when she's asked. See if you can get her attention first.'

Sir Gilles thumped on the door. 'M'selle! Count Etienne wishes to speak with you.'

A few moments passed, before Arlette's bright head appeared over the battlements.

'My lord?' her voice floated down, clear as a bell.

'Have you reconsidered? Will you come out, or do I have to drag you out?'

'I'm staying.'

'Is that your final word?'

'It is.'

Count Etienne gestured at the six troopers. They picked up the ram and approached the door.

'On my signal,' Count Etienne said, holding up his arm. He looked up at Arlette. 'Arlette, open this door, or by Christ, I'll do it for you.'

There was a pause, then, 'Hold, my lord,' she said. 'I'm coming down. There is something I'd like to discuss with you.'

Triumphant, Count Etienne exchanged glances with Gilles.

'I knew she wouldn't stay the course,' he said.

The bolt grated, the hinges creaked, and Arlette was framed in the doorway.

'Do come in, Count,' she said. 'I have something to show you.'

Inside, Count Etienne perched on a dusty bale of hay.

'Well, what is it? Do you capitulate?'

'Capitulate? Certainly not. But it's time that you knew that I have sent letters appealing for help to my stepmother. By now she will have distributed them. Here are some copies I made of them.'

The count looked bemusedly at the pieces of parchment Arlette had handed him. 'Letters? You sent letters? I swear you've sent none since you've been in here. The guards would have brought them to me.'

Arlette smiled. 'Yes, I thought that they might. That was why I sent the letters back with Father Josse on the day the news came concerning my father's troubles.'

'I beg your pardon?' Count Etienne held the letters out at arm's length, squinting to make out the writing.

'As you can see, I wrote to Eleanor enclosing a letter for

386

the Bishop of Vannes,' Arlette went on calmly. She pointed at one of the letters. 'And this one was for Queen Eleanor, and this for Duke Richard. Oh, and this was for the Pope. I wrote to him too.'

Count Etienne choked, and crushed the letters in his hand. 'You have written to the Pope?'

'Yes. And your friend the Bishop of Cahors. I didn't tell you before in case you found some way of retrieving my letters. But I'm telling you now, when they should have reached their destination safely.'

'You bitch!'

Arlette's blue gaze met his steadily. 'No, Count. I'm merely standing up for my family's rights. My father is in no position to defend me, so I must do the best I can myself. I have written those letters because I believe you are flouting the terms of the agreement you made with my father. Whatever the rights and wrongs of my father's current position, that agreement was legal. It is a binding contract, and you should honour it.'

The count drew in a sharp breath. 'And these letters will be well on their way?'

'Yes. So you see, you can't throw me on to the midden, and forget all about me. I won't let you.'

For a moment the silence was absolute, and then the count spoke, and his tone was harsh and unyielding.

'Very well, m'selle. Have it your way.' Throwing the letters on to the straw, he moved to the door. 'Gilles! Gilles!'

Sir Gilles stepped into the store-room. 'My lord?'

'Find the key for this place, and lock it from the outside. And set two guards on it.'

'Guards, my lord?'

'Mistress Arlette wants to be confined. Very well. Let her be confined. Properly.' Etienne threw a cold glance at Arlette. 'You can stay here till your hair turns grey, madam. I'll let you out if you swear to renounce our

387

betrothal, but not before. Do you understand? You'll stay here until you are prepared to swear that our betrothal agreement is void, and that you will drop all these actions that you have taken.'

'I'll be here a long time then,' Arlette said softly.

'That, madam, is entirely up to you.'

'The Pope knows I'm in here, Count. He'll get to hear of it if you maltreat me.'

Count Etienne ground his teeth, and slammed out of the tower.

After that they were occasionally brought trout from the river, or glazed ham, or pea soups with walnut bread. Once they were given pike with green sauce. Sometimes they were given milk, but this was not common as milk was usually reserved for children and infants. They had plenty of apples and pears. It seemed that Arlette's parting shot had gone home and the count did not want the Church to accuse him of starving Arlette de Roncier.

In fact Count Etienne left instructions that his prisoner and her maid should have access to food at all times, so they were never without fresh water, a loaf of bread and a jug or a bottle of wine. They never went hungry.

One day, not long after, a messenger had ridden into the bailey, and Arlette suddenly was allowed writing materials. She received a terse communication explaining that Count Etienne had granted her this privilege because the messenger had come from the Church courts, and that the Church had taken up her case. They wished her to restate her position.

Arlette took heart. She was not forgotten.

She trimmed her quill and used the opportunity to write more letters, expanding on her plight, to the most powerful people in Christendom. She chose the people she thought most likely to have a vested interest in seeing that justice was done, the ones that must see that if men were not able to honour their oaths the whole feudal system must crumble.

She wrote again to Queen Eleanor, and her son Duke Richard. She wrote to the Bishop of Vannes, and the Pope. She wrote most eloquently, withholding nothing. She wrote concerning the accusations laid against her father, and the fact that his lands in Brittany had been temporarily sequestrated pending a judgement. She mentioned her father's affliction, and Count Etienne's rejection of her. She pointed out to Queen Eleanor, her son and the churchmen that as her father was ill, she had no-one to champion her cause. This was why, she explained, she was championing herself.

When the second set of letters had been dispatched with the messenger, Arlette sat back to wait, certain that she would receive answers, and help, soon.

'Why did Count Etienne let you send those letters?' Clemence wondered. 'He could have destroyed them.'

'He wouldn't dare. He can't pretend I don't exist now so many people know that I am here. And he cannot pretend my marriage contract was never signed. There were too many witnesses. I know Sir Louis would probably deny anything to please his uncle, but what about the other witnesses? There's my father, Hamon le Moine, Father Josse, and my stepmother. He can't silence them all, especially now the Church is involved. He needs to be married so he can get an heir, but he needs the Church's blessing on his marriage. And until this case is settled that blessing will be witheld.'

She laughed. 'He thought I'd let him pack me off to Brittany. But I didn't, and now he's stuck with me. Thank God I sent those letters back with Father Josse.'

Locked away as she was from the heart of the castle, Arlette had thought to lose touch with events, but this was not the case. Voices carried a long way in the warm spring air, and it was not so far to the top of the tower. The bolt on the door to the tower had been rusty, but once greased, it was easy enough to use, and Arlette came to enjoy sitting or walking round the tower roof, partly to take a breath of fresh air, and partly because from there she had a bird's eye view of the castle. No one could enter or leave La Forteresse without her knowing it. She saw Gwionn Leclerc exercising Star. She saw him — bless him for the thought — exercising Yseult. Sometimes he would look up and, catching her eyes, would wave at her. She waved back.

Much of what went on at La Forteresse was discussed in the bailey, if not by the count or Sir Gilles, but by the guard or the grooms. So it was that in her first few weeks in the tower, Arlette learnt much about the day-to-day running of La Forteresse.

She knew the day Count Etienne decided to dismiss the minstrels. Grumbling at their loss of fortune, the three of them shuffled disconsolately through the gateway, their voices floating up to the roof where Arlette was taking the air.

'I thought we had our bread nicely buttered there,' the girl, Michelle said.

Arlette rose and, peering through a crenellation, saw the trio fully laden with flute and lute and harp dangling from their packs.

'Aye. But he only kept us on for the girl's sake, and now she's locked up in disgrace, so out we must go.'

'Do we go to Domme?' the girl asked.

Her father nodded. 'Aye. We'll try lining our purses with merchants' money in the market square.'

After that their voices faded, as the minstrels reached the fork in the road and took the way through La Forêt des Colombes. When they had gone, a subdued atmosphere fell over the castle, of heavy, tense expectancy, similar to the atmosphere one might feel on a summer's day before a storm broke.

The storm seemed a long while breaking.

Soon after the swifts had come back for the summer, and could be seen flying high over the Dordogne, Gosvin and Fulbert were on duty on the walkway. Fulbert was leaning on his spear, eyes half closed against the morning sun, while he tried to ignore his companion who was muttering darkly about unpaid debts.

'Come on, cough up,' Gosvin said, holding out his hand.

Fulbert opened an eye. 'Cough what up?'

Gosvin indicated the tower. 'That wager we had. It's been well over three weeks and she's not relented.'

'No, but she's sent letters abroad.'

'That doesn't count. The Lady Arlette herself has to come out. And she's not stepped across the threshold.'

Fulbert opened both eyes, and eased his shoulders. 'Play fair, Gosvin. You wagered she'd stay there a month. It's not been a month.'

'Soon will be. She's dug in all right.'

Fulbert grinned. 'So why are you worrying? When the month is up, you'll get your money.'

'I'd better.'

1187 flowed slowly by, and in the tower Arlette held to her word, and refused to leave.

The allowance of food continued as before.

The tower guards had firm instructions that if ever Arlette was to ask to come out they should march her straight to the count, where she would be made to sign a document releasing Count Etienne from his promise to marry her, after which she would be packed off to Brittany.

The girls were not cut off from daylight, having access to the tower roof from the upper chamber. The roof gave an unbroken view of the river and the flat, wooded valley which stretched out like a green carpet as far as the horizon. From there, Arlette continued to watch the comings and goings in the bailey. She could hear people talking, hens squawking, and pigs squealing. Sho could watch the horses clop across the drawbridge, listen to the clashing of steel on steel as Captain Gervase put his men through their paces – though all of these sounds were somewhat muted by the time they reached the top of Arlette's tower. She watched the world from afar, and after the first few months, discovered with surprise that she rather enjoyed her diluted and diminished world.

Father Theobald, the castle priest visited her, bringing her a copy of the Gospels that he himself had illustrated.

'When I was younger, of course,' he explained quietly and held out his hands for Arlette to see. They trembled like leaves in the autumn.

Arlette gave the priest a compassionate look. 'Doesn't the shaking ever stop?' she asked.

'No. Never. It's all I can do to keep my lord's accounts and write his letters.'

'I'm sorry,' Arlette said, bending her head over Father Theobald's jewel-bright Gospels. 'These are very beautiful.'

'Thank you, mistress.'

Noticing that the priest had stripped her of her title, Arlette sent him a sharp look, but said nothing. No one else was allowed in her tower, and she enjoyed his company and did not wish to alienate him.

A gentle soul, Father Theobald spent most of his time trying to persuade her to see the count's point of view. 'It's all about the land, my dear, try and understand. He needs more land.'

Arlette heard him out, and smiled sweetly at him, but would not budge an inch. She was waiting, she said, for the ruling of the Church. She would obey Holy Church, and no one else.

Sadly, Father Theobald left her.

Arlette read Father Theobald's Gospels.

She talked to Clemence. She did not see that Clemence should have to share her imprisonment, and accordingly sent one of the guards with a message to Count Etienne requesting that Clemence be allowed in and out of the tower. While Arlette knew that there was no danger of the count mistreating her since her case was now well-known and in the hands of the ecclesiastical courts, she half expected him to refuse this request. To her surprise Count Etienne agreed. Thus, while Arlette waited for Queen Eleanor, Duke Richard and the bishops to reply to her appeals Clemence brought in news from the outside world.

That summer Jerusalem fell, and the infidel Saladin captured King Guy. All of Christendom was up in arms. A tithe was imposed, the Saladin tithe, and a collection box was placed in every church in Christendom. The people loathed the tithe. Kings and noblemen flocked to join the crusade; Duke Richard was numbered among them.

Arlette wondered what he had done about her letter. She had not heard any news of her appeal for a long time.

Anna thought she would go mad at Kermaria with only Klara to talk to and baby Jean to play with.

After Barthélemy had left, the manor had seemed more of an empty shell than it had before he had arrived.

There were a few distractions which saved her sanity.

One day, when Anna was bathing baby Jean in the old horse trough, one of the carters who took Madalen's reeds into Vannes drove into the yard. He had a tale to tell, and as he and Madalen loaded the neat bundles of reeds and rushes on to his cart, he knew he had the perfect audience.

'There's some justice in this world, Madalen, my old

friend,' the carter opened. 'God's seen fit to strike de Roncier down.'

'What do you mean?' Anna demanded, lifting her dripping child from the trough and hastening to the cart. She wrapped Jean in the cloth she had ready for him. 'Is the count dead?'

Anna had not known the count, but she knew he was responsible for the destruction of Raymond's family. It had been he who had filled Raymond's soul with so much hate that Raymond had left her on his course of vengeance. She both loathed and feared him.

'No, he's not dead, but it's in my mind he would wish to be. I was told it happened after he had beaten a wench to death for refusing to lay with him.' The carter had been told no such thing, but he was a born storyteller, and every time he repeated his tale, he embellished it. 'He had a fit, and fell to the ground, foaming at the mouth. He's not moved since. Can't speak either, so I'm told.'

'It's less than he deserves,' Madalen said, mouth turned down by bitter memories.

'Oh, there's more. He and his countess have been turfed out of that filthy great castle. They're living on charity.'

When the carter left, Anna hastened to discuss the news at length with Klara who, if one were able to ignore her unremittingly doleful turn of mind, could prove to be a mine of information concerning Raymond and his family. Anna wished she had learnt of the count's misfortune before Barthélemy had left. Had Raymond heard this news? If he were part of Arlette de Roncier's entourage, how would this affect him? Would he come home?

Eventually, Anna grew bored with exchanging confidences with Klara, for Klara was repetitious, continually droning on about how wonderful it had been before Count François had sacked Kermaria. This news seemed to have brought it all back to her.

'Klara,' Anna said one day in exasperation. 'You're too

fond of looking back. Try looking forward.'

'But it'll never be the same again,' Klara moaned.

'No, I daresay it won't. It will be different, but that may not be a bad thing.'

'I liked it as it was.'

'Oh, Klara.'

By the end of the summer, Anna had quite lost patience with her companion.

Every day she walked with Jean over the bridge and looked down the road, straining her eyes as far as the bend. Her first, wildest hope was that Raymond would come home at last. Failing that, she prayed Barthélemy would return for the winter.

December arrived, bringing sharp frosts on its heels, but there was no sign of Barthélemy. They piled the fire in the hall as high as they could, and sat so close they were practically toasting, but as soon as they moved away from it, the cold nibbled at fingers and noses and toes. The hall had been designed to house a knight's retainers. They needed more people to keep in the warmth.

Anna went to visit Joel and Madalen in their cottage. The crack in the wall had been stuffed with reeds, but the moss had not relinquished its grip on the damp wall.

'I'd be very happy if you would move into the manor with me,' Anna said. 'It's very empty with only Klara and Jean and me.'

Brother and sister exchanged glances.

'The manor's drier than this,' Anna said persuasively. 'And the more of us there are living there, the warmer it will be. Think about it.'

'We don't need to think about it,' Joel said. 'Last winter the damp got into Madalen's lungs. It took her half the spring to shake it off. We'd be glad to keep you company — till Master Raymond gets back.'

Anna smiled. It did not look as though Barthélemy had found Raymond that summer. But she could spend this winter singing the songs he had taught her with Madalen and Joel.

And with God's help Barthélemy might find Raymond next summer.

Spring came.

Arlette had had no news from either of the Plantagenet rulers she had written to, or the bishops, or the Pope. She could do nothing but wait.

More time went by.

Clemence told her the great princes were warring amongst themselves.

King Philip invaded Northern Aquitaine, and Duke Richard ended up doing homage to the French king. His father King Henry was displeased, and the quarrel rumbled on into July 1189, ending only when King Henry died.

Arlette remained in her tower.

Duke Richard was now King of England, and King Philip's vassal for the Aquitaine. It was a complicated business.

Clemence brought Arlette all the gossip. She told her that a grudging respect was developing for her among the count's people. They had re-christened the tower 'Lady's Tower' in her honour.

Trooper Gosvin, who once did not have two pennies to rub together, had apparently found a mysterious source of income and become quite rich. It was thought that he would not remain at La Forteresse as a trooper much longer. He had ambitions to become a merchant.

At the beginning of August 1189, Sir Louis and Lady Petronilla had had a child, a son called William, and Lady Petronilla's crowing delight had apparently been too much for Count Etienne, who had galloped off after the child's christening and not stayed to partake in the celebrations afterwards. Lady Petronilla was said to have been laid low with a strange affliction that upset the balance of her mind. It took her several months to recover after the birth of her son.

Not content with having paved Paris – a paved city, imagine! – King Philip of France had extended his capital and had larger walls built to encircle it.

Oh, and a troubadour had arrived, called Barthélemy le Harpour. Clemence blushed when she told Arlette about the harper, and said that she thought he played very well; his songs must have impressed Sir Gilles, too, for the steward had asked him to stay at the castle for a week or so.

It was not easy for Barthélemy to find a moment for private conversation with the man the folk in La Forteresse knew as a squire, Gwionn Leclerc, but after a week at the castle, he ventured into Domme to size up the town as a source of future income.

A trio of musicians were established in the cliff-top market square overlooking the valley, and they were making a reasonable living, if the quality of their clothes and their instruments – all in mint condition – was anything to go by. The minstrels were perfectly civil, but Barthélemy was left in no doubt that this was their territory, and he should go elsewhere. On leaving the musicians, his attention was caught by the sound of a painted signboard creaking in a stray gust of wind. The sign bore a picture of two crossed swords. This was a hostelry, and one with a good reputation, if his memory served him: Les Deux Epées. A youth came to stand in the door of the stone-built inn. A prosperous town, many of Domme's houses and buildings were made from stone. The youth chucked a pail of water into a runnel at the edge of the square. A cloud of tiny blue butterflies appeared and alighted on the splash marks the water left on the drain, sipping the dirty water before the hot sun dried it up entirely.

Feeling thirsty himself, Barthélemy sauntered over and ducking his head under the low lintel, discovered that his luck was in.

There, sitting at a table by the door, sat the very man he wanted to speak to, Raymond Herevi, otherwise known as Gwionn Leclerc.

One glance told Barthélemy that Anna's lover had been there for some time, because his green eyes were hazy with a surfeit of wine, and his cheeks — especially the one with that ugly scar — were bright and flushed.

Waving for service, Barthélemy caught the attention of the potboy, the youth he had seen throwing water out in the square. About fourteen years of age, he had buck teeth and a distressingly spotty complexion. A dazzling white linen cloth was tied round his waist.

'A bottle of cider, if you have it,' Barthélemy said. As a native of Normandy, he had a sweet tooth and was partial to cider, but he was rarely able to indulge his preference. Good cider was not easy to come by outside his own duchy.

'Cider? Very good, sir,' came the brisk answer.

'You have it?'

The potboy's blemished chin inched up. 'All of Aquitaine knows of Les Deux Epées, sir, and our reputation is deserved. Of course we have cider.'

'Bring it over here.' Barthélemy waved at Gwionn's table. 'I'm joining my friend.'

At this, Gwionn Leclerc roused himself and regarded Barthélemy. His eyes were faintly hostile.

Barthélemy ignored this, sat down, and held out his hand.

'Barthélemy le Harpour, at your service. You'll have seen me at the castle.'

Gwionn Leclerc took the hand that was offered and shook it perfunctorily. 'Yes.'

'I've a message for you.'

'Oh?' The tone was bored, the eyes uninterested. 'Don't tell me my lady has finally decided to come down from her tower?'

'No. This message is from Brittany.'

The hazy, unfocused look vanished. The scar which cut across one lean, bronzed cheek was all at once more deeply graven. 'From Brittany, you say?'

Gratified to have won Gwionn's full attention, Barthélemy paused, drawing out the moment so he had time to assess Gwionn's reactions to the message. 'Yes,' he said, at last. 'It's taken me an age to find you, but I've a message from Anna, for Raymond Herevi.'

Gwionn Leclerc started, and threw a quick glance round the inn. 'Hush, man. Don't mention that name here, for pity's sake.'

Gwionn waited until Barthélemy's cider had been brought and paid for. Then the questions started.

'When did you see her? Is she well?'

'I've not seen her for over two years, since the spring of 1187. She was well then.'

Gwionn Leclerc's features relaxed, and the purple brightness that coloured his scar faded a shade. He swallowed.

'I'm glad. Christ, but I miss that girl. I was thinking about her before you came in.'

'You were? She was missing you when I saw her. She said to tell you she loved you. Will you be going back to Brittany to see her?'

'I can't.' They were the only people in the tavern from La Forteresse, but Gwionn lowered his voice till it was barely audible. 'I've unfinished business with de Roncier's daughter.'

'Leave it, man. Let it lie.' Barthélemy had prised the full tale of de Roncier's fall from power and his illness from Clemence. 'Your enemy can no longer harm

399

anyone. Leave his daughter alone.'

'I can't. She may give in any day. She must give in. It might be tomorrow—'

'Man, she's been up there for two years at least. Her maid tells me she'll never give up. You could waste your life waiting. Leastwise, she's innocent.'

'Innocent? I was innocent. I want her . . . I want her to suffer as I did. Anyway, what business is it of yours what I do?'

The squire's tone was so full of venom that Barthélemy blinked. 'Anna needs you.'

Gwionn turned tortured eyes on him. 'And I need her. God, I need her. But de Roncier killed my father, and I swore an oath to be avenged, don't you see? Only then can I be free.'

Barthélemy paused to sip from his leather tankard. The cider was good, better than any he had had outside Normandy.

He wiped his mouth with the back of his hand. 'She has your child, you know.'

Gwionn's hand snaked out, and caught at the neck of Barthélemy's tunic. His face was chalk-white.

'My child? Anna has my child?'

His surprise was genuine, Barthélemy would have sworn an oath on the relics of St Valérie herself. He watched as a slow beam of delight and pride spread across Gwionn's face.

'It's a boy. He was born more than two years ago, in November.' He did not see the need to tell Gwionn that he had helped deliver the babe himself. 'She called him Jean, after your father, I believe.'

'Jean,' Gwionn murmured. 'Jean.'

'He'll be three this year.'

'God, I've a son. Would that I could see them.'

'You love her?'

Gwionn looked affronted. 'Of course I love her.'

400

'But you won't go home. You hate more thoroughly than you love, I think.'

Gwionn didn't reply. His face hardened, and with a sinking feeling Barthélemy recognised that Gwionn Leclerc possessed the terrifying obduracy of a martyr. He would never allow himself to deviate from a road once he had set his feet upon it, however high the price. Even if the cost of sticking to that road be his life, or, God forgive him, his Anna's happiness, Gwionn Leclerc would pay it.

'You and the maid in the tower are a match for each other,' Barthélemy commented, lightly.

'What do you mean?' Gwionn demanded sharply.

'Both wilful. Both set on courses from which neither of you will deviate. It should be interesting to watch the outcome. Does she know you've your heart set upon revenge?'

Gwionn's eyes became green slits. 'If you breathe a word of this to a living soul,' he hissed, 'I'll have your tongue out and you'll never carol again.'

Alarmed by Gwionn's vehemence, Barthélemy held up a long-fingered harper's hand. 'Peace. Peace. So she doesn't know. Relax, man. I mean you no harm. There's no need for threats. Who would fetch Anna if you killed me?'

'I beg your pardon?'

Picking up his tankard, Barthélemy took another long draught of the sweet, golden cider, and eyed Gwionn over the rim.

'She's willing to come here. She wants to be with you.'

'I wish she could.' This with fervour.

'Do you? She could, you know. She has the most beautiful voice. She could be my trobiaritz. I'll fetch her for you, as long as you assure me you really care for her.'

'I do. By God, I do. My feelings for her are pure . . . uncomplicated. That means much to me.'

Barthélemy could sympathise with that. To a man as

401

twisted as Gwionn Leclerc, Anna's honest, clear love would be like finding a well in a desert. 'Very well. I'll go back to Brittany for the winter, and we'll set out next spring. You'll be here next summer?'

Gwionn Leclerc nodded. 'Where else can I go till I'm free of this?'

'You could try and forget it, as I suggested.'

'Don't you think I've tried? Christ, man, if I'd been able to do that I'd have been long gone. But I can't. Every time I look up at that tower I am reminded of what her father did to my family.'

'All the more reason for you to leave and go back to Brittany. Then you won't have to look at that tower.'

Gwionn shot Barthélemy a look that was almost pitying. 'You don't understand. How could you? If I'm honest I thought this would have been over years ago. I never thought she'd hold out so long. God knows where it will end. I have to see it through. But I'd be grateful if you would fetch Anna.' A thought seemed to strike him. 'You mustn't bring her into La Forteresse. Find her lodgings, and come alone. I'll meet her away from the castle. That de Roncier witch sees everything from the top of her tower.'

'I understand.'

Arlette was permitted to write at regular intervals to her stepmother at St Anne's Convent, and received regular answers, but there was no news of her plea to the Pope.

Apparently her father was neither better, nor worse. How long could a man's soul inhabit an empty shell of a body? He must be in purgatory. Eleanor told Arlette that there was as yet no news concerning his case either. Sir Hamon continued to manage the Huelgastel estates.

At La Forteresse life ran on much as usual. Arlette watched the comings and goings from the top of the tower.

Barthélemy le Harpour stayed a month and then left. She saw him loping energetically down the cliff path. She was yet to hear him play properly, only having caught the odd snatch of his repertoire as his songs floated up to her on the warm evening air.

Autumn approached, and Arlette put on her cloak when she climbed to the tower roof.

The swallows and swifts flew south for the winter.

Gwionn Leclerc continued to exercise Star and Yseult. He had taken an interest in swordmanship, and must have prevailed upon Captain Gervase de Limoges to train him. He did not show much aptitude at first, and Captain Gervase usually disarmed him effortlessly, but as the weeks passed, Arlette noticed an improvement in Gwionn's style. It took progressively longer for de Limoges to best him. Whereas at the beginning de Limoges had seemed to be toying with the squire, after a few months the duels became more serious. It was only a matter of time before Gwionn mastered the skill. Did the squire have his sights set on a knighthood, she wondered?

In 1190 King Richard set off for Palestine with King Philip. They quarrelled. Arlette realised Richard Plantagenet must have shelved her letters. So she asked for permission to write again, to his mother, Queen Eleanor, and because by now half of Christendom knew of Arlette's sojourn in the tower, Count Etienne had no choice but to allow her.

Barthélemy le Harpour came back.

He seemed to have made friends with Gwionn Leclerc the last time he was here, for no sooner had the harper arrived, than Gwionn Leclerc marched him into the stable. Minutes later they had saddled Star and galloped under the portcullis, with Barthélemy le Harpour riding pillion. They ripped along the road to Domme, faster than the devil himself.

* * *

Anna and three-year-old Jean were waiting for Gwionn in a clearing in la Forêt des Colombes.

Having combed her hair, and the dark curls of her child's, Anna sat on a log to wait. Her wordly goods — not that she had much — a spare bliaud and undergown, and an extra tunic for Jean — were tied in a bundle at her feet. The child rolled in the ferns and then, noticing the wood was full of butterflies, ran about chasing purple emperors and painted ladies, crying, 'Pretty! Pretty! Pretty!' Anna let him be. He was too young actually to catch any of them, and left the duller, speckled brown butterflies in peace. There was something to be said for being dull and unremarkable, Anna thought.

She was extremely nervous, so much so that her throat was dry. She had not seen her husband for four interminable years. She could hardly believe that she might see him today.

'Don't expect anything,' Barthélemy had warned her. 'He may have duties at La Forteresse that he can't leave. You might have to wait until tomorrow to see him.'

Dear Barthélemy. How she had come to rely on him. They had dealt well together while on the road. And Barthélemy had been right about her singing. When he had come back to Kermaria he had brought with him a collection of ballads, all of which were meant to be sung in the *langue d'oc* which was incomprehensible to Anna. They had spent that winter singing them. Anna had protested that she couldn't pass herself off as a trobiaritz because it would be a sham when she couldn't understand the *langue d'oc*. Grandly, Barthélemy had waved her objection aside.

'That's of no moment,' he had said. 'You may not understand what each individual word means, but I have explained the story behind each ballad. I don't quite understand how you do it, Anna, but you are very good at

404

singing them. You put your soul into it.'

Because Anna was desperate to see Raymond, she had done her best. Together she and Barthélemy had spent several months on foot, travelling all the way from Brittany singing as they went. And now she was here in the Aquitaine with Jean and, hopefully, today would see the end of their waiting.

It was hard living through these last few moments. For all Barthélemy's kindly-meant warning, Anna felt certain Raymond would come today. She seemed to have spent her life longing to see him. And now the moment was almost upon her. Would Raymond — she must remember to call him Gwionn here — look the same? What would he think of his son? What would Jean think of him?

Just then the sound of hoofbeats, staccato fast, entered the clearing. The hoofbeats came to an abrupt halt.

'Take the reins, Barthélemy,' said a beloved voice that sent shivers racing down Anna's spine.

She heard Raymond — Gwionn, she must call him Gwionn — come crashing through the bracken towards her. She tried to rise, but discovered her legs had turned to jelly.

'Anna! *Anna!*'

And then he was before her, with a few extra lines engraved around his eyes and mouth; and his eyes themselves? They shone bright as ever, hard as emeralds, and when they looked on her they softened.

Her nervousness dissolved, she regained the use of her legs and they flew into each other's arms.

'Raymond — Gwionn. Oh, Gwionn.'

They kissed feverishly; kissing lips, noses, cheeks, necks, both of them murmuring disjointed endearments, both of them trembling.

Anna's heart thumped like a tambour as she wound her fingers deep into Gwionn's hair. It was threaded here and there with a silver strand, but the texture was the same.

She breathed in his scent, and a slow warm glow spread through her whole body. So unfamiliar was this glow that it was a moment before she was able to identify it. She felt safe and happy for the first time in four years.

After some minutes, Anna became aware of a tugging at her skirts.

Jean was looking up at her, scowling. He had never seen anyone capable of stealing his mother's attention away from him so thoroughly. He disapproved.

Barthélemy strolled into the clearing.

'Mother?' Jean said, a little lordling who feared being displaced.

Gwionn drew apart from Anna and, keeping a secure hold of her hand, went down on his knees on the woodland floor to gaze at his son. Kneeling at her husband's side, Anna put her free arm about Jean and drew him close.

'You must be Jean,' Gwionn said, reaching out to touch one of his son's dark brown curls. 'I've been longing to meet you.'

Unmollified by this remark, the child's deep-set brown eyes were dark with suspicion.

'This is a very good friend of mine, Jean. His name is . . .' Anna hesitated ' . . . what should he call you?'

'I think Gwionn is best.'

'His name is Gwionn.'

Jean continued to scowl.

'Look, I've brought you a present,' Gwionn said. He thrust his hand inside his tunic, brought out an object wrapped in calico, and handed it to the child.

'For me?'

Jean had not had many presents in his short life.

'For you. Aren't you going to open it?'

The child needed no second bidding. The calico was cast aside to reveal a horse, an exquisite horse, lovingly carved in oiled and waxed ebony.

Anna caught her breath. 'It's lovely, Gwionn. Where did you get it?'

'I bought the wood from a merchant in Domme—'

'You carved it yourself?'

The horse was a marvel, a delicate black Arab, and Gwionn had captured it poised for flight, with the wind streaming through its mane and tail.

'A woodcarver at Vannes Cathedral would have been proud to have carved that,' Anna said. She wondered how long it would be before that flowing tail would be broken. It was almost too good for a child, an impractical present, but she loved Gwionn all the more for making the gesture.

'I had a few false starts,' Gwionn admitted, before asking anxiously, 'Does he like it?'

Anna laughed. 'You don't know much about children, do you? That silence tells all. He's struck dumb with amazement. He adores it. Don't you, Jean darling?'

Wordlessly, Jean nodded.

Barthélemy stepped forward. 'What's that you've got there, Jean, my lad?'

'Horse. Look.'

'Isn't that lovely? Would you like to sit on a real horse?'

'Yes.'

Barthélemy held out his hand. 'Come with me, and meet Star, and we'll let your mother and Gwionn catch up on their news.'

The harper and the child left the clearing.

Anna sighed and leaned against Gwionn.

'Did you ask Barthélemy to distract Jean for a while?' she asked.

'No.' Moving into a sitting position, Gwionn pulled Anna across his knees.

'Barthélemy's wonderful,' Anna went on. 'He always seems to know exactly what to do.'

'Mmm. He's a good man.' Gwionn seemed preoccupied

with the bodice of Anna's bliaud, which fastened below the neck in a complicated latticework of green ribbons.

'I thought you'd like it,' Anna said, smiling. 'I saw a similar dress on a lady in one of the halls we sang in, and her maid said the design had come back from the East.'

'How does it open?'

Anna blushed, and made as if to show him.

Gently he pushed her hand aside. 'No, let me discover it for myself. I'll untie this one first, and loosen it here . . . Now this one, and this one. There.'

Eyes on Anna's, Gwionn slid his hand into her bodice.

Anna sighed, and her mouth sought his. 'Gwionn . . .'

'Dear God, but you feel like heaven itself, Anna.'

Gwionn's hand caressed first one breast then the other. Anna moaned, and bit his chin.

Gwionn pushed Anna's bodice down.

'What, you'd take me here?' she asked, brown eyes sparkling. 'Practically in full view of the road?'

'Not quite,' And, picking Anna up, Gwionn carried her past the fallen log and fell with her into a clump of springy bracken. 'They can't see us here.' His lips sought hers.

'What if Barthélemy and Jean come back?'

'They won't. Barthélemy has more sense.'

Gwionn pushed up his wife's skirts.

It was some while before they spoke again, and when they did it was to agree that they must be parted no more.

Anna could enter La Forteresse, but to preserve Gwionn's secret identity, she must pose as Barthélemy's wife, and Jean as his son.

If, that is, Barthélemy was agreeable.

He was.

408

Chapter Nineteen

Watching from her tower later in the day, Arlette saw Gwionn Leclerc ride back with Barthélemy le Harpour.

Only this time it was not Barthélemy riding pillion behind Gwionn, but a young woman who looked ill-at-ease on horseback, and whose arms clung like ivy about the squire's waist. Barthélemy walked at Star's stirrup, carrying a little boy high on his shoulders — presumably this was his wife and child. It was queer how Gwionn — normally very fastidious with Star — had permitted the black gelding to be used as a packhorse, for the harper's back-pack and harp were stowed behind the saddle. Sir Ralph's squire must think much of the harper to permit him such liberties.

Arlette had always wondered why Gwionn Leclerc held himself apart from his fellow man. She was glad he had found some friends at last.

As Star clattered over the drawbridge, the young woman looked down into the ravine and shrieked, and gripped Gwionn Leclerc all the harder. Arlette wondered where Madame la Harpour and her child had been the last time Barthélemy had visited La Forteresse. Perhaps the child had been ailing, or too young to travel.

Barthélemy's wife turned out to be a trobiaritz, for that evening Arlette heard a strong, feminine voice float out of the hall in perfect harmony with Barthélemy's. When Arlette questioned Clemence, Clemence confirmed that the voice belonged to Madame le Harpour.

'They sound very well together,' Arlette commented.

'They do. They've impressed Count Etienne, who has a great love of music. He's asked them to stay.' Remembering the other musicians who the count dismissed, Clemence frowned. 'I wonder why he let the others go?'

'I can answer that,' Arlette said. 'His pride wouldn't let him keep them.'

'His pride?'

'When he arrived at La Forteresse, I expressed a liking for them. Busy playing the gallant, Count Etienne offered to keep them on for my sake. But when I crossed swords with him, and took my stand in this tower, the sight of them was a constant reminder of his broken word. He sent them away because they wouldn't allow him to forget that he had done a dishonourable thing in trying to set me aside.' Arlette laughed. 'I wonder if he still tries to justify his breaking of the terms of our betrothal contract? Clemence, have you noticed how it's apparently all right to act dishonourably to someone who is in a weak position?'

'I haven't thought about it in those terms.'

'I have. If I had had other relatives, powerful ones, who were perhaps close to the count, I would never have had to take a stand in this tower. But I only had my father, and once his position and wealth were called into question, I was left on my own. Weak and defenceless. And Count Etienne has the temerity to think of himself as a pious and honourable man!'

'Give it up Arlette. You're wasting your life—'

'Give it up? Never! I had a letter from the Bishop of Vannes last week, and he has agreed to write to the Pope again.' She gave a cynical laugh. 'Thank heavens that my belle-mère was a generous patron with regard to the rebuilding of his cathedral.'

Clemence's blue-grey eyes were sad. 'But nothing has

been settled, has it? You've not heard from Queen Eleanor?'

'Not yet. But I will.'

'Give it up, Arlette, please.'

'Never. I'll never give up. Right is on my side. I remember the wording of the terms. I'm bound to win, in the end.'

'Yes, but at what cost?' Clemence wondered. 'Are you willing to grow grey in this tower?'

And then Arlette gave Clemence one of her blank, uncomprehending looks, that made Clemence feel that they were speaking in different languages entirely.

'If it's God's will I grow grey here, then I'll grow grey.' She shrugged.

Clemence sighed. It was not a price that she would ever pay for a principle. She admired her mistress, but she would never understand her.

'Count Etienne has been inquiring whether you needed new gowns,' she said. 'I told him your old ones were worn, and he has given me money to buy stuffs at Domme. It won't buy luxuries, there'll be no Damascus silk, I'm afraid. But may I go?'

Arlette had a small store of money left, carefully hoarded for dire emergencies. It would not run to new gowns. She lifted a frayed sleeve and idly pulled at a loose thread. 'If you like.' She smiled. 'I've no use for Damascus silk here. Buy me two lengths of plain English wool.'

Startled by Arlette's agreement, Clemence lifted a brow. 'I thought you'd object to him clothing you.'

'You're forgetting. Count Etienne is my future husband. My father consigned me into his care, it's his duty to feed and clothe me. You may go to Domme.'

'Thank you. Sir Walter has agreed to escort me.'

Arlette's gaze became penetrating. 'You like Sir Walter, don't you?'

411

Blushing like a June rose, Clemence let herself out of the tower. She did like Sir Walter, very much, and if ever there was a time when she loved a boy called Morgan le Bihan, it had been in another life, and she had forgotten it.

In 1191 Arlette turned twenty and King Richard married Berengaria of Navarre.

Arlette continued to look down from her eyrie. She saw much of Gwionn Leclerc. Or was it that she simply noticed him more? He practised with the sword at every opportunity. And when he was not practising, he was often in the company of the harper, or the harper's wife and child. He looked happier than she had ever seen him. Latterly, Arlette never noticed the scar, and thought him quite handsome. Usually he would glance up at the tower roof, and if he saw her he would wave, for which Arlette was growing increasingly grateful. Madam le Harpour never looked up.

Arlette had her dark moments, her moments of self-doubt. At times she came to question her very existence. Not once did Count Etienne glance her way, and it was rare for any of his retainers to do so either these days. At the beginning, she had been a novelty, and all eyes had turned to her tower – the Lady's Tower. According to Clemence the tower was known far and wide as the Lady's Tower, but little mention was ever made of the lady within the walls of La Forteresse.

Count Etienne had forbidden it.

One day Clemence ran into the tower, eyes glowing, to tell her that Sir Walter had asked her to marry him.

Arlette was delighted, and the girls embraced.

'Oh, Clemence, I'm so pleased for you.'

'Thank you,' Clemence replied and, unexpectedly, her face clouded.

'Clemence? What is it? Aren't you happy?' Arlette asked, confused, for she knew how much Clemence had come to love Sir Walter.

Clemence twirled a strand of yellow hair around her finger. 'Of course I'm happy. And I would be ecstatic, if it were not for one thing.'

'What's that?'

'I wanted you to witness my wedding, but when Walter and I asked Count Etienne if he would release you just for the wedding, he refused. Oh, Arlette, can't you see? He'll never give in. And the Church court may not see it from your point of view. Supposing they side with the Count? You'll be stuck here for ever. I can't bear to see you wasting your life over this. Forget Count Etienne. He's simply not worth it.'

Arlette knew her face had grown hard.

'It's not the man I'm after, it's the principle that's at stake,' she said. 'My father's lands and position are irrelevant as far as my marriage contract is concerned.'

A tear glistened on Clemence's lashes.

'Oh, Arlette. Please. It's up to you. Your life doesn't have to be like this. Reconsider.'

'No.'

Clemence hung her head. 'Not even for my wedding?' she asked in a small voice.

'Not even for that.' Arlette made her voice soft. 'I'm sorry, Clemence, but I cannot surrender now. I know the Church will come to back me up. Do say you understand. I need your understanding. Please don't withold it, it's all I have.'

Clemence wiped her eyes with her sleeve and sniffed. 'I'll support you, Arlette, you should know that. But I cannot bear to see your life being wasted.'

'I have to do this.'

Clemence nodded, and smiled through her tears. 'I know. It's a shame you can't come to my wedding.'

'I'll be with you in spirit.'

And so she was, although the day of Clemence's marriage found her feeling especially lonely. Hardly anyone came near her tower all that long day.

It was as though the world had forgotten her, except for Gwionn Leclerc who waved at her when he went by.

Peculiarly strengthened by such bouts of despair, Arlette would emerge from them filled with energy and despatch another set of letters.

She would not let the world forget her. She would not be abandoned.

Once Clemence had married, Clemence's place was quite properly with her husband, Sir Walter. She moved into the keep to share his small knight's chamber. Count Etienne gave permission for Clemence to spend part of each day with Arlette — a sign that he knew the outside world had not forgotten her. Arlette did not view Count Etienne's generosity in this regard as a sign that he was weakening. Rather, it proved that he was aware the Church was pursuing her case. He did not want to lay himself open to accusations of mistreatment.

In March 1192 Petronilla Favell gave birth to another son, Laurence. Once again she was struck by the same mysterious, nervous condition that had struck her the previous time she had given birth, only this time it took her even longer to recover. Arlette learnt that it was almost a year before Lady Favell was able to pick up the threads of her life and become active once more.

Gwionn Leclerc was knighted by Count Etienne. The dubbing ceremony was held in the outer courtyard, and Arlette had a good view from her crow's nest. After his promotion, Sir Gwionn rode proudly under the portcullis, with a shining new sword safely housed in its scabbard. His special gilded spurs — only knights were entitled to wear these — flashed bravely in the sun. Arlette wondered if, now that he was a knight, Sir Gwionn would be so swollen with his own consequence that he would forget her. He was not.

When Star's hoofs struck the main causeway outside La Forteresse, he turned in his saddle as usual, and saluted her. His smile was both triumphant and beautiful, so beautiful it warmed Arlette's heart.

That same year King Richard was captured, and a massive ransom was demanded for his release.

The King was not freed until two years later in 1194. In February, at Candlemas, time, Queen Eleanor took her son's ransom and went to meet him. But before the Queen left, she re-read Arlette's letters. Arlette de Roncier intrigued her. She was astonishingly single-minded, given that she was a woman and God had apparently designed the world for men. The world was not kind to single-minded women. Queen Eleanor had learnt that long ago. Arlette de Roncier appeared to have a highly developed sense of justice, of honour. Again this was unusual in a woman. Queen Eleanor was reminded of herself as she had been when she was younger.

An indomitable woman, the Queen had spent several years confined in prison, and knew how loathsome it was. Like her son's subject, Arlette de Roncier, she had spoken out and stood by what she believed in when other women would have kept sensibly silent. She too had been punished. The Queen felt a strong sense of sympathy and admiration for Arlette de Roncier, and decided she had been imprisoned long enough. Using the Great Seal of England, as her son had empowered her, and her personal seal, she wrote to the bishops, directing them to write to Count Etienne Favell.

Then she went to meet her son.

Arlette was twenty-three years old.

415

She had held out in the Lady's Tower for seven long years without private conversation with anyone save Clemence and, briefly, with Father Theobald.

The news from Huelgastel was unchanged – Count François was still alive, but he was no better. While Arlette had been imprisoned in the tower, her father had been imprisoned in the shell of his own body. Eleanor seemed resigned to the fact that her father might never regain his health, and Arlette was beginning to fear she might never escape the tower.

But that autumn a letter came from the bishops for Count Etienne. It was brought by a special courier, who wore a fur-lined red velvet cloak, and had three long pheasant's feathers stuck in his cap. He had four bodyguards, and made a grand entrance, which was deliberate. The bishop's envoy wanted everyone to know that he had arrived.

From her look-out Arlette watched the show.

In the yard, the courier dismounted, and tossed his cloak to one of his bodyguards. Under the cloak he wore a padded jerkin, tightly nipped in at the waist, over a silk chainse. His belt had a silver buckle on it. His stockings were tight. Tossing his reins after his cloak, the bishop's envoy strutted towards the keep with two of his bodyguards.

He walked like a dancer, self-consciously, but with his head erect, and his hips slightly swaying. He held the bishops' letter very ostentatiously in one pale, beringed hand, to ensure that everyone had seen what he carried.

Several imposing red seals dangled from the letter. From her lofty vantage-point, Arlette saw them quite clearly.

At last, her answer had come.

When he had read the bishops' letter, Count Etienne stumped across the bailey, dismissed Arlette's guards, and unlocked the tower door.

'Madam? The ecclesiastical courts have reached a decision in our case. May I discuss it with you?'

'Of course. Come in.' Arlette wondered what decision the churchmen had come to. The count's green eyes were impenetrable when they rested on her, not kind and soft as they had been when she had first arrived at La Forteresse. Arlette could not tell from that whether she had won or lost.

It was the first time Arlette and the count had set eyes on each other at close quarters in seven years. Those seven years sat heavily on the count.

'You look older,' the count observed, following her train of thought. 'And prettier. Do I look older?'

Arlette smiled. 'Somewhat.' She indicated a stool, the best the ground-floor chamber of her tower had to offer. 'Do sit down, Count Etienne, and tell me the court's verdict.'

'Madam, you may rejoice,' the count said. 'You have won. The Church has given us one week in which to be married.' He looked very tired, and beneath the grey skin of his cheeks the bones of his skull were clearly visible.

'You agree with the bishops' ruling?'

'I have to, for my soul's sake. If at the end of a week we are not wed, I face excommunication. I've decided we'll be wed the day after tomorrow, if that's agreeable to you?'

'That's perfectly agreeable. Thank you, my lord count.' As Arlette examined the aged, sagging face before her, she was conscious that she should feel some triumph. Where was it? By rights she should be crowing like a cockerel, but suddenly all she could feel was pity for this tired old man. A quick calculation told her he must be fifty-eight.

For seven years she had watched and waited, striving to make him honour his promise to marry her. And now that she had succeeded, she should be jubilant. So why the hollow sensation in her belly? Why the urge to scream and run ten miles rather than bed with this sad, shrivelled creature who managed to be both proud and dejected all at once?

On impulse she took one of the count's hands. The skin was dry like a dead leaf, his fingers cold. 'My lord, I am content to have won my case,' she said. 'I have proved my point and my honour is satisfied. If it is still your will to set me aside then I will not force you to become my husband. Neither of us would benefit from an alliance founded on dislike and resentment.'

The count lifted his head, clearly startled. 'Madam, you misread me. I do not, and have never, disliked you. When I sought to put you aside, I sought merely to gain a more advantageous marriage. With power comes responsibility. Several hundred souls depend on me. I have to do my best for their sake as well as my own.'

The count pressed her fingers, and smiled, and as his lips parted, Arlette saw that the gaps in the count's teeth had grown large.

'I honour you for the stand that you have taken,' the count went on. 'At one time you angered me, but you have taught me much. I respect you for holding out for what you believed in. I see you as a woman of honour. There was never any other woman of whom I held that opinion, save our own Duchess Eleanor, Queen Mother of England.

'I would be honoured if you would become my wife,' the count continued. 'I would be proud if you would consent to become the mother of my children. In short, madam, you have become the only woman I could now marry. Will you marry me?'

Arlette swallowed. 'Count Etienne, I will.'

Not once had he named her by her title, as Lady Arlette, but that was of little account. He had his pride, and she had no wish to belittle him. All along she had sought

418

justice, and now she had it. Within one week, whatever the final outcome of the investigation concerning her father's alleged crime, Arlette would become the Countess Favell.

The count rubbed his dry hands together in a gesture of satisfaction. 'Good.' He took a thorough look around the room. 'Now that's agreed, let's see about moving you back to your chamber, eh?'

That day, Count Etienne sent a messenger to Favell Manor at La Roque Gageac, inviting Louis and Petronilla to the wedding.

Petronilla and Louis were on a split-log bench in the apple garth behind the manor, watching their sons, aged five and two, playing with the ripe fruit of which there was a glut that year. The elder boy, William, was collecting windfalls, stacking them neatly to form a cairn. Laurence was picking clover.

It was an idyllic scene, which lasted until William's little pyramid of apples was complete.

The moment Laurence saw what William had done, his eyes lit up. He toddled over to the apples and, before William realised what was in his brother's mind, Laurence had lifted a sturdy, plump leg and with one swift, accurate kick had destroyed William's carefully constructed pile. Then he sat down with a thump and looked around for approval.

For a moment William's mouth was round with disbelief. Then he began to scream. William could scream very loudly.

'Mama! Mama!' And, like a player who had been waiting for his cue, he fell down in the grass in a howling rage.

Sighing, Petronilla went to soothe her eldest. 'There, there, William. Never mind. Let me help you build another.'

419

'Laurence is bad. I hate Laurence!'

'No, you don't. He's only small. He doesn't know any better.'

'Papa should smack him.'

Over their son's head, husband and wife's gazes met.

'It was so peaceful a moment ago,' Petronilla said. 'Why does it always have to end in tears?'

She helped William start another pyramid and, when he was happily building, returned to the bench.

It was at this point that Count Etienne's messenger came into the orchard. He bowed, and handed Louis a scroll. 'Sir Louis. Lady Petronilla. I have the honour of bringing you an invitation to attend the nuptial mass of Count Etienne Favell and Arlette de Roncier.'

'What?' Petronilla all but choked. 'What did you say?'

The message was repeated.

Lips set, Petronilla heard it out. She glanced at the scroll which Louis was reading, and imperiously held out her hand. 'Let me see that.'

While she was reading, there came into her eyes an expression which was remarkably similar to the one in William's eyes when Laurence had kicked over the apples.

'Excuse me, Sir Louis,' Count Etienne's man said apologetically. 'But I'm to take back the answer.'

'Convey our congratulations to my uncle,' Louis said. 'And tell him we'd be delighted to attend.'

The messenger bowed and went out of the garth, clanging the gate.

Petronilla burst out, 'A plague on Arlette de Roncier! I thought we were safe. I thought he'd never have her, after she had defied him so openly.'

'Last time I spoke to my uncle, he did tell me how he was coming to admire her fortitude,' Louis answered mildly.

'Fortitude! Great *Christ*!' Petronilla looked at her sons.

Louis could see his wife needed time to adjust to this

turn of events. 'Petronilla,' his soft brown eyes were shadowed. 'You won't do anything rash, will you?'

'Rash?' Her grey eyes were wild, her tone high. 'What could I possibly do? They're to marry the day after tomorrow.'

'I don't know, my love. But sometimes you get a certain look on your face and it worries me. It reminds me of when you were ill.'

'But I'm not ill now.'

'No, my sweet, praise God you are not.'

At dawn on her wedding day, Arlette went to the chapel to pray. Generally, wedding ceremonies were short and, as was the custom, hers would take place outside the chapel at noon. For most people this brief exchange of vows was all that was necessary, but in Arlette's case − she was marrying a count not a commoner − more elaborate celebrations, including a nuptial mass, were in preparation.

The chapel at La Forteresse nestled alongside the keep, which dwarfed it, at the west end. The chapel's north wall seemed to grow out of the battlements overlooking the river. Built of the same fine gold stone as the keep, and roofed with grey lauzes − limestone slabs cut to form tiles − the interior of the chapel was simple. Here no saints marched along the walls, here were no golden stars twinkling down from an azure ceiling. Instead, a plain whitewash covered the walls. On one side of the altar, on a pedestal, an ancient painted Virgin rocked her child, as she had rocked it for over a hundred years. A plaster Joseph of the same era topped a pedestal opposite. The cross above the altar was simple, of carved and gilded wood. Great brass vases of tall white lilies and blue Michaelmas daisies stood on either side of the altar. An atmosphere of calm peace prevailed.

Arlette knelt before the altar. She had fasted for the

whole of the previous day, and already she felt slightly dizzy. Not that she minded being woolly-headed, if it kept her mind from dipping too deeply into some of her darker thoughts. For now her wedding day was upon her, she found herself increasingly concerned about what it would be like to have to sleep with Count Etienne. While in the tower, she had been so taken up with making the count stand by their betrothal, and all the legalities involved; her dowry, her position in society if her father was disgraced, and so on, that she had devoted little time to considering the physical aspect of their marriage. But now she was forced to think of these things, she had to admit that the idea revolted her.

She could have backed out of it. For all that he had tried to evade marrying her in the hope of marrying someone with money in their coffers, Count Etienne was a gentleman and would not have forced her. But this was what her father had wanted. This was why she had spent seven years in the tower. It was her destiny.

As she knelt before the altar, Arlette's stomach grumbled. Relieved by this diversion, her mind turned to food, and the feast that was to be held when the formalities of the ceremony and nuptial mass were over. She wondered what they would eat. Tantalising roasting smells had been wafting out of the cookhouse all morning. No doubt it would be richer fare than she had been allowed in her tower.

While Arlette tried to pray in the chapel, Petronilla Favell was riding in the direction of Domme, accompanied by her maid, Rose — a tall, angular woman, with deep-set brown eyes and lank greying hair hidden beneath her veil and barbette. Both woman wore flat embroidered caps. Lady Favell sat easily in her saddle, and her hands were relaxed on the reins. Rose sat awkwardly, with her teeth clenched and a bright spot of colour highlighting her cheekbones. Rose's thin body was tense, resisting every jolt and step along the way.

Their destination was a villager's hovel on the outer fringe of a hamlet which nestled in the la Forêt des Colombes, but it was no ordinary hovel.

When God had created the world, and formed the riverbed for the Dordogne, he had set it at the foot of a tall cliff which loomed over the gently undulating valley. The village was set at the top of the cliff, in a clearing in the trees. A track bore left towards the cliff.

Unerringly, Petronilla guided her horse towards it.

The track was wide enough to bear sure-footed horses in single file.

'We're not taking the horses down there, are we, my lady?' Rose asked, paling as she looked at the steep plunge to the river on her left hand. Rose did not like heights.

'Yes, we are. Don't worry, Rose. The track widens out ahead. See?'

Petronilla pointed ahead of them and, as she had said, the track broadened out into a wide ledge of plateau which ran along three-quarters of the way up the cliff.

Rose — who was by now gripping hard at the pommel of her saddle and trying not to notice the drop to the river — looked, and to her astonishment saw what appeared to be a cottage garden, for the ground had been dug over and various herbs and vegetables grew in well-organised rows on the plateau.

A swallowtail fluttered by. A wood-pigeon churred softly from the leaves of an alder which leaned out over the river as though it would trail its branches in the water.

The vegetable plot was bounded by trees and shrubs which clung to the crevices in the cliffside, effectively screening it from prying eyes. The only way one would ever find this place was if one had been told about it; one would never stumble across it by chance.

The ledge appeared to come to an abrupt end beyond the garden.

Petronilla drew rein and dismounted, and Rose did the same. Petronilla approached the edge of the ledge, and seemed to Rose to be looking along the cliff wall.

'My lady, do be careful, you might fall.'

'Over here, Rose. We go this way.'

Securing the horses' reins to a convenient root which jutted out of the cliff wall, Rose went over, and blinked at a complicated bridge of wood and rope. Posts had been driven into the rock-face, and a wooden walkway constructed along the very side of the cliff. Less than a foot wide, the walkway hung over the river and stopped at a large black hole in the cliff.

This was the entrance to the house they were visiting. It had been there for centuries, but its origins were shrouded in mystery.

'I'll not risk life and limb on that!' Rose declared, backing away.

Petronilla, who had not expected Rose to accompany her, shrugged, and set her foot on the rope bridge. It creaked, and she hesitated.

The inhabitant of the cave was an old woman called Lisette. The local wise-woman, Lisette was feared by some, and those who feared her called her La Sorcière – the sorceress. A rope ladder trailed down from the mouth of the cave to the water below. At the bottom, moored next to it, was a row-boat.

'Good day! Lisette? Are you in?' Petronilla called.

A round rosy face appeared in the entrance. Gossip had it that Lisette was in her sixtieth year, but her appearance belied this. Her face was unlined, and her blue eyes sparkled with life. Her bliaud was a forget-me-not blue which matched her eyes precisely. She wore no veil, and had wound her hair into plaits and pinned it on her head like a coronet. It was thick and lustrous. From her position on the rim of the ledge, Rose eyed La Sorcière's hair sourly. There were no grey hairs on La Sorcière's head.

'Lady Petronilla!' La Sorcière exclaimed. Her voice was as light as a child's. She stepped out of her cave and walked with a spring in her step down the swaying wooden path. 'It is an honour to see you.'

'You've let those saladings go to seed, Lisette,' Petronilla observed, pointing with her crop at the tiny garden.

La Sorcière's eyes sparkled. 'No, my lady. I have a use for the flowers. You came for some healing herbs?'

'I did. One of my servants has taken very ill, and my stocks are inadequate. I hoped you would be able to give me something to help.'

La Sorcière waved Petronilla up her precarious path. 'Come this way, my lady, and I'll see what I can do.'

'My thanks. Rose, you stay with the horses.'

Once in the cave, Petronilla ducked her head through the entrance and looked about her with sharp-eyed interest. It was cool out of the autumn sun. Petronilla had been here before, but each visit never failed to impress her with the orderliness of the place. With rushes on the floor, and a fire in the centre, La Sorcière's home should resemble a million other peasants' cots. It should look poor and mean and dirty and smell most vilely, but it did not. The smoke from the fire did not linger in the cave, but wound out through a crevice in the rock which pressed down over their heads.

Lisette's home smelt of fresh cut herbs, of lavender and rosemary and marjoram. The table was scrubbed so clean it was almost white. A jug of large-petalled daisies with yellow centres sat squarely in the middle, next to a loaf of bread. Bunches of herbs and flowers were tied up to dry on hooks that had been driven into its rocky roof, so many that you could not see the ceiling; and shelf after shelf had been carved from the walls, covering every available inch. Each shelf was a-jostle with corked bottles and stoppered jars and pill-boxes of every shape and size. Some of the jars were labelled.

One of the more extraordinary rumours concerning La Sorcière maintained that she had once intended to enter a nunnery but had quarrelled with the Mother Superior of the convent and had left before she had taken her vows. She was reputed to be able to read and write. Petronilla did not know whether there was any truth in the part of the story concerning La Sorcière's wish to take the veil, but the labels on those jars was proof positive that La Sorcière could indeed both read and write.

In one corner of the cave was an oak cupboard, whose door was secured with a piece of flax. The most potent and most dangerous of La Sorcière's remedies were kept in that corner cupboard, as Petronilla knew.

A duck waddled in and quacked in a desultory, well-fed manner. Lisette tore a hunk of bread from the loaf and tossed it through the entrance. The duck flapped out after it.

The sun made a lake of light on the floor.

'Would you care for some ale, my lady? It's freshly brewed.'

Petronilla shook her head. 'No. I can't stay long.'

'Very well, my lady. What is the nature of the problem?'

'It's Rose's husband, Tual. He's complaining of pains in his belly. He has a weak digestion.'

'Have you tried dill?'

'Dill has had no effect.'

'And fennel?'

'Yes, yes. I've tried all the usual remedies. He needs a good purgative.' Petronilla eyed the corner cupboard. She knew exactly what she was after, something to suppress sexual desire in a man. The leaves and bark of the willow

426

would be ideal, but she knew that the willow was something of a sacred plant to La Sorcière, and as such it would be kept in that cupboard. 'Perhaps you have something a little more potent? I thought perhaps . . . black bryony?'

Lisette frowned. 'Black bryony, my lady? That is a powerful herb. I only ever recommend black bryony for the most intransigent cases.'

Petronilla sighed. 'Sadly, Tual's case is intransigent. I've tried everything. But if you are worried that Rose might administer the wrong dose, let me reassure you on that. I'll administer it myself. I would like to give the poor man some ease.'

After a moment, Lisette nodded and, going to her cupboard, untied the door. 'Very well, my lady. If you are to administer the dose?'

'I will.'

'Black byrony is a strong purgative, but if you give your maid's husband too much, it will kill him. In large quantities it is a poison.'

'I understand. I will be very careful.'

La Sorcière moved to the light, and transferred a quantity of powder from one jar to another.

While she did this, Petronilla scanned the labels on the pots and bottles in the cupboard, and found what she wanted. Swift as lightning, her hand whipped out: it was the work of a moment to stow the pot she desired in the pouch hanging at her waist.

Lisette turned. 'This powder is taken from the root,' she explained, holding out a small vial containing the black byrony. 'The smallest pinch should suffice. The pain should go once his system is cleaned out. If it does not go, don't give it to him more than once a week. If he is still not better, I think the man should come to see me. Is that clear?'

Petronilla smiled. 'Certainly. But I think there will be

no need for that. I'm sure this will do the trick. My thanks, Lisette. Here, I have some money for you.'

'Thank you, Lady Favell.'

Arlette was dressing for her wedding.

During her seven years' incarceration in the Lady's Tower, clothes had become better cut, more pieces being used, and Arlette's wedding gown, which had been hastily stitched together by two long-suffering and by now red-eyed maids, was no exception. In a heavy, deep blue silk brocade, the bliaud was high-wasted with a scooped neckline. A white muslin undergown was to be worn with it; this would make the low neckline more modest. The gown had a full skirt which flared into a long train, the bodice had embroidered insets at the shoulders, and it had long pleated sleeves. Not normally one to place too much emphasis on clothing, Arlette fell in love with it on sight.

'Oh, Clemence! It's heavenly.'

Clemence grinned. It had been terrible for her to see her mistress stuck in the tower, and although she was aware Arlette had deep reservations about her marriage, she was delighted that Arlette had finally won her battle. Perhaps now she might find happiness.

'Count Etienne has sent you this belt to wear with it,' Clemence said.

'This is lovely too,' Arlette said, examining the gift, a delicate chain with gold filigree links and coloured beads set between the links.

'Will you be wearing your hair loose?'

'I will. It is my wedding day.'

Shortly after noon, Arlette sat at Count Etienne's side at La Forteresse high-table, scarcely able to believe that at last she was his countess. The short ceremony and nuptial mass had passed in a blur. Arlette gazed down the rows of trestles. She was the focus of attention. One by one, each of the faces found reason to turn in her direction. It was unnerving, but perfectly understandable. She was a curiosity. The people of La Forteressse des Aigles were anxious to see the woman who had lived among them for so long, yet had been so rarely glimpsed. They would soon lose interest in her.

Barthélemy le Harpour sat high in the minstrels' gallery, his wife at his side, singing a love song in the *langue d'oc* that was reputed to have been composed by Duke Richard himself.

At one of the trestles, a familiar face caught her eye, that of a fellow Breton, Gwionn Leclerc. Sir Gwionn had, by reason of his knighthood, moved a table closer to the dais during her sojourn in the tower, and sat where Sir Ralph used to sit. Sir Ralph had inherited a small apple-growing estate in Normandy, and while Arlette had been in the tower he had sent Clemence to ask her if he could quit her service. Arlette had released him, and Sir Ralph had left the Aquitaine. But she had Sir Walter, and Sir Gwionn, as she must now remember to address him, both men from her home. She was not quite alone here.

She hoped that the two knights would elect to stay. They could form her personal entourage. Catching Sir Gwionn's eyes, Arlette smiled.

The knight's mouth came up at one side in a lop-sided response which warmed Arlette's inside like the wine she was drinking. Holding her gaze, he raised his goblet to her, and drank. The knightly exercises must agree with him, for Sir Ralph's former squire looked very fit, broad shoulders straining against his tunic seams.

Arlette felt her cheeks grow hot, and hastily turned her attention on her new husband. He looked older than ever.

'Some more wine, Count?' she asked.

'That would be good.'

Arlette reached for the nearest bottle, but the count stayed her hand.

'No, not that one. We're having stuffed ham and jelly of quinces in a moment. My nephew and his wife have brought us a barrel of Beaune, which complements the ham perfectly. I'll have some of that. Will you join me?'

'No, thank you, my lord. I prefer something lighter.'

The feast continued throughout the warm autumn afternoon, and well into the evening. Arlette ate and drank sparingly, too nervous to do anything else; but nevertheless at the end of it her head was spinning.

Count Etienne noticed his bride had gone quiet.

'Are you all right, my dear?'

Arlette nodded.

The count reached for her hand and squeezed it. 'You're not nervous, I hope?'

Arlette flushed to the roots of her hair at his meaning, and lied. 'No my lord.'

'No need to be. If we sneak away quietly, without fuss, would that help?'

'I . . . I think so.'

'Come along then.'

And without another word, the count set his cup down on the trestle, rose, and led her from the hall. They had reached the stairs before anyone noticed. One of the guards let out a coarse shout.

Hearing the shout, Petronilla glanced up, frowning. She was wondering whether she had put enough of La Sorcière's willow into the count's wine-cup. The gift of the Beaune had been her idea, for Petronilla's father was a wine-merchant, and on pondering how to administer the drug, she had come to the conclusion that the wine that the count drank daily was the ideal carrier for it. It had been easy enough to doctor his cup, but Petronilla was uncertain as to the quantity she should use in the barrel. And she could hardly ask La Sorcière without arousing suspicion. So she would have to guess, based on the amount she had used today. Had she used sufficient?

She watched the count and countess sneak out of the hall, gave them a couple of minutes, and then followed them.

The count's door was warped and had a crack in it. If Petronilla peeped through the crack, she would soon discover if she had the dose right.

The count's bedchamber was the largest Arlette had seen, almost large enough to be a solar.

Two of the walls were clad in richly coloured tapestries. There was a fire, which had been lit to drive the moisture from the dank autumn air. The bed was huge and canopied and, despite her nervousness, Arlette felt a pang of recognition. It was similar to her father's great bed in Huelgastel. Arlette had not heard from Eleanor for some months, and had no news concerning either her father's health or the charges that had been laid against him. On the morrow she must write to her stepmother and tell her that she had become Countess Favell. Eleanor would tell her father. Would he, in his invalid state, be able to understand what she was telling him? Would it please him that Arlette had at last seen that Count Etienne honoured the marriage contract?

Throat dry, Arlette glanced at the white linen pillow before turning quickly away. She tugged at the lacings of her gown. Her stomach was full of butterflies.

The count was behind her, and both of them were standing on what appeared to be a tapestry of exotic design which must have been shipped from the East. Arlette had never seen one on a floor before, and for them to be walking on it seemed to be almost sacrilegious. But Arlette could not find her tongue to comment on this. She could hear the count disrobing, and was acutely conscious of his physical presence. His breathing sounded loud in the quiet of their chamber, where the only other sounds were the thumping of Arlette's heart and the crackling of the fire. She could not bring herself to look at him.

Her fingers were all thumbs, and the heavy brocade bliaud slid through her fingers and fell to the ground where it lay about her like a blue pool. Arlette bent to retrieve it.

'Leave it,' the count said, voice suddenly hoarse. 'Since I've not married you for your lands, as your father's case is not settled, I must have married you for yourself. I want to see you. Take off your shift.'

Briefly, Arlette searched her husband's eyes, hoping to find a trace of warmth and kindliness in them, such as she had seen when he had first welcomed her to La Forteresse. But she found none. Her heart sank. Ever since her release from the tower, Count Etienne had treated her courteously but coldly. Where was his warmth, his compassion? Had he lost his gentler qualities during her seven years in the tower?

Eyes fixed on her husband's, lest she should suddenly find the understanding that she needed, Arlette untied the laces at the neck of her gown. Her hands were shaking.

'Come on, come on,' Etienne said. Impatiently, he stepped forward, took hold of her gown at the neck, and pulled it over her shoulders.

There was a ripping noise as Arlette's undergown tore at the neck.

'My lord, you are ungentle.'

'Ungentle, am I?' Count Etienne gave an ugly laugh.

His green eyes ran up and down Arlette's naked body, until she felt like a cow at a market. No, it must be worse than that, she felt utterly humiliated.

'You would marry me,' he said, unemotionally. 'Nothing was said about being gentle that I recall.'

A flash of enlightenment left Arlette sick with dread. Count Etienne had not simply resented her standing up for herself and crossing him, he hated her for it. He had kept his hatred hidden until they had married, but he was

432

hiding it no more. This was to be his way of punishing her. A nightmare vision of a loveless, degrading marriage which endured for years formed in her mind's eye. Moving off the soft eastern carpet to the stone flags by the fire, Arlette vainly tried to cover her breasts with her hands. 'But, my lord,' she reminded him. 'When the order came from the bishops, I offered to release you from your promise. I—'

Another ugly laugh. 'For seven years you bruit it about all Christendom that you will have me, that you *must* have me because of the contract I made with your father. If you think after that I'd suffer your rejection. No, madam. You made your bed, and now you can damned well lie in it.'

Stepping out of his breeches, the count pulled off his chainse, and stood mother-naked before her.

'What, will you not look at me, madam? Will you not admire the fine husband that you have fought so long to win?'

He caught Arlette's chin in a cruel grip and turned her head to him. 'Open your eyes.'

Arlette did not comply immediately, and the grip tightened. Tears of fear and rage burned behind Arlette's eyelids. Her husband was an old man of fifty-eight, but he was still stronger than she was. There was little to be gained by resistance. If she angered him further he may come to beat her as her father had. She could hardly believe this was happening to her. She had thought him so kind at the beginning. Could he not find it in him to forgive her?

Reluctantly, she opened her eyes. She saw his belly, full and round with almost six decades of good food and wine in it. It sagged a little. She saw his pubic hair, which was greying. She saw his manhood. That sagged too, and Arlette was both surprised and relieved to see that as yet her husband was unaroused. He did not desire her.

Perhaps he did not find her pale skin pleasing.

She managed to wrench her chin free of his grip.

'Well, madam? Do you like what you see?'

Arlette went to the bed, flung back the covers and climbed in. If she did as he wished, if she tried to please him, it might yet work out for the best. 'I see my husband,' she said softly, and held out her hand. 'And I think it's time he came to bed.'

Count Etienne joined her.

Arlette smiled, put a hand on one of the count's shoulders, and lifted her lips to his.

The count grunted and took her in a firm hold. He pressed closer, and the stubble on his chin scratched her. Arlette was twenty-three, and yet this was the first time she had been kissed, or been tightly clasped in a man's arms. After the misunderstanding in the stable years ago, when her father had thrown poor Jehan out of Huelgastel because it looked as though she and Jehan had been kissing, Arlette had made sure that no one else had been put in a similar situation.

Count Etienne laid a hand on her breast. Arlette's skin looked white and dewy compared to his, and when she saw the age spots on the back of the count's hand, she was for an instant reminded of her father's freckled hands.

Her stomach tightened, and she had to steel herself not to pull away.

'What's the matter?' her husband asked, but she could see he was not concerned with her feelings, for his eyes were watching her nipple as his fingers stroked and caressed. He seemed to be waiting for something. She wished he would get on with it, so it would be over. His breathing was heavier than it had been a moment ago. She was not so innocent that she did not guess that that meant he was beginning to desire her.

Soon, soon it would be over.

Instinctively she arched her breast towards him, offering herself.

He glanced at her and, pushing her into the pillows, placed his lips around her nipple. He began to suck. It hurt, but not so much that it was unendurable. Arlette closed her eyes. For some reason she remembered the gaps in his teeth. Her skin shrank away from him. After a moment of this joyless suckling, the count lifted his head and gazed at her.

'Pleasure me, wife,' he said, guiding her hand to his flaccid manhood. He fell upon her nipple once more, sucking at it as though he were a babe whose mother had not fed it in a month.

Uncertain as to exactly what was involved in pleasuring him, Arlette did her best. But she could tell her best was not enough. She gave him no pleasure.

Some minutes passed. The count was perspiring. With a grunt he slid his body over hers, and rubbed himself against her. That did not seem to help either. Their sweat mingled. The grunting and rubbing and desperate pressing against her continued for some minutes. He thrust his hand between her legs, put his fingers inside her.

Arlette tensed herself for what must follow. He applied himself once more to her nipple, which by now was feeling quite sore. She wished he would take the other one.

After what seemed an eternity, Count Etienne lifted his head and looked at her, his eyes full of disdain. She gave him a nervous smile, unsure of what she should do.

The green eyes, so close to hers, narrowed. His weight was suffocating, his fingers still flicking her sore nipple. 'Don't laugh at me, you bitch.'

'Laugh? My lord, I'm not—'

With unexpected viciousness, he pinched her breast.

'Ouch! My lord!' Not understanding, Arlette gazed fearfully up at her husband, and watched the hot blood surge into his cheeks. So had her father looked when she

435

had angered him. So had François de Roncier looked when he took his belt to her. She wished she understood. 'Dear God,' she whispered. 'Not you, too.'

The fingers at her breast tightened, twisted her sore nipple. 'Don't ever laugh at me.'

'I'm not.' She tried to squirm away from her husband, but his body was sprawled over her. He was too heavy to escape.

One hand continued its torture of her breast. With the other he caught her by the hair. Tightened, twisted.

'Don't laugh at me.'

'I'm not laughing. I won't laugh. My lord!'

He fell on her again, and the pitiful heaving and pushing began all over until it seemed their bodies were so slimy and slippery they may as well have been swimming in a river of sweat. Thinking that a struggle would enrage him further, Arlette lay meekly under her husband. But he did not seem to like that.

He bit her breast.

She gasped. What did he want from her?

He jerked at her hair, bringing tears to her eyes.

She whimpered. Did he want her to cry? She'd do anything if it meant this would be over more quickly.

'That's better, bitch.'

And then she felt the difference, for he was pushing a hardness against her, a hardness that had not been there when he had not been hurting her. A moment later, and a hot, searing pain spread up from between her legs. She gasped.

'Moan. Bitch. Moan,' her husband said, each invasive thrust like a dagger splitting her apart.

At last she understood. Unable to become aroused when he was being gentle with her, her husband enjoyed tormenting her.

Her husband's manhood moved inside her, forcing, bruising, hurting.

'Moan, bitch.'

Arlette felt scalding tears slide out beneath her eyelids. She was married to a man who delighted in cruelty.

She moaned.

With a great, shuddering sigh, Count Etienne Favell let out a groan and was still.

Arlette was a virgin no more.

Outside the chamber room, Petronilla clenched her fists in fury, and resolved to double tomorrow's dose of willow in the count's wine.

Part Three

Death and Resurrection

And I saw a new heaven and a new earth:
for the first heaven and the first earth were passed away

Revelation 21:1

Chapter Twenty

Tossing and turning in one of the guest rooms, Petronilla did not sleep much that night. It was not sympathy for Arlette and the count's cruel treatment of her that kept her awake. She was frantic in case a child should result from Arlette and Etienne's union.

'Not enough,' she muttered, under her breath, in a sweat lest Etienne should try and take his wife again before she had managed to administer another, more powerful dose. 'I must contrive to give him more; I'll double the amount and see how that works.'

Petronilla and Louis were only invited to stay at La Forteresse for another week, then they planned to go back to La Roque-Gageac. Would a week be long enough for Petronilla to establish how much was the correct dose to render him incapable of having his wife? On one occasion when she had been purchasing remedies from La Sorcière, the woman had told her that everyone's bodies reacted differently to the herbs. Presumably if that was the case for medicines, the same went for poisons.

As the word 'poison' filtered through Petronilla's brain, a tiny shudder ran down her spine. She was not poisoning the count, merely trying to make it impossible for him to service his new wife. She had seen the row of deadlier drugs on La Sorcière's shelf, and had decided that she did not need them. Real poisons were too chancy. What if the body was examined and symptoms of the poison recognised? No, poisons were too dangerous. However, there was nothing to stop her using a herb that was usually considered harmless. After all, it was used daily in minute doses by apothecaries for treating flatulence and the like. Not many people were aware that in large quantities it would render a man impotent. Much safer. The count was old and would die soon in any case. She would not have to 'treat' him for long.

It was a form of security.

Petronilla thought it likely that even if Etienne took his wife ten times a night, she would not fall pregnant but she could not be positive. Count Etienne's other wives had remained childless. Petronilla had not meddled then. The count's first wife had been cold in her grave long before Petronilla had met Louis. And as for the second wife, Claudine, Petronilla had not interfered. Newly wed herself, and in awe of the count, the thought had occurred to her, of course, for from the beginning she had been ambitious for her husband; but she had not dared. She had not had her sons. Count Etienne must have rutted his first two wives – what Petronilla had seen pass between Etienne and Arlette could never be termed as love-making – in much the same manner as he rutted Arlette.

But Petronilla was older now, older and wiser. And she had William and Laurence, her beautiful sons, and while Louis may have turned out to be something of a disappointment, she could mould her sons in any shape she desired. She would bring them up to be worthy of her ambitions. For her two sons Petronilla would dare anything. She had to, for who else was there who would look to their interests? Louis never would. Petronilla was not prepared to bear the risk, however slim, that one day the count's seed might strengthen, and Arlette might become pregnant.

Thus it was imperative that Petronilla established the precise amount of willow leaves necessary to render

Etienne impotent before the end of the week.

Then she would be one step nearer Louis becoming count. In the dark, Petronilla's lips curved. Tomorrow, she would double the dose.

The next night, Count Etienne drank deep from the barrel of Beaune that his nephew and his wife had presented him with as part of his wedding gift.

Petronilla dogged the footsteps of the count and countess as they climbed to the second floor of the keep where the family bedchambers were situated, and hovered unnoticed half a circle below them on the stairs. They retired to their separate rooms. The count called for his page. His green eyes were bleary in the yellow torchlight, his features blurred with wine and fatigue. He looked very old.

'Marc! Marc?' His voice rose querulously. 'Devil take the boy. Always tripping over him when I don't want him and never there when I do.'

'I can help you, my lord,' Arlette said, coming back on to the landing.

'No. Don't trouble yourself. I've no need for you tonight. 'Marc! *Marc!*'

Just then, Marc — a long-limbed, uncoordinated lad of twelve, with a bush of dark hair and a rash of freckles smothering a solid, square face — came bounding up the stairs two at a time.

'Here I am, my lord.'

'Did you prepare my caudle tonight?' the count demanded.

A caudle was a hot nightcap made with honeyed sweet wine, spiced with ginger and saffron and thickened with ground almonds.

'Yes, my lord. It's by the fire.'

'Good boy.' Count Etienne looked a dismissal at his wife. 'Goodnight, madam.'

'Goodnight, my lord.'

The countess watched as her husband put a hand on Marc's shoulder for support and was led into his chamber.

Petronilla heard Arlette sigh — with relief? — before turning and disappearing into her own room.

Louis came up the stairs behind Petronilla.

'Coming?' he said, taking her hand with a smile.

'In a moment.' There was a door which linked the count's room with that of the countess, and if there was to be any nocturnal movement through it, Petronilla wanted to know. She jerked her head towards the privy. 'I need to pay a visit.'

Louis nodded, released Petronilla's hand, and continued up alone. 'I'll be waiting.'

Petronilla took up her station outside Count Etienne's chamber, and squinted through the crack in the door.

She saw the page, Marc, help the count disrobe, and settle him in his bed with his caudle. She heard him grunt as he hauled his pallet out from under the count's bed. Then the chamber went dark as he pinched the candles out. Marc's mattress, filled with chopped straw, rustled as he lay down on it. It was not likely that Count Etienne would call for his wife with his page sleeping in his chamber, but Petronilla wanted to be sure. If he were to try and take Arlette, Petronilla needed to know if he succeeded.

Ten minutes later, when the sound of gentle snoring came to her, Petronilla stole away to join her husband. Louis had not dipped too deeply into the barrel of Beaune. He may not yet be count but, praise the Lord, neither was he cruel or impotent.

At dinner the following evening the count did not drink as deeply as he had the previous night, but what he did drink came from the barrel of Beaune.

Petronilla realised that their gift of it to him had been

an inspiration. He drank the rich red wine with such greedy delight that, watching him, Petronilla came to the conclusion that she did not need worry when she and Louis went back to their home. All she had to do was ensure that Count Etienne had his wine from her father's cellar and no other. From this moment she would ensure his supply never ran dry.

When she had worked out the correct dosage, she would make a more precise calculation on the basis of the number of goblets of Beaune that Etienne was likely to drink at one sitting. She would mix the correct quantity of the herb into the barrel, and could quite safely leave the count to dose himself. There was no need to involve anyone else.

And if anyone else broached that barrel with the count? That was a possibility, but one she could shrug aside. Supposing Sir Walter drank a cup or two of the Beaune? The worst that would happen would be that Lady Clemence would find her husband not quite as responsive as usual. Or supposing Sir Gwionn drank some? That harper's slut who, rumour had it, shared her favours with the Breton knight, would have to turn to her cuckold of a husband for comfort. It would scarcely matter: Count Etienne was the only one who drank regularly and copiously of the wine.

With her plan fully formed, and knowing it to be sound, Petronilla had little doubt she would sleep well that night.

When everyone had retired, Petronilla made her usual excuse to Louis and took up her post outside the count's door.

That night Count Etienne and his young wife were to sleep together. Marc had been left in the hall, rolled up in his cloak by the fire.

Petronilla stuck her eye to the crack, and stretched her

ears to catch the slightest sound.

The count had his back to her and was blocking his sight of Arlette.

'Well, wench?' he said. 'What are you waiting for? You've your wifely duties to perform tonight. Strip.'

How harsh his voice sounded when he was in the privacy of his bedroom, Petronilla thought, how unlike his normal everyday voice.

He moved to the bed and sat, and Arlette came into Petronilla's line of vision, unlacing her gown with fingers that fumbled clumsily with the lacings. The girl was terrified, Petronilla realised, terrified of her husband. Who could blame her after a wedding night like the one she had endured? The nape of Petronilla's neck prickled. She felt uneasy. She did not want to watch this. She had to remind herself that it was all in a good cause. If she could get the correct dosage worked out, then Louis or William would be certain to be count. She shrugged aside her discomfiture.

Arlette's bliaud fell in a ring on the floor. Her shift followed. Carefully, the young countess stepped out of the ring and picked up her clothes, draping them over a coffer. She was young, slim, beautiful, and shook like a leaf in the height of a gale.

'Come here, wife. Help me off with my boots.'

Arlette padded slowly to the bed and, as she drew near, Petronilla saw the count's hand make a grab for one of her breasts.

Arlette gave a muted cry of pain.

Count Etienne smiled, took hold of her hair and hauled her face-down across his knees. He was still fully clothed. He pushed his hand between Arlette's legs.

Arlette's head was dangling, the blood rushing into her face which was all but obscured by her red hair, which snaked over her cheeks like bright flames in the candlelight. She whimpered; Petronilla caught a glimpse

446

of tormented blue eyes, and saw her take her lips between her teeth to stifle another cry.

'Dry as a bone,' Count Etienne complained. He pushed his wife roughly to the floor, and kicked her thigh with his boot. 'Kneel up, girl.'

'My lord?' Arlette knelt up on the eastern rug in front of her husband, and thrust back her hair. Red hair, white delicate skin, and the dark imprint of a boot on one thigh that was bruising even as Petronilla watched. 'What is it you want of me?'

Count Etienne shrugged off his tunic, cast his belt on to the bed, and untied the waist of his breeches. He took one of Arlette's hands and guided it to his crotch. 'Pleasure me. Come on, wench. I want to fill your belly with my seed. Make me big as a stallion and I'll ride you all night.'

She tried. Petronilla could see that. For several minutes the count's wife tried to tease her husband's flaccid penis into shape, while her husband mauled her breasts in a way that Petronilla guessed must be agonising. She was glad that Arlette didn't moan again. She was glad that Arlette's diligent ministrations failed to arouse her husband, for it meant that her herb was working. She had the dose aright.

Finally the count looked down at his limp member and swore.

'Use your mouth on me, girl.'

There was a moment's shocked silence.

'Pardon, my lord?'

He took a handful of that flaming hair and tried to force her head down. 'You heard me. Use your mouth.'

With a furious cry, Arlette wrenched herself free, and scrambled to her feet like a mad thing.

'No. No! I will do many things for you, Count, but I cannot do that.'

The count's face darkened and he reached for his belt.

Petronilla held her breath.

'Come here, girl.'

The long red snake-curls bounced and trembled as Arlette shook her head.

Count Etienne climbed to his feet, and his wife, naked as a babe, took to her heels.

She never made it to the door, fortunately for Petronilla, who would never have got out of sight in time if she had. The count was acrosss his chamber with the speed of a man half his age. In a trice he had tied his wife's hands behind her back with his belt and flung her, sobbing, across the bed.

'I'll teach you not to disobey me,' he said, and he cast about him for his riding crop. 'I'll teach you.'

Finding his crop he flexed it, once, twice.

Petronilla's skin crawled. Arlette looked so young, so helpless, trussed up on the bed. And, apart from the bruise on her thigh, her skin was unblemished, like a perfect white peach.

The crop whistled through the air. A red weal sprang up on Arlette's white buttocks.

Acid bile rushed into Petronilla's throat. She did not want to watch this. But she had to, lest the count's depravities enabled him to take her. She swallowed back the bile.

The crop lifted and fell. Lifted and fell.

Arlette never made a sound, which was a small blessing. Petronilla could not have stood it if she had cried out.

When the count dropped the crop, and kicked his wife from his bed, Petronilla was exhausted with the horror of it.

Exhausted, but triumphant. For however hard he beat her, however hard he had tried to work himself up to it, the count had not taken his wife.

The herb had done its work well. If only the countess would have her courses, and prove to her that the count's seed had not taken on that first night, Petronilla could retire to La Roque-Gageac happy in the knowledge that

448

Count Etienne's lands were all but hers.

Christmas tide crept up on them, and with it much noise and merriment.

Hounds barked and yelped and got underfoot as holly and yule logs were dragged into the hall by servants whose noses and cheeks were red with cold. They brought half the mud of the Dordogne in on their boots, soiling the rushes, but no one minded.

Wreaths were fashioned from the holly and nailed to the hall walls. Long lengths of dark, waxy ivy were plaited into thick ropes and suspended between the great tapestries. Bunches of mistletoe dangled from the wall-sconces and hung under the chandeliers which had been filled with slim white candles ready to cast their light over the trestles at the Christmas feast.

Up in the minstrel's gallery Barthélemy le Harpour was tuning his harp, and his black-haired wife, Anna, was practising an alba — a song to the dawn — which she was to sing after mass on Christmas Day.

The fire roared, yellow flames leaping a yard high or more; yet for all that, the air was chill and misted with people's breath as they went about their work. A cauldron of mulled wine was set in the hearth, cups and ladle at the ready, and the sweet fragrances of honey, cloves and cinnamon mingled with the smells of dog and humanity and woodsmoke.

It was Christmas Eve. Arlette stood beneath a ladder, supervising the hanging of the swags of ivy. She had a smile on her lips and a heart as heavy as lead. Her mind was elsewhere, dwelling on the harsh ironies of her life.

Sir Gwionn had entered the minstrels' gallery, and was talking to Anna le Harpour. Barthélemy took no notice, not even nodding at the knight. How strange. The knight bent his head close to that of the trobiaritz and, even from down in the body of the hall Arlette could see that Anna's cheeks were bright, her eyes sparkling with life as they never did when she spoke to her husband. Then Sir Gwionn bowed his head and took his leave of the gallery, but as he moved past Barthélemy le Harpour's wife, his hand rested fleetingly, with familiar affection, on the girl's hips.

Barthélemy le Harpour stared with intense concentration at the strings of his harp.

How peculiar. How very peculiar. Were Gwionn Leclerc and the girl lovers? And did her husband know?

'No, no, Véronique.' Arlette spoke tersely to the girl on the ladder, for half her mind was still caught up in the significance of the exchange that she had just witnessed between Sir Gwionn and Anna le Harpour. She wondered what it would be like to have someone who cared for you making love to you, instead of someone who hated you.

'Not like that, Véronique. Tie the ivy to the pole with the crimson ribbon. Here, you climb down, and I'll show you what I mean.' She rolled back her bell-shaped sleeves, glad she had put on the undergown with the long, wrist-hugging sleeves. It hid the marks on her wrists. Last night Count Etienne had tied her to the bed posts and beat her with more than usual vigour. She had fought hard to escape him. Her thighs ached, and her breasts and belly were sore. The count had been beating her more and more of late. He had mated with Arlette only that one time, three months ago on their wedding night, and since then had been frantic to repeat the experience; more frantic than ever when Arlette's courses had come and he knew that that one time was not going to be enough. He had not succeeded in his aim, and each time he tried he used more physical cruelty on Arlette in a vain attempt to arouse his flagging libido.

Recently Arlette had taken to wondering if Count Etienne's knights and retainers knew how the count treated his wife in private. For all that he raged at her, so far he had never struck at her face or hands. He had never left a mark on her that would be visible in public. And Arlette tried not to scream or cry out during those excruciating sessions with her husband. In public Count Etienne was the perfect, doting husband. Did Véronique know what she suffered? Did Sir Gilles, or her own knight, Sir Gwionn?

Arlette had come to hate her husband.

Should she complain? And if so to whom? What could anyone do to help her? And what would they say to her? She could visualise them staring at her in utter disbelief, and the look in their eyes would ask her how she dared complain when for seven years she had pitted her will against the count's to get this marriage. Seven years in the tower, and this was the result. She had never expected to find love; she had only hoped to have some power. But she had no power, only hatred, and breasts and thighs that throbbed and ached so that she was forced to move like an old woman, and could hardly climb this ladder to attach swags of ivy to a tapestry pole. She, who had once shinned up every tree in Huelgastel forest.

Arlette stretched up her arm and fixed the garland with the crimson ribbon. 'Like this, Véronique,' she said, tying the satin ribbon in a large shiny bow.

Recently Count Etienne had extended his torment to verbal abuse. He had taken to blaming her.

'It was not like this with my other wives,' he complained every time he failed to become aroused. 'At least I had pleasure out of them, and the chance of a babe. But with you there's nothing; no pleasure and, short of a miracle, not a hope of a babe.'

The idea of marrying Etienne had looked so promising when she had arrived from Brittany. He had been kind to her, genuinely kind. Did the count's cruelty all stem from the moment she defied him? Was his pride so great that he would brook no apology? They should have been able to make a fresh start. She could see that from his point of view she was to blame, but did his noble male arrogance so blind him that he could not see there were faults on his side too? Queen Eleanor and the churchmen had taken her part which was why they insisted he married her. Count Etienne had broken his word. If only they could have had a fresh start. If only . . .

Fiercely Arlette tied another ribbon to the tapestry pole. There would be no starting again. She detested her husband, because whatever the rights and wrongs of the past, what he did to her every night in their bedchamber was unforgiveable. There must be someone she could turn to. There must be some way she could escape.

A stir in the hall doorway drew her eyes. Lady Petronilla and Sir Louis had arrived, invited to join the Christmas festivities with their dreadful boys. Lady Petronilla had a proud, proprietorial arm over each of her sons. She saw Arlette and smiled, a gloating smile that said, 'Look at me. I have two sons, while you have none.'

Arlette sighed, and hopped off the ladder.

Véronique stood aside as Petronilla left her boys by the door and swept towards Arlette, skirts and rain-dampened cloak dragging in the rushes.

'My dear,' Petronilla cooed, tutting in gentle reproof. 'You must be careful. You mustn't work so hard.' She lowered her voice in confidentiality. 'You must remember, you may well be expecting.'

Arlette didn't respond to Petronilla's gambit. Petronilla was probing, too obviously, and she was not going to give her the satisfaction of an answer.

'Welcome to La Forteresse, Lady Petronilla,' she said coolly. 'I do hope your journey was not too tiring. Would a cup of mulled wine warm you?'

A disturbing light flared in Petronilla's pebble-grey eyes. Slowly and rather deliberately, Arlette thought, she peeled off her gloves, gloves which were of green kid and edged with ermine. Ermine was not usually worn by knights' ladies; a luxurious fur, it was generally reserved for princes and princesses, or counts and countesses.

'Some wine would be most welcome,' Petronilla said.

Arlette ushered her guest towards the fire, and ladled steaming spiced wine into a pewter goblet.

'What will you give the count for Christmas, Arlette?' Petronilla asked. 'We've brought him another barrel of that Beaune he's partial to.'

'Have you? He will be pleased. Only the other day the steward mentioned that the Beaune was nearly gone. I was going to order some more.'

For a moment Petronilla looked alarmed. 'You've no call to do that. It's my pleasure to keep the count supplied with the Beaune he likes.'

'Really, Petronilla, there's no need. We can order our own.'

Petronilla took a sup of her mulled wine and shrugged. 'It's no trouble. I get it from Father. What did you say you were giving the count?'

'I've drawn him a picture of the Benedictine Abbey at Sarlat. He's endowed the monks with some money to say masses for—'

An arched brow lifted. 'You can draw?'

'Yes. The picture's been done on the best quality vellum. I've used gold paint and—'

'You know your husband's bribing the monks to pray you give him a son,' Petronilla interrupted, not in the least interested in hearing about Arlette's gift. 'He'd prefer a son to a picture of the abbey.'

Petronilla spoke no less than the truth, and her cruel taunt brought a rush of hot blood to Arlette's cheeks. 'That remark would have been better left unsaid, Lady Petronilla,' Arlette said coldly.

Petronilla gave her a smile that would have cracked a glass mirror. 'I'm sorry, Countess, my tongue ran away

453

with me. Don't take offence, my dear. Please, let's be friends. It's Christmas, and we should all be merry together.'

'I'll show you to your room,' Arlette said and, head up, she left the hall.

Though Petronilla was confident that her potion was still effective, she wanted to see for herself.

Accordingly, she left her husband snoring in the feather bed that almost filled the best guest room, and headed for the count's door.

After ten minutes' peering through the crack she had seen enough. Her antaphrodisiac was working. The count was determinedly, manfully fighting the effects of the willow, but to no avail. However hard he tried to whip himself into a frenzy, he could not do it. Spreadeagled face down on the bed with her limbs tied to the bedposts, Arlette bore his raging and beatings in stoic silence. Watching her, lying there quite powerless while the count bounded around her, belt in hand – a grotesque naked satyr – an uncomfortable emotion made itself felt in Petronilla's breast. Recognising it as sympathy for the countess's plight – Petronilla was after all to blame for the count directing his anger at her – Petronilla turned away, sickened.

At that moment a hand fell on her shoulder. Her heart jumped.

It was Sir Gwionn Leclerc.

'Oh, it's you, Lady Petronilla,' Sir Gwionn said, pleasantly. 'I heard someone skulking about, and I wondered who it was.'

Gwionn had been on his way to fetch Anna from the hall. Most nights Anna slept there with Barthélemy and Jean – quite chastely, she assured him – as they had continued the charade of her being married to the harper. Since receiving his knighthood, Gwionn had been allocated the box-sized room on the third floor that had once belonged to Sir Ralph. Once or twice a week, he and Anna managed to share it together.

The liaison between Gwionn and Anna was common knowledge among the more wakeful of the servants and retainers who slept in the hall and heard her creeping out to Gwionn, but it was never mentioned openly, probably because of Barthélemy's popularity within the castle. Thinking Barthélemy ignorant of Anna and Gwionn's so-called illicit affair, they did not want to stir up trouble lest Barthélemy should leave La Forteresse. A freeman, Barthélemy was at liberty to leave whenever he wished.

Petronilla drew herself up to her full height and glared indignantly at the knight. 'I was not skulking, Sir Gwionn. I have simply mislaid one of my gilt hairpins. I thought it might have fallen on the stairs.'

Sir Gwionn lifted a flambeau from its bracket on the wall. 'Here, let me help you. It will glint in the torchlight. We should be able to find it.'

Dropping to his hands and knees, he scoured the landing and stairs.

'Thank you, Sir Gwionn,' Petronilla said. She pretended to join him in his search.

After a few minutes, Sir Gwionn lifted his head. 'Was it valuable, my lady?'

Petronilla turned her eyes from Sir Gwionn's disfiguring scar which time had failed to heal. 'Don't concern yourself any more, Sir Gwionn. I have more hairpins. It was just that I was positive I heard it fall about here. I must have been mistaken.' She gave a little tinkling laugh. 'I shall probably find it on my coffer next to my hairbrush.' She drifted up a couple of steps. 'But thank you for trying to find it for me.'

'My pleasure, my lady.'

Gwionn dropped the flambeau back in its bracket and watched Lady Favell sway round the twist in the stairs, a thoughtful smile on his lips. She must have a very low opinion of his intelligence if she thought he had been taken in with that yarn she had spun him about lost hairpins. If Lady Petronilla had lost anything, her maid Rose would have been the one sent to search for it.

No, when Gwionn had first seen her, Lady Petronilla had not been searching for any hairpins, gilt or otherwise. She had had her long nose pressed to Count Etienne's door.

Curiously, Gwionn approached the door and ran his fingers down the gap. What had she been looking at? Why should Petronilla Favell be interested in spying on the count in his chamber? If Lady Favell's tastes ran along voyeuristic lines, she would do better to come down to the hall any day of the week to watch the folk in the curtained-off married section bumping up and down beneath their cloaks. She would see nothing better in Count Etienne's chamber. The count was old, and his wife was naïve and inexperienced, as all noblewomen were when first married. She would have a poor show here.

So, if Lady Petronilla was not spying on the count for the quality of the display, she must have some other reason. Deciding it could not harm him to discover that reason, Gwionn leaned forwards and put his eye to the crack.

The count's bedchamber was ill-lit and thick with shadows; darker than the landing, the count's fire must almost have died, and he could not have more than one candle burning. Gradually, Gwionn's eyes adjusted to the light. The crack in the door was just large enough to give him a full view of the count's bed.

At first Gwionn did not register the full horror of what was transpiring in that room, but what he did see had his eyes out on stalks. He blinked, and shook his head in disbelief.

It was a scene such as he had never witnessed.

Arlette was lying face down on the bed, arms and legs stretched wide. Pillows had been heaped under her stomach so her body formed a little mountain and her buttocks were its peak. She was tied, *tied*, to the bedposts with cord; naked skin gleamed pearly white through the gloom. Her hair curled wildly over the mattress as though she had been tossing and turning. Her face Gwionn could not see, it was buried in the mattress.

The count was naked. He knelt up behind his wife, in a parody of prayer, butting at her from behind with his pelvis. But he must have had his pleasure of her already Gwionn concluded as he caught a glimpse of a limp, exhausted member.

Gwionn felt desire stir within him at the sight, and he straightened and let out a soundless whistle. He had misjudged the count, and his innocent little wife. Who would have thought de Roncier's daughter would have been able to inspire such an imaginative approach in a man as staid as the count. No wonder Petronilla had had her eyes glued to the door. It was a show such as Gwionn had never seen. He wondered whether Anna would permit him to tie her up like that. He would have to ask her.

Bending to the chink once more, Gwionn noticed other details that in the first shock of his surprise he had missed.

The count held a leather belt in one hand. Gwionn watched him push his pelvis towards his wife, and draw back. The belt was slashed across Arlette's buttocks. Gwionn noticed Arlette's buttocks clench, but she did not cry out. Stunned, Gwionn noted other marks on her buttocks, and across her back and shoulders. This was no game, as he had first supposed. This was torture.

Gwionn's erection subsided rapidly.

He was not watching a man and wife playing titillating bondage games for each other's pleasure.

Arlette was being beaten.

457

Odd, but that thought gave him no pleasure at all. His belly felt quite hollow.

Arlette Favell, née de Roncier, was being tortured in the most degrading way, and suddenly he wanted to help her. For years he had dreamed of visiting his revenge on her for the way her father had destroyed his. He should be dancing on top of the battlements to see her humiliated like this. Did this happen every night? Why did she not cry out?

Almost as if she sensed he was there on the landing, Arlette turned a piteous white face to the door.

Count Etienne butted his wife again. The belt snaked out, and another mark was added to those marring that perfect white body.

The blood began to pound in Gwionn's head. She may be de Roncier's daughter, but he could not stand by and watch this. He must intervene. He would do the same for anyone. he would do the same for a dog, for a mule . . .

He drew a deep breath, and lifted his hand to the latch.

'There you are, bitch,' he heard the count say. 'I've done with you. You can crawl back to your kennel.'

Gwionn stayed his hand and bent to the crack.

The count had freed his wife, and must have tipped her from the bed. She sprawled, a tangle of white limbs on an exotic eastern rug, sat up slowly, and hauled herself to her feet.

Moving like an old woman, she went from Gwionn's line of sight. After a few seconds he heard a door open, then close.

Count Etienne dropped his belt on the rug and, climbing into bed, pinched out the bedside candle.

Chapter Twenty-one

Every muscle aching, every limb bruised and battered, Arlette dragged herself across the matting in the adjoining chamber, a nightgown thrown round her shoulders. Her room was deserted, for she never permitted Véronique, who now acted as her maid in place of Clemence, to wait for her return from the count. How could she let the girl see that she came back in this state? She may be powerless to stop the count using her as he did, but she did have her pride.

A pot of tapers stood by the fire. Arlette fumbled for one, lit a candle, and sank down on to the sheepskin hearthrug to recover a little before she washed. She always washed when her husband had done with her.

She felt cold, as she always did afterwards. Throwing a couple of logs on to the fire, she watched the embers glowing through half-closed eyes, and felt the tears begin to flow as they usually did when she was safely in her own room. They dripped slowly down her cheeks, like blood from a wound that would not heal.

A sudden rush of air raised goosebumps on her skin. The click of a door closing had her heart thumping against her ribs. But she was too fatigued to move, save for clutching her robe more tightly to her chest, and too dispirited to raise her head from her contemplation of the flames.

'Have you not hurt me enough for one night?' she said.

'And have you forgotten your promise that my room should be my sanctuary?'

'My lady . . .'

Arlette recognised Gwionn Leclerc's voice at once.

'Sir Gwionn!' She looked up swiftly. Confused, and too exhausted to think straight, she rubbed her hand across her brow. Her eyes stung with more tears. 'What is it? Is there news concerning my father?'

'No, my lady. It's nothing like that.'

Gwionn Leclerc drew near and squatted down at her side, and as the logs that Arlette had added to the fire took hold, varying shades of gold flickered over the planes of his high cheekbones. The scar was dark. A pulse beat strongly in his neck.

'What is it, Sir Gwionn? You should not be here.'

'I know. I'm sorry, my lady.' Running his hand round his neck, Gwionn realised he was speaking the truth. 'I was concerned for you. Are you all right? Shall I summon your maid?'

'My maid. God, no!'

'You look . . . upset.' He wanted to help, but he did not know what to do. 'My lady, you need someone. I'll call Lady Clemence.' He made a move to go.

'No! Please—' She caught at his hand, anchoring him at her side. 'Clemence will be with her husband.'

'But, my lady, I must fetch someone. You're hurt. You need—'

He saw realisation dawn, and she stared at him, and he understood that she was appalled and shamed to her core.

'You know! Oh, God. You know what he's been doing to me!'

Silently, Gwionn nodded.

Arlette swallowed, and brushed aside a stray tear. 'How?'

Gwionn shifted uncomfortably. 'Never mind that. It's

460

enough that I know. Let me help you.'

Gwionn Leclerc's voice was gentle, a benediction after the torments Arlette had been suffering. She felt a sob rise up in her breast.

'No. Go away. I don't need you. I don't need anyone.' Jerkily she tore her gaze from his, and resumed her contemplation of the flames. Two more tears spilled over and ran down her cheeks. Arlette bit the inside of her mouth to control them, but it was hard because she had always liked Gwionn Leclerc and now she heard sympathy in his voice, and saw it reflected in his green eyes. It made her want to weep all the more. She had kept her humiliation from her maid. She had kept it even from Clemence. These past three months had shown her that some things one could not discuss even with one's best friend.

Count Etienne made her feel dirty, full of sin. He made her feel worthless. She knew how much he wanted a child, but in her heart she knew that what he did was wrong. There was no excusing it, but neither was there anything she could do about it. A man could do what he liked with his wife. They would say it was her duty to do as he wished. She may have risen to become a countess, but her lot was no better than that of any other married woman. She was a chattel of her husband's, to do with as he wished.

'I don't need anyone,' she repeated, as though to convince herself.

'Yes, you do. Let me help you.' Gwionn murmured. 'I won't tell anyone. You can trust me.' As Gwionn spoke he noticed with astonishment that his words rang true. What was he doing? He must remember who he was. This was François de Roncier's daughter, and he had vowed to have his revenge. He had vowed to seduce and ruin her, and now here he was wanting to comfort her.

He would unravel his tangled thoughts later. Right

461

now . . . Gwionn reached out and gently touched her on the shoulder. 'My lady—'

She looked at him, huge blue eyes swimming with tears. Her mouth was trembling, and her hair had fallen forwards, a golden river in the firelight which flowed down her breast.

Moving carefully, lest she should be startled, Gwionn pushed her hair from her face and lifted his forefinger to a faint mark at the side of her mouth. This mark would fade by morning, but there were others, elsewhere on her body, that would not. 'He has bruised you. Does this hurt?'

'A little.'

She vibrated with tension, like a drawn bowstring before release. Slowly, infinitely slowly, Gwionn looped a strand of hair round her ear. He let his fingers continue the slight movement to her neck, and rest there, light as thistledown.

She swallowed. Her eyes were clinging to his, and the hunger in them was almost painful to look at.

'My lady—'

With a soft, inarticulate sound, she turned towards him and buried her head on his chest. She began to cry.

Gwionn folded his arms about her and leaned his cheek against her head.

She was clinging to him now, slender fingers gripping the sleeves of his tunic, head pressed hard against him, and racked with great, shuddering sobs.

'Hush. Hush. You'll bring the count down on our ears.'

The sobs quietened.

A cramp in his thighs told him he had been in a crouch for long enough. Gwionn shifted.

Her grip tightened. 'Don't go. I'll be quiet.'

'I'm not going anywhere,' Gwionn assured her and, moving so he was sitting at his ease on the rug, he moved Arlette on to his knee to wait out the storm, rocking her like a babe in its cradle.

Her hair was thick and soft, softer than Anna's, and smelt of musk. If he shifted his head up and down he could feel her earlobe brush against his. The sobs were less passionate and were coming more easily. His tunic was damp with her crying. Absently he swayed to and fro, moving his head gently against hers. His earlobe warmed.

The sobbing stopped, and she heaved a great sigh.

Gwionn stroked her hair. He liked its bright colour, and the texture of it. He combed its tangled, sweat-damp length with his fingers. It had grown well past her waist and spilled out across the hearthrug. Gathering it together, he drew it carefully to one side, away from the fire, and admired it, unaware that she had pulled back slightly and was watching him. Her hair had lights that glinted and shimmered every bit as brightly as the fire.

Realising that she was watching him, he snatched his hand from her hair as though it were indeed bright flames and it had scorched him.

'I'm sorry, my lady. You have beautiful hair.'

'You think so? He hates it.' This last was said with some vehemence.

Gwionn touched her lips. 'Hush, my lady. We must whisper. Have you any idea what the count would do to me if he caught me in here?'

'What would he do?'

'Accuse me of adultery. He'd probably geld me,' Gwionn said bluntly.

She paled and drew back. 'You must go.'

He risked a grin. 'Don't you want me to stay?'

The colour raced back into her cheeks. 'Yes. No. I mean—'

Her confusion was adorable, but he must not tease her. 'What about your back?'

'My back?'

'Someone has to look at it. From what I could see it looked badly bruised.'

'But you can't—'

Gently setting her to one side, Gwionn stood and drew her to her feet. 'In that case I'll send for your maid, and she can do it.'

'No. I couldn't bear to see the pity in her eyes. Somehow with you it's all right. You do it.'

She moved to the bed and, unfastening the cord of her gown, lay down.

'I trust you,' she added.

'And I you, or I wouldn't risk being here.' Briskly, Gwionn came towards her and peeled the gown away. He was a knight, a fighting man, and he had watched his father being skewered on the sword of this girl's father. He had seen de Roncier instigate brutalities that would turn the stomach of the bravest man in Count Etienne's garrison, but the sight of the bruises and cuts on Arlette's slender, innocent body brought him no satisfaction. He hunted for the candle and set it down by the bed. The bruises were bad, both old and new ones, varying in hue from purple to yellow. It was a wonder that she could move at all.

'Christ, my lady, you're all the colours of the rainbow. And cut in one or two places. Let me bathe you.'

'Thank you.' Her voice was muffled. 'The ewer is on that coffer by the adjoining door.'

Gwionn found a sponge. 'I'll be as gentle as I can.'

Neither of them spoke while Gwionn sponged her, and for all that he tried not to hurt her, he was conscious that she had sunk her teeth into her lower lip. Her face was very drawn, and when he put the sponge aside he was certain his was too.

'Have you any soothing ointment?'

'On that shelf.' She pointed. 'There's a jar of arnica.'

He applied it liberally, wondering how the count could bring himself to hurt her. Arlette's back was made for stroking, for kissing, for loving . . . Realising his

464

thoughts were running away with him, he said prosaically, 'You'll need more of this.'

'I'll get it.'

'There, that's enough for now. You should rest more easily.' He covered her with her bedgown.

'Thank you, Gwionn.'

'Can I get you anything else?'

'No, thank you. Gwionn?'

'Mmm?'

'You won't tell anyone about this, will you?'

He stiffened. 'Haven't I promised?' He remembered Petronilla snooping on the landing. 'But if I were you I'd make a hanging to draw over the count's door. The wood's warped and there's a gap I could put my finger in. I noticed the light shining through − ' no need to mention Petronilla, it would only upset her further − 'and if I could see it, others might.'

Cheeks bright, she nodded, rolled on one side, and pushed herself up to a sitting position. She groaned.

Gwionn found himself wincing in sympathy.

'I hadn't noticed the gap,' she said. 'But I had felt the draught. I can always say it was because of the draught.'

He smiled. 'I'll bid you goodnight, my lady.'

'Goodnight, Gwionn. And thank you.'

Gwionn picked up her hand, kissed the back of it, and turned on his heel. At the door he glanced back. She had not moved, except to lift the hand he had kissed to her lips, for all the world as though she were returning his kiss.

He smiled, and softly closed the door.

He did not call Anna to his bed that night. Nor did he for the rest of the week for, even as he tried to focus on his desire for revenge, he was busy keeping watch for Arlette in case she should need him.

On the following evening, Arlette took up Gwionn's

465

suggestion and had a tapestry curtain draped across the door. It meant, though, that Gwionn was unable to find out if she needed him. On that occasion Gwionn solved the problem by simply entering her room and waiting for her by the fire. It was a chancy business, for if her maid had come in and started screeching, he would be hanging by his heels at the crossroads come dawn. He found he didn't want to stop and think about the implications of what he was doing. She might need him.

She had needed him, but not because the count had hurt her. Her bruises needed attention, and he could see that she needed his company.

He had calmed and soothed her, and tended to her back, and in her turn she had set his mind at rest by saying she had told her maid only to attend her if she was specifically bidden.

They had agreed that he was free to enter her room without knocking. It was more than his life was worth to be discovered knocking at the Countess Favell's door in the small hours.

On the third night Gwionn had entered to find Arlette already in her chamber.

'He doesn't want me tonight. He says he's full of remorse for what he has done—'

'Full of wine, more like,' Gwionn said.

She had shrugged. 'What's the difference? He's not going to hurt me tonight, that's all that matters to me. He's on his knees, praying. He seems to have decided that his impotence is because he incurred the anger of the Church – and therefore God's anger too – when he broke the terms of my betrothal agreement. He fears that God disapproves of him trying to have me set aside so he could make a more profitable marriage. He's begging God's forgiveness.'

'How's your back?'

'The same.'

'Let me see.'

Count Etienne supped well at the Twelfth Night feast, and when he retired he took his page, Marc, with him, a sign that Gwionn was beginning to learn meant that Arlette would have peace that night.

Nevertheless he waited till the noise of the revelries had quite faded, before slipping into her room without knocking, as they agreed he could do.

Arlette was sitting on the rug by her fire, a cat on her knee, a mug of mulled wine sitting on the hearthstone. Gwionn could smell the cinnamon. Her face brightened when she saw him.

'Gwionn! Come and sit down beside me,' she murmured easily. Since Gwionn had taken to tending to her back, she had lost all awkwardness with him, and spoke to him as she used to speak to Jehan; as she would to a brother. 'You can share my wine.'

'Thank you, my lady.' Gwionn sat down cross-legged at her side, and took a sip of the wine she had offered. He shared the feeling of ease that had sprung up between them and, despite himself, looked forward to their nightly rendezvous. It was becoming increasingly difficult for him to remember that she was de Roncier's daughter and he hated her; or that it would be ruin for both of them if they were discovered.

The wine was hot and sweet and very good. Gwionn enjoyed the warmth of it running down his throat, before he threw a pointed look at the connecting door between the count's chamber and Arlette's. 'I'd best not stay long.'

Stroking the cat with luxurious enjoyment, Arlette smiled. 'No. I don't want you having to face punishment on my account. Have you met Noella, Gwionn?'

'Noella?' He looked at the cat without much interest. To Gwionn a cat was a means of ridding the castle of rats and mice, and ranked scarcely higher than the rodents it was meant to destroy. 'I didn't know the cats here had names.'

'As a rule they don't. But this one stalked in here on Christmas Day and sat by my fire, proud as a princess. She eyed me as though I was a pauper in her domain. She wouldn't let me touch her at first. But I've won her over, don't you think?'

Noella sat, eyes closed, a contented ball of fur on Arlette's lap.

Gwionn nodded. 'She has a loud purr for a disdainful princess.'

'She does indeed.'

'And she's fat. Have you been feeding her?'

Arlette laughed.

Quick as a thought, Gwionn clapped his hand over her mouth to muffle the sound.

'Hush!'

Arlette took his wrist and pushed his hand away, still giggling. Her eyes were bright with a mixture of mockery and what looked to Gwionn like affection. His heart began to pound. He glanced at Arlette's lips. They looked soft and warm. She liked him, he knew she did. Suddenly, he ached to kiss her. Tonight, her whole demeanour was relaxed, one of slumbrous sensuality. Her hand was moving slowly across Noella's fur, caressing, enjoying, and all at once Gwionn wanted that hand to be moving soothingly across *his* hair, down *his* shoulders, across *his* chest . . .

'Noella's not fat,' she said. 'She's having kittens, you dolt.'

'Kittens? Oh, aye,' he responded vaguely. Then, sensing Arlette was looking at him expectantly, asked, 'When?'

'Any time, I should think.'

In the firelight, Arlette's hair was a golden nimbus about her head, her skin cream velvet.

Gwionn's loins stirred. Clumsily, he got up.

'I'd better go. You don't need me to look at your back, do you?'

'No.'

To his dismay, Arlette put the cat aside and came to her feet, to stand just before him. She tightened the belt of her nightgown. She was wearing nothing beneath it, as he knew from experience. He tried to quell the rush of lust that had overtaken him; for it was lust, he knew that. He did not care for the Countess Arlette Favell. He could not care for the Countess Arlette Favell. He cared for Anna, his wife. Only yesterday he had been in this room with Arlette, and had seen her naked body. He had anointed her fading bruises with the arnica unguent, and had managed to suppress his desires. But tonight . . .

Tonight he had to tear his eyes from the pale skin disappearing so tantalising into the plunging neckline of her robe. He tried not to think about her small breasts, which although he had not touched, he knew would fit precisely in the palm of his hands.

'He's not hurt me for over a week, not since that first time you came,' she spoke candidly. 'I'm much better. That first day you came, Gwionn, that was the worst. I think he shocked even himself, because a couple of days after that he confided that while he was at prayer it came to him that he must not lay the blame for his childlessness at my door.'

'I'm glad. I might have done something very foolish if it had continued.'

Her gaze warmed, and her lips curved. 'Would you? That would have been ill-advised, but I thank you for the thought.'

Gwionn had to get out of her chamber quickly. He turned for the door.

'Gwionn?' Her voice forced him to turn back. 'What's

the matter? Your mouth's all pursed up. Have I angered you?'

'Angered me? Jesu, Arlette, anger's the last thing on my mind.'

'What then? What is it?'

Her face was open, like a flower, a trusting, loving flower, that had seen the hand that was about to swoop down and pick it, and welcomed it. The ache in his groin was almost unbearable. No one, not even Anna, had ever managed to make him feel like this.

He could not resist her.

And all at once he found himself wondering if he should resist her. To take her now would be the most perfect revenge he could think of. He would make love to her with exquisite care. He would make quite certain that she fell headlong into love with him. It should be easy. She had only known abuse. If he took care with her . . . Afterwards, when she confessed her love, he would leave her. He would then break her heart, as her father had broken his. Simple. It was the most perfect revenge.

He reached for a tendril of red-gold hair. It curled round his finger like a vine. God, but she was lovely. He could see the promising curve of her breasts outlined against the fabric of her robe, and her long slender legs. Her eyes were enormous, drinking him in, in much the same way that he suspected he was drinking her in.

Before he considered his next action, one of his hands slid round her neck, and the other found her waist and gently caught her to him.

Smiling, she lifted her face to his. Their lips met.

He gave her an innocent kiss, the sort of kiss a young boy would give his first love.

How warm he is, Arlette thought. And how very gentle. She held herself still, the more to enjoy this new and pleasant sensation.

Slowly, delicately, Gwionn's lips were moving over

hers. So light she could hardly feel them. It was delightful, quite unlike the count.

From the moment their eyes had met over Noella, Arlette had been aware they were moving towards this kiss, but Gwionn's gentle delicacy and sensitivity to her wishes had surprised her. He kissed charmingly. She had expected, almost wanted, him to snatch him to her and kiss her till she was senseless. But this was better, so much better. How safe she felt with him. She put an arm around him, stroked his face, and when he drew his head back, gave him a shy but loving smile. She shifted slightly, and no sooner had she moved than his arms fell away. A question burned in his green eyes. Do you want more? they asked. One of his hands came up to stroke her earlobe.

Basking in the unaccustomed novelty of being kissed by a man who took note of her wishes, Arlette smiled her answer, took his hand, and their lips rejoined in another breathtakingly tender, beautiful kiss.

Contrary to his expectations, Gwionn was having difficulty controlling himself. His heart was pounding so loudly he was sure that the count would hear it and come running with half the castle guard in his wake. Arlette had begun to respond to his kisses, tentatively at first. Carefully, he teased her lips apart. Eagerly she pressed forward, and their teeth touched. She was so trusting, so welcoming, it almost hurt him to kiss her. A strange thought ran across his brain, that against him, Arlette was defenceless.

He ought not to do this.

Finding he had pitched in over his head, he disengaged, floundering. 'Arlette, we should not . . . We − ' luckily he caught the slip before it was out − 'you are married. This is dangerous territory we are treading on.'

Lightly, Arlette ran her fingertips over the planes of Gwionn's face, hovering for an instant over his scar. She stroked that too. She did not want to think about being married, not when Gwionn was holding her in his arms. Her pulse was racing for fear the count might walk in on them, but that only served to sharpen her feelings, adding a sharp sense of poignancy.

She felt right in Gwionn Leclerc's arms. She was where she belonged. Warm with happiness, Arlette tried to recall when she had last felt like this; not for years, certainly. This was what she had been looking for. Surely she had a right to snatch at a little happiness, even if it could not last?

And it could not last, cold logic told her that. She was the Countess Favell, and any carnal relationship with Gwionn Leclerc could only end in disaster.

'It would be worth it,' she murmured, to herself.

'What?'

'Never mind.' Exploring the length of his scar with her fingers, Arlette resolutely steered his mind down another avenue. She did not want to think about endings when they were just beginning. She had a right to some happiness, she would strive to keep him as long as she could. 'Does it hurt when I touch it?'

'No.' Gwionn's thoughts had tied themselves in knots. He desired Arlette, had wanted her for years, for revenge. If she had not saved him from drowning he would have seduced her years ago. Since she had saved him, he had regretted his missed opportunity, and spent much time berating himself for his weakness. And while Anna had been absent, nay, even while Anna had been with him, he had spent hours lying awake on his pallet dreaming of all the things he would do to Arlette should the opportunity ever come his way.

And here she was now, a plum in his arms, ripe and ready for the picking, and all he could think of was that he should protect her, that he should take control here, for she had been hurt enough . . .

'I would kiss your scar better if I could,' Arlette said, blissfully unaware of the irony in her words, blissfully unaware that a trooper from her father's garrison had put the scar there in the first place. A deep flush stole over her cheeks. 'You kiss very sweetly. I didn't know it could be so sweet to kiss a lover.'

'We're not lovers,' Gwionn said.

She pushed his hand into the neck of her gown, and placed it on her breast. Impossibly, her expression was trusting, innocent and seductive all at once. Her breast was warm, a perfect handful. Barely, Gwionn mastered the desire to press himself upon her.

'No. But we will be.'

Her candour disarmed him. Her eyes, dreamy in the flickering firelight, invited more kisses. Reason fled.

Gwionn abandoned all attempts to order his thoughts, and bent his head.

Arlette melted into his arms, quite without fear.

'Oh, Gwionn,' she murmured, when they next drew apart.

Feverishly, he fumbled at the sash round her waist, and her robe fell open.

'Arlette.' He swallowed, and reached for her. 'You're beautiful.'

'So are you,' she whispered with a smile.

Together they fell on to the rug, displacing a disgruntled Noella, who lumbered away.

'We've offended her,' Arlette said, smiling shyly at Gwionn.

'Forget Noella,' Gwionn said huskily, as he pushed the silken mass of her hair aside and found her earlobe with lips and tongue.

Arlette giggled softly, a warm throaty sound, full of joy. 'I like that.'

'Do you? What about this?'

'Mmm. Heaven.'

473

'And this?' He moved his hand down the warm curve of her body, gentle, unhurried.

'Oh, yes. God, yes.' A small moan of delight. 'Please don't stop.'

'I won't,' he murmured in her ear. 'Did anyone ever tell you how sweet you were?'

She shook her head.

His hand reached the triangle of red hair which sprung between her thighs, paused, and continued to its inevitable destination.

'Do you like that?' He made his voice a caress.

'Yes,' she gasped. 'Oh, yes. Oh. Gwionn. You must show me what you'd like me to do. Oh. Gwionn. Kiss me, Gwionn.'

Gwionn obliged.

'God, Gwionn, don't stop.' She murmured into his mouth. 'Don't ever, ever stop.'

Gwionn smiled.

Chapter Twenty-two

Arlette had never known anything like it. Gwionn Leclerc filled her thoughts to the exclusion of all else. He was kind, he was gentle, he was beautiful, and when he touched her the blood raced through her veins, and she felt more alive than she had ever felt before.

She could not get enough of him. She was greedy for his love, his kisses; for the reassuring weight of his body on her belly. In one night Gwionn Leclerc had converted her from a frightened, frigid girl, to a sensual woman who revelled in her sensuality. She was hungry for him, eager; it was as though she was making up for the months of maltreatment since her marriage and the long years of incarceration in the tower.

The lovers grew bold, and made love often in the candlelit chamber next to the count's. Fortunately luck was with them, for despite the folly of their forbidden liaison, neither of them spared a thought for the risks they were running. It was as though they had both been bewitched, and were caught in an enchantment so powerful that nothing was proof against it, neither duty, nor common sense, nor morality.

Arlette moved as though through a dream. She was Queen Guinevere; Gwionn her Lancelot. Count Etienne, naturally, was poor cuckolded King Arthur, except that, owing to his cruelty, Arlette felt disinclined to sympathise with him as she had when she had read of King Arthur in Wace's verses.

The spell Gwionn had cast upon her was overwhelming, so much so that she was conscious of only one fear — the fear of becoming pregnant by him.

On the Twelfth Night, when Gwionn and she had first become lovers, it had taken her by surprise. On that occasion they had not taken measures to ensure that she would not become pregnant. Arlette knew how to settle that fear, soaking a sponge in vinegar and inserting it before Gwionn came to her room. She never told her lover what she was doing, and the fact that he never once mentioned the possibility of their love bearing fruit only served to strengthen Arlette's conviction that Gwionn felt the effects of the enchantment as strongly as she.

Arlette had quite forgotten about the betraying exchange of gestures she had seen take place between Sir Gwionn and Anna le Harpour on the minstrels' gallery. And if she had recalled the gesture, so enthralled was she with her lover that she would have set it down to a passing infatuation on his part. Gwionn had her now. What need had he for the harper's wife?

Anna noticed the change in Gwionn at once. He did not stop calling her to his bed, but the calls became less frequent, and when she encouraged him to open up his heart, he became irritable and distant.

It did not take her long to work out the cause.

Gwionn and the countess were lovers. He was wreaking his revenge on Arlette de Roncier, as he had always vowed he would. Anna had not anticipated the effect it would have on her. Belittled by Gwionn's infidelity, a black despair took hold of her soul. Underneath the despair, a bitter anger was brewing.

She kept her anger bottled as long as she could, despite thinking that her husband should have abandoned his plans for revenge years ago. They were inappropriate.

Count François had undeniably perpetrated a great injustice against Gwionn's family, but Count François was being punished by God who had sent the paralysing sickness down on him.

This affair between the Countess Favell and her husband was no less than insanity. It had to stop. When Anna next had the chance, she would tell him as much.

After several nights during which she had lain awake, hoping to see her husband standing in the stairwell beckoning for her, she decided to take the initiative.

She tracked him down one evening after supper in the armoury, where he was discussing with Jacques Nares, the armourer, the design of an old German helmet Count Etienne had brought into La Forteresse as a curiosity. Both men were leaning on the scarred workbench lost in their conversation. The forge was banked down for the night. The amourer's two apprentices were still at their trestle emptying a wine-keg.

Anna caught Gwionn's eye, and signalled that she wanted a word. Then she hovered by the door waiting for him to finish his conversation.

'Listen, Jacques, the ventail on this old helmet is fixed.' Gwionn rapped it with his knuckles, and a tinny clang rang through the armoury.

Anna glanced curiously at the pegs on the armoury walls, and the shelves where the trappings of war had been stowed for the night. There were dozens of helmets and swords in racks. There were scores of pikeheads and polearms of an extraordinary variety of shapes and sizes, which had been thrown into boxes. Most were spearheads, plain and simple, but some were shaped like crosses, while others resembled hammers. There were maces with grim little spikes sticking out in all directions. There were axes and lances and crossbows and flails. It was a chilling array. Anna had no idea that man was so inventive when it came to discovering different ways of maiming or killing other people.

Jacques was talking. 'But all the ventails are fixed, Sir Gwionn, not just those in the older designs.'

'I know that, man. But have you tried to shout an order through one of those things?'

'No, sir.'

'Consider how much more convenient it would be if the knights could flip the ventail aside when not actually engaged. Why, the men might actually be able to hear what one said. Look, I'll demonstrate.'

Picking up the helmet from the workbench, Gwionn put it on.

'Can you hear me, Jacques?' he asked in muffled tones.

'Barely.'

Gwionn removed the helmet and dropped it on the workbench.

'Then you understand what I mean. And we're in a quiet armoury with you not two feet away from me. In the heat of battle, or even at a joust, there's much more din.'

Jacques nodded. 'I do see the problem. I'll experiment with some hinges tomorrow, and see what I can come up with.'

Gwionn slapped Jacques on the shoulder. 'Good man. I know you'll come up with something.'

'It might be better,' Jacques said, frowning thoughtfully at the German helmet, 'if I fix the hinges so the ventail lifts up rather than sideways. It should be possible without blocking your vision.' He brightened. 'I'll try it both ways, sir.'

'Jacques, you're a wonder,' Gwionn said and, smiling, strode out of the armoury.

His smile had faded by the time he reached Anna. 'What's the matter, Madame le Harpour?'

Anna resisted the urge to grind her teeth. She loathed it when he called her Madame le Harpour.

'I need to talk,' she said in a low voice.

'Can't it wait?'

'No.'

He sighed. 'Very well then. But I can't talk now. You must have a care for my position.'

'You are my husband,' Anna said softly.

'Yes. But in the eyes of everyone here you're married to Barthélemy. I'm a knight.'

Anna's urge to grind her teeth transformed itself into a violent desire to hit him. Instead, she smiled sweetly at her husband and said, 'Tonight then? You promise?'

'I promise.'

Giving her a curt little bow, Gwionn turned on his heel.

Anna thought it would be best if they made love before she broached the subject of the countess. She had thought it would strengthen the bond between them.

She was wrong.

Her husband made love to her as skilfully as ever, but Anna was wise enough to know that that in itself was no cause for rejoicing. After so many years, they each had an intimate knowledge of the workings of the other's body. Physically, everything was right. Mentally, it was all wrong. His soul wasn't in it. Gwionn was making all the right moves, and so was she, but it wasn't working.

Was his liaison with the countess more serious than she had thought? Had Gwionn come to feel affection for Arlette Favell? Was that why he had closed up like a clam?

His mind was certainly elsewhere. Anna might as well be a wooden doll for all the joy she was giving him.

When they had done, she began to speak.

'Gwionn? We need to talk.'

He groaned, rolling away from her. 'Must we? I'm tired.'

'You promised, Gwionn.'

A sigh. 'Oh, have it your own way.' Reluctantly, he rolled back and flashed her a jaundiced look. 'You're turning into a shrew, Anna.'

Anna was not going to be side-tracked into a quarrel. 'Gwionn, it's about the countess.'

He yawned. 'What about her?'

'You're her lover, aren't you?'

'And if I am? Would you be jealous?'

She laid a hand lightly on his chest, and stroked the brown hairs. 'Yes.'

His face lightened, and almost, he looked amused. He was pleased she was upset about it, Anna realised resentfully. He did not care that she hurt, but he was flattered to have had such an effect on her.

'There's no need for jealousy, Anna. You're my wife.'

'I think it should stop,' she said.

'Stop? Certainly not. I can't tell you how delicious it is to lie on de Roncier's daughter, and fuck her stupid. She's nothing but a whore at heart. She loves it.'

Anna frowned. 'I don't think you should talk about her like that. She seems likeable enough, and she's obviously growing fond of you. Her face can be very unguarded at times. I caught her watching you at dinner, and I think she loves you.'

'Good. It'll hurt her all the more when I stop.'

'Stop now. You've done enough. Think of the consequences if you are caught. It's adultery, Gwionn, adultery with a countess. You're breaking your oath of fealty to your lord. Every honourable man in the castle would condemn you. And you've not just yourself to consider. What about me and Jean? We need you whole.' She lowered her voice and put a proprietary hand on his manhood. 'I wouldn't want to lose any part of you.'

'Barthélemy would look after you both if anything happened to me,' Gwionn said.

'But I didn't marry Barthélemy. I married you. I love

480

you. It was a mistake to agree to act as Barthélemy's wife, I see that now.'

Strong fingers caught at her hand, green eyes pleaded. 'You won't betray me, Anna?'

'No. But I hate living a lie. It's all wrong. Jean is your son, and one you should be proud of—'

'I am proud of him.'

'Then when are you going to acknowledge him? Good God, Gwionn, with your background you'd think you should know what it does to a boy to have a father who won't ackowledge him. It warped you. And now you're doing exactly the same thing to Jean.'

'Not quite. I married you. My father did not marry my mother till before Philippe was born.'

Gwionn's mouth was a sulky line. He hated being cornered, Anna knew, but she felt strongly about this and pressed on recklessly. 'You're nit-picking, Gwionn.' She made an impatient gesture. 'You've not acknowledged Jean, and you should have. I'm beginning to regret having come here.'

'I'm not forcing you to stay. You're free to go whenever you like.'

Appalled, Anna was speechless for a moment. 'You don't mean that,' she said. 'You can't.'

Silence.

Anna covered her face in her hands, and removed them when she had her features under her control.

'This vow you have taken to revenge yourself on Arlette is only making your mind more twisted than ever.' She spoke as coolly as she could. 'I may well leave, because I can't bear to watch it. You must see that you should finish this affair with the countess. You're bound to be caught.'

Gwionn let out a short laugh. 'I disagree. We may never be caught. The way that old fool drinks himself into a stupor every night, she could entertain the whole garrison on the floor of his room and he'd snore through it.'

'Please end it, Gwionn. I'm begging you.'

'End it? Are you mad? When the job's only half done?'

Anna shook her head in bewilderment. 'Half done?' I don't understand.'

'I want my seed to grow in her belly. I want de Roncier's wench to bear my child. When I've accomplished that I'll consider the job done. Then I'll stop.'

Anna sank back into the pillow and stared at the ceiling.

'You like her. You're half in love with her,' she said in a dull voice.

He ruffled her hair. 'I hate her, my Anna, and have done for years.'

Turning her head, she looked searchingly into her husband's beautiful green eyes. 'Yes. I believe you do hate her. You hate her for being her father's daughter. But she must have some kind of hold over you other than desire, otherwise you'd come to your senses and see that this must stop. Half of you hates her and,' she swallowed, 'half of you loves her.'

He laughed, and to Anna's ears it was a laugh straight from hell.

Lying on her palliasse in the hall later that night, with Jean between herself and Barthélemy, Anna gazed unseeing up at the rafters. Her eyes were dry, and she felt vacant and empty as if wind could have blown right through her.

Barthélemy stirred, reached over Jean, and touched her arm.

'Are you all right, Anna?'

'Well enough.'

'A lovers' quarrel?'

Anna smiled sadly into the darkness. 'Yes. A lovers' quarrel.'

Barthélemy rolled away again. 'Well, if that's all it is,

you've no need to lie awake fretting half the night. Time heals all. He'll come round in the morning, I shouldn't wonder.'

'I hope so.'

And if he didn't come round? What then?

She could not stand to live like this for much longer. Turning on her side, she pulled the scratchy blanket up to her chin and wrapped her arms about her son. At least she had Jean. And Barthélemy.

The winter months flowed by with Arlette floating on a cloud of happiness.

The count had stopped being cruel to her. Occasionally he would make a feeble attempt to couple with her, but his growing obsession with religion and fear of God's judgement prevented him from hurting her, and he would soon abandon the task. He seemed to find the whole business of making love to her as distasteful as she found it with him.

No sooner had her husband dismissed her from his chamber and turned to his prayers, than Arlette had forgotten him, and flew joyfully into her lover's arms.

Sometimes Gwionn and Arlette made love in her chamber, sometimes in his. She felt passionately about her Breton knight, and the fear that they might at any moment be discovered added a thrill to the passion.

Arlette also had an intuition that this wild happiness could not last. She wanted to make the most of it.

Count Etienne was resorting more and more to prayer. He asked Arlette to join him in his intercessions.

'We should pray together for a son, my dear,' he said. 'God is more likely to hear two voices than one.'

Arlette had no choice but to agree, and so the charade began.

It took place every morning, after Mass.

483

The count and his countess remained behind in the chapel, kneeling side by side in their prie-dieu, and both – if the count only but knew it – prayed very different prayers.

The count folded his dry, veined hands together and prayed earnestly to become potent.

The countess fiddled with the beads of her rosary, and prayed, equally earnestly, that he should not. Further, she prayed that she should *not* conceive.

God did not answer the count's prayers.

He remained impotent.

God did not answer the countess's prayers either.

Duke Richard, back from his imprisonment in Germany, visited the Aquitaine and decided to build a chapel dedicated to St Martin at Limeuil. The count attended the ceremony of the laying of the foundation stone, and proffered a large endowment, thereby hoping to gain God's favour.

The count's prayers continued to go unheeded.

The ill-fated pilgrimage which took place in the spring of 1195 was Count Etienne's idea.

It grew as a natural development from his intercessions. No doubt he would not have thought of it if he had not been inspired by the chanson about Rocamadour that Barthélemy and his wife had sung one night.

The first Arlette heard of her husband's plan was at breakfast. Sir Louis and Lady Petronilla, who had come for a hunting trip, were present.

The meal was late that morning, and while they ate the steward went about his work, supervising the winding down of the three iron chandeliers from the ceiling in order that he might cut out the candle stubs and refill them. The stub-ends were thrown in a basket, so what was left of the wax could be melted down and re-used. As it was a lengthy and cumbersome business — as was lighting them — the chandeliers were only used on high days and Holy days.

Petronilla's two sons, William and Laurence, were playing like puppies in the rushes underneath the trestle. Both Sir Gilles and Sir Gwionn were with them, as was Marc, the count's page.

'I've decided that Arlette and I shall make a pilgrimage to Notre-Dame de Rocamadour,' the count announced good-humouredly, while waiting for Marc to cut him a slice of manchet loaf.

Arlette sat stiffly beside her husband, half expecting him to humiliate her publicly. It was scarcely credible that the genial man who smiled round the board was the same monster who had abused and hurt her a few months ago. Would any of them believe her if she told them? What would Lady Petronilla say if she knew? But Arlette knew the answer to that without asking. Lady Petronilla would not care two pins about how Count Etienne made love to his wife. That he made love to her at all might concern her, but not the manner in which he did it.

The count leaned towards her, and gave her one of the kindly smiles that she remembered from before her incarceration. Taking this to mean that he had no intention of humiliating her in the hall of his keep, Arlette smiled back. If she pleased him, all could be well between them, she was sure. She would make it right between them.

Courteously, eyes soft and apparently loving, Count Etienne replenished Arlette's silver goblet with watered wine. The goblet had been a wedding gift from Sir Gilles. When her husband was like this, Arlette was discovering that she could find it in her to like him. In company he was unfailingly attentive and amusing. She wished she could convince him that while she had had to make her stand over his breaking of their betrothal agreement, she regretted offending him. She wanted to heal the rift between them, and then he would always be like this, and would never revert to repeating the degrading rituals that had taken place after their marriage.

But if she did heal the rift between herself and Count Etienne, where would that leave her and Gwionn? That question seemed unanswerable. Life had become very confusing.

William roared past on hands and knees under the table and jostled Arlette's knee. Hearing her son – who could not hear him? – Lady Petronilla smiled complacently. Lady Petronilla's ambitions were for her boys.

Arlette did not care for that woman.

Though she despised the count for the way she had treated her in the past, Arlette was ready to forgive him, ready to try again. He was her husband, after all. If only she could give him a son. It would please him mightily but, almost more importantly would certainly put Lady Petronilla's nose out of joint. Seeing the malicious turn her thoughts were taking, Arlette pulled herself up, aghast. What was the matter with her? It was not like her to be so spiteful. Try as she might, though, she could not like Petronilla Favell.

Lady Petronilla's sharp grey eyes had fastened on the count, but she managed to make her voice as sweet as the honey that Count Etienne's page was spreading on his bread.

'A pilgrimage?' Petronilla purred. 'Why so, dear uncle? Do you have good news for us? Do you wish to give thanks that your wife has conceived?'

And the grey eyes slid with sly curiosity to Arlette.

Unsurprised by Lady Petronilla's uncivil behaviour, Arlette set her teeth. Lady Petronilla's question verged on the impertinent, but Arlette understood why she posed it. She had heard the rumours concerning her husband's impotence. Two wives in the grave and neither of them had quickened once. It happened often. There was her own stepmother as an example, but then with poor Eleanor everyone knew that the fault lay in her and not in her father. Arlette wondered whether Count Etienne had treated his previous wives as he had treated her after their wedding. Had his other wives suffered under his hands? Had they been sickly women? Or had it been the count's cruelty that had caused their untimely deaths? Arlette was not permitted to pursue that sobering line of thought, for the count answered Petronilla's question.

'I should have visited Rocamadour when we were first married,' he said. 'It is an oversight I intend to rectify by interceding to Notre-Dame de Rocamadour. I have offerings for Her. I shall beg Her for forgiveness for past sins and ask for Her blessing on my marriage so that this time,' his hand moved to cover Arlette's, 'it will be fruitful.'

The count had never forgotten that he had once forged an alliance with Henry the Young King who had died an ignominious death after plundering the shrine at Rocamadour. Count Etienne had played no part in that raid. At heart he had always had a religious cast of mind, and he had been disgusted by Henry the Young King's impiety. Since then he had been assailed by guilt. He did not feel any guilt regarding the political aspects of his alliance; it was Henry Plantagenet's sacrilege that sickened him, and the fact that he had once been involved with such an impious prince.

Petronilla's smile was frozen. 'Count, that is a wonderful idea,' she said, and even the cloying sweetness of her tones failed to mask her insincerity. What about the count's wine? If he went away, he would not have access to his Beaune. Somehow Petronilla must contrive to go with them. Though it was not likely that the count would give in to the lusts of the flesh while on a pilgrimage, when he would want to be chaste, he must have his medicine. Just in case.

Sir Gilles, sitting at the opposite end of the table to the woman whom he had once loved and hoped to marry, glanced swiftly in her direction and, equally swiftly, glanced away. Some days he was beginning to think he scarcely recognised her. She was so changed. Since the birth of her sons, Gilles had been unable to catch even a glimpse of the pretty merchant's daughter he had known. Instead he found himself regarding a woman he suspected was a predatory schemer capable of doing almost anything to achieve her ambitions.

Petronilla turned to her husband. 'Louis, don't you agree a pilgrimage is a wonderful idea?'

Louis nodded, and looked at the count. 'I should like to join you on your pilgrimage, uncle, if you don't object,' he said.

'Object? I'd be delighted, dear boy.'

'Petronilla, will you come?' Louis asked.

Petronilla, who had been staring at Arlette with a crease between her brows, glanced vaguely at Count Etienne. Recently Petronilla had noticed Sir Gwionn and the countess often had eyes for each other, and this had loosed a volley of suspicions in her mind and furnished her with another reason for wanting to accompany them.

'You say Countess Arlette is going with you?' Petronilla demanded, wondering if Sir Gwionn would travel with them. She hoped so, for then Petronilla would have ample opportunity to observe the two of them more closely. It would not do for Sir Gwionn and Arlette to become lovers. Sir Gwionn looked anything but impotent. If they did become lovers, Petronilla would not hesitate to expose them.

'Indeed.' Count Etienne picked up his bread. 'My wife must climb the steps and make her offering alongside me.'

Petronilla's brow cleared. 'I would love to go. I have

been longing to go to Rocamadour ever since I was a child. Father Nicholas told me about St Amadour's tomb, and the miraculous bell. I have always wanted to hear it ring.' Now all she wanted was for Sir Gwionn to go. Then she could keep an eye on him and the countess.

'The miraculous bell?'

Rocamadour was famed throughout Christendom as a holy place, and Arlette knew about its walnut statue of Our Lady, but she had not heard about any bell, miraculous or otherwise.

'Oh, my dear,' Petronilla yawned delicately. 'I thought everyone knew about the bell. It's ancient. Some say it was cast by Charlemagne. It hangs in the sanctuary of Notre-Dame, and when anyone in danger at sea invokes Our Lady's help, and promises to visit Rocamadour, the bell rings.'

'On its own?' Arlette asked. Petronilla's tale sounded extremely far-fetched. It sounded like the sort of yarn wily citizens might spin to draw gullible sea-faring pilgrims and their custom into Rocamadour.

'Yes.' Petronilla nodded. 'The bell rings quite on its own. Or rather it is rung by God's angels.'

Sir Gilles had lifted his eyes from the manchet loaf to watch Petronilla as she answered Arlette. His mouth twisted cynically.

Petronilla continued. 'When the canons and townsfolk hear the bell, they mark down the time and the day on which it has rung. And then, later, when the pilgrims from the ship pour in to give thanks, they are able to confirm the precise moment at which the Madonna saved them.'

'I could have done with knowing about that bell on my voyage here,' Arlette said, dryly. She glanced at Gwionn, and smiled. 'It might have saved Sir Gwionn and myself a wetting. However, Saint Radegonde did us very well.'

Petronilla, who had noted both glance and smile, put

489

on a shocked expression. 'My dear! I fear you do not take the story of the bell seriously enough. I know it is true. Father Nicholas is not a liar.'

Arlette smiled. 'It is a pretty tale,' she said politely.

Petronilla placed her clasped hands on the table. 'At any rate I have longed to go to Rocamadour.' She glanced pointedly at her sons, who were by the fireplace, whipping each other with rushes they had grubbed up from the floor. 'I have my own blessings to be thankful for, and alms to give.'

Sir Gilles' face – he had been listening to this exchange – darkened. He was not blinded by Petronilla's sudden show of piety, and if one was to judge by the nervous smile pinned to Louis Favell's lips, neither was her husband. These days Gilles barely exchanged two words with his former love, but he could see she was becoming more sly by the day. Petronilla looked as though she had mischief on her mind, and he was not the only one to suspect it.

She may be planning nothing, but Gilles made the decision that he too would take part in this pilgrimage. In Count Etienne's absence he would normally be left in charge of La Forteresse, but not this time. He feared for the count. He could not think what plot Petronilla could have turning in her head, but she was up to something.

This time, for Etienne's sake, Gilles must ensure that he went with him.

On a blue and white April day, the pilgrims agreed to meet in the bailey. They were going to make the most of a warm spell of weather.

The count insisted that everyone in his party put aside their fine linens and brocades, to don instead the drab homespun more usually worn by pilgrims.

'It's not the coarseness of the material I mind,' Petronilla said, dragging the itchy fabric away from her

490

body as she made her way irritably into the spring sunshine.

Weather like this always made Petronilla lazy, and the last thing she wanted was to spend a whole day – or possibly two whole days – riding to Rocamadour. Straightening both her spine and her resolve, she reminded herself of what was at stake. She had her two beautiful sons to consider. If it were not for them, she would be tempted to turn back and abandon the whole business; but for their sake she must put up with such petty inconveniences. She would do anything for her sons, and her determination that William should one day step into Count Etienne's shoes was growing daily. If ever there had been a time when she had been concerned about doctoring the count's wine, Petronilla had forgotten it.

She grimaced as she tugged at her gown. 'Just look at the colour, Louis. You have to agree it's too depressing for words. Don't you think it's depressing? Louis?'

Silently, Louis handed her a staff, and one of the wide-brimmed hats favoured by pilgrims for keeping the sun from their heads.

Petronilla regarded both staff and hat with distaste. 'And what am I meant to do with these, pray?'

'This is your walking stick,' Louis told her in a neutral tone. 'Pilgrims usually tie their pouches to the top so they can keep an eye on their valuables as they walk along.' Louis had discovered rather late in his marriage that there was another pleasure to be had from his wife apart from the ones he got from her in bed. He enjoyed teasing her. He enjoyed watching her squirm.

She was squirming now, inside, and her face was a picture of dismay. She lowered her voice to an urgent whisper. 'Louis? We are riding, aren't we? Don't tell me the old weasel's taken it into his head that we should walk to Rocamadour.'

It was over twenty miles to Rocamadour, a hard trudge

in the warming sun up and down winding, dusty roads, and Petronilla thought it quite unnecessary when they had perfectly good horses.

'A foot-soldier would think nothing of it,' Louis said, in the tone he adopted when William was being petulant.

'A foot-soldier? But I am not a foot-soldier.'

'I thought you wanted to come.'

'I do,' Petronilla declared firmly. 'You know I do. But to walk . . .'

Louis decided to put his wife out of her misery. He waved at the stables, where Jacob was leading out the horses. 'Put your mind at rest. We're riding. It will save us a couple of days. This jaunt will take the best part of a week as it is. There's trouble brewing between Philip of France and Duke Richard, and the count wants to be back as soon as he may.'

'Trouble between Philip and Richard? But Louis, didn't you tell me they called a truce?'

'They did. But my uncle doesn't trust either of them to keep it. The duke may make a call on his men at any time.'

'So the pilgrimage must be completed in as short a time as possible?'

'We'll be back before the week is out. Use your stick as a goad, if you wish, Petronilla. But don't lose it. When we arrive at Rocamadour, you'll need it to climb the steps to the shrine – unless you plan on going up on your knees.'

Petronilla shuddered. 'On my knees? No, I'll leave that to your uncle and his wife.'

Louis grinned. 'Here's your horse.' He cupped his hands to squire his wife on to a neat brown mare with one white stocking. 'And remember, you must wear that hat at all times.'

Ill-humouredly, Petronilla crammed the shapeless hat on to her head as Count Etienne and Countess Arlette emerged from the keep.

The young countess was wearing penitential robes, too,

and her hat. The dull colours looked good on her. And by some miracle, so too did the dreadful pilgrim's hat. Véronique had piled her mistress's hair up on top of her head, and covered it entirely with the hat. Here and there a red-gold curl peeped out. The Countess Favell looked enchanting, Petronilla observed sourly. And not the slightest bit uncomfortable in her vile, itchy robe.

Where was Sir Gwionn? She wanted to watch him. He had to come.

Petronilla knew that Father Theobald had heard all the pilgrims' confessions, and given them communion, but she did not know if Sir Gwionn had said his.

The custom was that when a pilgrim set out on his travels, all his belongings were guarded for him by the Church. Count Etienne had sent word to the Bishop of Périgord, as well as his personal friend the Bishop of Cahors. Two deacons had been sent – one from each of the bishops – to assist Father Theobald in discharging his responsibility for keeping La Forteresse safe for the few days the count would be absent. Carrying the bishops' authority, these men would stand in for Sir Gilles.

But Count Etienne was a soldier as well as a faithful man of the Church. He was practical. In these lawless times, might most often proved itself to be right, and to that end Count Etienne had put Sir Walter Venner in command of the castle guard and his troops. Sir Walter – though he thought of himself as Arlette's man – had sworn allegiance to the count before Arlette went into La Tour Brune. He had become highly trusted. He was to oversee discipline and Captain Gervase would assist.

The pilgrims assembling in the bailey looked impressive; for all that they wore the simple pilgrims' attire, the quality of their horses betrayed their high standing.

Sir Gilles and Sir Gwionn came out of the keep.

'Oh, is the Breton knight coming?' Petronilla asked, casually.

'I believe so. And Lady Clemence,' Louis answered.

That morning his uncle had decreed that the ladies could not take their maids with them. Louis braced himself to tell his wife this.

'Petronilla?'

'Mmm?'

She was watching the knights mount up.

'Count Etienne says that Rose and the other maids are to stay behind,' he said, waiting for an explosion. 'He says they would slow us down.'

But, astonishingly, Petronilla's lips curved in a smile. 'Quite right,' she said. 'Most likely they would.'

494

Chapter Twenty-three

Although it was a mere twenty miles as the crow flies to Rocamadour, the Pilgrim's Way followed the snaking curls of the river as it wound like a silver thread through the wooded valley, so the journey took double the time that it would if the Way had been made straight as an arrow like the old metalled Roman roads.

They were blessed by fine weather, and had two clear April days for their ride. It did not rain, and a gentle yellow sun warmed faces and shoulders.

The sun had brought other pilgrims out. A few rode as they did, but most trudged the Way on foot. Some of the more elderly or infirm were drawn upstream in gabares by draught-oxen, but since the Dordogne did not flow directly past Rocamadour, these last would finish the final leg of their journey in litters or carts which would be available for hire at Belcastel, where river and pilgrims took divergent paths.

Prayers were said, and offerings made at every shrine and church en route. Their pace was slow and measured.

Young leaves were unfurling on the poplars and alders which lined the riverbank. Crowfoot flowers glowed at the base of the trees, stalks entwining with tiny blue speed-wells. Brimstone butterflies crawled from their cocoons, dried their wings in the sun, and fluttered past in search of primroses. The blossom was bursting on the crab-apple trees, and Arlette saw her first swallow of the year.

But Arlette was not interested in the spring pageant which was confidently, inexorably unfolding all around her. She wanted time to stop. Her mind was turned in on itself, and she rode in an uncommunicative silence at her husband's side while a worm of worry gnawed inside her, insistent as an obsession.

She should have had her courses three weeks ago.

She could not be pregnant. She must not be pregnant.

Every time she and Gwionn had made love she had used the little sponge. She had prayed incessantly.

She could not be pregnant.

Litany-like, the phrase took on a life of its own and repeated itself over and over in time to the steady clopping of Yseult's hoofs.

She could not be pregnant. She must not be pregnant.

She tried to ignore Gwionn. Not because she was angry with him, no, she could not blame him. Like her, he had been blinded by passion. No, she ignored him because she did not want to be distracted by him until she knew what she could do.

If she were pregnant – which of course she wasn't – she did not think she could tell him, not yet. But who could she tell? She needed advice.

Covertly, she glanced at Clemence bouncing along riding pillion behind a squire on one of the count's horses. Clemence had never got to grips with riding, and since marrying a man who had acquired a destrier powerful enough to carry two, she never rode on her own if she could avoid it. Clemence was fortunate that Sir Walter had permitted her to ride behind him and so acquire the taste for riding pillion. Many knights would think it belittled them to have a woman clinging like a burr to their backs.

Arlette gave a soft sigh. This was another secret she could not confide to Clemence. If she were pregnant – and God grant that she was not – this was a cross she must bear alone for as long as she could.

God would help her. He had to, for she could not think of anyone else who would.

Count Etienne had only managed to make love to her properly that one time, on their wedding night. If she grew big with child, he would know it was not his. What would he do to her? At best she would be branded as an adulterer and set aside. At worst . . .

Her mind shied away from the tales she had heard of unfaithful wives who had been pressed to death; of women stoned from the town before the dogs were set upon them. But this was the twelfth century, and lately her husband had been acting the part of the civilised man in their bedchamber as well as in public. He had stopped hurting her. And even during the weeks when he had abused her, the count had never, ever humiliated her in public. It was cold comfort.

As the miles sailed past, Arlette fretted the hours away. It was quite possible that her time had been delayed because she had worried that her affair with Gwionn was going to be discovered. She might wake up tomorrow and feel the familiar ache in her belly, and know everything was going to be all right.

Gwionn trotted up on Star. Gwionn had another horse stabled at La Forteresse, given to him by Etienne, a hulking roan destrier called Titan, for Star was becoming old and was too fine-boned to carry him in the full panoply of a knight's armour. But Gwionn was lightly armed today, with only a leather gambeson over his tunic instead of his mail, and on such days he still enjoyed hacking about on Star. Every fibre of Arlette's being warmed in the proximity of his presence. She kept her gaze fixed on Yseult's plaited mane.

'Excuse me, my lord,' Gwionn addressed Etienne. 'Belcastel is just ahead. We leave the river here.'

'Thank you, Leclerc. How much further is it after that?'

'Two, maybe three miles.'

'Good. We'll make Rocamadour by nightfall?'

'Oh, easily, my lord.'

Arlette could feel Gwionn's eyes on her. 'You're not fatigued, I hope, Countess?' he asked, with polite formality, and when she peered sideways at him she saw his green eyes were concerned.

'No. I'm not tired, Sir Gwionn, but I shall be glad to reach Rocamadour,' Arlette answered.

Leaving the Dordogne at Belcastel where the sick pilgrims were transferred to their litters or waggons, the count's party proceeded across country until they reached another, smaller river, the Alzou. Once in the Alzou valley, they rode along the dip in the terrain which would lead them directly to the Ecclesiastical City. A white limestone cliff reared skywards on their left, and a pair of eagles circled in the heights. They must have a nest hidden in the rock-face.

Rocamadour was not yet in sight, but it was bound to lie around the next curve in the cliff, because a tented village had bloomed in the shade on the floor of the canyon – a tented village jostling with black-garbed pilgrims. Smoke spiralled upwards from scores of cooking fires, but there was no smell of roasted meats, only pea and bean stew, it being Lent. The tents completely obscured the grass at the bottom of the Alzou valley.

Beggars held out pitiful limbless hands, or threw back ragged hoods to display white, sightless eyes.

'Alms! In the name of blessed St Amadour, give us alms!' they cried.

Pedlars and hawkers weaved in and out of the pilgrims, selling bread, and wine, and the prized pilgrims' badges – the sportelles, or *senhals* as they were known in the *langue d'oc*.

Normally sale of these medallions was controlled by the abbots of Tulle, who administered the Ecclesiastical City, and levied profits on the badges. They should only have been sold in Rocamadour itself to pilgrims who had completed their pilgrimage, but the hawkers had smuggled them out, and must be selling them more cheaply than the monks, for they were going like hot cakes. Arlette reflected on the irony of people who were pious enough to contemplate going on pilgrimages buying unsanctified badges from hucksters.

The *senhals* were worn by the pilgrims as proof they had reached Rocamadour. The more renowned pilgrim sites all struck such insignia, and it was customary for pilgrims to sew them to their hats or cloaks. The Rocamadour *senhal* was oval in shape, and depicted the Virgin on a throne, with Jesus on her knee.

She saw that some of the pilgrims flaunted scallop shells, indicating they were returning from Santiago de Compostela; others wore the keys of St Peter, proudly proclaiming they had been to Rome. Those with all three badges walked down the rows of tents with a swagger. There was a pecking order among the pilgrims.

Arlette scanned the pilgrims for the palm insignia, which would signify that its bearer had been to the Holy City of all Holy Cities – Jerusalem itself. She did not see one of these.

A fellow with a tray of the unofficial *senhals* bounded up in front of Yseult, to wedge himself in between Arlette and Count Etienne. He had a mat of uncombed black hair which didn't look as though it had been washed in his lifetime, and a sour stink wafted up to Arlette's nostrils and served to confirm this. His grey tunic was fraying, and looked as though it would disintegrate if it were washed. A large and grubby wooden cross, tied on a leather thong banged against his chest as he hopped along.

'A sportelle, madame?' he asked, and grimy fingers with yellow, unkempt nails waved a silver badge under Arlette's nose. He gave her an impudent grin. The gap in the huckster's teeth matched the gap in her husband's.

'No, thank you,' Arlette answered, holding her breath because the smell was so foul, though she tried not to show her distaste.

'I've gold ones, if silver's beneath you, my lady.'

The huckster turned to Count Etienne who was looking down his nose at him.

'How about you, sir? A gold *senhal* for you?'

'No. We shall buy ours in the city itself,' Count Etienne said, without bothering to correct the man's mode of address. He heeled his mount to a trot.

Arlette did likewise.

But the huckster kept pace with them. 'You're missing a bargain,' the man panted, and his foul stench infested the air. 'Mine are cheap.'

Count Etienne signalled for Gwionn. 'Leclerc, get rid of this man, would you?'

Count Etienne applied his spurs to his horse's flanks and surged ahead with his wife at his side.

The huckster fell back and, turning her head, Arlette saw Gwionn shepherding him back into the tented village.

'We don't want his sweepings,' the count said after a few moments. 'There's no virtue in them.' He flashed her one of his rare smiles, and his eyes lighted in a way that reminded Arlette strongly of her lover. 'We'll buy ours in the city. If we cheat, our prayers won't be heard, and we want our prayers to be heard, don't we?'

'Yes, my lord,' Arlette agreed, with fervour. She felt like a Judas.

They rounded a curve, and there, set like a jewel into the centre of the cliff, was Rocamadour.

Confronting them was a mass of buildings on several levels, which seemed to have grown out of the rugged rockface. A tiered city. It was a beautiful, breathtaking sight, even though the light was beginning to fade, and the town was cloaked in shadows.

Arlette knew that the villagers — the smiths, the merchants, the traders, and tavern-keepers, those unconnected with the Church — lived in the smaller hotch-potch of houses on the lower levels, while the canons and monks of the Holy City occupied more pretentious buildings on the higher levels.

While Arlette had been preparing for her pilgrimage, Father Theobald had described the chapels and oratories that made up the Ecclesiastical City. Arlette had sharp eyes and was thus able to make educated guesses about the buildings in front of them. That insignificant little stone building, tucked under the vast overhanging rock, and appearing to be part of the rock itself, must be St Michael's chapel. Next to St Michael's, that larger building must be the chapel dedicated to Our Lady. Larger still was the basilica of St Sauveur. Poorer pilgrims were permitted to shelter in St Sauveur. Arlette could see St Amadour's church.

All of the chapels and oratories in the Holy City were stone built. Below the Holy City, on the lower levels, was the rest of the village where the lay folk lived, a slender skein of houses, mostly wooden, which twisted along the base of the cliff.

A town wall was in the process of being built, but there were great gaps in it that still needed filling.

Arlette lifted her eyes to the Holy City and stared greedily at the Lady chapel. It was there that the walnut statue of the Virgin was housed — the one that was supposed to work miracles. If anyone needed a miracle, she did.

She shot a guilty look at her husband. His eyes were fastened on the same place. Both of them were praying for very difficult miracles. Our Lady could not please them both.

She watched her husband cross himself, and waited till he had finished muttering.

'Will we go up to the chapel tonight?' she asked.

'Not tonight. There's an inn in the lower part of the village. We'll sleep there. I'm not as sprightly as I was once, my dear, and I intend to be properly rested before I climb the Via Sancta.'

The Via Sancta comprised of two hundred and thirty-three steps leading from the lower tiers to the more exulted ones, and it was customary for the most penitent of the pilgrims to ascend to the Holy City on their knees.

Arlette frowned, puzzled. Petronilla Favell had said something to the effect that anyone who mattered stayed at the abbot's palace.

'But Lady Petronilla told me she thought we would be staying at the abbot's palace.'

The count snorted. 'No doubt that's what she hoped. But the palace is aloft,' he pointed skywards, 'in the Holy City. Tonight we stay in the lower regions. Petronilla will have to curb her impatience until tomorrow. Then she can rest in the palace. If Our Lady could rest in a stable and give birth to her son, my nephew's wife can stand another night in an inn.'

Passing through the Porte Basse, and on to la rue de la Couronnerie, which was crowded with traffic, Count Etienne Favell and his wife were immediately accosted by a brace of serving men. Usually the count would have sent Sir Gwionn or Sir Gilles ahead to find them suitable lodgings, but both knights had become involved in an altercation with the huckster with the tray of illicit *senhals*, and had fallen behind, so Count Etienne decided to see to their lodgings himself.

'Are you going to the Holy City, my lord?' asked one, a groom with sparse ginger hair, sharp blue eyes and ears like cabbages. Like the *senhal* seller they had encountered in the tented village, this man did not know the count's

502

precise status, but he always called everyone on a fine horse 'my lord'.

'Tomorrow,' came Count Etienne's brief answer.

The groom's sharp blue eyes brightened.

'You'll need somewhere to stable your destrier, my lord.'

The other man, a hunchback with glossy, jet-black ringlets, and the most handsome face Arlette had ever seen, spoke up. 'And somewhere to rest, and eat, perhaps?'

'I'm fasting till tomorrow,' the count answered. 'But my wife will eat.'

Startled, for Count Etienne had softened his voice when he had referred to her, Arlette looked at her husband. He gave her a warm smile. Guilt rushed at her from all sides.

Meanwhile, the hunchback was dipping his head, a poignantly graceful gesture for one whose body was so warped. 'Of course, great lord. Will you take your ease, or keep a vigil?'

'We rest.' Count Etienne lifted a brow at the hunchback.

'I take it you represent one of these hostelries.'

'Yes, noble lord. L'Ange d'Or.' The hunchback indicated one of the inns.

The count ran his eyes over the yellow angel on the signboard sticking out into the street.

The Golden Angel was one of the few stone buildings on the lower levels. It had two storeys, and a red tiled roof, the older tiles' colour had faded and was obscured by dark, cushiony moss and pale green lichen. Here and there a bright, new tile indicated that the landlord kept his house in good repair.

A gutter directed the rainwater from the roof into a water butt which – now here was a real rarity – had a lid on it. The inn's door was painted the same bright yellow as the angel on the board, and flanked on the one hand with a small pot of rosemary, and on the other with a bay tree. There was the usual fly-blown pile of bones and rubbish out in the street, being picked over even as the count watched by an undernourished black mongel and two half-grown cats.

Having finished his cursory examination of the Golden Angel, Count Etienne turned to the two men. Their clothes were reasonably clean, and not too shabby.

The hunchback's dark eyes glinted, and Arlette realised that he had been amused by the count's scrutiny of them and their inn.

'Well, my lord? We're the best tavern in town. Stabling's round the back.'

'Always manned? The stables, I mean.' The count's mount was worth a fortune and he was not about to lose it.

'Yes, noble lord. Your horses will be safe with us.'

'Do you have a private bedchamber?'

'One, great lord. It's free as it happens.'

'Does it have a bed in it?'

The hunchback drew himself up as far as his misshapen body would permit.

'Of course, great lord.'

The count threw his reins at the groom, and prepared to dismount. 'We'll take it. There are others in my party. Look, you can see them riding through the Lower Gate. They can share the common room.' The count's eyes twinkled, and he winked with wicked enjoyment at Arlette. 'That should please Lady Petronilla,' he said, giving Arlette a tantalising glimpse of what he must have been in his prime, before bitterness and the lack of an heir had soured him.

Arlette put her hand to her mouth to hide her smile, and followed her husband into the inn.

Upstairs, in the low-ceiling bedchamber, Count Etienne threw his hat and cloak on to the bed and took his wife's hand.

504

'You know, my dear,' he said. 'I'm more sorry than I can say for the way that I treated you when we were first married. I do not understand what came over me. I felt as though I was possessed by demons. Will you forgive me?'

'Yes.'

'It will not happen again, not like that, I mean. I am resolved to approach you gently, or not at all,' he said, pausing expectantly for Arlette's response.

Arlette did not know what to say. She was relieved that she would no longer have to live in dread lest her husband hurt her. But he was yet to discover that she was pregnant by Gwionn Leclerc. Although the count had not acted violently towards her for some months, they had never spoken about his abuse of her, and the fear that he might revert to his former, callous behaviour had always been lurking at the back of Arlette's mind: under such circumstances she had fallen in love with Gwionn Leclerc without a qualm.

But now she simply said, 'Thank you, my lord.'

Count Etienne gave her a fond smile. 'Tomorrow, when we enter Our Lady's chapel, I shall pray for you to conceive my child. I cannot expect you to do so if I mistreat you, can I?'

'No, my lord.' So that was it. The remorse which the count's last speech engendered, died stillborn. It was not guilt that had prompted her husband to promise to treat her well, but self-interest. Always self-interest.

Count Etienne lifted her hand to his lips and kissed her knuckles. 'After tomorrow, everything will change,' he said.

Petronilla, who had been plagued with fleas in the common room of the L'Ange d'Or, woke early. Irritably, she scratched at a bite on her arm, and tried to get comfortable, but the straw mattress was unyielding and, try as she might, she could not beat the bumps out of it. It was like trying to sleep on the stubble in a harvested cornfield.

Last night Count Etienne had fasted, and Petronilla had racked her brains as to how she could get him to take his daily dose of willow — not that he would be likely to have his wife while he was on holy pilgrimage — but she wanted to be sure. Accordingly, Petronilla had had a night-cap of his favourite tipple laced with herbs and willow sent up to him. She hoped he had drunk it.

Beside her, Louis snuffled in his sleep. How could he sleep on this flea-ridden mattress? Petronilla wondered enviously.

She thought of her boys, whom she was missing, and wondered how they were. It would not be long before she could be united with them again, two days, maybe three. If she had not had to ensure the count had his willow ration, and watch Sir Gwionn and the countess, she would not have had to go through this farce. The sooner the count had completed his pilgrimage, the happier she would be.

Noticing another flea bite, this one on her thigh, Petronilla sighed, and began scratching anew.

The one joy this day seemed likely to offer was the fact that she would be able to watch Count Etienne and his countess wearing their knees out climbing the steps of the Via Sancta. They would be clad only in their undergarments. Petronilla was aware that some of the more zealous pilgrims were in the habit of further burdening themselves with great chains round their necks to atone for their sins, but she did not think it likely that Count Etienne would go that far. Still, the sight of him in his shirt-sleeves, and Arlette in her undertunic would be something. Even if the count insisted that she and Louis join him on the ascent to the Holy City, she would be able to relish the thought of Count Etienne struggling up the steps in order to father a child.

It would be some recompense for him having forced her to stay in the common chamber of a common tavern.

Back in La Forteresse, Anna and Barthélemy were having their first argument at one side of the hall.

'Anna, don't be a fool. Wait until he gets back,' Barthélemy said, *sotto voce.*

Anna yanked open the purse at her belt, tipped half a dozen coins into her hand, and counted them carefully.

'No. I've done all the waiting I'm going to do for that rat.'

'But he's your husband,' Barthélemy hissed. 'He's a knight. Think of Jean. His son.'

'I am thinking of Jean. What kind of a life is this for him, growing up thinking you're his father, when all the time his real father is buzzing round that bloody countess like a bee round a honey-pot?'

'But, Anna—'

'I've stood his insults long enough. I've been blind. I must have been, to have chased half-way across France to find him. If he'd loved me, he would have come back to get me. It's my fault. I should have realised when he never came back. But – ' her voice wavered, and then strengthened – 'I wanted him to love me so much, I couldn't see the truth, even though it was staring me in the face, plain as a pikestaff.'

'What if he does love you?'

Anna snatched up her spare bliaud and, rolling it into a tight bundle, rammed it into her pack. 'Love! That man doesn't know the meaning of the word. He's cold, Barthélemy, cold and heartless like a stone. If he loves anyone, he loves himself.'

She picked up Jean's tunic and leggings, and the ebony Arab that Gwionn had carved for his son fell out. It had lost half its tail, as she had known it would, but it remained Jean's most cherished possession. Anna stared blankly at it for a moment, set her jaw, and tossed the horse on top of her bliaud. She folded Jean's clothes with vicious efficiency, stuffed them in, and began wrenching at the strings of her back-pack.

Barthélemy watched her compassionately. He had wondered how long it would take for the scales to fall from Anna's eyes. He had been beginning to think it would take a lifetime. He had loved her for a long time, and had been content to wait patiently for this day. Later, he had hopes that she would be ready to hear his confession of love, but he knew that would not be for some while. He would have to let her wounds heal.

'You can't rush off on your own,' he said, mildly. 'Where will you go?'

'Back to Kermaria. I'm welcome there. So is Jean.'

Barthélemy nodded, crouched down, and began sorting through his belongings.

Anna blinked at him. 'Barthélemy?'

'Mmm?'

'What are you doing?'

He lifted his head. 'Packing for the journey, of course. You didn't think I'd let the two of you run off on your own, did you?'

Anna's brown eyes brimmed. 'But Barthélemy, you have a good place here, a nice little nest. I can't drag you away.'

Barthélemy's smile lit up his eyes. 'I'm a rolling stone, Anna. I don't belong in a nest!'

'Oh, Barthélemy,' she sniffed and knuckled away a large tear, 'you are a dear.'

Kneeling, Anna flung her arms about him and hugged him.

Gently, Barthélemy disengaged himself. He didn't want to be her dear. He wanted to be her darling.

'Go and find that son of yours while I finish packing.

He was pestering one of the grooms in the stables when I last saw him.'

The pilgrims met in la rue de la Couronnerie after a light breakfast which the count and his countess did not share.

Petronilla concealed a smile. As she had anticipated, the count was clad in a long linen chainse which almost reached his knees. His legs were bare. Unclothed, the calves of his legs were spindle-thin, the skin covered with a network of broken veins. He had knobbly knees — an old man's legs.

She was going to enjoy today. Petronilla turned expectantly to Arlette, certain she would look ridiculous in her shift. 'Good morning, Countess.'

'Good morning, Lady Petronilla.'

The countess was wearing a simply cut cream linen undergown, and her red hair swung loose down her back like a bride. She looked fresh and young, and heart-rendingly innocent. A slender lily with the dew still upon it. Petronilla remembered the humiliations she had witnessed Arlette endure in the count's bedchamber, and marvelled. Sir Gwionn was looking at the countess as though he could eat her, but he was not the only man to be regarding her in such a fashion. Sir Gilles — such a cold man these days — actually blushed when the countess greeted him. Petronilla's smile faded, along with her sense of happy expectancy. As if that was not enough, a baker's boy with a tray of fresh loaves walked past, and rubbed salt in the wound by whistling appreciatively.

'Come along, my dear.' The count took his wife's arm and limped off. 'To the steps.'

It took the best part of the morning to get the count and his wife into the Lady Chapel. Their progress was painfully slow because the count insisted on muttering

509

prayers at every step. At least it isn't raining, Petronilla thought, eyeing the sky.

Eventually they passed the half-way point, and the canon's dorter, and reached la Place des Senhals where the pilgrim's badges were made. Petronilla grew tired of standing. For a penny, Petronilla was able to persuade one of the craftsmen to let her sit on a stool in the shade of his workshop and rest.

'We could go on and say our own prayers at the top. We don't have to keep pace with my uncle,' Louis said.

'In a minute, in a minute,' Petronilla said, her attention snared by the sight of the craftsman's apprentice carefully pouring molten lead into a series of lozenze-shaped moulds. 'Oh, is that how you do it?' she said. 'I thought they were beaten into shape.'

'The cheap ones are, my lady,' the smith answered. 'But the ones that are authenticated by the abbot are all cast before they are struck.'

The heat from the furnace meant it was no less cool in the shade of the workshop than it was outside. Petronilla yawned, and fanned her face with a languid hand. Her stomach rumbled, and she thought longingly of her dinner.

'What materials do you use?' she asked.

'Gold, silver, tin, lead.' A wide smile split the artisan's face. 'Amulets to fit all purses, my lady.'

'I'll have a gold one,' Petronilla decided. 'Louis!'

Louis entered the workshop.

'Give me some coin, Louis. I'm having one of this good fellow's medals.'

The smith spread his hands in apology. 'I'm sorry, my lady, but I can't let you have one.'

She lifted a spare brow. 'What?'

'I'm obliged to hand all these to the monks of Tulle,' he explained. 'I'm not allowed to sell them. When you've climbed the steps, and made your confession before the

Miraculous Virgin, the priest will pronounce you purified, and then you may choose your *senhal*.'

Petronilla stood up. 'I see. So you refuse to sell me one?'

'I can't, my lady. If I did my license would be revoked.'

'It sounds very petty.'

'It's because of the dispute with the abbey of Marcilhac. They were issuing *senhals* too. Only,' the smith's voice was tinged with scorn, 'theirs were beaten. These are genuine.'

'And the only way I can get one is to climb the Via Sancta on my knees?'

'That's right, my lady.'

'It's quite the most stupid thing I've heard of,' Petronilla declared, and swept out into the street.

In the dingy, smoke-blackened interior of the Lady Chapel, hemmed in by other pilgrims as hot and sweaty as she, Arlette fastened her eyes on the elegant walnut statue on the altar, and prayed as though her life depended on it — which indeed it might if the count discovered her secret.

Our Lady must favour her prayers over the count's. Arlette did not have as much money as the count, she could not give as large an offering as he; but she remembered the parable of the widow's mite. If Our Lord had valued the widow's mite over those wealthier than her, surely His Mother would regard Arlette with compassion, and aid her.

'I know I have sinned, Sweet Lady,' Arlette prayed under her breath. 'But please help me. You know how he drove me to my sin. Gwionn Leclerc gave me great comfort. He was my friend. Let me not be pregnant yet. Let my courses come. I cannot have Gwionn Leclerc's baby. Help me, please. Show me a road to happiness.'

Dozens of carved wooden models hung on twine from the ceiling, offerings from grateful sailors who believed

511

they owed their lives to the Virgin. They swung gently to and fro in the light breeze which stole in through the studded oak door, all bearing witness to the miraculous powers of the bell and the icon on the altar.

Strengthened by the sight of these testimonies, a grain of hope took root in Arlette's mind, and suddenly, illogically, she knew her shameful secret would be safe.

Kneeling on Arlette's left was a middle-aged woman with thinning grey hair, a pasty complexion, and bad breath. She had entered the Lady Chapel on Arlette's heels and spent some time groaning and lamenting, and tugging at her hair and shift. Arlette was relieved when the angelus bell rang at noon.

'Hail Mary, full of grace . . .'

Concentrating on her prayers, Arlette fingered her rosary and murmured along with the priest and the rest of the pilgrims.

The pasty-faced woman wailed on.

Arlette tried to concentrate on the service.

'Blessed art thou among women, and blessed is the fruit of thy womb . . .'

The priest turned to the altar, picked up the aspergillum, and began to sprinkle holy water on the pilgrims nearest to him. A few drops fell on the count. A couple fell on Arlette.

Muttering the Ave Maria, the priest moved down the row, and more diamond drops sparkled down in bright arcs on to the heads of the fortunate few on the front rows. This done, he turned back to the altar and replaced the aspergillum.

Arlette had never prayed so hard in her life.

The count's party planned to spend their second night at Rocamadour in the abbot's palace, and when the count and Arlette had received their *senhal* from the priest in the Lady Chapel they made their way to the palace to wash

512

and change, for the count was finished with his fasting, and they had been invited to dine with the abbot later that evening.

Apart from the abbot's lodgings, which were luxuriously furnished with silken carpets on the floors and walls, and displayed silver plate on the side-boards, the palace was simpler than its name would suggest. A plainly furnished but comfortable building, with well-swept, stone flagged floors and long, cool corridors, it had an atmosphere of profound peace. Sandalled monks glided silently along the calm corridors, bent heads enveloped in their hoods, hands folded into the sleeves of their habits. Behind thick oak doors, distant bells tolled.

When the great portal closed behind them, shutting off the brightness and bustle of the Ecclesiastical City with its wailing, chain-laden pilgrims, it was like stepping into another world.

Men and women – even married people – were given separate accommodation in the abbot's palace and, to Arlette's delight she and Clemence were to share a chamber.

'Oh, Clemence, it is good to be with you again,' Arlette said when she had washed and put on a fresh shift and her soot-coloured pilgrim's robe. 'Since we've both been married, we hardly seem to have had a moment to talk.'

Clemence smiled warmly, and gave her friend a swift hug. 'Yes, it has been difficult. I've missed sharing confidences with you, too. I was worried about you after the wedding. You looked so sad, so pale. But I felt you didn't want to talk to me.'

'I didn't,' Arlette admitted. 'I was unhappy. There were . . . difficulties with the count.'

'You should have come to me,' Clemence said. 'A problem shared is a problem halved.'

'Not this one.'

Clemence looked hurt. 'Don't you trust me any more?'

'Oh, don't be such a goose, Clemence. Of course I trust you. It's just that I would have felt such a fool running to you and telling you that I regretted marrying the count. After so many years of fighting for it, I couldn't very well start complaining.' She smiled. 'Do say you understand.'

'I understand. But you could have come to me, you know. I wouldn't have mocked you.'

'I know. You are a true friend.' Arlette gazed into Clemence's honest blue-grey eyes, and wished she had the courage to share her current problems with her.

'Are your difficulties with the count resolved?' Clemence asked.

Arlette thought about her obsession with Gwionn Leclerc, which must come to an end, for both their sakes.

She thought about the baby that she was carrying, a cuckoo child since it was not her husband's. She could not hide that for ever.

She thought about Count Etienne, who had made a vow not to hurt her, but who had no idea as yet that he had been cuckolded.

'Some of my difficulties with the count are resolved,' she said, temporising. Sooner or later she would have to tell someone about the baby. Her stomach was as flat as a board at the moment, but for how much longer? She would rather Clemence was the first to know.

'Only some?' Clemence asked, and Arlette could see she had sensed that there was much Arlette was leaving unsaid. Arlette should have known she could not hoodwink Clemence.

'Oh, Clemence. There's more. Much more. Will you hear it?'

Clemence plumped down on the bed. 'We have all night.'

A door clanged deep in the palace, and then there was silence, a great waiting silence, which seemed to be full of ears, and all at once the peaceful atmosphere of the abbot's palace, which had had such a calming effect on Arlette's senses when she had first entered, seemed to stifle her.

She caught Clemence's hand. 'How long till we dine?'

'A little more than an hour. Why?'

'I must get out of here. Let's go for a walk. We can talk outside.'

The girls crossed Place St Amadour and entered a gloomy gallery – more of a tunnel – which passed underneath the Basilica of St Sauveur. The gallery led on to a terrace overlooking the Alzou canyon. A winding path veered off up the cliff.

'Does it lead to the summit?' Arlette asked.

'Yes. I went up this afternoon, while you were praying. You can see right down the valley from there, and when you look down on the Holy City it makes you feel as though you're a bird. It must be wonderful to be able to fly.'

Arlette stepped decisively on to the path. 'I'd like to see it.'

After a stiff climb they reached the top, and stepped on to what appeared to be a large square, or plateau. The plateau was thick with people, both pilgrims and townsfolk, all smiling and laughing as though it were Easter already, and their Lenten fasts were over.

Arlette groaned. 'I thought we'd be the only ones up here.'

'So did I. Oh, look! A dancing bear!'

Arlette looked and saw not one, but three dancing bears. Two of the bears' coats were mahogany brown, the third was honey-coloured. All were muzzled, and fairly small. Her father's great mastiff had been bigger than these.

A dumpy man with a leaf-green smock, baggy brown leggings, and a wide brimmed felt hat pulled down low over his face was plucking – none too expertly – on a psaltery. Evidently, the performance had only begun moments earlier, for people were in the process of converging on the bear-trainer and his bears from all corners of the lofty plateau.

The crowd surrounding the dancing bears swelled, and Arlette stood back, wanting to absorb the details of the square crowning the top of the rock.

Birch and beech, with here and there a stunted oak, had established rootholds on Rocamadour's crag. Near the cliffside, a broad swathe of trees had been felled. This felled area formed the square Arlette and the crowd were standing on.

Curious, Arlette skirted the edge of the bears' audience and walked to the margin of the cliff. A low wall which came up to her knees marked the perimeter of the square. At either end of the wall perched a watchtower, the nearest of which was manned by two guards. She peered over the edge.

'Careful, Arlette,' Clemence warned.

The rock plunged away in a sheer drop, so sheer that for a moment the bottom fell out of Arlette's stomach. It made her quite dizzy. She sat gingerly on the lip of the wall, gripping it with her hands.

The knot of people around the bears began to clap their hands and chant in time with the music. A dog began barking.

Fascinated with the view, Arlette leaned out over the wall. They were directly above the Holy City, which spread out below them clear as a map. There was the square in the middle, with its chapels and churches leading off it. Some of the chapels were obscured from sight by the vast overhang of rock beneath them. That other square, lying further to the right that was crammed with workshops, must be the Place des Senhals. The roofs of the workshops were shrunken by distance.

'You're right, Clemence. It is like flying. I can see the Angel.'

Clemence approached, and sat cautiously at her side. 'I don't know if you can. I think that's another house with a yellow door. The Angel's further to the right. But look, down there, you can see the river. Do you like it up here?'

'I love it.'

The clapping and chanting was getting faster and faster, drowning out entirely the sound of the psaltery. As the tempo increased, the dog's yapping grew more frenzied, and the group surrounding the bears drifted several yards in one direction, paused, and drifted slowly back again, like a dandelion clock that is being blown back and forth over the ground by the wind. Someone let out a shrill whistle.

The guards in the watchtower grounded their spears to watch the show.

'Arlette?'

'Mmm?'

'What was it you were going to tell me, back in the palace?'

Arlette drew in a deep breath, and checked to ensure no one was within earshot, but everyone else was stamping and shouting around the bears, except for a couple of pilgrims who had pushed their way out of the crowd and were wandering along the wall towards the far watchtower.

'It's very serious, Clemence,' Arlette opened. Then she paused, for Clemence did not appear to be listenening to her. Her eyes were fastened upon the couple.

Following her gaze, Arlette stiffened.

Even from the back she could recognise them. Even in their dull pilgrims' garb they were instantly recognisable.

One of the pilgrims was Count Etienne, and the other was Lady Petronilla. She was clinging to his arm. As Arlette and Clemence had done, they leaned over the

517

precipice, shuddered, and sat on the wall. Count Etienne disengaged himself.

Unconsciously, Arlette sighed. Her confession to Clemence would have to wait, she could not make it with her husband sitting not a hundred yards away. After bracing herself to make a clean breast of it, her husband's presence on the plateau was a frustrating coincidence; she was surprised that he was up here and not closeted with the abbot.

Following the bears' antics, the noisy crowd rolled as one across the square towards the cliff wall, and paused, virtually on the brink, all but blocking the girls' view of the count and Lady Petronilla. Someone hooted, and the crowd rolled back to the centre of the square.

As the crowd shifted, Lady Petronilla and Count Etienne hove back into view.

What happened next happened so swiftly that, had they not both witnessed it, Arlette and Clemence would not have believed the evidence of their own eyes.

Lady Petronilla, throwing a darting glance at the crowd, turned to face the count and shoved him hard in the chest so he tipped backwards over the wall and into the abyss. The last image Arlette had of her husband was of his hands jerking upwards in a futile reflex action as he tried to get a grip on thin air. His scream was the most chilling sound Arlette had ever heard.

Chapter Twenty-four

At the abbot's palace, in her cell-like chamber in the women's quarters of the guest wing, Petronilla was struggling with unfamiliar and complex emotions.

She had not planned to kill the count.

She had done so quite on impulse, and could only half believe what she had done.

She and the count had gone up the plateau separately, and met quite by chance when the bears began their performance. Seizing the chance to sing her sons' praises – Petronilla never passed up a chance for a private word with the count – Petronilla had linked arms with Etienne, and had drawn him away from the crowd. Dancing bears had not tied in with the count's current pious frame of mind, and it had been easier than usual to persuade him to listen to her.

It was when they were sitting on the wall above the precipice talking about William, that she heard the voice. It was in her head. It was very clear.

'Push him. Push him,' the voice said, 'and all your worries are over. Louis will become count, and after him William.'

The voice had so startled Petronilla that for a moment or two she had quite lost the thread of the conversation.

'Push him. Push him,' the voice repeated, insistently.

Petronilla had shaken her head, and the voice had fallen silent. But the damage had been done. As she resumed her conversation with the count, she could not help noticing how slim was the wall on which they were perched.

Her gaze had swept around the square, and she had seen only the people clustered round the performers. The bears and the man with his psaltery had all their attention. No one was interested in her and the count. She doubted any of them had even noticed their existence.

She had leaned back and eyed the drop. It was dizzying. He would be certain to die.

And all she had to do was give him a sharp push . . .

Petronilla's blood had begun to rush in her ears. Her heart had thumped. And, drawing in a huge breath, she'd glanced once more round the square, turned to him and pushed him over.

There. Done. In a second. He'd screamed, but there had been no witnesses, and anyone would scream if they had tripped and inadvertently fallen into that great pit of space.

She'd got up to see where he'd landed, but had had to sit down again almost at once, for her legs were shaking like aspens, and she was afraid she'd be over that cliff herself if she did not sit down.

Louis was count.

At last she was Countess Favell, and William, her beloved eldest son would one day be count.

She had had to forgo her supper, of course, once the distressing news had been brought to the abbot's palace. But supper was a small price to pay.

She was Countess Favell.

She had committed a black sin. One that she could never confess, and be shrived of; but it was worth it.

She was Countess Favell.

A soft knock on the door interrupted her musings.

'Yes?'

The latch lifted, and a monk was framed in the doorway, head lost in his cowl.

'Countess Arlette would like to see you, my lady,' he said.

Making a mental note to correct the monk's mode of address in future, Petronilla rose.

'Poor lady,' she said, in a sympathetic voice. 'I expect she wants comforting.'

Petronilla stalked proudly through the door of Arlette's bedchamber, and closed the door with a snap. The candle guttered. She was countess. She no longer had any need to defer to the Breton chit. She would be courteous, but lofty, as befitted her new status.

The count's widow, who had been seated on the bed, rose as she entered. Her companion, Lady Clemence, was with her.

Petronilla sailed forwards, hands outstretched in a generous gesture of sympathy. 'My dear! This must be dreadful for you. And to think we had such high hopes of this pilgrimage. What a tragic end to it.'

'Yes. It is very tragic,' Arlette replied quietly.

She had not taken Petronilla's hands so, after a moment Petronilla clasped them instead to her bosom.

'We will look after you,' Petronilla declared grandly. 'We understand your father's case is unresolved, and I'd like you to know that you may rely on our hospitality.'

Arlette said nothing, and lifted her gaze to the cross on the wall of the cell. For the first time Petronilla noticed that Arlette's eyes were hard and her mouth thin. She looked pinched and cold and very determined, but what could she have to be determined about? She must be mistaking bitterness for determination.

Because Petronilla found the ensuing silence awkward, she filled it. 'The Favells would not take it out on a woman merely because she was unfortunate enough not to bear children,' she went on, generously. 'I know Louis will agree with me when I say that you will always have a place at La Forteresse. A wicked turn of fate may have made my husband count and me his countess, but we will not simply cast you off.'

Arlette and Clemence exchanged looks that Petronilla could not interpret, but which she was sure she did not like.

'There's something I have to tell you, Lady Petronilla,' Arlette said, sweetly. 'Before you start to crow.'

'Crow?' Petronilla lifted her chin a notch. 'You are insolent! I think you are forgetting that you are speaking to the Countess Favell.'

'Countess? You?' Arlette laughed. 'I think it will be some time before that bright day dawns.'

'What do you mean?' Petronilla frowned. 'Count Etienne is dead. He has no direct heir. In that case Louis inherits.'

A slow, triumphant smile warmed Arlette's pinched features. Petronilla's spine prickled. A sense of foreboding came over her.

'But he does have an heir.' Arlette covered her belly with her hands. 'I am with child.'

Petronilla felt as though someone had punched her in the head. Her thoughts flew in all directions, so she could not grasp any of them.

'What?' Stupidly, she stuttered. 'What did you say?'

'I'm going to have a baby.'

Several moments went by. 'But you can't be!' Petronilla cried, eventually. 'You can't be!'

Another small, triumphant smile. 'But I am.'

Petronilla's lips worked while she concentrated on one important point. She had thought her potion had worked. She was *sure* her potion had worked. 'You can't be with child,' she blurted. 'That was the *raison d'être* of this pilgrimage. The count was praying for you to conceive.'

Arlette nodded, easily. 'That's true. He was. And when we left La Forteresse, I had an inkling I might be pregnant, but it was too early for me to say anything. I did not want to raise his hopes without good reason. I decided that a few extra prayers would not go amiss in any case.' She lowered her head, shielding her eyes from Petronilla. 'My main regret is that the count never knew.' She crossed herself. 'He would have liked to know that he was to be a father.'

Petronilla stared with unconcealed loathing at the count's widow. 'You adulterous slut! If you're pregnant, it's not the count's brat you've got in there!'

Arlette raised a tawny brow. 'Not the count's? Don't be ridiculous. Of course it's the count's.'

'No, it's not! It can't be. It must have been someone else.' Petronilla brought her face close to that of Arlette's so she could watch her reaction. 'Count Etienne couldn't have performed if Venus herself had spread her legs for him. You're nothing but a harlot. Who was it? Sir Gwionn? Sir Gilles?'

'I forgive you these slanders,' the count's widow responded complacently, outwardly unmoved by Petronilla's accusation. 'You are overwrought.'

Petronilla's palms itched to slap her. 'I'll not let this rest, madam,' she managed to speak through clenched teeth. 'I'll not let your bastard rob me of my title.'

'*Your* title? Lady Petronilla, I suggest you sit down. There's something I insist we discuss.'

The widow's voice, though low, had a menacing edge to it.

'I have nothing more to say,' Petronilla declared loftily. She headed for the door.

Arlette got there first; without using force, Petronilla was unable to get past.

'You'll not go till I've done,' Arlette said, in that soft voice that Petronilla now recognised had a thread of steel running through it. 'I want to discuss my husband's murder.'

'M . . . murder?'

'Yes. Murder.'

Wondering how much Arlette knew, Petronilla tried to order her thoughts. Thus far, Arlette had given no hint that Petronilla was implicated. She felt rather like a fly who had blundered unexpectedly into a spider's web. It would be difficult to wriggle free, but with a little delicate manoeuvring, she was certain she could do it.

Recovering swiftly, Petronilla said, 'What *are* you talking about?'

Arlette gave Petronilla a smile that would have frozen hell over.

'I've made it quite plain. I wish to discuss my husband's murder.'

'Oh, my dear,' Petronilla said, deciding a ladle full of sympathy might not go amiss. 'I fear grief is addling your wits. No one knows how your husband died. No one saw it happen. It appears he took a walk and tripped by the cliff wall. His death was an accident, a tragic accident.'

'It was no accident. It was cold-blooded murder.'

The widow's look of determination was becoming more pronounced by the minute, accentuated by the fine lines which had appeared round her mouth, caused no doubt by the tension in that lying smile of hers.

A knot of apprehension began to form in Petronilla's stomach. 'My dear, are you aware of the serious nature of your accusation?' she said as coolly as she could.

The count's widow exchanged another of those meaningful and extremely worrying looks with her companion. 'Yes. Murder is a hanging offence.'

The web was tightening.

'But no one saw anything,' Petronilla spoke as confidently as she could. 'I was told that the people on the cliff-top were watching some players.'

'A man with three bears and a psaltery.'

Petronilla's mouth was dry, but she resisted the need to

swallow. Arlette's chilling smile enlarged. Her eyes, Petronilla noticed, were untouched by it.

'Not all of the people on the cliff were watching the bears, my lady,' Arlette said. 'I wasn't.'

Petronilla licked her lips. 'Wh . . . what were you doing?'

'Watching you.'

'As God is my witness, I wasn't there!'

'Do not lie, my lady. You can't make me disbelieve the evidence of my own eyes. I saw you. You were talking to the count. You pushed him over.'

'You're the liar,' Petronilla said, battling for calm. 'You're jealous of my good fortune, and you seek to destroy me. I always knew you hated me. From the first moment you arrived, you have done your best to turn the count against me and my husband.'

Arlette shook her head, almost sadly. 'No. I never hated you. Jealousy is a province I leave entirely to you, my lady. But I did see you push my husband to his death.'

'Liar!' She straightened her shoulders. 'It would be your word against mine. One woman's against another. Impasse, I think, on that score. But I intend to voice my suspicions concerning the babe's father.'

'I wouldn't if I were you.'

'Why?'

'Because there is another witness.'

Petronilla's heart lurched sickeningly as, all at once, she saw the full extent of the trap she had walked into.

Eyes wide, she turned fearful eyes on Arlette's companion.

Lady Clemence dipped her head in assent. 'Yes, Lady Petronilla,' she said, gently. 'I too saw you on the rock above the city. I too saw you kill Count Etienne.' There was a catch in her voice. 'Oh, that poor man . . . I'll never forget that scream . . .'

A painful silence gripped the room.

Outside the cell, the bell rang to summon the monks to compline. A door slammed, and the candles flickered in a sudden draught.

'Stalemate, I think,' the count's widow murmured.

Outwitted, and silenced by a paralysing combination of fury and frustration, Petronilla glared at the woman whom she would always regard as her mortal enemy.

Her dreams lay in tatters about her. For years she had longed for the count's death in order that Louis could succeed to the title. And now she had seen to it that the count was at last dead, the path should have been clear for Louis and William. But, no, her plans had to be thwarted by a Breton strumpet who she knew − she just *knew* − had been indulging in a little extra-marital copulation. The child was *not* Count Etienne's. She'd wager her son's life on that. But, certain as she was, Petronilla could do nothing. If she breathed a word of her suspicions concerning the child's parentage, the countess would not hesitate to lay charges for murder against her.

It was indeed stalemate.

'You *bitch*!' she got out, quivering with hatred and resentment.

'I suggest you keep your voice down, Lady Petronilla,' Arlette said tranquilly. 'You'll burn the good monks' ears.'

Petronilla's breast heaved.

'Goodnight, Lady Petronilla,' Arlette added. 'Sleep well.'

'You'll have to step warily, Arlette,' Clemence warned, when Petronilla's footsteps had faded. 'You've made an enemy tonight.'

'I know.' Wearily, Arlette flopped on to the bed. 'I'm very grateful to you for standing by me. She'll not forgive you, either.'

526

Clemence shrugged. 'She's a murderess, and ought to be brought to justice.'

'We're holding a sword over her head,' Arlette said. 'Life for her will be a living hell. She was prepared to kill for her ambition. Now, every day, she'll eat her heart out over what she has lost.'

'Isn't it fortunate that you should have been pregnant after all?' Clemence said thoughtfully. 'You'll be able to keep your position without having a husband.'

Arlette's eyelids were drooping. She was bone-weary. So much had happened that day that she could hardly keep pace with events. The shock of Etienne's death had been swiftly followed by the realisation that she and her unborn child were safe. If the count was dead no-one need know that the baby she carried was not his. She had had to steel herself to face the interview with Lady Petronilla, and had been hard pressed to keep her temper. But she had, by a hair's breadth.

And Clemence was right, Arlette was in a most unusual position. Briefly, Arlette considered telling Clemence the full truth concerning the child. Clearly, Clemence did not take Petronilla's accusations about adultery seriously.

'There is a precedent,' Arlette said, sleepily. 'Duchess Constance kept her title when Duke Geoffrey died.'

Clemence wrinkled her nose. 'The Duchess remarried, didn't she? After Arthur was born.'

'Did she? Perhaps I'll marry too, when my child is born.'

Arlette fell silent, thinking. Only that afternoon in Notre-Dame Chapel she had prayed for a way out of the maze in which she found herself. And now she was free, but the price paid for her freedom had been high. Her husband was dead. She found his death difficult to accept, even though she had witnessed it with her own eyes.

By murdering the count, Petronilla had freed her; for if he had lived, Count Etienne would have been within his

527

rights to have her set aside because of her adultery — women had been pressed to death for less. But Petronilla had given Arlette and her baby a reprieve. They were not completely out of the woods, for problems remained, but their immediate safety was assured. And to think that Arlette had been seconds away from a full confession to Clemence when the count had died . . .

Her thoughts ran on. Only Gwionn knew the truth about the baby's parentage. Could he be relied upon to keep the secret? It flashed in on Arlette that perhaps she and Gwionn could marry, but she did not allow herself to dwell on that thought. It was too soon to think of remarriage — with anyone.

Her first priority must be to ensure her baby's safety, and a hasty, ill-considered marriage might put that at risk. She was the Countess Favell, and as her husband's widow was a tenant of Duke Richard's. Until her baby was born, Arlette would be very careful not to put a foot wrong. She would do nothing to alienate the powers that be.

She was still fully clothed, but against all the odds, Arlette drifted into a deep, restorative sleep.

It was four days before Count Etienne's funeral cortège wound in through the gates of La Forteresse.

Gwionn, who smelt a rat and was eager to ferret it out, had ridden in the vanguard of the funeral train the whole day.

But finding a moment to speak confidentially with the countess was not easy, and he resigned himself to having to wait.

In the rear of the cortège the count's widow — shrouded in black muslin veils so he could not so much as exchange glances with her — had been constantly hedged about. Sir Gilles, for instance, once he had overcome his shock at Count Etienne's death, had not left Arlette's side. Under the castellan's eagle eyes, Gwionn had managed to pass on a simple expression of sympathy, but that was all.

It was very puzzling.

With the count dead, and no heir, Sir Louis and his odious wife should be cock-a-hoop. Yet Sir Louis was subdued, and his wife sullen. Was there some impediment to their succession?

The most likely impediment would have been if the count had fathered an heir on Arlette.

But that, as he knew, was impossible.

A crazy, tantalising thought took root in Gwionn's mind, and all the way back to La Forteresse it grew apace, tormenting him every step of the way.

Had he finally succeeded in giving Arlette a child?

God knows he had tried most diligently. He had begun to think she was barren, for as far as he knew Arlette had never taken precautions against pregnancy as Anna had done. No, Arlette was surely far too unsophisticated to be privy to such tricks.

Was the Countess Favell carrying his child?

Every time Gwionn asked himself the question a surge of primitive elation filled him.

And by the time the cortège passed under the portcullis, he was sure she was; and that she must be intending to pass his child off as Favell's.

Gwionn would make no hasty decisions.

He had waited for his revenge for a long time.

He would not spoil it at the eleventh hour.

When the count's coffin had been taken to the chapel, and the vigil begun, Gwionn went in search of Anna. He couldn't see any of her belongings in the hall. Neither were Barthélemy and Jean anywhere to be found.

He looked in the chest in his room, where Anna sometimes left a silken scarf or a veil. Nothing.

Back in the hall, he accosted Arlette's maid, Véronique,

who was beetling past, bowed under the weight of a heavy roll of black samite.

'Have you seen Barthélemy le Harpour?'

'He's gone, sir,' Véronique said, resting the end of the roll of cloth on a trestle, and panting slightly.

'Gone? But where?'

Véronique's eyes were blank. 'I don't know, sir. Looking for more work, I suppose.'

'And Anna — Madame le Harpour? What of her?'

'She went with him, naturally.'

'What?'

'They are man and wife, sir.'

Becoming aware that Véronique was regarding him with a very puzzled expression, Gwionn pulled his scattered wits together.

'Yes. Yes. Naturally. And they've taken the boy?'

'Yes, sir. Is that all? Lady Clemence asked me to take this to the chapel, and—'

'Yes. Thank you, Véronique,' Gwionn mumbled. 'You may go.'

After ascertaining that Anna had not left him a message with anyone else, Gwionn made his way back to his room and shut the door. Flinging himself on his narrow bed, he tried to assess his feelings. This did not come naturally to him, for his feelings always seemed to be tangled up one with another. It was like groping his way through a mist.

He ought to feel some grief at Anna's desertion of him, but after an hour's deep reflection he came to the conclusion that he didn't. Perhaps he didn't have any feelings. Had they all been bludgeoned out of him that day Arlette's father had butchered his?

He had thought he loved Anna, had thought they understood each other, and that she would always stand by him. He had accepted her love for him as absolute, unconditional. It was something of a shock, a blow to his pride, to discover that it was not. At the least Anna should

530

have left a message for him; after all, she was his wife and Jean was his son.

But Gwionn had withstood worse knocks than this, and Anna's defection might yet be turned to his advantage.

All at once the mist cleared, and Gwionn realised that he did feel something. He felt free, and that feeling was exhilarating.

With Anna and Barthélemy gone, no one in La Forteresse knew his true identity — not that the Raymond Herevi who had married Anna had existed for many a year. Raymond had become Sir Gwionn Leclerc, and without Anna's inhibiting presence he could fulfil his destiny.

Gwionn would miss Anna's calmness. He would miss being loved and he would miss their easy loving, but he was confident he could find that elsewhere.

Not dissatisfied with recent events, Gwionn smiled and put his hands behind his head. He could see what lay ahead. He would have to be patient, but the first step must be to discover if Arlette was going to have his child. If she were pregnant, there would be an official announcement.

All in all it was a good thing Anna had gone. It was indeed an ill wind that blew no one any good.

Riders had been dispatched from Rocamadour with news of the count's death and, two days later, when the Bishops of Cahors and Périgord arrived wearing their jet black copes and mitres, and with half a dozen priests dancing attendance, the funeral was held. Crows round a corpse.

Gwionn stood to attention as the count's coffin was lowered through the chapel floor into the deep, velvety darkness of the Favell vault. The Favell tomb had been carved out of the limestone rock on which the castle had been built. A series of labyrinthine passages led to smaller, sealed chambers underneath the chapel; in times of siege, people or treasure could be hidden in these secret chambers.

This was to be Count Etienne Favell's last resting place.

His widow kept her head bowed while the funeral rites were completed, and after the service the Bishop of Cahors led her from the chapel.

Gwionn had yet to have any private talk with her, but he learnt afterwards that she had spent several hours closeted with the bishop in the solar. He was more than ever certain that a public announcement was imminent, and that the bishop would make it.

That afternoon, Gwionn was summoned to the solar.

Lady Clemence was sewing in the lofty window seat overlooking the river, and Arlette sat at the table before a scroll of parchment. She was trimming her quill, frowning in concentration.

Gwionn stared, temporarily off his stride, for he had quite forgotten that Arlette could write, and the sight of a woman with a pen in hand had discomposed him. He stared at the letter, which opened,

'Dearest Eleanor, your loving step-daughter begs
you to both weep and rejoice with her . . .'

Arlette lifted her head and smiled at him, her formal lady-of-the-manor smile. 'Ah, Sir Gwionn. I have a favour to ask you.'

Gwionn bowed, politely. 'I am yours to command, my lady.'

'It's about Yseult. As you know, my mare grew older during the years of my confinement.'

'I did my best to care for her.'

She gave him another smile. 'I know that, Sir Gwionn, and I thank you for it. But the fact remains that she is no longer as sprightly as she was. I am not intending to put

Yseult out to grass, but I shall be needing a younger mare. Something with a little more stamina. Yseult would lag too far behind in the chase, and I like to be out with the leaders. She's a fine horse, but she's too dainty to drive hard.'

Gwionn did some swift reckoning. The hunting season began at Midsummer. Arlette could not be with child if she was considering hunting.

But Lady Clemence had glanced up sharply at Arlette's words. She put an end to his calculations.

'Arlette?' she said, with a severe frown which did not sit well on her pretty, placid face. 'You're not thinking of hunting this year? Not in your condition.' Then she gave a gasp of horror, and a pink tide washed across her cheeks. 'Oh, Arlette. Forgive me. I should not have spoken. Nothing's been said yet, has it?'

'It doesn't matter, Clemence. The bishop and I were planning to make the announcement this evening,' Arlette said, soothingly. 'I am perfectly happy for Sir Gwionn to hear the news a littler earlier than the others.'

Arlette's gaze locked with Gwionn's and her blue eyes sparkled. All at once he realised that Arlette had wanted, indeed expected her beloved but impetuous Clemence to speak out at the mention of the hunt, and betray her condition.

It was her way of informing him that she *was* pregnant, and that the child was his.

As he smiled into her wide, pleased eyes — eyes that were begging for him to collude with her, he did some swift reckoning. Arlette believed she knew him, but she scarcely knew him at all. What would she do if she realised his mind was set on revenge, and had been for as long as he had known her? She was entirely at his mercy. At last Gwionn had a de Roncier where he wanted her. He could do it, he knew he could. All he had to do was to speak out, and Arlette Favell would be brought to her knees.

He could destroy her.

But if he did that would hurt his own child.

How odd, that such a thought should spring to mind. Anticipating such a scene as this, Gwionn had run through it many times in his head, and not once had it occurred to him to consider the fate of any child he might father on Arlette. His dream had come true, but he had not realised how his whole viewpoint would alter when it did.

Perhaps his revenge would be more thorough if he kept his own counsel, let her bear the child, and pass it off as the count's. Yes, that was an alternative, a far more subtle route; one that would ensure that his child, be it son or daughter, would inherit Count Favell's estate. And for all that he had waited long to be revenged upon Arlette, Gwionn was discovering that the revenge which did not harm her appealed the most. Stunned by this realisation, he hoped that he had not been so foolish as to fall in love with her. No, he could not possibly have done.

Put baldly, the choice before him was either to destroy Arlette Favell, and wreck his child's good fortune, or collude with her for the sake of that child.

An enthralling thought struck him. If the law-courts cleared François de Roncier of treason, the child might inherit the de Roncier lands too . . . Now there was a thought to conjure with. If he let Arlette pursue her course it would practically guarantee that a grandchild of Jean St Clair would lord it over the entire de Roncier county.

What justice.

'Permit me to be the first to congratulate you, my lady,' he said.

Relief sprang into Arlette's eyes. She swayed towards him but, giving a surreptitious glance at Lady Clemence, checked. Her gaze warmed, and became a loving caress, such as his Anna used to give him, and Gwionn had no doubt that if it were not for the restraining presence of

Lady Clemence, the Countess Arlette would be in his arms.

And there was another consideration. If Arlette Favell did love him, and her look admitted as much, it was just possible she might be persuaded to marry him, despite the difference in their stations. All this could be his. That way, he could steward the estate for their child. He gave her one of his gentle smiles, for of all the smiles in his arsenal, he knew she responded best to the gentle ones.

'Thank you, Sir Gwionn.' Arlette lowered her voice to a rapid whisper. 'I wanted you to know before . . . before the official announcement.' She raised her voice again. 'Will you help me choose a mare?'

Lady Clemence dropped her sewing on a cushion. 'You're not going hunting this year, Arlette,' she said. 'I shall forbid you.'

'Rest easy, my friend, this year I forgo the hunt. I'm merely asking for Sir Gwionn's help in choosing a younger mare. One that can be trained for next year's season.'

'I'd be delighted,' Gwionn said. 'We can try the market at Domme. Failing that, I could ride into Sarlat.'

'Oh, Sir Gwionn. You're very kind. I hoped I could rely on you. I shall need a reliable man, now my husband is gone.'

The question in her eyes was unmistakable.

Gwionn bowed gallantly, and laid a hand on his heart. 'Countess, I will protect your life, and that of your child's, with my own.'

Her smile was brilliant.

'Why, thank you, Sir Gwionn. I was praying you'd say that.'

As the months passed and the Countess Favell grew great with child, Gwionn came to admire her.

He intended to woo her, and win her hand in marriage but, as her belly swelled, he held back.

The cryptic conversation they had had in the solar, and the bishop's announcing of an heir for Count Etienne, had confirmed that she intended the child should be passed off as Etienne Favell's, but other than that her mind was closed to him. She kept her distance, which was, he acknowledged, a sensible precaution, for if her plan was to succeed she could not afford for tongues to start clacking. They had been extraordinarily lucky not to have been discovered when the count was alive, but to risk discovery when she had staked everything on their child was insanity.

Thus Gwionn had no option but to bide his time. Not that he minded. He would continue to do so until the child was born, alive. In any case, there was little to be gained in proceeding too quickly with his wooing, for the Countess Arlette was only clinging to her title on account of her unborn child. If anything happened to that child, she stood to lose everything to Sir Louis and Lady Petronilla. Why should he waste time wooing and winning Arlette's hand when the babe's death would mean she was worthless to him? He didn't love her. He couldn't love de Roncier's daughter.

Arlette Favell's value to Gwionn lay in her producing a normal healthy child: a boy in preference, but a girl would do.

Meanwhile, the whole of the Aquitaine was balanced on a knife edge.

Duke Richard, being jealous of the power of the neighbouring barony of Beynac, had seized Beynac castle and had given it to his infamous mercenary captain, Mercadier. It was a lesson to the other lords and barons in the Aquitaine, who learned from it to keep their heads down and keep quiet.

Mercadier's reputation was as black as sin; that autumn, bands of his mercenaries took to marauding the countryside: raping, pillaging, stealing, murdering.

No one was safe.

'What is Duke Richard thinking of?' Arlette asked Sir Gilles, who was sharing a trencher with her at table one night. 'He can't think that he's winning loyalty by installing Mercadier at Beynac.'

Spearing a piece of baked perch with his knife, Sir Gilles flipped it on to their trencher. 'Mercadier's tenancy of Beynac is only partly to do with ensuring our loyalty,' he said. 'Mercadier has fought for the duke for years, and has long cherished an ambition for a castle of his own. Beynac is his prize.'

Arlette ran a slender finger round the rim of her goblet, frowning. 'But it can't go on. It's like living in the midst of a war. Jacob informed me a gang of his cut-throats raped a girl in La Roque-Gageac market square last week, in broad day with half the townsfolk peering through their shutters and no one daring to stand up to them. Is that true, do you think?'

Gwionn, who had been reaching for the platter, looked up. 'It's true,' he confirmed. 'I heard the same tale from Louis Favell. It was the blacksmith's daughter. She drowned herself after, in the river, for shame.'

'No!' Arlette looked shocked. 'I'm not having that happening here.'

'They wouldn't come here, Countess,' Sir Gilles hastened to reassure her. 'We're too well fortified. They're lazy cowards at heart; mostly they attack the undefended villages. They're after easy pickings.'

'You're probably right,' Arlette said, 'but we must not become complacent. Sir Gilles, I'd like you to do a full inventory of the contents of the armoury.'

'Yes, my lady.'

'Lady Clemence and I will check we have enough caskets of salt beef, and sacks of flour in the vault—'

'I doubt they'd lay seige to us,' Sir Gilles said.

'Nevertheless, we'll run no risks. Sir Gwionn?'

'Countess?'

'I'd be grateful if you'd help me with the accounts. Father Theobald is too old for the task, and I've discovered a few discrepancies in them.'

'Yes, my lady.' Gwionn agreed pleasantly, for though the clerk's job was one no knight should stoop to, it would mean that he would have a cast-iron excuse for seeking Arlette out, and he could proceed with his wooing of her. Subtly, of course. He did not want to risk their adultery being discovered any more than she did. But he was equally keen that she should not forget him.

December came. Arlette's baby was due any day.

On St Lucy's Day the knights arranged a bow and stable hunt, for foxes, but they managed to kill a boar as well and there was great rejoicing. Afterwards, Arlette and Clemence were summoned to the hall, where they had to endure a blow-by-blow account of a chase they had not been able to take part in, and were forced to exclaim over the limp carcasses laid out on the trestle.

'Pay your debts, Venner. That's a hunting knife you owe me,' Sir Gilles said, flushed with triumph. The boar had been his kill. 'I told you there was a boar in the area. I saw its spoor last week, but you swore blind they were stale. You said I was mad to take my boar spear along. Thank Christ I did or that brute would have gored the hounds. He ran half-way up the shaft as it was.'

'God, listen to the man bragging,' Sir Walter answered, glumly taking his knife from his belt and passing it to the castellan. 'It's only a small boar.'

Sir Gilles's chest swelled. 'Small? Small? Just look at the brute. It almost spitted that black rache.'

Arlette stepped forwards, rubbing the small of her back, for it was aching just as it did when her courses were about to start. 'It's a very fine boar, Sir Gilles,' she acknowledged with a smile. 'We'll enjoy it.'

There were three foxes too, with fine, soft brushes dangling over the edge of the table. The knights had acted as beaters, driving the foxes into the fire of the archers. The foxes were not for eating by those in the castle, although the animals would be skinned and their pelts cured. The arrows had been removed, but red stained splotches on the fur marked the points where the arrows had struck.

Arlette went to sit down and stroked one of the foxes. It was a pretty creature. 'It's a shame they had to die when we don't eat them,' she said, looking at the wound the arrow had made.

At that moment the hall door crashed back on its hinges, admitting an icy blast of air, along with Sir Louis, Lady Petronilla and their two sons. The boys were squabbling vociferously over possession of a slingshot. Lady Petronilla's maid, Rose, and a manservant followed with their trunks.

Arlette repressed a sigh.

As was traditional, she had invited the count's family for Christmas, but they were ten days early. Arlette had not expected them until Christmas Eve when she hoped her baby would have been born. Now Arlette knew what she was capable of, she had not wanted Petronilla Favell anywhere near her during her confinement or the birth. Ignoring the ache in her back, Arlette made as if to heave herself on to her feet.

Gently Clemence pushed her back. 'Receive them sitting,' she said.

Petronilla swooped down on them. 'Oh, what a bore. We missed a hunt,' she said, tossing her plumed velvet hat down beside the foxes. 'Louis, we missed a hunt.'

Louis, who was already engaging Sir Gilles in a conversation comparing bows made from yew and bows made from boxwood, grunted.

Petronilla turned to Arlette, and ran her steel grey eyes over her appraisingly. 'Good day, madam,' she said.

Since the count's death, Petronilla often refused to address Arlette as 'my lady' or 'countess', a discourtesy Arlette chose to ignore.

'Welcome, Petronilla,' Arlette said. She wished her backache would go away, and she wished Petronilla Favell at the other side of Christendom, at least till her baby had a firm hold on this world, but neither of her wishes looked as though they were going to be granted. 'You look to be in good health.'

Petronilla's charcoal-darkened brows snapped together. She glared at Arlette's belly, declaring bluntly, 'And I see you've managed to last thus far. You're bigger than I thought you'd be. I'll own I didn't think you'd carry it full term.'

'No? Well I have. I . . . Oh, Lord . . .' Arlette broke off as a wave of pain swept up from her back, up and round her abdomen.

Clemence spang to her side, hands outstretched. 'Arlette? Are you . . . ? Is it . . . ?'

Arlette drew in a deep, shuddering breath. 'Yes. I think . . . oh, God.' She paused, clinging on to Clemence's hands while the pain – which had become a weird tension centring on her belly – intensified. Gradually it faded, and she sighed. 'Yes. I think it's happening.'

Briskly Lady Petronilla loosed her cloak and called for Rose, who was returning empty-handed from the guest chamber where she had taken Lady Petronilla's travelling chest.

'Here, Rose, find Véronique,' Petronilla said. 'Tell her that madame is being brought to bed. Get her to send for the midwife—'

'Excuse me, my lady,' Arlette broke in, slightly breathlessly, because another pain was sweeping over her.

She might be in labour and the outcome might be uncertain, but she would not stand for Petronilla ordering her servants about as though she did not exist. 'Lady Clemence knows what to do. She is in charge here. You,' she managed to smile, 'are my guest.'

For a second Petronilla looked totally bemused. 'But, Countess, you're in labour. You must accept my help.'

Women always rallied round when a baby was being born, and while the labour lasted, old grievances were forgotten and hatchets were buried. But Arlette was determined: she did not trust Petronilla Favell.

Arlette struggled to her feet.

Sir Gilles and Sir Gwionn leapt to her assistance, but Sir Gwionn reached her first.

'You can help me most, Lady Petronilla,' Arlette gasped, 'if you entertain the menfolk.'

Petronilla glowered.

Arlette's fingers, white with tension, clung to Gwionn's arm. 'Will you do that, Lady Petronilla?'

'Of course she will,' Sir Louis broke in. 'Glad to help, aren't you, my dove?'

'Delighted,' Petronilla responded, tight-lipped.

Between them, Clemence and Gwionn assisted Arlette to her room, where Véronique was already waiting for them.

The bedcovers were turned back. The birthing chair was in place before the fire, and a painted screen had been brought in. It stood to one side. In the depths of Arlette's mind, a disturbing memory stirred and was still. This was no time to remember ghosts.

Arlette's breathing was coming in short, sharp bursts.

Gwionn threw an uneasy glance at the birthing chair. With its cut-away seat and its high back and arms, it put him in mind of an instrument of torture from a dungeon. It looked out of place in Arlette's chamber. Uneasily, he turned to go.

'Sir Gwionn,' Arlette's voice, threaded with pain, held him back. Her eyes were huge and anxious.

'My lady?'

'Don't let Petronilla in here, will you? However persuasive she might become.'

'Rest easy, my lady. You're quite safe. I wouldn't let her attend this birth if she were the last woman on earth.'

Arlette smiled and, lying back on her bed, submitted herself to Clemence's capable and loving hands.

Chapter Twenty-five

Leaving the ferry boat behind him in the estuary, Father Yann trudged along the narrow, soggy trackway which meandered through the marshes to the manor at Kermaria.

It was raining; a slow, steady, unremitting drizzle which soaked through his cloak and hood. If he walked briskly, he could ward off the chill. These days an incipient stiffness in his joints make brisk walking something of a penance, but he found he could increase his pace by dangling a carrot in front of his nose, telling himself that if he strode out he would reach the manor in time for supper. Anna — if the rumour was true and she had returned — would give him a hot meal, and that would put him right in a trice.

On reaching the main track where it forked left for Kermaria, Father Yann saw a man striding ahead of him. The man had a wheat sack folded over his head as a makeshift hood, and was whistling a tune that Father Yann recognised as being one of the the bawdier marching songs returning crusaders had brought back from Palestine. As he was clearly heading for the manor, Father Yann hailed him.

'Ho there!'

The whistling stopped, and the man turned, to reveal a pleasant, open face. He was in his twenties, and had merry blue eyes and a mouth made for laughing. Thick brown curls clung wetly to his skull.

'Good day, Father. You coming my way?' he asked, pleasantly.

Father Yann caught up with him. 'I trust so. I'm looking for Anna. I heard she's back.'

Was it his imagination or had some of the joy evaporated from the young man's eyes to be replaced by a look of wariness?

'She's back.'

'And well, I hope?'

'Yes.'

'And Jean? Is her son with her?'

'Yes.'

Warned by the curt, almost surly replies the young man gave him, which to Father Yann's mind jarred most peculiarly with his candid face, the priest tried to phrase his next question delicately. 'And did . . . did anyone else come back with her?'

The young man stopped, put his hands on his hips and turned to confront Father Yann.

'Yes. Someone did come back with her. Me.'

'You?' Under cover of his sodden cloak, Father Yann's hand crept to the cold comfort of his cross. Something was wrong here. Very wrong. 'But who are you, my son?'

Disregarding the rain, the young man swept the sacking from his head in a parody of a courtly bow. 'Barthélemy le Harpour, at your service.

'Father, I hope you've not come to make difficulties for Anna, because if you have I warn you I shall insist you turn around and go back where you came from. She's been very unhappy, and now I . . . we . . .'

The young man broke off, and ran a long-fingered hand through his damp, dishevelled hair. His blue eyes were confused, pleading, desperate, but above all determined.

'She's happy now, you see,' he said. 'At last she's let me make her happy.'

'You're lovers?' Father Yann asked bluntly. He was not shocked: in his lifetime he had noted that not all the couples whose vows had been sanctified by Holy Church found happiness; but he was concerned. If Raymond Herevi was alive this was adultery, which he should not condone. The young man before him did not strike him as evil. Anxious, yes. But evil, most definitely no.

'No. Yes.' Barthélemy spread his hands as though to prevent the priest from proceeding down the path. 'Oh, hell. Leave us alone. Please, Father. She suffered so much before. And now she's happy with me. We're both happy. I don't want any pontificating priest to spoil it.'

'Where's her husband?' Father Yann had to ask. 'Where's Raymond Herevi? Is he dead?'

'Dead? No, he's not dead. But he might as well be as far as Anna is concerned.'

Father Yann put a hand on the young harper's sleeve, but seeing a belligerent light flare in those expressive blue eyes, thought better of it and removed it. 'What do you mean, he might as well be dead? Young man, I think you'd better explain yourself.'

Barthélemy le Harpour cast a hunted look over his shoulder.

They had almost reached the bridge over the moat, and the entrance to the yard. The gates, which Father Yann noticed had been repaired and painted, were open. Ahead of them, just visible through the gap in the moss-clad wall, stood the ruined manor. Its outline was blurred by the drizzle and shreds of an evening mist which was rolling off the marsh. Grey smoke gusted from the square chimney, and hung in dark drifts over the roof.

Father Yann's stomach rumbled. 'Listen, young man. I'm not as young as I was, and I've trod a weary road to see that Anna's thriving,' Father Yann said. 'I'll not go till I've seen her.'

Barthélemy le Harpour gave him a long, hard look. 'If I

can convince you she's happy, will you promise to let us be?'

'Yes. If I can see her with my own eyes, and judge her happiness for myself,' Father Yann agreed.

Barthélemy gave a resigned sigh. 'Very well. But I'll take you into one of the old outbuildings first. I don't mean to be inhospitable, but there are a few things I ought to explain before you see Anna.'

Later, Barthélemy ushered Father Yann quietly into the hall, and for a moment or two the men hovered in the doorway, watching.

Anna had drawn a stool up to the tiled fireplace, and was gently admonishing her son − how he had shot up! − who was turning a spit in the fire. The spit had a goose on it, which had probably been poached from the marsh.

Father Yann's mouth watered.

'No, Jean,' Anna was saying. 'You must keep it moving. Remember last night you complained yours was burnt? Most likely you forgot to baste it too.'

At that moment Barthélemy clicked the door shut, and her head whipped round. Father Yann hung back in the shadows to observe her, unobserved.

The face that turned to the door was unguarded, and her eyes went directly to her lover's.

Anna looked radiant. There was no question of it. She was older, naturally, but her eyes were bright, her smile soft and loving. She wore her contentment like a cloak, a woman who loves and knows her love is returned. One glance at it was confirmation that the harper had not been lying when he had said Anna was happy. Father Yann racked his brains. Had he seen her wear that look before, when he had married her to Raymond Herevi? He could not recall it. All he remembered was seeing her eyes fill with hungry longing every time she looked at her husband. And after, when Raymond had gone, that same look would reappear whenever she mentioned him. The priest had thought her devoted. But seeing her now, relaxed as never before, and looking more fulfilled than the brightly coloured Madonna in St Peter's cathedral, Father Yann realised that what he had mistaken for devotion must have been desperation. Too naïve himself, he had not realised what that hungry, famished look had meant. Anna must have known, in some shadowy recess of her soul, that Raymond Herevi did not love her wholeheartedly, and never would.

Suddenly becoming aware of the priest, Anna lost colour.

'F . . . Father Yann,' she stuttered, swallowing. 'I . . . I wasn't expecting you, but you're welcome, of course.' Recovering, she pushed herself to her feet, and crossed the floor. 'Let me take your cloak, and find you a stool. You need to dry off.'

Barthélemy went to Anna's side, drew her to him, and hugged her.

She turned puzzled eyes on her love. 'Barthélemy?'

'It's all right, Anna,' Barthélemy said, reassuringly. 'There's no need to pretend. I've been saying my confession. Father Yann knows everything—'

Anna dragged herself out of Barthélemy's arms. 'But he'll tell the bishop!'

'No, my dear,' Father Yann said, quickly. 'I won't do that.'

'You don't condemn us?'

Chafing his hands together to warm them, Father Yann stepped towards the fire. 'No. I can't condone your actions, but I've learnt tolerance in my old age. If you're happy with this young man . . .'

Anna gave Barthélemy a loving smile, and moving close again she linked her arm with his. 'I am happy, Father, very happy.'

547

'. . . and if he sees you and your son are cared for . . .'

'I will, Father,' Barthélemy assured him, earnestly.

'. . . I'll not breathe a word about Raymond Herevi.' He sniffed the air appreciatively. 'That goose smells very good,' he said.

Anna took the hint. 'You'll stay for supper, I hope, Father?'

'Try and prevent me.'

Arlette's baby, a healthy boy with a shock of red hair exactly like his mother's, was born just before midnight.

Clemence took the news down to the solar, where those with a vested interest in the outcome of the birth had repaired after supper in hopes of being the first to hear. Her head was muzzy with fatigue, for although the birth had been easy for Arlette, the strain of worrying had tired her.

She pushed open the door.

Lady Petronilla had appropriated the high-backed chair, and had dragged it before the fire. She sat tall and still, proud as a peacock. Her husband stood like her consort at her side.

Sir Gwionn perched on the edge of the table, swinging a long, leather-encased leg to and fro, apparently engrossed in a conversation between Sir Gilles and Clemence's husband, Walter. Clemence noticed a tray on the table. On it was a plate of sweetmeats, which was full, and two wine bottles, both of which were empty.

At her entrance five pairs of eyes turned towards her.

Gwionn Leclerc's cheeks were unusually pale, his scar was a bold red line in the candlelight. His eyes were dark and had sunk into their sockets.

'It's over,' Clemence said, moving towards the haven of her husband's arms.

Walter came to meet her half-way and, drawing her to

him, proffered his wine-cup. 'It's hot, and spiced, and very restoring,' he said.

Clemence took a swift sip.

'Well?' Petronilla's harsh voice cut through the expectant hush like a knife. Her fingers were curled like claws round the arms of the chair. All tension, she was gripping so tightly that Clemence could see the bones through her white skin.

'Well?' Petronilla repeated. 'Tell us. Quickly.'

'A boy. The countess has a beautiful baby boy.'

Sir Gwionn stirred. 'And the countess?' His voice was husky with fatigue.

Clemence gave him a warm look. 'She's well and—'

Petronilla cut in. 'The babe is healthy?'

'Indeed he is. He has beautiful hair, just like the countess.' Clemence smiled reminiscently. 'He has a lusty pair of lungs on him, and already he's suckling.'

It had been bad enough to hear that Arlette's baby was a son and living, but Petronilla took the news that the countess was feeding him herself like a blow to the heart. Over the months she had prayed long and hard for this baby to die, but in case her prayers were not heeded, she had made contingency plans which involved a wet-nurse who would be in her pay.

'Surely the countess is not feeding the child?' Petronilla asked. 'Why should she bother when wet-nurses are two a penny? She'll be worn out. Why, I'd earmarked a girl in La Roque-Gageac as the babe's wet-nurse. A good girl, of sound background,' she added as an afterthought. The common view was that a baby absorbed the wet-nurse's morals along with her milk.

Gwionn Leclerc straightened abruptly. His hands were bunched at his side. For a moment Clemence thought he was going to speak, but when he did not, she answered Petronilla.

'The countess has decided she will feed her baby herself,' she said.

Petronilla lifted a supercilious brow. 'Like a common peasant?'

'If Our Lady fed the infant Jesus, I am sure Arlette Favell can feed her daughter,' Clemence said.

Gwionn Leclerc let his breath out in a hiss, and smiled. 'Convey my congratulations to the countess,' he said.

Lady Petronilla shot the knight a look of black fury. A moment later, she had rearranged her features, and her face was a blank mask. Head up, she rose and sailed from the room.

Louis, who suspected he knew what was going through his wife's calculating mind, watched her go uneasily. He was disappointed, naturally, that his uncle's wife had been brought to bed of a live male child. It meant he would never become count. But he had made it plain to Petronilla often enough that he was not prepared to fight for the privilege. He did not want the responsibility of starting what must devolve into yet another minor war in the Aquitaine. With Mercadier and his mercenaries lodged at Beynac, the region was troubled enough.

If God had seen fit to bless his uncle by giving him a son for his heir, he would not argue with that. And now that the news was beginning to sink in, he realised that disappointment was not the only emotion in his mind. He felt relief too. He was glad that his uncle had left an heir behind him. If truth be told, Louis was quite content with running his manor. That was enough for him.

Catching the blue eyes of Countess Arlette's castellan on him, Louis decided that this was a good a time as any to make a clean breast of things.

'Forgive my wife's brusqueness, Sir Gilles,' he said. 'She has long cherished ambitions on my behalf. Ambitions that I myself do not share.'

The blue eyes narrowed.

Sir Gilles' position in La Forteresse was clear. There were always difficulties when a man's heir was born posthumously. As Count Etienne's castellan, it was his duty to support the countess and her son should the count's nephew decide to cause trouble.

'You won't oppose the child inheriting?' he asked.

'Not I,' Louis said.

Sir Gilles's expression relaxed. 'May I make a suggestion?'

'Please do.'

'Look to your wife, Favell.'

Louis nodded. 'I will. It may have taken me a while, but I've got her measure now. I thought it would be safe to let her have her head, but from henceforth I'll be keeping her on a very tight rein.'

'Wise man,' Gilles approved.

'Will you convey our congratulations to the countess, Lady Clemence?'

'Of course, Sir Louis.'

Louis Favell bowed, and followed his wife to the guest chamber.

Father Theobald insisted that Arlette's son be baptised within three days. He was christened Lucien Robert in honour of the saint upon whose day he was born, and in remembrance of Arlette's grandfather.

Arlette lost herself in caring for her baby. Christmas came, and although Arlette came down to the hall while Lucien was sleeping and tried to take part in the festivities, they seemed unreal to her and passed as though in a dream.

She continued to feed Lucien, but frequently her duties required her elsewhere, so Clemence brought a nurse for Lucien in from Domme. The nurse washed the child, and changed his linen, and watched over him while she slept — never was a child so carefully guarded — but she was not a wet-nurse. Though it caused many raised eyebrows, Arlette continued to insist she fed her baby herself.

Clemence came to speak to her while she was feeding Lucien in her chamber.

'Arlette, it's time you were churched.'

Arlette knew that, having survived childbirth, she was expected to attend a ceremony of thanksgiving and give an offering to God. This she accepted, but the notion that women's bodies were unclean after having given birth to a child, and that husbands could not have intercourse with their wives until after they were purified by the church, rather rankled.

She pulled a face. 'I've always thought it something of an insult that the church enjoins us to go forth and be fruitful, and then when we do it declares us unclean. Besides, I've no husband impatient for his rights.'

'Nevertheless. It's time. Now Christmas is past, Sir Gilles is ready to advise you concerning your next husband. He asked me to sound you out to see if you would meet him for a formal discussion on the subject.'

'Next husband?' Arlette had spent the past few weeks entirely wrapped up in caring for Lucien, and thoughts of marriage had not crossed her mind. It was too soon to think of marriage.

'I understand two noblemen have already been making inquiries,' Clemence went on. 'Didn't he tell you?'

'Yes. But I can't say I paid him much attention.' Arlette lowered her gaze to the child at her breast, and tenderly stroked the red-gold head. She loved watching her child blissfully sucking at her breast, so confident of his right to be there. He was so helpless. So trusting. She loved the sensual innocence of the rosebud mouth tugging at her nipple, she loved the warm feeling it engendered – a feeling which reached to her core. And to think most

552

noblewomen farmed their children out on a wet-nurse.

'What's the hurry?' Arlette murmured. 'I'm not certain I want to get married again in any case.'

'You don't want to get married?' Clemence laughed. 'Don't be naïve. What have your wishes got to do with it? You're a count's widow and he,' she jerked her thumb at the suckling child, 'will need a guardian. They won't let you remain unwed for long. You know that. The Favell lands are extensive: Duke Richard will want reassurance that you're not going to marry someone unsympathetic to his rule, and the best way to do that is to marry you to one of his men.'

Arlette frowned, for Gwionn Leclerc's scarred face had jumped unbidden into her consciousness. 'If I marry again, Clemence, I tell you it will be someone of my own choosing.'

Clemence came to sit beside her on the bed, and gently took hold of one of Lucien's tiny feet which had emerged from its swaddling. She sighed. 'They'll never let you choose your own husband, you know that. Sir Gilles has letters from two suitors, both of whom have the duke's blessing.'

'How old are they?' Arlette asked, idly. She did not want to take this seriously.

'One of them, Sir Baldwin Deville, is forty-five, but the other is older.'

'More old men,' Arlette dismissed her suitors with a wave of her hand before moving Lucien to her other breast. 'I won't have either of them.'

'But, Arlette—'

Arlette thought of Gwionn's tall, straight body. The real father of her child was young and handsome, despite his scarred face.

'If I must have a husband, I'll have a young one.'

'Sir Gilles favours Sir Baldwin,' Clemence told her. 'You'll find it hard to persuade him otherwise.'

Arlette shot her friend a penetrating look. 'Sir Gilles is serious about this?'

'Yes. If you hadn't been so involved with Lucien, you'd have seen this for yourself.'

'I won't do it, you know. I'll never marry a man who is not my choice. I've done it once, but I won't make that mistake again.'

Clemence spread her hands in a gesture of helplessness. 'I don't see how you can avoid it. If Duke Richard recommends this man—'

Lucien had fallen asleep at Arlette's breast, head lolling and mouth rimmed with white milk. Arlette drew the edges of her gown together and wiped Lucien's mouth with a muslin cloth. This done she gazed thoughtfully into the fire.

'I have it!' she exclaimed.

Clemence, who had heard that particular tone of voice before, and knew it spelled trouble, regarded her with wary blue yes. 'Yes?'

'It's time we went home.'

Clemence blinked. 'Home? You mean to Brittany?'

'Yes. Oh, don't look like that, Clemence. I've not visited my father since we came here.'

'Your father's too ill to know you.'

'I know. Eleanor's last letter said his condition had worsened. He can't last much longer. I should like to show him his grandson before he dies.'

'Sir Gilles won't like it.'

'He can't stop me. We won't be gone long.'

'And your suitors?'

Arlette smiled. 'They'll have to wait till I've seen my father. When I come back I'll consider my suitors, but not before.'

'Will you tell Sir Gilles about this?' Clemence asked. 'I think it would be best coming from you.'

'Naturally. You can arrange the churching.'

Her tone gave Clemence pause.

'Arlette, you've something up your sleeve, haven't you?'

Arlette stretched her eyes wide. 'Up my sleeve? Whatever are you talking about? I want to see my father. Is that so remarkable?'

Given the way François de Roncier had treated his daughter, Clemence thought it was nothing less than miraculous. But she said nothing, and after giving her friend a final, searching glance, she went to find Father Theobald to discuss Arlette's churching.

Throughout January, Arlette kept Sir Gilles at bay on the matter of her marriage, with vague promises to give the subject her full attention in spring-time when Lucien was older.

But by February a rider galloped in on a lathered horse with a letter for Arlette from Eleanor de Roncier. The letter contained important news which only served to strengthen her resolve to visit her family.

The Feast of St Hilary, 1196

Dearest Daughter, before God I am your loving friend.

Although I am grieved that I cannot report any improvement in your father's condition, my heart is lighter since I last wrote to you.

The Bishop of Vannes came to the convent today to celebrate Mass, and he brought with him a missive from the law-courts. They have come to a ruling on your father's case concerning the allegations that were made against him with regard to Duke Geoffrey's death nearly ten years ago. They have, thanks be to God, decided that there is insufficient evidence against him.

Apparently the entire case rests on the word of
one man — and the man is a mere knight at that.
It is one man's word against another, and when
the honour of two men is put in the balance, the
word of a count — even an invalid — weighs
more heavily than that of a knight. I believe your
grandmother must have influenced the verdict, for
she did not hesitate to take up the cudgels to clear
her son's name, and rushed in and spoke most
vehemently on his behalf. I also maintain this
conflict has restored some of your grandmother's
youth, for she has regained an enthusiasm for life
which seemed lost after the death of Count
Robert.

So we are to return to Huelgastel, in triumph,
and your father is exonerated completely. Thus
you are, once more, Huelgastel's heiress.

I had hoped that your father might recover
when he heard that he had been cleared of all
blame, but he has moved neither hand nor foot
since I told him. I fear he is beyond earthly help.

Count Etienne's man, Sir Gilles, will be pressing
you to wed again. Your grandmother bids me tell
you to weigh your decision most carefully. She
would have me remind you that your son, Lucien,
will ultimately be master of both La Forteresse
and Huelgastel, and any man you marry must be
a trustworthy guardian — a steward with no
personal ambition which might turn him against
your son and prevent him from handing over the
lands in their entirety.

Your grandmother has also expressed a desire to
see you, which I share.

Your grandmother is an extraordinary woman,
and quite indefatigable. I swear she will live for
ever. She is well into her sixties, and the good

news concerning our reinstatement only came this morning, but already she is packing and anxious to go home. I declare she had commanded her tiring woman to unearth the trunks before the news was half-way out of the bishop's mouth. But Huelgastel is where she belongs, and she has been restless within these walls, like a caged lioness.

For myself, I shall be sad to leave St Anne's. Although I have known great sorrow here for the state of your father's health, I have also found great peace. The days march past in orderly fashion, with no great alarms, and it suits my temperament. It is very calming, very restoring. One's soul can flower and blossom as it will.

To my mind a nun's lot is an enviable one.

Ah, well. Back to Huelgastel. Your grandmother tells me that Sir Hamon le Moine has discharged his duty honourably and maintained the castle and lands impeccably. Sadly, Sir Hamon admits to becoming forgetful, and has declared his days as seneschal are numbered. His wife, Lady Deneza, whom you will remember, had been put in charge of the domestic arrangements. She was called to God last autumn, and since then Sir Hamon's mental capacities have diminished rapidly. I believe his eldest son, Jehan, has returned and has been helping his father run the estate. Jehan has won his spurs, and come back a knight. Was he not a childhood playmate of yours?

My prayers, as ever, are for you and your son. He must make you so happy.

When you next write, send your messenger to Huelgastel. I pray he will bring word that you are to come and greet your family and look over your inheritance.

May the lord Jesu bless you and keep you.

Your loving belle-mère,
Eleanor de Roncier, Countess.

Sitting back thoughtfully to digest the contents of
Eleanor's letter, Arlette noticed her stepmother had styled
herself countess and sealed the letter with the de Roncier
seal. Rigidly scrupulous, Eleanor had disdained use of
both title and seal while her father's honour lay in the
balance, but now was free to employ them again.

For her grandmother's sake, Arlette was glad her father
was to be restored to Huelgastel. But it would be a bitter
triumph with François being brought back on a litter. She
wondered how aware her father was about what was
happening. If he was as sick as Eleanor's letters suggested,
he would be ruler of Huelgastel in name only. Who would
be real ruler? Sir Hamon was too old. And Eleanor was
interested only in God. Her grandmother would no doubt
run the household, despite her age. But she would have
Jehan to help her.

Arlette was pleased to hear that Jehan had come back.
He was clever, and even as a child he had had a highly
developed sense of responsibility. He would make a good
seneschal.

He was both kind and diligent, like Sir Gilles.

As she thought of Sir Gilles, Arlette held down a sigh. It
had become imperative that she go to Huelgastel as soon
as the weather warmed. Sir Gilles would not like the idea,
and she foresaw lengthy discussions, but when Arlette
showed him her letter, he would have no option but to
agree to her going.

At last the days began to lengthen.

Arlette was in the hall, supervising its spring cleaning
when Sir Gilles strode up to her. 'Excuse me, my lady.

May I have a private word with you?' he said.

Arlette knew what Sir Gilles wanted to discuss with her. Her marriage. Of late the castellan seemed to have become obsessed with that topic. Realising that he was only doing his duty as he saw it, Arlette suppressed her irritation and gave him a smile. 'Of course.'

Sir Gilles escorted her into the chapel, where they sat on a bench.

'My lady, I think you're aware of what I'd like to discuss with you . . .'

'My marriage.'

Sir Gilles nodded. 'You should make a decision soon, my lady. Your suitors grow impatient.'

'I appreciate your concern, Sir Gilles. It is indeed an important decision, but it is one I will not make without consulting my family.'

'Do you still plan to visit them?'

'Yes.'

A puzzled frown creased Sir Gilles' brow. 'I understood your father was so ill that he was unable to speak.'

'That is so. But my grandmother and my stepmother are still able to advise me. I should like to discuss this matter with them. It is more than a mere whim on my part, Sir Gilles, it is a necessity. You will appreciate that Lucien is now heir to Huelgastel as well as La Forteresse?'

'Yes, my lady.'

'I shall be leaving quite soon. Lady Clemence is to accompany me. We shall not require a great train. Sir Gwionn Leclerc and half a dozen men-at-arms will suffice.'

'Will Sir Walter be accompanying you and his wife, my lady?'

'No.' For some reason Arlette could not fathom, Sir Walter had elected to remain behind at La Forteresse. Clemence had tried to persuade her husband to change his mind. Usually she was successful at this, but on this occasion she failed. After reassuring Clemence that their visit to Brittany would be short, and that she would soon be reunited with her husband, Arlette had dismissed Sir Walter's obduracy from her mind. Duty often caused knights and their wives to be separated. 'Sir Walter wishes to remain here.'

Accepting this, Sir Gilles nodded. 'How long will you be gone, my lady?'

'That will depend largely on what I discover at Huelgastel. But in my absence I am placing this castle and the estate management entirely in your hands, Sir Gilles.'

'Thank you, my lady. You will let me know if you come to a decision regarding your choice of husband?'

Arlette inclined her head. 'I shall keep you fully informed, by messenger. And in return, I shall expect to be told all that happens here.'

'Naturally. When do you plan to go?'

Arlette paused to consider. 'After Easter, when the weather is warmer. I'm taking Lucien to show to his grandfather, and I don't want to risk him getting ill.'

Chapter Twenty-six

Huelgastel, May, 1196

For the first time in almost ten years, Arlette walked into Huelgastel solar. It was mid-afternoon, and as she was but newly arrived from the Aquitaine, her cloak was still about her shoulders. She carried her son in her arms.

The solar was empty. Arlette found herself gazing at the familiar herons who stalked majestically around the walls. The frieze was a weak echo of its former self: the colours were grimed and faded, the herons had lost their sharpness, and the bold red chevrons on the roof beams which arrowed towards the apex were buried beneath years of smoke and soot.

The hand of time had left its mark everywhere, but on her way to the solar Arlette had noticed improvements as well as deterioration. The stables, which had been put into the charge of Aubrey and Olier when she had been a child, had been altered beyond recognition. The building had been enlarged and six new stalls had been squeezed in under the guards' walkway. Repairs had been made to the armoury, quite recent repairs, if one compared the dark, more seasoned wood with the newly adzed white timbers. Flags had been laid in the bailey. This much Arlette had gleaned while striding through the yard with Lucien. As Eleanor had intimated in her letter, Sir Hamon and Jehan had obviously discharged their caretaking responsibilities diligently.

On their arrival at the stables, Arlette had not recognised the groom who had handed her from her horse. She had yet to see anyone she knew.

Once in the domestic buildings, the ravages of time were more apparent. In the hall, everything needed a good scrub and polish. The hangings were dirty and frayed. The display of Saracens' blades still had pride of place on the wall, but they had dulled, and spiders had woven gossamer threads between them. The pewter on the sideboard was coated with a film of dust. Arlette knew that Lady Deneza, Sir Hamon's wife, had died the previous autumn, but Eleanor and Marie had brought her father back from the convent some months ago, and both hall and solar bore evidence of their long absence from the castle. Had Lady Deneza lost heart before she died? And why had Eleanor and Marie not set things right? Was Arlette's father sicker than she had been led to believe?

'Eleanor! Eleanor!' Arlette called, turning for the corridor which led from the solar to the chapel and family apartments.

She had written to her stepmother informing her of their likely date of arrival, but the journey had been uneventful and swift. They were early.

Wandering into the cool twilight of the passage, Arlette heard a door slam in one of the chambers above.

'Eleanor! It's Arlette! I'm home!'

Home. Even after all these years, Huelgastel remained home to her.

She heard a rustle of skirts, and the quick pad of slippered feet on the cold stone floors, and Eleanor was before her, smiling her gentle smile.

She hadn't aged a day. Her pale complexion was unlined, and her fine hair had been scraped firmly back, so it was completely lost to sight beneath the severest barbette and wimple Arlette had seen outside a nunnery. Her gown was plain and dark, her veil was of simple bleached linen, and a silver cross banged against her breast.

'Arlette! My dear child, it is good to see you. You look so well. Is this your son?'

Leading Arlette back into the light of the solar, Eleanor's pale eyes gazed wistfully at Lucien. He was awake, and regarded the newcomer with great interest before focusing on the shiny cross on Eleanor's breast.

'Yes, this is Lucien.' Arlette held her child out for her stepmother to take.

Reverently, Eleanor took him from her. 'He's beautiful,' she breathed. 'And what gorgeous green eyes he has. He must have those from his father.'

'Yes. The colour of his eyes only changed quite recently.'

Fondly, Eleanor stroked the red crest of hair. 'But his fiery crown he inherits from you. Oh, he's lovely, Arlette. Quite perfect. But so tiny.'

Arlette smiled. 'He's growing fast. He's over four months old.'

Lucien put out a chubby fist and clutched at Eleanor's cross. To Arlette's horror, after examining it for a few moments, he put it in his mouth, and began to suck it noisily.

'Oh!' Arlette flushed with embarrassment, and made as if to retrieve the cross. 'I'm sorry, Eleanor.'

To Arlette's surprise, Eleanor stayed her hand. 'Let him be. He does no harm.'

Watching her stepmother's downbent head and indulgent smile, Arlette felt her heart twist in sympathy for her, as it was borne in on her that if God had gifted Eleanor with her father's child, she would have evolved into an entirely different person. Motherhood would have distracted her from her obsessive devotion to religion. Motherhood would have been her salvation.

Unconsciously, Arlette sighed.

Hearing the sigh and misinterpreting its cause, Eleanor

looked up guiltily. 'My apologies, Arlette. How selfish I'm being. You want to see your father.' She paused, and seemed to be seeking the right words. 'Your grandmother is with him. We're afraid to leave him alone. I should warn you, Arlette, in recent days his condition has worsened.'

'How so?'

Eleanor handed Lucien back to Arlette. 'For the past few years, although your father could not speak, he had no difficulty moving his eyes, or swallowing, so I could feed him. I always fed him myself. But lately – ' Eleanor stopped to clear her throat – 'lately he's lost even that ability. He's fading before our eyes. It's a miracle he's alive.'

By common consent the two women began making their way to the corridor.

'What about broth? Can't he eat that?' Arlette suggested.

'I thought of that. He chokes. It's horrible.'

Eleanor turned and pressed Arlette's hand. 'I'm so glad you're back. It can only be a matter of time. Father Josse sees him daily. If his condition worsens he'll be given the last rites. Your father will be glad to see his grandson.'

'Do you think he is aware of what is happening? Will he understand that Lucien is his grandson?'

'Oh, he knows.' Eleanor's voice was bleak. 'That is the tragedy of it. You only have to take one look at his eyes to realise that he is fully conscious of everything that happens to him.'

'Poor Papa.'

'Yes. It is quite dreadful to watch him. He is a man in torment.'

Though Eleanor's warning should have forearmed her, Arlette was quite unprepared for the sight and sensations that accosted her in François de Roncier's bedchamber.

A brazier, full of glowing embers, and a blazing fire, filled the room with suffocating heat. A sickly smell lodged in her nostrils. A branch of rosemary had been flung into the fire to sweeten the air, but the clean, sharp scent of the burning herb was tainted with another, less pleasant aroma. The heavy, oppressive stink of death. Arlette recognised it and shuddered. She had come across it once before, in this very room, before her mother had died. Last time she had not known what it signified. This time she did.

As she crossed the chamber, her skirt hushed across the rushes. An elderly woman clad in sombre widow's garb was sitting on a stool by the bedside, one claw-like hand clutching a silver-topped walking stick. The woman glanced up, and drew Arlette's gaze from the spectre in the bed. Her shoulders were stooped with age, she was shrunken so her widow's gown swamped her, but her head was tilted at a proud angle. Her face was lined and the skin hung in folds about her withered cheeks, but her dark eyes glittered and her nose jutted – the beak of a hawk. Though Marie de Roncier had aged, she had not lost any of her haughty beauty.

'Arlette?' The dowager countess leaned forwards on her stick, black eyes blinking in the direction of the door. 'Is that you?' Her voice, strong and commanding as ever, creaked like an ill-oiled gate.

'Her sight is going,' Eleanor explained in a whisper.

Ignoring for the time being the motionless figure in the bed, Arlette went to kneel before her grandmother.

'Yes. It's Arlette, Grandmère. I've come to stay for a while.'

She kissed her grandmother's bloodless cheek.

'You're three days early,' Marie said, with that abrupt, almost impolite directness of manner that tore away the years.

Arlette hid a reminiscent smile. Her grandmother had

not changed. 'I know. We made good time. Will you forgive me?'

The black eyes softened. 'Forgive you? Don't talk foolishly, girl. Who's this?'

'This is Lucien, your great-grandson.'

A shaking, skeletal hand reached out and stroked the baby's cheek.

Lucien gurgled happily, and clutched his great-grandmother's talon of a finger.

'He likes you, Grandmère,' Arlette said.

Marie tutted and shook her finger. Lucien smiled. 'He has a good grip,' she pronounced gently and, despite herself, an answering smile lifted the edges of her severe mouth. 'And he has your father's hair.'

'Yes, Grandmère,' Arlette said, thanking God for her son's sunny nature. Lucien was revelling in the attention of these strangers, and he continued to oblige by cooing and burbling like a wood pigeon.

The dowager countess's smile enlarged. 'Your Lucien is charming, child, and I'm delighted to meet him before the light goes from my eyes completely.'

'Oh, Grandmère—'

'No pity, child. No pity. Pity serves no purpose. At least I've learnt to hop about with my sticks,' Marie said, and the creaking harshness was back in her tone. She disengaged herself from her great-grandson. 'Besides, your father has more need of pity than I. Look to your father, child.'

Arlette drew in a deep breath and, rising, faced the bed.

Count François de Roncier, the man who had been fierce enough to best every knight in his castle in single combat, and who had once tamed the wildest horse in the duchy, had barely enough body on him to make a mound in the coverlet. He had lost most of his hair, and what he had left clung to his skull in wispy red clumps. His cheeks were hollow, his eyes sunk back into their sockets and, save for a scattering of freckles – relics from the days he had ridden in the sunlight – his skin was the colour of dirty bone. The arm and hand protruding from his nightgown were wasted. Count François resembled a corpse – the corpse of a ninety-year-old man. He was forty-four.

Remembering that Eleanor believed her father's faculties were intact, Arlette managed to school her features to hide her shock. Seeing her father's hazel eyes were open, she leaned over the bed.

'Hello, Papa.'

He blinked, but other than that not a muscle moved.

Arlette swallowed. 'It's Arlette, Papa. I've brought your grandson to you.'

François blinked.

It was unnerving trying to speak to someone who could not respond. 'Eleanor, he blinked at me,' Arlette said. 'Does that mean he hears me?'

Eleanor came to stand at her side. 'Yes. It's the only movement he has left. One blink signifies yes, or his agreement to whatever you have said. Two blinks signify no.'

Arlette leaned over her father with Lucien. 'This is your grandson, Papa. This is Lucien Robert Favell.'

François blinked. His eyes moistened.

'Eleanor, Papa is starting to cry,' Arlette said, distressed. 'I've made him unhappy.' She picked up her baby and hugged him to her chest.

Eleanor, scrutinising her husband's still face, counted two blinks. 'No. Those are tears of happiness, Arlette. You've made him happy. Show Lucien to him again.'

There was a lump in Arlette's throat as she obliged. 'This is Lucien, Papa. Your grandson.'

François blinked. A tear rolled down his fleshless cheeks. Eleanor wiped it away.

567

'That's enough for now, Arlette,' she said. 'He tires very easily. Let me show you to your room.'

Arlette found a smile and put it on. 'There's no need for that, Eleanor, I remember the way.'

Gwionn was thinking about Anna, his wife. He had not yet forgiven her for leaving him without telling him where she was going. He had a suspicion she had taken their son to Kermaria and, now he was back in Brittany within a stone's throw of his father's old manor, it would be the work of day to ride out there and put his theory to the test. But something was holding him back.

Arlette.

Arlette Favell, née de Roncier, the mother of his second son, was holding him back. She loved him, of that he was confident, and she loved their son. She would ensure the child's succession to both the Favell, and the de Roncier, county. She did not need him. He had served — in every way — his purpose.

That rankled.

He had served his purpose and Arlette had no further use for him. He could of course threaten to denounce her, but if he did so he would jeopardise his own son's succession, and it was a far more effective revenge to have his son inherit the lands that de Roncier killed Gwionn's father to keep. He was revenged more thoroughly if he kept a still tongue in his mouth.

So why did he continue to stay in the lion's den? The lion was old and crippled and would roar no more. The lion was no longer a fit adversary for him. The game was over. He had won.

Why did he not wish to return to claim Anna?

Why the continuing obsession with Arlette?

It was Arlette, with her wide blue eyes, and her shy smile, who haunted his every thought. In his mind's eye he saw her trailing red hair and her slender white body.

Memories of the forbidden sweetness of her supple limbs as they entwined with his crept into his dreams, crept into every waking thought.

He wanted her.

Since their son's birth, Arlette had kept him at arm's length. Very politely, naturally, it was not that she had avoided him or shut him out. On the contrary, on the journey to Huelgastel she had sought him out and spoken with him at length on such diverse subjects as hunting, keeping accounts, horse-breaking, even swordsmanship – a subject no woman had ever broached with him before. She even confessed to having had a liking for archery when she was younger. She had asked him how mail-coats were made, and had listened with every sign of attention to his answer, but nonetheless, he had been kept very firmly at an arm's length. She, who had borne him a son.

He knew she loved him. He wanted her.

He would have her once more, but not because he loved her. He would see if there was anything else he could get out of her.

After that he would set out for Kermaria.

Arlette met Clemence in the solar.

'What news of your father?' she asked.

Arlette shook her head. 'He looks like a death's head.' She sighed, and a wave of utter exhaustion swept over her. The long ride, and fretting lest Lucien took ill on the journey had taken their toll on her. Since giving birth Arlette had found she needed rest more than any other time in her life. The journey itself was enough to tire her, but finding her father sunk so low had come as the final blow. Though Eleanor's letter had tried to prepare her, Arlette had not realised the full implications of his condition. For all that knew he was sick, her father had lived on in her mind as a vital, energetic being. She remembered him as he had been in his prime. It was hard to reconcile the man she remembered with the lifeless thing lying in her father's bedchamber.

Clemence eyed her shrewdly. 'You don't look much better,' she said, with the frankness of an old, trusted friend.

'I do feel tired.'

Clemence took charge. 'Go and rest. It will do you good.'

'I can't. My father might take a turn for the worse. Besides,' a wave of her arm encompassed the solar, 'look around you. My grandmother's eyes are going, she can't see what needs doing, and Eleanor has obviously been too taken up with nursing my father to keep house properly. There's much to be done. I can't rest.'

Clemence took her arm. 'Nonsense. Listen to me, Arlette. You'll be no good to that baby of yours if you get too tired. Your milk will dry up. Go and rest.'

'But what about all this?'

'Leave it to me. I know what should be done. And if your father needs you, I'll call you.'

'I haven't seen Sir Hamon yet, or Jehan,' Arlette said, wistfully. 'I should like to see Jehan.'

'Later. When you've rested.' Clemence gave her a little push in the small of her back. 'Off you go. And if you dare reappear before two hours are up, I'll send you straight back.'

Arlette lay resting on the bed she had once shared with Clemence. Beside her, in the de Roncier crib, Lucien lay on his back, sound asleep. His hands were flung back beside his head, tiny fists loosely curled. His cheeks were faintly pink, his lips smiling. Arlette had lain her son there herself, when he had fallen asleep while she had been feeding him.

Véronique had been sent down with a pile of dirty linen

that needed boiling, and no doubt Clemence would enlist her help scouring Huelgastel.

Arlette was exhausted. Closing her eyes, she waited for sleep to claim her. While she waited her mind whirred.

She felt bad about not helping Clemence. She hoped Clemence would not offend Sir Hamon and Jehan by taking charge of the domestic arrangements. It appeared that the seneschal and his son had done their duty with regard to matters military, but since Lady Deneza had died the domestic arrangements had suffered. It was not to be expected that the men would wield any influence over what was traditionally regarded as the woman's area. Arlette wondered who had been put in charge of solar and hall since her family had come back from St Anne's. Lena, her grandmother's maid?

A heavy lassitude spread through her limbs. It was not unpleasant. She yawned.

Dreamily, she wondered where Clemence would sleep. As Sir Walter was not with them, her friend could share this room with her as they had done when they were girls. Failing that, there was a barrel-vaulted storage recess with a narrow window slit a couple of turns below Arlette's chamber. Clemence could have that if she had a mind for privacy. Arlette remembered Clemence's former sweetheart, Morgan le Bihan. Was he still in charge of Huelgastel mews? As sleep began to steal over her, Arlette wondered if Clemence had seen him. When she woke up, she must remember to enquire.

The click of the door-latch woke her.

The sound of the bolt being slowly drawn across made her open her eyes.

She found herself gazing at the broad back of a man with tousled, chestnut-brown hair She knew him immediately. It was Gwionn Leclerc.

She sat up so abruptly that her head swam.

'Gwionn! You shouldn't be in here! And why are you locking that door?'

He put a lean finger to his lips and drew near to the bed. 'Hush. We'd best whisper. I'm sorry to disturb you, but I had to talk to you. I'm glad our son is sleeping.'

'You mustn't speak of him as our son, not even to me. It's too risky.' Concerned, Arlette gave him a faint frown and shook the last vestiges of sleep from her head. 'Are you certain you weren't seen? If you were, the scandal could destroy everything we have worked for. It would cast doubts on Lucien's parentage, and then we'd have nothing.'

He smiled reassuringly. 'I wasn't seen.' Dropping to his knees on the matting by the bed, he took her hand and raised it to his lips. Arlette had missed the intimacies they had once shared, and was seized with a sudden longing to cling to him, but that she must not do. For the sake of their child, she must get Gwionn from her bedchamber as quickly as possible.

'I had to see you,' Gwionn said, and his voice was seduction itself. 'I find this pretence that we must be separate intolerable. The journey here has been a cruel penance for me; seeing you so near each day, and yet unable to touch you. I want to touch you. Arlette, let me touch you.'

With his every word, Arlette knew she was weakening, but she steeled herself to remove her hand from his hold. But Gwionn held it fast.

'It's for the best,' she said as firmly as she was able. 'For Lucien's sake.'

'But what about me? Do my wishes count for nothing? You are attracted to me. Do you love me?'

Arlette looked away, but Gwionn caught her chin and brought her head round to his. His eyes were very dark. 'You do love me.'

Hot, betraying colour stung Arlette's neck and cheeks.

She had not been brought up to consider her feelings important, but neither could she bring herself to deny it. He had helped her in her hour of need, and she had grown fond of him, and come to rely on him. She cared about him. Was that not love? But she had been taught that duty must always come before love.

'I . . . I am attracted to you, very much,' she admitted. 'You have been kind to me, and were a good friend when I needed one—'

'And now I'm cast out, is that it?' he asked. 'You have a child, *our* child, and I am nothing to you. You act as though I were a stranger.'

Arlette caught Gwionn's forearm, wanting to make him understand. 'How can you say that? I have to treat you like any other knight in my entourage. I have no choice. It's for Lucien.'

He stared searchingly into her eyes. 'I want you, Arlette. I love you. I want to marry you.'

'M . . . marry?'

'Yes. Why not? You'll have to marry again. Sir Gilles mentioned suitors. You don't want another greybeard in your bed, do you?'

Shuddering, Arlette gave him a rueful smile. 'You know my answer to that.'

'Well then, why not marry me?' A touching expression of uncertainty shadowed his face. 'You do love me, don't you?'

Arlette swallowed. 'I think perhaps I do. My heart beats fast at the sight of you. It always has. Certainly no other man has been as gentle to me as you. If you had not cared for me when the count . . . when the count . . . I don't know what I would have done. I was at my wit's end.'

'Let me care for you for ever, Arlette. Marry me.'

Loving fingers stroked her cheek, found her earlobe and softly, tenderly caressed it.

'You are not . . . the duke has not approved you,' she pointed out.

'We're in Brittany, on lands that are yours by right of birth, not marriage. Here you may marry whom you like.'

Gwionn's argument was at best tenuous, and both of them knew it. Duchess Constance, who ruled the Duchy of Brittany on behalf of her nine-year-old son, Arthur, should have an interest in Arlette's choice of husband, especially since François de Roncier had once been accused of treason. But in practice, the counts of Brittany were as fiercely independent as the counts of the Aquitaine. Had François been hale enough to approve of a marriage between Gwionn and Arlette, the duchess would have little option but to swallow it, no matter how bitter a pill. But with the count so weak, if Arlette chose a husband who met with Eleanor and her grandmother's approval, no-one would be likely to object to the marriage.

Arlette was tempted by Gwionn's proposal. Gradually, she had come to love him. His was the face that she sought every morning when she came down to the hall to break her fast. He was young and handsome, and she knew that he would give her no unpleasant surprises on their wedding night. He would not hurt her. True, he was only a knight, and it was unusual for a countess to marry a knight, but it was not impossible. Men could, and did, rise through the ranks.

He had seen the hesitation on her face and pressed on with another point. 'Marry anyone else, and you'll be storing up problems for the future.'

'What do you mean?'

He shrugged. 'I should have thought it was obvious. Your husband might be very kind and considerate to Lucien at the beginning. But the moment you and your new husband have a child, you husband will look at Lucien – his step-child – with entirely different eyes. He will develop ambitions for the child of his loins. He will look at Lucien and see an interloper. He will see the one thing that stands between his child inheriting all your lands. He will come to hate our son — he might even murder him.'

Arlette was silent. This was an argument more telling than all the rest put together. It was a problem that had occurred to her, but her mind had shied away from Gwionn's grim conclusion, not wanting to see it.

She glanced fearfully at the child in the crib. 'Murder? Surely not?' But even as the words were out of her mouth, Arlette called Petronilla Favell to mind. When she had first seen Petronilla in her Byzantine finery, she had recognised ambition in the woman, but it had never crossed her mind that one day that same ambition would drive her to murder.

'Marry me,' Gwionn murmured, persuasively. 'I will protect our son.'

Gwionn leaned towards her, his face hovering an inch from hers. In anticipation of his kiss, Arlette closed her eyes. She didn't know what to say, but she did want his kiss. She ached for it, and more besides. It had been a long time since they had made love.

'You want me,' he muttered in a satisfied tone. And as his lips met hers, his hand moved to cover a breast.

Arlette pressed towards him with a little moan of surrender.

Hearing it, Gwionn lifted his lips from hers, and the longing in his eyes made her heart miss a beat.

'Can you move over on that bed? My knees are finding this floor something of an ordeal.'

Arlette smiled, and sat up. 'One moment,' she said and, padding across the floor to one of her travelling chests, she flipped back the lid, and drew out a yellow imported sponge and a dark, corked bottle.

Gwionn, who had been stripping off his clothes, frowned.

'What's the matter, Gwionn,' Arlette asked, puzzled by his expression. 'You must have seen your other women use one of these.' She poured the vinegar on to the sponge. 'It stops babies coming, at least it does most of the time. It didn't stop Lucien.'

Gwionn's green eyes were full of astonishment and, though she did not realise it, anger.

'You mean you used one before?' he got out.

'Mmm.'

Arlette bent and put her lips to his.

Gwionn could feel her milk-filled breasts press against his chest through the fabric of her gown. His hands moved of their own accord to cradle their new, heavy weight. So she had tried to stop his baby being born, had she? All that time and he never knew. Still, it hadn't worked, had it?

Setting his anger aside, Gwionn gave himself up to the moment.

Their passion, having been dammed up for so long, was easily spent.

Afterwards, Gwionn lay back on Arlette's pillows with a sigh of contentment and pulled her into the crook of his arm. Her eyelids were drooping languorously, like a cat that had been lying too long in the sun. Twining a red-gold curl round his fingers, Gwionn regarded her thoughtfully. There was something magical about making love to Arlette, something which was missing when he made love to Anna, and he could not pin it down.

He was married to Anna, whom he had always regarded as his true mate. Anna knew everything about him, and had accepted him for himself. And in many respects Anna was more sensual than Arlette. Yet there was an added spice, an extra frisson, in having Arlette which his

576

earthy Anna had never given him.

Was it merely the fact that forbidden fruits taste sweeter? Was it really that simple?

He should not have Arlette because he was Anna's husband. But when he did have her it was glorious. He lost himself completely. Every time. Her shy delight, and the touch of fear in the back of her eyes, which said, 'Please don't hurt me. I know you won't hurt me', was more powerful than any love potion any warlock could concoct.

He dropped a kiss on the top of Arlette's head, and tightened his grip on her, as he finally faced the truth which he had been avoiding for months.

He loved her.

He had blithely mentioned marriage as a ploy to inveigle her into his arms, and had not had the slightest intention of following his suggestion through. He had thought it amusing to think that she might consent. He had liked to imagine marrying her, and had seen them dividing their time between their estates in the Aquitaine and in Brittany. He would have had the satisfaction of seeing his son grow up to inherit all of de Roncier's lands as well as Etienne Favell's. He had thought revenge was all he cared about, but he had been deceiving himself with his imaginings.

He loved her.

And now he had admitted to himself that he did love the daughter of the man who had murdered his father, what was he to do? Should he commit the sin of bigamy in order to marry the woman he loved? If he did, he would never be able to answer to his real name again. Raymond Herevi woud be dead. It would be worth it.

And Anna? He was fond of her, but fondness was not love. This Arlette had taught him. He would have to cut Anna out of his thoughts, but that should not be too difficult, not if he had Arlette. Anna had betrayed him.

Anna had run off with Barthélemy. Anna deserved to be forgotten.

It occurred to Gwionn that Arlette had not replied to his proposal. Uncertain as to what he would do if she accepted, he said, 'You never answered me.'

'What?'

Her voice was slurred and sleepy.

'You never answered me. Will you marry me?'

She gave a contented giggle, and her hand slid down to his penis which stirred at her touch.

She lifted her head, and smiling blue eyes met his. 'I thought I answered you clearly enough,' she said, kissing his chest. 'But in case you've misunderstood, I'll spell it out for you. I'll marry you, and gladly. I'll speak to Eleanor tonight, and we'll put it to my father.'

Gwionn swallowed, and mentally cast Anna into the outer darkness. 'I thought your father was fading fast and couldn't speak.'

Some of the light went out of her eyes. 'He is. But Eleanor knows how to communicate with him. I want him to witness our marriage, so if he's agreeable, I'll ask Father Josse to marry us in the chapel tomorrow morning.'

Father Yann had had second thoughts with regard to Anna and her liaison with Barthélemy le Harpour.

While he had been a guest at Kermaria, breaking their bread, it had seemed only natural that Anna should be permitted to find happiness with the harper. At Kermaria it had been impossible to gaze into Anna's dark, contented eyes and to tell her that what she was doing was wrong, and that he and the Church could not possibly condone it.

He had come to regret what he realised was moral weakness on his part, and wished that he had spoken out there and then.

578

The weeks had run past, and the priest had hoped that time would have eased the pricking of his conscience. This did not happen. On the contrary, every day found him increasingly disturbed by Anna's infidelity. He wished he had been strong and had not left Anna and Barthélemy with the impression that one could lightly set aside one's marriage vows and cleave to another.

At the time, Father Yann had been thinking only of Anna's happiness, and it had been abundantly clear that the harper, even though not wed to the girl, had shown her far more devotion and consideration than Raymond Herevi ever had. He was not a cruel man, and certainly Anna's happiness ought to be considered, but once away from Anna and the influence of her shining eyes, Father Yann's conscience would not leave him alone.

Anna and Raymond Herevi were man and wife. He had heard them make the vows which bound them together for eternity in the porch of his own church at Locmariaquer. At the very least it was incumbent upon him to try and bring about some sort of reconciliation. Added to that was the not inconsiderable point that Barthélemy le Harpour had no rights to the manor and desmesne at Kermaria. In the absence of Sir Jean's legitimate son, Philippe, that land was more properly Raymond's.

Such thoughts had brought Father Yann to Vannes where he had discussed the case – omitting names, naturally – with one of the bishop's own clerics.

The cleric was quite clear as to what Father Yann should do. Father Yann should strive to find the woman's missing husband, and do his best to see them reunited.

Accordingly, Father Yann borrowed one of the bishop's mules. He would set out of Huelgastel the very next day, where he hoped that Father Josse would throw some light on the whereabouts of one Gwionn Leclerc, known more properly to him as Raymond Herevi.

* * *

François was lying on his bed, imprisoned in the body that had betrayed him.

Outside, dark had fallen, and his grandmother's one-time maidservant, Lena, had taken over on 'sentry duty' as he called it in the lonely recesses of his mind. She had lighted the candle at his bedside, and the wall-sconces by the fireplace. She had built up the fire – Lena always banked it higher than anyone else, it was as if her sixth sense told her that he was chilled to his marrow. François knew, though, that however high the fire and however tall the flames, he would never be warm again.

He longed to be able to speak. He prayed to be able to speak. Just one sentence. He would tell Lena to have pity on him. He would tell her to let the fire die down, and hasten his end.

And as for the candles, François hated them too.

He longed for the dark. But ever since his paralysis he had not been allowed a moment's darkness. There were always candles, just as there were always sentries, loving, smothering sentries, who watched in vain for the merest flicker of a muscle in his useless, wasted flesh.

François knew they watched in vain. As his illness had progressed he had felt less and less in contact with his body. It was as though his mind was a bird and his body was its cage. He might flutter about inside it, and rage to be free, but the bars of the cage held firm. However much he beat his wings he could not fly away.

One day, soon, he must fly free.

François had three senses left, but they came and went like the ever-changing tides. At times his hearing was acute. His sight likewise. His sense of smell was usually keen.

He could not see Lena, sewing at his side, because they had set his head towards that gruesome cross of Eleanor's. The crucifix hung, lurid as the day it had been painted, on the wall opposite the bed. But he could smell Lena. She

580

had a warm, slightly sweaty smell which he did not dislike. It was better than the foul miasma which came from his own, corrupting flesh.

François liked Lena. He always had, but it shamed him that she should have to baby him. In another lifetime, a healthy young man whose second wife had proved less welcoming than his first, had turned to Lena for consolation.

The flickering light cast unearthly shadows on Eleanor's Christ writhing in its death throes. It seemed to mock him. Christ's death throes, François recalled bitterly, had only lasted three hours. His seemed to last an eternity.

He closed his eyes and shut the repellent crucifix out — today was a good day for seeing and hearing — and let his thoughts run on. What else could he do but think?

The sight of his daughter and grandson that afternoon had given him quite a jolt.

Over the years, Eleanor had read all Arlette's letters to him, so he was fully aware of the difficulties his daughter had faced when the finger of suspicion had been pointed at him and the rest of her dowry had been withheld from her fiancé. François had been fully apprised of her confinement in the tower. He knew about her letters of appeal, and he knew about her final triumph.

He was proud of Arlette, who had, in the end, proved to be almost as good as a son. And she had given him the heir that he had craved. That glimpse he had had of Lucien had shown him a handsome babe. A babe with noble blood in his veins — and a sturdy body. A survivor.

For the second time that evening, François found himself wishing he could utter just one more sentence. He wanted to tell Arlette that he was proud of her. Suddenly he was filled with a piercing sadness. He wanted to tell his daughter that he loved her. And now he never would. It was enough to make a man cry.

Just then a sound on the stairwell dragged his attention from his thoughts. Two people entered the chamber. He recognised his wife's footsteps, but could not move his head to confirm this. Was it Arlette who accompanied Eleanor? Someone else had come up with them, but they remained on the landing.

'Thank you, Lena, you may go,' François heard Eleanor say. 'I will relieve you.'

'Madame.'

There was a rustle of fabric and a sense of emptiness emanated from the stool by his bed. Lena had gone.

Arlette's face appeared in front of his. She gave him a smile that melted his heart. She was a grand girl. Clearly his disciplining of her when she had been an unruly child had not been in vain. If only he could speak. If only . . .

Her smile vanished. 'Oh, Eleanor, look, how sad,' Arlette murmured and, stooping over him, she wiped his nerveless cheeks with the sleeve of her gown. 'Papa's crying.'

Am I crying, François wondered? He hadn't known.

He tried to smile, though he knew it was futile.

'Papa? Can you hear me?'

François blinked once.

'I've something very important I'd like to discuss with you.'

Arlette waited expectantly.

He blinked.

'I'd like to marry again. Only this time I'd like to marry someone of my own choosing. Papa, would you mind?'

Several thoughts rushed in on François at the same moment. Firstly, that she ought to marry someone who could bring them more lands, and consequently more security. Old habits died hard. And secondly, that that person's honour should be unimpeachable – it would have to be to safeguard Lucien's rights. But the last thought that rushed in on François was that he would be

582

dead soon, and he wanted to give his daughter a gift. Something to demonstrate his love for her, and his pride at what she had become. Muzzled as he was by his illness, he could not openly speak of his feelings. But he could gift her with this, he could bow to her wish and see her marry the man of her choice. Arlette's first, dutiful, marriage with Count Etienne, though it had astonished everyone by being fruitful, must have been difficult. Count Etienne would not have thanked his bride for forcing his hand and humbling him in the eyes of the world.

Suddenly, more than anything, François wanted his daughter to have the happiness that he had had with Joan. This was his chance of demonstrating his love for her.

He wondered who it was she wanted to marry.

She read his mind.

'Papa, the man I have chosen is outside, waiting to meet you. Do you want to meet him?'

François blinked, once.

Smiling, Arlette pulled back, and dipped out of his line of vision.

'Come in, Gwionn. My father would like to meet you,' he heard her say. 'Papa, this is Sir Gwionn Leclerc. You may remember seeing him before I went to La Forteresse. He was Sir Ralph's squire. He's become a knight, and I love him.'

A man bent over the bed, a handsome man with a cynical face and vicious scar which puckered up the right side of his face − doubtless a memento of some shady skirmish. His eyes were cold and unnaturally bright green. They were fringed with thick lashes. He had sensual lips, which were unsmiling. François supposed he was nervous. He estimated Sir Gwionn's age to be about thirty, and if the man's face was anything to go by, he looked more than capable of acting as Arlette's consort. His battle-scarred features were vaguely familiar, but without Arlette's introduction, François doubted he would have recognised him. All those years ago he had had few thoughts to spare for knights' squires.

'Gwionn, this is my father, Count François de Roncier,' Arlette said, punctiliously observing the courtesies. She nudged her knight. 'Say something, Gwionn. Ask him.'

Sir Gwionn cleared his throat. 'Count, I should like your daughter Arlette's hand in marriage. I have asked her, and she has done me the honour of accepting me. My lord, may we marry?'

'Oh, please, Papa. Please say yes.'

François didn't hesitate. He blinked once.

Arlette flung herself across his chest and hugged him. François could not remember the last time she had done that. Through a mist of tears he looked at his daughter's radiant face.

'Can it be tomorrow, Papa?'

Again, he blinked, but at that point his wife intervened.

'You're too hasty, Arlette. Marriages can't be arranged overnight,' Eleanor said, repressively.

Arlette straightened. For commoners, that might be true, but she had been wife to one count and was daughter of another. Anything could be arranged if her father willed it. 'But Eleanor,' she lowered her voice, 'I do so want Papa to witness this marriage. And you told me . . .'

She left her sentence hanging, but she did not have to complete it. Every person in the room, including François, knew that he did not have much longer to live. In a few weeks' time, no, in a few days' time, François de Roncier would not be able to witness anything.

Setting her misgivings aside, Eleanor sighed. To the last she would be the dutiful wife. 'Very well, Arlette. If your father agrees. I'll go and see Father Josse. But you know what they say about May weddings – they're ill-omened.'

'I'm surprised to hear you give ear to superstitious flummery, Eleanor,' Arlette said. She leaned over François. 'Papa?'

584

François blinked, and received another hug as his reward.

Chapter Twenty-seven

Father Yann's borrowed mule plodded alone amiably enough until he reached the point where the road began to climb up through the forest towards Huelgastel.

No sooner had the bishop's mule set his hoofs on the incline, than it grew roots and refused to budge. Muttering to himself about being too long in the tooth to be undertaking such jaunts, Father Yann dismounted, and hauled the mule the rest of the way.

In the bailey, his eyes fell on a groom, idling against a water butt chewing a stalk of straw. With relief he handed his mutinous mule to the groom, explained he had come from Locmariaquer, and asked to see Father Josse.

The groom squinted at the sun which was peeping out behind a snowy drift of clouds. 'He'll be in the chapel by now,' the groom said, removing the straw. 'On account of the wedding.'

'Wedding? What wedding?' Father Yann asked, beating the dust from his well-worn grey habit.

'It's the Little Lady's wedding.'

'Little Lady?'

'Arlette Favell — Count François' daughter. They're allowing her to marry again.' The straw went back in the groom's mouth.

For no reason that Father Yann could think of, he went cold all over. 'Who's her husband to be?'

The groom grinned, and spoke through the straw. 'A

knight from her household. One Sir Gwionn Leclerc.'

Father Yann's heart flipped over. And for the first time since his ordination he swore. 'Christ, no! The bastard! The lying, hypocritical, shiftless bastard!'

The straw dropped from the groom's gaping mouth as the priest from Locmariaquer gathered his faded grey habit into his hands and began to run across the bailey as fast as his ageing legs would carry him.

Reaching the chapel, Father Yann paused neither to draw breath nor to ponder on the enormity of what he was about to do. He burst through the door faster than the stone from the sling which David had used to fell Goliath.

One raking glance of the vaulted chamber where several haloed saints processed around the chapel walls was sufficient to tell him that the worst had happened.

He was too late.

Father Josse stood by the altar under a blue, star-spattered ceiling, facing a couple whose hands were tightly clasped. There was a shining new ring on the woman's finger, and Father Josse had his hand lifted for the final blessing.

The woman was wearing a simple, high-waisted green damask gown, with a silver girdle and a delicate beaded belt. Her head was uncovered, and white bridal lilies adorned her shining red hair, hair which had been dressed and coiled round her head like a coronet. This must be the Little Lady the groom spoke of, Arlette Favell. She was smiling. Her companion, a hand-span taller than she, Father Yann recognised instantly.

There were others present, three veiled ladies, and their serving women, and a handful of knights. Father Yann nodded nervously at Sir Hamon, surmising that the tall knight with dark curly hair at his side was his son, Sir Jehan. A motionless invalid was propped up on a palliasse that had been squeezed in next to a prie-dieu; this must be

Count François de Roncier. Ignoring the astonishment on everyone's faces, Father Yann lurched forwards. He might only be a lowly parish priest, and unused to such exalted company, but he knew right from wrong and he must speak out.

'Stop! This must stop,' he cried.

Everyone stared at him. Raymond Herevi had the grace to blanche. He dropped the woman's hand and stepped backwards.

Father Josse calmly finished the benediction.

'This marriage is prohibited!' Father Yann declared, in ringing pulpit tones that should have been audible in the bailey.

'Prohibited?' It was the red-haired woman who spoke. Her smile had dimmed. 'What do you mean, Father?'

Composedly, Father Josse folded his hands together in the sleeves of his vestments. 'Yes, you must explain yourself, brother. You should know better than to storm in and interrupt one of God's holy sacraments.'

'I do not do it lightly, believe me,' Father Yann said earnestly, recalling with a sense of dread that this barrel-vaulted chapel was at the heart of the de Roncier kingdom. 'But that man,' he pointed at Raymond Herevi, 'cannot marry that woman.'

'You mean they are related?' Father Josse asked, clear brow clouding. 'I was not aware of that, but if there are grounds for suspecting consanguinity, then naturally we must investigate them.'

The Little Lady turned bemused blue eyes on Raymond Herevi. 'Gwionn? What is this? What does this priest mean? Are we related?' She tried to reclaim his hand, but he shook it off. 'Gwionn?'

Surmising from her tone, and the confusion writ large on her face, that the Little Lady was not colluding with Raymond Herevi, and was an innocent, Father Yann stepped towards her, pity in his heart. 'Madame, it is true that this man is related to you. He is a cousin of sorts.'

'A cousin?' The redhead turned back to Raymond Herevi. 'Gwionn, what does this priest mean?'

Raymond might once have viewed his marriage to Arlette solely as the victorious culmination of years of campaigning, but now he saw it more as a pathway to happiness. The moment Father Yann had hurtled through the door, Raymond realised that his life had just fallen apart. Both his own personal happiness and absolute victory over his old enemy, de Roncier, had been snatched from his grasp. He laughed, in a desperate attempt to bluff his way out, and salvage what he could from the wreckage of his life.

'The man's mad, Arlette. Either that or drunk. I'm no cousin of yours.'

'Don't lie!' Father Yann's finger jabbed the air accusingly. 'You are Raymond Herevi, son of Sir Jean St Clair, and you are marrying this woman out of spite.'

At mention of the names Raymond Herevi and Jean St Clair, a choking noise came from the invalid on the mattress. With a low cry, one of the women stooped to attend him.

Frantic, Raymond Herevi ignored this and turned his green gaze on the woman he had deceived, but whom he loved. 'This man's lying, Arlette. I'm Gwionn Leclerc. I've never heard of any Raymond Herevi.'

'I can prove it,' Father Yann was not going to give up. 'I have witnesses who will testify as to your true identity, but that is not the main drawback to this wedding, Raymond, as well you know.'

The red haired 'bride' was gazing at her 'husband' as though she had never seen him before. She looked at Father Yann. 'And what is the main drawback, Father?'

Gently Father Yann took her by the hand. 'He already has a wife, whom he has abandoned.'

Her eyes dilated, and she drew in a sharp breath.

'Gwionn? Already married?'

'Yes. I'm sorry, my child.'

'You could be mistaken?'

The hope on her face was pitiful. 'There's no mistake. I married them myself. Ten years ago in my parish at Locmariaquer. His wife's name is Anna, and they have a lovely boy, Jean.'

A defeated, shuttered look settled on Arlette's features. 'Madam le Harpour,' she murmured. She straightened her shoulders. 'Gwionn? No, your name is Raymond, is it not? Raymond, is this true? Are you married to her?'

Raymond swallowed. Save for his scar his cheeks were waxen. He had broken Church law by marrying Arlette, and now that everyone in this chapel knew that, the most prudent course would be for him to take to his heels lest he should be arrested. But he did not want to go. Arlette's eyes were fixed on him, confused, and clouded with hurt and betrayal. Suddenly it was very important that she understood.

'Arlette, I do love you. It's true that I came seeking revenge, at first. But that was before I knew you. I came to love you. I want to marry you. What could I do?'

'So it *is* true.' She closed her eyes. 'Oh, Gwionn – Raymond – if only you had told me the truth.'

'The truth wouldn't have won you. I wanted you. Can't you see? Oh, Arlette, always remember I love you.' He reclaimed her hand and, kissing it, looked intently at her. He must go, and quickly, but he had to know his son would be safe. 'And Lucien?' he muttered.

'Count Etienne's son will be quite safe,' she said understanding his unspoken question. 'You need never lose sleep on that score.'

Giving Arlette one last twisted smile Raymond said, 'So I've been granted my revenge, but not my love. Farewell, my love.'

Arlette gave a broken sob.

Tearing his eyes from her, Raymond pushed clumsily past Arlette and the two priests, and barged through the open door. His footsteps could be heard receding down the corridor.

The woman who had been bending over the invalid lifted her head, and turned a pale, piteous face towards the figures frozen by the altar. Father Yann recognised her as Eleanor de Roncier.

'Arlette, come here,' Eleanor said on a muffled sob. She thrust her veil back over her shoulders. 'This revelation has been too much for your father. He is dead.'

Jehan le Moine, the tall knight who had witnessed the wedding alongside his father, Sir Hamon, glanced searchingly at the Little Lady's appalled face, and dashed out after Raymond Herevi.

Alone at last, her three hours' vigil at her father's coffin over, Arlette left the chapel where her bridal lilies lay on her father's cold breast.

Numb to her soul, she crept up the circling stairs towards the tower chamber where Véronique had passed the night watching Lucien. There were a couple of hours left before dawn. With luck, if Lucien was quiet, Arlette would get some rest.

As she approached the landing, she saw a shadowy figure leaning against the wall. The figure moved into the light of a flambeau.

'Jehan!'

Jehan le Moine bowed over her hand. 'Excuse me, my lady, may I speak with you?'

Arlette had barely had time to do more than smile at her former playmate since she had arrived in Huelgastel, for which she felt guilty, but she was worn to the bone, and could think only of the quiet and relative solitude of her room.

'Can it not wait until morning?' she asked, smiling an apology.

'Assuredly. It was only that I was concerned you might be wondering where Raymond Herevi went.'

Arlette shot Jehan a sharp, grateful look. 'I was wondering. But my mind's a tangle. And with my father's death there has not been time to think about him.'

'I'll be brief. You must be exhausted. When Raymond Herevi left the chapel, he went to his quarters and took up his helm and sword. Then he went straight to the stables. He saddled Star and headed east—'

'East? Are you certain he went east?' Arlette asked, puzzled. Father Yann had explained about Raymond's connections with Kermaria, and that his wife was lodged there. Kermaria lay to the west of Vannes. 'I thought he would go west. He might have doubled back . . .'

'He didn't,' Jehan said shortly.

'Oh?'

'I followed him,' Jehan confessed, and deep colour flooded his cheeks. 'I intended to thrash him within an inch of his life for the way he deceived you.'

'But you didn't?'

'No.' Jehan's dark eyes regarded her sombrely. 'But he's gone. East. I thought you'd like to know.'

'Thank you, Jehan.'

Bowing briefly over Arlette's hand, Jehan slipped away.

If Gwionn – Arlette corrected herself – if Raymond had not gone to Kermaria, where had he gone?

He had left his most valuable possession, his roan destrier, Titan, together with various other trappings of his knighthood behind at La Forteresse. It was more than likely that he was racing hot-foot to claim them before there was time to send word to Sir Gilles that as a dishonourable man he should be stripped of his knighthood. She would not send word.

593

She still loved him, she could not help that. There was a pain in her heart that would take some time to heal. He had betrayed her, but one part of her still wanted him.

If only he had been free, if only . . .

Arlette took hold of herself, and forced herself to be realistic. All those years Gwionn had been with her as Sir Ralph's squire and then as her knight he had been plotting and scheming for her downfall. It chilled her to the core to think that her loving Gwionn could have been so cold and calculating. He was all twisted up inside, and though she thought she loved him, she realised she had hardly known him. There was a sense in which it had all been her father's fault. If he had not attacked Jean St Clair at Kermaria, she would never have met Gwionn Leclerc.

Though she felt betrayed, Arlette did not want revenge. Revenge only bred hatred and chaos, and she had seen enough of both to last her a lifetime. Let him take his belongings, and get out of her life. It was probably best if she never set eyes on him again.

Shaking her head, Arlette opened the door of her chamber.

Véronique was sitting on the bed, chin in hand, staring blankly at a candle in the wall sconce.

Lucien was quiet.

'Thank you, Véronique, you may leave,' Arlette said, peering at her son in the crib. Oblivious of the day's terrible events, Lucien was sleeping the deep sleep of the innocent.

Véronique hesitated. 'Lady Clemence said you weren't to be left, my lady. She thought the company might cheer you.'

Dear Clemence, Arlette thought, always thinking of me, but could she not see that today's griefs were too many and too mighty to be held at bay solely by the presence of Véronique?

Aloud she said, 'That was very thoughtful of her,

594

Véronique, but I should prefer to spend this night alone with my son.'

'But, my lady—'

'You may go, Véronique,' Arlette said, firmly.

When the girl had gone, Arlette sat on the edge of the bed and pulled Lucien's crib towards her.

'Well, my boy. We're on our own from now on,' she whispered. 'You have lost your father, and I have lost mine.'

Lucien slept on, and after rocking the cradle for a while, Arlette kicked off her shoes and stretched herself out on the bedcovers.

There was a gnawing ache in her belly, which her mind associated with Gwionn. Gwionn — no, she must remember: his name was not Gwionn but Raymond. Raymond had gone. When he had collected his destrier, would he go back to his real wife, to Anna? How had that woman stood all those years at La Forteresse pretending to be married to the harper when all the time she was married to Gwionn? What kind of love would lead a woman to do that?

And Arlette, blinded by her own attraction to Gwionn — it was so hard to remember he was Raymond — had never guessed the truth. Now she thought of it, Gwionn had seemed upset when they had returned from Rocamadour to find that the harper and Anna had left. Had Anna finally tired of waiting? Had her love run out? Would he return to her one day only to find that he had been rejected? She sighed. She would never know, and she ought not to think about him any more.

But it was well-nigh impossible to keep her mind from straying back to him. Where would he go? Would he start anew? She wished him well, but a nagging doubt surfaced. All the time she had known him he had been wrestling with demons from the past. And now he was running away, but it was more than the past he was running away from this time. He was running away from himself.

It was incredible to think that he had been married all along, that Father Yann had married him ten years ago, before he had set foot in Huelgastel. What a fool she had been to fall for a man who was at best a cheat and a liar. And at worst . . .

Arlette would rather not think about the worst. It was sufficient to know that she had been deceived by him.

But she *had* loved him and, for all that it had been a sham at the beginning, she was certain that lately he had come to love her. But how strange, that she had not even known his true name.

She remembered how he had comforted her when Etienne had hurt her. That had been good.

With a pang of regret for something beautiful and fragile that has been lost and will never be regained, Arlette also remembered their love-making, and the loving look she had seen in his eyes. She had not dreamed that. No, it had not all been hate and betrayal. It had had its beauty too, and one thing she was certain about – in the confused tangle of emotions in Gwionn's mind, there was love for her. He had admitted it, and publicly. It must have choked him to admit that he had a fondness for the daughter of his old enemy.

But most importantly, Gwionn had given her Lucien. That was something real to thank God for.

She sat up and lovingly rearranged her son's coverlet. 'Your father, my boy, was a rogue, but you shall never know it from me.'

Her thoughts ran on. The last thing Gwionn had said to her was that he had been granted his revenge, but not his love. He had left her reluctantly, but he had had the satisfaction of knowing that his son would one day lord it over her father's lands.

Relaxing back into her pillows, Arlette closed her eyes.

Justice of a sort had been achieved. Years ago her father had destroyed Jean St Clair in a quarrel over a few acres of land. Now Jean St Clair's grandson would inherit it all, lock, stock and barrel.

Arlette opened a weary eye, squinted at the ceiling, and addressed the Almighty.

'Is that what this has all been about? Have You been seeing that justice prevails?'

She closed her eyes again, wondering what would become of them all.

Eleanor looked set on becoming a nun. It was all her stepmother had ever really wanted.

And her grandmother? Arlette's lips curved. That formidable lady was likely to outlive them all. She would be able to advise Arlette on the running of Huelgastel — if she did not take over completely!

And Clemence? Clemence had her husband. She would fill the solar with her children.

And Arlette?

Arlette would stand alone. But not completely alone. Her grandmother would stand by her. And she could rely on Clemence and Jehan. She would not think about marrying again, not for a long, long time. A Penelope, she would resist Sir Gilles and his suitors, however much Duke Richard approved of them. Never again would she be rushed into anything. She had had enough of husbands for the time being.

Ever since her mother had died Arlette had placed the responsibility for her happiness in others' hands. As a child she had pinned her happiness on winning her father's approval. Then she had hoped that marriage with Count Etienne would do the trick, and finally she had pinned her hopes on Gwionn Leclerc. Now she knew that no one could help her.

It was down to her.

She was twenty-five years old. It had taken her over

twenty years to discover this daunting but liberating truth.

The winter of her life was over . . . And the spring was about to begin.

PAULINE BENTLEY

Rogues & Players

A colourful saga of the Elizabethan Age

Gabriellen is the strong-willed daughter of Esmond Angel, a renowned playwright and manager of Lord Barpham's troupe of travelling players. In Gabriellen's eyes no man can match her father, in wit, personality or presence. He is her hero. Until she meets and falls in love with Jack Stoneham, an ambitious and daredevil privateer. Gabriellen also befriends Mark Rowan, a Welsh horsebreeder who travels the country fairs and is Queen Elizabeth's spy who discovers plots against her life.

Jack finds favour at the court, and, aware of the Queen's penchant for unattached men, keeps his affair with Gabriellen a secret, refusing to marry her even when she is with child. Furious at this treatment, Gabriellen joins her father's troupe and finds some comfort in her growing talent as a writer; her father's eyesight is failing and he relies upon her help, though it must not become known, for a woman succeeding in the male-dominated world of the playhouse would meet with prejudice and persecution. But Esmond Angel is not all he seems and his links with the London criminal Underworld draw Gabriellen into danger...

Rogues and Players is full of the atmosphere and colour of the Elizabethan age; reflecting the bawdiness, religious fervour, ambition and intrigue of the time – encompassing the defeat of the Armada and culminating in the disastrous rebellion of the Earl of Essex.

FICTION/SAGA   0 7472 3979 7

A selection of bestsellers from Headline

THE GIRL FROM COTTON LANE	Harry Bowling	£5.99 ☐
MAYFIELD	Joy Chambers	£5.99 ☐
DANGEROUS LADY	Martina Cole	£4.99 ☐
DON'T CRY ALONE	Josephine Cox	£5.99 ☐
DIAMONDS IN DANBY WALK	Pamela Evans	£4.99 ☐
STARS	Kathryn Harvey	£5.99 ☐
THIS TIME NEXT YEAR	Evelyn Hood	£4.99 ☐
LOVE, COME NO MORE	Adam Kennedy	£5.99 ☐
AN IMPOSSIBLE WOMAN	James Mitchell	£5.99 ☐
FORBIDDEN FEELINGS	Una-Mary Parker	£5.99 ☐
A WOMAN POSSESSED	Malcolm Ross	£5.99 ☐
THE FEATHER AND THE STONE	Patricia Shaw	£4.99 ☐
WYCHWOOD	E V Thompson	£4.99 ☐
ADAM'S DAUGHTERS	Elizabeth Villars	£4.99 ☐

All Headline books are available at your local bookshop or newsagent, or can be ordered direct from the publisher. Just tick the titles you want and fill in the form below. Prices and availability subject to change without notice.

Headline Book Publishing PLC, Cash Sales Department, Bookpoint, 39 Milton Park, Abingdon, OXON, OX14 4TD, UK. If you have a credit card you may order by telephone — 0235 831700.

Please enclose a cheque or postal order made payable to Bookpoint Ltd to the value of the cover price and allow the following for postage and packing:
UK & BFPO: £1.00 for the first book, 50p for the second book and 30p for each additional book ordered up to a maximum charge of £3.00.
OVERSEAS & EIRE: £2.00 for the first book, £1.00 for the second book and 50p for each additional book.

Name ....

Address ....

....

....

If you would prefer to pay by credit card, please complete:
Please debit my Visa/Access/Diner's Card/American Express (delete as applicable) card no:

							·									

Signature ....Expiry Date ....·